THE RISING OF THE MOON

'The period details are fascinating and the language fast-paced . . . this novel brings us a compelling combination of love, war and idealism. It is a long, intense and epic story that is very well worth reading.'

Books Ireland

'The best work of its kind since Leon Uris' *Trinity* published a decade ago.'

Irish Post

'This book, as well as being a first rate novel, is a mine of original historical research. No Irish, British, American or Canadian's library, will be complete without a copy.'

Irish Democrat

'Exciting . . . *The Rising of the Moon* is an epic tale of war and love, of passion and idealism.'

The Cork Examiner

'Ellis enhances this chronicle's inherent drama by exploring the personalities and motivations of combatants on both sides. The hardiness of idealistic beliefs and the appalling ferocity of warfare are strikingly depicted.'

Publishers Weekly

'This well-written, thoroughly researched novel is rich in historical and military details. It is the story of an intense young man's coming of age, but also an intriguing and readable tale about a little-known incident in American history.'

Maria A. Perez-Stable

The Rising of the Moon

By the same author

THE LIBERTY TREE

THE RISING OF THE MOON

A Novel of The Fenian Invasion of Canada

Peter Berresford Ellis

A Methuen Paperback

A Methuen Paperback

THE RISING OF THE MOON

British Library Cataloguing in Publication Data

Ellis, Peter Berresford
The rising of the moon: a novel of
the Fenian invasion of Canada.
I. Title
823'.914[F]   PR6055.L49/

ISBN 0-413-17990-7

First published in Great Britain 1987
by Methuen London Ltd
This edition published 1988
by Methuen London Ltd
11 New Fetter Lane, London EC4P 4EE

Printed and bound in Great Britain by
Richard Clay Ltd, Bungay, Suffolk

There beside the singing river
That dark mass of men was seen.
Far above their shining weapons
Hung our own beloved Green.
Death to every foe and traitor!
Forward! Strike the marching tune
And hurrah me boys for Freedom!
'Tis the Rising of the Moon!

Ballad of the Irish Rising of 1798

Acknowledgments

Most of the events in *The Rising of the Moon* are a matter of history and public record. Many of the scenes were created around historical incidents and people for the purpose of fiction. In pursuing my researches in Ireland, Canada, the United States and England, I had to study countless books, articles, documents and other papers – both primary and secondary source material – too numerous to list as a bibliography. I also found myself owing a debt of gratitude to many people. This book would not exist in its fullness without their interest, advice and enthusiastic encouragement.

I would particularly like to place on record my thanks to Mrs Margaret E. Teal of the Ridgeway Battlefield Museum, Ontario; to David Owen and Tim O'Shaughnessy of Fort Erie; Professor Hereward Senior of McGill University, Montréal; Maria Soteriades-Matakias of Montréal; Elizabeth McNair of St Lawrence College Library (University of Ottawa), Cornwall, Ontario; Mary Kate Brennan of Buffalo, New York; William H. Loos, Rare Book Room, Buffalo and Erie County Public Library, New York; Barbara M. Soper, Librarian, History Department, Buffalo and Erie County Public Library, New York; Rebecca Koontz of Williamsville, New York; Ronald Paszek, Superintendent, Holy Cross Cemetery, Lackawanna, New York; Judith A. Quinn of New York City; Bill and Jessica Hart of New York City; The Irish-American Cultural Institute, St Paul, Minnesota; P. B. Boylan, Department of Archives, National Army Museum, London; Dave Holder of 'Shiloh'; Pádraig Ó Conchúir; Mary O'Sullivan Cardiff, who attended the 'birth' and gave me invaluable obstetric advice; very especially to John Carson, research organizer extraordinary, my chauffeur and companion on one memorable trip to Fort Erie and Buffalo; to Shirley Carson, for her warm Canadian hospitality;

and to my wife, Dorothy, who accompanied me on my first trip to Ridgeway and Fort Erie. Finally, I dedicate this work in memory of my father who first stirred my youthful interest in the tragic history of *Roisín Dubh*.

Chapter 1

It was obvious that they were brothers in spite of the differences in their ages. They shared the same square shape of head with an aggressive thrusting jaw; the same prominent, thinly arched nose; the same green-flecked amber eyes and the same broad, sloping forehead and sun-bleached light brown hair. But here the similarities ended.

Gavin Devlin was the eldest and more sturdily built than John-Joe. He carried himself with a military erectness which comes with several years of service. His worn and faded blue uniform sat naturally and comfortably on his muscle-hardened frame. His captain's insignia stood in aged, bleached gold on his shoulders while his battered sword scabbard brushed his high boots which, like his belt and holster leather, were cracked and stained in service. Yet the shabbiness of his uniform did not hide the aura of quiet authority, the impression of a man used to command and to being obeyed. It was when one peered closely at Gavin Devlin that his youth became apparent for he was only in his mid-twenties. It was a youthfulness in years only. Manhood had come too quickly and the harsh experience had left its scars in the deep etched lines which creased his eyes and mouth. The square set of his shoulders was betrayed by the tautness of the muscles in his neck, showing where his nerves were drawn tight by the ordeal of war. The most striking difference between him and his young brother had something to do with the inner quality of the eyes. Both brothers shared the same colouring but Gavin's eyes were deepset with a tired, haunted look, burning with some curious fathomless fire. The grimness was reinforced by the thin line which was his mouth, pressed tight to deny its natural humour. Every few moments his right hand would move to ease the sling in which his bandaged left arm rested against his chest. The movement was an automatic, nervous plucking. The preoccupation of his gaze showed that he was unaware of the gesture, of its regularity; unaware, too, of the occasional glance of sympathy from the milling people around him.

The younger brother, John-Joe, was no more than eighteen years old. He also wore the uniform of the Union Army but the bright, untarnished gold of his second-lieutenant's insignia proclaimed his recent commission and the spotless blue of his uniform was new and sharply pressed. His leather belt, holster and silver scabbard were all resplendent with polish and a man might have shaved in the mirror of his black leather boots. His gilt buttons flashed in the afternoon sun and, unlike his brother, he wore gloves of dazzling white. The boy's face matched his uniform, unmarred and fresh. There were no lines of experience on his fair, flushed features. His smile came quickly, the eyes shone in excited merriment. His actions were swift and decisive, giving the impression of a young hound quivering with anticipation for the orders of his master.

'Damn it, Gavin!' he exclaimed with a high, youthful laugh. 'Is the Brigade never going to come?'

The brothers stood among the large crowds clustered outside the imposing granite of the Treasury Building, a short distance from the White House grounds, watching the lines of marching soldiers moving in an endless rhythmic column, like some gigantic blue serpent, down Pennsylvania Avenue from the direction of the Capitol.

John-Joe pressed forward a little, raising himself on tip-toe to get a better view across the heads of the people at the serried ranks with their bands and battle-flags.

'Have some patience, John-Joe,' replied Gavin. 'They'll be here. Don't forget the entire Army of the Potomac has to march by.'

'I wish I were marching with them,' John-Joe said, resting back on his heels. Then he swung self-consciouly to his brother, his eyes dropping to Gavin's sling. 'Sorry. I guess that's selfish of me,' he said contritely. 'You are the one who should be marching. You've fought with the Brigade for three years. I'm not even officially posted to it until Friday.'

Gavin contrived to shrug with his good shoulder.

'I think it was a lucky thing that I stopped a Reb ball down at Sayler's Creek last month otherwise I would have to march. I don't really care for six hours of drill parade in this heat.' There was a thin smile on his lips.

The day was excessively warm with the inevitable stifling humidity that the citizens of Washington had come to accept with bad grace; a day that warned of the oppressive heat of summer to come.

'You're not serious,' John-Joe dismissed with a chuckle. 'Not to have marched in the victory parade . . . well, at least you've seen action. I didn't even get my posting from training camp until the war was practically over.' His voice held a note of regret. 'If only the Rebs had fought on, just for a few more weeks until. . . .'

They heard the music first above the clamour of the cheering crowds. The tune was jaunty; a swaggering, saucy air that rose above the noise of the 'hurrahs' and yells of delight. The high fluted pitch of the fifes and the bragging flourish of the drums caused necks to crane, heads to turn.

> Our hearts, so stout, have got us fame
> For soon 'tis known from whence we came;
> Where'er we go they dread the name
> Of Garryowen in glory.

A voice called enthusiastically, 'It's the Irish Brigade! The Irish Brigade is coming!'

The cheers rose and were redoubled as the band swaggered by and the green banners of the Brigade came into view. At the head of the column a large flag of silk cracked in the soft breeze: an Irish harp with a wreath of shamrocks with the words *Erin go bragh* – Ireland for ever – embroidered in gold on a field of rich emerald green. Behind the colour party, sitting punctiliously on his white horse, came the brigadier, Robert Nugent, with his staff behind him. Then came the standards of the 69th New York with the men stepping in jaunty time to the music of 'Garryowen'. Behind them came the other regiments: the 88th New York, who called themselves 'Mrs Meagher's Own' after the wife of the Irish revolutionary, Thomas Francis Meagher, who had been the prime mover in the formation of the Brigade at the start of the war; then the 63rd New York; and finally the 28th Massachusetts.

The crowds roared with delight as the Brigade stepped lightly along the broad avenue which fronted the lawns of the White House, where a great platform had been raised from which the President and his cabinet could take the salute. As the marching men approached the stand, the banners dipped and a silver shimmer of swords sparkled as the officers swung them to the salute. With a single crack, a thousand palms smacked the wooden stocks of their rifles as the men brought them from their shoulders in honour of the President who, rising to his feet, swept off his hat to place it over his heart in acknowledgment.

The cheers became deafening. The Irish Brigade! Who had not heard of it? It had been foremost in almost all the major encounters of the war and was acknowledged the most effective and colourful unit of the entire Union Army. Officially they were listed as the 2nd Brigade, 1st Division of General Andrew Humphrey's 2nd Army Corps, part of Major-General George Meade's Army of the Potomac. However, they answered simply to the Irish Brigade and their standards, their battle cries and their flamboyant marching to the music of their motherland left one in no doubt who they were.

With the other regiments, divisions and corps of the Army of the Potomac, the Brigade had been waiting since dawn this Tuesday, 23 May 1865, to take their place in the grand review to celebrate the victory of the Union Army over the Confederacy. From ten o'clock that morning 65,000 men in companies, regiments, brigades and divisions had swung down from the white-painted Capitol, following their bands and emblems between the White House and the Ellipse to pass in front of the newly installed President. Tomorrow, Wednesday, it would be the turn of the army of General William Sherman to parade with its battle honours. The capital was bursting with crowds eager to witness the historic occasion. The windows of every building lining the route, the doorstep and sidewalks, indeed, every possible vantage point, were athrong with the crowds. More people had flocked into the city of Washington to see the victory parades than had ever come to see the inauguration of a president. The crowds were, in general, good natured and out for enjoyment after the four years of bitter hardship and sacrifice. They lost no opportunity to express their enthusiastic relief and joy at the ending of the war. During these last two months the secessionist Confederate States had collapsed but the Union had paid dearly for its victory. Newspapers were already trying to make final assessments of the casualties and claiming that the Union Army had lost 359,528 killed and 272,175 wounded compared to the Confederacy's 280,000 dead and just over 100,000 wounded. Then there were the civilian costs, the damage to property and commerce and the ensuing bitterness between the North and South, which could not be so easily assessed. The North was hopelessly in debt now and the South was economically ruined.

Gavin Devlin found himself standing mentally aloof from the wildly cheering masses around him, viewing the grand parade with a cynicism that the experience of war had borne and hardened. Watching the fluttering banners and marching lines of men, listening to the swaggering thunder of the drums and fluting of the pipes, he found himself wondering whether there really was anything to celebrate in such a victory as the Union had won.

The previous month, on 9 April, General Robert E. Lee had surrendered his Confederate Army of North Virginia to the Union Army's commander-in-chief, Ulysses S. Grant, at Appomattox Court House in Virginia. The surrender had heralded the final days of the Confederacy. It was not until the end of April that General Joe Johnston's army had capitulated to General Sherman in North Carolina and then, on 4 May, General Richard Taylor's troops east of the Mississippi had laid down their arms. On 11 May Jefferson Davis, the President of the Confederate States, had been captured by Union cavalry. The capture came as both a relief and an embarrassment. It was well known on Capitol Hill that the government had hoped that Davis would escape into exile and oblivion. Now the Union had no ordinary prisoner on its hands. Most people expected that Davis would be tried for High Treason and executed. There was a popular ditty sung in the streets with the refrain, 'We'll hang Jeff Davis from a sour-apple tree!' Wiser men on Capitol Hill knew that the execution of Davis would provide a martyr for the South and a new rallying point which would prevent any hopes of a quick reconciliation between the States. In these closing weeks of May, however, the conflict seemed finally over. There was only one Confederate Army in the field which had not surrendered to the Union; this was the trans-Mississippi army of General Edmund Kirby Smith but his agreement to surrender terms was expected daily.

John-Joe had moved forward towards the front of the throng, waving his hat high above his head and yelling until his voice cracked in excitement. Gavin found he could not share the mood as he stood staring across the heads of the waving people to the faces of the marching men. Most of them were youthful replacements who had scarcely seen battle, youngsters like John-Joe, though here and there he saw the tired, gaunt visage of veterans moving like ghosts among the living. One thing all the faces shared was the expression of unfathomable relief that the war was over; finally over . . . and, perhaps, there was a touch of something else on their features. Surprise; surprise that they were still alive when so many thousands were dead and wounded.

The majority of the soldiers of the Irish Brigade were comparatively new recruits. Gavin felt ancient as he observed them going by. During the May and June of the previous year the Irish Brigade had been so decimated that there had been talk of re-grouping it as a single battalion. The casualties during the terrible fighting in the Wilderness, at Spottsylvania and at Cold Harbor had been severe. Of the Brigade's ten officers ranking major and above, all had been casualties – six killed outright and the rest badly wounded. The Brigade had known heavy losses in the previous years of the war but never had there been such a wastage of men as during those few weeks of living nightmare, of fighting alternated by forced marches as the strength of the Brigade drained away through death, wounds and disease. Gavin shivered slightly as he recalled the slaughter at Cold Harbor. Bayonets matched against a withering Confederate artillery barrage. The brigadier, Richard Byrne, had fallen mortally wounded during the first charge leading the way with the 28th Massuchusetts. Of the 310 men of the 28th Massachusetts who had rushed forward, only eight men had survived. The new brigadier, Pat Kelly, had been killed a few days later leading another bayonet charge against the murderous artillery. Finally, the senior surviving officer, a captain, was appointed acting-brigadier until the Brigade could be withdrawn from the battle lines. Out of the five regiments that had constituted the Brigade there were not enough survivors to create a full-strength battalion. Gavin was still astonished that he had survived unscathed; at least, untouched in any physical sense for he was still haunted by the screams and cries of the dying and by the vision of hell that he had seen. Nearly a year afterwards, he would awake at night with the sounds of those screams in his ears and the vision of men dying in helpless agony. For three days the wounded had lain untended at Cold Harbor before a ceasefire could be arranged in order to remove them. They had died by the thousands and their ghosts still tormented Gavin.

The Brigade had been withdrawn to recuperate and Tom Smyth had been given command, managing to bring it back to strength, although the Brigade now consisted of four regiments in place of its previous five. Then Robert Nugent had taken command to lead the Brigade through the fierce fighting of the 'Twelve Days Campaign' of late March, which had culminated in Lee's surrender at Appomattox. It had been a bitter campaign of running battles, of weary marches through the mud and slush of war-torn Virginia. Pawns sacrificed by the move of a distant hand until, three days before Lee's surrender, Gavin had taken a Confederate musket ball in his upper left arm at a place called Sayler's Creek. The ball had torn part of the muscle and he had been lucky not to loose the arm. It was still giving him pain but he was slowly recovering. Now, watching his brother's enthusiastic, cheering figure, he felt glad that John-Joe would not have to experience such a vicious growth to manhood. He had missed the hideousness of war's reality and now all that was left was the unsubstantial tinsel of pomp and circumstance.

'Devlin!'

A firm hand gripped his good arm from behind and Gavin started from his revery and turned. An officer with the blue tabs of the medical corps stood smiling at him.

'I thought I recognized you, Devlin.'

The surgeon-captain was about thirty years old, a pleasant-faced handsome man with blond hair and twinkling blue eyes. Gavin recognized him immediately. He had been in charge of the field hospital at Petersburg where Gavin had been treated after receiving his wound.

'Captain Taylor, isn't it?'

Taylor nodded in acknowledgment. 'How's the arm? On the mend, I trust?'

Gavin's right hand touched the sling momentarily. 'It still pains me a little,' he confessed.

'Bound to,' agreed the surgeon-captain cheerfully. 'But another few weeks and you'll be fine. Take my word. The removal of the ball was neatly done. Neatly done. You'll soon be mending again.'

Gavin felt awkward at the man's blitheness and he turned the conversation from his wound. 'Are you in Washington to see the parade?'

Taylor's head shook emphatically. 'No. I am posted to the military hospital at Georgetown. It's my last posting, thank God! I'm due for demobilization next month and then . . . then I'm heading back to Upper Canada to set myself up again as a country doctor in a nice, quiet township by Lake Erie. Hope to marry, too.' He smiled self-consciously. 'The only gunshot wounds that I intend to treat from now on are when a farmer shoots himself in the foot instead of hitting a rabbit.'

Gavin returned the man's grin. 'I didn't realize that you were a Canadian.'

'Not originally. I was twenty-three when I settled there fresh out of medical school in England. It's a good country.' He paused. 'But what about you, Devlin? You'll be due for demobilization soon.

What are you going to do now? Weren't you a lawyer before the war?'

Gavin shook his head, 'I joined up before I was called to the Bar, but just after I finished law school. I guess I'll go home to New York and go back to law, though.'

'Get yourself a lucrative law practice, Devlin,' Taylor advised approvingly. 'Who knows where that might lead? Law to politics, politics to the White House. Several of your presidents have arrived by that road.'

'Not me,' Gavin grimaced. 'You have to be born in this country to be president. I was born in Ireland.'

'Ah! Of course,' Taylor said. 'I'd forgotten. You are in the 69th New York. The Irish Brigade.' He turned his head towards the marching columns. 'I wondered why you were watching them march by.'

'It's not the reason,' Gavin said quickly. 'I wasn't keen to see the parade. My brother insisted we come. He was posted to the Brigade this week.'

'Lucky fellow,' Taylor sighed enviously. 'At least he's missed the war.'

'I don't believe he thinks that he's lucky,' Gavin replied, nodding to where John-Joe was pressing forward, waving his hat and still cheering. Taylor took in the young man's enthusiasm and shook his head, almost sadly.

'I suppose we were all young once, before the war,' he mused. Then he turned a disapproving glance on the yelling crowds about them. 'It's not my business but I do think that President Johnson could have forgone a victory celebration in the circumstances. Someone once said that whoever overcame his enemy by force had conquered only half of his foe. I bet if Abe Lincoln had been alive he would have avoided rubbing the Southerners' faces in it and stopped the victory parades and celebrations.'

Gavin stared at Taylor in astonishment. Taylor had just articulated the thoughts that had been in the back of his mind ever since the adjutant-general had issued the orders for the parade five days before. It was not only a question of celebrating the military defeat of the South, which would surely embitter the people further and perhaps harden the animosities that Lincoln had always sought to avoid, but Gavin also felt it wrong to celebrate at a time when the country should be mourning for its murdered leader. While the celebratory flags and bunting flew from almost every house, hotel and store in the capital, the flags on all official and public buildings were still at half-mast and draped in mourning black. Amidst the cheering and martial music, Gavin found it hard to accept that it was only a few weeks ago, on Good Friday, that President Abraham Lincoln had been shot while sitting in a box at Ford's Theater watching the last act of a popular melodrama. He had died the next morning without regaining consciousness and the news of the assassination had stunned the North, flushed on the threshold of victory.

Lincoln had not been the only member of the administration singled out for assassination. Secretary of state William H. Seward, a former governor of New York and a friend of the Irish Brigade, had been badly wounded. A man had gained entrance into his house, drew a knife and attempted to stab him to death. Rumour had it that Vice-President Andrew Johnson and the commander-in-chief, General Grant, were also on the assassins' list.

Conspiracy was the word on everyone's lips. The man who had killed Lincoln, an actor named Booth, had been shot to death in Virginia a few days afterwards. Lewis Paine, the man who had attacked Seward, had been arrested and seven others, implicated in the assassination attempts, had been rounded up. But who had been behind the Good Friday conspirators? The Confederacy? Popular reaction had been to blame the South although the more discerning minds had asked why the South, in the process of surrendering in chaos and collapse, would want to murder Lincoln, especially when Lincoln was the only man preaching reconciliation between the States rather than retribution? Of course, it had been suggested that the assassins were merely a self-appointed group of Southern fanatics. Nevertheless, other rumours began to spread.

Some saw the hand of Vice-President Johnson behind the conspirators. Few people liked Johnson. He had been born in North Carolina but represented Tennessee in the Senate at the start of the war and became the only Southern senator who had not seceded with his State before the start of the war. The kindest remark Northerners had to say of him was that Johnson was a man who knew on which side his bread was buttered. It had come as a shock to most people when Lincoln, the Republican, beginning his campaign for a second term in office during the fall of 1864, had replaced Hannibal Hamlin with Johnson, the Democrat, on the ticket as Vice-President. Lincoln had, by all accounts, made the decision as a concession to the hard-line 'war' Democrats. Not only was Johnson a preacher of retribution – 'treason is a crime and must be made odious!' was his constant cry to Lincoln's appeal for charity towards the South – but he was a reputed drunkard, violent in language and bellicose in temper. A mercurial character, impetuous and inconstant. Some on Capitol Hill whispered of Johnson's delusions of grandeur and jealousy of Lincoln. Now that he had assumed the office of President, his belligerency was helping to harden attitudes towards the defeated South.

However, for every rumour which favoured Johnson as the architect of the assassination conspiracy, there were two rumours which laid the same charge against the secretary for war, Edwin M. Stanton. As the likely chief assassin, Stanton was a popular choice among the officers of the army, especially among the generals who had dealt directly with him. He was pugnacious and egocentric; a man of volatile temper with a malignant vengeful attitude to those who dared oppose him. He never questioned the right of his own actions nor his authority and had no hesitation in acting without advising other members of the executive, not even the President. He was impervious to the feelings of others. Most of the general staff had fallen foul of the secretary for war at some time. It was well known that Stanton believed the South should be made to pay for the war and was a supporter of Johnson's retribution argument. Newspapers were certainly happy to drop veiled hints about Stanton's involvement in the conspiracy as recompense for the feud which the secretary for war had conducted against them. Stanton had no time for newspapers and had introduced censorship at an early stage, closing newspapers that broke his rules, arresting editors, threatening proprietors and banning correspondents from the war zones. At one point he had issued orders for a reporter named Henry Wing of the *New York Tribune* to be shot for refusing to hand over a dispatch he had written for his newspaper. It was only just being revealed that Stanton had persistently misled the public about the war by altering casualty figures. In the case of Grant's despatches on his failure to take Petersburg in the June of '64, Stanton had purposely altered the casualty figures to one-third of what they actually were. It was now disclosed that Stanton had tried to prevent the publication of the Union's surrender of Harper's Ferry to the Confederacy and, having delayed the news for twenty-four hours, he insisted only 4,000 troops had surrendered instead of 11,200. With the war over, newspapers could get their revenge on Stanton by raising certain questions about the assassination of Lincoln. Why, for example, had Stanton ordered the withdrawal of troops guarding the bridge over the Potomac to the South on the night of the assassination? Why had Stanton failed to provide an adequate bodyguard for President Lincoln at Ford's Theater? And when Lincoln had finally expired at 7.20 a.m. on Saturday, 15 April, had there been a grim satisfaction when Stanton pronounced, 'Now he belongs to the ages'? Those near the reviewing stand on the White House lawns had noted with grim pleasure that when General Sherman had mounted the stand to be introduced to the new President and his cabinet he had deliberately refused to take Stanton's proffered hand.

Victory and peace? Or was there a new war beginning?

Gavin became aware that someone was calling to him. He focused on the elated features of his young brother.

'Didn't you see the Brigade? Weren't. . . .' John-Joe became aware of the surgeon-captain standing beside his brother and he replaced his hat and assumed a posture more becoming to an officer of the Union Army. 'I beg your pardon, sir.'

Taylor smiled indulgently. 'That's all right, son. They do make a pretty spectacle.'

'Captain Taylor, this is my brother, Lieutenant John-Joe Devlin,' Gavin introduced.

John-Joe managed to execute a formal salute in spite of the jostling crowds. The surgeon-captain returned it gravely although there was a flicker of amusement in his eyes.

'Captain Taylor was in charge of the field hospital where I had the Reb ball dug out of my arm,' explained Gavin.

John-Joe's eyes fell on the tabs of the medical corps, apparently noticing them for the first time. Taylor's smile broadened as he saw the slight change in the young man's posture.

'I'm just the fellow who sews everyone back together again so that they can have another attempt to cut each other to pieces,' he said, not disguising the cynicism in his voice.

The young lieutenant frowned slightly, holding his head to one side as he listened to Taylor's accent. 'Are you English?'

'That's right, son. You've a good ear for accents. I was fondly imagining that I'd lost mine during the seven years I've been over here.'

Gavin, watching his brother, was perplexed at the conflict of expressions which chased themselves across the young man's face. There was a strange hostility mirrored there which worried him. It was an abrupt open antagonism which must have been obvious to Taylor as well. Gavin coughed nervously to draw the surgeon-captain's attention.

'We have to get back to quarters, Taylor. It was good to see you again. Thanks for. . . .' His hand strayed to the sling again. 'I hope I won't have need of your services in the future.'

Taylor took his hand, 'If you do,' he grinned, 'then, as a civilian doctor I shall have to charge you for them.'

Gavin turned to find his brother already moving rapidly away through the mass of people. He found himself hard pressed to catch up with him.

'Hey! What's the hurry?'

'Sorry,' John-Joe muttered, dropping back to a more easy stride.

'From the look on your face,' ventured Gavin, 'I would suspect that you have discovered Captain Taylor has some acutely contagious disease.'

'What do you mean?' frowned his brother uncertainly.

'It was obvious that you couldn't stand the man. Why? Do you know him from some place else?'

'What makes you say that?'

'Why so goddam sour, then? You can't dislike someone at first sight for no apparent reason.'

'The man was English.'

Gavin halted in the middle of the pushing stream of people, staring at his brother in astonishment. 'What?' he said, moving to catch up again. 'Is that it? Is that why you dislike him?'

'Isn't it enough?' returned John-Joe sullenly.

Gavin abruptly hauled his brother into a doorway where they would not block the path of the shoving crowds.

'You'd better explain this to me,' he said. 'How come you hate the English?'

'Have you forgotten that we're Irish?' John-Joe thrust out his jaw pugnaciously.

Gavin stood for a moment in bewildered silence. Then he said quietly, 'You were scarcely a year old when you came to this country, John-Joe. I was only a few years older. We are Americans. This is where we were brought up.'

'Irish-Americans!' retorted John-Joe.

Gavin breathed deeply. 'And that qualifies you to be unsociable to every Englishman you meet, does it?' He did not hide the sneer in his voice. 'Do you realize that Taylor probably saved me from dying of blood poisoning or, at least, saved my arm? You've never seen a field hospital, have you? It's like a slaughter yard where overworked surgeons will saw off an arm or a leg because they don't have time to probe for bullets and, even if they do succeed in removing a ball, it's a ten to one bet that mortification will set in and they don't have the medicants to spare. At least Taylor cared enough to save me from that.'

'The act of one Englishman doesn't wipe out the debt of blood we owe to the rest of them,' John-Joe's teeth were clenched. 'Haven't you learnt enough of our history not to hate everything English? Isn't Ireland ruled by Englishmen by right of conquest? An Englishman might have saved your life but look at the countless Irish people that they have slaughtered to perpetuate their conquest. Tyrants and braggarts every damned one of them!'

Gavin shook his head slowly, surprised at the vehemence in his brother's voice. 'It sounds as if you are a candidate for the Fenian recruiting officer.'

John-Joe's eyes flashed momentarily and there was an imperceptible squaring of his shoulders. 'If you want to know,' he said defiantly, 'I've already joined the Irish Republican Brotherhood. I joined a circle last year before I left New York for the training camp.'

Gavin was not really surprised. The majority of soldiers in the Irish Brigade were members of the Brotherhood; the Fenians they called themselves after the legendary *Fianna* of ancient Ireland, a group of mythological warriors who served as the High King's bodyguard.

'So, my fine brother,' he nodded slowly. 'You are a Fenian!' He sighed in deep resignation. 'Jesus, Mary and Joseph! One war is scarcely over and you are already preaching another.'

'The only reason why the Irish fought in this war was to get military training to fight the English,' returned John-Joe. 'That's why Meagher formed the Irish Brigade. I thought that you would have been among the first Fenian recruits knowing Pa's stories of the Famine years and. . . .'

'Spare me Pa's maudlin reminiscences of the old country and how he fought the English back in '48,' interrupted Gavin. 'I know it all. And I also know that I live in America. What happens in Ireland is the business of the Irish who live there, not mine.' He paused and then uttered a bark that was neither laughter nor exclamation and reached forward to link his arm with his young brother's. 'Hell, John-Joe! Let's not argue politics. We shouldn't be quarrelling today.'

John-Joe grimaced. 'We shouldn't be arguing at all, Gavin,' he agreed.

'That's right. On a day like this we should be heading for the nearest bar and getting drunk. Have you ever been drunk yet?'

'A few times,' John-Joe smiled. There was a youthful boasting to his confession.

'Everyone in Washington will be drunk tonight, so let's go and join them.' Gavin guided John-Joe out through the throng in the direction of Massachusetts Avenue.

'Where are we going?'

'I thought we'd try Phelan's Billiard Rooms. Most places will be packed fit to bursting but we ought to be able to squeeze in there. It's up by Union Station.'

John-Joe glanced at his brother. 'I know it. Are you sure you don't mind Phelan's? It's a Fenian meeting place.' The jibe in his voice was unmistakable.

Gavin swung in annoyance, gripping his brother's shoulder with his good hand.

'Let's clear this matter once and for all, John-Joe,' he said with quiet firmness. 'Let's get it straight. I am indifferent to the Brotherhood. They have a right to their opinions but I have a right to mine. I know all about the high hopes they have of liberating Ireland, of the old dream of establishing the Irish Republic. Isn't every man in the Brigade a member of the Brotherhood, more or less? When I first joined the Brigade, when Meagher was in command, he told me that it would be used as the nucleus of an Irish army of liberation when the war was over. I remember Meagher saying that if only one in ten men of the Brigade survived the war, then the military experience gained by that one man would be of more service in Ireland's fight for freedom than the entire ten without military service. I told him then that I had joined to fight for the Union. I am an American. Well, the war is over and I suppose Meagher and his friends will continue with their grand scheme to liberate Ireland. I wish them luck. But I am going home. I've had my share of war. I've seen enough fighting and heard enough stirring calls for liberty or death to last me a lifetime.'

'Doesn't the freedom of Ireland mean anything to you?' pressed John-Joe.

'Sure it does,' responded Gavin. 'The freedom of every individual and every nation means a great deal to me. If the politicians have told us the truth, we've been fighting for people's freedom during these last four years. It's why I fought: to obtain the emancipation of the slaves and to maintain the Union. Remember what Lincoln said? The doctrine of self-government is right, absolutely and eternally right. Of course I believe that Ireland should be free to govern herself. But only the Irish people can accomplish that. Not a bunch of hot-headed emigrés.'

Gavin dropped his hold on his young brother and began to walk away. He paused after a few steps and turned back with a conciliatory grin on his face. 'Come on, John-Joe. Let's forget politics. Let's get drunk.'

Chapter 2

The wind was brisk and easterly, blowing across the straining ferry as it churned its way through the choppy waters of the Hudson, ploughing from Jersey City to the Liberty Street Pier on Manhattan Island. On the small starboard walkway, atop the fomidable side-paddle which was whisking the waters in a froth below, Gavin and John-Joe stood huddled from the wind watching the approach of the city skyline with mixed emotion. At the southern end of the island the houses grew more clustered and rose to incredible heights the like of which was not mirrored in any other city that they had seen in their travels with the army. They could smell the smoke of coal fires as the wind carried the odours of the city across the water to them. New York! The great port of the New World with its mass of ocean-going vessels, its high-masted schooners and clippers, its whalers, sheltering en route for the ports of New England, its grain ships, collier brigs, trawlers and coasters. All hard packed around the piers and wharves which clustered around the southern end of the island. Standing further off shore, beyond the guns of Castle Williams, a few warships swung idly at anchor, their gunports closed, masts bereft of sails. Stern and silent sentinels over the largest collection of trading and merchantmen ever assembled in a single port. New York! And they were coming home.

At the end of June the Irish Brigade had been disbanded and its regiments entrained back to their cities of origin for official demobilization. The Irish Brigade went with the thanks of the commander-in-chief, General Grant, if not with the wholehearted gratitude of the nation, for there were still many who entertained a general prejudice towards Irish immigrants and their mainly Catholic religion. Grant had said that no one who had seen the Irish Brigade go into action against all odds could doubt Irish tenacity, courage and loyalty. Any general instructing the Brigade to hold his flank rested easy in the knowledge that the flank would be secured. There were some in government who smiled maliciously at Grant's fulsome praise. Wasn't Grant's mother from Dungannon, in County Tyrone?

Well, the Brigade cared little of what others might think. Among their fellow soldiers they had achieved a reputation for light-hearted courage, open-handed hospitality and loyalty to the Union. Many of their officers and men had been offered positions in the regular army and Brigadier Nugent had announced his intention of accepting. But the majority of the Brigade had declined. The regular army held no exciting prospects for them. There would be little to do except the chores of garrison duty among the resentful populations of the South or, at most, some excitement among the Indian tribes of the West.

There were many of the Brigade who saw the end of the war as simply a pause; a reminder of the unfinished business they had promised to undertake – the project for the liberation of Ireland. They, the members of the Brotherhood, were in the majority. But there were others, Gavin Devlin among them, who merely wanted to return home to pick up the pieces of their civilian lives again. Men who sought to escape the fanfare of official welcomes and return to their homes as quietly as possible. That was why Gavin had insisted on returning separately from the rest of the Brigade, taking the train to Jersey City and, from the railroad depot's wharf, entering the city by the Hudson River ferry to escape the platitudes and the parades. Only John-Joe's loyalty to his brother made him forego the ceremonies and accompany him. Now John-Joe was seizing his arm as the ferry edged into the pier.

'Look, there's Pa waiting to meet us, Gavin!'

John-Joe turned, yelling and waving.

Gavin caught sight of his father sitting in a barouche peering up as the ferry moved closer. Doctor Manus Devlin had hardly changed during the year since Gavin had last seen him. He was a stocky man who, in his middle fifties, was now running to fat. His bright blue suit seemed bursting at the seams as he sat, slightly hunched forward in the seat of the carriage. His tall, black silk hat was pushed well back from his perspiring forehead, allowing strands of his greying-brown hair to spill across his face. He shared his sons' facial compositions and amber eyes. Every now and then he wiped a giant kerchief across the sweating brow as he sought to combat the stifling heat of the city's summer.

Gavin felt an emotional pang at seeing him. He was always confused about his feelings towards his father for they moved from love to anger and contempt with such swiftness that he was never sure exactly what his attitudes were and, finally, he found himself feeling guilty at his confusion. His contempt arose from his belief that his father lived solely in the past, existing with the bitterness of failure and exile; a man who constantly had to seek justification for being an immigrant and found his redemption in a shrill anglophobia. In fact, during the last few weeks, Gavin had been building a growing anger towards his father as being responsible for John-Joe's conversion to the Brotherhood. For ever since Gavin could remember, he and John-Joe had been raised on Manus Devlin's views of Irish history and tales of insurrection and defeat. Yet Manus Devlin had secured a good life for himself and his family in New York City. The city needed doctors with good experience and Manus Devlin was certainly a good doctor. He had done well for himself and now ran a large house in Greenwich Lane employing three servants. He endowed both his sons with an adequate allowance to supplement their meagre army pay, and he was well connected through numerous Irish patriotic and Catholic societies. Yet instead of enjoying the success of the New World, Manus Devlin seemed burdened by the memories of failure in the old one. Here was another basic difference between the two brothers. While John-Joe thrived on the stories of Ireland, Gavin was more interested in the country in which he had been raised. To him Ireland was simply a strange, foreign place and the English – well, he supposed they were no better nor worse than any other nation.

'Hey, Gavin! Come on!' John-Joe was pushing him along the deck.

'Careful!' protested Gavin, easing his left arm away from his brother's grip. 'I may have this arm out of a sling but it's still tender.' John-Joe did not hear him, he had gone racing ahead to pick up their valises.

Manus Devlin was grinning as he waited for them at the coach. John-Joe was the first to reach him, tossing his valise to the ground and swinging his father almost off his feet.

'Damn it, son!' cried Manus in protest, clutching a hand to the barouche's side to steady himself. 'Steady now!'

'It's been an age since I left home,' cried John-Joe exuberantly. 'I'd hardly have known you.'

'Seven months to be exact,' sniffed the coachman in disapproval as he stood holding the horses.

John-Joe glanced to the burly, red-headed man and grinned. 'Still as sour as ever, eh, Patsy-Mike?'

Patsy-Mike had served Manus Devlin for the last ten years. There was no ceremony between the Devlins and their servants. They were all one family. Patsy-Mike's usually woebegone face grew even longer.

'Guess they didn't teach you any better manners in that army of yours,' he said. 'You ain't much different.'

'Neither am I,' replied John-Joe cheerfully.

Having disentangled himself from John-Joe, Manus Devlin turned to gaze at his eldest son; a slight shadow crossed his face, gone too soon to identify it as hurt or disappointment. There was a reserve between them unlike the immediate physical warmth that existed between him and John-Joe.

Gavin held out his hand. 'Hello, Pa,' he said quietly.

Manus Devlin took his son's hand and gripped it firmly. 'Good to see you home again, Gavin. Are you well? Is the wound healing?'

'It's well enough.'

'I could take a look at it when we get back to the house.'

'It's all right.'

The corners of Manus Devlin's mouth turned down momentarily. Then Patsy-Mike broke the awkwardness by chuckling. 'Guess he's probably got a notion how much you charge, doctor.'

Gavin glanced at the red-haired coachman and a look of understanding passed between them. Patsy-Mike always sensed the unease between him and his father. 'Glad to see you well, Patsy-Mike,' Gavin smiled.

The man inclined his head in acknowledgment. 'Glad to see you safe home, Master Gavin.'

Manus Devlin was suddenly all bustle. 'You're mother is waiting for us at the house. Let's put these bags up and get going, eh?'

'Is mother well?' asked Gavin.

'In the prime of health, son. The prime. But it's far too hot for her to come waiting around the wharves.'

It was certainly hot even for New York in summer. Spring and summer in the city were always called the immigrant season, the time when the great ocean-going ships came flooding in to land their cargoes of humanity at the offshore islands that acted as quarantine stations. The heat also guaranteed that it was fever time. Try as the city authorities would, every season epidemics of typhus, typhoid and cholera would erupt among the poor quarters and spread rapidly through the city. The richer people could move to the north, leaving the danger behind, to take up residence in the small country mansions that many had built beyond the great new park which had been constructed in the centre of the island. Work on this central park had only commenced a few years before the war and the wealthy had flocked to buy or build their houses around its more healthy borders, away from the overcrowded streets at the southern end of the island.

Manus Devlin and his sons clambered into the barouche while Patsy-Mike climbed up on the box and flicked the long whip sending the horse trotting along Liberty Street towards Broadway.

'Well, boys,' Manus Devlin sat back and gazed at his two sons opposite him. 'Home from the wars. Ma and I are proud of you both. The entire city of New York is proud of you. And we're all proud of the Brigade.'

'Hell, Pa,' John-Joe protested sheepishly. 'I didn't even hear a shot fired in anger. By the time I left training camp and joined the Brigade it was all over.'

Manus Devlin patted his youngest son sympathetically. 'But you were an officer of the Irish Brigade, a lieutenant, and no one can argue about that. That's going to count for a lot one of these days, eh, Gavin.'

Gavin stirred uneasily, not sure what his father meant. But John-Joe was already chatting on obliviously.

'At least I saw the victory parades in Washington, Pa. That was wonderful. You should have seen the Irish Brigade marching with its banners and its band and the whole country looking on with the President and all the generals.'

Manus Devlin smiled absently, his eyes, slightly brooding, on his eldest son. 'There's going to be a Fourth of July celebration in honour of the officers of the Brigade at the St Nicholas Hotel. The Manhattan Circle of the Brotherhood are organizing it. I hope you'll both be there.'

The question was directed at Gavin but it was John-Joe who answered. 'Of course we will.'

Gavin was aware of his father's gaze, still awaiting the answer. He felt sweaty and irritable with his father. He knew Manus Devlin was a member of the Brotherhood and, without putting it in words, his father was suggesting that he had a duty to attend the function in order not to let him down before people. He bit his lip.

'I guess I've forgotten just how stifling New York is in July,' he said, trying to avoid his father's look of reproach and censure.

He turned to stare at the familiar buildings as the coach began to move off along the great rutted highway. In spite of the tremendous wealth contained in the city, the streets, in most places, were merely dirt tracks. The winter rains forced the mud into rock hard ruts and even on a thoroughfare such as Broadway stagecoach horses had been known to slip and break their legs. New York was primitive in many ways – a ferocious and barbarous city which was a combination of a rough frontier town, with slums worse than any European seaport, and a wealth that was inconceivable. It was the centre of an abundant prosperity where immense mansions stood whose owners boasted exquisite carriages and fine horses and whose wives bedecked themselves in breathless displays of jewellery and gowns of the latest European mode. Yet side by side, by the mansions of the rich, stood the squalid tenements and hovels of the poor. Most of the slums stood near the harbour wharves where the fine old houses of rich merchants had been deserted, the owners moving to the better situated palaces beyond the crowded confines of the southern end of the island. These houses were now taken over and had degenerated into filthy tenements while even old churches and chapels and every damp cellar in the area were filled with immigrant families. Here were countless human rookeries amidst the labyrinths of darkened alleyways along which vile and disgusting smells permeated. Gavin knew that among those dark caverns, side by side with the homes of families, there existed slaughter-houses, bone-boiling factories, horse-skinners and glue-makers, whose nauseating trades, among the swarming warrens of people, spread disease and death on the hot summer air. Even factories making *loco foco*, the self-igniting matches, could carry on their work unimpeded allowing their noxious fumes to suffocate the weak and ill.

The city was bursting at its seams and yet, each spring and summer, immigrants would still pour into it in their tens of thousands. Physically confined to the south, the east and the west, the city was forced to spread rapidly northwards. As a boy Gavin could remember when the neighbourhood of 50th Street had been considered the limit of the city's expansion; he could recall the protests when the city extended across the pauper's cemetery at 50th and Fourth Avenue and the cemetery had become such a danger to the health of those encamping across it that it had to be dug up and removed, coffin by coffin and bone by bone.

Manus Devlin's talk of the old country had been of the dear green isle across the water. Of an Emerald Isle in which there were rolling mountains and majestic green glens edged in the russet of heather through which stately rivers pushed from lochs of deepest blue. A veritable paradise. From Manus Devlin he had learnt that the Gaels of Ireland were hospitable gentlefolk who held their word to be inviolable; a people where honour and hospitality counted for more than anything. But Gavin had seen the world of the New York Irish immigrant; a hideous world. He had often pondered how strange it was that while other immigrants usually passed through the city to find space and peace in the virgin lands to the west, or in the smaller, more manageable cities, the Irish remained huddled a few yards from where they had first set foot in the new country. Here was a people who, supposedly, and by all the stories he had been told, had hungered and thirsted for their rural idyll in Ireland, for their lands and farms, who had tried to hold their mountains, glens, rivers and lakes, even to the cost of blood; a people who for centuries had sought to drive the English devil from their Eden. But here, in New York, they had decided to sink into the condition of miserable town tenants with whose squalor even European seaports would hardly present a disturbing comparison.

He glanced at his father, smiling and chatting to John-Joe. Sometimes he wondered whether his father could come from the same nation as those unfortunate creatures who haunted the slums of New York. No; he did Manus Devlin an injustice. He felt stirred by guilt to compensate again for his hostility to his father. The reason why Manus Devlin had brought his family to New York was because he had fought against poverty and oppression. Back in the '40s, a blight had hit the potato crops of Ireland, rendering them useless as food. The failure had been turned into an artificial famine by the callousness of the absentee English landlords, backed by the English administrators of Ireland. When the potato crop had failed, they had refused to allow the Irish to use the abundant crops of wheat, corn and oats and demanded that these crops be sent out of Ireland to be sold for the landlords' profits, in addition, forcing the Irish to pay rents for their pitiful small holdings or be evicted by police and military. The Irish had died in their hundreds of thousands or fled the country in equal amounts. In a few years the Irish population had decreased by two-and-a-half millions. Such a situation gave rise to support for a new attempt to drive the English from the country and there arose the Young Ireland movement, pledged to establish a democratic republic. Manus Devlin, who had a small country practice in West Cork, had joined the rebels. But the rebels were badly organized with no military command, no headquarters, no specific plan of insurrection, no store of munitions or accurate information about their enemies. When word came for the rising, all had been confusion. Although 6,000 men armed with pikes, pitchforks and ancient fowling pieces, gathered to march against the military barracks at Mullinahone and Ballingarry, they were hardly a threat to the might of the English empire. Within a week the insurrection of '48 was over and its leaders captured or fled. Among those who managed to get passage on a ship bound for British North America was Manus Devlin with his wife and his two young sons. From British North America it had been easy to cross the border into New York. Gavin reflected that he had to give his father his due. He had fought and failed. Where he disagreed with his father was in his making a religion out of that failure.

His father still talked about fighting to free Ireland. Looking at the streets around the harbour athrong with Irish immigrants, Gavin wondered whether the priorities were wrong. Would it not be better to free the Irish in New York? And yet what was it that enslaved them? What was it that condemned them to such misery? Why were they apparently predestined as the victims of poverty and disease, of the swindlers and bullies who preyed on them as soon as they came ashore? Stunned by the hurly-burly of arrival, how many Irish men and women, frightened and confused, had been taken in hand by quick talking 'runners' who promised them cheap lodgings, taking them to houses amidst the slums where they were systematically robbed, bullied, cheated, detained by force until they were discarded, helpless in the immensity of the strange city. Bludgeoned by their reception, was it a wonder that pain, disappointment, bereavement – the terrible price of suffering – had to be dulled by *uisce beatha*, whiskey, the water of life? Yet the water of life only sedated feeling until a life of suffering was ended by a premature death. Was it a wonder that the name of an Irishman and a drunkard had become synonymous and the people of America saw the Irish simply as a drunken, fighting, law-breaking rabble whose clannishness not only united them in penury but isolated them as well?

He found himself giving another guilty glance towards his father, suddenly recalling a time when a city official had attacked Manus Devlin on Irish vices. His father had turned to the man with a frown of anger.

'You sound like the English, sir,' he had sneered. 'So the Irish are ignorant, wild, raggedly-clothed peasants? Well, perhaps the English, having forbidden the Irish for generations to go to school, have become entitled to taunt them with their ignorance. Having deprived the Irish of their lands, their goods, their trades and professions, perhaps the English have a right magnanimously to mock their poverty. That is their right as conquerors, sir. But you have only the right of ignorance!'

Gavin sighed.

The yelping of dogs brought him back to his surroundings again. A pack of dogs of all shapes and sizes were running hither and thither across the road, causing Patsy-Mike to haul back on his reins and let out a stream of colourful oaths. Groups of small boys carrying clubs were giving chase, yelling at the top of their voices.

'Damned dogs!' snapped Manus Devlin.

Gavin had forgotten how numerous dogs were in the city, especially during the summer when the heat drove many of them mad. Hundreds of dogs, frothing at the mouth, became yet another menace on the streets, transmitting viruses mainly to children. Gangs of boys found employment during these months by chasing them and beating their brains out with cudgels and sticks in order to collect the fifty cents reward offered for every carcass by the City Health Inspector. Dogs weren't the only animals to menace the streets, for hogs and pigs were often found roaming and many a starving pig had attacked children. Even on Broadway itself, cows, oxen and forlorn-looking mules roamed uncontrolled.

Gavin realized that his father was looking at him in expectation. He had been asked a question. 'I'm sorry, Pa, my mind was elsewhere.'

'I just wanted to make sure that you will attend the celebration.' Manus Devlin said. 'Your mother will be going along as well.'

More blackmail. Gavin sighed. 'Yes. I'll come.'

There was relief on his father's face. 'Excellent. Your mother will be pleased.' It was his way of saying that he was pleased. 'She'll enjoy showing off her two sons in the Irish Brigade.'

Gavin was about to retort that the war was over; that the Irish Brigade was disbanded but, before he could begin to articulate the anger which welled up, Patsy-Mike had turned the carriage into the tree-lined avenue of prosperous houses and halted it.

John-Joe was already scrambling from the barouche crying excitedly, 'Look, Gavin! We're home! We're home!'

Chapter 3

The house on Greenwich Lane was a mock-Georgian style red brick building, one of a row of similarly built structures in a small thoroughfare which ran at an angle from Sixth Avenue through to 13th Street. It was a select residential street containing the homes of merchants, lawyers and doctors. Manus Devlin had moved his family into the house a few months after its construction ten years before as a reflection of his new-found prosperity. It was his badge of genteel elegance, the hopeful attainment of every immigrant.

As the carriage came to halt before the steps, the great oak door was flung open and Bridget, the Devlins' maid, hovered on the top step. Although her hands were demurely folded in front of her starched linen apron, her figure quivered in her excitement. She was a tall girl of twenty-five, with black hair tucked under her maid's cap which, pinned as it might be, escaped here and there in rebellious streaks. Hers was a translucent skin covered in freckles. Her blue eyes twinkled in perpetual amusement. Her facial muscles could never attain immobility and her lips were always twitching with humour. She had been with the Devlins ever since stepping off the immigrant ship from Liverpool some nine years ago. She was a gawky Kerry girl who somehow filled the role of an elder sister to Gavin and John-Joe, even though, in reality, she was younger by nearly a year to Gavin. Bridget had never been able to attain the sedate attitude Manus Devlin expected in a maid and now no one cared. Bridget was simply Bridget and her fun-loving hoot of laughter was recognized along the entire block. She tried hard to stand in a proper, decorous attitude, waiting while they disembarked from the barouche but a few seconds was all she could manage before she cast dignity to the winds and yelled over her shoulder: 'They're here, ma'am! The boys are home!' Then she came flying down the steps to fling herself at the brothers.

'Master Gavin! Master John-Joe! Why, yous look a sight and there's no lie in that. Look how grow'd yous both are!'

John-Joe wriggled out of her embrace grinning. 'Come on, Biddy,' he said, using his pet name for the girl. 'I've only been away seven months.'

Gavin, smiling as well, nodded. 'And I was home on leave a year ago. I can't have changed that much.'

Bridget chuckled and rolled her eyes. 'That's a time too long, I'm telling yous. Your Ma is waiting in the drawing room and cook and I have prepared such a feast. Oh, and several people have been calling by and asking when yous are coming home and. . . .'

Manus Devlin coughed in annoyance.

'*Ciúnas, a Bhríd!*' he said irritably. '*Tá tú ag geabaireacht.*'

Bridget stopped her prattling and threw a hint of a curtsy in the doctor's direction at the same time as contriving to give a broad wink to the boys. The rebuke did not seem to upset her.

Manus Devlin had a habit of speaking Irish to Bridget and sometimes to Patsy-Mike but he would never use the language with his wife or allow his sons to gain any knowledge of it. Inevitably the boys had picked up a few odd words and phrases by listening to the chattering of Bridget and Patsy-Mike but they would never repeat anything in front of their father. Gavin had done so only once when he was twelve years old and was not likely to repeat the experience. He had picked up a phrase from one of the maids who had just been pinched on the bottom by a forward errand boy. '*Scread Mhaidine ort!*' the indignant maid had yelled. '*Cacamas!*' Gavin had remembered the words, whispering them over and over to himself for several days, without understanding their meaning. A few days later an old friend of his father, a Young Ireland comrade, had been visiting and both men had retired to Manus Devlin's study to engage in reminiscences over their whiskey. Gavin had entered the study, seeking to impress his father, and solemnly pronounced the words. His father had risen red faced and angry with a hand raised ready to strike but the friend had held him back.

'The boy doesn't know what he's said, Manus,' the man smiled resorting to English. 'You can't punish him for something he doesn't know.' Then the man turned to the wide-eyed, fearful Gavin, shaking his head although his eyes twinkled with merriment. 'What you've said, *garsún*, is bad – very bad. It's a curse and you should never use it.' Then he glanced back to Manus. 'If the boy wants to know the language, why don't you teach him some Irish?'

Manus Devlin had grimaced disapprovingly.

'What good will it be to the boy? Will it help him earn his keep?'

'But there's more to it than that. It's the language of his people.'

'And for how much longer? The way English is spreading in the old country, the language will soon be lost. O'Connell always said it would be a good thing too. One has to be realistic about it.'

'O'Connell! The Liberator!' The words had been a sneer on the lips of his father's friend. 'A traitor to his people if ever there was one. When I was a boy, and in spite of the English Penal Laws, two-thirds of the country spoke Irish. Yet O'Connell, himself an Irish-speaker, would only address his audiences in English and call for the death of the language.'

'Irish political freedom is more important than saving a language,' retorted Manus Devlin.

His friend had shaken his head sadly. 'Manus! Manus! Wasn't it part of our Young Ireland programme to prevent the destruction of our language? Didn't Tom Davis say that a people without their own language is only half a nation? Didn't he say that a nation should guard its language more than its territory? Language is a sure barrier against conquest and assimilation; a more important frontier than fortresses or rivers.'

'Tom Davis was an idealist.'

'And we were not? Isn't Irish freedom an ideal?'

'That's different. Besides, in America we speak English but we are different and separate to England.'

'But isn't the country developing her own brand of English? Sure, it's only at the infant stage but she's maturing and the language is growing and moving away. By the time all her immigrants have gone down into the melting pot they will have derived a new language, and it will be as distinct from English as French, Spanish, Italian and Portuguese are from their common Latin progenitor.'

Manus Devlin had suddenly noticed Gavin still standing wide-eyed. 'Get off out,' he snapped, though not unkindly. 'But don't let me hear you speaking a word of Irish again.'

As Gavin had shut the study door he had heard the friend saying, 'It's all right, Manus. The boy couldn't understand what we were talking about.'

Although Gavin had not understood the nuances of the argument between his father and his father's friend, he had understood the basic conflict, for Gavin was a reflective and sensitive child. Ever since witnessing the argument he had never resolved the apparent contradiction in his father's outlook. Why did his father prattle about the necessity for Ireland to be independent from England if he wanted the Irish to forget their language and become English?

Bridget had run into the house to prepare the way while Patsy-Mike took the barouche round to the small stable at the rear.

Aideen Devlin was waiting to welcome her sons home in the drawing room. It seemed to both Gavin and John-Joe that she never changed with the passing of the years. She was a constant factor in their lives. Her face was soft and pleasant, the eyes grey and stoically serene. A heavy weave of brown hair, sparkling with gold, swept high on her head. Her whole attitude was one of calm repose. Nothing ever flustered her; she had never been known to lose her temper or display anger. Long suffering was the term that Gavin had come to think of in connection with his mother. Even when Manus Devlin over-indulged himself, which was a certainty on St Patrick's Day, she never seemed angry or put out. She was an intensely practical woman and it was thanks to that practicality that the family had survived the first grim year in America. She had been careful, frugal, and an anchor to Manus Devlin's more mercurial nature. The Devlins had survived therefore and grown prosperous.

Neither Gavin nor John-Joe had ever heard their mother speak about the old country. Her practicality was to make the best of the new country and never once look back to Ireland. She allowed Manus Devlin to do all the maudlin sighing for the past and what might have been. Aideen Devlin understood her husband thoroughly and supported him but never once indulged him. She was the foundation of the family; the security which had allowed Gavin and John-Joe to pass moderately unscathed through the unstable life and perilous changes of their early years.

She greeted her sons with a warm and equal affection, neither pressing them for news nor opinions, simply showing happiness in the knowledge of their safe homecoming.

Manus Devlin strutted about demanding Bridget serve the supper immediately and seeming not to hear when she replied it would take a moment to finish the preparations.

John-Joe was already enjoying himself, launching into accounts of life at his training camp, of the characters, the incidents and the numerous soldiers' tales which Gavin had heard all too often. Gavin sat quietly, now and then catching his mother's gentle searching eyes and giving her a reassuring smile. He was very much like his mother in character, practical and determined once his mind was made up. John-Joe seemed to have inherited his father's blustery and argumentative temper.

'Rosaleen McHale will be at the Fourth of July celebration, Gavin,' his mother said abruptly, seizing a lull in John-Joe's reminiscences.

Gavin coloured slightly in surprise. He had been pushing the subject of Rosaleen McHale to the back of his mind during these past few weeks. Indeed, he had tried to avoid thinking about any aspect of his future although he knew it was inevitable that the subject would soon arise once he came home.

His father misinterpreted his discomfiture and chuckled. 'We mustn't push the boy. He'll be making the announcement soon, I dare say.'

Gavin saw John-Joe throw him a sympathetic glance. Rosaleen McHale was the daughter of Stead McHale, a New York lawyer, whose firm McHale and Gogarty was a prosperous business on Chatham Street which specialized in corporation law. Stead McHale had lectured on the subject to Gavin's class at law school and had been impressed so much by his responses that he had invited him to dinner at his home. Gavin remembered little except his meeting with Rosie McHale and from then on he had been 'paying court' to her. She was a few years younger than he was, attractive and vivacious. During the war, Gavin had always made a point of visiting her during his irregular leaves from the front. An unspoken understanding had grown up that, when the war ended, they would be formally engaged and marry. In preparation, Stead McHale had already written to Gavin to offer him a position in the firm of McHale and Gogarty with the prospect of a junior partnership once he was called to the Bar. There would be time to consider and talk about the situation, Stead McHale had added, when he came home.

Aideen Devlin smiled gently. 'You take your time, son,' she advised. 'No one is hurrying you.'

Gavin decided to retire early that evening. He felt uncomfortable and wanted time to think and so he left John-Joe still recounting his brief military experiences to the appreciative audience of his father and went upstairs to the room he shared with his brother. Laying on his bed he found himself thinking about his father and brother; of his father's Irish patriotism and of John-Joe's self-proclaimed Fenianism. He sighed irritably. Why was he haunted by this Irishness when all he wanted to be was an American? In spite of himself, he found the childhood memories filtering back and they were vague enough. Vague and precious few.

He recalled a green valley opening to a large blue inlet of sea with steep russet-coloured mountains rising on every side. He recalled small whitewashed cottages dotted among the rich green fields on the valley floor and a gushing stream which traced the valley to the sea. There was a house which childhood memory made into a giant, mystical castle. He recalled smells too. Pungent herbs and flowers and the sweetness of newly cut grass. Another memory was of a woman who sang softly in pleasant, melodious tones, though he could not recall the words or the exact tune. There was the memory of skirts rustling and the odour of violets which he always associated with his mother. His father was a dark suited shadow always seeming to carry a leather bag. He recalled the stink of leather which went hand in hand with the faint reek of alcohol both of which smells he associated with his father. In fact, the sour tang of leather was the predominant smell from his childhood; the leather of the seats of the small one-horse buggy, the leather of the harness and trappings.

There was a sharper memory. Bodies lying along the roads, half-hidden in the hedgerows. Naked, livid bodies with bones that seemed to burst through tightly stretched skins. Eyes wide and lifeless, gazing towards the blue skies. To this vision was coupled the memory of a soft moaning of women and the plaintive wail of children. It was probably about that time that his father had gone away for a while. There was a vague feeling of tension in the atmosphere, of his mother's nervousness and irritability. Then there was yet another memory. First came the sound of banging. A scream. Then a splintering of wood. A door was smashed and strangers in redcoats and white breeches burst through it. They milled around, giants with harsh pale faces and wild eyes, screaming in awesome tones. They were threatening. He felt his mother gripping him against the hard cloth of her skirts and he smelt the odour of violets more strongly than ever.

Or . . . being roused at night; shaken urgently awake. The faint smell of leather. Out of the blackness came his father's voice. Whispering. Softly whispering. Then the perfume of violets. The faint cry of his baby brother. The lurching coach. Again the stink of leather and the jangle of a harness.

A new smell now; the tang of salt water, the wild perfume of the sea winds. The creak and groan of wood. The pitch and toss of an unfamiliar motion.

That was all his memories of Ireland. And that was more than he wanted to remember; more than he felt comfortable with. He was an American now.

The next afternoon Gavin went for a walk through the humid sunbaked streets of the city. It was inevitable that his footsteps should lead him down to Lafayette Place to pause outside the tall whitewashed mansion of Stead McHale. He knew that McHale himself would be at his office or in his club and it was an even bet whether Mrs McHale would be at home or not. It was Rosaleen he wanted to see.

A thin negro in butler's livery opened the door. Gavin did not recognize the man as one of McHale's regular servants and guessed he was new to the household.

'Is Mrs McHale or Miss McHale at home?'

The man's face was immobile. He carried himself with all the polished attributes of an English servant.

'Mrs McHale is out, sir. I believe Miss McHale is in. Shall I say who is enquiring?'

Gavin had no visiting cards and felt awkward. 'Captain Devlin.'

The butler nodded and swung the door shut, leaving Gavin hesitating on the porch. The door opened after a while and the servant gazed at him with a new interest.

'Miss McHale is in the garden at the back of the house, sir. Shall I show you? . . .'

'I know the way.' Gavin turned oblivious to the slightly raised eyebrows and moved swiftly down the steps, along beside the house into the garden. The lawns that stretched behind the house were fairly large as town houses went. At the far end stood a belvedere raised in eastern style on a wooden octagonal frame with a platform floor that was open through the trellis work. It was the new fashion among town house owners to have a place in the garden to use for a soirée. Belvederes or gazebos, as they were called, were very popular and the McHales believed in keeping up with the latest fashions.

Rosie McHale came running towards him. She gave a gurgle of delight as she flung herself into his arms, and her mouth sought his without any sense of shame. The fierceness of her embrace was something new to Gavin and surprised him. She broke away breathlessly and stared up at him, her eyes laughing defiance. She was as he remembered, as though the intervening year had never happened: a small, delicately boned girl whose white shoulders merged into soft arms and small pale hands. Her head was proportionately small, the face almost heart-shaped, but carried proudly. Her hair was of raven blackness, shimmering almost blue in contrast to her pale eyes whose colour was changeable like the sea. Her mouth was a little too broad. The red of the cosmetic she had applied made this fact more noticeable.

'You've been a long time away at your rotten war,' she greeted. Without waiting for an answer, she seized his hand and drew him towards the belvedere. 'Come and sit with me and tell me all your news.'

Feeling awkward, Gavin allowed himself to be dragged to the wooden seat, piled with cushions, which rested in the summer-house. She pulled him down to sit close to her, then turned to ring a hand bell with a shattering vigour. A moment later a heavily built negress came scurrying out of the house. The old woman saw Gavin and her eyes crinkled in a smile of recognition.

'Good to see you home, Captain Devlin.'

'Thanks, Beulah,' Gavin smiled in reply. 'Good to see you keeping well.'

Beulah had been with the McHale's since Mrs McHale had been a young bride.

'We want some cold lemonade,' ordered Rosaleen; turning to Gavin impatiently as the old woman turned and hurried away.

'Shall I go and fetch the lemonade from the kitchen?' asked Gavin, feeling a moment of embarrassment. 'It's a hot day for an old woman to be hurrying about.'

Rosaleen stared in momentary surprise. 'Beulah can manage,' she replied shortly. Then, eagerness in her voice, 'When did you arrive home, Gavin? Are you back for good? We heard that you had been wounded. Are you recovered? Was it bad? Was . . . ?'

He held up his hand to staunch the deluge of questions. 'John-Joe and I arrived back yesterday. I wasn't badly hurt. The wound is almost healed.' His right hand had strayed automatically to his left shoulder. 'I took a piece of lead in my shoulder but it's fine now, really it is. As for being back for good, why, from tomorrow, the Fourth of July, I shall be a civilian again. That's the date for the official disbandment of the Brigade.'

She nodded her dark hair vigorously. 'I know. There's a big celebration at the St Nicholas Hotel. I was praying that you'd be home for it, Gavin. Everyone who is anyone is going to be there. Senators, Congressmen, councillors, the mayor . . . why, just about everyone.' Her eyes suddenly dropped to his threadbare uniform and blinked in disapproval. 'You are not going to wear that shabby old thing, are you? All the officers in New York have smart uniforms.'

Gavin grinned cynically. 'Where we were, there wasn't much time to care about keeping our uniforms nice and smart.'

She did not understand but went on, 'Well, just so long as you have something better to wear. Everyone will be expecting the officers to turn out in their best with their medals and all. If you come looking like a tramp, Gavin, I shall die! And I won't dance with you at all.'

Her eyes were smiling and Gavin was unsure how seriously he should take her. The thought made him realize, with some abruptness of clarity, that there were many times when he did not know if Rosaleen was being serious or simply mocking him. On several occasions he had found himself surprised, even a little shocked, at her more impossible comments. He never knew if she meant them or whether she was trying to provoke a reaction.

Beulah was hurrying across the lawn as fast as her girth would allow bearing a tray with glasses and a pitcher of lemonade. Gavin stood up and moved to help her set down the tray.

'Have you missed me?' Rosaleen asked coquettishly as the old servant returned to her kitchen.

Gavin, pouring the lemonade, answered promptly, 'Of course.'

He was thinking that Rosie McHale had changed since he had first met her when she was sixteen. She had had the spontaneity of youth then; an eagerness to know about things, to experience things and to enjoy that experience. Although their meetings, walks, picnics and other outings were conducted under the eye of Mrs McHale or some suitable chaperon, Rosaleen was able to demonstrate a zest for life whose exuberance captivated his quieter spirit, appealing to his reserved nature. The liaison was one that Stead McHale did his best to encourage. Rosie was his only child and McHale's law firm needed an heir. Now the war was over, everyone was assuming that Gavin would marry Rosie and accept McHale's offer to join the firm. Indeed, on his last leave Gavin had actually given Rosaleen a ring; not a proper engagement ring but a token. He had come to think of his future in terms of being Rosaleen's husband and a junior partner in McHale's law firm and yet, during the last year especially, he had been irritated by some inexpressible reservation which lurked at the back of his mind. Was it that he had changed or had Rosaleen?

'What are you thinking?'

Gavin blinked and brought his gaze to Rosaleen's pale eyes. 'Sorry?'

'I said, what are you thinking about?'

'Oh,' he fumbled for words. 'I was just thinking how long the war has lasted. How things have altered.'

'Well, the rotten old war is over now,' she dismissed lightly. 'We can start making our own plans.'

Gavin knew that she expected him to say something, something about the engagement, the future, but he took refuge in sipping his glass of lemonade.

'Daddy will be at the celebration,' she continued after a slight pause. 'He's waiting to hear what you have to say about his offer. He told me all about it, of course.'

'Well,' Gavin forced a smile, 'there's no hurry to make decisions.'

Rosaleen arched her brows. 'No hurry? After four years? That's a long time, Gavin Devlin. I've been waiting for four years. I should say there is a hurry. I want everything now before I am too old to enjoy it.'

'You are only twenty-one, Rosie,' Gavin reproved with a smile.

'At twenty-one most girls are married with children.' She paused and a sudden look of horror overcame her features. 'Not that I want children right away,' she added hastily. 'Maybe not ever. Horrible things, babies. Kitty-Ann had one a few months ago and when I went to visit her I nearly died!' She shuddered at the memory. 'No, I won't have a baby yet. I'm much too young for that. I want to live first and have a big house of my own with plenty of servants and give balls and soirées. . . .'

Gavin suppressed a shudder. Maybe he'd been too long away in the army but the idea made him feel panic.

'I think you are looking too far ahead, Rosie,' he said quietly. 'I'm not even a lawyer yet. It will take at least six months before I can be called to the Bar, that is if I'm lucky.'

Rosaleen chuckled and waved her hand dismissively. 'I've talked it over with Daddy. He'll pay for our first house. It will be a wedding present. And then, with what you will earn as a junior partner. . . .'

Gavin digested her announcement and interrupted, 'I want to pay my own way.'

'Of course you do,' she smiled winningly. 'But we must be realistic, Gavin. It would take ages before you were able to afford a house that way. Why, I'd be an old woman. Shame on you for mocking me so! Pay your own way, indeed!' She shook her head with a smile. 'Anyway,' she went on brightly. 'I've talked it all over with Daddy and he's agreed. There's a house for sale on Amity

Street, just at the back of Washington Square. It's ours as soon as we fix up the arrangements.'

'I can't accept that,' Gavin blurted.

'Nonsense!' Rosaleen was obliviously smug to his protest. 'It's all settled. With you away in the army I have had little else to do except make plans.'

Gavin was quiet. He felt a helplessness as if he were in a stream being borne forward by a remorseless current, thrown against rocks and scraping through rapids, powerless to escape. Rosaleen *had* changed. The vivacious uncomplicated girl had grown up. The exuberance of youth now seemed simply a frivolousness towards the things he considered serious. Did he recognize in her a hard determination to be assured of the comforts of life? In that Rosaleen was surely no different to most of the girls within his social ambit. Yet he had thought she was different. Despite the years of exchanging bright, chatty letters while he was away, they hardly knew one another. Her former eagerness with life which had attracted him now appeared simply as wilfulness. Ah, surely he was being unfair? He could not make such judgments in so short a space of time. Time! That was it.

'I need some time to think about things, Rosie,' he said. 'We both need more time to discuss our plans. . . .'

He felt her bewildered gaze as he dropped his eyes to the glass in his hand.

'I don't understand,' she said. 'We've known each other for five years, Gavin. That's more than time enough to know what we both want out of life.'

He put the lemonade glass back on the table and sighed. 'Do you realize that this is the first time we've talked without your mother or some chaperon hovering in the background, Rosie?' he asked. 'We've only met with others about. We need to be able to meet privately more often and talk about ourselves and what we want without other people influencing us.'

She giggled and put her head on one side.

'I'm sure I don't know what you are suggesting, Gavin. I think that you are being improper,' she said primly.

Gavin bit his lip in indignation. He wanted her to understand. 'I've been away a long time, Rosie. I've seen things. . . . Some things that I took for granted before the war I can no longer accept. I. . . . Look, what I mean is that we should be in each other's company much more before we rush into making plans and . . .'

He saw that her face was suddenly full of suspicion.

'Are you trying to tell me that you want to delay the marriage?' There was a tremor in her voice, a dangerous glint in her pale eyes.

'Damn it, no!' His voice was harsh with frustration; frustration with himself rather than at her, at not knowing what he, himself really wanted.

She stared at him with puzzled eyes, never having seen him so vexed before.

He rose to his feet awkwardly. 'I'd better go, Rosie.'

He hesitated. 'All I want is for the both of us to be happy. I don't want other people arranging things for us until I am ready.'

Rosaleen half shrugged. 'Daddy will expect to talk to you at the celebration ball tomorrow.'

'Shall I call for you and escort you to the ball?' Gavin asked, deflecting the implied question.

She sprang to her feet with an expression of annoyance. 'Daddy will be taking Mummy and I to the ball so I will see you there.' She turned away to the house and then paused. 'I think you are being very strange, Gavin,' she said over her shoulder. 'I hope you'll be more yourself tomorrow.'

She turned and ran lightly over the lawn to the house leaving him to see himself out of the garden. He turned, feeling depressed, unsure of himself. Perhaps everything would be clearer in his mind tomorrow evening.

Chapter 4

The Devlins gathered at seven o'clock in the hall of the house in Greenwich Lane. Gavin and John-Joe had turned out in their best dress uniforms which Bridget had spent hours preparing, sharply pressing the trousers and jackets, polishing the gilt buttons and gold epaulettes of rank and ensuring the scarlette sashes around which their sword belts were buckled were clean and properly folded. Their boots, too, had been highly polished. Gavin had to borrow a pair of John-Joe's white gloves to complete his dress. The brothers were the first to arrive in the hall with John-Joe nervously peering at the mirror and adjusting his uniform, brushing invisible specks from it. Manus Devlin arrived next dressed in a black broadcloth suit with a fine white ruffled shirt and black tie. The jacket and trousers were smartly tailored but gave him an air strangely at odds with his corpulent physique. He seemed agitated and kept peering at his fob watch.

At last Aideen Devlin came down the stairs. She wore a sober russet gown, slightly hooped in the modern fashion, with a shawl to match draped across her arms. Her gloves came well above the elbows. Her shoulders were covered in lace and she wore a necklace of three rows of pearls ending in a pendant of silver mounted with matching pearls.

'Mother!' exclaimed John-Joe. 'I swear you look like a young girl. You'll be the most dazzling woman at the ball. You must reserve the first waltz for me.'

Aideen Devlin chuckled happily at her youngest son. 'You're a flatterer, John-Joe,' she admonished, 'just like your father.'

'And his father has a prior claim,' added Manus Devlin. 'The first waltz is mine, Aideen. I'll have no young whipper-snappers cutting me out. Not even my own son!'

Aideen smiled contentedly at her husband. 'The first waltz it shall be, Manus. Now where did I put my handbag?'

Manus was already shouting for Bridget. 'Where's Patsy-Mike and the carriage. *Cá bhfuil Patsy-Mike anois?*'

'Isn't yer man at the door with the carriage now?' came Bridget's irritated protest.

In a sudden bustle, Manus Devlin herded his family into the street where Patsy-Mike and the barouche were waiting. Manus Devlin handed his wife up and waited while she sank to the velvet cushions, nestling the folds of her dress around her, gathering in the waves of silk. The doctor climbed in beside her while John-Joe and Gavin settled opposite. Patsy-Mike shut the door, flicked a coin to the urchin who had been holding the horse's head, climbed up on the box and urged the animal off at a steady trot towards Sixth Avenue.

Aideen glanced across to Gavin in the gloomy interior of the carriage. 'I saw Mrs McHale this morning, Gavin. Is everything all right between Rosaleen and yourself?'

Gavin stirred uncomfortably. 'Why do you ask?'

'Oh, it's just that she thought tonight would have been an ideal opportunity to make an announcement, what with the whole city being there.'

John-Joe eased the tension by giving a chuckle. 'You'll have to give Gavin a chance, Ma,' he said. 'He's been a long time away and I don't think he realizes that the war is over yet.'

'Too much time wasted,' grunted Manus Devlin. 'Time to get yourself sorted out, eh, Gavin? I think McHale's offer is a good one.'

'Please, Pa,' Gavin said, stifling an inward groan. 'I just need a little time to readjust.'

'Of course you do, Gavin.' Aideen Devlin reached forward, bringing the scent of violets to his nostrils, and patted his arm. 'You can have all the time in the world. No one is forcing you. Isn't that right, Manus?'

'Eh?' Manus Devlin hesitated and then nodded. 'Sure. Take as much time as you want. The arm is healing well, is it?'

Gavin sighed. 'Yes. It's healing well, Pa.'

Patsy-Mike eased the barouche across Sixth Avenue and set it at a steady pace along 8th Street before turning right on to Broadway to halt before the architectural elegance of the St Nicholas Hotel. The imposing façade had been completed twelve years before at the exorbitant cost of one million dollars and had become a centre for every prestigious occasion in the city. There was already a string of carriages lining up to deposit their passengers in front of the brightly lit foyer whose portals, indeed, the entire frontage of the hotel, were hung with bunting and Union flags. A placard announced, 'Grand Victory and Fourth of July Celebration in honour of the Irish Brigade.' Even as Patsy-Mike brought the carriage to a halt outside the lofty entrance they could hear the strains of a waltz drifting out on the early evening air.

The foyer was crowded with people newly arrived checking their coats, cloaks and hats, walking sticks and swords. A harassed man in hotel livery was trying his best to cope with the throng. They moved in a body up the curving grand staircase. On each stair stood ornate pots of rubber plants, coleus, geranium, hydrangea, oleander and elephant ear, giving a rustic odour to the occasion. On the first floor they moved into a majestic ballroom of white and gold with gilded cornices and white painted doors which held panels of rococo flowers. Bunting was strewn around the walls, with small Union flags and portraits of Abe Lincoln, Andrew Johnson and Tom Meagher, the founder of the Irish Brigade. Above a platform at the far end of the room, on which a small orchestra was playing enthusiastically among flowers of many hues and varieties, hung a large 'Stars and Stripes' next to a large tricolour of green, white and orange. It was the flag symbolizing the unity of the people of Ireland which had been presented to the Young Ireland movement in 1848 by Alphonse de Lamartine, the president of the French Republic, the design of which had been taken from the French tricolour.

The ballroom was lit with seven candelabras with the seventh, a five-tiered monster, in the centre, giving the room a bright yet flickering light. It was the smells that made an immediate impact on Gavin as he stared at the throng who either stood or milled around the edges of the room or swirled madly across the dance floor. The odours of flowers mingled with the fragrance of muti-scented perfume sachets, of cologne water and hair pomade, all topped by the bitter smell of burning bayberry candles.

The orchestra were playing a slow waltz and Manus Devlin lead his wife into the colourful movement of people, drifting away on the tide of dancers. Gavin peered round, his eyes searching for Rosaleen. He had not realized just how many people would be at the celebration. There was an abundance of uniforms to be seen: uniforms of all colours and designs, with shiny brass buttons, dazzling gold braid, tinkling epaulettes, scarlet sashes and red and yellow stripes on trousers. Uniforms with black polished boots trimmed with braid.

The movement and rustle of fans emanated mainly from the elderly women seated around the edges of the room, chaperons mainly watching their young charges with disinterest, objects of sexual lethargy, engaged only in gossip and criticism of those around them. Anxious-faced matrons stood or sat as the mood took them watching plaintively for prospective partners. Only the young girls seemed to be throroughly enjoying themselves. They reminded Gavin of a horde of bright butterflies. They swarmed in little huddles, their voices high and giggling. Now and then an occasional hoot of laughter would set an embarrassed would-be partner flushing. As they drifted by him, Gavin felt an uneasy stirring as he glimpsed a hint of little soft white breasts emerging from lace flounces. Some of the girls stared boldly at him, as they did at every young man in uniform that took their fancy, before casting their eyes downward and bringing up their fans to cover their mouths. There seemed no end to their abundance; of girls with red hair, or dark hair smoothly sleeked from the ears into chignons; of blondes with golden curls swept back into saucy styles; and of auburn tresses twirled into sparkling earbobs which tossed and danced as their owners pirouetted on the ballroom floor. A few bolder spirits wore tea roses tucked behind their ears in imitation of Spanish ladies of quality.

'Well now!' called a voice. 'Gavin! John-Joe!' They turned as a priest clad in a black cassock and roman cap came pushing through the crowd to them. Father John MacMahon was in his late forties, a man of medium height with steel-grey hair and a sharp scrutinizing gaze. He had served as one of the chaplains of the Irish Brigade although the Devlins had known him far longer than the war years. He was a frequent visitor to the house in Greenwich Lane and served on several Irish patriotic committees with Manus Devlin.

'Good evening, Father,' Gavin greeted him as the priest halted, reached into his pocket and hauled forth a large kerchief with which he proceeded to mop the perspiration from his forehead.

'It's hot enough,' he remarked in his strong County Monaghan accent. Years of living in New York had not dulled its tones. His eyes wandered across to the girls and then back to the brothers with a wicked grin in them. 'Ah, didn't I see you looking now?' he said as they averted their gaze in embarrassment. 'Well, if it weren't for me cloth wouldn't I be measuring a pace or so with one of those young fillies myself? Angels! Angels, every one.'

'I suppose so, Father,' smiled Gavin.

Father MacMahon guffawed good naturedly and dug an elbow in

his side. 'There's me forgetting. It's only one girl that you'll have eyes for tonight, isn't that right? I thought I saw Rosie McHale in the Supper Room across the hall.'

'Thank you, Father.' Gavin was about to turn away when the priest caught him gently by the arm.

'If you have some time within the next few days, Gavin, I'd like to see you for a talk. I've moved into the presbytery at the Church of Holy Innocent on Thirty-Seventh Street.'

'Of course, Father,' Gavin frowned hesitantly. 'What do you want to see me about?'

Gavin was not a church-goer, much to his mother's regret. If he had been asked, he would have claimed to be a Catholic but he also admitted that he was not a good one. He entertained a cynicism about the church which had also grown out of his war experiences although he respected MacMahon. But he looked upon Father MacMahon and the other chaplains of the Irish Brigade as exceptions to the priestly calling rather than the rule. They had endured all the hardship of war with the men, sharing the terrors of the battlefront by acting as medical orderlies under fire.

Father MacMahon obviously did not want to elaborate on the subject for he said, 'Just a chat, when you have time, Gavin.' Then he turned to John-Joe with a smile. 'And aren't you proud of John-Joe? I'll bet your father means to organize a royal send-off.'

Gavin looked bewildered. 'Send off?'

John-Joe was flushing with embarrassment.

'Surely. When is it that you are leaving, John-Joe? Is it next week?'

'Yes, Father,' he replied, running a tongue nervously over his lips, embarrassed before Gavin.

'Well, we'll all be down at the wharf to see you off, that's for sure. Now get about enjoying yourselves.' The priest's eyes danced towards the girls again and he grinned. 'Angels! Angels, every one.'

He was gone pushing his way through the throng, his voice raised in new greetings.

Gavin was left staring at his brother. 'What's all this about, John-Joe? What did Father MacMahon mean? Where are you off to?'

John-Joe bit his lip. 'I wasn't planning to tell anyone until this weekend, Gavin.'

'Tell what?' pressed his brother.

Suddenly irritated by the loudness of the music and oppressiveness of the ballroom, Gavin seized hold of John-Joe's arm and propelled him outside on to the landing. 'Tell what?' he repeated.

John-Joe stared defiantly at Gavin for a moment. 'I'm off to Ireland, Gavin,' he said softly.

Gavin's mouth opened in astonishment. It took him a moment or two to find his voice. 'You are what?'

John-Joe motioned with his hand, a curious defensive gesture. 'I'm off to Ireland.'

'But why? For what?' demanded Gavin.

'I told you. . . .' John-Joe lowered his voice. 'I told you I was in the Brotherhood. There's 150 officers going to Ireland to help train and organize the Brotherhood there.'

Gavin rubbed a hand through his hair trying to gather his thoughts. 'Whose hare-brained scheme is this?'

'It's no hare-brained scheme,' retorted John-Joe in annoyance. 'The whole thing has been planned by General Halpin and General Millen. I'm leaving with a group commanded by Colonel O'Sullivan Burke next week.'

Gavin bit his lip. He knew the officers John-Joe had mentioned.

'You see, Gavin, there are good men in the undertaking. Reputable men. The Brotherhood needs trained officers in Ireland.'

Gavin stared at John-Joe in dismay. 'Do you know what you are doing, John-Joe?'

His brother drew himself up. 'I'm not a fool.'

Gavin gripped his arm sharply. 'Damn it! You may get killed. You may be caught and thrown into an English jail or worse.'

'I'm prepared to take that chance. I took an oath when I joined the Brotherhood. I knew what it meant and I am prepared to keep it.'

They stood glowering at each other for a moment and then Gavin said, 'We'll have to talk about this later. This is not the time nor the place.'

'You'll not get me to change my mind,' his brother assured him swinging back into the ballroom.

Gavin stood gathering his thoughts a moment before turning towards the Supper Room. The room was less crowded than the ballroom. There were long, white linen-topped trestle tables forming a triumph of gluttony. Amidst a sparkle of glittering crystal dishes stood large silver tureens filled with a limpid soup, tinted burnt amber; there were boned woodcock, turkey, *chaud froids* of veal and dishes of varied fish, crab and lobster. Arranged on other tables were blancmanges, pastries, cakes and ice creams. Liveried attendants hovered everywhere with trays bearing glasses of champagne and wine.

Rosaleen McHale was surrounded by half-a-dozen young men who vied for her attention, bearing all manner of dainties to please her palette. She laughed at one and now another, chiding them or praising them as her flitful mood took her. Her flickering eyes saw him approaching and a broad smile spread over her features causing the would-be beaus to glare at him in unconcealed jealousy.

'Gavin! You've come at last! What an age you've been!'

She turned to the others, dismissing them airily. 'Thank you for your attentions, gentlemen, but my fiancé has arrived at last.' Then she turned, 'I've been waiting impatiently for you to dance with me.' She was already dragging him back towards the ballroom chattering on in her musical soprano. 'You don't know how bored I have been, just waiting for you to come and rescue me.'

'I don't believe you,' he found himself saying.

She pouted; there was something wilful in her pursed mouth. 'Are you jealous?'

'Have I cause to be?' he countered.

'I'd like you to be jealous, Gavin. Come . . . oh!'

They had pushed into the ballroom and were just taking the floor when the music stopped. A portly master-of-ceremonies had climbed to the platform and was waving his arms for silence.

'Ladies and gentlemen, for your entertainment . . . the nightingale of New York, Mrs Shelagh Keogh, who will sing for you while you draw breath from your strenuous activities on the dance floor.'

There was a burst of good-humoured applause as a solidly built middle-aged lady ascended the platform and came forward. A sharp clearing of her throat and a regal nod to the leader of the orchestra preceded her launch into an old Irish ballad.

While going the road to sweet Athy,
Hurroo! Hurroo!
While going the road to sweet Athy,
Hurroo! Hurroo!
While going the road to sweet Athy,
A stick in my hand and a drop in my eye,
A doleful damsel I heard cry;
Och, Johnny, I hardly knew ye!
With drums and guns, and guns and drums
The enemy nearly slew ye,
My darling dear, you look so queer,
Och, Johnny, I hardly knew ye!

The audience began to stamp their feet to the rhythm and voices began to join her. But during the war years the balladeers had changed the wording of the song and, although Mrs Keogh struggled magnificently to keep to the original version, the people insisted on singing the new, popular chorus.

> When Johnny comes marching home again,
> Hurroo! Hurroo!
> We'll give him a hearty welcome then,
> Hurroo! Hurroo!

Gavin felt embarrassment for the singer as the chorus vibrated around him. It seemed odd that a ballad about the tragedy of war had suddenly been transformed into a paean of victory. Yet the original version had been the wrong thing to sing at the wrong time. People still wanted to revel in victory and he saw Mrs Keogh shrug and accept the fact with good grace, her resonant tones joining in: '*When Johnny comes marching home again. . . .*'

Mrs Keogh went through two more popular ballads and then there was a pause while the musicians refreshed themselves.

'The dancing should begin again in a moment,' Rosaleen said. 'Oh, here's Daddy.' Her eyes focused across Gavin's shoulder and he swung round as Stead McHale came up.

'Welcome home, my boy,' breezed the lawyer, seizing his hand and pumping it. He was a tall and lean man with a prominent nose giving him a Mediterranean appearance. It was obvious where Rosaleen drew her raven hair from, although she had her mother's pale eyes, for Stead McHale had dark restive orbs that went with his swarthy skin. He could easily have been a Spanish Don. The story had it, and it seemed that McHale had been instrumental in helping it to spread, that his grandfather had served in the Hibernia Regiment of the Irish Brigade of the Royal Spanish Army when Colonel Arturo O'Neill attacked the English at Pensacola in support of the American rebels. It was part of the story that Grandfather McHale had married a Spanish *senorita* of wealth and prominence while the regiment was campaigning in Florida and that the Spanish influence had found paramountcy in the family features.

'Your father told me that you had been wounded, Gavin. Nothing serious, I trust?'

Gavin shrugged awkwardly. 'I took a ball in my shoulder, sir, but it is healing well enough now.'

'Excellent! Excellent!' enthused McHale. 'When will we see you at the house? Mrs McHale and I are looking forward to a long talk about your experiences. The nation owes a great debt to boys like you, Gavin. A great debt. Yes, surely it does.' McHale caught his daughter's glance and turned back with a chuckle. 'I am reminded that we have the future to discuss as well as the past.'

Gavin felt embarrassed and licked his lips nervously. All he could do was say, 'Yes, sir.'

'Splendid. But that's men's talk and I doubt if this is a good time or place. Why not come and see me one lunch time at my club? I always lunch there. . . . The Athenaeum on Madison Avenue. Come along one day next week. We'll talk things over then.'

'Yes sir,' Gavin responded.

McHale nodded and smiled. 'Now you two young people enjoy yourselves. I must look around for Mrs McHale. I've deserted her long enough.' The lawyer waved expansively and pushed away like a tall ship sailing through rough waters.

Rosaleen was tugging at Gavin's arm in annoyance. 'Come on, Gavin, before the music finishes.'

Gavin, aware that the orchestra was playing a waltz, took her carefully in his arms. 'It's years since I tried to dance a waltz,' he said nervously.

'It's easy, you'll not forget,' she smiled back.

Gavin counted silently as they moved cautiously into the whirling dancers. One, two, three, one, two, three, dip, swing, three; turn, two, three, again, two, three. The rhythm came almost naturally back to him and soon he caught himself drifting to the melody. The dance eventually ended and Gavin led her back to the edge of the floor, obtained two glasses of champagne from a passing waiter and guided her out on to the verandah. The night air was warm, the temperature hardly different to that inside. There was an empty wicker chair near the balustrade and Rosaleen flopped into it, reaching up an eager hand for the champagne glass whose contents she proceeded to swallow in almost eager gulps.

'I need this,' she sighed and then, catching his eye, added, 'you look disapproving.'

Gavin shrugged. 'It's best to sip champagne. It's potent stuff, Rosie.'

She chuckled gaily. 'It's not the first drink I've had this evening.'

He realized it must be true. Not that she was drunk but she was certainly high spirited and the alcohol seemed to enhance her skittish mood.

'When are you going to see Daddy?' she demanded.

'He asked me to go next week but there is plenty of time.'

'Time?' she sighed impatiently. 'Since you've returned, Gavin, all I've heard you say is there is plenty of time. Of course there isn't. Don't you know how long it takes to organize a wedding? There's so much to do. The house, the ceremony, invitation lists . . . why it will take months.'

'Months?' Gavin felt a panic.

'Daddy is determined that it will be the grandest wedding this old city has ever seen. And there'll be a honeymoon in Niagara . . . that's my idea. They say the Falls at Niagara are the grandest thing and quite the vogue for honeymooners.'

Gavin felt the irritation growing. 'Do I have a say in all this?' He sounded bitter but he could not disguise his voice. For four years the army had told him what to do and where to go. He thought it would be different when he returned to being a civilian. Now he was being told again. Rosaleen did not appear to notice the sharp tone in his voice. Perhaps the champagne had deadened her senses.

'Of course you do, Gavin. But I knew you would have no objections and Daddy says he can afford it. After all, he wants to please me.'

There was a cough at Gavin's elbow. He turned to find a fair-haired man in a major's uniform standing by.

'My dance, Miss McHale. Had you forgotten?'

Rosaleen came to her feet with a laugh. 'Why Major Kincaid. I'm truly sorry. I think I did forget. Gavin, please excuse me. I promised this dance to Major Kincaid.'

Kincaid smirked. 'The privilege of rank, captain,' he said as he led Rosaleen back into the ballroom.

Biting his lip, Gavin sat down on the stone parapet, one leg swinging as an expression of his annoyance. He was confused. He wanted time to think, to reflect. Why did everyone insist on pushing him into what they wanted him to do. John-Joe; his father; Rosaleen and Stead McHale. They were all making his mind up for him, giving him no opportunity to make his own decisions. He was still brooding about it when Rosaleen came tripping back.

'Gavin, have you forgiven me?' She bent towards him and her lips brushed his forehead.

'There's nothing to forgive,' he said, trying to sound indifferent.

'Oh, I think so. You see, while I was waiting for you I had to promise a few of the more insistent beaus that I would reserve some dances for them.' She took out her dance book and waved it like a totem.

He frowned. He had thought she meant something else. 'That's hardly . . .' he paused and picked up one of her favourite words, 'hardly proper.'

She flushed slightly. 'Soon we'll be married and then I won't be able to go dancing at all,' she replied. 'Don't be petty about it. I've reserved some dances for you.' She suddenly waved at a young man who was approaching them purposefully. 'I must go. The third dance after this one. Remember, Gavin.'

He watched her move off with exasperation. Angrily he signalled to a waiter for another drink, this time taking a straight whiskey. He wished he could understand his confusion. A year ago he had been sure of what he wanted. Marriage with Rosaleen and a practice in law. But that had been before the nightmares started; the grim nightmares about the dead and dying. The nightmares which brought a thousand unanswerable questions into his brooding thoughts. He wanted people to leave him alone for a while, just a while in which he could catch his breath, think and come to his own decisions. He set down his empty glass. He should forget the nightmares. He had to forget them. If only he did not have the feeling he was being oppressed by a conspiracy of others to govern his life for him.

He rose and went to stand at the doors of the ballroom, watching the swirling mass beyond. John-Joe was dancing with some pretty girl who was blushing and giggling furiously as he whirled her around the floor. Gavin found a frown of annoyance coming to his face. John-Joe was so young, too full of youthful idealism and enthusiasm. Idealism should be born of reason and reflection. John-Joe's was the mawkish romanticism created by his father's tales of old Ireland and the failures turned glorious by the maudlin reminiscences of those who had tried to justify their failure.

Rosaleen came swirling into his vision, dancing with her youthful partner, her laughing face flung back to gaze at him as if fully absorbed in his attentions. Resentfully, Gavin turned from the lines of spectators. He was not going to draw attention to himself by letting people see him watching Rosaleen McHale dance with every man at the ball.

Chapter 5

'The bishop has given me new marching orders,' Father MacMahon was telling Manus and Aideen Devlin as Gavin joined his parents in a corner of the ballroom. 'He wants me to become priest of a parish called Anderson in Madison County, Indiana. He's given me a year to settle all my affairs in the city and move there. I suspect that he hopes to bury me away where I can't embarrass the Church by my political activities.'

Father MacMahon noticed that Gavin had joined them and gave him a searching glance. 'Have you torn yourself away from Rosaleen already, Gavin?' he asked ingenuously. 'There's nothing wrong, I trust?'

Gavin coloured slightly. 'Nothing's wrong,' he said, annoyed at this attention.

Manus Devlin had spotted Rosaleen across the floor, giggling with the young man as they stepped through a polka.

'In my young days one's fiancée did not dance with other men,' growled Manus.

Father MacMahon saw Gavin's expression darken and said hurriedly, 'Well, times change, Manus. Indeed they do. And wouldn't it be a sad world if they didn't?'

'Anyway,' Gavin muttered, 'we are not engaged yet.'

Manus Devlin was about to say something else when the orchestra abruptly stopped and the master-of-ceremonies, whom Gavin did not know but was apparently some local merchant who was chairman of the organizing committee for the celebration, climbed on to the platform and called for quiet.

'*Céad míle fáilte!* A hundred thousand welcomes, ladies and gentlemen. Tonight is a celebration. It is a threefold celebration. Firstly, we celebrate the victory of our armies and rejoice in the unity of these United States of ours.' Loud cheers and enthusiastic applauses greeted him.

'Secondly, we celebrate the Fourth of July, the anniversary when the United States became free from the yoke of England!' The cheering was redoubled.

'Thirdly, we celebrate the return of our boys . . . the return of the Irish Brigade!' The applause was wild with whistling, stomping and cheering. When it died away, the perspiring man nervously fingered his collar as if it were too tight and raised a hand as if to bestow a priestly blessing.

'But, my friends, we must not forget, as we celebrate, why Thomas Meagher formed the Irish Brigade at the commencement of this war. Tom Meagher formed the Brigade to defend the unity of this mighty republic. That was his immediate objective. In recruiting for the Irish Brigade he pointed out that this republic was the mainstay of human freedom the world over. It has given to our people an asylum and a chance to live freely in honour, pursuing the professions denied to us in our motherland. When this republic became threatened with disruption, it was Tom Meagher who said it was the duty of every liberty-loving Irish man and woman to prevent such a calamity at all hazards. Above all, Tom Meagher said, it was the duty of all Irish citizens of this republic, especially those who aspire to establish a similar form of government in our motherland, to join up and defend these United States of America. It was a duty not just to the United States but to Ireland as well. Irish men and women could not hope to succeed in their effort to make Ireland a free country, an independent republic, without the moral and material aid of the liberty-loving citizens of these United States. But that aid would not be forthcoming if the United States could not preserve her institutions of liberty from destruction. The immediate aim was to preserve the union!'

The master of ceremonies paused, carried away by the paraphrased eloquence of Meagher's words.

'My friends, the Irish people answered the call. The union is preserved and the Irish Brigade have distinguished themselves. Now there is a greater task facing the Irish people, the main task for which Meagher sought to prepare us . . . that task is the liberty of the motherland!'

From a low growl, rising to a deafening cheer, the applause rose on all sides. Waving his hands in the excitement the master of ceremonies' voice rose above the frenzied clapping, 'Yes, there is unfinished business for the Irish Brigade. . . .' He managed to get no farther and had to wait until the cheering died away again before continuing. 'General Meagher is unable to be with us tonight. I can tell you that President Johnson has invited him to become the governor of Montana Territory. . . .'

More cheers and cries of: 'Hurrah for Meagher! Hurrah for Meagher of the Sword.'

Meagher of the Sword! It was the name which Meagher had earned as a leader of the Young Ireland uprising when he told the people of Ireland that 'the enemy we have to deal with can understand no arguments from you but the point of swords'. Condemned to death and then having his sentenced commuted to transportation for life, Meagher had made an amazing escape from the penal colony in Tasmania, arriving in New York in 1852. Meagher of the Sword, the dashing personification of the legendary *Fianna*.

'In the place of General Meagher tonight we have a man who you all know,' went on the master-of-ceremonies. 'He is a man in whom the destiny of our poor motherland now rests. . . .' The man paused tantalizingly. A tall, slightly stooping figure in the uniform of a Union Army colonel moved on to the platform as the master-of-ceremonies shouted, 'Colonel John O'Mahoney!'

As if on cue, the orchestra swung into a wild chorus of 'The wearing of the green!'

Gavin stared with interest in spite of his proclaimed indifference to the Brotherhood. Everyone in the Irish community knew of John O'Mahoney, the undisputed leader of the Irish Republican Brotherhood in America. Like many of the leaders who had escaped the aftermath of the Young Ireland uprising, O'Mahoney had initially fled to Paris before settling in New York. He was from Limerick, scarcely fifty years old now but still with jet black hair, a broad, high forehead and piercing dark eyes, though with a slight cast in his left one. He was clothed in the shabbiest of uniforms and he looked more like a scholar than a soldier. The truth was, he was a scholar, a graduate of Trinity College, Dublin, a classicist who had published just before the war a translation of Seathrún Céitinn's mammoth history of Ireland *Foras Feasa ar Eirinn*, the first popular history of the Irish completed in 1634. It had been O'Mahoney who had reminded members of the Irish Republican Brotherhood, which he had helped to form in 1857, 'to make Ireland an independent democratic republic', of the *Fianna*, the legendary warriors of Ireland. The members of the Brotherhood eagerly adopted the title, becoming Fenians.

O'Mahoney stood head slightly bowed, his dark eyes staring

around the ballroom, waiting quietly while the patriotic chorus died away.

'Friends,' he spoke so quietly that most people began to strain forward to listen. 'I do not mean to interrupt the festivities of the evening more than I can. I wish you to enjoy this evening.' He paused and allowed a small spatter of applause to punctuate his message.

'As the chairman of these proceedings has said, my friends, the Irish Brigade has been disbanded from the Union Army having covered itself in glory. It has been disbanded from the Union Army but not from the Irish Army of Liberty. There is unfinished business for it to conduct.' He paused again and stroked his nose as if seeking to collect his thoughts.

'There is little for me to add except that the time is coming when we shall act, when Ireland will once more take its place among the nations of the world. To achieve that aim, the Brotherhood needs money. I make an appeal to every true-hearted Irish man and woman here tonight, indeed, to every lover of liberty whatever their nationality. Ireland needs your support. Members of the Brotherhood will be moving among you to make collections. Please donate as generously as you can. That is all I have to say.'

The applause was rather puzzled, perhaps a little disappointed. Many had been expecting O'Mahoney to deliver some more stirring appeal.

Then the master-of-ceremonies was back again, mopping at his brow with a large kerchief.

'Before we carry on with the dancing, I have another speaker to introduce to you. He is a man known to many of you. Ladies and gentlemen, New York's own William Randall Roberts.'

The applause was polite now, restrained, as a short statured man with a dark spade-shaped beard and neatly brushed dark hair made his way to the edge of the platform. He was in his mid-thirties and he wore the uniform of a colonel of militia, a brevet rank bestowed on him for organizing the New York militia during the war. Whereas O'Mahoney's uniform had been threadbare and hung uneasily on his lanky form, Roberts was well turned out with glittering braid and polished boots and bright red sash. He carried himself with a sharp decisive manner. He was originally from Mitchelstown, in County Cork, and had come to New York when he was nineteen years old. It was said that his store on the Bowery had already made him a millionaire. Gavin had seen him once or twice before because Manus

Devlin served on the committee of the Knights of St Patrick of which patriotic society Roberts was president. In the last year or two, Roberts had become known as one of the more pugnacious spokesmen of the Irish Republican Brotherhood.

'I do not wish to prolong these speeches,' Roberts began, his voice slightly hectoring. 'But in supporting John O'Mahoney in asking for a collection to support the cause of Irish liberty, I think you should know what the principles of the Irish Republican Brotherhood are. . . .'

Gavin gave an inward groan. He had heard it so many times before.

A voice cried: 'To free Ireland! That's the only principle, isn't it?'

Roberts stood, hands on hips, nodding his head and smiling. 'Indeed, my friends. But I must say something further. It has been the misfortune of our people that our conquerors have transmitted to the world nearly all that the world knows of our history and character. We are the victims of a relentless and long-continued persecution. We have been represented by our rulers in a light best calculated to subserve their own interests and to screen the immorality of their usurped authority over our people who, though cut down by armed force, trodden underfoot by an unscrupulous imperial power, have never ceased to struggle for their rights, have never for an instant surrendered their claim to that independence which is the true life of a nation, as slavery, whether voluntary or accepted, is its virtual death.'

Gavin looked towards the door of the Supper Room, then hesitated. Everyone was watching Roberts expectantly and he realized it would be bad manners if he left his father's side in the middle of such a speech. He turned back with a resigned air feeling that he had heard too many great patriotic speeches from Fenians to be moved by them.

'Irish history has been falsified. Our attempts to free ourselves have been deliberately misconstrued. Our motives and sentiments have been misrepresented by the agents of our conquerors who profit from our misery and enslavement. Large proportions of our fellow men have come to view us through this distorted medium and have come to regard us as a people not only incapable of self-government but actually unfit to be entrusted with the management of our own affairs. To remove this erroneous notion and to stop the continued falsifications about us, the Irish Republican Brotherhood was formed to represent the aspiration of freedom for the people of Ireland.'

Roberts paused. There was a stillness in the hall which had not been present before. This was a reaction to Roberts with which all the applause for O'Mahoney and the patriotic singing could not compare. Even Gavin felt the power of Roberts's personality, vibrant and exhorting, as he used words like a virtuoso coaxing music from an instrument.

'We, in the Brotherhood, believe and declare that freedom – which is the right to life, liberty and the pursuit of happiness – is inherent in every creature. However individuals, by crime or violation of the laws passed for the well-being of society, may forfeit any portion of these rights, the enslavement of a homogeneous people, either by a foreign power or domestic tyranny, cannot, under any circumstances, be justified. The God of Nature placed between the English and the Irish nations not only the distinction of national character but also natural barriers which have written on imperishable record the claim of our people to an independent national existence.

'Not one generation of our people, the people of Ireland, have voluntarily agreed to surrender their rights as free men and women. They have never ceased to protest and struggle against the plunder of their national rights. From age to age, the legacy of patriotic effort has been transmitted from sire to son, from mother to daughter. The battlefield, the dungeon and the scaffold have proved the fidelity with which the sacred trust has been discharged.'

Roberts paused again, apparently gauging the feeling of his audience. The atmosphere was electric. Roberts stood knowing that he had them in his hands, animating them with the desires that fired his own being, transmitting those fires through the music of his voice.

'The Irish Republican Brotherhood has been organized to demand, aye, and to achieve, what so many of our people have attempted before – the liberation of our people from the domination of England. We demand it in the name of every man and woman of Irish origin throughout the world, without distinction of creed or class or political ideology. We claim the land of our fathers and mothers for the benefit of the people whose birthright it is, who love it with a filial affection and who have earned it in the sweat of their brows. Theirs is the right to live upon it, possess it and enjoy it!'

The applause resounded in such strength, with such fervour, that Gavin felt the building vibrating to its wild thunder. Roberts stood, nodding at the effect of his oratory, letting the applause roll around him.

'We seek injury to no man or woman. Our quarrel is with the

government of the nation which has robbed us of our liberty, which has murdered our people for the glorification of their empire and which has sustained its presence in our poor country by tyranny and usurpation. If, in our onward march to liberty, any such oppose us arrayed under the flag of our oppressors, which has been the symbol of slavery in Ireland and is the ensign of the enemy of liberty in many lands across the face of this earth, on their heads, not ours, be the consequence. We ask only for justice for our people. We ask for the vindication of that principle which requires that no alien power shall rule a people by right of conquest. We demand that the alien power which governs us shall no longer be permitted, undisturbed, to devour our substance while those who produce it by their toil wither and pine in bondage which at once destroys their bodies and debases their souls.

'Our watchword is – Ireland free! Ireland a republic! And when we have liberated our people, when Ireland's free will and action are untrammelled and unquestioned, for the freedom and elevation and the happiness of humanity across the world shall we stand. We seek freedom and the Rights of Man for all peoples; we abhor faction and sectionalism which has been deliberately fostered among our people by our conquerors. We make no reservation, we tolerate no distinction that would divide the people of Ireland. Our cause is not only the cause of a nation striving for its independence, it is the effort of enslaved humanity to emancipate itself from the thraldom and debasement of feudal tyranny.

'The elevation of a downtrodden people is a benefit conferred on the whole family of nations and of none might this be said more truly than of Ireland. From her position and resources, Ireland – once free – is capable not only of rendering her own population happy and prosperous but of defusing, by example and influence, the spirit of independence throughout the world, wherever her scattered children are to be found. For the sake of common humanity, then, the advancement of which we seek is an ideal to be supported. We ask for the good wishes of all liberty-loving people and the active aid of Ireland's children and, most especially, the aid and influence of this great American republic which the children of Ireland have helped to form. The Irish Republican Brotherhood now commits itself to the great struggle – the liberty of the Irish people!'

Roberts turned abruptly and strode rapidly from the platform before the audience realized he had finished. There was but a second's pause and then the cheering and thunder of applause erupted once again. The orchestra attempted to strike up another chorus of 'The wearing of the green' but it was drowned by the enthusiasm of the people. Some were so moved by Roberts's oratory that they paused to wipe their eyes. Gavin had found himself momentarily under Roberts's hypnotic spell. Of course, what Roberts said was right, was moral and just. No nation should be ruled by another by right of conquest. But that was the problem of the Irish people. He was an American now. He had no right to fight Ireland's battles. Even so . . . he almost wished he could share his brother's idealistic enthusiasm. It was some time before the master-of-ceremonies could restore order and the orchestra was able to play a quiet waltz to restore calm to the ardour of the people.

'A grand speech, wasn't it?' cried Father MacMahon turning to catch Manus Devlin by the arm with a squeeze of delight.

'It takes more than speeches to make a revolution,' commented a man standing close to Manus Devlin. They turned to stare at the stranger, a lieutenant-colonel in his early thirties, who was standing in the company of an attractive young woman. The lieutenant-colonel was a thickset man with powerfully built, rather broad shoulders. He had hard but pleasant features, tousled fair hair, a thick moustache under which sharp white teeth glinted in a humorous grin and its mocking humour was mirrored in his grey eyes. He was undoubtedly handsome although his skin was slightly swarthy and the overall impression Gavin had was that the man would not appear out of place in the costume of a buccaneer or an old-fashioned pirate.

Manus Devlin scowled at him. 'I do not have the pleasure of your acquaintance, sir, but Colonel Roberts is well known to me. He has made an excellent oration and means every word he utters.'

'Yet it will take more than sound and fury to free Ireland, sir,' replied the officer unabashed.

Manus Devlin's face reddened and he opened his mouth, his eyes growing fiery. He hesitated as if searching for the right words.

'Colonel Roberts is a man to back words with action. By indicating that you believe the contrary you insult a worthy man. An apology is called for.'

The colonel's humorous smile broadened although the lady who accompanied him looked worried and laid a restraining hand on his arm. 'You are too sensitive, sir,' he said evenly.

Manus Devlin ground his teeth and took a step forward but Gavin caught his father by the arm. It was then that Colonel Roberts pushed himself, smiling, into their circle.

'Steady, Manus,' he said. 'Thank you for a spirited defence but you must forgive my friend, John. He's been too long at war to appreciate the art of oratory.'

To their astonishment he laid a friendly hand on the young colonel's arm and shook his head in mild rebuke.

Manus stared from Roberts to the lieutenant-colonel and coloured. 'I didn't think this officer could be acquainted with you, William,' he muttered. 'From what he said. . . .' Manus' voice trailed off.

Roberts turned, still smiling and greeted the company, bending low over Aideen Devlin's hand, nodding to Father MacMahon and shaking Gavin's hand.

'Now allow me to introduce Colonel John O'Neill, late of the 7th Michigan Cavalry. And this lovely lady,' bowing slightly to the woman accompanying the young colonel, 'is Mrs Mary O'Neill. They are staying with me for a week or two while they visit New York.'

Aideen Devlin smiled at Mrs O'Neill. 'Have you come far?'

'From Nashville, Tennessee.'

Manus shook hands stiffly with O'Neill. 'I had no idea that you were acquainted with Colonel Roberts,' he said gruffly. 'I should have taken your remarks less seriously, colonel.'

'Oh,' O'Neill grinned wickedly, the piratical gleam in his eye, 'but they are meant seriously, doctor. I have heard some very fine speeches from all manner of patriots in my time but that is all. Talk and more talk.'

'Action cannot take place before organization, John, as I have already explained,' Roberts said with a rueful shake of his head.

'Certainly,' O'Neill replied with a cynical smile. 'O'Mahoney has been organizing the Brotherhood in America since '57. Last January, so it was reported, a great convention was held with 348 delegates representing Fenian circles or branches. It was claimed that the Union Army alone contained 14,000 Fenians paying their dollar on enrolment and ten cents a week subscription. And I've heard that the Reb army had as many in its ranks. A Fenian Sisterhood has been launched. O'Mahoney promises support to the revolutionaries in Ireland – support in men, arms and money. In Ireland we are told that the Fenian movement has also been organized and grown considerably and that it is led by a mysterious personality known to the people as *An Seabhac Siúlach* – the Wandering Hawk – who will soon appear with a mighty army to throw the English out of Ireland. This person, if he exists, has reached mythological propensities in the minds of our people. So far it is all talk. When there is action, then I shall join the Brotherhood.'

Mrs O'Neill, blushing slightly in embarrassment, whispered: 'Do not excite yourself, John.'

Manus Devlin, his face crimson, snorted indignantly. 'I trust your stay with Colonel Roberts will persuade you to the view that there can be no action without thorough organization, young man.' He glanced round and his eyes met Aideen Devlin's. He hesitated and then said gruffly, 'If you will excuse my wife and myself, it is time for us to repair to the Supper Room.'

With a jerk of his head, he held out his arm for Aideen Devlin to take and they moved off.

O'Neill sighed and glanced at Gavin. 'Your father takes these things seriously, captain.'

'So far as politics and Ireland are concerned, he does,' agreed Gavin.

'Manus is a good man, John,' Roberts said. 'My father knew him in Cork in the old days. He was with him at the fight at Ballingarry in '48. You should respect his opinions.'

O'Neill nodded. 'A man has a right to his opinions. But that's an argument that works both ways.' He winced slightly and Mrs O'Neill looked anxious.

'Is it the wound, John? does it trouble you?'

O'Neill gathered himself together and looked discomfited. He forced a pained smile to his lips. 'It is nothing. But perhaps we should take a turn on the verandah, Mary. Excuse us, gentlemen.'

He inclined his head to the company and walked away with his wife supporting him slightly.

'O'Neill was wounded at Nashville last December,' Roberts explained, filling the silent curiosity. 'He served in Scholfield's Corps. They lost 4,000 men in the taking of Nashville.'

Father MacMahon was watching the O'Neills' exit. 'They certainly make a handsome couple.'

Roberts smiled curiously at the priest. 'Mrs O'Neill was a Sister of Mercy.'

Father MacMahon raised an eyebrow. 'When O'Neill was badly wounded at Nashville, Mrs O'Neill was a Sister of Mercy in the hospital where he was taken. She was his nurse. A few months ago she renounced her vows and married him,' explained Roberts.

'I still say they are a handsome couple,' Father MacMahon responded.

Gavin thought he detected a hidden rebuke in the words.

'He seems very self-opinionated,' interposed Gavin. 'Usually men who urge belligerent action do not know much of war.'

Roberts shook his head. 'That's not true in John's case. He was in the army long before the war started. He fought in the Mormon War in Utah and, I believe, in some Indian campaigns. The 7th Michigan were fighting Morgan's Raiders and he gave a good account of himself there. O'Neill's a fine soldier. If the rhetoric of the Brotherhood is to succeed then it needs to be backed with young men like O'Neill.'

'O'Neill is originally an Ulsterman, if I hear his accent right,' Father MacMahon observed.

'From Monaghan, the same county as yourself, Father. Where else should an O'Neill be from?' grinned Roberts, referring to the fact that the ancient clan lands of the O'Neills had always been in Ulster.

'You appear to think he has a point, though?' pressed Father MacMahon.

'In saying that the Brotherhood is long on rhetoric and short on action?' queried Roberts. 'Well, let me put it this way. O'Mahoney, our president, is an ascetic. A scholar. There is nothing wrong in that except that I don't trust ascetics in politics. Do you know that O'Mahoney lives in near poverty in this city, determined to sacrifice everything for the cause? He declines to receive any assistance from the Brotherhood's funds in any shape or form. He seems to care nothing for personal success and position in life.'

Father MacMahon smiled gently. 'I seem to recall our Lord followed a similar course,' he rebuked.

'You think it is more to his credit than discredit?' asked Roberts.

'I know O'Mahoney to be a man totally absorbed with the idea of insurrection in Ireland and with freeing the people of Ireland.'

Roberts made a dismissive gesture. 'He is also a man who lacks judgment, Father. He will part with his last cent to anyone who approaches him with a woeful tale. Surely, I will grant you, that he is a dreamer of lofty idealism. He's a combination of seer and ancient Celtic chieftain. But he lacks judgment of men and loves flattery. He surrounds himself with an imbecile pack who are no use whatever to our cause and who will betray him when he can no longer serve their interests. Yes, O'Mahoney is simply a good natured soul who loves listening to flattering tales of himself; to tales of the chieftains of old without taking a single lesson from their misfortunes and ultimate extinction. He's about as qualified to lead the Irish revolution as Lamartine was to lead the French one.'

Father MacMahon smiled encouragingly. 'And you have some ideas how the leadership of the Brotherhood should be changed?'

Roberts nodded immediately. 'When it comes to revolution, Father, it needs a pragmatist, a practical man and one with good business sense.'

'In short, Colonel Roberts,' Father MacMahon's voice held a subtle note of irony, 'someone like yourself?'

Roberts was not offended at his tone. 'In short, Father,' he replied evenly, 'someone who will be elected to govern the Brotherhood democratically, with a democratic cabinet to advise him. O'Mahoney formed this movement but since then he has led it by self-appointment only. It is time to change the constitution of the Brotherhood.'

'Well, you will be able to test your judgment at the next convention where I suppose you will put such proposals to the vote?'

'Indeed, I will,' replied Roberts vigorously.

Gavin had followed the exchange with interest but felt like an outsider eavesdropping on matters that interested but did not concern him.

'Gavin! I've been hunting all over for you!'

He turned, somewhat guiltily, as Rosaleen came gliding up with a frown on her pert features. She glanced with a sudden smile at Father MacMahon and Colonel Roberts. 'Forgive us, gentlemen, Gavin promised me this dance.'

She grabbed his arm and he followed her obediently on to the floor.

'The next three dances are reserved for you,' she smiled brightly as they swirled away in time to a waltz. They didn't talk much, giving themselves over to enjoying the dance. And when the orchestra finished the waltz it moved straight on to a reel which prevented any conversation because of the constant partner changes. The third dance was a polka which also precluded conversation and when Gavin was finally about to suggest some supper another young officer came up to claim the waltz which followed.

Chapter 6

Gavin made his way to the Supper Room and ate sparingly of the buffet but was more liberal with the champagne. He found a few former comrades from the Brigade who had discovered a card game and insisted that he accompany them. The game was being held on an upper floor in someone's suite. It seemed to belong to a colonel from some cavalry regiment who was stretched drunk and oblivious on his bed. The table was stacked high with army back pay and empty bottles of whiskey as, with shouting and laughter, the cards were shuffled. There were four men at the table but a dozen others crowded around waiting for their turn to take a hand. There were a number of giggling women in the room who were obviously not official guests but who had been smuggled in from the more unsalubrious taverns in the neighbourhood south of Broadway. Gavin took a hand, won it and withdrew immediately to the shouts and catcalls of his companions. A buxom woman lurched towards him, her hot breath against his ear whispering a proposition. He shook his head with a smile whereupon her bad imitation of a refined accent was displaced by a vocabulary that a Bowery costermonger would have found difficult to improve upon.

Increasingly bored and irritated by the evening, Gavin returned to the ballroom. Manus and Aideen Devlin had already left, although John-Joe was still dancing. Gavin presumed that his brother had changed his partner but all the young girls looked the same to him. He found Rosaleen just as she was leaving the floor.

'Shall I escort you home, Rosie?' he asked.

'It's much too early,' she protested. 'Anyway, Daddy is on the organizing committee and feels that it is his and Mummy's duty to stay until the end.'

'I am tired,' he sighed. 'I'm going home.'

'I will go home with my parents anyway,' she replied in an offhand fashion. 'Besides, I'm booked for the next two dances. Are you sure that you won't stay for a dance later?'

He shook his head, feeling guilty at the pouting of her lips.

She reached forward and touched him lightly on the arm. 'I hope you'll pass through this grouchy mood, Gavin. The war's over. It's time to have some fun.' She hesitated. 'Will you call by tomorrow afternoon? For tea. We can discuss what you are going to say to Daddy.'

Before he had time to answer, she had swung to wave at someone across the ballroom floor and, with a brief smile in his direction, had flounced away. Gavin ground his teeth and then gave a mental shrug. Perhaps it was just as well. He would not have been able to check the irritation at her assumption that he would seek her approval of what he was to say to Stead McHale. He felt tired; not just with the lateness of the hour but generally; tired with his apparent inability to control his own life, to stop events and other people controlling him. He shook his head. Tomorrow. He would sort things out tomorrow. It was too late to think now. The girls, he noticed, had become quieter, their faces had grown livid, their breathing was heavy in the now stifling atmosphere of the ballroom which was induced by the smokey light as the candles on the chandeliers burnt down, flickered and died. His melancholia had become a depression. He found himself yearning for the quiet of the open fields, the calm of a bivouac by some gushing stream. He wanted air; fresh air and open spaces and not the enclosed oppression of the city.

He left the ballroom and made his way down the grand staircase to the foyer of the hotel. He asked for his sword and coat from the sleepy-eyed liveried attendant and walked to the entrance. He paused for a moment on the top step to draw a cheroot from his case, receiving a light from the uniformed doorman who wished him a 'Good morning, cap'n.' He glanced down Broadway. The sky was, indeed, paling and there was a movement in the street. A garbage cart eased its way down the centre of the road followed by a manure cart around which half-a-dozen men moved dutifully with shovels clearing the road. The task was usually performed twice daily in order to keep the streets of the city clean. Gavin exhaled deeply, shook his head when the doorman asked if he wanted a hackney, and decided he needed the long walk home. He craved the cool, crisp morning air to clear his head. He needed time to think.

'Spare a dime for a war veteran, cap'n?'

He noticed half a dozen beggars moving expectantly towards him.

He felt awkward and began to grope in his pocket for loose pennies. It was, however, the nerve-tingling screech of ungreased wheels and the rattle of wood on the sidewalk that made him glance up. One of the beggars was approaching closely, seated on a small wooden cart so low to the sidewalk that its means of propulsion was the hands of the hunched figure who sat on it. The reason for this method of transport was immediately obvious. The man had no legs; both seemed to have been severed above the knees. The screeching cart halted a yard or so away. From the light shining from the foyer of the hotel Gavin saw an outstretched arm encased in a frayed and tattered Union Army jacket. His eyes were fascinated by the dirty, grasping, claw-like hand that was thrust towards him.

'Spare a dime, cap'n?'

The voice was made monotone by the numerous times the beggar must have repeated the phrase but it still could not disguise the faint resonance of an Irish accent. There was something oddly familiar about the voice and the hunched figure. Gavin stared down into a gaunt face, dirty and unshaven. Pale, hunger-starved eyes stared back. Sweat stood on the man's brow in spite of the early morning chill, perhaps the product of the manual propulsion of the creaking wooden cart. The pale eyes seemed to stare through him.

'War veteran of the Irish Brigade, cap'n. Spare a dime?'

Some recognition was stirring within Gavin's mind. 'What regiment?' he demanded.

'Sixty-nineth New York,' came the reply promptly.

Memory came back. 'Quinlan! Sergeant Jack Quinlan!'

The pale eyes flickered uncertainly. 'That's me.' The voice was defensive.

'Quinlan! It's me – Captain Devlin . . . I mean, I was a lieutenant when. . . .' He paused awkwardly.

For a moment recognition came into the eyes and then faded again. 'Ah.' Then, 'Spare a dime, cap'n?'

Devlin bit his lip and glanced to the two awkward stumps. 'I'm sorry to see you like this, Quinlan.'

His memory stirred uneasily. Jack Quinlan. Sergeant Jack Quinlan. Cold Harbor, June '64. Was that really only a year ago? Quinlan was twenty-four years old then. A tall man with red hair and a deep baritone voice. He had been an excellent singer and a good dancer, leading off the jigs and reels at the regimental dances. Jack Quinlan. A bright young man; a bright future. Cold Harbor, June '64. The Irish Brigade had been thrown against the Reb artillery of General

Anderson; thrown across the bogs and swamps until they were forced back . . . or what was left of them. Some 10,000 Union soldiers dead and wounded left on the field. And Sergeant Jack Quinlan had led them into the darkness.

'Ready the flag!' His voice had been eager and full of youth. Vibrant with hope. The green banner had been borne bravely in his hands as he had moved forward shouting the rallying cry in that deep baritone voice of his.

'Ready the flag!'

'Spare a dime, cap'n?'

'Cold Harbor, wasn't it?' Gavin asked, gazing at the broken wreck before him. Quinlan should have been twenty-five years old now but his tightly stretched pale skin, his nervously moving adam's apple, jerking up and down in his scrawny neck, and general appearance made him seem old. He could have been sixty or seventy hunched there on his cart. There were deep shadows under his eyes that were not formed by the pale, eerie light of dawn but by dark blotches on his pale skin.

'Eh?'

'I was with the Brigade at Cold Harbor. That's where you lost your legs.'

The thin lips twisted and then straightened. 'Reckon I did, cap'n.'

'But you fought well. You served the Brigade well. You must have received something for your service?'

'Sure,' the voice was still a monotone. 'They give me a silver medal. I had to sell that about last Thanksgiving.'

'But a pension,' pressed Gavin. 'There must have been a pension . . . ?'

There came a rasping sound. It was meant to be a chuckle. 'Them folks up at regimental headquarters told me there were nearly 300,000 wounded veterans like me and where would the money come from? Pension!' Quinlan became suddenly animated for a moment, leaning forward and spitting on the pavement in his frustrated fury. 'How am I expected to keep a wife? Better I be dead, cap'n; better that than be like this. I'm no use to her. The kid . . . the kid died just before March. Better that a Reb shell had killed me so that she could make a new life than be tied to me crippled like this.'

As abruptly as the anger came, it vanished leaving the hunched beggar in an attitude of resignation. He made to turn away.

Gavin dug into his pocket and found a silver dollar. 'Take this, Quinlan.'

He thrust it into the man's top pocket. There was a muttering from the other beggars who had been watching the proceedings with a speculative eye. Gavin was sure that they had not seen the value of the coin he had given Quinlan and so he dug for a handful of pennies and sent them scattering across the sidewalk. While there was a scramble for them he leaned close to Quinlan.

'Where do you live?' he demanded. 'I'll see what I can do to help.'

The expressionless eyes turned to him. 'You'll find us down Bayard, back of the Bowery.'

The hunched figure turned the wooden cart with amazing dexterity, thrusting his hands against the sidewalk and moving rapidly away. Gavin stared at the receding shadow, listening to the squeak and thump of the wooden wheels until it faded away. In his mind there came a faint echo of the song that Mrs Keogh had struggled so valiantly to sing that evening.

> You haven't an arm and you haven't a leg
> Hurroo! Hurroo!
> You haven't an arm and you haven't a leg
> Hurroo! Hurroo!
> You haven't an arm and you haven't a leg
> You're an eyeless, noseless, chickenless egg;
> You'll have to be put with a bowl to beg.
> Och, Johnny, I hardly knew ye.

Gavin shuddered in the chill morning air and turned down Broadway.

Chapter 7

Gavin did not see John-Joe until the next evening when they were dressing to go down to dinner. He had wanted to speak about his brother's trip to Ireland but John-Joe had not been home until the evening when Gavin had returned from Rosaleen McHale's house. That visit had already put Gavin in an irritable mood. What should have been a pleasant afternoon had turned into a couple of hours of verbal fencing and growing frustration as Gavin found himself unable to articulate his anxiety over the future. He had left Rosaleen in an angry mood. As soon as he saw his brother he brought up the question of the Irish trip.

'It's all settled, Gavin,' John-Joe said defensively. 'There's nothing to talk about.'

'I think there is,' Gavin replied moodily. 'Don't you realize that you'll be going to a strange country? You will be a foreigner there.'

John-Joe chuckled. 'A foreigner in the land where I was born?'

'That's right. You were a baby when we left Ireland. It's not even as if we had any family or friends left there now.'

'I have friends,' snapped John-Joe. 'And the Brotherhood will be my family.'

'The Brotherhood!' Gavin ground his teeth, his own frustration and irritability causing him to vent his spleen on his brother. 'For God's sake, John-Joe, don't you realize that you are involved in something dangerous? It's all very well being romantic about revolutions. Pa can afford to sit here, a few thousand miles away from Ireland and preach about fighting for liberty. His dreams are enough to sustain him. But you . . . you're young, John-Joe. You've a life to live, not to throw away. You might be imprisoned or killed.'

John-Joe grew angry in turn. 'I've told you that I'm prepared for that. It would be a noble thing to die fighting for Irish freedom.'

'Noble?' Gavin sneered. 'There's nothing noble about death. And death might not come on a battlefield. It might come on some cold, grey morning on a foreign scaffold for a people who probably won't give a damn about you, even if they knew your name or why you were doing it.'

'You are wasting your breath, Gavin. I am leaving the day after tomorrow.'

Later that evening, still irritable and moody, Gavin found his father in the study. 'Won't you forbid John-Joe to go on this stupid trip to Ireland?' he demanded without preamble.

Manus Devlin stared at his eldest son in surprise, a faint flush coming to his cheeks. 'For what reason?' he demanded, his jaw thrusting out aggressively.

'Because it's wrong.'

'Is it wrong that John-Joe has volunteered to help fight for the liberation of his own people?'

'His own people? What does John-Joe know of Ireland and its people?'

'He knows what I have told him and, like you, he has grown up in an Irish family.' Manus Devlin reached for a cigar and toyed with it before lighting it. 'Gavin, what John-Joe is doing has given me more pride than anything either of you boys have done until now. My generation failed to free Ireland. It is up to the next generation. He has made me proud, fiercely proud, that I have sired a son who will take up where I left off. I honour him.'

His amber eyes burned with a strange fire as he stared at Gavin. 'Politics forced us here. English politics. And here I live in exile waiting for the day when the English are gone from Ireland so that I might return to die in the land in which I was born and raised. John-Joe is a credit to me, to his people.'

Gavin was stung by the rebuke from his father. 'How noble!' he sneered angrily. 'Sacrificing for his people, eh? A few streets from here are his people. I can show you them – starving and dying, living in squalid sickness and disease. Irish people for the most part. Is John-Joe fighting to free them?'

Manus Devlin banged his fist on the desk with a violence that startled Gavin. His father's face had become a mask of fury. He had never seen such vehemence before. Usually his arguments with his father were always controlled, quiet affairs in which there was merely verbal fencing without emotion, only suppressed belligerence.

'Yes, John-Joe will be fighting to free them,' Manus Devlin said. In spite of the fury in his face, his voice was forcibly controlled. 'You say that a few streets from here are Irish people living in sickness and poverty? You say that they are our people? I accept that, Gavin. But who put them there? Who forced them to migrate in their tens of thousands. Ireland is a beautiful little country. A score of years ago its population stood at eight million and it was producing enough food, wool and flax, to feed and clothe eighteen millions. Yet why do the Irish leave their little island, leave in such numbers to starve and die in foreign cities?' His voice was almost a hypnotic monotone. 'There is one culprit, Gavin, one never failing source of all the evils of Ireland and her people. That is its connection with England; the English conquest and English rule.'

Gavin shrugged indifferently.

It was always the same old story. The English. He had been hearing the story of the English conquest ever since he could remember. His whole life was coloured by the fact that he had been born Irish and the Irish had been conquered by the English. All the Irish were governed by laws made by the English far away in their own country. Not only that, but Gavin had been taught that he had been born an Irish Catholic and Irish Catholics were only just emerging from an easement of certain rules called the Penal Laws which took charge of every Irish Catholic from his cradle to his grave. Irish Catholic children could have no education. Irish Catholics were excluded from every profession, except the medical profession, and from all official positions without exception; Irish Catholics were forbidden to exercise trade or commerce in any corporate town; Irish Catholics were legally disqualified to hold leases of land for a longer tenure than thirty-one years and also disqualified from inheriting the lands of Protestant relations; Irish Catholic priests could not celebrate mass under severe penalties but any priest who recanted his beliefs secured a pension from the English Government; an Irish Catholic child could, while under age, convert to Protestantism and reduce his father to a tenant in his own home. All this Gavin had been taught. He had learnt that generation after generation the Irish people had risen up against the English overlords to free themselves only to be crushed. He had learnt that his great-grandfather had been hanged during the uprising of 1798 and his grandfather had served a prison sentence in the aftermath of the insurrection of 1803. His father, Manus Devlin, had grown up in a slightly more liberal society which saw the passing of the Catholic Emancipation Act in 1829. Manus had forsaken the republican ideology to which his family had adhered and began to follow the 'Liberator', Daniel O'Connell, who had secured Catholic Emancipation and was intent on securing a Repeal of the Union. But O'Connell had failed and Manus Devlin had returned to the revolutionary Young Ireland movement. Their failure became his failure. And now Manus Devlin was intent on passing on the torch to his sons. With Gavin he had failed but with John-Joe. . . .

'I am fed up hearing about Ireland and her suffering,' breathed Gavin. 'We are living in America now.'

Manus Devlin's eyes narrowed. 'If you don't respect my view of politics, son,' he said quietly, 'then hear me as a doctor. All my life I have been fighting disease and sickness. It has been my lot merely to treat the symptoms, to deal with the outward manifestations of the disease. At times, I would have gladly given everything I had if I could have found the cause, the root of the disease.'

'What has that to do with what we are talking about?' demanded Gavin, bewildered.

'Just this. Of course one could go out into the streets and help the poor, help the sick, help the people in their disease and poverty. But is that going to stop immigration? Is that going to halt the flood gates which expel Irish people in their thousands from their own country? That is dealing with symptoms. I applaud John-Joe because he is going to deal with the cause. Ireland free and independent, Ireland in control of its own destiny and wealth, Ireland nurturing its people . . . that will stop the disease and poverty.'

Gavin blinked. 'That's a dream,' he said, unwillingly impressed.

'Everything man has ever achieved has started as a dream,' smiled his father. 'John-Joe goes with my blessing and that of his mother. I hope he will go with your blessing as well, Gavin.'

The earth was wet, an icy, clinging mud in which he had lain for what seemed an eternity. It was cold and soft like the bodies of the dead among which he had taken shelter. Cold and soft and stinking with a sickly odour; an odour like old earth, stale and full of death. The sky above was black, not just black with the shadows of the night, but black with heavy, rolling clouds which obscured the stars and the moon. It was quiet. Deathly quiet. The only sound was the rising stertorous breathing of the men who lay in the icy mud with him; who crouched among the barren waste of leafless trees; who, unseen, peopled the formless, desolate landscape. Far down the eastern horizon a thin bar of grey light began to expand.

Far off a bugle sounded. Then it began. The end of the world. The rain of destruction. Before him the hills belched bright yellow and red flame and there came the loud explosion of cannon fire, cracking one after another and followed by the screaming of shells, the secondary explosions and all was chaos; an inferno from which there was no escape. Men screamed in pain and fear. Others tried to bury themselves in the mud, under the rotting corpses as if seeking their protection. Mud mingled with wet blood, sticky, clinging. Limbs, torn from the bodies of both dead and living, were flung in abandoned fashion across the field.

He crouched in a tight ball. An explosion near him showered him with mud and something wet and soft hit him against the side of the head. He reached out to wipe his face and felt the sticky lump of still warm flesh, which caused him to retch violently.

The cannonade went on . . . and on . . . and on, the sound ringing in his ears, exploding against his vibrating eardrums until he could no longer think, no longer hear. Yet he could hear; he could hear the screams and cries of the men around him. He began to shiver, not knowing whether it was from the icy coldness of the mud or from fear. The enemy cannonade continued to rake their lines and still no one gave the order to move, no one called for them to move forward nor to withdraw. Anything would be better than being shot to pieces. Anything to escape the fearful rain of death and destruction which poured over their huddled forms.

Then a bugle sounded. He found it odd that he could hear such a small thing as a bugle against the thunder and roar of the cannonade.

A voice called, 'Ready the flag!' A calm, resonant voice. A musical baritone of a voice.

'Ready the flag!'

They began scrambling through the mud in the half-night, the sharp thorns of bushes tearing at them like anxious hands. Bayonets glinted, swords flashed as the light of dawn edged over the distant horizon.

'Ready the flag!'

There came a crack as the wind took the silk battle emblem, lashing it on its pole like a stock whip. The cannonade continued, mowing men down in their hundreds as they stood waiting, like hounds waiting to be unleashed. The bugle sounded far off.

'Forward! Forward!'

Yelling incoherently, crying in relief, in desperation, in anger and in fear, they swept forward, moving line after line, rank after rank. The shadows of the enemy soldiers awaiting in the dark, rifles and bayonets at the ready, were better than the remorseless cannon shells which poured down on them.

'Ready the flag!'

Gavin woke up, his face bathed in sweat. His room was pale with the grey light of dawn filtering through the curtains. He reached up a hand to wipe his brow and turned to stare at the quiet outline of his brother sleeping on the far side of the room they shared.

'Ready the flag!' The voice had been that of Sergeant Jack Quinlan. He recalled it now. The deep baritone which had led so much of the entertainments in the camp. Poor Jack Quinlan. Gavin recalled the haunted eyes, the claw-like hand. 'Can you spare a dime?' 'Ready the flag!' He shuddered and turned over, trying to snatch back a few more moments of oblivion.

In the end Gavin went with his father down to Hoboken Pier to see John-Joe off on the first stage of his journey to Ireland. In spite of the differences in their character, in spite of the disagreements, there was a real affection between the brothers. Gavin felt protective and anxious. He still blamed John-Joe's romantic idealism on the careful fostering of his father. But Gavin was, deep within him, realistic enough to know that everyone had to live their lives as they saw fit. Wasn't that the very thing that he was demanding? His father, Rosaleen and Stead McHale were trying to shape his own life when he wanted to shape it for himself. How could he demand that right for himself while trying to impose his own ideas on his young brother? Everyone had to find and follow their own path.

The first stage of John-Joe's journey was in a coaster which would take him and his companions to Boston where they would embark on an ocean-going vessel for the city of Cork in southern Ireland. Aideen Devlin had made her own private farewell to her youngest son and refused to come down to the pierhead. It was left to Manus Devlin to keep up a light chatter about the sights and wonders which John-Joe would see in Ireland.

As Patsy-Mike turned the carriage down Canal Street to Hoboken Pier they heard the sounds of a band and then saw a small crowd of people waving the green banners and flags of the Brotherhood.

'It looks like it's going to be a fine send-off,' smiled Manus Devlin.

Gavin stared aghast. 'This is madness,' he breathed. 'Why doesn't O'Mahoney send the British a telegraph to let them know when you are arriving?'

John-Joe grinned. 'The English will never bother their heads about what we do in New York. They're far too complacent. Besides, this is just a show, an opportunity to wave the flag and collect money. When we really set off for Ireland it will be in disguise and in different ships.'

Gavin was not reassured. 'Why warn them at all? It's not a game that you're playing, John-Joe.'

Manus Devlin glanced with irritation at Gavin. 'John-Joe knows it.'

A group of men, mostly still clad in the uniform of the Union Army, stood self-consciously on the pierhead. The band was playing 'Garryowen' and the small crowd were waving and cheering. The carriage stopped and Gavin jumped out and took down John-Joe's valise. As his brother climbed out, followed by Manus Devlin, Father MacMahon came bustling up and began to make introductions. There were a couple of generals, two colonels and many of lesser rank. Gavin stared around, curious at the excitement and enthusiasm. Someone, Gavin was not sure whom, climbed on a box and made a stirring speech. He ground his teeth impatiently as he listened to the same dreams, the same accusations, the aspirations of love of country, of freedom, liberty, democracy and, when it was over, the band struck up again. A lady, dressed in a violent green taffetta, was handed up on to the wooden box. It was Mrs Keogh, looking older and paler in the sunlight. Her breath came in deep gasps as she strove to obtain her loudest resonance.

> Will you come to the bower o'er the free boundless ocean,
> Where stupendous waves move in thunderous motion;
> Where the mermaids are seen and the wild tempest gathers
> To love Erin the green, the dear land of our fathers,
> Will you come, will you, will you, will you come to the bower?

The emotion of the song was catching. The invitation to the Fenians of America to return to Ireland had become a popular rallying song during the last year. A stirring, evocative arousal of the soul of the exile. The people gathered on Hoboken Pier raised their voices to its promise and its commitment.

> Will you come and awake our dear land from its slumber
> And her fetters we will break links that long did encumber
> And the air will resound with hosannas to greet you,
> On the shore will be found gallant Irishmen to meet you,
> Will you come, will you, will you, will you come to the bower?

Gavin wondered how much John-Joe really believed in that invitation. He glanced at his young brother, singing with flushed face and eager eyes. Then the song was ended. John-Joe was gripping his hand, embracing him fiercely and was gone; gone down to the ship along with the others to the cheers and the thunderous strains of 'Garryowen'. Gavin waited in silence with Patsy-Mike while his father stood at the end of the pier, waving to the old coaster until it pulled out of sight down the river, weathering the headland to move towards the wild grey Atlantic before turning north to Boston.

Will you come and awake our dear land from its slumber?

They rode home to the house on Greenwich Lane in moody silence, each imprisoned in his own thoughts.

Chapter 8

It was after he had returned from Hoboken Pier that he was stirred by the memory of Jack Quinlan. He was immediately full of self-reproach for he had promised to visit the man and see what he could do to help him. Quinlan seemed to symbolize all that was wrong with New York, with its slums and poverty. That was why he felt guilty about him, why he wanted to help him. He dredged his memory for the address Quinlan had given him and hailed a hackney. 'Bayard, back of the Bowery.'

The driver cast a dubious eye at him. 'Sure you want to go down there, cap'n? Ain't really your sort of place.'

'Bayard is where I said,' confirmed Gavin, mentally reminding himself that it was high time he bought some civilian clothes now that he was officially out of the army. He had grown too used to wearing his uniform.

The cabby shrugged indifferently. 'It's all the same to me. Leastways, don't expect me to wait for you, cap'n. Not down there.'

'I pay you a dollar an hour or fifty cents a mile with seventy-five cents an hour waiting. It says so on your price board there. I can't see anything about you choosing where you want to go or where you will wait,' Gavin retorted.

'Jesus, captain,' protested the man. 'Have a heart. Bayard can be pretty bad trouble.'

'Let's get going,' Gavin said, ignoring the protest.

Bayard was an immigrant area, a small space crammed with tenement houses which huddled between warehouses and storage rooms. It was a short stretch of dingy buildings and broken cobblestones which could boast of no legitimate business whatsoever. There were more 'barrel houses' than tenement blocks where a man could get all the liquor he could drink for five cents and where the bordellos and gin mills did a thriving trade. From dawn to dusk the area slept off its debauches but from dusk until dawn the streets were crowded with all manner of people seeking diversion. In their turn these people were sought by a horde of hustlers, prostitutes, pick-pockets and thieves of varying description. Drunkards and brawlers went openly through the area with cudgels and knives. Among the darkened buildings a variety of sports were to be found from dog fights to the more popular rat hunts. A prize of as much as one hundred dollars would be offered for any dog who could kill sixty full-sized rats in five minutes. The cabby was right: Bayard could be pretty bad trouble.

Gavin relented and paid the nervous cabby off in the Bowery and walked down the street wondering how he could find exactly where Quinlan hung out. He turned into a tavern and pushed through the crowd to the bar. The accents were as diverse as the languages were numerous but the sour-faced barman seemed to have no trouble coping with the linguistic problem. A burly man was ordering drinks, '*Zwei Gläser Bier bitte. . . . Wir haben es eilig.*' 'Coming up, mister,' replied the barman pouring the beer and, at the same time, fending off an aggrieved Italian who was shouting. '*La prego di rispondermi quando la interrogo!*' 'Sure, mister,' the barman did not blink. 'But when I've finished with this other guy.' Adding to the bedlam of immigrant languages, a red-faced Irishman pushed his way up. '*Dia anseo isteach . . . pionta, más é do thoil é.*' Again the barman took it in his stride. 'Okay, Mick, but give me a minute.' Gavin leaned across the bar.

'Do you know where Jack Quinlan lives?'

The barman glanced up in the process of drawing the beer. 'Who?'

'Quinlan, a legless beggar in a wooden pushcart.'

The barman shrugged. 'Plenty of beggars, legless and otherwise, around here, captain.'

A hand tugged at his sleeve. It was the red-faced Irishman. '*An bhfuil Gaeilge agat?*'

Gavin could only guess at the question. 'No. Sorry, I don't speak Irish.'

'*Is cuma,*' the man shrugged. 'It does not matter. I have some English. Is it Quinlan that you seek?'

'Do you know where he lives?'

The man smiled and winked broadly. '*Tá tart orm. . . .* I have a thirst, captain.'

Gavin slipped a quarter into the man's hand and was shown to the door. The man pointed across the street.

'An teach mór; gabh ar dheis ansin . . . the big house, turn there *ar dheis . . . dheis* . . .' He made several gestures to the right.

Gavin nodded his thanks and began to move away as the Irishman turned back. He could hear him calling loudly, '*Ba mhaith liom gloine leanna anois!*' And heard the barman's imperturbable answer, 'Yeah, Mick, the beer's coming up now.'

The four-storeyed tenement to which he was directed was dark and dirty. Garbage spread across the sidewalk while the children scrambled happily among it watched by bare-legged, emaciated-looking women, who sat on the steps of the building chattering in shrill Italian.

Their conversation faltered as they watched him approach and they began to whisper to each other, giggling and nudging each other in a lewd manner. Beyond them the darkened lobby seemed threatening. It stank of unfamiliar cooking smells and the stench of urine. He paused while his eyes grew accustomed to the darkness and, in the gloom, he saw a stretch of darkened doors along a dingy corridor. He hesitated and turned back to the women on the steps.

'Where will I find Jack Quinlan?'

They stared up at him and then at each other. '*Che cosa dice lei?*' demanded a moon-faced woman, grinning.

Gavin shrugged and pressed again, 'Quinlan. Jack Quinlan. Does he live here?'

The moon-faced woman gestured indifferently. '*Che cosa le abbisogna?*'

One of her companions suddenly giggled. '*Ceenlanda, la Irlandese.*'

'*Ah,*' nodded the first woman. '*Ceenlanda. Chi va lei cercondo – Ceenlanda?*'

Gavin suddenly realized what she was saying, *Ceenlanda*. Quinlan. He nodded vigorously.

'*Si, si,*' the moon-faced woman was happy now. '*Signora Ceenlanda. Passi da questa parte. La porte che lei cerca è la prima a sinistra. Là.*'

Gavin looked helplessly at her. 'What?'

'*Ceenlanda!*' snapped the woman impatiently. '*Là! Là!*'

There was no mistaking the jabbing motion of her finger to the first door on the left of the hallway.

'Thank you,' he muttered.

'*Chi è?*'

He moved to the paint peeling door and knocked. A voice called out; a woman's voice. He decided it was an invitation to enter.

The room was small and just as squalid as the exterior of the tenement. There was a smell of burning wax from candles, mixed with the sour odour of boiled cabbage. There was another musty smell that he could not place. But in spite of the squalidness of the room it was kept fairly neat. There was a bed in a corner which, while the sheets were none too clean, judging from the area which was turned down, was tidy enough. In a corner a piece of string held up a threadbare curtain which covered a small wardrobe. Gavin caught sight of a blue army jacket and the golden chevrons of a sergeant's insignia. There was also a table in the room, a bare wooden table with three wooden chairs.

It was strange that the room should have had the first impact on him rather than its occupant, a slight figure which stood before the bed. The figure was so slight that it was almost a wraith without corporal existence. Only the voice drew his eyes towards it.

'Well, we don't get too many officers down here. Who recommended you, captain?'

He heard the note of false lasciviouness.

Gavin met the eyes first. They were deep blue and bright, almost violet in colour. He had never seen such eyes before; deep, captivating and yet strangely expressionless, almost as if they were dead. The face was attractive, no doubt of that. A small, delicately boned face with a high forehead, a tiny nose and rather thin lips, but attractive nevertheless. It was almost the face of a young girl; almost. Yet the pale, freckled skin was stretched too tightly and the harsh lines of experience showed deeply at the corners of the mouth and under the eyes. The hair was not quite red, a mass of ginger weaving strands of spun-gold within it. It fell to her shoulders around an enhancing white neck which was perhaps a little too long, a little too thin. The figure would in normal circumstances have been well proportioned, well developed, but there was a slightness about it that seemed to indicate a degree of emaciation. Hunger seemed to sit on the woman. Woman? No! His first reaction had been right for, in spite of the scars of experience, she was no more than a girl. She stood watching him, hands on hips, her pelvis thrust slightly forward, shoulders back – a provocative stance which was unnatural. Her lips were parted in a smile of welcome but it was a facial gesture only, without feeling.

'Well, captain, are you going to stand there all day? Come in. It's a dollar in advance and two dollars for half an hour.'

Gavin felt his cheeks burning. His years in the army had left him without illusions. He was certainly no angel but there was something obscene, unexpectedly obscene about the offer.

'I'm looking for Jack Quinlan,' he said slowly.

The reaction on the girl's face was as if he had physically slapped her. She blinked and her provocative stance disintegrated, her hands falling to her sides, her lips trembling.

'Why? Who are you?'

A realization began to dawn in Gavin's mind. 'Are you Mrs Quinlan?'

'What if I am?' The voice was full of antagonism.

'I'm sorry . . . where's your husband?'

'Jack's dead.' The words were thrown out angrily. It was Gavin's turn to blink.

'But I only saw him a few days ago,' Gavin began.

The girl's lips were set in a thin line. He could see the muscles in her face fighting for control. 'The peelers said it was an accident. He was run over trying to cross the street.'

'I'm sorry.' It sounded so meaningless.

'Who are you, anyway?' she demanded, smothering a small cough.

'My name is Devlin. Captain Gavin Devlin. I was in your husband's regiment.'

Her face was immobile. 'What do you want?'

Gavin spread his hands in an helpless gesture. 'I saw your husband a few days ago. I said that I would try to help him.'

The girl's jaw thrust out. 'You're too late. He's dead. Dead and buried.'

'I'm sorry.' Again it was a meaningless phrase. 'You were his wife, weren't you?' He wanted to be absolutely sure.

'I'm Nora Quinlan, yes.' Her voice was full of scorn; anger and scorn. 'And don't think that I don't know what is in your mind, captain. Quinlan's wife is a common slut, a prostitute. How bad that would look for the regiment. How could she let her husband down, let the Irish Brigade down? Isn't that it?'

He shifted uncomfortably. He had been thinking something along those lines. 'I was wondering how old you were, Mrs Quinlan,' he parried.

She raised an eyebrow to emphasize her scorn. 'I'll be twenty next month.'

Nineteen years old! Sweet Jesus! Nineteen and a widow. Gavin gestured around the room. 'Haven't you any family here to look after you?'

'I came out from Ireland to marry Jack. He came here a year before I did. We'd been sweethearts in our village but there was no work there. Jack's family had been evicted from their cabin. So Jack came to New York. Then he sent for me. He said that he had a good job, enough money for us to live on. I didn't know that he had gone to be a soldier. I came here and found him in a fine Yankee uniform and a war going on. We married and were two weeks together before he joined his regiment. Aye, for two weeks I had a whole man.'

Gavin bit his lip, staring at her. She had folded her arms across the top of her stomach. Her eyes were dangerously bright. 'It's what he wanted. Marriage, I mean. He set me up in a room.'

'Here?'

She shook her head. 'When the money ceased, after he was discharged from the army, we had to move here because it was all we could afford. I was with child by the time he came back from the war. It lived three weeks before it died. I didn't even know Jack had been wounded until he came home. They brought him back to me, half a man. What did they give him, his fine American army? A few dollars and a silver medal.' She was reciting without feeling, without emotion, as if her mind had left her body.

'Couldn't you have found some work?' demanded Gavin. 'Surely any work was better than. . . .' He let his voice trail off in response to the anger in her face.

'Work?' she sneered. 'In Ireland we were told that you only had to walk the streets of New York and pick up the silver dollars from the sidewalk. What work? The whole world has come here looking for work.' She coughed in her anger, paused to recover and let out a long, shuddering sigh.

'We needed money. Jack couldn't get out at all at that time. They say that the first time you sell yourself to a man, it is difficult. They say that after the first time it gets easier. It is not true. The first time is easy. It gets difficult with each succeeding time. That was the only work that I was able to get in this place.'

'Perhaps you could have gone back to Ireland,' Gavin ventured.

The scorn was back in her voice. 'Do you know how hard life is in Ireland? My family was only too glad to see me go with the hope that I would send back money to them. And where would the ship money come from to have taken us home? Better to be a whore in New York than a whore in Dublin. At least in a strange city, in a strange land, there's no shame.'

'How did the accident happen?' Gavin asked, deciding to change the subject which had become embarrassing to him.

'They told me he was crossing Broadway, coming home. A dray came down the street. With that damned cart of his, he couldn't get out of the way in time. The peelers said that he had been killed outright, thanks be to God!'

It was the first time that the name of God had come to her lips. Gavin felt its use was automatic, without meaning.

'A dray?' he pressed. 'Who owned the dray? Who was at fault?'

She stared at him. 'You sound like a lawyer, captain.'

'I was going to be one before the war,' he acknowledged. 'I mean to be one now. Were you offered compensation?'

She threw back her head and chuckled mirthlessly. 'Compensation? Who'd pay the likes of me compensation?'

'If the dray was at fault then you are entitled to it. Tell me when this happened and exactly where it happened and I'll make enquiries for you.'

Nora Quinlan gazed at him puzzled for a moment. 'You'll not make a big fee out of me, captain,' she sneered. 'No one does anything for nothing. So what do you want? Me?' she smiled cynically. 'No, I doubt if you have any need to buy a woman.'

Gavin's face reddened. 'Jack Quinlan served in my regiment. I promised to help him.'

'Even so, Jack hardly moved in the same circle as you did, captain. So why would you be doing something for nothing?'

Gavin hesitated. He didn't know what motivated him. He felt confused and he was annoyed by his confusion. 'Let's say that it is something for me.'

Nora Quinlan's eyes narrowed. 'You feel guilty because you survived the war and Jack didn't, is that it?'

Gavin was surprised that the girl could even begin to articulate the confusion in his mind. He did not reply.

'Jack was killed near the Canal Street horse-car stop in Broadway, just near the terminus. It was the day before yesterday about noon.'

Gavin nodded. 'How about the burial?'

'I managed to get him a five-dollar burial at Calvary Cemetery yesterday.'

Calvary was the main Catholic cemetery across the East River at Newtown. Gavin fumbled in his pocket and counted out five silver dollars. Nora Quinlan stared at him unemotionally.

'Take them back, captain,' she said quietly. 'I'll do my own burying.'

'But. . . .' Gavin began.

Her eyes flashed for a moment. 'Do you want me, captain? I'm prepared to earn the money.'

'All right, Mrs Quinlan,' Gavin said patiently, scooping back the money. 'I'll be making some enquiries and see what can be done. I'll come back and tell you what is happening just as soon as I can.'

She did not say anything; just stood in the same spot on which she had been standing when he had entered, not moving, just standing staring at him. He turned out of the squalid little room, out of the dark, vile-smelling tenement block and through the cackling women on the doorstep. One of them called out to him in a voice that was coarse and suggestive but he ignored it. He strode quickly away, up the street to the Bowery and kept going along Canal Street away from the slums, away from the poverty and the nightmare of sordidness.

His mind was full of thoughts of handsome Jack Quinlan; Sergeant Jack Quinlan.

Ready the flag! The rousing baritone; the waving green banner; the broad shoulders flung back as the charge began. Ready the flag! Spare a dime! The gaunt, hunched figure on the wooden cart, squeaking down the street. And cutting through the images came the face of the girl, of the innocence that was now filled with experience and anger.

> Where are the legs with which you run?
> Hurroo! Hurroo!
> Where are the legs with which you run?
> Hurroo! Hurroo!
> Where are the legs with which you run
> When you went to carry a gun?
> Indeed your dancing days are done
> Och, Johnny, I hardly knew ye!

Damn it! Why did that song keep haunting him? Why did it keep pounding in his head?

Chapter 9

'Gavin!'

The imperious tone of Rosaleen McHale rang across the marble front of Stewart's Store at the north-east corner of Broadway and Chambers. The outing was not what Gavin had intended. He had merely wanted to take Rosaleen for a quiet drive through the newly constructed Central Park in order to discuss his apprehensions. Nearly a week had passed and he had not been able to bring himself to see Stead McHale. When he had arrived at the McHale mansion he found the girl full of her own plans and she assumed peremptory command of the expedition, insisting on going to Stewart's Store in order to choose materials for a new dress. Beulah came along as chaperone.

'Gavin!' she cried again as she skipped lightly from the carriage and made her way across the sidewalk to the store.

Gavin glanced at the elderly servant. 'Why don't you wait in the carriage, Beulah, until we come out?'

The old woman's face crinkled in worry. 'I should follow Missy Rosie, sir.'

'Now what's going to happen to Miss Rosie in a store, Beulah?' Gavin smiled reassuringly. 'You take it easy now. We'll be back soon.'

Beulah nodded, obviously relieved at not being dragged around the store. 'I take it mighty kindly of you, Captain Devlin,' she said.

Gavin guessed that Rosaleen did not appreciate that Beulah was not so young and active as she used to be. He always felt vaguely uncomfortable at the remote and indifferent attitude which the McHale's displayed towards their servants. In the Devlin household Bridget and Patsy-Mike were part of the family rather than hired help. He followed the girl into the store and found her flitting from one pile of material to another exclaiming in a loud voice. Anxious-faced assistants converged on her.

'There you are, Gavin,' she frowned. 'I thought you had deserted me. Where is Beulah?'

'I told her to stay in the carriage until we came out. I'll carry your purchases. The reason I wanted to take you out today was so that we could talk without anyone else around.'

She bit her lip and seemed about to say something but there was a hollow cough behind them and a pale-faced, elderly assistant, seemingly clad in black mourning, inclined his head. 'May I be of service?'

'Show me your silks,' Rosaleen commanded, turning to the problem in hand.

They followed the assistant into the interior of the store. Gavin suppressed a sigh as Rosaleen started to chat, criticize and study, head to one side, as the assistant began to go through the materials. Gavin eased himself into a chair and watched while the girl smiled at this pattern, sneered at that. No, this was not what Gavin had intended. He had wanted to go somewhere quiet, away from the influence of the McHale household, somewhere he could gather his thoughts and explain to Rosie some of the anxieties he had, some of the half-formed ideas for the future. Now he suddenly had the strangest thought; he saw himself sitting mesmerized as if watching a beautiful multi-plumed bird, dancing on a branch and singing enticingly. He stirred uncomfortably. Was he mocking Rosaleen? He should not mock her . . . didn't he love her? It was odd how strangely detached he had become since his return. He had been in love with Rosie McHale until last year. *In love*. But loving someone was not quite the same thing. You had to know someone to love them. He had never thought much about it during the war. The war seemed to make everything different. Life became telescoped by war as if there was no time to think nor to plan. All emotion was compressed and was used up so quickly in case death came and life was wasted. Maybe he had been like that. A young man in war needed a young woman to yearn for, to come back to.

He pulled a cheroot from his pocket and lit it, puffing gently as he watched Rosaleen surrounded by harassed assistants, ordering, praising and criticizing. His eyes fell on the ring she wore which he had given her a year ago as a token. It was a silver-mounted piece of polished Connemara marble shaped as two hearts entangled. It seemed to him as if someone else had bought it. Out of the drifting chaos of his thoughts one idea was beginning to form with some clarity. He wanted to make his own way in life and not rely on gifts from Stead McHale. The experiences of the war had made him somehow different, a stranger to the comfortable world of wealthy New York society. It was not his world; not his people. After he had been wounded at Sayler's Creek he had spent two weeks laying on his back in the field hospital thinking about the injustice and poverty he had witnessed and had stirred with a growing passion that he must do something about it. Exactly what he could do he did not know. Whatever it must be, the world of the McHales now appeared superficial by comparison.

He clung to the belief that Rosaleen would understand once he was able to talk to her about it. Certainly the exuberant Rosie of his youth would be able to share his new dream. Or was memory playing him false? He closed his eyes and for a moment tried to imagine her face as he had first known it, as he had carried it with him during the war years. Innocent? Yes. Alive, eager, too. He tried to conjure that face back. The image that formed was not quite right. He saw small, pinched features, white translucent skin, red hair and bright violet eyes. He grunted in perplexity. He was visualizing the features of Nora Quinlan. He opened his eyes and shifted his weight uncomfortably.

Nora Quinlan had been in his mind several times during the last few days. He had promised to find out some details about Sergeant Jack Quinlan's death but he had not done so yet. He had spent the time buying civilian clothes and adjusting himself to the fact of not wearing uniform for the first time in four years. He felt more guilty about not fulfilling his promise to Nora Quinlan than his avoidance of Stead McHale and the discussion about his future. He really ought to make enquiries about the facts of Quinlan's death. If there was some way of raising some compensation for the girl, it might help to ease her out of the depressing life she was being forced to lead.

'Gavin!' Rosaleen's voice penetrated his thoughts. He glanced up with a guilty start. 'I've asked you twice about this colour. I declare, you were sitting there daydreaming.'

'Sorry,' Gavin replied, scrambling to his feet. He hardly glanced at the material in the girl's hands. 'It's fine.'

Rosaleen pursed her lips in contemplation. 'Are you sure? You're not just saying that to please me? You know how I must have the truth? It's not too yellow, is it?'

Gavin looked beyond Rosaleen and saw the pleading in the

assistant's eyes. 'Not at all,' he said more firmly. 'It's an excellent choice.'

Rosaleen hesitated and then turned back to the assistant. 'Nevertheless,' she said, 'let's see the other roll – the blue one – just to make sure. I don't want to make a mistake, do I?'

Gavin sat down again suppressing a sigh.

He had some difficulty in finding police headquarters as it had been moved to a new building on Mulberry Street, between Bleeker and Houston, during the war years. It was a new imposing five-storey building of white Westchester marble taking up the entire block to Mott Street. Gavin entered and told the sergeant at the desk the purpose of his visit. The man was not particularly helpful.

'We are pretty busy, counsellor. . . .' he began when Gavin asked to see the police record of the incident.

'Devlin!' A hand fell on his shoulder and he turned to face a grinning man in the uniform of a police sergeant. His hair was a riot of ginger curls.

'Hello, Murphy,' Gavin returned the grin as he recognized the man. 'So you've gone back to the old job?'

Murphy had been a policeman before joining the 69th New York as a junior officer. 'You couldn't keep me away,' nodded Murphy. 'What brings you down to headquarters, Devlin?'

Gavin explained.

'Ah, I recall you were a lawyer.' Murphy turned to the desk sergeant. 'I'll take the counsellor to the record morgue, Harry, okay?'

The desk sergeant shrugged indifferently and turned back to his ledgers. Gavin followed Murphy to a room which had nothing in it but a few tables and chairs. The ginger-haired policeman left him there for a few moments, returning with a folder. The single slip of paper was not helpful. A dray belonging to the Delancey Meat Packing Company on Rutger had run over a beggar later identified as Jack Quinlan who resided on Bayard. The driver of the dray had told the police that the beggar, on a hand-propelled cart, had crossed over the street between the horse-cars straight into his path. It was an accident but the main fault lay with the beggar. Gavin pursed his lips in disappointment.

'Not what you had hoped for?' Murphy asked sympathetically.

Gavin pushed the folder back to him. 'I was hoping that there would be grounds for compensation,' he confessed.

Murphy frowned and glanced at the report. 'There's a lot of

beggars in New York. They are dying of exposure or in fights every day. What makes this one special?'

'Doesn't the name mean anything to you?'

'Quinlan? Jack Quinlan. Should it?'

'Sergeant Jack Quinlan. He carried the regimental colours at Cold Harbor. That's where he had his legs blown from under him.'

Murphy whistled softly. 'Poor bastard. I didn't know him, though. I joined the regiment after Cold Harbor.'

Gavin had forgotten. He sighed and stood up. 'Quinlan has a nineteen year old widow.'

'It's bad luck, Devlin,' Murphy stroked his nose ruefully. 'But there's a lot of other fellows in the same position. Still, you could go and see the owners of the dray. They might give some donation as a patriotic gesture, if you explained the circumstances. Trouble is, there are too many cases like it in this city.'

Gavin nodded slowly. He knew that fact too well.

'Oh, Devlin,' Murphy said as he turned from the room. 'There's also the Irish Emigrant Society over on Chambers. They might be able to help her out. Have you tried there?'

He shook his head, 'No, but thanks for the information.'

'That's okay. We'll probably see each other again in the course of business, eh, counsellor?'

Gavin raised his hand in farewell and left the police headquarters. He was thinking about Nora Quinlan again. Nora Quinlan married at eighteen; welcoming back her hero husband, her legless hero-husband; her penniless hero-husband.

> With drums and guns, and guns and drums
> The enemy nearly slew ye . . .

That damned song stirred again in his mind. The enemy *nearly* slew Jack Quinlan but his own people had succeeded.

Gavin rode the City Railroad, the horse-drawn cars, across to Division Street and then walked down Rutger until he found the tall red brick building with a big painted sign 'Delancey Meat Packing Company'. He was directed up to a suite of offices which were above the warehouses. The main office contained only two people. A harassed-looking clerk was obviously in charge, sitting behind a desk checking papers. He was a little man with a large moustache, balding head, in shirt and waistcoat. Gavin noticed that the cuffs of the shirt were frayed and dirty. The other occupant sat in a comfortable chair near a window reading a newspaper. He looked more like a customer than an employee for he was quite well dressed.

Gavin handed the clerk his newly printed visiting card and explained the nature of his business. The clerk looked more harassed and indecisive. He stared at the card.

'Are you a lawyer, mister . . . er . . . Devlin?'

There was nothing to indicate it on the visiting card which Gavin had presented. But Gavin nodded.

The clerk scratched his pate. 'I have no authority to discuss such a matter. I will find out if someone will see you.'

Gavin smiled patiently. 'If you would be so kind.'

The clerk scurried away and Gavin turned to gaze indifferently out of the window. From the corner of his eyes he saw that the man reading the newspaper had lowered it slightly and was examining him from curiously bright-green eyes set in a thin, almost hawk-like face made ugly by thick, bulbous lips. He was well dressed and from this angle Gavin observed that he carried a hand gun in a shoulder holster beneath his jacket. Gavin ignored the man's open scrutiny and stared down from the window into a yard where the carcasses of meat were being off-loaded from a wagon which had obviously transported them from the wharf at the bottom of Rutger Street, bringing them up to the meat packing plant below. He watched in disapproval at the clumsy way the men were handling the sides of butchered meat, letting them drop on to the dirty cobbles of the yard, sometimes to be kicked about by boisterous workmen.

'Mister Delancey Junior, one of our directors, is in his office, Mister Devlin,' the rasping voice of the clerk sounded behind him. 'Will you come this way?'

Gavin turned after the man and followed him along a dark oak-panelled passageway into a large, brightly lit office. It was well furnished and held an opulence that made the clerk's office look like a hovel. It was carpeted with matching burgundy drapes and prints hanging from the wood panelling. Gavin noticed it was on the opposite side of the building to the meat packing yards below. The windows opened to the more pleasant vista of Madison Street. Behind the ornate oak desk a young man sat chewing at an expensive Havana cigar. He rose to his feet as Gavin was shown in and extended a limp hand.

'Mister Devlin?' He waved to a chair in front of the desk before dropping back into his. 'I'm Brock Delancey.'

Gavin had a momentary feeling that he should recognize the name.

Brock Delancey was about the same age as Gavin. He was undoubtedly handsome, a broad pale face and curly soft brown hair. There was something hard about the eyes and the compression of the mouth. He was dressed in a light blue suit trimmed in deeper blue with a white ruffled shirt and a fashionable grey silk cravat and waistcoat. He sat back and stared expectantly at Gavin with the self-assuredness of money and position. Gavin's immediate reaction was the thought that he was someone's spoilt son.

'My clerk says you want to see me about someone called Quinlan, Mister Devlin?'

The voice was soft, well modulated, the smile superficially friendly.

'That's right,' Gavin agreed. 'Sergeant Jack Quinlan. He was run over and killed by one of your drays a week ago.'

Brock Delancey frowned and rested his cigar on an ashtray.

'I can't recall. . . .' he began. His eyes narrowed and he stood up and walked to a cabinet and flicked through some papers, returning with a single sheet and re-seating himself at the desk.

'You're talking about the beggar who got himself killed wheeling his cart right under one of my drays?' Delancey asked, tapping the piece of paper. 'The matter was reported to the police. The death of another Bowery bum who couldn't take care of himself.'

Gavin bit his lip.

'Sergeant Quinlan lost his legs at Cold Harbor. He was wounded leading a charge of the 69th New York.'

Delancey shrugged indifferently. 'Many people were wounded in the war, counsellor. What is your interest in the death of this beggar?'

'Jack Quinlan served his country honourably, was wounded for it. I've seen the police report about the accident in which he died. But Quinlan left a young widow. I was hoping that your company might feel some obligation.'

Delancey smiled tightly. 'If you have studied the facts you will have discovered that this company was in no way to blame for the accident, counsellor. The truth of it is that Quinlan was entirely to blame. He might have injured our horses. Our responsibilities are clear. They do not extend to giving charity.'

'I was not thinking of legal responsibility, Delancey,' Gavin replied, 'but moral responsibility.'

Delancey suddenly threw back his head and barked with laughter. 'You are in the wrong place, counsellor. I run a business and not a charitable institution of which there are many in this city. I suggest you try one of them.'

There was a cold finality in Brock Delancey's voice which made Gavin realize it would be hopeless to appeal further to the man.

'Thank you for your time, Mister Delancey,' he said as he left the office and followed the dark corridor back into the clerk's room. The harassed little man gave him a worried glance as he passed through and he was also aware of the scrutiny of the hawk-faced man in the corner. He went down the stairs and passed out into the brightness of Rutger Street. He had taken a dislike to Delancey, although he realized it was hardly rational. Delancey was well within his rights. He had no legal responsibilities towards Jack Quinlan. It was an accident with the burden of cause on Quinlan himself. If Delancey could see the pathetic pale face of Nora Quinlan and realize the hopelessness of her situation. . . . No, that would probably not matter to a businessman like Brock Delancey. Yet he wondered why it mattered so much to himself.

Chapter 10

Nora Quinlan's eyes widened in surprise as she recognized him.

'Can I come in?' Gavin asked, taking off his hat.

She opened the door wider and stood back to allow him to enter the room. He carried a small picnic basket which he placed on the bare wood table. She closed the door and stared down at it without moving. 'I'm not looking for charity,' she said after a moment, her voice ending in a nervous cough.

'Good. I'm not offering it,' he replied cheerfully. 'I wanted to eat so I brought a basket of food along with me. You can share it.'

Her eyes met his and for a moment anger bridled there. Then she relaxed and gave a long sigh of resignation. 'Very well, Captain Devlin. Shall I make you some tea?'

He smiled. 'That's a good offer . . . may I call you Nora?'

She shrugged indifferently.

'Mind if I sit, Nora?'

She gestured to the bed. 'That's the only comfortable seat in the room, Captain,' she replied.

'Call me Gavin,' he said, seating himself at the end of the bed and watching while she busied herself with the kettle.

'Why did you come back?' she asked eventually with some hostility in her voice.

'I told you. I found out who the dray belonged to and went to see them.'

'And?'

'I was hoping to get some form of compensation.'

Her mouth quirked but she said nothing. When he did not say anything more she interpreted his silence correctly. 'I didn't think there would be any compensation. So why did you come back?'

Gavin tried to summon a satisfactory reason. 'Jack Quinlan was in my regiment.'

'I imagine a lot of people served in Jack's regiment. They have not come here. What exactly is it that you want?'

'Must I want something?' countered Gavin.

'Everyone wants something.'

'You are cynical, Nora,' Gavin said.

'I have no understanding of that word.'

He smiled. 'To be cynical is to be doubting, sceptical, distrustful, suspicious. . . .'

'No need to quote a dictionary at me,' she sniffed, preparing the teapot. 'Besides, you would be sin . . . sin. . . .' she fought for the word.

'Cynical,' supplied Gavin.

'Yes, you'd be that if you lived here, down on Bayard, instead of in some big house with servants.'

'How do you know I live in a house with servants?' he asked.

She gave him a scornful glance.

'Isn't it written all over you? You've probably never had to want for anything in your life.'

He watched her in silence as she finished making the tea. When she had poured it into the cups, he asked, 'Nora, what do *you* want?'

The abruptness of the question caused her to stare for a moment in surprise. 'Me? What do I want?'

'Yes. What do you want now most of all?'

She shrugged. 'Money, I suppose.'

'How much? Enough to go back to Ireland?'

She looked at him suspiciously. 'What's behind this?'

'Don't keep being distrustful,' Gavin sighed. 'Why are you so suspicious? What do you take me for?'

'To be sure, I don't know what I take you for, captain. I don't even know what it is that you want of me.'

Gavin realized that he did not know the answer to that question himself. All he knew was that he had a desire to help Nora Quinlan and he told her so. 'A person like you should not be in this position,' he ended weakly.

'What could I do?' There was anger in her retort. 'Jack crippled and no money in the house. What was left for me to do? First I went round the big houses begging for work. Then I managed to get a job in a tavern and, because I wouldn't indulge a drunken customer, he reported me to the owner claiming that I had short-changed him. I was thrown out. What could I do? Tell me that?'

'I'm not reproaching you,' Gavin said hastily. 'I just want to help.'

'But why?' She thrust her face pugnaciously towards him. 'If you want to sleep with me it will only cost you two dollars and you don't have to go through all this fuss.'

'It's not that. . . .' Gavin flushed unhappily.

'Then what is it? Why do you want to help me? There are hundreds of Jack and Nora Quinlans in this city.'

'Hell!' His voice was suddenly harsh and caused her to start in surprise. 'I don't know why. Don't keep asking. I just feel that I have to, that's all.'

She watched him curiously for a moment and then shrugged. 'Your tea will be cold.'

'Do you want to go home?' he asked, after he had taken a sip.

'Home?'

'To Ireland.'

'To County Cavan? That's not home for me any more.'

'Then maybe I could get you a job here; perhaps a housemaid or something like that.'

'I told you, I'm not looking for charity,' she jerked up her chin again.

'It's not charity,' he insisted.

She stared at him with her fathomless violet eyes and shook her head in bewilderment. 'You're a strange man, Captain Devlin. A strange man, right enough.' Her eyes searched his face. 'I don't understand you at all.'

There came a sharp tap on the door. A colour suddenly tinged her cheeks and she looked towards him uncertainly. 'It may be a customer,' she said hesitantly. 'I'm sorry. . . .'

Gavin felt a pang of irrational anger. 'I'll pay for your time,' he said brusquely, hurtfully.

The tapping came again and she rose to the door. 'What is it?' she called. She opened the door and hesitated. 'Oh, it's you.'

From where he was seated Gavin could not see the man who apparently stood at the door. 'Percentage time, sister,' came a soft masculine drawl.

Nora turned silently to the mantelpiece of the room. The man did not follow her or step into the room.

'One dollar fifty,' she said counting out some coins.

'That's a drop on last week, sister. The boss ain't gonna like it.'

'It's all I've earned,' protested the girl.

'Then you'd better get out on the streets and start rooting for more work. One dollar fifty, indeed!'

Gavin heard steps receding down the hall. The girl went to close the door but Gavin moved from the end of the bed and peered out. He could only see the black shadow of a man disappearing into the sunlight. He waited a few seconds and then hurried to the front of the tenement. There were the usual group of Italian women seated on the steps talking in shrill voices to each other. He squinted in the daylight.

Across the street he saw a tall figure striding away. He caught the glint of burnished copper hair and the cut of the smart suit. While he could not see the face, he recognized the suit and the man's build. It was the same man who had been sitting in the outer office at Delancey's Meat Packing Company. He drew back and returned to the girl's room. She was staring at him oddly.

'What was that about?' she demanded.

'Who was that man?'

'Is it any of your business?' she countered.

'I think so.' His voice was tight and its tone caused her to frown.

'He's the man who calls to pick up my percentage, that's who,' she said defensively. 'He comes regular as clockwork, every Wednesday at noon.'

'Percentage?' Gavin pressed. 'Of your earnings?'

'What else?' she smiled without mirth.

'You mean he's your pimp?'

She coughed nervously. 'No. Protection, that's what. Do you think this is a city of free enterprise? I don't have a pimp but everyone has to pay protection. Every week Hogan comes along and collects ten per cent of all earnings from every girl working the streets around here. In return we are protected from people moving in from other territories.'

'And if you don't pay?'

Nora Quinlan grunted. 'Only one girl refused since I've been here. She claimed her pimp would do all the protecting she needed. The pimp was found in the East River.'

Gavin stared at her. 'How could that man run this racket?'

'He's only a collector, stupid,' Nora Quinlan scoffed. 'I wouldn't like to fool around with whoever is behind him.'

'Do you know who is behind him?'

She shook her head. 'I don't want to. It isn't healthy to ask questions.'

Gavin exhaled slowly. It was a strange coincidence that he had seen the man – Hogan, Nora had called him – in the office of the company whose dray had killed Jack Quinlan. He wondered what connection Hogan had with the company.

'Well,' Nora Quinlan interrupted his thoughts, 'are you eating or not?'

She laid out the sandwiches and cakes that he had brought with him and poured fresh cups of tea. He forced a smile and pushed both Hogan and the Delancey Meat Packing Company into the back of his mind, sitting there and prompting the girl to talk about herself. As she relaxed it was as if a dam had been breached. She talked about Ireland, the village in County Cavan where she and Jack Quinlan had grown up together. She talked of Jack's dreams of making money, of getting a good job. Of his saving to afford the ship money and his departure from Queenstown for New York. There was no doubt that she had been in love with Jack Quinlan, with his burning ambition to escape from the claustrophobia of the village. There had been tales of the gold that could be picked up simply by walking the streets of New York. The months had gone by, months of yearning, of solitude, and then came Jack Quinlan's letter with her ship money, money to buy her passage to New York. They had two weeks of happiness before Jack Quinlan rejoined his regiment and then the dreams turned to nightmares.

Gavin, noticing the passing of the time, finally stood up. 'Will you trust me, Nora?' he asked.

'Trust you, for what?' she countered.

'I want to help you. I want you to believe that. I will try to find you a job, something to take you out of this. May I come back and visit?'

Her lips turned down cynically. 'I have a lot of visitors, captain.'

He drew in his breath in exasperation. 'You know I don't mean that.'

She raised a shoulder and let it fall indifferently. 'Come when you want. It makes no odds.'

He saw the small look of hurt and hopelessness in her eyes, wanted to try to comfort her in some way, but all he could say was, 'I'll come back soon.'

As he was walking slowly back towards the Bowery his thoughts turned again to Hogan and he bit his lip. On the Bowery he paused to buy a newspaper and checked through the advertisements, found what he wanted and took the street cars to Cedar Street. It did not take him long to find a small office outside of which hung a board,

'Gabriel Symes, Investigations'. He pushed in and found a ferret-faced little man sprawled in a chair, tilted back against a wall scanning the society column of the *New York Tribune*. He put down the newspaper and straightened up as Gavin entered.

'What can I do for you, mister?' He had a breathless voice with the faint suspicion of a wheeze.

'Mister Symes?'

The man grimaced and waved an encompassing arm. 'That's what the notice says, mister.'

'Then I want to employ you.'

'Sit down, mister. Didn't think you came in just to pass the time o' day. Divorce enquiry, is it?'

'No.'

Symes raised his eyebrows in interest.

'It's a simple job,' Gavin began. 'Following someone and finding out about their business.'

The ferret-faced man drew a pad and pencil towards him and pursed his lips. 'Go on, mister,' he invited.

Gavin gave him a detailed description of Hogan. He also gave him the address of Nora Quinlan's room. 'This man goes there at noon every Wednesday. I want to know why, who else he sees and who he finally reports to.'

Symes looked dubious and scratched his chin. 'Sounds like a percentage man, mister.'

'And if he is?'

'Then the job might be dangerous. Bayard isn't exactly a healthy place to make enquiries in.'

'You'll be paid for the risks,' Gavin assured him, drawing out his pocketbook and laying some coins on the desk. 'Here's ten dollars in advance. The man calls on a Wednesday. That's a week from now. I'll return here on the Thursday morning to hear your report.'

Symes pocketed the cash. 'Fair enough but I need to know who you are, mister.'

Gavin handed him one of his visiting cards. Symes glanced at it.

'All right, mister,' he said. 'I'll have a report for you by next Thursday.'

He tossed and turned hearing the noise of the bombardment and unable to escape from the inevitable hail of death in the bleak light of dawn.

Ready the flag!

Jack Quinlan's baritone rose, strong and firm, his tall figure was powerful against the faint light of dawn, his handsome features seemed as if they were lit by an uncanny fire, the features clearly defined in silhouette against the sky, the clean-shaven jaw pushing towards the enemy in an attitude of defiance. In his hand, held tightly, was the flagstaff with the silk snapping and cracking in the breeze.

They moved forward in lines, in serried ranks, across the icy flats, their feet squelching in the wet earth, their forward motion was slow, painfully slow, over the swampy ground. Shadows ran towards him. He saw the bright flash of bayonets, saw the gleaming eyes, flashing specks with white borders, the blazing masks of hate as the enemy ran towards him, lips curled in bestial snarls, teeth and bare gums showing in masks of death.

Forward!

He wanted to turn but the mud held him in place. He screamed, trying to fend off the jabbing actions of the long, gleaming bayonets. He tried to reach forward with his hands, tried to tear the blades from his stomach but they jabbed in, thrusting sharply with red blood spurting over the ground before him. Yet he felt no pain; no pain at all.

A bugle sounded from afar joined by others until they rose in a great fanfare which then died away like the soft sigh of a summer's breeze.

He blinked in puzzlement and the scene was changed.

He lay down on a warm green sward bathed in the soft gold of the sun. Beside him, running over weed-veined rocks was a gurgling stream whose silver waters sparkled and played in the light.

Her voice was but a gurgling echo of the stream and he turned his head into the gold mist created by the sun through the rising damp of the trees and foliage.

She stood there by his side, looking down with a wistful expression, a lovely apparition sent to be a moment's ornament.

He gazed at the eyes first, clear, deep blue like violet. Her small delicately boned face with its high forehead, tiny nose and thin lips – though not sulkily thin, the pale freckled skin and the hair which was not quite red but a mass of dark gingery curls, weaving strands of spun gold and falling to her soft white shoulders, tugged by the gentle hands of the morning breeze.

She was Fand, the ancient Irish goddess, the wife of Manannán Mac Lir, god of the oceans. Yes, she was Fand, the Pearl of Beauty.

'What is it that you want, Captain Devlin?' Her voice was a soft soprano.

'It is you that I want,' he gasped painfully.

She flung back her hair, shaking its flaming curls and laughing. 'For two dollars?'

'I want you!' He tried to rise, stretching out a hand towards her but somehow she slid from his searching grasp like some ethereal spirit.

'The new is ever sweet, the old is often sour,' she taunted.

He strove to rise again only to be met by the stark figure on a small wooden cart, the bloody stumps dripping red on the green emerald grass, a claw-like hand held towards him.

'Spare a dime? Spare a dime?'

He opened his mouth to scream at the haunted eyes that accused him. He tried to turn his head away but they were all about him now . . . shadowy figures in grey uniforms, each holding a bright new musket and bayonet which glittered and sparkled, each flickering bayonet pointed down at his stomach.

'Spare a dime!' they chanted in unison.

He tried to shield himself but Quinlan's rich baritone suddenly called, 'Ready the flag!'

Like a congregation answering the priest, their voices rose. 'Ready the flag!' The bayonets thrust forward. Gavin screamed, his hands held out to fend them off. . . .

A few moments passed as he stared into the darkness of his bedroom, hands stretched out, eyes flitting from one shadow to another. A light flickered outside, there was a tap on his door. It opened and his mother stood there, a gown wrapped around her, a lamp in one hand. Behind her came Manus Devlin rubbing the sleep from his eyes.

'What is it, son?' Aideen Devlin asked. 'What's wrong?'

Gavin lay back, feeling the sweat pouring from his brow.

'Nothing. . . . Just a nightmare, I suppose.'

Manus Devlin grunted and disappeared but his mother came and sat on the edge of his bed, placing the lamp on the bedside table. She reached out a cool hand and touched his forehead. For a moment Gavin was a small boy again.

'Would you like me to get you something to drink?'

He smiled up at her. 'I'll be all right, Ma,' he said. 'It was just a bad dream, that's all.'

Chapter 11

Gabriel Symes was sitting behind his desk puffing on a foul-smelling cigar when Gavin entered his office. The investigator glanced up and his ferret face twisted in a smile. 'Morning mister,' he said, nodding to a chair.

'Did you find out anything?' Gavin demanded without preamble.

Symes nodded. There seemed something nervous about the gesture. 'Sure did. Ain't gonna trust putting it to no paper, though. Not me. And it'll cost,' his eyes narrowed in speculation as he gazed at Gavin. 'It'll cost you fifty. Plus the ten you advanced me last week,' he added hastily.

Gavin stared at the man for a moment. 'Let's hear it. If it's worth it then I'll pay you fifty.'

'Plus the ten?'

'Plus the ten,' Gavin affirmed.

'Guess I ain't got much to lose, either way,' Symes sighed. 'Okay. Yesterday I went up Bayard. I picked up your man, Hogan, without any trouble. Kept a safe distance because there were a couple of bowsies with him. Tough guys carrying cudgels. Ain't no one gonna mess with that man. Saw him do the rounds of the girls. He's a percentage collector right enough, not just from the girls but from the bars and boarding houses. After I finished following him I made a few discreet enquiries. Hogan collects for most of the rackets around the docks. It's a pretty big operation. Makes me break out in a cold sweat just thinking of it.'

Gavin sighed irritably. 'You're not telling me anything I hadn't guessed.'

'Hold hard, mister,' Symes protested. 'I ain't finished yet. Your man Hogan completed his day with a pretty big leather bag of money. He rode a street car to Broadway, his shadows following him and me hanging on behind. He dismissed his men up near City

Hall and then went straight into the Astor House Hotel. Now that's a mite tricky. I wonder whether to follow or just hang about outside.'

Gavin eased forward on his chair. 'What did you do?'

'Went inside,' grinned Symes. 'Your man was in the hotel bar talking with another man. He left ten minutes later minus the bag of money. The other man picks it up and then he leaves. This time the man has a carriage and a liveried coachman, too. Goes uptown. I managed to pick up a hackney . . . I did tell you expenses are extra?' he added anxiously.

Gavin waved him to continue.

'The carriage drives uptown to one of them big mansion places by the new park.'

'What did this man look like?'

Symes smiled in self-satisfaction. 'Getting your money's worth now, eh, cap'n?'

'What did he look like.'

'Young, early twenties, blond hair; no, more a light brown. Smartly dressed.'

Gavin sat back, eyes wide, as he recognized the description. He whistled softly through his teeth.

Symes smiled complacently. 'I guess you already know that the house belongs to Senator Delancey?'

'Senator? You've just described a man called Delancey to me,' Gavin said. 'But he can't be a senator.'

Symes chuckled. 'No, but his dad is. The young guy is Brock Delancey. He helps run his dad's businesses. You must have heard of the senator, though . . . owns a good slice of Manhattan and Long Island too. Also owns some slave plantations in Delaware or maybe it's Maryland.'

Gavin smiled condescendingly. 'You're behind the times, Mister Symes. Slavery was abolished back in 1863 with Lincoln's proclamation,' he corrected. 'No one has slave plantations any more.'

The little detective looked up in amusement. 'Ain't no one told the senator then. No, mister, abolition only applied to the Reb states of the south.'

Gavin stared at him in disbelief. 'But emancipation was what the war was all about.'

'Might have been what your war was about, mister,' replied Symes, 'but so far as Democrats like Senator Delancey are concerned it was to preserve the Union, not to destroy slavery. Do you think the slave states of Kentucky, Missouri, Maryland and Delaware would have thrown in their lot with the Union against the Confederacy if they were fighting simply to abolish slavery?' The little man shook his head.

'But Lincoln's abolition bill . . . ?' protested Gavin.

'Applied to the Rebs not to the North. But, I'll grant you that there are some radical hotheads in Congress trying to get an amendment through to bring abolition into force all over the States. They'll probably succeed but not if the Senator and his supporters have their way.'

Gavin shook his head trying to absorb the overthrow of an idea that he had simply taken for granted.

'About Delancey. . . .' Symes reminded him.

Gavin tried to bring his mind back to the business in hand.

'Do you think Brock Delancey is in business for himself?'

Symes chuckled. 'Your guess is as good as mine, mister. My guess being that he's just an errand boy for his dad. You can't build up the racket that he appears to be running without a lot of expertise and friends in high places. Know what I mean?'

Gavin stood up slowly and counted some bills from his pocketbook. Symes watched him greedily.

'This also buys your silence, Symes,' Gavin said. 'Forget everything you've told me.'

The ferret-faced man nodded eagerly. 'You don't have to tell me, mister. The Delancey family are pretty powerful in this burg. I don't wanna get stepped on. So, if it's all the same with you, you never consulted me and I never worked for you. All right?'

Gavin nodded. Outside it occurred to him that he had found a mission. The half-formed thoughts about wanting to do something about the misery of the immigrant slums had bothered him for some time. Now he had been presented with an opportunity to do something. The Delancey family were profiting from the slums, from the poverty, misery and crime. They were a pestilence and he wanted to destroy them; wanted to smash their complacent empire. He stood hesitating, wondering how he should set about this momentous task. He needed advice. Perhaps it was high time he accepted Stead McHale's invitation to go to talk about his future as a lawyer. Perhaps Stead McHale would advise and lend his support to expose the rackets.

McHale's club was the Athenaeum on the corner of Madison Avenue and East 25th Street. It was a centre for politicians, lawyers, newspaper proprietors and others who controlled the city. One didn't apply for membership of this exclusive club until one was invited to join. Gavin was certainly not a member and, before he was allowed through the hallowed portals, a liveried youth bearing a silver tray with his visiting card had to be despatched into the inner sanctuary of the club in search of McHale while Gavin fretted on the plush carpet of the reception hall. After what seemed an age the youth returned with a note for the receptionist. The man smiled bleakly and instructed Gavin to follow the youth. He was led through walnut-panelled corridors to a large room of dark oak and red leather chairs and couches.

He saw McHale at once, standing before the ornate marble fireplace nursing a brandy glass and talking to a rotund, prosperous-looking man dressed somewhat ostentatiously in the new fashion of tailored trousers and a brightly coloured waistcoat beneath a frock coat. McHale smiled at Gavin and the man, following the lawyer's gaze, nodded his farewell. Gavin caught McHale's respectful, 'Goodbye, Senator. Best of luck with the Bill.'

Stead McHale took Gavin's hand briefly and asked him what he wanted to drink, at the same time indicating a couple of red leather-padded armchairs nearby. McHale eased his girth into the chair opposite Gavin as he ordered a whiskey for Gavin and a brandy for himself.

'You seem to have been avoiding us of late, Gavin,' he said sorrowfully. 'I had hoped we could have finalized all our plans by now. Rosie is getting quite fretful.'

'It's been hard to adjust since I returned, sir,' Gavin countered.

'Understandable, my boy. Understandable. But time waits for no man, they say.'

McHale produced a silver cigar case and thrust it towards Gavin. He declined. McHale took an Havana from the case, cut it with almost ostentatious respect and lit it. The waiter slid silently up with their drinks.

'Here's to the future, Gavin. I'm glad that you've come to see me. Now we can get things sorted out and put Rosie's mind at ease.'

'Well, sir,' Gavin began hesitantly. 'It is certainly about the future I want to talk.'

'Naturally,' McHale smiled thinly. 'We must talk about you joining the firm. No problem there. You took an excellent degree in law, my boy. Six months' practical experience with McHale and Gogarty and I can guarantee that you'll pass the Bar Examination. Then my offer of a junior partnership still stands.'

'I'm grateful, sir,' Gavin was still hesitant. 'I really do want to go into law.'

McHale raised an eyebrow as he caught the inflection in Gavin's voice. 'You say that as if there is some problem? Is there?' His tone sharpened.

'Perhaps if I tell you the full story, sir? Then you'll be able to advise me. But, if you don't mind, I won't give you the names, not just yet. Let's see what you feel about the story first.'

Stead McHale waved his cigar in invitation.

Cautiously at first, then with growing fervour as he warmed to the subject, Gavin began to tell the story of Jack and Nora Quinlan.

'But,' McHale interrupted, 'the firm who owns the dray is not legally responsible under law for the man's death, Gavin. You can see that, surely?'

'Yes. I've read the police report. I was hoping to make an appeal to moral responsibility.'

'Morality and law don't mix, son. If you can't get them on a point of law, then you can forget the morality.'

'But,' Gavin leaned forward, 'there is something else about this company. The owners are involved in organized crime.'

McHale raised his eyebrows; 'How do you make that out?' he demanded.

Briefly, without mentioning Symes by name, Gavin recounted what the detective had discovered. Gavin also kept back the name of Delancey.

McHale shook his head dubiously. 'But can you prove it, son?' he asked. 'You claim that the owner of this company is engaged in running waterfront protection rackets, is collecting percentages off prostitution and is involved in the runner system. Fine. But can you prove it? Can you prove that the man is in control of most of the crime on the waterfront? It's a pretty big accusation and without proof. . . .' he shrugged.

'All I have to go on is what I've told you, sir,' Gavin said. 'That's the reason I came to see you. I know that I have to get tangible proof. I want to ask your advice as to how I should proceed.'

McHale pursed his lips thoughtfully. 'It's not the sort of law our firm handles, Gavin. You know that. We only deal with criminal law if it affects our established clientèle and then we sub-contract to a criminal lawyer. We deal only in business law.'

'I know that, Mister McHale,' Gavin said. 'But I want to collect evidence about these people to pass on to the police.'

'What you are saying, son,' McHale stroked his nose thoughtfully, 'is that you want to become a one-man crusade against this meat packing company. You'd just be operating out of public interest. Well, let me tell you, son, public interest doesn't put beans in your belly.' He leaned forward, his eyes serious. 'Look, son, I know how you feel. There's a lot wrong with our city. It's new, it's young, vibrant and growing. One of these days it will be the biggest city in the world. We already have a million citizens, we're bigger than most European cities. But we still have to be given time to adjust and grow. I know how you must feel. I used to be angry when I was young and saw people in distress but life's like that. You must think of your own future . . . indeed, of Rosie's future, too. You won't make a fortune by pursuing will o' the wisps. You just have to be more practical about life, Gavin. Now, if you were a multi-millionaire with money to burn, I'd say, yes; sure, go ahead if you want to be a philanthropist. Pursue the public interest. But, son, you don't have money and there ain't no money in public interest.'

Gavin was dismayed and confused at McHale's reaction.

'I don't see it like that, sir,' he said stubbornly. 'These people need to be caught and prosecuted.'

McHale sighed. 'Who are the people involved, anyway?' He paused to relight his cigar. 'What's the name of the meat packing company?'

'My evidence so far implicates Brock Delancey but I believe that it is his father who is behind the entire business.'

McHale choked over his cigar, coughing and spluttering so much that he had to signal the waiter for some water. Finally he turned white faced and tight lipped to Gavin.

'Are you crazy, boy?' he said hoarsely.

Gavin was startled by the vehemence of his expression. 'What do you mean?'

'Christ's sake! The *Delancey* family! You are talking about *Senator* Delancey!'

'I know they have wealth and political position but . . .'

'That's saying the least. Senator Delancey owns a considerable portion of this goddam city. Delancey is big money, son. He owns factories, mills and cotton plantations. Politically, as a Democrat, he's very close to President Johnson.'

'All the more reason to expose him.'

McHale's eyes narrowed.

'You'll stand no chance against Delancey if you start to spread those sort of tales about him, son,' he said coldly. 'He will crush you without even noticing you.'

'You seem to know a lot about the Delanceys,' Gavin bridled.

'Damn right!' nodded McHale, leaning back in his chair. 'Senator Delancey has been my client for fifteen years. If it had not been for Delancey and his connections I would not have had a law firm in the first place. That was the Senator you saw me talking to when you came in, boy.'

Gavin's face was immobile with shock. 'You are Delancey's lawyer?' he asked slowly.

'And a close friend. The Senator and his son have been frequent guests at my house as you would have known if you hadn't been away during the war.'

'I see,' Gavin's mind was working furiously. Then he said firmly, staring McHale straight in the eyes; 'That still doesn't alter my opinion nor my intention.'

McHale watched him stand up. He reached forward to catch the sleeve of Gavin's jacket; 'Look, boy, I've known your pa for a long time. I've served on Irish patriotic committees with him. You and your family are our kind of people. Rosie's firmly set on you, son. Hell, I've offered you a junior partnership. Wouldn't do for Rosie's husband to go through the struggle that I had to when I set up in practice. Now, son, I know the war alters a young man's perceptions. There's a lot of young men who have returned from the war determined to change the world. They'll grow out of it. So will you. You can't go riding around the city on a white horse. The war is over. Drop this crazy notion of yours because you will be the one who is destroyed. Settle down to earning your living. Think of Rosie.'

Gavin gazed down at the lawyer coldly. 'You'll forgive me if I leave you, Mister McHale. I suddenly feel the need for a bath.'

He swung on his heel and left the club.

He didn't know what made him take the direction he did. He left the Athenaeum buried in angry thoughts; angry and confused. He had been outraged to learn that McHale was involved with the Delanceys. Not only involved but McHale obviously had some idea of the shadier dealings of the Senator. McHale had obviously opted for the easy life – to see no evil nor hear no evil. It made him grow speechless with the indignation born of youthful idealism which he would never have admitted was every bit as passionate as John-Joe's idealism about Ireland. He walked rapidly through the streets to ease his anger and confusion. It was only when he found himself on 37th Street that he realized the direction in which he was unconsciously heading. He saw the dark outline of the Church of Holy Innocent and wondered whether it was pure coincidence or whether he had been led there by the feeling of guilt. He had promised Father MacMahon at the celebration dance that he would call in to see him. That had been over a fortnight ago. Next to the church stood the presbytery and, as Gavin approached it, he saw MacMahon himself stooping on the doorstep, tending some flowers in a wooden tub. The priest straightened and caught sight of Gavin. 'You've caught me at my vice, son.'

Gavin looked at the tubs of flowers that spread on the presbytery steps. 'I didn't realize that you were a gardener, Father.'

'Amateur. Strictly amateur,' replied MacMahon dusting his cassock. 'Let's go inside and feed the inner man.' He led Gavin into the cool interior of the presbytery, leading the way directly to the kitchen and drawing a bottle from a cupboard.

'This came by the *City of Cork* on her last run over,' he winked. 'It's the genuine article.' He poured two glasses reverently. '*Sláinte*!' He raised his own glass and allowed the amber liquid to flow back in one gulp.

'Here's health!' responded Gavin, sipping at his.

'Isn't it grand stuff?' smiled the priest. 'Cost me a pretty penny. But isn't there a saying; *is milis fuisce, ach is searbh a íoc*? Whiskey is sweet but paying for it is bitter.'

'I'll not argue,' replied Gavin solemnly.

MacMahon refilled their glasses and then motioned Gavin to take a chair while he lowered himself into an old leather-backed rocker near the kitchen range.

'You said you wanted to talk with me, Father,' prompted Gavin as he settled himself.

MacMahon nodded, sipping slowly at his second glass. 'I've known your pa, Manus Devlin, for a number of years, Gavin. I know he's proud of John-Joe going off to fight for Ireland.'

'I don't approve of that, Father,' Gavin interrupted sharply.

'So I've heard. Manus told me your views. That's why I wanted to see you. I wondered if you were entirely set against the Brotherhood?'

'I'm simply indifferent to it, Father. I believe in Irish freedom . . . is there anyone who cares for the progress of mankind who doesn't believe all nations should be free? But it's a matter of choice. I'm an American.'

'An Irish-American,' corrected MacMahon. 'Gavin, the Brotherhood needs men like you.'

'The Brotherhood doesn't need me, nor I the Brotherhood, Father. There are more things of immediate concern in this city than pursuing the dreams of Irish liberation. There are people in this city, Irish people, too, who need liberating just as much as the people in Ireland.'

MacMahon raised his eyes to Gavin and peered intently at him. 'Ah, you have fire in your belly, Gavin. I can recognize it. The Brotherhood can bring about the freedom of its immigrants just as much as it can encompass the freedom of its people at home.'

'I don't follow you, Father.'

'If Ireland was free then there would be no need for immigrants to come here in their droves to live in squalor and poverty. And if the social programme of the Brotherhood were put into practice, then Ireland would become an example to the world.'

Gavin smiled wanly. 'That's what Pa has said, more or less. It's a debatable point.'

'It's a point that I'd like you to think about, Gavin,' the priest pressed. 'The Brotherhood needs men of intelligence and professional skills not just military ability. It needs men who possess legal training. Now, there is a job available at headquarters in the city. . . .'

Gavin frowned. 'I didn't know you were a Fenian recruiting officer, Father.'

'The call to serve comes in many guises, Gavin,' MacMahon smiled softly.

'According to Archbishop Hughes, priests shouldn't play politics.'

'Well, I'm not playing,' Father MacMahon chuckled. 'Besides, son, a priest is also a man. Politics is the mechanics by which man lives and, indeed, isn't the Church itself a political movement?'

'The Hierarchy have always denounced the Brotherhood and said God must be placed above politics,' Gavin replied.

'Are they to tell God what He should do?' mused MacMahon. 'Above politics? According to the Book of Psalms, God defends the cause of the poor, delivers those in need and overthrows the oppressors. That's hardly keeping His nose out of politics. If you read the fifth chapter of Ephesians, God enjoins people not to take a passive role against those that govern in darkness but to fight and expose them. God is hardly keeping out of politics so why should I reject His example?'

'In spite of the pronouncements of the Hierarchy?'

'The Hierarchy are playing politics themselves,' MacMahon said. 'Haven't they always been out of step with the Irish people when it came to politics? They think that they can protect the Church by playing the obedient child to the conqueror, ingratiating themselves and begging crumbs from the rich man's table. That's not the Church which our Lord founded.'

Gavin sighed; 'Well, Father, Ireland must take care of herself. It is not my fight. My fight is for the people of the city I live in.' He hesitated. 'For example, Father, what would you do if you found that someone, under a cloak of respectability, someone in high public office, was actually running all the crime imaginable in this city? What would you do if you had no one to help you, no one to advise you nor power to fight with? Would you say, that's the way it is? Would you say, I am too weak to do anything about it and walk away?'

'That's the same question that Jesus put to his followers, son. It's the same question that made me join the Brotherhood because I decided to stand and fight tyranny and while you fight tyranny, no matter where you are, you don't stand alone.'

Gavin rose to his feet and put down his empty glass. 'Thanks for the drink, Father.'

MacMahon rose with him. 'If you ever need my advice, Gavin, you know where to find me.'

He followed Gavin to the porch of the presbytery. Gavin paused and smiled at the wooden tubs of flowers. 'I wish all vice resulted in such beauty, Father.'

Father MacMahon patted him on the shoulder; 'Good luck, son.'

Chapter 12

Nora Quinlan gazed in astonishment as Gavin entered her room and announced his intentions. She stared in silence, her brows creased as if she had not heard properly.

'I'm taking you out,' Gavin repeated. 'A Sunday outing. Now get your hat and come and let's go. We'll do anything you want to do. Ride a street car up to the new park; call in to see Barnum's Old American Museum on Ann Street or visit the circus on 14th or Kelly and Leon's Minstrel show . . .' he halted breathlessly. 'The decision is yours.'

The girl continued to gaze at him, her expression changing from astonishment to suspicion.

'All right,' he said when she still made no reply, 'if you won't make up your mind, I'll do it for you. We'll start by Sunday lunch in the Gramercy Park Hotel and then we'll have an afternooon stroll in the park. Have you ever been for a Sunday stroll in Gramercy Park?'

Nora Quinlan shook her head slowly. Then she said: 'What if your friends see you with me?'

'They'll be envious,' smiled Gavin.

'Envious?' her voice filled with bitter ridicule. 'Envious of you walking out with a . . . whore?'

Gavin flushed at the jibe. His intention was to get the girl away from the penury of Bayard with its violence and crime and disease. He wanted to show her that another world existed in New York; a happier world, a place where people could laugh and enjoy themselves.

'Are you coming or not?' he demanded gruffly.

He saw her eyes widen a little at the angry set of his jaw. She hesitated and shrugged. 'I've nothing else to do,' she muttered defiantly. She drew on an old wollen shawl and a small straw bonnet and followed Gavin out of the dreary tenement block. The Italian women nudged and chuckled among themselves as Gavin offered the girl his arm.

'You said that you'll take me anywhere I want?' Nora suddenly asked.

Gavin nodded.

'Then,' he noticed that her expression had become wistful, 'I'd like to take a street car up to the new cathedral.'

'St Patrick's?'

'Yes. I'd . . . I'd like to light a candle for Jack.'

'Very well,' Gavin agreed. 'And after the cathedral we'll go to Gramercy Park for lunch.'

They walked slowly up to the Bowery and caught a street car, making two changes before arriving at the great sandstone Gothic frontage of the Catholic Cathedral of St Patrick on Fifth Avenue. The girl's eyes grew round as she surveyed the massive towers which pushed towards the heavens.

'I've never seen it before,' she whispered. 'I've heard about it but never seen it. I thought there were many beautiful churches in Ireland but there's nothing compared to this. Why, I bet even St Peter's in Rome isn't so grand!'

Gavin grinned indulgently, letting the girl lead him up the steps to the tall doors. In the great gloomy vaulted interior the mass was being sung by a choir whose voices seemed to echo and re-echo through the vastness of the building. The choir had reached the *Sanctus* and their voices surged with force. Nora turned to him with a shy smile. 'I'll not be long.'

He watched her move to the centre aisle, kneel and genuflect to the High Altar, bowing her head for a moment or two in prayer. Then she rose and walked to the side chapel, dropping a coin noisily in a box, removing a candle and walking to the bank of spluttering, flickering candles which stood before the image of the Madonna. She lit it and pressed it into place before kneeling down, genuflecting again and bowing her head. When she rejoined him her eyes were misty with tears. She smiled at him but said nothing. Gavin felt a tremendous desire to take the girl in his arms, to comfort her and protect her from the world. It took him a moment to control the surge of feeling and then he held out his arm; 'Now, Mrs Quinlan,' he said, his voice oddly strangled, 'let's go to have some lunch. I'm famished.' She did not apparently notice the curious tone in his voice but meekly took his arm.

He turned with her down the steps of the cathedral. At the foot of the steps, where a carriage had just deposited them, Stead McHale, his wife and Rosaleen, were staring up at him, mouths momentarily agape. Stead McHale was the first to react. His face assumed a mask of burning maliciousness that rivalled a gargoyle in the twisting of its features. He whispered something to his wife whose eyes dropped away and assumed a frosty look. McHale took Rosaleen firmly by the arm and they moved up the steps. Only Rosaleen gazed from Nora to Gavin with an expression of bewildered hurt. Feeling helpless to deal with the situation, Gavin merely removed his hat but they swept by. The great door of the cathedral swung shut with a bang that seemed to shatter the resounding notes of the *Agnus Dei* which had drifted out.

'Were they friends of yours?'

Gavin brought himself back to reality. 'Friends?' He bit his lip. 'Not exactly.'

'But the girl . . .' Nora pressed perceptively. 'She looked as though she has been more than a friend.'

Gavin sighed. 'I thought she was . . . once.'

'What happened?' Her interest was genuine.

'I'm not sure, Nora,' he said brusquely. 'I don't even know whether whatever it was that happened happened to her or to me.'

Hearing the tone in his voice she did not bother to press further.

Gavin dismissed Rosie and her parents from his mind and assumed a false gaiety which eventually became a genuine feeling. The rest of the day passed with pleasant rapidity. He did not even mention Hogan nor Brock Delancey nor his resolve to gather evidence against him. He had made the decision with qualms. It was almost as if his decisions were being made for him by some other force, a destiny of which he was being a prisoner. He had known, after his meeting with Stead McHale at the Athenaeum, that he was closing a door on the future which had been planned for him. He had already reached the decision that his engagement to Rosaleen was a mistake but he had not yet found the courage to tell the girl. He assumed that Stead McHale had already done so on his behalf. It was the matter of telling his father and mother that was going to be difficult. As for how he would survive until a new opening in a law firm came up, well, he had his army back pay to last him a while. But that Sunday he dismissed all these thoughts and gave himself over to making the day enjoyable, avoiding any further tension. Nora and he finished the evening with a dinner at French's opposite the City Hall. The girl had never dined out in style before and was not a little awed by the magnificence of the restaurant. When Gavin escorted her back to her tiny room her eyes were dancing with laughter and she whirled happily to collapse on the end of the bed, throwing off her bonnet and shawl.

'If I live to be one hundred, Gavin Devlin, I don't think that I shall enjoy a day so much.'

'I hope you are wrong,' Gavin said sharing her happiness. 'I hope you'll have many more fine days in your life, Nora.'

Her eyes grew serious as she gazed up at him, the faint cloud of suspicion creeping into them. 'Why are you doing this for me, Gavin Devlin?' she asked quietly. 'What is it that you want from me?'

Gavin hesitated, raised a shoulder and let it fall eloquently.

'I guess I don't know that myself,' he replied gruffly. 'Good night, Nora. I'll be in touch soon.'

He hurried from her room, swinging out of the dark, smelling tenement block with a feeling of unease. Unease with himself. Unease with the lack of understanding of his own emotions.

Manus Devlin emerged from his study as Gavin was coming down to breakfast the next day.

'Can I have a word before you go out, son?'

Gavin nodded wondering whether Stead McHale had already broken the news. He followed Manus into his study and swung the door shut behind him.

'Take a seat,' Manus invited him.

Gavin dropped into a chair while his father established himself behind his desk. 'I understand things are not working out with McHale?'

Gavin groaned inwardly. So Stead McHale had been in touch. 'It's a bit complicated, Pa,' he said.

Manus Devlin stared thoughtfully at his eldest son. 'There's some trouble between you and Rosaleen, isn't there?'

Gavin grimaced.

'Another woman?' asked his father.

Gavin hesitated briefly and shook his head.

'There's a saying that it is always a rough path to the bridal bed,' Manus smiled.

'Rosaleen and I have changed during these last few years, Pa,' Gavin replied, feeling he ought to try to explain matters. 'We're different people, wanting different things out of life.'

'Is that you or her speaking?'

'Me, I guess.'

'I heard that you had a difference of opinion with Stead McHale. I'm not going to ask what it was about, son. But if you don't go into McHale's law firm, what will you do?'

'I want to take up law right enough, Pa. But not on McHale's terms. There are ethical reasons why I can't join McHale.'

'Ethical, eh?' Manus Devlin picked up a pen and toyed with it for a few seconds. 'I want you to make the right decision, son. You had a good record in the army. You've a good law degree, too. You can have a pick of jobs. Just make sure that you make the right decision.'

Gavin gave a small smile. 'I think I'm doing that, Pa.'

'You remember that before the war I used to go north for a month or so during the summer?' Manus asked, as though changing the subject.

Gavin nodded. Ever since his father had settled in New York and established his practice, he had formed a regular ritual of going on a hunting trip every summer into the Wilderness of Lower Canada beyond Québec City. But it was a trip which he had not made since the first shots of the war had rung out at Fort Sumter four years ago.

'I was planning,' Manus Devlin was saying, 'that after the war was over, you, John-Joe and I would make that trip together. The first time all of us would be together, the very first summer the war was over. You were both too young to come with me before the war.' He hesitated and looked slightly nervous. 'Would you come with me, Gavin? We could go at the end of the month and spend all August up there. I was hoping we could all have gone . . . John-Joe and you . . . well, what do you say?'

Gavin felt awkward. It was as if his father was scared of rejection. He felt he wanted to please him but the idea of spending a month in the wilderness right now, at this time when he wanted to start work finding out about the Delanceys. . . .

'I'd like to very much, Pa,' he said with some reserve. 'But could I let you know in a day or two?' Perhaps he would be able to think of some valid excuse by then.

'Of course, Gavin,' his father was on the defensive now. 'Don't worry if you can't make it. I just thought it might be a good idea to give you some time to readjust, to sort out in your mind what you want to do. See what you feel in a few days' time.'

Bridget entered abruptly. Her face looked troubled.

'Excuse me, doctor,' she said to Manus before turning to Gavin.

'It's Miss Rosaleen, Master Gavin. She seems a wee bit upset. I've put her in the drawing room.'

Gavin rose, biting his lip. He had wanted more time to prepare for this encounter.

Rosaleen McHale stood stiffly before the mantlepiece above which Manus Devlin's portrait of President Andrew Jackson stared down disapprovingly on the proceedings. The President had been chosen to dominate the drawing room as Manus claimed Jackson to be the first Irish President of the United States. Jackson's parents had come from County Antrim and Jackson had been fond of telling people how they had only just made it to the shores of America before his birth, otherwise, as no president could be born outside the United States, he would have been disqualified from office. The bleak disapproval on Andy Jackson's face was mirrored on that of Rosaleen McHale before him.

'I've come to hear an explanation, Gavin,' her voice was taut, full of suppressed emotion.

'Explanation?' repeated Gavin, wanting time to collect his thoughts.

Her lips thinned slightly. 'Daddy told me about his talk with you at his club. You insulted some friends of his and also insulted him. That was bad enough. But I was not prepared for the shameful behaviour of yesterday; yesterday on the steps of the cathedral of all places where everyone could see!'

'Shameful behaviour?' Gavin felt a flush on his cheeks. 'I was escorting the widow of a member of my regiment to the cathedral. What is there that is shameful in that, Rosie?'

Her eyes blazed in anger. 'Liar!' she stamped her foot. 'Daddy said she was some Bowery prostitute. How could you be so wicked, so vile? As if no one would know that you were flaunting down Fifth Avenue with a common whore! How dare you insult me so?' She went on, unheeding his darkening features. 'Daddy told me that you were spreading malicious lies about his friend, Senator Delancey, and his son, Brock. Brock and his father have visited many times with us. The Delanceys are a grand family. I cannot understand why you should pick on them. I know you have been acting strangely since your return, but I thought you just had to be given time to settle down. I don't know what you are doing, Gavin, but you seem to have deliberately set out to insult both me and Daddy.'

Gavin waited until she had paused for breath and then said slowly;

'That I have not, Rosaleen. But if your father is associated with Delanceys' rackets, then he will fall with the Delanceys as well.'

Rosaleen raised her flushed features. Gavin did not allow her time to interrupt.

'As for insulting you, Rosie, that's not so. Maybe we've both changed, though. We've grown up differently. Maybe everything has changed and there is no going back. I loved you once, was *in love* with you. But I am my own man, Rosie. I cannot be told how and where I am to lead my life. The life I want to lead is obviously not the life that you and your father want me to lead. Ever since I came back I began to realize that we were making a mistake about our marriage.'

Her mouth formed a twisted 'o', then her jaw snapped shut.

'How dare you insult me to my face?' She fumbled in her bag, took out a small box and threw it across the room so that it almost hit him. It thudded against the wall and the small silver ring, the polished Connemara marble of two hearts entangled, dropped on to the floor.

'There is your ring back and here,' she drew forth some letters and dropped them beside the ring, 'are your beastly letters. Vile things. There can be nothing more between us.'

'The Rosie I thought I knew would have listened to what I had to say about the Delanceys before judging things. I doubt whether there was much between us in the first place if I could have been so wrong about you.'

She stared at him for a moment in astonishment. He suddenly felt genuinely sorry that he was not able to communicate with her. Scarlet in anger, she turned to the door.

'Rosie,' he called softly, 'give your father a message from me. I mean it seriously.' She halted at the door waiting, her back still turned to him. 'Tell him that when a ship sinks then the rats usually sink with it. He'll know what I mean.'

She threw him a glance of hatred. 'You're unspeakable! Daddy will come round here and horsewhip you.'

'I doubt it,' he replied. 'That would require guts.'

With an inarticulate cry of indignation, Rosie McHale flounced from the room. A moment latter, Gavin heard the street door slam. Curiously, the only emotion he felt was relief.

For a moment he stared down at the bundle of letters and the ring, then bent and gathered them up. He was aware of his mother standing at the door, her eyes wide with worry.

'I heard Rosie leave.'

He forced a smile. 'I shan't be marrying her, Ma. And I shan't be joining McHale's law firm.'

Aideen Devlin waited as if in expectation of some further explanation. 'Then what are you going to do?' she prompted.

Gavin shrugged. 'Find out what I should be doing and then go and do it,' he replied, giving her a swift peck on the cheek before taking the letters out to the kitchen range and burning them.

Chapter 13

Gavin picked up a copy of the *New York Daily Tribune* on his way to the barber's shop. There was a customer already in the chair when he went in so he sat down and began to scan the paper. It was full of reports of the possible trial for High Treason of Jefferson Davies, the Confederate President. But it was the small paragraph, almost insignificantly placed, that caught his eye. It caused him to feel a sudden coldness as if an icy wind had blown through the door.

> Found in the East River last night, the body of Gabriel Symes, a private detective, who was formerly in the Metropolitan Police of this city. Symes had been brutally beaten and indications are that his attackers then threw him into the river where he drowned. Mister Symes was instrumental in bringing many malefactors to justice and it is imagined that he met his unhappy end as a vengeance killing.

Gavin put down his newspaper and, almost in a dream, allowed himself to be beckoned into the barber's chair. Was it a simple coincidence? Surely, Brock Delancey . . . ? He shivered. He wondered whether he should go straight away to the police with his story. No. He needed advice before he made an official approach. As he left the barber's shop he recalled the freckle-faced, ginger-haired police sergeant, Murphy, who had served with him in the Brigade. He dropped into Lovejoy's Hotel, opposite City Hall, and wrote a note to Murphy asking to meet him for a drink. He sent a boy directly to police headquarters promising him fifty cents if he returned with Murphy's reply.

Murphy met Gavin in the bar of Lovejoy's later that evening and sat toying with his drink while Gavin poured out his story. As Gavin spoke he saw the policeman's body growing increasingly tense and his initial smile had frozen into a thin line, almost a mirthless mask.

'What should I do, Murphy?' demanded Gavin as he finished his story.

'Do?' Murphy's voice was a harsh whisper. 'Forget it!'

Gavin looked at him, not understanding for a moment.

'Devlin, this is the Delancey family that you are accusing, not some two-bit hoodlum.'

'So what?' demanded Gavin. 'All the more reason to do something.'

'So what?' echoed Murphy, staring at him as if he were insane. 'The Delancey family own a good chunk of this turf, boy.' He gestured through the window to the imposing edifice of City Hall across Park Row. 'See that building? Old man Delancey has only got to whisper to the mayor and the mayor would have that pile of stones gift wrapped and given to Delancey on a silver platter.'

'Everyone has told me they are powerful. I know that otherwise I wouldn't be asking your advice, Murphy. If they killed poor little Symes, or had him killed, it means they are running scared. I want to know how I fight them.'

Murphy shifted uncomfortably. 'You don't fight them, Devlin. You don't fight the Delanceys. You just avoid them.'

'Avoid them?' Gavin was indignant. 'Avoid them when they are running some of the most vicious sordid rackets in this city? They must be destroyed not avoided.'

Murphy gazed directly into Gavin's eyes. 'Do you think that no one knows the Delanceys down at headquarters? Do you think no one knows that they pick up percentages on the tenements, boarding houses and brothels along the waterfront?' His voice was quiet. 'Listen, Devlin, and wake up to reality . . . the Delanceys can pay off the Commissioner, the General Superintendent and most of the force. . . .'

Gavin stared back coldly. 'Are you saying that the police are paid off by Delancey?'

Murphy shrugged. 'Take it which way you like but just don't go to the City force with any tales about the Delanceys and expect them to be acted upon. Besides that, it wouldn't be a healthy thing to do.'

Gavin banged his fist in anger on the bar top. 'Jesus, Murphy! These are your people that the Delanceys are hurting,' he said between clenched teeth.

Murphy grimaced indifferently. 'My people? They ceased to be my people when I put on this uniform, Devlin. I'm an American police officer.'

Gavin felt a stirring of guilt. Your people. My people. Immigrants. Irish immigrants.

Murphy reached forward and laid a hand on Devlin's arm. 'You know the rules, Devlin. You've been in the war. The strong survive, the weak perish. It's a law of nature. So far as I see it, the Irish here get what they deserve. All they care about is whiskey and political argument. People like the Delanceys are just more intelligent than most. They know how to use those passions. The Senator remains in the Senate by handing out a glass of free whiskey to his voters. If the voter behaves himself, he may get a job or a hand out at political headquarters. If not. . . .' He made a negative gesture. 'As for the rest, Devlin, it's up to them to survive or go under.'

Gavin breathed out slowly. 'You'll be telling me that you don't care if the Delanceys murder, rob or cheat because they have money and privilege with a voice in city hall and the Senate,' sneered Gavin.

Murphy shrugged again. 'If that's the system, then I have to make the best of it. I'm not out to change the world, Devlin. I just want to survive.'

'Jesus!' swore Gavin in disgust as he rose to his feet.

Murphy glared up in anger. 'What gives you the right to be so bloody pious, Devlin?' he demanded. 'You're just a damned Teig along with the rest of us with the exception that your old man made a bit more money so that you didn't have to beg or work along with the likes of me. You can afford to be bloody sanctimonious. Well listen, your dad hasn't got the political know-how or enough money to finance your confrontation with the likes of the Delanceys so take my advice – don't try it.'

Gavin's eyes narrowed. 'Is that a threat, Murphy?' he asked coldly. 'Are you threatening me?'

'I'm advising you for your best interests, Devlin. Don't mess with the Delanceys.'

He ran screaming through the icy mud of the fields, his hands clasped to his ears as he tried to shut out the wailing shriek of the shells and the roar of the cannonade. He ran crying in fear through the stark burnt wilderness, amidst the swirling grey acrid smoke of the guns and flickering fire of explosions. He ran until he burst out of the forest on to a quiet plain of green through which a small silver creek babbled and chattered its way across a bed of shining pebbles, cool and fragrant amidst the small field trefoils and multi-coloured flowers. He staggered across the plain until he collapsed at the edge of the creek.

She was standing there, standing waiting for him. The green mantle of precious silk fluttered in the morning breeze, spangled with stars of red gold. Her eyes were violet blue, clear and cloudless like dew drops on the top of a blade of grass. Her cheeks were reddened like roses and gold rings were the tight curls of her red-gold hair. She was fairer to look upon than swans at dusk upon a silver river. She bent and smiled, brushing his lips with her own red ones, sweet like honey mingled with wine.

'What is it that you want, Captain Devlin?' she whispered softly.

'You!' he cried. 'I know now that it is you I want.'

She smiled softly. 'I am the Tara of women. I am an untrodden path. I am your desire. I am the unobtainable. Your hand must renounce what your heart yearns for, Captain Devlin.'

The explosion blew him backwards in the cold mud.

Ready the flag! Jack Quinlan's baritone rang out. They were moving forward in lines now, in their serried ranks, running through the mud, the icy cold mud, until they reached the ditch and threw themselves forward to escape the thunder and roar of the cannonade.

The gaunt figure with the haunted eyes crouched in the ditch before him on a wooden cart, a skeletal hand outstretched. The black hungry eyes devoured him. 'Spare a dime?'

He awoke with a start, dry mouthed and fearful. There was a momentary comfort in knowing that it was only a dream: a comfort before he stared into the moody blackness about him.

Manus Devlin was still finishing his breakfast when he went down the next morning.

'Have you thought any more about our trip, Gavin?'

Gavin suppressed a desire to snap in irritation. 'I'm pretty involved with something right now, Pa,' he said.

Manus Devlin looked troubled. 'I saw Stead McHale last night at the Athenaeum Club. He talked in riddles for a while. He wanted to warn me, it seems. Said you were getting into something out of your depth, Something dangerous.'

'I don't want to discuss it, Pa,' Gavin said shortly.

Manus Devlin looked hurt. 'That's your choice, son. According to McHale you are going around making wild accusations against a valued client and friend of his.'

'The accusations are true,' Gavin said.

'McHale also said something which upset me, son. He claimed that you had become involved with a Bowery prostitute and were actually flaunting the relationship.'

'That's a lie!' snapped Gavin. 'If you must know, it began with me trying to help the widow of a sergeant who served in my regiment. She had fallen on hard times because of his death.'

'Prostitution?' queried Manus Devlin.

'It was a choice between starvation or survival.'

There was an uneasy silence between them for a moment. Then Manus prompted; 'I think I have some right to know, Gavin.'

Gavin told him briefly. 'By accident I discovered who was behind the rackets down on Bayard. The rackets that are run by respectable people – prostitution, the runners system, protection, robbery, you name it. I didn't fight these last four years for scum like the Delanceys to live in luxury on the suffering of others.'

Manus met Gavin's eyes and held them. 'You told McHale about the Delanceys?'

Gavin chuckled sardonically. 'I told Stead McHale, yes.'

Manus whistled softly. 'I wish you had come to me, son. I could have told you that Senator Delancey and his son Brock were frequent visitors to McHale's household. McHale has represented the Senator for ten or maybe fifteen years.'

'I found that out,' Gavin said bitterly. 'I told a police friend of mine, too. It seems that the Senator has control over the city police force as well.'

Manus' eyes widened a little. 'Then you are in a dangerous business, son. At least McHale was right in warning me about that.' He exhaled deeply. 'I'll not advise you one way or the other, son. It's your business. I was your age when I first went into Repeal politics in Ireland. That was at a time when everyone was warning me to stay out, when the Orangemen and the Unionist bully boys were going about the country beating up the likes of anyone who dared utter a word against the Union. I didn't listen to those who told me to keep out of Repeal politics. I don't expect you will take any notice if I told you to stay out of this. But I do say – be careful, son.'

Gavin suddenly felt close, very close to his father. He felt a curious desire to embrace him for the first time in many years. Instead he smiled softly and said, 'Thanks, Pa. I will.'

Manus Devlin stood up and moved to the door, pausing on the threshold and glancing back to his eldest son. 'All the same, what will you do?' he asked. 'McHale has more than enough influence to stop you getting in any other law firm in this city. I don't doubt he'll do that.'

'McHale doesn't control the law in every state, Pa,' replied Gavin.

'You mean you might move out of the city?'

'Maybe. I don't know. I haven't finished with the Delanceys yet. I am going to work down at the Law Library to see whether I can find any means of proceeding with a legal action.'

'Like I said, son,' Manus Devlin said slowly, 'I'm not offering you advice. Sometimes, though, newspapers can do things in this country which no one else can do.'

Gavin tried to fathom his meaning.

'Hal Geary now, he owns the *Commercial Tribune* and is a supporter of the Brotherhood. He might hear you out if you mention my name.' Manus Devlin smiled briefly before he closed the door after him.

Arriving at Printing House Square, Gavin handed his visiting card to a messenger and was immediately escorted to the offices of the proprietor of the *Daily Commercial Tribune*. Hal Geary was a thin, hard-faced man, whose tight features were softened by humorous blue eyes. He shook hands, a brief, cold handshake, and gestured for Gavin to be seated.

'I know your father well, son. Served on several committees with him as a matter of fact. A good Democrat. Now what is it that I can do for you?'

Gavin told him, telling his story slowly and with precision. Geary's face became expressionless, even the eyes grew cold. At the end of Gavin's story the newspaperman leant back in his chair and drummed his fingers on the table for a while.

'Stead McHale has a reputation as one of the finest business lawyers in the city. He donates considerable sums of money to various charities, to the Democratic Party and to Irish organizations. There's some talk of him running for mayor in a year or maybe two years' time. He'd have my support if he did so.'

Gavin felt his faint hope sink. 'I appreciate just how well placed the Delancey family are,' he said bitterly.

Geary didn't rise to the insult. 'So you've come back from the wars to change the world, eh, son?' he said softly.

'We hold these truths to be self-evident,' sneered Gavin, rising to his feet, 'that all men are created equal; that they are endowed by their Creator with certain inalienable rights; that among these are life, liberty and the pursuit of happiness. That to secure these rights, governments are instituted among men, deriving their just powers from the consent of the governed.'

Geary's mouth quirked in response. 'So you can recite the Declaration of Independence, son. That's good. Most of the people living down on Bayard haven't even heard of it.'

Gavin turned towards the door; 'I don't want to waste your time. . . .'

'Hold it, son!' Geary was still sitting stretched behind his desk but the sharpness in his voice called Gavin back. 'Listen, son, you've failed to pursue the Delancey family with the law and so you want me, rather this newspaper, to take up the crusade against the Delanceys and their ilk? Is that right?'

Gavin spread his hands. 'I guess so.'

Geary's eyes twinkled again. 'You want me to reveal their crimes to the people of this city and have them hounded out of politics?'

'Will you?' demanded Gavin.

'No, sir!' Geary replied with alacrity. 'But let me add my advice to that which you have undoubtedly received from Stead McHale and from your friend in the police force. Leave the Delanceys alone. Concentrate on your own life. Leave crusading to those who are best able to handle it.'

'Like you?' sneered Gavin. 'A big, powerful newspaper owner who is too scared to go after a crook because he has the prefix Senator against his name.'

Geary took the insult straight-faced. 'There's little room for idealists in the real world.'

Gavin bridled. 'You'll forgive me if I remark that I thought the war, in which over 600,000 Americans have been killed, was fought because of an ideal.'

Geary picked up a cheroot, lit it, and blew the smoke across the desk towards Gavin. 'Son, I don't rightly know of one war that was fought over ideals. Wars are fought for power or money, usually both.'

'Wasn't the emancipation of the slaves an ideal?' cried Gavin. 'Wasn't that the best and purest ideal man ever fought over?'

Geary inclined his head wearily. 'You reckon that was what the war was about, eh son?'

'What else?'

The newspaper owner allowed himself a cynical smile, the first time his lips betrayed an emotion. 'Slavery, son, was just an incidental issue. The war was about the Union. The Union first and last, the Union to maintain the financial viability of these United States and the power that Union brings with it.'

Gavin twisted his lips in disbelief.

'Come on, boy,' snapped Geary. 'The Union was everything. It's to the Union that we Americans owe our freedom, our safety and our respect abroad . . . the Union makes us strong. The Union was born out of the necessities of disordered finance, prostrate commerce and ruined credit. When we ran down the Union Jack and hauled up our own flag, we sprang forward with a new life, a new financial prosperity which is the copious fountain of our national, social and personal happiness. One day this continent will be united from eastern seaboard to western seaboard, north to south. Then, by God, the world will tremble at our name. When we won our freedom from England we were a nation of four millions. Today we are closer to forty millions and we are respected because of our power and our strength. The war was fought to retain that power and strength.'

Gavin gestured impatiently. 'Were so many people deluded then? Was freedom for the slaves no issue at all?'

'The anti-slavery lobby was a rallying cry. Abe Lincoln used it, that's all.' Geary jabbed his cheroot towards one of the frames that hung on the walls of his office. It contained a piece of handwritten paper. 'Go and take a look at it, son. Tell me what it is.'

Gavin saw it was a letter dated from the White House the previous year. The signature was Lincoln's.

'Read it, son,' pressed Geary.

Gavin cleared his throat. '"My . . . my paramount object is to save the Union and is not either to save or destroy slavery . . .",' Gavin glanced at the newspaper proprietor, then turned back to the letter. '"If I could save the Union without freeing any slave, I would do it, and if I could save it by freeing all the slaves, I would do it; and if I could save it by freeing some and leaving others alone, I would also do that. What I do about slavery and the coloured race I do because it helps to save the Union and what I forbear, I forbear, because I do not believe it would help to save the Union".'

'You see, son,' interrupted Geary, 'if Abe had thought slavery was in the interests of the Union he would have been right down there in Richmond alongside Jeff Davies, rooting for slavery.'

'And the moral issue?' demanded Gavin coldly.

'The moral issue is power, son. Some have it, some don't.'

'You make power sound like the ultimate goal for man to strive for?'

'So it is, son. The advantage of power is that you can do what you want with it. Power is pleasure which helps to alleviate the pain of life.'

'What about using power for the common good?'

Geary chuckled. 'There you go sounding like these new fangled communists out of Europe. If you want to survive, son, be a pragmatist.'

'So you'll do nothing about the Delanceys?'

Geary shrugged. 'Not unless I find myself with a greater power than they. That's the rules of the game, son. The Delancey family are powerful. You can't fight power unless you have an equal or greater power. Power only retreats against power.'

Gavin frowned. 'I think you are a dishonest man, Mister Geary,' he said slowly. 'You will only posture and take moral attitudes when your opponent is weaker.'

He turned to leave the office.

'That's pragmatism, son,' Geary called after him. 'That's being realistic.'

Chapter 14

'Devlin! Gavin Devlin!'

Gavin was just emerging from the New York Law Institute Library on Chambers, just behind City Hall, when the shout arrested him. The library was just closing as it was six o'clock in the evening and there were only a few people on the street. He turned and saw the flushed features of Sergeant Murphy. Murphy pushed his way up and halted, his face worried.

'I've been looking all over town for you, Devlin.'

'Don't tell me that you've changed your mind about the Delanceys?' Gavin smiled cynically.

'I'm no mug, Devlin,' Murphy replied sharply. 'But it was about the Delanceys that I've come to warn you.'

Gavin raised an eyebrow. 'Warn me?'

'Word is out on the street that certain people have been told to give you a little demonstration in minding your own business.'

'What's that supposed to mean?' Gavin asked.

'Christ sake! What do you think it means? Take some advice, Devlin. Clear out of the city for a while. Back off from chasing the Delanceys. And for God's sake, don't say that it was me who warned you.'

Murphy swung away abruptly and walked swiftly down the street.

Aideen Devlin was being served by Bridget when Gavin entered the breakfast room the next morning. The remains of a meal at his father's place indicated that Manus Devlin was already in his surgery. Gavin moved to his mother's place and kissed her lightly on the forehead before turning to help himself to coffee from the sideboard. His mother was reading a letter.

'It's from John-Joe,' she glanced up. 'He's arrived in Queenstown and says that he will be on his way to Dublin soon.'

Gavin sat down and glanced across with interest.
'Anything else?' he prompted.
'No,' Aideen Devlin shook her head. 'Just that he has arrived safely and is with friends. He sends his love to all of us and will write when he can.'
Bridget turned from the sideboard. 'Kidneys, Master Gavin?'
'Whatever you care to put on my plate, Bridget,' replied Gavin gravely sipping at his coffee. Bridget gave him a glance of disapproval.
Aideen had placed the letter by her plate and was examining her eldest son quietly.
'Your father is leaving for his trip to Lower Canada tomorrow, Gavin,' she said after a while. 'He'll be away for a month.'
Bridget pushed a plate before him and nodded her head to Aideen before leaving the room. She had piled enough kidneys on it for three people.
'He was disappointed that you could not go with him, Gavin.'
'I simply can't afford a month of hunting and fishing just now, Ma,' Gavin protested.
Aideen sighed deeply. 'Your father was looking forward to this first summer after the war. He wanted to take John-Joe and you on a hunting trip. Your father has a great love of the wilds, of the hunt . . . even when we were in Ireland.'
Gavin pursed his lips. 'Well, he was not disappointed when John-Joe decided to go to Ireland instead.'
His mother heard the accusation in his voice and regarded him with her gentle, forgiving expression. 'I don't begrudge him his pride in John-Joe, Gavin. No more should you. Ah, but you are like your father in certain ways.'
Gavin bent to his breakfast, saying nothing.
'Manus is a man of strong conviction, Gavin. Ever since he was a student at the College of Surgeons he was a man of firm ideals. He was full of hope, Dedicated. He was so like you.'
Gavin stared up in surprise. 'I would have thought that description fitted John-Joe, not me.'
Aideen Devlin shook her head. 'Both my sons are idealistic, each in their own way. John-Joe is enthusiastic, eager, youthful; you are more stolid, slow to fire but when you are a-fired there is no quenching you.'
'Pa should not have allowed John-Joe to go to Ireland,' Gavin said flatly.

'How could he stop him?' demanded his mother. 'How could he when John-Joe was going to attempt the very things that your father had failed to accomplish? You don't know with what passion your father cares for the Irish people. It was because of that passion that he has had to spend eighteen years in exile here.'

'Is that really how he sees it – exile?' Gavin asked. 'Is that how you see it, Ma?'

Aideen smiled softly. 'I have come to accept this life. It's a good life. I've made my home here and brought my children up. God send that I see my grandchildren grow up also. But your father. . . . Well, I was always a rival to *Roisín Dubh*, his Ireland. He was so in love with her that he had to sacrifice himself for her. I don't begrudge him . . . not really. Better to be in love with Ireland than another woman.'

Her eyes were suspiciously bright.

Gavin came round the table to her side and squeezed her hand. 'This is my home, Ma. America. I can't make it otherwise. I can't share John-Joe's dream of Ireland with Pa. Maybe that's why Pa favours John-Joe.'

Aideen sniffed and blew her nose on a small piece of linen. 'Your father loves you both equally,' she rebuked. 'He worried about you constantly when you were at war, just as now he worries about John-Joe. He wants your love, Gavin . . . above all he needs your respect.'

'He's always had my love,' Gavin said, gazing at the table. 'But I cannot be part of his world. His world is 3,000 miles away across an ocean. My world is here.'

'I understand that,' Aideen said sadly. 'I understand you both. If only you two would speak with each other instead of at each other. Why not go north with him, Gavin? Just this once; this one hunting trip. It would mean so much to him.'

Gavin shook his head. 'I have to do what I feel I must.' He bent to kiss her. As he left the room she called out; 'At least will you go to the railroad depot to see him off?'

'I will, Ma,' he called across his shoulder not wishing to see the tears in his mother's eyes.

He left the Law Institute Library at the usual time that evening and turned down Chambers. At the corner of the street he paused to light a cheroot and wave away some urchins who were begging for pennies. It was then he became aware of two men on the other side of the street. He turned to meet their gaze. His heart skipped a beat as he caught the pale eyes of the copper-haired man called Hogan. The man saw his start of recognition and his bulbous lips parted in a savage grin. The second man was raw-boned, not dressed so well, but was a big, powerfully-built man who carried a wooden stick in his hand. They began to cross the street towards him. He turned and began to hurry along the sidewalk hearing their footsteps quickening behind him.

'Devlin!'

A panic stirred within him.

'Devlin! We've a message for you!'

The mocking call made him cold with fear. An alleyway loomed up ahead and he darted into it and began to run. The rasping breath and heavy tread of his pursuers echoed after him. He ran down the stinking dark warren between the tall tenement buildings, across vile garbage which the inhabitants had simply thrown from the doors to rot and decay.

'Git round the other way, Kylie!' he heard a voice cry. 'Cut him off!'

Gavin skidded and banged into a rotting wooden door whose lock seemed to tear away from the wood, sending him sprawling into the black interior of a building which was full of snarling dogs and screaming children. A shrill female voice began to shout at him in a language he could not understand. The atmosphere was so hot and stuffy that he retched as he clambered to his feet.

Hogan stood silhouetted in the door.

Without thinking, Gavin lashed out with his foot, catching the man on the thigh just as he aimed a blow with his stick. The cudgel caught Gavin a glancing blow on the side of the head, momentarily stunning him. He staggered back, slipping on something. The slip caused him to miss the full impact of Hogan's second blow, allowing him time to recover his balance. With a cry, Gavin twisted and hit out with his fist, catching the man on the side of the head, causing him to grunt in pain. Then Gavin leapt back through the door, away from the bedlam of cries and screams and yelping dogs. He staggered back along the alley, his breath coming in heavy gasps. There were faint cries behind him. He paused at the entrance to the street, reaching up a hand to feel something sticky on his forehead. The cudgel had grazed him. He drew himself up and walked quickly away, darting down the first turning he came to and doubling back again until he found himself outside the Astor House Hotel. He did not hesitate but strode through the foyer into the washroom to tidy himself up. Afterwards he went into the bar and ordered a drink.

For the first time it struck home how isolated he was. Murphy had been right. The police force were not going to help him. Neither was Geary with all the power of his newspaper nor McHale and his law firm. Power only retreats before power. Geary had said that. So what could he do? Was he deluding himself, spending his days in the Law Institute Library, trying to puzzle out a legal method of attacking the impregnable Delancey castle?

The laughter from beyond the screen which separated the bar of the Astor House Hotel from the lounge was vaguely familiar. Gavin moved across to peer beyond it.

Brock Delancey was seated at a table in the far corner with Stead McHale. With them sat a very fashionably dressed woman whose features, for a moment, were hidden by an elegant hat. She was giggling nervously as she sipped a colourful-looking concoction from a tall glass. Gavin did not need to see her face to recognize Rosaleen McHale. He ground his teeth bitterly as he stared at the bland lawyer with his giggling daughter and the handsome, smiling profile of Brock Delancey. His first reaction was to turn and leave but he found himself under the spell of a welling anger which he could not control. Instead of leaving he walked to their table.

Stead McHale saw him coming first and whispered something to Delancey. Delancey met his gaze, his smiling features growing serious. Rosaleen, observing their expression, glanced up and was startled.

'Well, it's Captain Devlin, isn't it?' Brock Delancey spoke first in his softly modulated voice.

Stead McHale bit his lip uneasily as he watched Gavin's expression.

'I fell in with a couple of your friends a while back, Delancey,' Gavin said evenly. 'Hogan was one. I think he called the other man Kylie.'

Delancey's eyes narrowed slightly. 'I don't recall any business acquaintances of those names. However, I hope the exchange was profitable?'

'Sure,' Gavin said in grim humour. 'They convinced me what a dirty specimen of human excreta you are.'

Rosaleen let out a wail while Stead McHale sprang to his feet, his face white. 'You'd better leave before I have you removed, you young whippersnapper,' he exploded. 'You can't talk to Mister Delancey in that manner.'

Delancey raised a hand and McHale fell silent. 'You'll have to give me satisfaction for that, Devlin,' his voice was almost a hushed whisper. The lounge had grown silent and people were turning to stare.

'You mean you want to send your thugs and bully boys after me again? What will it be next – shall I be beaten up and thrown in the river like poor Symes?'

Rosie McHale was staring at him an expression of incomprehension making her face seem like a clown's mask. Delancey had come to his feet now, his face working. The hotel manager had appeared, anxious faced. 'Is there any trouble, Mister Delancey?'

Delancey teetered for a moment, fighting for self-control and then, assuming it, studiously straightened his jacket.

'This person is being offensive to my party and myself,' he said coldly. 'Have him thrown out.'

The manager waved to a couple of liveried footmen who were hurrying across the lounge.

'I'll have satisfaction one way or another, Devlin,' whispered Delancey so that only Gavin could hear.

It happened so quickly that no one could believe it. Gavin poised himself lightly on the balls of his feet and eased back, suddenly thrusting his fist forward like a piston, smacking against Delancey's jaw. The man went flying backwards, crashing over his chair and hitting his head on the oak-pannelling behind. He was knocked out cold. Rosaleen McHale began to raise her voice in a cry of hysteria while her father dropped to his knees beside Delancey's body. The manager grabbed at Gavin but he offered no resistance.

Stead McHale glared up. 'You've gone too far, boy. Too far.'

A hand tightened on Gavin's arm and spun him round. He found himself staring into the almost incredulous face of Sergeant Murphy.

'I'll take care of this man,' snapped Murphy to the manager and his doormen. He propelled Gavin swiftly out of the lounge, through the lobby and into the street outside.

'For Christ sake!' hissed Murphy. 'What the hell did you do a stupid thing like that for?'

'I met up with two of Delancey's boys a short while ago.'

Murphy gazed at him, catching sight of the faint discolouration on Gavin's temple. 'How come they left it at that?' he mused grimly.

'They didn't have an option,' replied Gavin with a ghost of a smile.

Murphy shook his head in disbelief. 'They'll kill you now for sure, you damned fool.' He began to compel Gavin to move forward away from the hotel.

'Are you charging me?'

Murphy shrugged. 'With what?'

'Delancey might prefer a charge of assault.'

'No. Brock Delancey likes to savour his own vengeance, Devlin. He'll have your guts nailed on his wall.'

'Then I'll have to disappoint him.'

Murphy paused in mid-stride and faced Gavin. 'You can only do that by getting out of the city and staying away until this has blown over.'

'You might have some good advice there, Murphy.'

'Damned right I have. Get going.'

Gavin nodded his thanks and walked swiftly away. By the time he had walked a dozen paces he had made up his mind that he would be accompanying his father on his extended hunting trip. A month would be about right for things to die down. But he still had not finished with Brock Delancey and his father, not by a long chalk. His first thought was to send a note to Nora Quinlan telling her that he was going away for a while and sending her a gift of money. Then he wondered whether the gift would be misinterpreted. He turned and found a hackney and persuaded the driver to take him down to Bayard and then wait for him in a bar on the Bowery. As he entered the familiar tenement building he saw that the door of Nora Quinlan's room was open and a small, rotund little man pushed out with a smirk to Gavin. Gavin knocked softly and entered. Nora was sitting on the edge of her bed, a shawl draped around her naked body. She flushed when she saw him and her eyes fell away as if she were ashamed.

'I had to see you,' he said defensively. 'I have to go away for a few weeks. Maybe four weeks.'

She glanced up again and saw the bruise on his forehead. 'What happened?'

Gavin raised a hand to his temple and smiled ruefully. 'Nothing.'

'Are you in trouble?' she pressed.

'Nothing that will not blow over.'

Nora Quinlan coughed nervously. 'Why did you come here?'

'I didn't want you to think that I'd gone away and . . . well, I just wanted to tell you that I'll be back.'

She raised her eyes wearily to him. 'What is it that you want from me, Gavin Devlin?'

If there were truth in dreams then he must be honest. 'I believe that I want you, Nora Quinlan.'

Her gaze faltered and fell and she sat in silence awhile, gazing down as if absorbed by the sight of her bare feet.

'Look, Nora,' he moved to her and bent down before her so that he could gaze up into her eyes. 'I don't know the truth of it. I don't understand my own feelings but I do know that you've come to mean a great deal to me. I want you, Nora. But not for payment. I want you because I need you. I need you because I love you.'

Her violet eyes flickered at him and dropped again. 'You don't have it backwards, Gavin Devlin?' she whispered. 'You don't love me because you need me?'

'When I return in a month we'll sort it all out. That's a promise.'

'I could almost believe it,' she sighed.

For the first time he suddenly noticed the bright sparkle of tears in her eyes. 'I'll be away for a month, only a month,' he assured her.

'I'd like to think of you coming back because I'm so afraid of loneliness.' Her voice was a whisper. A sudden confession.

'I'll be back. Look,' he reached into his pocket and hauled some coins on to the table. 'There's . . .' he quickly counted. 'Twenty-one dollars here. It's not much but it will help until I get back.'

She was suddenly sobbing, a series of sobs which ended in a rasping cough.

'I'd get something to ease that cough,' he muttered helplessly.

She drew herself up and tried to smile. 'It's only a stomach cough. I've had it for a while.'

'Well, look after yourself.' He reached out a hand and stroked her cheek softly. She swayed slightly and closed her eyes. He was aware of her nakedness, the soft curve of her throat, of her rounded shoulders and breasts. The sudden tension of his hand against her cheek caused her eyes to flutter open. He let his hand move down to caress her neck, moving downwards . . . Then she wrenched back.

'No, no, no!' she cried, making him start. 'You're spoiling it! Spoiling it! It's dirty!' She turned away, her thin body convulsed in sobs.

'I love you, Nora,' he said bewilderedly.

'You can't. You mustn't.'

Gavin moved gently to her, taking her heaving shoulders in his hands. 'I wouldn't do a thing to hurt you.'

She pulled away, coughing slightly. Her hand wiped the tears from her cheek with a rough gesture of annoyance. 'You'd better go now.' Her voice was dull, lifeless.

He hesitated and nodded. 'Things will be different when I get back. We'll sort things out.' His voice was full of reassurance and optimism.

She didn't reply but simply sat on the end of the bed staring down at the floor.

Chapter 15

The city of Montréal spread on its large island around the majestic peak of the extinct volcano from which it took its name when the Breton explorer Jacques Cartier had exclaimed, 'It's a royal mountain . . . *un mont réal*!' As cities on the American continent went, it was an old city which had started life as a missionary settlement in 1608. By the time of the English conquest in 1759 it possessed 5,000 inhabitants mostly occupied with an extensive fur trade. Now it had altered beyond belief. Its newly completed railway connections with the rest of the continent, its banking facilities and its shipping links which made it the largest grain port in the world, had turned it into a considerable centre of commerce. For a short time it had been the capital of the united provinces of Upper and Lower Canada until, in 1849, French-Canadian rebels had burnt down the parliament buildings.

Manus and Gavin Devlin had arrived by train across the new Victoria Bridge and taken a *calèche* to the small hôtel which Manus Devlin had already booked. Gavin was amazed at the gracious beauty of the city as the carriage swept through small cobbled streets, by sidewalk cafés where flower sellers tried to attract attention and *chansonniers* drew small crowds while they sang the latest ballads. Everywhere the voices were French.

'It's another world,' he whispered to his father as he gazed up at the tall buildings and imposing chateaux which seemed so foreign to his eye, so unlike anything he had seen before.

'Guess it is, son,' smiled Manus Devlin. 'You might be in Paris, France.'

'Except for those,' Gavin nodded to where a company of red-coated soldiers were marching in file, flat footed down the cobbled street, the leather of their shoes banging and causing heads to turn with stares of sullen resentment.

'I'm glad you decided to make this trip with me, Gavin,' Manus Devlin suddenly said. It was the first time he had commented on Gavin's abrupt change of plan. He hesitated but before he could say anything more the *calèche* had pulled up in a narrow street and a door had been thrown open by a large woman whose fleshy face was wreathed in smiles. She came out waving her hands and letting forth a voluble stream of French. To Gavin's surprise, his father replied in kind. His French was slightly halting but nonetheless fluent for that.

'This is Madame de Calvet,' Manus Devlin said. The woman was nodding and smiling at Gavin. 'I don't expect you can remember her? Soon after we arrived from Ireland we spent several weeks here before we went on to New York.'

Gavin tried to dredge up childhood memories but none came. He knew that he had few memories of Ireland and hardly any of the family's journey and arrival in New York. It was as if he had purposely cut off such memories. New York was his home. Nothing seemed to exist before it.

'When I come back to Montréal, I always stay with Madame de Calvet,' Manus Devlin was saying.

Madame de Calvet ran a rooming house, a *pension* as it was called locally, and she had hot baths and, more importantly, hot food waiting for them after their long train journey. The food was delicious, bowls of onion soup topped with melted cheese. After the meal, Manus Devlin offered to show Gavin something of the city before evening. It was a pleasant walk, through the narrow streets, moving to the more spacious thoroughfares where fine chateaux, Catholic churches and the great twin-towered cathedral of Nôtre Dame rose imposing. Doctor Devlin was particular in pointing out that the cathedral had been designed by an Irish architect, James O'Donnell.

After some time had passed, Gavin noticed that his father kept checking his pocket watch and he asked him what was the matter.

'Matter of fact, I have a call to make.' Manus Devlin hesitated. 'I have no objection to you being with me if you give me your word that you will remain silent and then forget all about the matter.'

Gavin frowned, searching his father's face. 'It sounds mysterious,' he said.

'It's politics, son.'

Gavin smiled. 'The Brotherhood?'

His father nodded.

'Well,' grinned Gavin, 'so long as you don't expect me to hold a pike or build a barricade.'

'It's no matter for flippancy,' Manus Devlin replied disapprovingly.

'Sorry.' Gavin was contrite. He wondered whether his father was seeking to impress him by his melodramatic attitude.

'I have to meet some gentlemen,' his father said. 'I do not know them and I would certainly feel more comfortable if you were alongside me.'

Gavin could see that his father was serious and he nodded slowly.

'Are you expecting trouble?' he asked.

'I don't know what to expect.'

'All right Pa,' Gavin said. 'I'll come along and look fierce for you.'

Doctor Devlin suddenly grinned. He turned and lead the way through a maze of small streets, stopping a few times to consult a piece of paper, and then pausing before a particular door. It was opened by a pleasant-faced woman who questioned him in French.

'*Bonsoir, madame,*' Manus Devlin replied. '*Paul et Louise, comment vont-ils?*'

A worried expression crossed the woman's features. '*Paul va fort bien mais Louise est malade, monsieur.*'

'*Est-ce que c'est grave, madame?*'

'*No, ce n'est pas grave.*'

'*Bien.*'

'*Comment t'appelles-tu, monsieur?*'

'*Je suis Finn.*'

'*Ah, Monsieur Finn.*'

The door swung open and she beckoned them inside. Gavin's knowledge of French was limited to that which a harassed schoolmaster had tried to impart to him in his boyhood. He knew enough to gather that the strange conversation in which his father had enquired after the health of Paul and Louise and identified himself as 'Monsieur Finn' must be some bizarre password system. The woman led them up a rickety wood staircase to an upper room where two men were sitting over a bottle of wine. They gazed suspiciously as they entered. The woman spoke rapidly. One of the men, a tall, swarthy faced individual with a long moustache and a blue serge suit, which made Gavin think of him as a sea captain, rose and stretched out his hand to Manus Devlin.

'Welcome to Montréal, Monsieur Finn. We've been expecting you.' His dark eyes flashed to Gavin in question.

'My son,' Manus replied to the unasked question. 'Captain . . . Finn.'

'*Je te présente mon ami, Henri,*' the man nodded to his silent companion. '*Je m'appelle Paul.* We can talk in English if you want,' he offered.

'Thank you. It might be easier. It is a few years since last I was in Montréal.'

The man, Paul, gestured for them to be seated and took two glasses from a cupboard, pouring wine for each of them. Manus Devlin brought forth a bulky envelope and placed it on the table. Paul read through the papers slowly and then passed them to his still silent, but watchful, companion.

'You know what is the contents of these letters?'

Doctor Devlin nodded.

'Your movement is interested in the state of politics in French-Canada. Note, I say French-Canada not Lower Canada nor British North America.'

'I note it,' Doctor Devlin assured him gravely.

Gavin was sitting trying to mask his feelings. He had presumed that his father was merely acting as a courier between the Brotherhood's headquarters in New York and a local Brotherhood circle in Montréal.

'*Alors!*' The man, Paul, smiled. 'The main question which your movement poses is what would be our position if it sought control over a port on this side of the border from which to establish an Irish Republic-in-exile and launch attacks against the English? That is a grandiose scheme, *mon ami.*'

Gavin started in surprise. Was the Brotherhood proposing an invasion of British North America?

'At the moment,' his father was saying, disarmingly, 'it is not a scheme but merely a sounding out of possibilities.'

Paul scratched his nose thoughtfully and glanced to his companion. 'Just over one hundred years ago the English took this land by force. Our own mother country sold us to the English interest. We do not forget. My father was one of the *Patriotes* who fought at St Denis in 1837 – one of those who was hanged by the English. We rose up to proclaim our republic. We failed. But one day we shall have a free Québec which is not bound to the whims of our English overlords.'

Manus Devlin leant forward. 'That is the aim of the Irish Republican Brotherhood, M'sieur Paul. The Brotherhood believes that a unity of your people and mine could bring about this great work. I have been asked to collect your reactions to the proposals outlined in these letters and take them back with me to my headquarters.'

Paul pursed his lips. 'We must have time to consider,' he said.

'I am passing up country for three or four weeks and will return through Montréal. Is that time enough?'

'Time enough,' agreed the man. 'Do not expect much from the French-Canadian constitutionalists such as *Le Parti Rouge*. Although the party is lead by former *Patriotes*, men like Louis-Joseph Papineau, who claim they wish to see a radical republic established here in French-Canada. They have been unnerved by the failure of 1837. We, of *L'Mouvement Pour Lá Republiqué*, would not have the same reservations. *Alors*, Monsieur Finn, we will discuss this more fully on your return.'

They all rose to their feet, shook hands, and Gavin followed his father back to the street. As they made their way back to Madame de Calvet's rooming house Gavin asked, 'Is the Brotherhood serious?'

Manus Devlin raised an eyebrow. 'I thought you agreed to forget that visit?'

'But it's a crazy scheme, even for the Brotherhood.'

Manus Devlin sniffed. 'I thought you weren't interested in the Brotherhood or its schemes, Gavin?'

'I can't fail to have some interest in it when it's all around me, Pa. It touches my life every day.'

Manus Devlin was quiet for a moment and then he said, 'You were nine years old when I brought you here, Gavin. You ought to remember something of your childhood, about arriving here.'

'I remember the continuous smell of salt water and the rocking motion of the waves,' Gavin replied. 'I remember being sick a lot of the time. I remember, also, that we landed on an island where there was some sort of camp. There were a lot of people there who were ill. Maybe it was a quarantine station like they have in New York. I recall a long journey afterwards but that's all.'

'How the mind of a child selects its memories for storing to adulthood,' sighed Manus Devlin. 'How it eliminates the bad ones and retains the pleasant ones. Can you remember your two uncles, my brothers, their wives and children who came across in the same ship with us?'

Gavin's eyes widened at the question and he shook his head. His father had never mentioned any relatives before. He thought hard. He could just remember a little girl who used to play with him. He recalled some kindly adults on the ship but he couldn't remember their faces.

'You never mentioned relatives before, Pa,' he said.

Manus Devlin bit his lip reflectively. 'No, I didn't. I'll tell you about them when we go north. Tomorrow we'll be taking a boat down river to Québec city. It will take a couple of days to get there.'

They reached Madame de Calvet's house and Manus Devlin turned in immediately without saying any more and leaving Gavin with a sense of annoyance and frustrated curiosity.

Quite early the next morning they went down to the old stone quay on the river front and found a small sailing vessel which plied a trade between Montréal and Québec, running goods and passengers between the two cities along the broad sweep of the St Lawrence. It was a small, square-sterned barque which belonged to a Scotsman. They managed to secure a cabin for the two-day trip. At midday exactly the barque pulled away from the quay, the faint breeze flapping her sails, and slowly, so slowly, the vessel moved through the short, choppy waters, along the blue highway whose banks were lined with dark clusters of conifers.

As they stood near the prow of the dipping vessel, which cut through the blue waters, Gavin remarked, 'It's a beautiful river.'

'We sailed down here when you were a boy,' Manus Devlin replied. 'Have you no memory of it?'

Gavin shook his head. 'You would think that I could not have forgotten such a sight like this.'

'You would,' agreed his father dryly.

Gavin caught the sharp note of rebuke. He stirred uneasily. It was true. He could not remember. Only vague disjointed scenes stirred in his mind; scenes which made no sense. He gave up trying to put them into some order after a while and leant back to watch the sweeping scenery open before him as the sprightly little ship tacked and bobbed its way along the broad river. Strangely, while the vista did not bring memories of his boyhood to him it brought a vision of Nora Quinlan. He felt a painful longing for her company, wishing the girl could see such magnificent beauty for surely this was the real America, not the crowded slums of New York city with its terrible odours. Ah, but perhaps that was real, too? But which was more real? He had the recurring nightmare last night; the dream about Jack Quinlan and Nora. Nora, clad in a green mantle – Fand the Pearl of Beauty, the Queen of the Otherworld. Fand the Unobtainable. It was his mother who had taught him the stories from Irish mythology.

He wondered why it was that he dreamt of Nora in the role of Fand, wife of Manannán Mac Lir, the Ocean God?

They finally reached Québec. Whereas Montréal was impressive, Québec simply took his breath away. It was a towering citadel above the river with its ancient walls and frowning fortress, black cannons poking out aggressively and red-coated sentinels pacing the battlements. The barque sailed in under the tall cliffs to edge into the quays of the lower town, for the city was built on two levels. Manus Devlin had told his son that they would spend a night in the city, pick up a guide named Olivier Plamondon and move down river beyond the city before striking into the interior. Looking at the city, Gavin wished they could spend more time there.

Doctor Devlin seemed to know his way about and from the quay he hailed a *calèche*, the inevitable two-wheeled vehicle, whose driver barely gave them time to climb aboard before he cried '*Marchez donc!*' and flicked his whip above the head of his horse, sending it rattling up the steep streets, swaying the carriage so dangerously that Gavin was compelled to cling on to the side with both hands. They had reserved a room in a hotel called the St Louis and Manus Devlin only gave Gavin time to wash before he took him out to show him the ancient city from the walls. Before them the St Lawrence rolled grandly between shores studded with townships, moving to the north-east where it would eventually empty into the Atlantic. Below them, by the shore of the lower town, warehouses and wharves stretched. They stood some 300 feet above the lower town where the upper town nestled on a bluff just below the fortress called the Citadel, guarded by strong walls designed to resist any assault and massive gates which had been removed after the English conquest. Manus took an obvious delight in showing Gavin the pleasures of the city, in conducting him along the breezy esplanade. Only once did he say; 'A pity John-Joe isn't here.'

Québec gave Gavin an impression of cleanliness and of crystal clearness in the sharp light of the northerly clime. His father was pleased with Gavin's reactions and happy they were sharing a pleasure together. After lunch they hailed a *calèche* outside their hotel. There were numerous carriages plying for hire there and the drivers, grim-faced French-Canadians, seemed to identify them immediately as visitors from south of the border for they surrounded them like a flock of geese, underbidding each other in an effort to get their custom. Once the carriage had been selected, though, the others moved off. Manus Devlin had negotiated a tour of Montmorenci for a fare of five dollars. He explained to Gavin that there was a spectacular cataract there. The driver took them at a rattling pace down through the streets of the lower town, across the St Charles, no more than a wide creek on the northern shore of the St Lawrence, and then along the road through Beauport, through three toll gates. Doctor Devlin pointed out the Beauport Asylum for the Insane and the house where General Montcalm, who commanded the French at Québec, had lived before he met his death at the battle whose outcome lost France this part of the continent. A drive of an hour took them to the Montmorenci river. They left the carriage at an hotel and walked along a pleasant river path to the long flight of steps that lead to the foot of the falls.

'Seventy feet high,' Manus Devlin smiled. 'In winter the ice freezes the falls.'

His father had been right. It was spectacular and very beautiful.

'The French call it *La Vache* – The Cow.'

'Why?'

'Some say it's because of the white foaming waters reminding people of milk, others that the noise of the falls can be heard in the city like the distant lowing of a cow.'

'It's a beautiful country, Pa,' Gavin said as they drove back to the city. 'Did you never think of settling here when we arrived from Ireland? You seem to like it very much.'

'It was a thought,' Manus Devlin agreed. 'Many Irish have settled here. You'll find a lot of Irish who have become assimilated into the French-speaking communities now. It wasn't for me, though. This country is still ruled by Englishmen.'

Chapter 16

Olivier Plamondon was a short, thickset man of swarthy appearance. He was taciturn and spoke only in answer to a direct question. He met them on the quayside of the lower town clad in ancient buckskins and a 'coon skin cap looking like a figure out of the early pioneering days. Both Manus and Gavin had changed their city clothes, storing their trunks at the hotel, and carrying only essentials in canvas bags. Plamondon had a large birchwood canoe waiting for them, a *canoe de Bouleau* he called it. It was a large affair in which they were to sit on pinewood slats. It sat on the water like a duck. It was already loaded with equipment and sporting guns.

Plamondon spoke no English and his French was so accented that Gavin could not understand him at all. Only his father could converse freely. He saw the guide examine their bush clothes with a critical eye before placing the bundles into the canoe. Manus Devlin volunteered to man the paddles with Plamondon because Gavin had no experience in canoes at all. The canoe moved away from the quays with a speed that left Gavin breathless, pulling away into the broad river towards the Ile d'Orléans, taking the northerly passage. The island was large and fertile and Gavin saw evidence of cultivation. It was pleasant to relax and do nothing, watching the thickset shoulders of the French-Canadian rippling with muscle as he dug the paddle into the water. Leaving the large island behind them they sped on towards a spot where bullrushes covered broad mud flats and where swarms of snowgeese gathered. Large ocean-going vessels, tall-masted schooners and even a squat, aggressive-looking British battleship, its ensigns flying proudly, moved past them down the great sea road of British North America. Gavin had seen many such ships in the harbour of New York but here, along this beautiful river, it was as if they intruded, as if they had no right to be here.

'We'll be camping tonight on that island ahead of us,' called Manus

Devlin behind him. 'It's called Ile aux Grues, the island of cranes. Does it seem familiar to you?'

'Should it?' asked Gavin staring at the approaching dark shape of the island.

'We had to live there six months.'

Gavin's eyes widened. He did remember an island. An encampment where there had been many people who had been sick.

'I wanted to bring you and John-Joe here,' his father was saying. 'I thought it might help to explain my feelings for Ireland.'

'How would coming to this spot explain that?' demanded Gavin.

'You'll see, son.'

They fell silent again as the island drew nearer and Plamondon guided the canoe to land, bumping its nose into the soft mud of the embankment. They climbed out, unloaded and drew the canoe out of the water. Plamondon began to prepare the encampment while Gavin examined his surroundings. It was like a paradise with trees and shrubs growing close to the water's edge, mirrored in the summer blue water of the river, which twisted around the numerous rocky bays. The ground rose from the shoreline with emerald green grasses coloured by innumerable wild flowers. Among the tall conifers Gavin could see the white of a small church and nearby a number of white-washed buildings, low, single storey buildings. The place was deserted.

Manus Devlin was watching Gavin's face with a curious expression. 'Isn't it a beautiful place, son?'

Gavin smiled his agreement. 'It's how I envisage paradise, Pa. Look at those forest glades and the groves of wild flowers. I vaguely recall being on an island but I can't remember anything as beautiful as this. Why,' he chuckled, 'we should have stayed here.'

Manus Devlin's lips twitched slightly. 'Many did, son, but we were lucky.'

Gavin frowned in bewilderment at the hidden meaning in his father's voice.

Manus Devlin muttered something to Plamondon and then took Gavin's arm. 'Come with me.'

He turned across the springy turf, along a small pathway which skirted the group of buildings.

'Quarantine buildings,' he grunted as he saw Gavin examining them. They were all empty and boarded up. So was the church. They moved up a rise behind the buildings and there Manus Devlin halted. Beyond was a fairly open strip of green but the ground rose in a series of vast humps like hillocks. They were too regular and uniform to be natural.

'What are they?' demanded Gavin.

'Mass graves,' replied his father.

Gavin stared down. 'But there must be hundreds buried down there.'

Manus Devlin smiled thinly. 'Thousands,' he corrected. 'It will never be truly known how many Irish men, women and children lay huddled beneath the soil of this island, Gavin. I have heard it placed as low as 6,000, an average estimate of 20,000 and the highest estimate of 100,000.'

Gavin stared at the grassy mounds trying to imagine 100,000 dead. 'But why?' he said.

His father sat down on a boulder. 'Back in '48 when we came to America, towards what was to be the end of the brutal famine years, this island had been made into a quarantine station. Thousands of our people were trying to escape from the conditions in Ireland, from death by malnutrition and its attendant diseases. Ships bringing timber to England, instead of returning empty to the ports of British North America, would collect cargoes of our people who wanted to migrate. We called them "coffin ships" because our people died in them by the hundreds.'

Gavin shrugged. 'The fever should have been confined and fought in Ireland.'

Manus Devlin's face twitched but he retained his composure. 'It was not fever out of Ireland that killed our people in those "coffin ships". Healthy people starting the voyage would be dead by the end of it. Our people were more often than not battened down below decks like animals, below decks where wood had been stored and where, in the sawdust and refuse, there lived germs which produced a new sickness and disease. The hopes and aspirations of thousands of our people ended here on this island, ended under those mounds which you see down there.'

Manus Devlin gestured back down the rise to the buildings. 'That was the hospital – *hospital*!' His tone was bitter. 'There were no beds. The bedding was spread on the ground and soon became soaked from the perspiration, excreta and body odours – full of disease. Inside the buildings there was hardly any ventilation and the smell was intolerable. The cold nights finished off those who could not squeeze inside. The beds were always full, sometimes two and three to a bed, filled without distinction of age or sex. People died from lack of water because there was no one to nurse them. Doctors and nurses who volunteered to treat the cases of fever, of typhus and bacilliary dysentry died. I knew four doctors out of Ireland who died while I was here. Relatives simply abandoned relatives. Robbing the corpses which lay unattended was a common enough pastime.'

Gavin gazed around at the verdant tranquility, listening to the summer sounds of birds and the soft whisper of the river around the island. He tried hard to dredge back the memories, the vague recall of an encampment, of people lying sick around him.

'We took a ship from Queenstown and arrived here during the summer. There were thirty vessels waiting off the island on the day we arrived. If a ship had fever aboard then the captain had to put in near to the island to offload the sick. Many captains refused to row the sick ashore. I have seen sailors simply toss the sick over the side. Those who could swim ashore were hauled out of the water and nursed as best as possible. Most people did not reach the shore. Often they would drown on the very bank, unable to scramble up through the soft mud. We were always hauling bodies out of the water.'

Gavin found his body had become cold, listening to the suppressed emotion of his father's memories.

'We were lucky, your mother, you two boys and I. We were untainted by fever. My two brothers were already showing signs of it and Phelim's wife, poor Moira, had already died during the voyage. Our captain was more humane than most. We had a boat to take us to the shore . . . at a price, of course. When they discovered that I was a doctor they put me to work immediately.'

Manus Devlin ran his tongue over his drying lips. 'You've been in war, son. You must know what it is like to hear people screaming for water. God, what a terrible sound that is. This island was like a scene from the *Inferno*. I saw a young boy walking by who suddenly sat down under a tree as if to rest for a moment. When I noticed that he was there some hours later I went across to find him dead. He had simply sat down and died. There was a child lying, abandoned, by the hospital door, covered in vermin. It had no hope.'

Gavin shook his head. 'I can't recall any of this.'

'You were young,' nodded his father. 'Perhaps it is part of survival for a young child to shut such things from its mind.'

'How did we survive it?'

'Being a doctor I had certain privileges. I managed to get a tent and keep you all away from the quarantine houses. I took every precaution I knew to prevent you all from catching the fever. But it didn't prevent my brothers and their families from dying. First Phelim died in my arms; then Paudeen; then Paudeen's wife and the children, one by one.'

'Are they buried down there?'

Manus Devlin nodded. His eyes were dangerously bright. 'Thousands of Irish men, women and children are buried on this island, Gavin,' he said, with a sudden catch in his throat. 'The thing is to remember why. Why it had to be. They were fleeing from an artificial famine induced by the absentee English landlords who rule their country, they were fleeing from the foreign tyrannical laws which govern them.'

Gavin had heard many stories from his father about the English conquests of Ireland, of the continual fight to win liberty and independence, but, looking at the green hummocks in this pleasant, forgotten, little islet in the St Lawrence, he became aware of a feeling of poignancy about what it really meant.

'You must hate the English very much, Pa,' he said quietly.

Manus Devlin reached for a kerchief to blow his nose. 'The English? I hate their government in Ireland. I hate the English landlords, their soldiers and their politicians lording it over our people.'

'But that is not the English people,' pointed out Gavin.

Manus Devlin forced a smile. 'No,' he said thoughtfully. 'You've a wise head, son. A government with its sepulchre of privileges does not constitute a people, neither does a conquering army. Perhaps one should feel sorry for the English; a nation which enslaves other nations cannot itself be free. . . .'

He stared down the rise towards the green hummocks. 'But here, Gavin, here, where so many thousands of our people lie in pitiful, unmarked mass graves – where even their names are forgotten – I cannot help feeling a raging torrent against the complacency of a nation that has allowed such crimes to be committed in its name with its passive condonment.'

The weeks passed rapidly. Olivier Plamondon was a good guide. He knew his woodcraft and did not waste a single word or gesture. As they moved north he found good hunting among the caribou, the large grey deer which were quite distinct from the common red deer known to Gavin. Great herds of caribou ranged through the wilderness as far south as the shores of the St Lawrence, tramping through the spruce woods, across mountains bare of trees where rocky ground was carpeted with furze, moss and blueberry bushes. They seemed to live on the moss, sedges, lichens and grasses. Gavin observed that, unlike red deer, both sexes had antlers, although those of the cows were much smaller. Their grey coats gave them a buoyancy in water and they had an outstanding swimming ability which took them across the most rapid currents. Their feet were round and broad for walking on the boggy tundra and the herds were continually moving.

Plamondon had urged them to camp among the dry grey larch stubble in an area of the wilderness which rendered the place like a muddy desolation. They saw a small herd of caribou on their first foray from the camp but they were already on the move and caught wind of their approach. While the vision of the caribou was apparently defective, their sense of smell was extremely acute. They returned to camp disappointed although there came some momentary excitement when they saw a black bear feasting off some blueberry bushes near the campsite. But the animal, spotting them, simply ambled off.

That night in camp they heard a frightening banshee howl.

'*Carcajeu*,' replied Plamondon in response to Manus Devlin's question.

'A wolf,' explained Manus to Gavin. 'The Indians call them *kekwararkis* up here.'

His father had not mentioned any more about the Ile aux Grues, or Grosse Isle as the English pronounced it, since they had left it five days before. But it was now that Manus Devlin brought up the subject of the Brotherhood again.

'Father MacMahon told me that the Brotherhood had offered you a job,' he said abruptly.

Gavin stared into the leaping flames of the campfire.

'If you have completely finished with Stead McHale, then the Brotherhood needs some trained legal minds and they are willing to pay a small salary. It would get you started.'

'I have to finish the work I have begun,' Gavin replied.

Manus Devlin was silent a while. 'The Delanceys are very powerful people,' he eventually observed.

Gavin grinned cynically. 'And power retreats only before a greater power, is that it?'

'Something like that.'

'If that's what you preach, Pa, it isn't what you practise.'

Manus Devlin raised an eyebrow in query. 'How do you make that out, son?'

'The Brotherhood. That's the example. Is the Brotherhood stronger than the empire of England? The Brotherhood is pitting itself against the vast resources of a great empire because it believes it is fighting for what is morally right.'

'I see your point,' accepted Manus Devlin. 'However, I know that the only reason you came away with me was because things became awkward for you in New York. I have contacts, too, Gavin. I heard about the incident with Brock Delancey at the Astor House Hotel. If you would accept some advice, I'd say don't return to New York for a while. The Delanceys are capable of holding a grudge for years.'

'I have to return, Pa,' Gavin replied.

Manus Devlin grimaced at the finality in his son's voice. 'Well, let me put this thought in your mind, son; one man can't bring down the Delancey empire any more than one man can bring down the empire of England. If you joined the Brotherhood it would put you in contact with people who would be of great help to you . . . politicians, lawyers and newspapermen. You would find a protection in their ranks as well as assistance to fight social evil. That is what the Brotherhood stands for. Just think about that job that Father MacMahon suggested to you.'

The next day Plamondon led them through a swamp bringing them out by a foaming brook which roared loudly over black rocks and lichen-veined boulders amongst overhanging trees. He had brought them upwind of a caribou herd and now gestured for them to take their shots. Manus Devlin allowed Gavin to make the first shot and he managed to bring down a cow of about 300 pounds, sending the others stampeding off before Manus could make his kill. Without a word Plamondon set to work dressing the slaughtered beast, opening and emptying the body cavities to allow the animal to cool quickly. Gavin offered to help him but Plamondon gave a quick, almost irritable, shake of his swarthy head. The French-Canadian knew his job, brandishing his glinting hunting knife with a dexterous ease.

He dragged the animal over on its back, heaving its head up on to a small bank of earth. Then he took some pieces of rope from his pockets and secured each of the four legs to nearby branches so that the carcass was anchored on its back. As Gavin went to help him secure a hind leg, reaching forward to grasp it, Plamondon grabbed his hand and pushed it away, letting forth a stream of voluble French. Behind him, Manus Devlin, cleaning his gun, chuckled.

'He is telling you that you mustn't touch the musk glands just below the hocks. See where those dark tufts of hair are? The glands give off an oil with an odour that can taint your hands.'

Gavin stood back respectfully and watched the expertise of the hunter.

Plamondon cut quickly around the anus and rectum of the beast, slicing the skin from the pelvic bone to the rib cage, cutting upwards carefully so that the intestines were not punctured. The wall of tissue separating the stomach and intestines from the lungs and heart was also cut. Then he reached up to grasp the windpipe and gullet. With these cut free, Plamondon was able to free the internal organs from the mesentery tissues as he pulled. He dragged the offal away from the carcase after sorting out the heart and liver.

When it came to the musk glands, the French-Canadian pinched them with finger and thumb, sliding his sharp knife under them and cutting right through along the base. He removed the glands and threw them away, cleaning his hands in the brook to ensure that they and his knife were clean before returning to the meat. Observing Gavin watching his movements, he muttered a few words. Manus Devlin said, 'He says that some people prefer to cut the glands out first before dressing the animal. He says that is fine if water is near but it is far better not to take the chance of contaminating your hands or knife.'

While Manus Devlin was translating, Plamondon rolled the caribou on its side and cut deeply into the back of the neck, behind the shoulders, right to within a few inches of the antlers. Then from this point he began to cut the carcass into manageable pieces of meat. Gavin noticed that he cut out the piece where his bullet had penetrated and threw it away.

'Plamondon knows his business,' nodded his father. 'Never leave game on the ground because the meat can sour quickly. The best way, if the animal is not too large, is to quarter and hang it. Keep it off the ground, keep it away from the sun.'

Gavin smiled at his father. 'I hadn't realized that you knew so much about woodcraft.'

'Sometimes one has to know a lot about many different things if you want to survive,' Manus Devlin shrugged.

Plamondon was wrapping the pieces of meat in strips of cheese cloth which he carried in his knapsack. They all carried pieces of the carcass back to camp to hoist them into a nearby tree.

That night Gavin had another nightmare.

A rattling cart was being dragged along by a galloping horse across the mud flats where he stood. The horse was blood flecked, screaming in exertion as it floundered across the mud, the cart dragging, minus a wheel. It bounced, creaking and straining, lifting as it thumped against a hidden rock so that the entire cart threatened to turn over. There was no driver, just a bloody mess of flesh sprawled over the driver's box. It plunged on until it reached the river and disappeared in a threshing whirlpool of foam. The din and clatter of battle suddenly receded with the light of the day.

He was walking back across the mud flats, shoulders bent, back amidst the silent dead and the screaming wounded. He passed a pile of corpses thrown together in a heap and paused to watch in fearful fascination as a hand clawed through the pile, out of the twisted bloody flesh – a claw-like hand which suddenly thrust towards him while a voice cried, 'Spare a dime?'

He stared for a moment in horror at the clawing hand and then turned, running quickly across the mud flats until he found a green warm sward and threw himself down on its comforting mattress. He lay panting, listening to the gurgle of the gushing creek. When he raised his eyes she was sitting nearby, her mantle of soft green silk fluttering in the breeze. She sat throwing wild primroses into the water and watching them bob away in the white chattering current. Then she turned and smiled softly at him.

'What do you want, Captain Devlin?'

'I want you.'

'It costs two dollars.'

'No, no, that is not what I want. I want you.'

'What am I?'

He hesitated, 'You are . . . you are. . . .'

She threw back her head and chuckled, her voice an echo of the gurgling stream. 'How can you have me when you do not know me?'

She rose, shaking her head, and walked to where the gaunt man sat waiting for her on his wooden cart. He stared accusingly, the bloody stumps of his legs thrust forward, his claw-like hand reaching out. 'Spare a dime?' Then there came the shriek of a falling shell and everything was enveloped in a reddy blackness.

When he woke up he found his father bending over him, and Plamondon gazing anxiously over Manus Devlin's shoulder.

'Are you all right, son?'

Gavin wiped the sweat from his brow. 'Sure, it's just a dream.'

Manus Devlin pursed his lips. 'A dream, eh? It seems you've been having quite a few of these dreams since you came back from the war.'

Gavin nodded slowly. Then his father said, 'Does this Nora Quinlan mean more to you than what you have told me?'

Gavin started. He had told his father everything except how he felt for Jack Quinlan's widow. He was about to make a denial but his father said, 'You muttered a lot about her in your sleep, son.'

'I guess that I am in love with her, Pa,' Gavin replied.

Manus stared at him a moment and bit his lip. Then he turned to Plamondon and said something. The French-Canadian nodded and returned to his bed on the far side of the fire. Manus Devlin turned back to his son. 'What does she feel about you?'

Gavin shrugged. 'I don't really know. She is suspicious of all men. Life has made her that way.'

'You told me she was a prostitute.'

'It's not her choosing,' Gavin flushed.

'It's not some infatuation? Are you serious, son?'

He nodded.

'You wouldn't have a chance of making a life in New York. You know what society there is like. The gossip and scandal would break your mother's heart.'

'I recall that Christ said that prostitutes were more qualified for heaven than some priests,' retorted Gavin.

His father exhaled deeply. 'I know the quotation, Gavin. It's from Matthew's Gospel. However, it doesn't solve the problem.'

'You disapprove.'

Manus shook his head. 'I've lived long enough not to make judgments in these matters, son. I'll tell you this, though: it seems that you have given yourself two problems in New York. The Delanceys and this girl.'

'Have you any advice?' Gavin had not meant to sound hectoring but it came out that way.

His father stood up and threw some more wood on the campfire before turning back to his bed. 'It's a big country, Gavin,' he said slowly. 'A big country.'

Chapter 17

They arrived back in New York in the third week of September to the stifling heat and the hubbub which clashed with their nerves in contrast to the peace of the wilderness and even the clean, bright cities of Québec and Montréal. They had left the silent Olivier Plamondon at Québec and taken the barque back to Montréal where Manus Devlin had kept his appointment with the man called Paul. Little had been said at the meeting but letters for the Brotherhood's leadership had been passed across. It was only on the train back to the city that Manus Devlin again raised the matter of Nora Quinlan with Gavin.

'It would be wise,' he urged 'if you didn't tell your mother about this until you have had time to make some firm decisions.'

'I'll go straight to see Nora when we arrive,' Gavin told him.

'Remember, son, it is a decision that can't be taken in isolation. Find out what the girl wants as well as taking account of what you want. And another thing . . . take care of yourself. I don't think the Delanceys are the sort to forgive and forget within a few weeks.'

Gavin was full of excitement when he arrived at the drab tenement carrying a basket of food and a bottle of wine. He strode through the gossiping Italian women, oblivious of their habitual lewd gestures and sly smiles and tapped on the girl's door.

It opened immediately.

The girl who stood there was a tall blonde wearing a faded gown which barely covered her. She was pale skinned and had a kind of lascivious attractiveness which seemed somehow coarse and suggestive. Her lips were thick and sulky and her eyes carried dark shadows beneath them. She stared speculatively at Gavin and said, 'Two dollars, in advance, handsome.'

Gavin took a moment to recover from his surprise.

'Where's Nora?' he demanded. 'Nora Quinlan?'

The girl arched an eyebrow. 'Never heard of her, love. You coming in or not?'

'She lived here. This is her room.'

'This is my room. Stop wasting time. Time's money.'

'An Irish girl named Nora Quinlan lives here,' he said tightly. 'Where is she?'

The girl grimaced at the anger in his voice. 'I've been living here just over a week, mister,' she said sulkily.

'Then what happened to the girl who lived here before you did?'

'I don't know.' Seeing Gavin's blackening brows, she turned and thumped on the wall. A door opened further along the passageway and a plump girl clad in a threadbare wrap came out, standing with folded arms and a cigarette in her mouth.

'What is it, Aggie?'

'He's asking for the girl who used to live here.'

The plump girl removed her cigarette and spat. It was such an obscene gesture that he could hardly suppress a shudder, even with his mind full of anxiety.

'What's wrong with Aggie, mister? Ain't she your type?'

'I'm looking for Nora Quinlan,' Gavin repeated.

The plump girl shrugged. 'She's probably dead by now?'

The shock of her words caused Gavin to reach forward to catch hold of the doorpost. 'What?' his voice was harsh.

'They took her off. She got some sort of fever.'

'They? Who are they?' he snapped.

'How the hell do I know?' retorted the woman. 'Pauper's hospital people most like.' She turned back into her room slamming the door behind her.

Gavin leaned back, eyes closed for a moment. When he opened them the blonde girl was still gazing speculatively at him.

'Sure you won't come inside, handsome? I'm much better at it than her. Betcha!'

He swore violently and turned away.

It was the next day, on the advice of Manus Devlin, that Gavin tracked Nora down to the imposing façade of St Vincent's Hospital on West 11th Street run by the Sisters of Charity. The main ward rooms were given over to the care of the impoverished sick and the interior comforts were sacrificed to maintaining an imposing frontage, for within the place was shabby: a bleak, draughty interior whose gloomy rooms and corridors were made terrifying by gaunt-faced nuns, figures of fear in black habits and clacking beads. Occasionally a doctor appeared among them, indifferent, always hurrying. The hospital echoed to the moans of the sick, sighing like a wind, sometimes punctuated with a piercing shriek of pain. To be poor in the city was considered a crime but to be poor and sick was a crime that was unforgivable, which made the attitude of contempt and casual cruelty of the nursing staff towards their patients accepted as natural behaviour.

A thin-lipped Sister of Charity sniffed with disapproval as she checked the records.

'Quinlan, Mrs Nora Quinlan. She was admitted two weeks ago. Consumption. Are you the husband? We have it on record that she was a widow.'

Gavin found himself colouring. 'I am acting as her lawyer,' he lied. 'Her husband, Sergeant Jack Quinlan, was killed a few months ago.'

The Sister's face wavered between an expression of surprise and suspicion. 'Very well, I will take you to the ward. This way.'

He followed her along the cold, echoing corridors until she pushed him into a large but gloomy room. There was a bed in a dark corner. One of many. He hesitated when the Sister pointed towards it and departed. It seemed as if a child lay there, perhaps a large doll. Yet it was a person, a thin skeleton of a person lying under a rough, dirty grey blanket that seemed far too heavy for the body to support, weighing down on it so that it seemed to push it down hard on the thin straw mattress. For a moment all that Gavin could recognize was the red glints of hair which spread on the dirty greying pillow.

Summoning his failing courage, Gavin moved across to stand at the foot of the tiny rough wood bed and gazed down at the face, so white, so translucent that the blue of the veins showed clearly on the forehead. The skin seemed more tightly stretched than ever, the lips drawn back so that the gums and teeth showed from that once pretty mouth.

'Nora!' His voice was a whispered cry.

She did not stir; did not flutter her dark lids.

Gavin moved round to the bedside and knelt on the dusty floor beside the wooden cot.

'Nora!' His voice was more urgent and seemed to pierce the girl's mind.

A breath rattled in her throat. 'Jack?'

For a moment Gavin wondered if the sound had come from her. 'Nora, it's me . . . Gavin. Gavin Devlin.'

The eyelids flickered, the eyes moved in search of him. God! How those bright violet eyes had faded. The teeth bared as the lips twisted into a parody of a smile.

'Jack!' she breathed.

He felt tears springing hotly to his eyes and tried to fight them back.

'Jack . . . I'm so . . . so frightened.'

He reached forward and found her claw-like, cold hand and pressed it gently, fearing undue pressure would crush its tiny, pathetic existence.

'Here,' he whispered. 'I'm here. I've come back like I promised.'

The girl's eyes tried to focus on him. 'It's so frightening to be . . . alone.'

'You're not alone any more. I'm with you,' he declared.

She did not seem to hear him. Her breath came in gasps as she tried to suck oxygen from the stifling air.

'Remember . . . remember the lover's seat by the roadside? The one by the little blue lake at the foot of the meadow . . . where the hills rolled and climbed like sea in winter, almost tumbling on top of each other?'

She paused in her rambling, making a rasping noise in her throat, croaking painfully. It took a moment for Gavin to realize that it was meant to be a chuckle.

'I long for home, Jack. I wish we'd never left Ireland. The dark roads and burnt earth rising out of the valleys . . . I miss them here. Take me back, Jack. I want to see the primroses bloom amidst the heather again. There is nothing for us here . . . nothing. It is so cold, so grey. I will never be well here. Take me back so that I can grow well again. I am so lonely and frightened here.'

She gripped his hand with a sudden desperate, almost inconceivable strength. He was surprised that such strength could exist in her frail, spent frame.

'Jack, I love no one but you. Haven't I followed you across the world for love? I'll love no one else.'

He choked back a sob of grief and whispered, 'Easy, Nora. I'll take you back. I promise.'

She was seized by a paroxysm of coughing which racked her thin body so violently that he thought she must surely be ripped apart by the ferocity of it. Then it passed leaving her bathed in sweat, so weak that she could scarce struggle for breath. After a while she lay quietly, so quiet as if she were in a deep, peaceful sleep. He rose and left her.

At the reception desk he asked the same thin-lipped Sister: 'Can anything be done for Mrs Quinlan?'

The Sister's face was still cold and disapproving. 'All that can be done is being done for her.'

'If it's a question of money . . . ?' he began.

There was a flicker of interest. 'Does Mrs Quinlan have money?'

'It can be raised.'

For a moment an expression of pity passed across the woman's face. 'Save your money, young man. It will make no difference.'

'I'll come tomorrow morning. Perhaps I can speak with a doctor here?'

'It will make no difference.'

'I'll come tomorrow morning.'

That evening he asked Manus Devlin if he would go to the hospital with him and examine Nora Quinlan. His father had no hesitation.

'You say the hospital told you it was consumption? You mean pulmonary tuberculosis?'

Gavin shrugged, blaming himself for not recognizing anything was wrong when now he recalled all the times Nora Quinlan had coughed and he had dismissed it as merely nervousness.

'Consumption was all they said,' he replied.

There was a different Sister on duty the next morning when Gavin and Manus Devlin went to the hospital. She was a homely faced woman who kept smiling nervously and then tried to hide the smile, remembering the strictures of her order.

Nora Quinlan had died before dawn. Gavin allowed his father to take him to a bench and get him seated. He heard his father turn back to the Sister, identify himself as a doctor and begin asking a series of technical questions which he could not understand. All he knew was that Nora Quinlan had gone whimpering into that eternal dark night, frightened and alone. She had wanted love; had wanted to stay alive in the warmth of the sun among the people who had cared for her and whom she wanted to care for – among friends. She was only nineteen years old and she had died alone and penniless; isolated from everyone she had known, everything she had known. A widow at nineteen, alone in a strange city, thousands of miles from her home, she had gone crying to her death in the dark of a poor ward.

Gavin felt a sudden hysterical impulse to clench his fists and physically attack someone or something. He was aware that the Sister was gazing at him. Did he want to see her? She was being laid out for a pauper's funeral. No, no, no! He could not bring himself to gaze on that tiny, pathetic shell that had once been so alive. He could not bear that pain.

A pauper's funeral?

'She should be buried with her husband,' he found himself saying coldly. 'Sergeant Jack Quinlan in Calvary Cemetery, Newtown.'

The Sister of Charity was uneasy. 'It costs money. Five dollars.'

'Bury her with her husband!' Gavin found himself shouting wildly. 'For Christ's sake don't bury her alone. She was frightened of being alone!'

His father was whispering to the Sister and then he felt Manus Devlin's strong hand on his arm, firm but kindly, guiding him from the hospital.

The earth was icy cold, the mud clung like anxious hands to his shivering body as he lay stretched against it. The smell of the earth was a sickly odour, like the stench of decaying corpses, the purient smell of decomposing flesh. The earth was full of death. Above him the night was black, clouds like swirling shadows, hid the stars and the moon. It was quiet, deathly quiet. Far off a bugle sounded. Then, what he feared most, began. The thunder of explosions, regular and monotonous. The belch of flame and roar of the enemy's cannonades resounded with every shell aimed at him, screaming in like devils from an unspeakable hell. Explosions erupted all around him. Then, as he knew it would, a figure stood up.

Ready the flag!

Jack Quinlan's rich baritone urged the men onwards. But men screamed in fear and pain as explosion after explosion rocked the earth around them, showering everything with mud and wet, sticky flesh; limbs torn from bodies and flung in abandoned fashion. He pressed closer to the earth trying to avoid the shrieking cannonade.

Ready the flag!

The bugle sounded. In lines, in serried ranks, they began to move with the morning breeze now cracking the silk of their battle flags. Drums beat the marching pace, the single monotonous beat, as they moved forward into the darkness, rifles held forward, bayonets glinting in the rising light. The bugle sounded again and like a damburst they went on, shrieking, crying, weeping incoherently as they began to run forward with the mud clawing at them as if it was aiding their foe in holding back the charge. Still the remorseless cannonade poured among them.

Ready the flag!

The voice of Jack Quinlan rose to a scream.

Gavin was suddenly all alone; all alone on the green sward by the gushing silver creek. And she was kneeling by his side, smiling down as he lay on his back on the warm earth. Her eyes were sorrowful, deep violet yet edged with a curious softness. Her small, delicately boned face with its high forehead, tiny nose and thin lips were framed in hair that was not quite red but a mass of dark ginger curls weaving strands of spun gold, falling on her soft white shoulders that emerged from the green shimmering silk of her gown.

'Are you Fand the Pearl of Beauty?' he asked slowly.

She chuckled, her voice an echo of the gushing of the stream. 'You *know* who I am, Captain Devlin,' she mocked.

'You are . . . you are. . . .'

'If you do not know that you cannot have me.'

'But I do want you!'

She laughed again. 'For two dollars?'

'I want you!'

Laughing, she bent towards him, her mouth opening slightly and then . . . the red splashed across her body, blood spurting from the green of her mantle and she fell without a sound on the ground beside him. He tried to struggle upwards and found himself meeting the haunted, accusing eyes of Jack Quinlan. He sat before him, a stark figure on his small wooden cart, the bloody stumps dripping red on the green grass, a claw-like hand thrust towards him.

Spare a dime?

He opened his mouth to scream at those haunted eyes and tried to turn his head away. Her frail body was stretched now across his bloody stumps and the cart was receding backwards into the blackness of the battle. Above the crash and roar of the cannonade he could hear Jack Quinlan's voice, Spare a dime? Spare a dime?

The sky had darkened considerably and the rain was sheeting down as the 10th Street ferry edged towards the jetty. The ceremony at Calvary Cemetery, across the river at Newtown on Long Island, had been brief. Manus Devlin had offered to accompany his son but Gavin had declined, perhaps a little too sharply. It was something he had to do alone and Manus Devlin accepted that. But the young priest, fresh from the seminary, had gabbled through the burial service. Apart from the priest and the two grave diggers, only Gavin stood by the soaking muddy hole his eyes on the small pine wood coffin. 'In the sure and certain hope. . . .' Poor Nora Quinlan had been anything but sure and certain. She had been frightened and alone. Now, as her wasted body was lowered into the muddy earth, the young priest mumbled and mispronounced his Latin phrases without understanding, without compassion.

It was nearly ended when Gavin raised his eyes to the young priest and said, 'Recite Psalm Ten for me, Father. For . . . for her.'

The priest flushed and hesitated. He only had his *Missal* in his hand and could not remember the words.

Gavin bent to scoop up a handful of mud and gazed down at the coffin, almost obscured by the falling rain and mud.

'Why standest thou afar off, O God!' His voice was full of bitterness, causing the priest to draw his brows together in a frown and the grave diggers to exchange a glance. Gavin ground his teeth trying to recall the elusive words. 'Why standest thou afar off, O Lord? Why hidest thou thyself in times of trouble? The wicked in his pride doth persecute the poor. Let them. . . .' He hesitated, his voice suddenly choking. 'Let them be taken in the devices that they have imagined.' His voice rose in anger as he threw down the handful of mud on the rain-soaked coffin. He stared down for a moment with the wind whipping at his face, mingling with the tears in his eyes. Then he strode from the cemetery without a backward glance.

Now as the ferry edged against the 10th Street pierhead he realized that the time had come to make a decision about his life.

Chapter 18

Within a week Gavin had joined the Irish Republican Brotherhood and accepted the full-time job which had been offered him through the intervention of Father John MacMahon. His reasons for joining were complex and had much to do with his father's suggestion that, if he wished to continue to build up a case against the Delanceys, then the Brotherhood was a large and powerful organization that would put him in contact with numerous people – politicians, lawyers and newspapermen – who held a common social belief of creating a world where the Delanceys, or people like them, could not exist. For this reason, rather than being swayed by the rhetoric of the struggle for an Irish Republic, did Gavin throw himself into the work which the Brotherhood offered him. The work was actually very boring and mainly concerned the ways and means of raising money to finance the movement from membership subscriptions to lotteries, dances and sales of work. These funds then had to be converted into gold coinage or passed through various bank accounts and, by varied paths, sent to the organization in Ireland itself. In this, Gavin's knowledge of law, particularly of business law, was invaluable but the work did not stir a passionate interest in him.

Manus Devlin was proud that Gavin had finally joined the Brotherhood though he seemed to appreciate his son's unspoken reasons. He was quietly supportive to his son, realizing that the death of Nora Quinlan had wrought some inner change in him. No mention of her was ever made to Aideen Devlin. However, Aideen sensed the change in the relationship between her eldest son and her husband, of the new bond between them, and wondered about the reason for it, wondered and thanked God for it.

In the initial weeks of his work for the Brotherhood, Gavin found himself with little time on his hands to think about the Delanceys for the work sent him on several trips out of the city, mainly to the state capital at Albany where the secret headquarters of the military wing of the Brotherhood was. A General Staff had been set up and regiments had been established throughout the country, recruited mainly from the veterans of both Union and Confederate armies. Military training was still given with the aim that the soldiers of the Brotherhood would be able to be transported across the Atlantic to Ireland to take part in the coming insurrection. To this end the Brotherhood were already negotiating with the Navy Department to purchase two surplus warships that were currently laid up at the Brooklyn docks. Gavin, at the same time as taking the Fenian oath to join the Brotherhood, had accepted a commission as 'staff captain' into the military wing, although he considered himself more of a book-keeper and messenger than a revolutionary, more of a paid organizer than a rebel.

It was, of course, in Ireland that the insurrection was to be organized and where the Military Council of the Brotherhood, led by the mysterious *An Seabhac Siúlach* – The Wandering Hawk, were awaiting for the right moment to put the plan into operation. The news from the Military Council was that the uprising would take place before the year ended and the Brotherhood of America anxiously scanned the pages of the newspapers awaiting the declaration of an Irish Republic. But the only news from Ireland was of the arrival of more and more regiments of the British army and the raising of a large local militia from Unionists and Orangemen. Then came news which shocked the Brotherhood. The offices of the *Irish People*, the journal of the Brotherhood in Ireland, had been raided. The English had acted suddenly and effectively. Leaders of the Brotherhood were being arrested, including several of the Irish-American officers who had gone to train the insurrectionists, and the jails were filling. There was anxiety about John-Joe in the Devlin household as the reports came in.

A convention of the Brotherhood in America was called in Philadelphia early in October with 600 delegates attending. It was Father MacMahon who returned to New York with a report of the working of the biggest Fenian convention ever held. The news from Ireland had stirred the American Brotherhood up to independent action. Delegates decided that the movement could no longer be governed by John O'Mahoney acting as a virtual dictator nor should it be merely a subservient organization to the Brotherhood in Ireland. While there was enough respect for the scholarly O'Mahoney to re-elect him as president, a new constitution was adopted making this an accountable office with the inauguration of a senate of fifteen members which, in turn, would elect a president of the senate who would be vice-president to O'Mahoney. Ultimate power, however, would reside in the congress of the Brotherhood and congressmen would consist of delegates elected from each 'centre' or branch of the movement across the country.

It came as little surprise to Gavin to learn that the president of the senate was to be William Randall Roberts, the New York businessman who had made such a stirring speech at the Fourth of July celebration. Roberts lost no time in appointing a cabinet which included the posts of roving ambassador and a bond secretary to organize the issue of bonds of the Irish Republic as a means of raising new finance, the bonds to be redeemed when the Irish Republic became a fact. A secretary for war was appointed. The position of secretary for war went, by unanimous approval, to Major-General 'Fighting Tom' Sweeny. Sweeny was already a hero-figure among the Irish Americans. Born in Cork, he had arrived in New York with his widowed mother at the age of twelve. He commenced his career by working in a law publishing firm before joining the army to fight in the Mexican War, winning his spurs at Vera Cruz and losing his right arm at Churubusco. The loss of his arm did not handicap him and he remained in the 2nd US Infantry and fought in the Indian Wars. The start of the Civil War saw him fighting with his regiment for the Union at Wilson's Creek, Missouri, where he was carried wounded from the field. His stamina was extraordinary and five months later he was colonel of the 52nd Illinois. Two months after that he was wounded again. Recovering, he was appointed brigadier in General Wallace's division as it swept against the Confederate General Beauregard at Shiloh, sustaining severe casualties including the loss of Wallace himself. 'Fighting Tom' commanded his brigade at Corinth and then advanced to command a division of the XVI Corps of General Renville Dodge during Sherman's campaign against Atlanta in which the Union Army sustained 21,656 casualties. General Dodge subsequently preferred charges against Sweeny for insubordination but he was acquitted during a court martial and appointed major-general of militia. Now, at the age of forty-six, 'Fighting Tom' Sweeny was passionately committed to the establishment of an Irish Republic and he was not content to watch from a distance. He declared that the American Brotherhood could not simply be a commissariat for the Irish Brotherhood. The Fenian organization in Ireland had been effectively crippled. The news of the arrests in Ireland demonstrated that a rising there was out of the question for the time being. In America there were thousands of trained Irish soldiers who had joined the Brotherhood. Immediate action should be taken before inactivity took its toll.

At the convention there were in attendance forty-four delegates from the provinces of British North America led by Michael Murphy of Toronto, claiming to represent 125,000 members of the Brotherhood. Murphy and his delegates cut impressive figures. It also gave Roberts and Sweeny the lead they wanted. The Irish must strike where England was weakest; they must secure themselves a homeland on the American continent, an independent territory on which to raise the Irish flag, an independent territory from where the Irish could gather strength and international recognition. Then they could launch an attack on English rule in Ireland. What better than to seize the territory which England claimed in North America but which she would not defend as tenaciously as she would a territory near her heartland?

Roberts, the orator, warmed to this theme. British North America was already in turmoil. There were two major territories – Upper Canada and Lower Canada which had been united back in '41 but were bitterly antagonistic to each other, divided between the French-Canadians of Lower Canada and the English-dominated areas of Upper Canada. These territories had already attempted to set up independent republics in '37, a rising that the English had ruthlessly crushed. Among the French-Canadians there was strong opposition to English rule. Papineau, who had led the attempt to establish a French-Canadian republic in '37, was now leader of a strong political movement, the *Parti Rouge*. Having fled to the United States and then to Paris after the suppression of the uprising, Papineau had been pardoned ten years later, had returned and established his constitutional party which sought a separation of Lower Canada, Québec as the French called it, and the establishment of a radical republican government even as the Brotherhood wanted established in Ireland. Many sections of the *Parti Rouge*, he added, wanted Québec to become a member of the United States. There were even groups who were committed to the establishment of a French-Canadian republic by more extreme methods. And what of the unrest in Upper Canada where there were not only considerable numbers of Irish but even more Scots – Scots who had fled there after the English suppression of the 1820 uprising in Scotland? Had not William Lyon Mackenzie, who had declared the republic of Upper Canada in arms in '37, been a veteran of the 1820 uprising in Scotland? Such people and their descendants would surely have no love for England?

And what of the rest of British North America? What of New Brunswick, Prince Edward Island and Nova Scotia? Did he have to remind delegates that Nova Scotia was a stronghold of the Scottish Gaelic language – a sister language to their own Irish Gaelic? Why was that? Because the English, with their ruthless clearances of people from the glens of Scotland, had pursued the same genocidal policies against the Scots as they had against the Irish. And what of Newfoundland? Was that not known to the Irish as *Talamh an Éisc* – the Land of Fish – where so many of their countrymen now found sanctuary and where the old language continued? And beyond Lake Superior to the west, why there it was simply an unclaimed wilderness governed by the Hudson Bay Company of London.

Since the war between the States, the English, and those loyal to their empire, had become afraid of the United States, for England had no wish to see a strong unified nation on the North American continent. Had not England supported the Confederacy during the war in the hope that the United States would simply wither away into petty, warring factions? Well, the Union had been preserved and now England was afraid for her territories in the north; so afraid that a union of these provinces was being advocated – a Dominion of Canada under the British Crown. The scheme was receiving widespread opposition. The provinces of British North America would never agree to such a union. Here was England's weakest point; here was where the Brotherhood should strike.

The convention stirred with excitement.

Roberts had prepared his arguments well. The army of the Irish Republican Brotherhood would march north across the border, they would seize control of a portion of the British North American territory, working with allies who they would obviously find there. They would establish an Irish Republic-in-Exile with access to the Atlantic from which Fenian ships could be sent out against England. Indeed, the territory could even become a bargaining pawn for the eventual freedom of Ireland.

The convention rose with enthusiasm.

O'Mahoney attempted to quash the support. The resources of the Brotherhood, he cried desperately, should be used for armed intervention in Ireland in support of an uprising. In Ireland only.

But the delegations from the British North American provinces had risen to give their ardent support to Roberts' plan. All the Irish in Canada were opposed to the union of the provinces and would throw themselves wholeheartedly behind the scheme. O'Mahoney looked helplessly on while the convention passed a unanimous resolution ordering General Sweeny to investigate the possibilities of the military aspects of the plan and draw up a scheme for an invasion of British North America for the purposes of establishing an Irish Republic-in-Exile. The convention broke up with a new enthusiasm.

The plan quickly received support from many quarters, even appealing to Americans with no Irish connections at all but who remembered the support England had given to the Confederacy, supplying it with new warships such as the *Alabama* and the *Florida* and allowing British North America to be used as a safe haven for Confederate irregulars to strike at the United States. These Confederates were able to raid shipping on the Great Lakes and even cross the border in force to strike at northern towns and military installations. When Confederate irregulars had raided and burned the border town of St Albans, Vermont, Union General John Dix had ordered his commanders to pursue the retreating raiders into Lower Canada and haul them back across the border without deference to British neutrality. England had been the Confederacy's leading supplier of arms and munitions during the war. Indeed, had not the English Tories been forced to rule in coalition with the Liberals, it was obvious that England would have declared war on the United States in support of Jefferson Davis's Richmond Government. When Richmond fell, the Union soldiers had greeted the event with a ditty containing the line, 'Johnny Bull, we'll settle next with you!' The *New York Herald*, which had its finger close to the political pulse in Washington, was able to comment a few days after the Philadelphia Convention:

> In Canada the Fenians will establish a provisional government and operate for the deliverance of Ireland. The United States will play the neutral game, precisely like Great Britain in our present contest with the rebels. Under the color of neutrality, the Fenians will send out a swarm of armed vessels to cruise against English merchantmen, filling the seas, as it were, with Fenian *Alabamas* and *Floridas*. They will all be perfectly proper under the precedent established by Great Britain in building ships to prey upon American commerce. England will find, before many years, that the neutrality game is one that two nations can play at.

The Brotherhood had strong political lobbies both in the Senate and Congress and it was mainly due to the powerful voice of Democrat

Congressman Sydenham Elnathan Ancona of Pennsylvania that Roberts and Sweeny secured a meeting with President Andrew Johnson and secretary of state William Seward. Roberts began the proceedings by being somewhat flattering to the President, reminding him that his own grandfather came from County Antrim in search of religious freedom and played his part in the War of Independence. Then he came directly to the heart of the matter, asking what Johnson's attitude would be if the Irish Republican Brotherhood invaded British territory on the North American continent and established an Irish Republic-in-Exile?

The President stroked his nose thoughtfully before replying. 'The Irish-American community virtually form an Irish nation outside their own sorrowful country,' he said slowly, as if weighing each word. 'Perhaps that is justification enough for them to seize a territory, raise an Irish flag above it and declare a Republic-in-Exile. Perhaps it is justification for using that territory as a base from which to fight for the liberty of their motherland. There are certainly precedents for what you propose. Many Americans, soldiers of fortune mainly, have set out to claim territory in central America in order to further the financial and political welfare of this nation of ours. . . .' He smiled briefly. 'I can bring to mind, gentlemen, the activities of William Walker who, you may recall, led an army into Nicaragua just before the war and established himself as president of that republic.'

Johnson shuffled among the papers on his desk. 'I have, in fact, received word from our representatives in Buenos Aires of an attempt to establish a new state around the Chubut River in Patagonia by Welsh colonists. This summer, so my agent informs me, Welsh colonists have established themselves on the Chubut, raised their own flag, established a senate and declared themselves to be a free and independent Welsh nation. Of course, the Argentine government claim jurisdiction over Patagonia so it will remain to be seen just how long this new settlement will exist. But,' he smiled, 'there are precedents to your plan.'

Roberts and Sweeny exchanged glances, unsure of what the President was saying. They pressed him further.

'Gentlemen, shall I say that the attitude of my administration is that it will recognize accomplished facts? I think that is clear enough?'

Roberts and Sweeny thought it was. They had only to cross the border, seize a territory and declare an Irish Republic-in-Exile and

President Johnson would recognize it as a legitimate government and state.

They pressed him again. Would he release John Mitchel, jailed as an active and leading Confederate, who in their estimation was vital to the cause of Irish freedom? Roberts had already persuaded his senate that Mitchel was the only man who could act as the Brotherhood's ambassador. The President glanced at them in surprise. Mitchel was something of a *cause célèbre*. The son of an Ulster Presbyterian minister, he had become a lawyer before being involved as a leader of the Young Irelanders. Sentenced to fourteen years transportation he had made a spectacular escape from Van Dieman's Land and, safe in New York, had published his *Jail Journal* which had been hailed a classic of revolutionary literature. But to the astonishment of the majority of his fellow Irishmen, Mitchel believed in the institution of slavery with all the Biblical literalism of his Ulster Protestant upbringing. When asked how he could justify the slavery of a fellow being, possessed of an immortal soul, he replied complacently that Moses and the Prophets had done so. When asked if he would send a fugitive slave back to his or her master he had replied, assuredly, Paul the Apostle sent back the absconding Onesimus. Then Mitchel had rounded on the Abolitionists and asked, 'Are you better Christians than He who founded Christianity, better lovers of liberty than the Greeks who invented it, better Republicans than Washington or Jefferson and all the Republicans of old?' When his astounded compatriots pointed to the Constitution and the inalienable right of every human being to life, liberty and the pursuit of happiness, Mitchel had merely dismissed them as dupes of cant, saying that no human being ever had or could have such inalienable rights.

How could he demand liberty for his own conquered nation when he denied it to other peoples, demanded his compatriots? The liberty he sought for Ireland, he replied, was the sort of liberty the slave-holding Corcyraens asserted against Corinth, the liberty of the slave-owning Corinthians fought for against Rome and the slave-holding Americans wrested from England. The Irish exiles had pleaded with Mitchel 'to come back to them' but he had scornfully replied, 'Come back to you? Why, when was I ever amongst you?' He left his newly acquired home in New York and moved to Knoxville, Tennessee, and when the war between the States commenced he threw himself passionately into the cause of the Confederacy in whose service his eldest son and his youngest son gave their lives. At the end of the war he had been placed in jail, recanting none of his unpopular notions.

Yet for all his beliefs Roberts recognized in Mitchel a man of passion, of almost frenzied activity, a man who had become something of a hero in Europe, especially in France. Roberts knew that Mitchel was too much of an individualist to work at Fenian headquarters and his views on slavery would inevitably lead him into conflict with the Brotherhood whose views were entirely opposite. However, he wanted to use Mitchel's unboundable energy as a fiscal agent in Europe and ambassador to the sympathetic French government, most of whom were personally known to him.

President Johnson, glancing at Seward, said he would look into the matter of Mitchel's release adding, 'I cannot ignore the express desire of so important a segment of the American community as you represent, gentlemen.'

He did not. Within a few days after the meeting, the fifty-year old Mitchel had been released in New York. After a few more days Mitchel was on board *L'Europe* bound for France. In his journal he reflected:

> The language of Andrew Johnson to the deputation of that body (the Fenians), respecting my release, leads me to think that the United States' government may really contemplate the policy of permitting, or at least conniving at, any enterprise the Irish-Americans may undertake. All through the war they have been buoyed up by this hope, and have been directly encouraged to entertain it – that when the South should be effectually subdued they would be let loose upon England. The Fenian organization has spread like wildfire through the army, and there are now many thousands of disbanded soldiers who would desire nothing in the world so much as the chance of embarking on board a few transport ships for the shores of Ireland. The ferocious language held against England, both in Congress and in the Press, on account of the fitting out of Confederate cruisers in British ports, and the consequent widely spread destruction of American shipping, all this makes it natural to believe that the Washington government might be perfectly willing to use such a powerful and zealous force as these mustered-out Irish soldiers, and might look on while they work their will.

In a few weeks William Randall Roberts had achieved far more for the Irish Republican Brotherhood in America – giving it a respectability and a prestige as well as a sense of immediate purpose – than all the years of O'Mahoney's self-appointed leadership. There was a tremendous surge of hope among the Irish people. Never since the days of the United Irishmen had an Irish Republican movement been so strong, numbered so many trained men, had so much financial support and achieved the benign backing of a powerful government.

Chapter 19

Manus and Gavin Devlin supported Roberts's scheme from two widely differing points of view. Manus Devlin's support was an emotional adherence to action, any action. Gavin saw the scheme as the pragmatic approach that Roberts had suggested at the Fourth of July celebration. Judging from the information at hand, and Gavin had personally witnessed the resentment of the French-Canadians, the plan was entirely workable. Whereas it was simply a dream to transport thousands of troops, munitions and supplies across the Atlantic to Ireland in the face of the watchdogs of the Royal Navy, it was entirely feasible to march a Fenian army across the border, seize territory and use it as a hostage for Irish freedom. Horace Greeley's powerful *New York Tribune* thought it good strategy, so did James Gordon Bennett's *New York Herald* and the *Irish-American*, the most influential of the Irish community newspapers. Roberts was certainly not lacking in energy in his swift re-organization of the Brotherhood.

Gavin was set a task almost immediately Roberts arrived back from his meeting with President Johnson in Washington. He was to negotiate the rental of the old Moffat Mansion on Union Square as the new headquarters building. Gavin was able to achieve this with a deposit of $6,000 and a rent of $1,000 a month. It was an excellent piece of propaganda for the secretariat of the Brotherhood to be housed in visible splendour. However, there were dissenting voices. John O'Mahoney, still titular president of the Brotherhood and still influential, was highly critical of the new headquarters. He was becoming more petulant as he watched power slipping from his grasp. He had began to oppose everything the senate suggested on principal. Spending such money on hiring the Moffat Mansion was a criminal waste, he argued. The senate merely over-ruled him and O'Mahoney had left the meeting, red-faced with fury and muttering under his breath.

The same evening as that senate meeting, just after 8 p.m., Gavin left the building. His mind was preoccupied with the contemplation of how a man as intelligent as O'Mahoney could be so full of vain glory, so willing to sacrifice the movement to personal prestige. It was dark and the gas lamps were lit along the square. There was a promise of a cold night to come, mist was rising as the warmth of the sidewalks and buildings were chilled by the darkness of the evening. He halted for a moment by the elegant iron railings which surrounded the bronze equestrian figure of Washington whose right arm was flung out towards the square's three-acre park. There were a few people about and no sign of a hackney. He was aware, however, of an enclosed carriage swinging by the statue and pulling up alongside him. Aware, too late, of a figure behind him and a revolver shoved against his ribs.

'Keep quiet and get in!' snapped a voice.

He was propelled into the blackness of the carriage. Someone was already seated in the interior and the figure with the revolver was scrambling in behind him. The door slammed and the carriage jerked forward, swaying as its driver urged his horses rapidly through the streets.

'What do you want?' he demanded, trying to peer at his captors in the darkness. 'I've no money.'

There was a rasping cough. 'Shut yer yap, cap'n,' snapped a voice.

'Who are you?'

A street lamp flashing by shone its light momentarily into the interior of the carriage. Gavin had a brief glimpse of one of the men but a brief glimpse was enough. His body went to ice.

'Hogan!'

'I said, "shut up!"'

Gavin tried to lick his dry lips. 'This won't get you anywhere,' he said attempting to hide his nervousness.

Hogan's companion who had done most of the talking wheezed with laughter. 'It's getting me a hundred bucks, cap'n.'

It was then Hogan spoke for the first time. 'Shut up. You, too, Devlin.'

There was a brittleness in his voice which made Gavin save his breath. He wondered where he was being taken. To see Brock Delancey? He thought not. The carriage seemed to be travelling eastwards. After a while he smelt the salt tang of the East River and felt the carriage shuddering over a hollow-sounding road. He guessed they had hit the timber wharves along the waterfront. The carriage halted abruptly and they hauled him out. He peered round quickly. He had been right. They were on a deserted quayside of rotting wood which poked out into the river. Beyond them dark warehouses stretched gloomily away. There were no signs of anybody else nor any welcoming lights from a waterfront tavern.

'Get it over with quickly,' snapped Hogan's voice.

Gavin tensed his body. 'You can't do this, Hogan,' he protested helplessly.

The other man shoved him backwards. 'Get over there, cap'n,' he grunted. 'Get over there by the edge of the wharf. You'll be going for a swim shortly and it would save us the trouble of having to carry you across.'

He realized there was no appeal to these grim shadows and now he understood exactly what had happened to poor Symes. He edged backwards to the end of the wharf, watching the moonlight catch the dull metal of the pistol that his assailant held. His mind worked a split second before the crack of the pistol. He threw himself backwards, hoping the tide was in sufficiently to break his fall so that he would not break his back on the mud flats. The crash of his body against the icy water came as a relief but knocked the breath from him. He felt a searing pain cross his temple and, with detached astonishment, realized that he had been grazed by the bullet. Gulping air he plunged under the water and struck out. Something seemed to explode near him. He held his breath until he could stand it no longer and rose for air. Without waiting to check on his assailants he dived once more and, when he emerged again, he could hear nothing except the swirling of water. He drifted along with the current for a while but his head was painful and he felt faint. He decided to strike out for the nearest wharves. He found a ladder and began to haul himself up.

'What the 'ell . . . ?' demanded a voice as he heaved himself on to the quay. The voice seemed to come from a long way away. He wanted to find out who it belonged to but he passed out. It must have only been for a few moments because he came round with a dark figure bending over him.

''Strewth! You're alive! Thought you were a goner.'

Gavin frowned as he tried to focus. 'You're English,' he groaned feeling it to be a silly observation.

''Sright, mate,' came the reply. 'And you've hurt yerself bad. Yer head is bleeding.'

Gavin tried to make his mind work. It was no good going to

Greenwich Lane. Delancey's men would probably be watching for him there. 'Can you get me to Father MacMahon? Thirty-Seventh Street. Church of Holy Innocent.'

'Yer a Roman Catholic,' came the voice cheerfully. 'Yer don't want a priest. Yer ain't gonna die.'

'Get me to Father MacMahon.' Gavin mumbled, feeling he was going to pass out again. 'Get a cab. He'll pay. Give you a dollar, too.'

His last memory of the voice was it saying, 'Yeah, I've heard that before.' Then darkness overtook him.

He rushed forward in the deafening mêlée of heat and smoke and wild cries of terror from the wounded, among the struggling pain-racked bodies. Only the dead were still; only the dead were quiet. The serried ranks poured forward across the mud flats, across the cold mud which clung so pleadingly to their legs as if trying to halt their progress. They poured forward in a broken confusion, muskets and bayonets held fearfully before them, forward into the cannonade which no power on earth could resist; forward in a wave of overwhelming panic, the contagion spreading along their lines.

Ready the flag!

Jack Quinlan's voice was a tuneful baritone of glee. They plunged into the shallows of a river, splashing frantically. Then he stumbled and fell, fell deep in the swirling eddies of the river, felt the ice water washing over his mouth as he gasped for air. He tried to hold his head above water but he was being pushed under. He threshed out with his hands.

And she, she laughing, hauled him on the warm dry river bank as easily as if he had been a baby. 'You have forgotten me, Gavin Devlin,' she said in accusation.

He mumbled and fought for breath.

'Yes, yes. You have forgotten me while you played with your war.' She stood up and walked slowly away. He tried to reach after her and from his frantically working mouth all the sound he could produce was, Spare a dime! Spare a dime! She glanced carelessly back over her white shoulder and her voice was an echo of the gurgling water beside him.

When he opened his eyes he was in a warm bed and the anxious face of Father MacMahon was staring down at him.

'*Buíochas le Dia*!' he muttered. 'You've taken a hard crack on your skull, Gavin. And two dollars and a cab fair I had to pay for you.'

Gavin groaned. 'What time is it?'

'You've been here since last night,' replied Father MacMahon. 'It's nearly time for the midday Angelus.'

'Do my father and mother know where I am?'

'I haven't had time to see them. I thought I'd wait until you recovered consciousness. What was it? Were you beaten up?'

'In a manner of speaking,' Gavin sighed. 'Can you bring my father here without my mother knowing?'

The priest nodded but looked puzzled.

'I'll explain to you both together,' Gavin promised.

Manus Devlin was adamant as soon as he had listened to the story. 'The Brotherhood must get Gavin out of the city,' he said to Father MacMahon.

Gavin, still lying in bed his head bandaged, looked from his father to the priest and back again. 'But there must be some way of dealing with the Delanceys now? I could swear out a warrant for attempted murder and. . . .'

Father MacMahon shrugged. 'No, your father is right, Gavin. It's only your word against the Delanceys. At best, you are a witness against Hogan but who is to say whether this man was acting for Brock Delancey? There's no way you can fight them yet. It's better that you leave the city for a good, long while.'

'What of Hogan?' demanded Gavin.

Father MacMahon glanced at Manus Devlin and stroked his nose thoughtfully. 'Hogan's a different matter,' he said slowly. 'I'll drop a word about Hogan in certain quarters. But there is no way we can tackle the Delanceys.'

Gavin bit his lip with a sigh of exasperation. 'I'd almost forgotten the Delanceys and what vermin they are. I became too involved with the Brotherhood. I nearly forgot why I joined it. . . .'

Manus Devlin leaned across the end of the bedstead. 'Listen, son, the Brotherhood holds out the best hope that you've got for some protection against the Delanceys and their bully boys. Don't forget that.' He hesitated as if regretting speaking so sharply.

Gavin smiled. 'I'll not forget, Pa.'

Father MacMahon nodded slightly. 'Manus, you go home and pack a bag for the boy. Tell Aideen that he has been sent away on behalf of the organization. I'll go to see Roberts and try to make that less of a lie to save myself a penance.'

Manus gazed thoughtfully at his son. 'Will you be all right to travel?' he asked.

It was the priest who answered confidently. 'Give him a day or two and he'll be as fresh as a newborn babe.'

It was Father MacMahon who returned with the news first. It had been agreed that Gavin would be transferred to the military wing of the Brotherhood and join General Sweeny's staff up in Albany, the State capital.

'I have a friend, Father FitzGerald, who runs a small retreat in Albany,' smiled Father MacMahon. 'I'll take you up there myself when you're better. You'll be able to rest there and won't have to undergo the hazard of staying at an hotel or boarding house which might bring you to the attention of the Delanceys.'

'I don't want to be hiding for the rest of my life,' protested Gavin.

'Neither shall you,' Father MacMahon assured him. 'We'll find a way of dealing with the Delanceys but we need time to do it. You'll be fine along with Father FitzGerald.'

'So long as I'm not expected to attend mass every day,' Gavin said hastily.

Father MacMahon sighed, his face troubled. 'I always knew that you were not what is called a good Catholic, Gavin.'

'You know I'm no Catholic at all except by accident of birth. I've seen too much suffering in this world, too many people have died, for me to be able to believe that an all-good omnipotent deity has charge of the affairs of mankind.'

'God is omnipotent, Gavin, but man has free will.'

'In that case, the argument is more horrendous. If there is an omnipotent God who therefore knows what mankind will do before they do it, yet sits back and lets it happen, then to call such a being all-good is obscene.'

'You don't shock me, Gavin,' the priest replied sadly.

'I'm not trying to shock you, Father,' Gavin said. 'But don't expect me to waste my time and energy in trying to persuade myself to believe in a God.'

Father MacMahon shook his head in sorrow. 'Maybe the priest in me is a little shocked at that, Gavin. But I know you to be a moral person. That's important. So I'll tell you this, the next best thing, if you don't want to spend your time making yourself believe in God, is to live your life well, live it morally, work for the good so that

God will come to believe in you.' He rose and brushed down his cassock. 'And now,' he grinned easily, 'I'll have to give myself a penance of two decades of the rosary for preaching such heresy.'

That evening Gavin's father came back to the presbytery. He carried a valise of clothes and a large parcel. 'Your mother said that I was to give this to you with her love, son.'

Gavin eased himself up in the bed and stared at the package a moment before opening it. Inside were his army boots, brightly polished, his sword belt and holster, with his sword and revolver. Underneath them was a neatly folded dark green uniform with gold trimming and a green peaked cap. He stared in amazement. The uniform was modelled on the Union Army infantry uniform except for its colouring, the brass buttons and insignia. Each brass button had a small wreath of shamrocks on it with the letters 'IRA' in the centre. The insignia carried the legend *Na Fianna Éireann* picked out in gold lettering. The shoulder blazes had captain's bars in them. Gavin was astounded.

'Your mother has been working on this uniform ever since she knew that you had joined the Brotherhood and accepted a commission,' his father said proudly. 'It's the uniform of the army of a free Ireland, the Irish Republican Army.'

'It's a bit premature, isn't it?' Gavin replied, carefully replacing it in the parcel.

Father MacMahon chuckled. 'Not a bit. You'll be the best-dressed officer on General Sweeny's staff.'

Gavin raised a cynical eye. 'And the only one in uniform?'

'The designs for the uniform were approved of some time ago by the Brotherhood,' Manus snapped gruffly. 'If the Brotherhood is to become a belligerent army then, by the laws of civilization, it has to adopt a uniform and battle flags. All the officers and men who can afford uniforms are having them made to the approved design which your mother has spent hours following.'

Gavin smiled gently and laid a hand on his father's arm. 'Thank mother for me, Pa. Tell her . . . I am very proud and grateful for her gift.'

Manus Devlin gripped his eldest son's hand. 'Watch out for yourself, Gavin. I'll keep in touch through Father MacMahon.' He hesitated and glanced down at the uniform. 'Wear it with honour, son.'

Chapter 20

John-Joe Devlin gazed out of the tenement window across the drab grey roofs of Dublin which were made more grey by the rising smoke of thousands of fires seeking to warm the cold November morning. There was no curtain at the single attic window of the room which he rented and shared with Tom Bawn. It was not a large room and the sloping roof made it seem even more restricted than it actually was. There was space for two cot beds, a chair, a lumpy couch and a table. A curtained-off area served as a wardrobe for both of them while a small cast-iron stove gave out an inadequate heat although, with patience, a kettle could be boiled on it. The room was brown, a deep yellowing brown, which came from long years of neglect. There was no carpet, just splintering wooden boards and a piece of sacking placed by the beds which served to prevent them inflicting injuries to their feet when John-Joe or Tom Bawn clambered from bed in the morning. It was, all in all, a dismal and depressing place.

There were many tenement buildings in this quarter of Dublin, south of the river and within an easy walk of Dublin Castle, the seat of imperial government in Ireland. The area was crammed with hundreds of ancient, decaying, four-storey buildings in which thousands of families had to exist in a single room no bigger than the one John-Joe and Tom Bawn occupied. Many of the buildings were actually condemned as being unsafe and unfit for human habitation. Since John-Joe had arrived in the city, one of the buildings had collapsed killing several of its unfortunate tenants. Unlike his brother, Gavin, John-Joe had isolated himself from the slums of New York and therefore the warrens of Dublin were a foreign country to him, a strange and frightening world: dirty, squalid, an over-populated ghetto of narrow, disreputable streets, lined on both sides with cheap lodging houses or dirty tenement blocks.

The man from the Brotherhood, who had met him from the train which had brought him directly from Cork, had conducted him straightway to the attic room, introduced him to Tom Bawn and told him he would stay there under the name John Duffy until further orders. Even though it had been late when he had arrived, the streets had been crowded with brawling, drunken men and women. John-Joe had felt repelled at the sight. But it was the smells that remained with him more than anything. Loathsome odours rose from the gutters which were running, open sewers whose odious contents spilled over the pavements and under doors, spreading a murky torrent of offal, animal and vegetable, in every state of putrefaction. The smell was like nothing he had encountered before. Disease and death were a constant companion in these areas. Tom Bawn, who had been a student both in Dublin and in Paris, was inclined to quote statistics and he informed him that the city's death rate was equivalent to Calcutta, a city infested with plague and cholera. Even Moscow, groaning under Tsarist tyranny, had a lower death rate than Dublin where, out of every one hundred babies born, fourteen did not survive two weeks of their birth.

It was a terrible shock for John-Joe. Where was the emerald green isle? The island of saints and scholars? The beautiful vistas that his father had told him of with sighing longing? Instead he found a harsh and cruel society; a frightful and miserable existence where death came as a blessed release from suffering. It was Tom Bawn, the student of statistics, who had told him that Dublin had not always been such a terrible place. In fact, the Dublin of over-crowded slums, of poverty and death, had not existed twenty years before. It had become like this only during the famine years, those four short terrible years when Ireland had lost one-and-a-half million people from death caused by the diseases brought on by malnutrition and a further one million from migration, only during those years had the cities of Ireland swollen to unmanageable sizes. John-Joe had tried to visualize what the loss of two-and-a-half million people would be in physical terms and gave up. The attempt left him physically sick and burning with a hot anger. The famine in Ireland had been artificially induced. The potato crop had failed, true; yet Ireland was producing barley, oats and corn to feed not just eight millions but eighteen millions. Every famine relief ship captain rushing into the ports of Ireland could not believe the fact that six ships to their one were leaving the ports bearing cargoes of grain. The absentee landlords of England demanded their rents and the peasants of Ireland, faced with eviction and inevitable death, were forced to sell their produce to the landlords while their children cried in hunger. Immense herds of cattle, flocks of sheep and hogs, were shipped continuously from every one of Ireland's thirteen ports, bound for England, while thousands of people died on the roadside for want of food. The landlords enjoyed their wealth in England while the Irish nation began to vanish from the land. A Royal Duke felt moved to comment on the plight of the Irish; 'We all know that Irishmen can live upon anything, and there is plenty of grass in the fields. . . .'

Thousands had poured into the towns hoping to escape the hunger of the countryside and many remained in Dublin. They stayed in the expectation of work but resigned to a life of penury. In such circumstances prostitution flourished and the unfortunate women from the terrible slum areas flocked nightly to the quayside taverns, or to the thoroughfares of O'Connell and Grafton Streets in order to earn a living; prostitutes were even allowed on board the ships in the Dublin docks to entertain the crews. Beggars were everywhere, especially former servicemen without arms, legs, eyes, all clad in tatters of their former uniforms in which they had helped to establish England's empire. The streets were also crowded with children, children of all ages from a few years and upwards, who seem to have no permanent home nor parents and who begged and hawked for a living from passers-by. It was the children who haunted John-Joe; children with cramped, lined faces and burning eyes like shrivelled and stunted old men and women – aged by their suffering and the prospect of death even before they had learnt how to live. They seemed lacking in animation, wandering like silent wraiths through the city, hands held in a mute call for alms; joyless, voiceless shadows. That was the unnerving thing about the children – their quietness. Even the dogs slunk behind them, fleshless creatures with vertebrae protruding like a bone saw. They glared hungrily with burning, wolfish eyes, watching avidly; their tongues twisting nervously around rotting canines as they debated whether or not to attack before slinking back into the shadows of the houses.

Will you come and awake our dear land from its slumber . . . ?

John-Joe felt bitter as the words of the song echoed in his mind. Dublin had made him burn with a rage which no recounting of Ireland's sad history had made him feel. He raged against the fat little Queen who sat smugly on her throne surrounded by the pomp and circumstance of a vaunted empire, secure in her wealth and power, believing in her divine right, in the moral right of her imperial power. She resided over a world in slavery; over poverty, death and nations chained to produce wealth for a small élite of her people. The sight of the poor of Dublin stirred John-Joe as nothing had ever stirred him before; stirred him into an angry passion which made him throb with a desire to strike a blow against the tyranny which had produced such degradation, such hopelessness and such frightful savagery. He found himself hating the English administration in Ireland for its barbarous indifference, its complacency and the egotism which justified its rule.

He turned back from the window and stared moodily around the attic room. He was full of anger and he was bored. When he had arrived in Queenstown, Cork, he had expected to be training men in the use of arms, expected an insurgent army to be gathered waiting, expected the blow against English rule to occur momentarily. Instead he had been ordered to Dublin. His only companion was Tom Bawn, a fair-haired man about five years older than himself. He had studied at Trinity, graduated from the Sorbonne and still spent most of his time studying. He was loquacious only when talking of Irish history otherwise he was a somewhat taciturn companion. That Tom Bawn was not his real name was obvious.

The weeks had passed with nothing to relieve the boredom, the claustrophobic boredom of the attic. They did not leave the tenement except at night when Tom Bawn would take him on walking tours of the city, pointing out the position of each military barracks, the bridges over the river, the main routes out of Dublin and above all the forbidding grey walls of Dublin Castle, the seat and symbol of English rule. Tom Bawn occasionally went to meet a contact in the Brotherhood to seek 'orders' but the message he brought back was always the same. Wait. It had been a pale-faced Tom Bawn who had come back to the attic room one day in September with the news that the offices of the *Irish People*, the Brotherhood's newspaper, had been raided. A strong force of police and military had broken into the offices, seized books, manuscripts, papers and the founts of type. Most importantly, they had seized lists of subscribers. The English had acted suddenly and effectively. Within days the jails were filling with the leadership of the Brotherhood and several of the Irish-American officers who had shipped over with John-Joe.

'We must rise up now,' cried Tom Bawn as he paced the room in anxiety, 'We must strike now while we still have an organization.

The Young Irelanders failed because they left it too late. We must strike now!'

At least there was still hope for, try as the authorities would, they had not found the hiding place of the Brotherhood's leader – the mysterious *An Seabhac Siúlach*, the Wandering Hawk. However, they had discovered his identity, naming him as James Stephens, a Young Irelander who had been wounded in the uprising of '48. Stephens had managed to escape in the aftermath of the rising and reached Paris where he had lived for some years, devoting himself to a study of politics and literature. His knowledge of French was so fluent that he had been chosen to translate *David Copperfield* and *Martin Chuzzlewit* into French, earning the critical praise and the admiration of their author Charles Dickens. For years Stephens had worked secretly and tirelessly to build up the Brotherhood in Ireland, co-ordinating its activities among Irish exiles, particularly in America. But now . . . now the secret was out. There was no disguising the blow which had been dealt against the Brotherhood. In spite of Tom Bawn's enthusiasm for an immediate rising, the Brotherhood would need time to recover and reorganize.

During October the weeks passed even more slowly. John-Joe became nervous that the house might be raided as reports of arrests of Irish-American officers were frequent. Then the alarms began to die away and November arrived. John-Joe's boredom grew into frustration which made him irritable to the point where he reached a decision to return home. *Home*! The thought struck him forcibly that New York was home. Three months couped up in a Dublin attic, with only nocturnal walks to relieve the boredom, had taught him that he was an American. He was homesick, homesick for his family, his friends . . . his home.

Tom Bawn came into the room, his face flushed, his eyes moving nervously from side to side. He heeled the door shut and stood for a moment, his breath coming in short gasps as he sought to recover from the exertion of the climb to the attic.

'He's caught, John,' Tom Bawn said slowly, sinking on to his cot. 'Jesus, Mary and Joseph, they've got *An Seabhac Siúlach*!'

John-Joe stared at him numbly. It had probably been a matter of time but even so it came as a shock. *An Seabhac Siúlach*, the Wandering Hawk! The leader of the Brotherhood! The embodiment of all the hopes of Ireland!

'What's happened?' whispered John-Joe.

'The police picked him up early this morning with Charlie Kickham, who edited the *Irish People*. What a mess!'

He swung off the cot and went to the table. A half-full bottle of whiskey stood there. He filled a glass and tossed it back.

'I urged action! I urged it back in September. Now it's too late. The country will fall apart again. They'll be no rising.'

John-Joe was silent. Tom Bawn looked at him bitterly. 'You can hardly move through the streets with the number of military patrols now. There's spies and informers everywhere.'

'How did they get him?'

'Spies and informers. Traitors that are the curse of Ireland. Apparently Stephens had been hiding out at Sandymount, just a mile or two from here. Someone informed on him. Colonel Lake and his men surrounded the house and broke in before a warning could be given. There's four men along with Stephens who have been arrested and taken to the Castle. They say that Inspector Dawson and Hughes identified Stephens.' He banged his hand, striking his balled fist on the table top and causing the glasses and the bottle to jump. 'Damn them! Traitors and scum, police and informers, the curse of Ireland!'

'Is it the end of the Brotherhood?' asked John-Joe.

Tom Bawn stared up at him, his pale eyes alight with a strange fire. 'Are you game for action?'

'But what . . . ?'

'Action, *mo bhuachaill!* Can you drive a sidecar?'

'You mean one of those buggies I've seen out on the streets?'

'Aye, a jaunting car.'

'Sure,' John-Joe frowned, 'I've often driven our family buggy back home.'

'*Maith an fear*! Good man!' He turned to his cot and, lifting the mattress, pulled a small brown paper package from underneath. Seated at the table he tore off the wrappings. The black gun metal glinted in the light. The heavy Colt revolver lay polished and oiled. Alongside it was a box of ammunition. John-Joe stared from the gun to Tom Bawn.

'What do you mean to do?'

The fair-haired man laughed grimly. 'We must show them that the Brotherhood has teeth. Dawson and Hughes identified Stephens. They betrayed him to their English masters. We'll teach them to play Judas.'

'You mean that you plan to murder them?' John-Joe felt a cold breath of fear as he watched Tom Bawn load the gun.

'Retribution is the word, *mo bhuachaill*. Assassination. Isn't that what you came over here to teach us, how to kill people?'

'On a battlefield, yes, but this. . . .'

Tom Bawn went to the window and gestured theatrically. 'There's our battlefield, out there on the streets. We have to fight in the only way our enemies allow us, so don't give me your grand notions of battlefields, death and glory. Do you think that we like fighting from the cover of hedgerows and fences? Wouldn't it be grand if it were like the old days, like Vinegar Hill when army moved against army? Surely the English generals would love that. They crushed the flower of the Irish armies at Aughrim of the Slaughter and they have expected us to curl up like a dutiful dog at England's feet. But we still fight and we'll fight on our terms.'

John-Joe stared at his intense red face and wondered whether it was his passion or the drink talking.

'Are you with me, John-Joe?'

'What do you mean to do?'

Tom Bawn took a map from his pocket and thrust it on the table before the young American and seated himself beside him. 'See here, by the Castle? This is Exchange Court. It's the headquarters of the traitors who call themselves the Irish Constabulary. Tomorrow at eleven o'clock Dawson and Hughes are due to report for duty. . . .'

'How do you know?' interrupted John-Joe.

Tom Bawn grinned. 'The English are not the only ones to have informers. My information is accurate, *mo bhuachaill*, don't doubt it. Now,' he jabbed with a finger. 'I'll be standing here, on the opposite side of the road to the police headquarters. You will be in the sidecar and parked here in Dame Street. Be in position by five minutes to eleven. At a minute before eleven you will begin to move slowly along the road. If I am still waiting drive on and park beyond me. However, if I know my men, they'll be on time. I'll get them as they enter the headquarters. You pick me up and we'll be away down the road. You'll take a straight route to Bull Alley and turn in. A friend will be waiting to take the sidecar and then we'll separate, on foot, and double back behind Dublin Castle. You'll take this road, walking leisurely through St Stephens Green and Merrion Square back here to the room. Understand?'

John-Joe nodded. 'The Brotherhood has approved this?' he asked.

Tom Bawn chuckled as if tremendously amused by the question. 'Would I be doing this if I didn't have the backing of the organization?'

John-Joe shrugged. 'And all I have to do is drive the buggy?' he pressed.

'*Ceart go leor*. Right enough.'

John-Joe felt a sense of relief. 'It seems easy enough,' he said. 'But where do we get the buggy from?'

'It's all arranged, *mo bhuachaill*. It will be waiting for you on the City Quay opposite the Customs House. You'll collect it at half-past ten from a man called Dillon.' Tom Bawn smiled. 'For once the peelers will get a taste of their own medicine, *marbhfháisc orthu!*'

John-Joe felt a sense of fear. Yet here was action. Here, at last, was a means through which he could contribute a blow for the cause. But he was appalled at the prospect of cold-blooded murder, an assassination. Whatever Tom Bawn called it, it was still killing. Yet what difference was that to leading a charge across a battlefield against an enemy prepared and ready? It did not feel right somehow. It did not seem like an act of heroic, glorious revolution. They talked the plan over in detail for some time, ate a sparse supper and finally went to bed. John-Joe had little sleep. He twisted and turned fitfully. Surely this was not how soldiers felt on the night before they went into battle?

The imposing edifice of the old Irish Parliament building, once the focus of political and social life in the country until the abolition of the Irish Parliament in 1801, dominated the view along Dame Street. John-Joe was glad it was a cold day, a grey overcast day with icy, sleeting rain flurries. It had given him the excuse to muffle himself in a large greatcoat and wrap a scarf over his face, pulling a hat well down on his head, without exciting any curiosity or suspicion from those passing along the street. He sat watching the minutes tick by while his horse bent its head to a nearby trough of water. He had one scare when a man accosted him and demanded to know if he were plying for hire but the man had accepted John-Joe's negative shake of the head and moved off.

Two members of the Irish Constabulary strolled by on the far side of the street and he followed their progress nervously, watching their casual pace, shoulders back, proud in their green-black uniforms with their sword-bayonets slapping against their legs and their Enfield rifles slung across their shoulders. It was true that the police in New York were armed but they only carried side-arms. In Ireland the police were a fully accoutred military force with side-arms, rifles, bayonets and swords and even supported by properly trained cavalry units. One could actually buy a commission in the Irish Constabulary in the same way as one could buy a commission in the British Army. Tom Bawn had told him that the presence of the Constabulary in Dublin was only a recent innovation, a precaution against the awaited rising of the Brotherhood. The city was usually patrolled by the Dublin Metropolitan Police who were a normal, civil police force, unlike the military organization of the Constabulary. Since he had landed in Ireland, John-Joe realized that the country was an armed camp. The Constabulary was everywhere and one could not walk far, either in town or country, without encountering armed soldiers, hussars, dragoons and marching infantry. England kept a regular army of 26,000 troops in Ireland. There were 6,000 regular troops stationed in the Dublin garrisons alone. That was not including the militia forces which mustered a further 12,000 troops. Military coercion was apparently the only way England could exert her will and govern Ireland.

A sudden panic seized John-Joe. He had been daydreaming too long. He glanced at his watch and then sent the sidecar moving forwards over the cobbles. He had no time for nervousness now. He must concentrate on doing his bit. He swung the buggy round a corner and spotted Tom Bawn immediately. He was leaning against a wall smoking a cigarette as if he were simply huddling from the soft drizzle which was now falling. John-Joe began to relax. The policemen had not come, perhaps they would not come. Perhaps the information was not accurate.

He was twenty yards away from Tom Bawn when he saw the fair-haired man suddenly throw his cigarette away. His hand went streaking to his overcoat pocket. The revolver was out in a moment and he was running to the centre of the road. Standing there in the open, he fired two shots in rapid succession. John-Joe's eyes flickered in the direction Tom Bawn's smoking gun was pointing. He saw two men falling on the steps of a building. Then he was having to restrain the horse, which reared and lashed out in fright with its forelegs. He spent a few precious seconds bringing the animal under control and, by the time he had done so, Tom Bawn was swinging himself up.

'Get going! For Christ's sake, get going!' His face was animated.

John-Joe whipped the reins and sent the horse plunging forward over the cobbles. There was a crack behind them and something whined close by. He was dimly aware of shouts, a piercing shriek, and shadows were springing out of the way of the swaying buggy.

'Turn down here!' cried Tom Bawn.

John-Joe yanked the reins nearly bringing the vehicle tumbling over. As it was, it raised itself on one wheel, gave a lurch and swung back again. With Tom Bawn yelling instructions they swung through a maze of tiny streets until his companion told him to slow down. They went on at a pace which did not excite comment through several more streets before entering a small mews. An elderly, unsmiling man, sprung forward and started to unhitch the horse without a word to either of them.

Tom Bawn leapt down, wiping the sweat from his face.

'*Maith an fear*!' he grinned fiercely. 'That was a damned fine drive, *mo bhuachaill*. Now we split up. You know the route home?'

'Through St Stephens Green and Merrion Square,' nodded John-Joe.

Tom Bawn flicked up a hand in salute and went striding off rapidly. John-Joe waited a moment, still trying to stop his heart pounding, and then he forced himself to stroll casually out of the mews. It all seemed so unreal. It was almost as if nothing had happened. Yet two men had fallen on the steps of the police headquarters. Two policemen, his enemies, but two men, two human beings. He was now an assassin . . . a murderer. And what had been achieved by the death of those two men? Were they really the enemy? He suddenly remembered an old farmer saying that if you kill one dog, the master buys another. So long as there was a master there would be other dogs. He didn't feel like a hero fighting for the revolution, he didn't feel like a soldier. Only if one killed hundreds, in companies, to the sound of a trumpet was one a hero.

Chapter 21

They toasted each other with whiskey in the safety of their attic room. Tom Bawn had arrived before John-Joe and he was giggling hysterically to ease the tension within him. The laughter was infectious, causing John-Joe to forget his fears, anxiety and moral self-recriminations. They had struck a blow in the shadow of Dublin Castle itself, the heart of the imperial administration, and the adrenalin of victory aroused a childish glee. And after they had exhausted themselves pummelling each other in jubilation, the lack of sleep and apprehensions of the day overcame them. They lay back on their cots and each fell into a debilitating sleep of utter fatique.

John-Joe's first awareness that strangers were in the room was when he was shaken roughly awake. An elderly man with heavy, graven features, was bending over him. John-Joe started from the bed, his heart beating rapidly.

'Steady, Duffy,' cautioned the man.

Fear clawed at his heart as he glanced for his companion. Tom Bawn was standing by the bed, rubbing the sleep from his eyes looking bewildered.

'Caught like sleeping babes,' jeered the man who had woken him. 'Sleeping and no one on watch.'

For the first time John-Joe saw that the man had a companion who stood by the table. He was a young man who carried himself with a military bearing. He was examining Tom Bawn and John-Joe with bright, intense eyes. There was a grim sense of character in the man's firm, iron set of his jaw. He had a dark complexion and carried his solid, stocky build, with an aggressive attitude.

'A bright pair, eh?' sneered the elderly man.

John-Joe's face was bathed with perspiration. He had no doubt that his captors were the police.

'Well, Tom Bawn?' The young man's voice was a pistol crack. 'Do you know me?'

Tom Bawn shifted his weight awkwardly. 'I've seen you at headquarters,' he muttered.

'Mister Devoy represents the Military Council,' reproved the elderly man.

John-Joe's mouth slackened. He stared at the two men. Were they not the police?

'Who gave approval for the action which you took this morning, Tom Bawn?'

John-Joe's companion raised his head defiantly. 'It was necessary,' he replied.

'Necessary?' There was an uneasy coldness in the young man's voice.

'We can't sit back and allow them to ride roughshod over us. *An Seabhac Siúlach* is betrayed by his own countrymen. Where is the promised rising? The months pass and all we have are promises. Then our leaders are arrested one by one. We can't sit back. We can't give up.'

'You have not answered my question,' the young man said evenly.

Tom Bawn shrugged. 'I took it on myself.'

John-Joe glanced at his companion in surprised, amazed how easy Tom Bawn had lied to him that the Brotherhood had approved the action.

'You involved Dillon and Madden in your hare-brained scheme as well as Duffy here.'

'We succeeded,' replied Tom Bawn sullenly.

The man, Devoy, bit his lip and his eyes became bright pin-points. 'Succeeded?' he sneered. 'You were a damned fool. You were recognized. The police are looking for you by your real name.'

'How . . . ?' gasped Tom Bawn.

Devoy made a cutting gesture with his hand. 'You were identified. Our contacts at police headquarters told us.' There was a suppressed fury in his voice. 'The Brotherhood must have discipline. Lack of discipline is what has brought us to our knees in the past. Our foe is wise and his strength lies in the unquesting obedience of his soldiery; in their discipline and strength of arms. We cannot afford anarchy in the face of organized strength.'

'But. . . .'

'There's a ship leaving the North Wall at dawn. It's bound for Liverpool. In two days' time there is a ship for Boston. Séamus will make sure you get the ferry and get you tickets and an allowance to cover your expenses until you get to America.'

Tom Bawn stared helplessly. 'But I. . . .'

'The matter has been decided. It is an order from the Military Council,' snapped Devoy. 'It would only be a matter of time before they found you and you know too much about the organization for safety's sake. You'll not get any mercy from the English except a short piece of hemp rope. Get your things together. You'll stay with Séamus tonight.'

John-Joe finally found his voice. 'What about me?' he asked.

Devoy turned his gaze at him. His voice softened a little. 'At least you took the trouble to cover your face, Duffy. You were not identified and the police have no clue as to your identity. If they track Tom Bawn to these rooms they will have the name John Duffy but little else.'

'I was in on the . . . the assassination. . . .'

'He did what I told him,' Tom Bawn interrupted. 'He was acting on my orders and thought they came from the Brotherhood.'

Devoy nodded and smiled briefly. 'I thought that was the case. No blame attaches itself to you, Duffy. We will give you a new name, John Roe, and change your residence.'

John-Joe hesitated. 'Look,' his voice was blunt. 'I've been in Ireland for three months. I came to train men. To take part in an uprising. I've been driven bored with inaction. . . .'

Devoy suddenly chuckled. 'If it's action you want, Devlin, then we might be able to provide some shortly. I heard a good report of the manner in which you carried yourself this morning. We can use a cool-headed man. In the meantime, pack your things. I'll take you to the next safe house.'

On the steps of the tenement John-Joe gripped the hand of his erstwhile companion in brief farewell. He felt a strange sense of personal loss as the fair-haired young man strode away with the man Séamus. He had been closeted in the same room with him for three months and felt an awkward bond of companionship. Now Tom Bawn seemed a forlorn, slightly bowed figure, clutching a carpet bag, going into exile like so many thousands before him; exile until liberty or until death.

John-Joe's new companion, the man Devoy, took him to a tavern in a cul-de-sac near Merrion Square run by a man named Curran. To John-Joe's surprise the tavern seemed a favourite meeting spot for soldiers but, as Peter Curran told him, when John-Joe expressed alarm at the fact, he was safer there than at any other spot. It was two days later that Devoy came for him.

'Do you have a warm coat?' he demanded without preamble. 'There's a frost outside.'

'Where are we going?' asked John-Joe when they were seated in a carriage, swaying across the cobbles.

Devlin passed across a pocket book with some papers. 'Your name is Ed White. You are an American newspaper reporter representing the *New York Herald* These papers will identify you should the need arise. Say nothing unless you have to.'

The carriage halted outside an imposing building where, to John-Joe's consternation, there were police and soldiers in armed abundance. They stood guard all around with bayonets fixed. Devoy seemed to ignore them entirely and hurried up the wide stone steps to a door. A stoney-faced uniformed inspector of police came forward, glancing swiftly at Devoy and then to John-Joe, before opening the door.

'This way,' he grunted.

Bewildered, John-Joe followed his companion and the police officer through sombre wood-pannelled corridors until they turned through two swing doors. They were in a crowded courtroom. The inspector motioned them to the side behind the packed public benches. Further down in the well of the courtroom were some bewigged lawyers in black robes while, facing the court, a sallow-faced man sat gazing balefully out. 'That's Stronge, the Chief Magistrate,' whispered Devoy. The man was just concluding a speech.

'. . . I therefore see nothing to prevent me setting the date for your trial as of the twenty-seventh of November and hereby order your committal, until that date, to the confines of the Richmond Jail. I would earnestly entreat you, in view of the grave charges with which you are now faced, to employ a member of the legal profession to represent your interests in this matter. Do you understand, James Stephens?'

Stephens! John-Joe found himself craning forward with curiosity to gaze upon the man in the dock. Stephens – the mysterious 'Wandering Hawk' – the undisputed leader of the Brotherhood. At first glance John-Joe was disappointed. The man did not strike an imposing figure. He was about average height, almost stout with broad shoulders. His fair hair was balding and he wore a sandy beard tinged with grey. Yet there was some vitality about the man, some infectious aura as he stood straight, almost defiantly in the dock, his high cheek-boned head well back, his chin thrust forward.

'I feel bound to say in justification of, rather than with a view to my own reputation, that I have employed no lawyer or attorney in this case. . . .' His soft rolling accent had a mesmerizing effect on the court. There was silence in the room, not even an occasional cough or clearing of a throat. '. . . And I mean to employ none because in making a plea of any kind or filing my defence,' he suddenly smiled disarmingly, 'I am not particularly well up on those legal terms – I should be recognizing English law in Ireland. I deliberately and conscientiously repudiate the existence of that law in Ireland.'

There was a gasp in the courtroom. The atmosphere became electric.

'I repudiate its right or even its existence in Ireland,' repeated Stephens, raising his voice a tone. 'I defy and despise any punishment it can inflict on me. I have spoken!'

There was a moment of silence in the court before the dry tones of the magistrate cut through the tension. 'I hope you will reflect on this matter. Remove the prisoner.'

Devoy caught John-Joe by the sleeve and, proceded by the police inspector, they left the court and were in the carriage again.

Devoy heaved a sigh. 'Do you think you'll recognize Stephens again?' he asked John-Joe.

John-Joe nodded, bewildered.

'Good. I told you that I might provide you with some action. We are going to rescue Stephens out of Richmond Jail.'

That evening a dozen men gathered in a small upstairs parlour in Curran's tavern. Apart from Devoy, John-Joe knew only one of the men in the room, a flamboyant personality in his early thirties with piercing eyes, a broad forehead and a spade beard. Colonel Tom Kelly was one of the Irish-American officers. He originally hailed from Galway before settling in New York. During the war he had served in the 10th Ohio and had been wounded at the bloody battle of Missionary Ridge when his regiment had to lead a charge up a bleak mountainside against General Braxton Bragg's Confederate forces. Kelly was quick and decisive in his movements and his abilities had, apparently, been recognized by the Brotherhood in Ireland for he was now filling the post as chief-of-staff to the Military Council. As such, Kelly was in charge of all military operations and he came quickly to the point of the meeting.

'You men have been chosen to act as the rescue party to release James Stephens from Richmond Jail,' he announced.

'The Military Council,' Devoy added, 'has concluded that Stephens is irreplaceable to the Brotherhood. The very name *An Seabhac Siúlach* has aroused the country to a fever of anticipation. If we abandoned him to his death at the hands of English law, or, at least, to exile or penal servitude for life, it will be a crippling blow to our organization. Of course we have able men to replace him, but Stephens has become a symbol to the Irish nation and if the English can arrest and deal with him with impunity it will put back the cause of Irish liberty for a century.'

One of the men seated next to John-Joe shook his head. 'Richmond Jail is the strongest in the country. There is an armed guard there and Portobello Barracks is only fifteen minutes walk away.'

'There is a garrison of 6,000 troops in Dublin,' protested another man. 'How could we hope to spirit Stephens away?'

'Figures can impress people to any action or inaction,' Kelly retorted. 'Yes, there are 6,000 regular troops in the Dublin garrison. But let's remember this, my friends, half of the militia are loyal to our cause and many of the regular troops, the Irish regiments, have taken the Fenian oath.'

'If we rescue Stephens it will create the biggest stir in years and make the English look ridiculous,' added Devoy.

'What are the orders, colonel?' asked the man who had raised the first objection.

Kelly smiled, taking out a cheroot and lighting it with a flourish.

'Are we agreed, gentlemen? Do you all volunteer for this task?'

There was a general mutter of approval.

'We have to do but little,' Kelly said confidently. 'In a day or two we shall gather at a rendezvous to be decided. At the appointed hour we shall position ourselves outside the prison. On a signal, we will throw a rope ladder over the prison wall and Stephens will join us. How he will get out of his cell and into the prison yard will not concern you. Your job will be to act as bodyguard and prevent any pursuit. If all goes well, Devoy and I will escort Stephens to a safe house while the rest of you disperse.'

'It sounds simple, colonel,' said one man.

Kelly grinned broadly. 'The best plans generally are, my friend.'

'Isn't it too simple?' demanded the man seated next to John-Joe. 'Didn't I hear that Governor Marquess has instructed the keys of Stephens' cell and of the door of the corridor approaching the cell to be removed to his office each night and locked in a special safe under armed guard? And didn't I hear that a loyalist prisoner has been placed in the next cell with instructions to raise an alarm if anything suspicious is heard?'

'Our enemies are very kind to us,' mused Devoy. 'They seek to awe us by telling us how impossible it is to rescue Stephens. They seek to impress us by telling us how well he is guarded. We must thank them for the information because forewarned is forearmed.'

Chapter 22

James Stephens's trial was scheduled to start on Monday, 27 November. It was on the preceding Friday that John-Joe received the word from Devoy to meet him and the rescue party at Lynch's tavern in Camden Street. They gathered there just before midnight. Devoy had brought a rope ladder and some rope and a lead weight but there was some consternation because it had been discovered that the revolvers, with which they were to arm themselves, had not been delivered to Lynch's as promised. One of the men had to take a carriage and set off to collect them, which plunged both Devoy and Colonel Kelly into an ill-temper until he returned. Finally, they set off in ones and twos towards the imposing structure of Richmond Jail. The night was dark and cold with the rain blowing in sheeting gusts. Colonel Kelly had ordered the men to rendezvous at the southern wall of the prison which fronted the banks of a canal where a road ran between the high brick walls and the bank lined with clusters of tall dark elms.

'Beyond the wall is the governor's garden,' Kelly whispered, as they gathered around him. 'Our man will be coming out over that wall.'

John-Joe felt the same dry-mouthed excitement that he had experienced in Dame Street. 'How will he signal?' he asked.

'By throwing a handful of gravel across the wall. When we hear the gravel strike the ground, we will heave the rope ladder across the wall for him to climb over.' Kelly glanced at his watch. 'It's fifteen minutes before one o'clock. We'd best take up our positions and, for the sake of God, no talking and no smoking.'

He split the dozen men to post lookouts across the canal bridge in the direction of the military barracks of Portobello. Other men he stationed among the elms along the prison walls. John-Joe took up his position with Devoy in the shade of a tall elm which gave a little shelter from the gusting rain. Behind them on the dark waters of the canal inquisitive ducks splashed now and then. The canal formed the southern loop of the Grand Canal from the west, curving through Dublin to join the Liffy near its mouth. It was a busy stretch of water in daytime but now it was dark and deserted except for the ducks whose splashing and occasional piercing quacks caused the watchers to start with nervousness. Time passed and all was quiet, each man straining their ears to listen for the sound of the handful of gravel which stood between a man's freedom and ultimately between his life or death.

Back in Lynch's, while waiting for the man to return with the revolvers, John-Joe had asked Devoy; 'How will it be done? Can you tell me now?'

Devoy had smiled. 'There is no reason why not, Devlin. You may recall the police inspector who let us into the courtroom?'

John-Joe nodded.

'Well, the Brotherhood has men who are highly placed in police headquarters and in Dublin Castle. The inspector is one of several of our men who keep us informed. One of his brothers is a hospital steward in Richmond Jail and the night warder is one of our men also.'

'What will happen?'

'Governor Marquess thinks that the keys to Stephens's cell are safe under guard in his private safe. What he doesn't know is that our warder friend has made wax impressions of the keys. Duplicates have been cut. The hospital steward will take the duplicate keys, enter the wing where Stephens is confined and release him from his cell.'

'Isn't it true that there is a loyalist prisoner in the next cell who has been bribed to signal if he hears anything?' asked John-Joe.

Devoy chuckled dryly. 'It has already been suggested to the man that whoever can enter one cell without trouble can enter his cell and slit his throat while he sleeps. We will not have to worry about him.'

'What then?'

'Our man will take Stephens into the prison yard. There is a high wall which separates the exercise yard from the governor's garden and the garden is separated from where we are by the high wall you see before you. A ladder will be in place in the exercise yard. Once in the garden he will throw a handful of gravel across and we will throw over the rope ladder.'

Devoy made it sound so easy. Now as they waited, the tension grew. It seemed they had been waiting hours but it was only about three-quarters of an hour. The rain ceased falling and the dark figure of Colonel Kelly appeared behind them.

'Thanks be to God,' he whispered. 'I was scared the rain would drown the noise of the gravel. It must be nearly time.'

As if on cue there came a sudden splatter like heavy raindrops from the darkness.

'Christ!' Kelly hissed. 'The signal! Where's the rope ladder?'

Two men detached themselves from their hiding place. They ran quickly across the road, throwing up the weight attached to the guide rope. It snaked up into the darkness. There was an agonizing pause and then the rope ladder, attached to the guide rope, moved slowly upwards.

'He's coming! He's coming!' hissed a man and Colonel Kelly swore at him, ordering him to be silent.

A moment later a shadow appeared on top of the wall ten feet above them. The figure paused, down came the ladder and the figure scrambled downwards, falling the last few feet and landing awkwardly. Kelly and Devoy bent to help the man to his feet. There was a pause, a silent hug between Devoy, Kelly and the stocky shadow, and then they were hurrying down the road towards the canal bridge where an enclosed carriage stood waiting. John-Joe felt a wild desire to run as he trotted after Kelly, Devoy and their charge. The driver was already on the box and said nothing as the four of them scrambled inside while the remaining men dispersed quickly to a pre-arranged plan. As John-Joe slammed the carriage door shut, it jolted forward and set off at a quick trot towards central Dublin.

'Best change out of that prison garb, James,' Devoy said picking up a bag from under the seat and pushing it across. 'Jane sent these things for you.'

Stephens reached for the bag. 'Is my wife well?'

It was Colonel Kelly who replied. 'She is staying with her sister at Mrs Butler's house. That will be your final destination but, for the time being, you'll stay with the Bolans.'

Stephens began to strip off the rough-spun prison shirt. He suddenly peered at John-Joe for the first time. 'I don't know you, do I?'

Devoy performed the hurried introduction. 'A pleasure to meet you in the circumstances, lieutenant,' grinned Stephens.

'Were there any problems, James?' Devoy asked.

'None to speak of until Breslin took me to the prison yard,'

Stephens replied. 'The ladder which had been placed there was too short. No one had thought to measure the damned wall. I nearly wept with frustration. But Breslin decided to get hold of Byrne, the warder. They actually carried a table out of the warders' room and stood it under the wall of the yard. Then we balanced the ladder on it while I shinned up. I had to drop down the other side. I hope I landed in the governor's prize marrows,' he added with a grin.

'Will Byrne carry out the rest of the plan as arranged?' demanded Colonel Kelly.

'He'll place a number of false keys in the doors of the other cells and dress up the scene to give the impression that it was an "outside" job. Then he will start on his scheduled rounds about four o'clock at which time he will "discover" my empty cell and raise the alarm. All hell will be let loose in Dublin then, gentlemen.' Stephens succeeded in wriggling into his trousers. 'Ah, I feel more civilized now.'

Colonel Kelly glanced at him worriedly. 'Are you still intent on staying in Dublin? I wish you would let us get you out of the country. It will be safer.'

Stephens shook his head emphatically. 'No; I am the leader of the Brotherhood. My job is here, in Ireland. I must be here if the rising is to succeed.'

John-Joe leaned forward excitedly. 'When will that be, sir?' he demanded.

'Soon, my boy, soon,' Stephens replied with a vague smile. 'The day is coming. The day is coming soon.'

It was five o'clock when John-Joe returned to Curran's tavern and went straight to his bed where he fell into a fitful sleep. Once he half-awoke to the sound of a bugle and the noise of a body of horsemen passing along Clare Street from which the cul-de-sac, where Curran's tavern stood, cut off. He finally rose well after the noon hour and found Curran, grinning from ear to ear, was ready with a hot breakfast and the latest news.

'The military have been going mad since dawn,' he chuckled as he brought the tray into John-Joe's room. 'The entire Dublin garrison have been roused and is marching up and down not knowing where to go. The hussars and dragoons have been galloping about the streets as distracted as a dog without a tail. Boy, boy! Dublin will be remembering this day for many a long year. There's a reward of a thousand pounds offered already for Stephens.'

John-Joe ate his meal and dozed again during the afternoon.

At about four o'clock the noise and clatter of horsemen halted in the cul-de-sac outside and there was a banging on the street door.

John-Joe leapt from his bed in panic as a voice resounded; 'Open! In the Queen's name!'

He glanced around desperately wondering whether to scramble up to the roof and escape that way. Then he realized how impossible it would be for the little tavern was dwarfed on either side by the taller Georgian houses of the neighbourhood. He felt cold as he listened to the clink of spurs and swords. The soldiers were spilling into the tavern. He opened his door a crack and peered to the head of the stairs.

He heard a nasal English drawl saying, 'Sorry to inconvenience you, Mister Curran. Orders are orders. Every tavern in Dublin has to be searched.'

Then a trooper was clattering up the stairs and before John-Joe could start back the hussar was on the landing staring straight at him. To his surprise the man deliberately winked at him, paused and then turned down again with a clatter. He heard a voice saying, 'Nothing above, sir. I've taken a look.'

The drawl of the English officer acknowledged the report. Then the hussars were gone. He heard the jingle and clatter of their horses move off. As John-Joe leaned in bewilderment against the door jamb Curran came hurrying up the stairs with a grin.

'Were you seen?'

'A hussar came up the stairs and . . . winked at me. I don't understand.'

'Don't worry,' Curran chuckled. 'We've plenty of friends in the 10th Hussars. A lot of the men have taken the Fenian oath . . . not that Colonel Bakers knows, God save him!'

'I'd like a drink,' John-Joe said weakly.

'That you may have and I'll bring some food directly,' replied Curran.

At eight o'clock that evening Devoy arrived at the tavern and came straight to John-Joe's room. 'Dublin has gone mad with joy,' smiled Devoy, throwing himself down into a chair. 'The name of the Fenians is on everyone's lips and, by God, if Stephens gave the word to rise now, I don't doubt the people would come out against the English with their bare hands.'

'Is Stephens safe?'

'Safe enough and not far from here.'

'Will he give the word for the rising?'

A troubled expression crossed Devoy's face. 'No, not yet,' there was a hesitation about his voice. He sat frowning for a moment and then he forced a smile. 'You should have seen the shenanigans in Dublin this day. The military and the police didn't know what to do nor where to look. A number of our sympathizers, who are known to the authorities, have had their houses raided. Several people have been arrested but the arrests have been random. They even have Royal Navy ships outside Dublin harbour stopping and searching all the vessels putting out to sea. Sir Hugh Ross, the English commander, has proclaimed a state of readiness in case of a rising and the Viceroy has issued rewards.'

'Why don't we strike now then?' demanded John-Joe. 'With the people behind us, it is the perfect time.'

Again there was a shadow on Devoy's face. 'Stephens is a cautious man. He wants all the conditions to be perfect before giving the word. We have to succeed this time. It must not be a failure. We have had too many failures in Ireland . . . oh, grand failures, I'll grant you, but a failure is a failure for all that.'

'It's the waiting that irritates me,' confessed John-Joe. 'I didn't expect it to be like this when I came from America. I thought I would be training men, thought the rising would be a matter of weeks away. The day Tom Bawn came up with his scheme I was going to ask to be relieved of duty so that I could return to America.'

Devoy gave him a searching glance. 'I can understand your frustration, Devlin. I was in the army myself . . . the French Foreign Legion to be precise.'

John-Joe was surprised and said so.

'By the time I left university I was already a member of the Brotherhood. Four years ago I joined the Legion and went to Algiers to learn something of the military art in order to prepare myself for the rising. I know what the frustration of waiting feels like.'

'At least Tom Bawn hit the enemy where it hurt.'

'It was wrong. Individual assassinations won't help us, especially killing Irishmen who serve the English Crown. England will always find plenty of men to take their thirty pieces of silver. Not every Irish man and woman pulsates with indignation at the subservience of their people. That's the way of it, Devlin. Like it or not. Only by discipline and concerted action can we shake loose from England's stranglehold.'

'Are you telling me that I am to be cooped up again, simply

waiting?' John-Joe demanded. 'If so, it's better I return to New York. . . .'

Devoy held up a hand, shaking his head. 'There is a job for you, if you'll take it. It means going out of Dublin for a while, which is probably better in the circumstances. Anyone with an American accent is being arrested and interrogated now.'

'What's the job?'

'Training a company of men in the use of arms; giving them some military knowledge.'

John-Joe smiled broadly. 'That's what I came here for,' he said. 'Where will I go?'

'Tomorrow you'll be taking the train to Mullingar. At the station there a friend will meet you with a horse. Your ultimate destination is a village in the Meath hills. Curran will see you safe to Broadstone Station. You'll be disguised as a seminarian, a trainee priest. Maynooth, the Catholic seminary, is on the same railway line as Mullingar so that when you buy a ticket you'll buy one to Maynooth. Curran will also buy you a ticket for Mullingar and give it to you just before you board the train. In that way, your journey ought to excite no interest from the police who will be watching the station.'

'How will I recognize the person at Mullingar?'

'He will recognize you. When you come out of the station entrance you will take off your hat. Wipe your brow with a handkerchief, replace your hat, drop your handkerchief and then bend down to pick it up.'

'It sounds rather theatrical,' John-Joe smiled.

Devoy's face was serious. 'Such theatrics will save our lives.' Devoy rose to his feet and held out his hand. 'The Brotherhood has need of good men with military training like yourself. Train your company well. From time to time you will receive orders from the Military Council through our area commander in Meath. You'll be introduced to him by the friend who meets you in Mullingar. He's a good man. Above all, let me counsel patience. The word for the rising will be given soon. That I guarantee.'

John-Joe felt Devoy's firm grip and gazed into the young man's resolute eyes with a feeling of reassurance. With such leaders as Devoy the movement was bound to prevail.

Chapter 23

John-Joe was met at the small brick railway station of Mullingar by a man who introduced himself as Dualta Hanrahan. He was a few years older than John-Joe, a broad-framed man with corn-coloured hair and startling blue eyes. He had a florid, fleshy face which carried an expression of permanent amusement, as if everything he saw about him surprised and amused him at the same time. He was dressed for the country and gave the appearance of being an ostler. It was an assessment which Dualta Hanrahan later confirmed by telling John-Joe that he worked at an hotel in Kells.

'Do you ride?' he asked after the ritual of recognition had been performed.

John-Joe assured him that he did.

'I have the nags hitched across the way . . . Father,' grinned the man.

John-Joe felt uncomfortable and conspicuous in his seminarian's clothes and tugged awkwardly at his collar as he followed the broad-shouldered man to the hitching rail. The horses that he had brought with him were strong and willing. Dualta confessed that he had borrowed them from the hotel as he secured John-Joe's valise to the saddle of one of them. He turned and gazed at John-Joe with amusement, staring at his boots until John-Joe demanded whether something was wrong.

'*M'anam*!' chuckled Dualta. 'Wasn't I told that all Americans wore squared-toed shoes? The peelers do be looking for strangers who wear such boots because they swear they be Americans and therefore Fenians. They say 'tis the Yankee fashion.'

John-Joe laughed. 'Well, I brought these in a shop in Grafton Street, Dublin, not two weeks since so I reckon I'll not excite curiosity.'

Dualta nodded. 'You'll do, Father,' he emphasized slyly. Then he climbed on his horse and waited until John-Joe mounted. 'We'll take the road to Castlepollard, just north of here. Mullingar is packed with soldiers and po'lis. I'm thinking that the sooner we're away the better.'

John-Joe had already observed that the station yard was full of red-coated soldiers and, as they turned out into the main street, the town was no better.

'Is it a garrison town?' he asked.

Dualta shook his head. 'The soldiers have been encamped about the town since September because of rumours of a rising.'

They fell silent until they had left the town behind them and, once on the open country road, Dualta increased the pace to a steady trot along a well-used road which threaded its way through two small lakelets and into a forest.

'Do you know Irish?' demanded Dualta suddenly.

John-Joe shook his head.

'*Is cuma*, no matter,' shrugged the big ostler. 'But the place where you'll be is Irish-speaking. Some of the old folks there have no understanding of the English. But you should be able to get along fine. Perhaps you'll learn some Irish yourself.'

'I'd like that,' John-Joe replied. 'You speak the language yourself, I suppose?'

'*Buíochas le Dia*, thanks be to God,' nodded Dualta. 'English has not chased the language out of this part of the country yet. And when Irish is dead entirely then what's the use of saying we are any different to Englishmen? Our language is the pulse of our soul.'

'Where exactly are we going?' asked John-Joe turning the conversation.

'A village in the hills of Meath called An Bhaile Dearg.'

John-Joe tried to repeat the sounds.

'The English call it Ballyderrick. Now there you have it, my point about language. Ballyderrick! *A thiarcais!* What does Ballyderrick mean? It's gibberish. It has no soul. No identity. But An Bhaile Dearg now. . . .'

'What does it mean?'

'The Red Town. And when the sun is lying on the mountains, just before it moves below them, you can see the meaning of the name.'

Dualta suddenly reined in, his eyes narrowing.

Almost without warning a column of a score or more of riders and horses came cantering around a bend in the road. They were English lancers, sitting upright in tight blue uniforms with red and gold frogging and brass-faced helmets with bobbing silken tassles. Their eyes were held rigidly to their front. White-gloved hands held the upright lances whose butts rested in their stirrups. Little standards fluttered bravely from each wooden shaft. At their head rode a young officer, one hand gripping the reins of his steed, the other a fist on his thigh, just above his sword which slapped at the withers of his black mare. He glanced at Dualta and his eyes flickered over John-Joe. Then the column cantered passed, mud flying from the hooves of their horses, using up so much of the road that both Dualta and John-Joe were almost forced into a ditch to give them passage.

'*Mo thóin libh!*' muttered Dualta glancing after them. John-Joe did not understand the words but he sensed their inflection, Dualta glanced back at him. 'There's a sheltered spot to our left, before we skirt Lough Derravaragh, where I would recommend you change out of those seminarian clothes.'

'I won't be sorry to do that,' confessed John-Joe.

'I've brought some plain country garb with me, good riding breeches and boots and a thick coat to keep out the winter chill.'

'I have a suit . . .' began John-Joe.

Dualta grinned. 'A city suit?' he jeered. '*M'anam!* Why not call in at the nearest barracks and give yourself up?'

John-Joe bit his lip, accepting the rebuke. They continued in silence for a while until they reached the spot, a small clearing, where John-Joe stripped off and put on the clothes Dualta had brought. They were rough homespuns but warm and comfortable. Dualta eyed him critically and nodded.

'You'll do,' he grunted as he climbed back on his horse.

Bundling the seminarian clothes into his valise, John-Joe swung up. 'Is it far to this place – Ballyderrick?' he asked.

'An Bhaile Dearg,' corrected his companion softly. 'No, not far.'

'Do you know anything about this company that I am to train?' pressed John-Joe.

Dualta grinned broadly. 'Indeed. I am the captain of it.'

John-Joe's eyes widened a fraction. 'Are there any former soldiers among the men?'

'I served two years in the militia, rank of corporal. That's all. The rest are farm boys. Good men.'

'How many?'

'A dozen.'

'Do you have arms?'

Dualta smiled. 'That we do. Three Springfield muzzle-loaders which were part of a Yankee shipment,' he said proudly. 'We have two breechloading Enfields which we borrowed from the militia barracks and we have two Sharps breechloaders. We also have four revolvers and three fowling guns as well as half-a-dozen pikes and a couple of swords.'

John-Joe stared at him in amazement. 'You expect to take on the English soldiers with those? What about ammunition?'

'We have ammunition for most of the guns except the Springfields.'

John-Joe shook his head wonderingly. 'It's hardly an impressive armoury,' he said. 'The English are now arming themselves with repeating rifles, Sniders and Enfields.'

'We'll be able to hold our own,' Dualta said defensively.

John-Joe pursed his lips cynically. 'Going into battle with a muzzle loader against a repeating rifle is like going up against field artillery with pikes.' He hesitated. 'If the word for the rising came, do you know what your company is meant to do?'

'Surely,' Dualta nodded. 'I am to gather my men and ride to join our forces at Kells. Mister O'Malley is our local commander and his job will be to secure the barracks and crossroads there. Kells stands on a road which the English would use to rush reinforcements along to Dublin if their garrison there is threatened.'

John-Joe nodded. 'I suppose you have a map of the area?'

Dualta made an affirmative gesture.

'Don't worry,' he said. 'We may have little in arms and ammunition but we have a great strength of purpose.'

'I don't doubt it,' John-Joe replied. 'But weapons are a better security for success. This local commander of yours. . . . O'Malley? What's he like?'

'You'll be meeting with him soon. He's a good man. He served in the *Patricios*.'

'The what?' John-Joe frowned.

'Sure, you come from America and haven't heard of the *Patricios*? The Irish Legion of St Patrick which fought for the Republic of Mexico during the war with the United States.'

John-Joe shook his head. 'I've never heard of them.'

Dualta shrugged as if he doubted John-Joe's assertion.

They had emerged from the woods now and were climbing into some low hills with valleys stretching away into the distance, a vista of beauty in spite of the harsh light of early winter. John-Joe had the impression of a well-wooded, fertile country.

'It's the best cattle country in Ireland,' Dualta said, gesturing around. 'This is the county of Meath.'

They came to the shoulder of a broad hill and halted to let their horses rest for a while, leaning forward in their saddles to gaze upon a pleasant, green valley stretching away below. It was a valley of deep green grass meadows and evergreen forests that looked inviting and fresh in spite of the cold of winter. A well-kept road ran through it. Dominating the entire valley, however, was a great house; a tall imposing building with a colonnade frontage which reminded John-Joe of some of the great mansions built by southern plantation owners. The house stood a pale ochre colour with tall windows and it was four storeys in height. Outhouses and barns surrounded the place and about a mile away, connected by a roadway, stood a smaller lodge house.

'A grand sight, isn't it?' Dualta glanced at John-Joe.

'Pretty impressive,' he agreed.

'That's Castle Carrick. Don't the English have a habit of calling every wee house they build in Ireland a castle?'

'Who owns it?'

'Lord Mountcarrick, but we haven't seen a Mountcarrick on these lands in over a hundred years. It's said that they have a huge fine house in London. Mountcarrick is what they call an "absentee"; his estates, which stretch as far as you can see from this spot, are run by his agent, Captain Francis Dashfort. Dashfort is lord of the manor here, the law of the land and the sole arbiter of all our fates.'

'That's feudalism,' scoffed John-Joe.

'It's the way things are,' replied Dualta.

Steam was rising from their horses in the cold air and Dualta patted his beast on the neck.

'They have a good sweat on them. We'd best get along to An Bhaile Dearg before they take cold.'

'Is it far?' asked John-Joe as Dualta led the way along the track.

'Four miles across the valley on the other side of that tall mountain. That's Slieve na Callaigh. It means the Hag's Mountain in English but even the English use the Irish name. It's an ancient spot. The great fair of Tailltean was held on its slopes and they say it's where the great law-giver, Ollamh Fodhla, is buried.'

'Who was he?'

'The *seanchaí*, the old storytellers, will tell you that he was the eighteenth High King of Ireland who ruled here a thousand years before the birth of Christ. It was he who ordered all the laws of

Ireland to be set down in writing. Sure, everywhere you go in the county of Meath, the land is riddled with ghosts of the past, with ancient fortresses and palaces. This was the land of the High Kings of Ireland. Now it's the land of Lord Mountcarrick, governed on his behalf by Captain Dashfort. The High Kings of Ireland are no more but we have English lords a-plenty. An Bhaile Dearg marks the western boundary of the Mountcarrick estate.'

John-Joe glanced uncertainly at his companion. 'Do you mean Lord Mountcarrick owns the village as well?'

Dualta chuckled loudly. '*M'anam!* Mountcarrick's estate includes seven villages and all of them paying rent to him, or rather to Dashfort.'

'But the small farms that we have passed from time to time, surely the people own their own lands there?'

'I can tell that you are a stranger to Ireland,' Dualta smiled sadly. 'The Irish have only a precious hold on the land they occupy. No small farmer owns land. There are a few estates in the hands of Catholic Anglo-Irish families but over ninety per cent of the land is owned by the English, whether they be colonists or absentee landlords. The Irish who work the land can be evicted at a moment's notice on the whim of the landlord or his agent. The Irish are landless and dispossessed while living in the boundaries of their own country.'

They were moving across the valley floor now, along the trackway which passed through a wood silent with winter cold and only an occasional hardy bird to sound its lonely call. The shot caused their horses to buck and shy. It took them a moment to get them under control. A man emerged from the shrubbery a short distance away with the carcass of a red fox in one hand and a sporting gun tucked under his arm. He halted as if in surprise at seeing them. Two more men came out of the undergrowth and drew up behind the first man. The first was obviously the leader of the trio, a tall man, well dressed with an erect bearing. He had a broad, pale face with watery eyes of an almost indiscernible colour, light but scarcely blue. His hair was fair, almost bleached, and he wore long sideburns that came down his cheeks to nearly form a beard. His expression, as he examined Dualta and John-Joe, was one of arrogance. Here was a man who needed no lessons in self-assurance. The other two men seemed to be stewards or gamekeepers.

'Act dumb,' hissed Dualta from the corner of his mouth as he swept off his hat with an extravagant flourish and edged his horse forward.

'God save your honours!' he cried.

John-Joe was astonished to hear his accent somehow thicken.

The pallid-faced man gazed at Dualta with distaste. 'Who are you? What are you doing riding through my woods?'

One of the stewards leaned forward, his eyes narrowing. 'Tis Hanrahan, sir, the ostler from the Green House Hotel in Kells. I mind him well.'

'Sure you do, Connor, you being a discerning man,' smiled Dualta.

'Hanrahan, is it?' snapped the man with the red fox.

'The same, your honour,' confirmed Dualta gaily. 'And were we not riding to see our cousin in An Bhaile Dearg, with your honour's permission?'

The man sniffed. 'And who's that with you?'

'That would be my cousin Seán-Seosamh Ó Doibhlín from the county of Tyrone, my second cousin on my mother's side. Ah, and save the poor body, but he has a speech affliction and not a word does he utter.'

John-Joe tried to look like an imbecile as the gaze of the pallid man fell upon him.

'On your way then, Hanrahan. And tell those at Ballyderrick that I am watching for poachers. I know that someone is setting traps in my woods. If I catch them . . . *when* I catch them . . . then it'll not just be a whipping and eviction but they'll be beating hemp in the Drogheda Bridewell.'

'God bless and save your honour,' replied Dualta with another flourish of his hat.

When they had ridden out of ear-shot, John-Joe hissed; 'Who the hell were those people?'

'That was our lord and master in these parts, Captain Francis Dashfort. The weasel-faced man with him was his manager Thady Connor and the other,' he shrugged, 'just one of the estate workers.'

'Why did you put on that act?' pressed John-Joe. 'You sounded like a half-wit or some character out of a playhouse.'

Dualta chuckled. 'Sure, the English think that every Irishman is just an ignorant peasant with no knowledge at him. What harm does it do to keep them set in their prejudice? They will know better when the day of the rising comes. *Scread Mhaidine oraibh!*' He spat across his shoulder.

'I'm not sure it was right to pretend that I was dumb,' John-Joe said.

'God save us!' Dualta rolled his eyes. 'And what would you have done once Dashfort had heard your nice Yankee accent? Don't you know that he is not only the landlord here but the justice of the peace? You Americans are being hunted the length and breadth of the country and you want to have a nice conversation with Captain Dashfort?'

'I could have imitated an Irish accent,' replied John-Joe.

Dualta grinned. 'Let's hear it,' he challenged.

'Sure, indeed, and I'll be after going the road to Ballyderrick this moment,' John-Joe made an attempt at the accent.

Dualta looked pained. '*A thiarcais!* That's enough to give you away if not to the English themselves then to their informers and spies. Don't you know that you cannot say "I *will* be after" because it makes no sense? When an Irishman says, in English, I *am* after doing something then it means that he has done it . . . *after*, don't you see? If we have to speak the tongue of the conqueror let's try to retain something of ourselves in it; let's sing it to our own tune.'

John-Joe looked chagrined. 'I thought I sounded pretty good,' he said lamely.

His companion shook his head vigorously. 'If you get questioned by the authorities, it would be best to pretend that you have a speech impediment. An Irishman will spot you as an American for sure and Judas is a common companion in this country.'

'All right,' John-Joe said. 'But wouldn't it be better to stick to my proper name?'

Dualta gazed at him pityingly. 'And didn't I give them your proper name in its proper Irish form? If you want to learn the language, better you learn the Irish form Ó Doibhlín, not the anglicized distortion Devlin. And if you tell people that you hail from County Tyrone or Sligo then you can't go amiss for that's the Ó Doibhlín clan land and with so many of them in the area it will be hard for a body to check up on you.'

John-Joe sighed. He realized just how much a foreigner in this land he really was.

Suddenly Dualta gestured in front of him. 'Well, here we are. Here's An Bhaile Dearg.'

Chapter 24

To call An Bhaile Dearg a village was perhaps to do it more honour than it deserved. The place was built in an untidy heap at a crossroads, or rather where two muddy trackways intersected, one moving due east to west and the other crossing north-east to south-west at a slight angle. They were unpaved tracks. The entire village consisted of less than a dozen buildings, which huddled into the earth as if seeking protection from the fierce winds which swept across the bleak mountain. It nestled down amidst the heather beyond the stands of elms, conifers and bare oaks which afforded some protection to the buildings' eastern sides. The backs of the houses were planted firmly northwards against the slope of the mountain beyond. Some of the roofs of the buildings were of sedged thatch while a few were thatched in straw. Most of them were constructed of large stones, the poorer types packed with mud while a few were limed, packed and washed with yellow lime over the entire exposed surface. Smoke rose thick and grey from several chimneys and, in a few instances, snaked through unglassed windows which were simply deepset holes in the stone walls. A pall of thick grey smoke blew from the village before the gusting wind.

Dualta led the way, trotting his horse down the hillside and, as they grew nearer, John-Joe could make out small patches of cultivated land with a few signs of livestock; gaunt, slab-sided cows; a bull tethered in a pasture beyond the village; a motley collection of sheep and several goats; a few pigs and a concourse of hens strutting about where small children romped and played. A few women stood at their doors watching their approach with grey, impassive faces and suspicious eyes. Dualta greeted them cheerfully in Irish and had his greetings solemnly returned. He halted before a large squat stone cottage at the far end of the village. It displayed some signs of comparative prosperity by the fact that the windows were glazed and the roof was of straw thatch.

'You'll be staying here with Peadar Finucane and his wife,' Dualta informed John-Joe as he swung down from his horse. 'Peadar and his wife have no English but they have a niece in the village who will translate for you.'

John-Joe was troubled about the prospect. 'Do you live in the village?'

Dualta shook his head. 'I live at the hotel where I work in Kells. It's not great work but it is better than slaving on the land, thanks be to God.'

As John-Joe dismounted a small, silver-haired man with a face which spoke much of the outdoor life and hard, back-breaking work, came out. His expression was pleasant enough. He was dressed in country style with breeches made of brown corduroy into which a shirt of white linen was tucked and fastened by a leather belt. A loose wool jacket was worn over the shirt while on his feet were stockings of white knitted wool and heavy boots. He greeted Dualta in Irish and a rapid conversation was exchanged before they both turned to John-Joe.

'This is Peadar Finucane, John-Joe.'

'*Dia duit*,' smiled the man.

'Good day,' replied John-Joe, feeling the awkwardness that comes when one stands in the presence of a person whose language one has no knowledge of.

'*Tá an lá go dona. An bhfuil tú fuar?*'

'He says that it is a bad day,' translated Dualta. 'Are you cold?'

John-Joe smiled and shook his head. 'I'm still warm from the ride.'

Dualta translated again and the man gazed up at the sky. '*Ach, tá sé ag cur fearthainne anois. Isteach libh!*'

'He says that it's started to rain now so he asks us to go inside,' smiled Dualta.

John-Joe hauled his bag from the horse and followed Dualta into the dark interior of the cottage. Here was the same austerity as he had witnessed in the slums of Dublin, although the harsh poverty seemed more palatable in the countryside. The inside of the cottage, the *bothán* or cabin as he heard it called, mirrored the great rectangle of its outside. Most of the rafters were exposed and at each end a wooden ladder ran up to an open loft. He came to learn that the large loft was called *an lochta* and this served as the main store room. The smaller loft, the *cúllochta*, had been set aside for his bedroom, a room in which he had to keep company with all manner of strange objects gathered by the Finucanes over the years. The ground floor of the *bothán* was divided into one very large room which was the living room, kitchen and dining room combined, while a tiny room under the small loft was the Finucanes' own bedroom and which they proudly called *an seómra* or 'the room'.

The ground floor was of earth hardened by decades, if not centuries, of constant use. On this rush mats provided the only insulation from the winter chills that crept in. There was a hearth of stone from which a great open chimney rose and through which the light of day shone dimly down through the smoke from the turf fire, which was constantly alight. Across the fire hung a gallows-shaped affair of iron with a swinging arm on which a kettle of water perpetually dangled to heat. All the food was prepared by simmering from this arm. John-Joe noticed that the furniture of the place was simple, almost crude in construction. A wooden dresser, damp and riddled with woodworm, a thick pine table which not only served as the dining table but the place where food was prepared, where the sewing and mending was done or any other chore that needed such a surface. There were a few wooden chairs around this table while, along one wall of the room, a long, high-backed bench, a settle, was constructed in order to provide a storage space under its seat.

The walls were lime-washed, a gloomy yellowing colour and garish religious pictures hung as wall decorations, bright-painted pictures that were harsh to the eye. The one decoration which seemed at odds to the religious works was an ancient flintlock musket whose metal shone and whose wooden stock was polished with obvious care. John-Joe noticed that the dresser had shelves which contained some books. When he was able to find time to examine them, he found that one was an old Irish-English Dictionary, published in Paris in 1768 by its compiler, a Doctor O'Brien. Another of the Irish books had been published in Louvain in 1618 which, he discovered, was a book of religious meditations. It was Dualta who explained that during the Penal Years, when attempts had been made to root out Irish, most of the books in the language had to be published in European cities such as Brussels, Paris, Lisbon and particularly in Louvain where an Irish printing press had been established as early as 1611. From these presses, books, such as dictionaries, grammars, religious works, histories and poetry, were smuggled into Ireland to keep its language and ancient literature alive. Peadar Finucane also had a novel on his bookshelf which John-Joe recognized as one he had read in English a few years before: an Irish version of Maria Edgeworth's *Castle Rackrent*, published by the Ulster Gaelic Society of Belfast forty years before. When Dualta had said that Peadar Finucane could not speak English he had, and he cursed himself for his anglicized mentality, dismissed Finucane as a poor illiterate peasant. He subsequently realized that Peadar Finucane was a highly literate man in his own language.

The strongest impression which the Finucane *bothán* had on John-Joe was the smell, the chesty smell of smoke which seemed to cling to everything. Together with the sooty fumes were the odours of cooking, the sharp smell of boiled cabbage and pork. It was a warm, comfortable smell.

John-Joe grinned as his eyes rested on the ancient polished flintlock above the fireplace. 'I hope that isn't one of the guns that I am expected to train your lads with.'

Peadar Finucane saw the gesture and glanced enquiringly at Dualta.

'That gun was carried by Peadar's father when he was a young man in the '98 uprising,' Dualta replied solemnly. 'Peadar is fiercely proud of it although the triggering mechanism has been shattered.'

Peadar Finucane nodded eagerly as Dualta spoke and burst into rapid Irish.

'His father carried the gun during the battle of Tara,' translated Dualta. 'It was a grand fight, he says. Our lads gathered on the summit of the Hill of Tara and raised their standards there. The whole of County Meath came out during that rising. They were poorly armed, of course. Pikes, reaping hooks, spits, fowling pieces and a few muskets and swords. The royal hill of Tara was chosen as a rallying point because of what it means to us. You see, Tara is the site of the palace of the old High Kings of Ireland. The English soldiers marched on Tara. In spite of their artillery and cavalry, our boys fought all day and well into the night. But the cannon did for them in the end. The next morning found 350 Irish patriots dead on the hill.'

John-Joe gazed at the flintlock with a new respect.

'The old man is fiercely proud to have you under his roof,' Dualta added gently. 'He'll give you his last penny and, if needed, his life as well.'

'I understand,' John-Joe smiled and nodded to the old man. 'Thank him for me.'

'You can lend him a hand with the hard work on his land in thanks,' Dualta said. 'Don't do it as a favour. The people here are terribly proud and independent. They all know who you are, by the way. The villagers, that is, and you can trust them all with your life. The only person to be wary of is Thady Connor but he rarely comes to the village. If he does, avoid him. He's a bastard and he's friendly with the Constabulary.'

Dualta turned and spoke rapidly with the old man before turning back to John-Joe.

'I'll be leaving now. You are in good hands.'

John-Joe felt a moment of panic. 'How will I communicate? Didn't you say the old man had a niece who spoke English?'

'She will be here soon . . . she and Peadar's wife are visiting relatives. Don't worry. You'll be fine.'

'When will I see you again? When will we start the training?' pressed John-Joe.

'Within a few days,' Dualta assured him. 'I will arrange a meeting of our company. In the meantime, rest and get to know how the land lies in these parts. Sure, you might even learn some of the *fíor teanga na hÉireann.*'

John-Joe supposed Dualta meant Irish but before he could ask the man had raised a hand in farewell and left. John-Joe watched from the window as the burly, florid-faced man rode off leading John-Joe's estwhile mount behind him.

The old man coughed nervously and pointed to a chair near the fire. '*Suí síos.*'

It was impossible to misinterpret his meaning and John-Joe sat with a self-conscious smile.

'*Ar mhaith leat cupán tae?*'

'Sorry?'

The old man pointed to the simmering kettle and then to a tea pot. '*Tae?*' He pronounced the word carefully.

John-Joe's eyes brightened. 'Oh . . . tea. Thank you.'

Finucane filled the pot and stirred it, letting it stand a moment while he fetched a cup. He poured the liquid, added milk and pushed it across.

'Is goot?' he asked as John-Joe took a cautious sip. It was a moment before John-Joe realized that the old man had used English words.

'Ah . . . is it good?' He nodded. 'Very good.' He tried to scrape his memory. 'Gaw maw.'

Finucane frowned. 'Gaw maw? Ah. . . .' His eyes softened. '*Go maith.* Goot. *Go maith.*' He slapped his thigh with delight.

An uneasy silence fell between them, each trying to find a way of forming another small communication but before a feasible thought occurred to either the door burst open. A middle-aged woman in a long black country cloak came in, saw John-Joe, who rose hesitantly, and spoke rapidly to the old man. She was a handsome woman with fair hair, now showing grey flecks, but her face still had a quality of youth and vibrance in it. Her eyes were blue, dashed with specks of green although John-Joe wondered whether it might be a trick of the light. She had broad, strong features tinged a little with the lines of poverty and hard work which was a distinctive feature of country people. Peadar Finucane finished replying and turned to John-Joe.

'*Mo bhean*,' he said, keeping the words distinct. '*Mo bhean*.'

John-Joe felt helpless.

'My uncle is introducing his wife, Nuala Finucane,' came a soft voice from the door.

John-Joe turned. A second woman entered, removing her heavy cloak of home-spun wool, letting it slide from her slim shoulders. She was a younger version of the middle-aged woman, a girl certainly no older than himself. She stood in the doorway with the silver droplets of rain sparkling in her gold-spun hair. She was tall, taller than even Peadar Finucane, and slim. John-Joe noticed the pale elegance of the girl's face, the naturally red lips, the high sweep of the cheekbones and the bright blue of her eyes which gazed at him in mild curiosity. In spite of her tallness her figure was well shaped, clad in a blouse which was held tight to the waist by a black bodice. A billowing skirt of apple green came half way down to her shins. John-Joe gaped; a goddess who was the soul of Ireland! It was as if the girl had stepped out of one of the books of Irish legends which he had read as a boy. She could have been Áine, the ancient Irish goddess of love. He realized that they were all staring at him, waiting for him to say something.

'I'm sorry?' he mumbled.

'I'm Murna Finucane,' smiled the girl. 'My uncle was introducing his wife, my aunt Nuala.'

'I'm happy to meet you,' he smiled hesitantly, glancing from the elderly woman back to the girl. 'Tell your aunt that I hope that I am not putting her to any trouble. I appreciate the hospitality and am very grateful.'

The girl translated, her voice a soft, musical soprano. John-Joe felt mesmerized by her singing accents.

'My aunt says that you are most welcome. There is no trouble. And my uncle says that you are a long way from your home in

America and so you must now look upon this house as you would your own.'

'I cannot thank him enough,' John-Joe said, adding with a frown of seriousness; 'Does he know the risk that he is taking, the risk that all of you are taking, in sheltering me?'

Murna Finucane shrugged. 'Everyone in this village supports the Brotherhood. Yet our risk is smaller than yours. We are proud to help.'

Nuala Finucane had started to busy herself at the fire while her husband seated himself and took out a long clay pipe and tin of tobacco. He shoved the tin towards John-Joe with a look of query. John-Joe smiled and shook his head, watching the old man fill and light his pipe. The girl was storing things in the cupboard which had evidently been brought back from their trip. There were a few brief exchanges in Irish and a merry peal of laughter from the girl.

John-Joe stirred uncomfortably. 'I'm sorry I don't speak Irish,' he muttered. Then, 'I had no idea that so many people still spoke the language.'

Murna smiled across the room. 'It is not so widely spoken as it was before the Great Hunger. It is still strong in this area though. Where is it that you come from?'

'I was born in Cork,' John-Joe replied. 'But I was only a year old when my parents left for America. I was raised in New York.'

'Is New York a big city . . . as big as Dublin?' asked the girl.

John-Joe grinned. 'Even bigger,' he assured her.

'I've not been farther than Kells,' shrugged Murna. 'That was big enough.'

The old man interrupted with an obvious question. 'Perhaps you would teach me some Irish?' suggested John-Joe after the girl had explained to her uncle what was being said.

'If I am able,' replied Murna. 'But you will find that there are not many people in An Bhaile Dearg who have no English at all, only the old ones. And I shall be near to translate for you.'

'But I'd like to learn the language. After all . . . it is . . .' He wanted to say 'my language' but that sounded too melodramatic.

Nuala Finucane said something and the girl echoed; 'The evening meal is ready.'

Peadar Finucane stood up, his hand going to his pocket. Then he hesitated and glanced with a troubled eye at John-Joe. He muttered something. Murna smiled apologetically.

'It is the custom in this house to say a decade of the rosary before the evening meal,' she explained. 'My uncle wonders if you would object.'

John-Joe frowned at the request. 'Why would I object?' he asked wonderingly.

The girl shrugged. 'My uncle wonders if there be Catholics in that New York of yours.'

John-Joe chuckled and drew out the rosary beads which had been a parting gift from his mother. Finucane's gaze relaxed as he saw the beads and, smiling, he took John-Joe by the arm and guided him to a place at the table.

Chapter 25

It was three days before Dualta Hanrahan came back; three days in which John-Joe tried to adjust to the strangeness of his new surroundings and to the dreary weather with its persistent rain falling in icy cold gusts. While the land below the mountain, Slieve na Callaigh, was fertile enough, few things grew in the dead of winter. Generally, it appeared as a bleak landscape with a constant wind coming off the mountain and moaning through the leafless oaks of the forests which spread in a kind of solemn borderland around the cultivated fields. In most of the fields frosts were breaking up the stubble and causing the ploughing to be delayed. Here and there patches of numerous evergreens gave contrast and colour against the tall gaunt black oaks and elms.

Everyone in An Bhaile Dearg worked on the vast estate of Lord Mountcarrick. The estate had large, fertile fields providing crops of wheat, barley and oats, but its main source of income was the fine cattle herds that ran on its pastures. The woods, too, were also put to use not only to provide fuel but to sell to timber merchants in Drogheda, the main county town at the mouth of the River Boyne. The village lay on the western edge of the Mountcarrick estate. Each cabin was allowed to cultivate a patch of land for the growing of food for the family. This land was mainly carved out of the stony mountainside and was of poor quality compared with the rich fields further down the valley. The villagers grew mostly root crops because the winds would tear away any wheat or barley and therefore the staple diet was inevitably potatoes. The few animals owned by the villagers were poor beasts; the cows were gaunt and slab-sided and the few sheep appeared little different. Only the pigs managed to survive the harsh conditions but even these were lean compared to some John-Joe had seen. Red meat was a luxury for fowl was a common dish. The proximity of the woods provided the villagers with a bird called *colmán coille*, which he recognized as a wood pigeon. They nested in the bushes and trees and were trapped to be prepared into appetizing dishes. The trapping was done surreptitiously because the woods were part of the estate and any villager caught in the act was considered by Captain Dashfort, the estate manager, to be a poacher and punished accordingly. Dashfort ran the estate like an autocrat of old, a remote foreign despot whose every whim became law. Each family in An Bhaile Dearg had to pay rent to the Mountcarrick estate for the privilege of living in their cabins and using their patch of land. Sometimes this rent took up the entire amount that the estate paid them in wages for their work and they were forced to sell some of their own produce to pay the difference. To ensure that the rent was paid seemed to be the sole ambition of every villager for, if it was not, then eviction would surely follow and after eviction poverty and death were not far removed.

The villagers were friendly to John-Joe, smiling and greeting him with shy, warm greetings as if acknowledging his secret and demonstrating their support. But no one bothered him by seeking to engage him in conversation and he, in turn, was too unsure and shy to speak with them first. Peadar and Nuala Finucane were hospitable to a fault but he found it hard trying to talk with them constantly through the interpretation of their niece Murna.

The girl lived a smaller *bothán* a short distance down the hill from the Finucanes. Her parents were dead and both had apparently died from a fever which had ravaged the county in '59. Murna's brother, Enda, nine years her senior, had become the tenant of the cabin, working on the Mountcarrick estate. He, with the help of the Finucanes, had raised Murna. Then, eighteen months ago, just after Murna's seventeenth birthday, Enda Finucane had walked to Kells and enlisted in the British Army. He had rejected the unremitting destitution of rural drudgery and announced his ambition to see something of the world. They had not heard from him since he joined up. Thady Connor, Captain Dashfort's overseer, had already warned the girl that she must be prepared to leave the cabin as soon as Dashfort had a new tenant-worker to move in for although generations of Finucanes had lived there there was no security of tenure and only estate workers could rent the pitiful cabins. It was, as John-Joe found out, a harsh world.

Most of the three days, while he waited for Dualta Hanrahan to appear, he spent in Murna's company. In truth, he felt that he had fallen in love with the girl with all the suppressed intensity of youth.

She was eighteen, and, to his eye, her face seemed to carry some ethereal, unworldly beauty. It was not a sensual attractiveness, not a physical comeliness which he had seen with many Irish girls. On the other hand her features were not entirely without perceptiveness. There was a wisdom in her eyes that countered the innocence of her features. He fought for a long time to find the right word to describe it. A purity. That's what it was. He was happy with the word. A purity. He grew to delight in her company and in the fact that his heart beat more rapidly every time she entered the room.

It was the second day that Murna took him for a walk across the shoulder of Slieve na Callaigh to show him a vantage point to view the countryside. It was cold but the wind had dropped. Around them the gorse grew close to the ground among numerous grey stones, many of which John-Joe noticed seemed to have been placed by man in upright positions.

'Were they put up by the farmers for shelters?' he asked.

The girl chuckled softly. 'They've stood like this for thousands of years. It is said that they mark the graves of our ancestors in olden times. It is a very ancient place.'

'Dualta told me it was called Hag's Mountain in English.'

'On the plain below us, the ancient fair of Aonach Tailltean was held in the days when the High Kings ruled the land,' she nodded. 'Meath is an old province, full of history.'

'I thought Meath was a county?' frowned John-Joe. 'There are only four provinces in Ireland, surely?'

'In the days of Tuathal Inghlachtal, Tuathal the Acceptable, who was High King for three decades in the second century of Christ, it was decided that a fifth province be created in Ireland. There were four provinces, as you say. Uladh that is Ulster; Laighlin that is Leinster; An Mhumhain that is Munster and Connachta, a name which the English could pronounce and so it remains as Connacht. Each province had its king and from the provincial kings was chosen the *Ard Rí na hÉireann*, the High King of Ireland. Tuathal, when he was High King, thought it was unfair that a High King should have to rule both his own province and the entire country. He suggested that the High King should have a special province where he could hold court and that this province would be the seat of the High Kings no matter from what province he came. Thus any jealousy between the provinces would be eliminated. A middle province was created and called by that name – Mí, the middle province. When the English came they pronounced it Meath and divided it into two counties – Meath and Westmeath. But this was the estate of the High Kings, the fifth and middle province of Ireland.'

The girl suddenly laughed. 'Here is an Irish lesson for you. From the date of the creation of the fifth province the Irish word for a province has become *cuige* which means "a fifth".'

John-Joe stared at the girl. 'How do you know all this?' he asked admiringly.

Murna frowned in surprise. 'Everyone knows these things. We listen to the *seanchaí*, the old storyteller. There is little else to do in the long evenings of winter.'

She turned and pointed across the valleys. 'In Meath and Westmeath you will find the remains of the great palaces of our ancient High Kings. You came by way of Mullingar, didn't you? Well, nine miles to the west is the hill of Uisneach where the High King would summon the assembly of all the provincial kings and their chieftains together with the Brehons, who were the law-givers. They would gather by Aill-na-Mireen, the Stone of Divisions, which is still there today. Uisneach was one of the four great royal palaces.'

'I've only heard of Tara,' confessed John-Joe.

She nodded. 'And there is Tailltean, which the English call Teltown, and Tlachtga, which they call the Hill of Ward.'

The vista of countless valleys and rivers running eastward to the sea, fringed with heavy woodland, was beautiful and breathtaking even in the grey light of a winter's day. John-Joe felt a sense of mystery, of mythology and ancient history. It was through these same valleys, across these mountains, that the men of Ireland had marched northward to do battle against the warrior-god Cúchulain who, single-handed, defended the pass into Ulster. And from Ulster, through these valleys, marched the armies of The O'Neill to harry and defeat the soldiers of Elizabeth of England; and, again, somewhere to the east, along the broad stretch of river Boyne, which cut through the countryside, came the armies of William of Orange and James II to do battle one hot day in July. John-Joe breathed in the romantic atmosphere, imagining the fabulous clashes and the passionate hopes of the people. He stood in silent hero-worship of the land about him, his eyes soft and dreamy meditating on the visionary hopes of his knight-errant perfectionism. Ireland would be free again; he would free it.

'It's a beautiful spot, a holy spot,' he whispered.

Murna grimaced. 'It's not what the farmers say,' she replied. 'It's great enough in the sheltered valleys but up here. . . .'

John-Joe shook his head. 'I meant remembering the great deeds that were once done here.'

'Well,' the girl smiled, 'great deeds do not feed the people today. It's no different starving here than starving in some other place.'

John-Joe felt slightly hurt, almost as if she had uttered some blasphemy. He sighed. He supposed that he could not expect everyone to have the same vision. Yet how he loved this land; he felt in sudden communion with his ancestors. Yes, he would free this land.

He was already impatient when Dualta Hanrahan came to the village and took him to an old barn about a quarter of a mile away which was set deep in a wooded grove. It was known as Ó Buachalla's barn although Ó Buachalla had long since died and the place was used to shelter the communal cattle of the village during the intemperate winter weather. Seven young men had gathered there most of whom he had already seen about the village. They greeted John-Joe shyly. All spoke English out of respect for John-Joe. Dualta explained that the others who made up the company of a dozen men were working that evening. Under some straw at one end of the barn, two of the men removed some earth and revealed a small cavity filled with objects wrapped in sackcloth.

'This is our arsenal,' Dualta said proudly as they unwrapped the sacking and displayed one of the muskets that lay hidden there.

John-Joe took the weapon and examined it critically, trying to recall his weeks of training at the infantry depot. The block was rusty and the mechanism was stiff.

'Let's see all the weapons,' he grunted.

They sat round and watched quietly, as if he were conducting some mystic religious ceremony. He took each weapon and examined it thoroughly. Finally he sat back and shook his head sadly.

'What's the matter?' demanded Dualta with a frown.

'I would say that the best way to commit suicide would be to attempt to fire one of these guns,' he said.

Dualta grimaced.

'How so?'

'Each of these weapons is rusty. Almost corroded. When was the last time you cleaned them?'

It was a young man, Seán Ó Cleirigh, who lived opposite the Finucanes' *bothán*, who replied.

'We haven't cleaned them since we had them. We don't know how.'

'I thought as much,' sighed John-Joe glancing at Dualta.

Dualta did not meet his gaze.

'Very well. The first lesson will be this: you are soldiers. To a soldier a musket or rifle is his best friend. It stands between him and death. He must take care of it. He must love it.'

He gazed at their puzzled faces and realized the enormity of the task that he was undertaking. He had to take this group of enthusiastic farm lads and turn them into a disciplined fighting force. It had taken him six weeks of basic training to begin to understand about military discipline; six weeks of full-time training in a camp with properly trained officers and supplies. How could he train this bunch of lads by the light of a candle in an old barn with weapons that were almost worse than useless?

'We will start,' he said, 'by learning how to clean our weapons; by cleaning them and keeping them clean. If a gun is dirty it could blow up in your face and kill you.'

Seán Ó Cleirigh looked disappointed. 'When do we get to be shown how to use them?' he asked.

'When I am satisfied that you know how to look after them,' snapped John-Joe.

He saw them glance at Dualta. After all, he was their captain. John-Joe looked at the man who nodded slightly.

'John-Joe is the commander until he is satisfied that we know how to be soldiers,' he conceded.

It was agreed that they would gather every third day for two to three hours. As the days began to progress and the muskets and rifles grew clean, John-Joe began to explain about the mechanisms, how to disassemble and rebuild the weapons and how best to use them. It did not matter whether these boys were able to salute or form fours; what mattered was that they could obey orders, shoot straight and move in proper formation on command. They had taken to heart the lessons of cleaning and every meeting started with an inspection of the weapons. John-Joe spent a lot of time instructing on trigger pressing, being annoyed that there was little enough ammunition to give them practical experience. Of course, there was the additional worry that the noise of shooting would attract unwelcome attention so he contented himself with lectures on the effects of individual sniping and on volley fire. And between his training sessions, John-Joe devoted himself to acquiring a knowledge of Irish, working when he could in Peadar Finucane's patch of land or helping to repair thatch and generally making himself useful in the village.

Saturday evenings were the great social occasions of village life.

The villagers would crowd into one another's houses for what they called a *céilí*, a grand social evening of dancing, singing and, when food would allow, feasting. Murna told him that during summer there would be dancing in the centre of the village but winter was a time for storytelling, tales of ancient times long, long before the coming of the English. There were those who retained memories of the old tales who would recite them and, if a word or pause was out of place, a member of the audience would correct it for, it seemed, everyone possessed such knowledge. And between the stories came the songs and poems. Someone played an ancient fiddle, another had a whistle made of oat-straw, a traditional shepherd's pipe, while another had *bodhrán*, a winnowing drum of goatskin. Yet another played a *bosca-ceoil*, a concertina, and another had a *uillinn*-pipe which was a bagpipe through which the air was pumped by means of a bellow activated under the arm of the player and so named 'elbow-pipe'. The music was beautiful and created an emotional reaction deep in John-Joe's soul. Murna sung on these occasions with a sweet soprano voice that echoed as pure as a bell. John-Joe loved listening to her singing the ancient songs even though he had no understanding of them until the words were explained to him.

On the first *céilí* he attended, it was Murna who sang a special song for him and in which everyone joined in a lusty chorus:

Oró! Sé do bheatha 'bhaile!
Bhfearr liom thú ná céad bó bainne
Oró! Sé do bheatha 'bhaile!
Anois ar theacht a' tsamhraidh.

Ho there! Welcome home!
Better you than a hundred cows.
Ho there! Welcome home!
Now our summer comes to us.

It was at that first *céilí* that John-Joe asked her what her name meant.

'I am named after *Murna na Muinéal Báine*,' she smiled and then chuckled at his perplexed face. 'Murna of the White Neck who was wedded to Cumhal and bore his son Fionn. Now surely you have heard of Fionn Mac Cumhal the greatest leader of the Fianna?'

'Finn Mac Cool?' He rendered the name into the English phonetics of his childhood. 'Was Murna the mother of Finn?'

'You seemed impressed at that,' she observed.

He coloured for he had been weaving youthful fantasies. Murna was the mother of the leader of the ancient Fenians and it somehow merged with his daydream of Murna as the personification of all that he was struggling for.

'Tell me about Murna,' he invited, turning her observation.

'*Murna na Muinéal Báine*? Little enough to tell.'

A man nearby, overhearing, called out: 'Tell the tale of Murna and Fionn. Tell it in English for the stranger to hear.' He raised his voice to the others. '*Cíunas anois, tá scéal le hinsint aici*!'

A quiet fell and Murna sat forward on her chair.

'*Murna na Muinéal Báine* was a granddaughter of Nuada of the Silver Arm and she married Cumhal, the chieftain of Clan Bascna who was overthrown and slain at a battle at Cnoc, a place which the English now call Castleknock near Dublin. After the battle, Murna took refuge in the forests around Slieve Bloom where she bore Cumhal's child and called him Demna. But as he grew up, Demna was so fair and handsome that he became known as "The Fair One" – Fionn. They say that it was on account of the whiteness of his skin and his golden hair. As a boy Fionn learnt the accomplishments of poetry and science from the druid Finegas who dwelt not far from here on the banks of the Boyne. In a pool of the river, under boughs of hazel, lived Fintan, the Salmon of Knowledge. Finegas had sought to catch this salmon many a time for it was known that whosoever ate of it would enjoy all the wisdom of the ages. He had failed until the day when Fionn became his pupil. Then Finegas caught Fintan, the Salmon of Knowledge, and gave it to Fionn to cook, bidding him to eat none of it.

'When Fionn brought the cooked salmon to Finegas the old druid saw that there was a change in the countenance of the boy and he demanded to know whether Fionn had ate of the salmon. Fionn denied it but added that as he was turning the spit over the fire his thumb brushed the salmon and had been burnt so that he put his thumb into his mouth. Whereupon Finegas told him that he must now eat of the salmon for it was so prophesied. Fionn ate and became wise and strong and whenever he felt in need of knowledge all he had to do was place his thumb in his mouth and the knowledge was his.

'His mother, Murna, married again to become wife of the King of Ciarraí. Fionn went off to Tara to ask the High King if he could take service in his bodyguard. That was when Cormac Mac Art was High King and when Goll Mac Morna was leader of the Fianna, the bodyguard of the High King. It was at a time when Tara was troubled by a demon who came at nightfall and attacked the city throwing fire balls against it and setting it on fire. None could do battle with him for as he came the demon played on a harp so sweetly that the music made all the warriors fall into the sleep of forgetfulness.

'Fionn went to the High King and said he would slay the demon if the High King made him leader of the Fianna and make him chieftain of his father's clan, Clan Bascna, which had suffered sorely since his father's death at Cnoc. The High King was impressed and gave his word.

'Now there was a man called Fiacha who had been a comrade of Fionn's father and who was possessed of a magic spear with a head of bronze and rivets of Arabian gold. The spear head was kept laced in a leather case for when the naked blade was laid against the forehead of a man it filled him with such a battle fury and a strength that he became invincible in every combat. Fiacha gave Fionn this spear and taught him the use of it.

'So Fionn took the spear and went to the great ramparts of Tara to await the coming of the demon. As soon as he heard the notes of the demon's harp and felt drowsiness overtaking him, he laid the spear-head against his brow and the magic of the demon came to naught. The demon fled before him, all the way to Slieve Fuad, which is now Slieve Gallion in County Armagh. Fionn slew the demon there and carried its head back to Tara. And Cormac called the Fenians together and set Fionn over them as their leader. They all swore fealty to him and Fionn Mac Cumhal became their greatest chieftain.'

She paused and cries of approval resounded from her audience. John-Joe sat enraptured. She met his eyes for a moment and held them before dropping her gaze away with a shy smile on her face.

It was a week afterwards that Dualta took John-Joe to meet O'Malley, the local commander of the military wing of the Brotherhood, in a small forest clearing not far from the village. He was a tall, angular man with a frizz of light brown hair, wild and curly like a field of wheat. His eyes were green and mesmeric. His pale skin was flushed across the cheeks and he carried his humour on his face, a broad smile which hardly left him. He was in his early fifties but the cut of his well-tailored clothes did not conceal the suppleness of his body, the muscles of which a younger man might be proud. Dualta respectfully addressed him as *múinteoir* which John-Joe discovered meant 'teacher' for, in fact, O'Malley was a schoolteacher in Kells.

They sat under a tree and O'Malley and Dualta took out their pipes and proceeded to light up.

'You have lookouts posted, Dualta?' asked O'Malley.

'I have, *múinteoir*.'

'Then we can talk in peace.' O'Malley turned to John-Joe. 'How soon will Dualta's company be ready?'

'Ready for what?' countered John-Joe. 'It is hard to train a band under such conditions and with archaic weapons. If I had ammunition to use for practise it would be better.'

'Ammunition is scarce and costly. Besides, the noise of shots would bring out every spy and informer in the county. There's a military barracks not so far away. When the time comes that is the place that must be captured by Dualta's company. If the barracks isn't secured then it will dominate the road from the north and the English can pass their cavalry along it, south to Dublin.'

'Dualta has shown me the barracks.'

O'Malley glanced at John-Joe with a whimsical smile. 'You are young to have been an officer in the Federal Army.'

'I'm nineteen,' replied John-Joe in annoyance.

'No great age. I was fighting your army before you were born.'

'Dualta told me that you fought for the Mexicans.'

O'Malley smiled reflectively. 'My grandfather was a colonel of the Ultonia Regiment in the Irish Brigade of the Spanish Army. I studied at Valladolid thinking to become a priest. But being young and adventurous I went to Mexico and was there when the war between the Mexican Republic and the United States broke out.'

'Wasn't it about some territory?' hazarded John-Joe. 'Didn't the Mexicans claim that the land between the Rio Grande and the Nuecas belonged to them?'

O'Malley took the pipe out of his mouth and roared with laughter. 'The reverse, *mo bhuachaill*. It was the Americans who claimed that land from Mexico. But no matter. America declared war on Mexico in '46. I think it was May. There were many of us who believed that the American case was unjust and that to force the issue by war was an evil. I joined the Mexican Army and when the Mexicans raised a battalion of Irish recruits called the Legion of St Patrick, *Los Patricios*, I joined it. Many of the soldiers had actually served in the Federal Army like John O'Reilly who was the commander of the battalion.'

'I've never heard of them,' confessed John-Joe.

'No, perhaps you wouldn't. The Americans treated us harshly, more harshly than the Mexicans. We fought a bitter war. I was at

Buena Vista when nearly 2,000 of our men were cut to pieces by artillery. That was just before General Santa Anna, the Mexican commander, decided to make himself President of Mexico. Then came Churubusco. Now, that *was* a battle. There were many thousands of casualties. Our battalion was hemmed in within a convent and it was the flag of the *Patricios* that was the last left flying on the field. The Americans took many of us prisoners and everyone who was found to have served in the American army were immediately court-martialled for, it was claimed, they were deserters. Out of our battalion fifty men were condemned to death, including O'Reilly himself. They hanged sixteen at San Angel and four more on the following day at Mixcoac. But it was those who were hanged at Tacubaya that I remember most. That was the day when the Americans stormed Chapultepec. They brought thirty of the *Patricios* seated on carts with nooses around their necks within sight of the battlefield. The American officers told them that they would be hanged immediately the American flag appeared over the fortress they were storming. So they were.'

'Why weren't you hanged?' demanded John-Joe.

'There was no way they could find an excuse for doing so. I was not a citizen of the United States, nor had I ever lived there. They were trying to punish all those Irish who had lived in America before joining the Mexican forces. Those who they did not execute received fifty lashes on their backs with a rawhide whip. Then they were branded on the right hip with the letter "D" two inches high. They were made to wear an iron yoke weighing eight pounds with three prongs, each one a full foot in length, around their necks. Finally they were condemned to hard labour while the American army remained in occupation in Mexico. Yes, *mo bhuachaill*, I've seen war and what men can do to each other.'

He shook himself and relit his pipe. 'That's the trouble with the Irish, always caught up in other people's wars instead of concentrating on their own war of liberation. It's a pathetic business. In fact, all war is a monstrous evil. Glory! What's glorious about a lonely death in some muddy field with the guts hanging out of you?'

John-Joe was surprised. 'But you are committed to a war to drive the English out of Ireland,' he protested.

'That doesn't mean that I must have illusions about it,' O'Malley replied sharply. 'There is an old Spanish proverb: let him who does not know war, go to war. Having said that, I know that if the representatives of our nation went, cap in hand, to the Vice-regal

Lodge in Dublin and said to the English lieutenant-governor; "Please, sir, would you kindly remove yourself, your administration and your army from our country because we would like to govern ourselves?", then the English would roar with laughter and clap those representatives in jail or hang them. To get rid of the gun it is necessary to take up the gun. I am ready to fight. But I don't claim there is any glory in it, *mo bhuachaill*. There is no elevating human quality about it. It is a job; a job to be done and finished with so that the people of this country can start living a proper life again.'

'My views do not coincide with your own, sir,' John-Joe retorted. 'I believe there is a glory about fighting evil and there is a nobility in hating oppression and, in hating it, striving to overthrow it.'

O'Malley smiled. 'War is like prostitution, *mo bhuachaill*. Both are the slaves of desperation.'

Sitting listening to them, Dualta moved uneasily. '*M'anam*! You would think the two of you are on opposing sides.'

O'Malley knocked out his pipe. 'There's room for idealism as well as realism,' he said. 'It is simply a question of knowing which is which.'

He put his pipe in his pocket, and was abruptly serious. 'The Military Council are still functioning in Dublin, Devlin. I have to make regular reports on the state of things in the county in preparation for the rising. You say Dualta's company need more training?'

John-Joe nodded.

Dualta bit his lip and looked embarrassed.

'*An Seabhac Siúlach* promised that the rising would be this year. It will be Christmas soon. There is precious little time left,' John-Joe said.

O'Malley rose to his feet. 'The day will come, I'm sure of that. Keep on with the work, Devlin. The day will come soon.'

Chapter 26

Every Sunday the people of An Bhaile Dearg, together with people from the neighbouring villages, would trudge across the bare fields, through a desolate, wind-torn landscape, in order to attend mass. The villages on the Mountcarrick estate were not big enough to support a priest and the people had to tramp five miles to the church. It was accepted that John-Joe would not attend mass regularly for the authorities were still watching for suspicious-looking strangers, particularly Americans. But the weeks of December had sped by and Christmas Eve fell on a Sunday. John-Joe decided to accompany the Finucanes to the morning mass.

He walked a little apart from the others in case he was observed, stopped and questioned by the Constabulary. Here and there across the dreary landscape, walking among the leafless oaks, were small groups of people, families, individuals, all with a purpose about them as they converged on a small grey stone church tucked in a corner of a valley. John-Joe was surprised at how crowded the place was. He was fortunate enough to be able to slip inside the building for many had to cluster around the door to hear the priest, a thin, gaunt-looking man with black glaring eyes and sharp features. The man's voice, as he intoned the Latin formulas of the mass, was strident, almost bellicose. The people huddled before him, obediently chanting the responses in subdued monotones which acted as a counterpoint to his rising accents. Then an expectant hush descended as he climbed the steps to the lectern to deliver his sermon.

'*In nomine patris, et fili, et spiritus sancti* . . . amen,' he muttered, raising his black staring eyes to the congregation. Unsmiling, angry looking, he let his gaze travel slowly over the faces before him. So slowly, so intently, that John-Joe felt a wild desire to rise and run out of the building.

When he finally spoke John-Joe was surprised that he began in

English and continued in English. He glanced round, seeing the concentrated look on the faces of the people as they sought to follow the man's harsh accent. He felt a little sad for he saw people from An Bhaile Dearg who he knew possessed no word of English pretending to follow the sermon, nodding slowly to the rising and falling and the pause of the priest's voice as if they understood perfectly. John-Joe suddenly realized that they were ashamed to admit their ignorance of English; not to understand the language had been made into a stigma by the civil authorities and that stigma was being enforced by the ecclesiastical powers. The young man's heart went out to them as they sat silently letting the wrath of the priest's voice engulf them in unintelligible sounds.

'Does not the Epistle of the Blessed Paul, chapter 13, say: Every person must submit to the supreme authorities. There is no authority but by act of God, and the existing authorities are instituted by him; consequently anyone who rebels against authority is resisting a divine institution, and those who so resist have themselves to thank for the punishment they will receive. For government, a terror to crime, has no terrors for good behaviour. You wish to have no fear of the authorities? Then continue to do right and you will have their approval, for they are God's agents working for your good. But if you are doing wrong, then you will have cause to fear them; it is not for nothing that they hold the power of the sword, for they are God's agents of punishment, for retribution on the offender. That is why you are obliged to submit. It is an obligation imposed not merely by fear of retribution but by conscience. That is also why you pay taxes. The authorities are in God's service and to these duties they devote their energies.

'Discharge your obligations to all men, pay tax and toll, and give reverence and respect to those to whom they are due.'

The priest paused and glared around him, his lips thinning.

'There is in this land, this fair and happy country of ours, misguided souls who tempt eternal damnation; souls who are led by a group of evil, seditious men. These are people who resist the powers, who resist the legitimate powers set over them. They behave contrary to all the tenets of the Blessed Gospels and the teachings of our Holy Mother Church.'

He stopped, coughing slightly.

'These wicked men call themselves Fenians, a brotherhood of evil and corruption! You have all listened to me on several occasions reading the pastoral letters of Archbishop Cullen of Dublin. Now I must say again, these men are a canker in our land. They claim that their land, their property, their country, has been stolen and say that they will fight to reclaim it. The very act itself is contrary to the will of God. Does not the Blessed Luke say that if a man takes what you own, do not ask him to return it?'

John-Joe sat staring at the priest in amazement, his blood tingling with indignation.

'Does not Hebrews say that you must accept the plundering of your property with joy because there is a better and more lasting possession awaiting for you in heaven?'

The priest drew his brows together, leaning forward to almost physically project himself into the congregation.

'I say this, the men who call themselves Fenians are an affront both to God and His Church and they must be destroyed. I warn the foolish youths of this parish to shun those who would enticed them into such illegal organizations. Talk of an armed rebellion against our legitimate government is a blasphemy. Isn't it clear enough in the words of Christ – render unto Caesar the things that be Caesar's. . . . ? I implore the youth of this parish that, should they be approached, should they know of someone spreading the evils of sedition and treason, which is an abomination in the eyes of God, go straightway to the authorities and report the malefactor.'

John-Joe moved uneasily and heard a slight murmur from some of those seated around him. The priest, in the fervour of his sermon, was oblivious to the soft response.

'If I must condemn the foolish youths who have joined this wicked conspiracy, then I must say a word about the prime movers in all this mischief. How much must we not execrate the conduct of these designing villains who have been entrapping innocent youth and organizing this work of crime? Thank God they are not our people or, if they ever were, they have lost the Irish character in the cities of America.'

John-Joe felt his face was brilliant red, hot with the flush of embarrassment and anger.

'I speak of those who call themselves Irish-Americans. What animal is that? I know of the Irish people; good, honest, obedient to their rightful masters. I know of Americans, a mixture of many nationalities who, as we have seen in recent years, do not even agree on the method of their own government. It is these Americans who have come to pollute our land with sedition; men who claim to be Irish or of Irish descent; men who wish to take advantage of the good nature of our people, gathering money from them so that they might live in luxury instead of by honest toil.'

John-Joe sat feeling sick now, revolted at the tirade of the priest, outraged by his claims against the Brotherhood. That an Irish priest could preach such things seemed an unbelievable affront to his congregation.

'Beyond even these are criminals of far deeper guilt,' the priest was continuing. 'There are men who, while they send their dupes into danger, fatten on the spoils in New York and in Paris. These are the execrable swindlers who care not to endanger their own necks but endanger the necks of men that trust them. They care not how many are murdered by the rebel or hanged by the strong arm of the law provided they can get a supply of dollars either for their pleasures or their wants. I preached to you last Sunday on the eternity of Hell's torments. But when I look down into the fathomless depth of this infamy called Fenianism I say that Hell is not hot enough nor eternity long enough to punish such miscreants.'

The silence in the church was almost deathly and the priest stopped as if becoming aware of it for the first time. Here and there rose a muttered whisper as someone vainly tried to translate for those who spoke no English. The priest bit his lip, muttered an incantation in Latin and turned away to the altar.

After a while the people began to drift away from the church, returning to their homes. John-Joe had a feeling that people who knew him were refusing to meet his eye, averting their gaze. Only Murna smiled briefly at him. He felt a surge of panic wondering whether there were those who would obey the priest and betray him to the authorities.

'Hello, Devlin.'

He jerked his head nervously at the bluff greeting. He was surprised to meet the rubicund stare of O'Malley. The man was leading a horse by the bridle.

'I'll walk with you if I may,' he said, falling in step with him.

'Are you sure you want to be seen with me . . . there might be spies?' John-Joe asked nervously.

'*Amaidí*! Nonsense! We're all friends here.'

'Are we?'

O'Malley chuckled. 'You thought Father Shenton's sermon was a little fierce?'

'Fierce?' snorted John-Joe. 'Is the man in the pay of the English?'

'Does that surprise you?'

'The clergy are Irish. I would have thought that they would have been on the side of their own people against those who are oppressing them.'

'Listen, *mo bhuachaill*, you ought to know the history of our Holy Mother Church. It's a temporal organization claiming spiritual domination. In Ireland, after the Penal Laws, the Church has always consistently and strongly opposed those who sought to overturn England's conquest. Obedience to the temporal ruler, obedience to God. Those are the tenets of the Church.'

'But why?' demanded John-Joe as they walked along the path to Slieve na Callaigh. 'How can the Church here be so different to the Church back. . . .' He hesitated.

'You were going to say "back home"?' O'Malley grinned. 'You came here thinking this was your home and now you are not so sure, is that it?'

John-Joe nodded.

'I had a different image of Ireland when I was in New York,' he admitted.

'Well, *mo bhuachaill*, perhaps the Church is not so different here as in New York. It is only that we have a different set of masters and the Church gives its loyalty and obedience to whoever is in power.'

'You make the Church sound like a whore,' protested John-Joe.

O'Malley nodded thoughtfully. 'Perhaps she is. When the English introduced the Penal Laws after the Williamite Conquest, the Church tried to woo the English, seeking toleration if not recognition. After all, hadn't the Pope been William's ally and helped pay for his military conquest of Ireland?'

'But the Orangemen say they overthrew the Pope and the Catholics at the Boyne?' protested John-Joe.

O'Malley gave a sharp bark of laughter. 'If they did, it was with the financial and military support of the Pope acting under the League of Augsburg. William's victory at the Boyne was celebrated with a *Te Deum* in St Peter's in Rome and in all the major Catholic cathedrals in Europe! Let the Orangemen indulge their fantasies, the Church is a whore.' He paused a moment and then continued. 'After the Williamite Conquest and William's about-face on his promise to grant religious liberty to Catholics and Dissenting Protestants, the Catholic hierarchy thought that if they showed obedience then the English would drop them a few crumbs in reward for being good servants. Any misbehaviour on the part of the Church would be punished by a stricter enforcement of the Penal Laws. The Church proved right in that; as the clergy endeavoured to prove themselves good, loyal citizens, the English granted them the occasional relief measure as a reward for good behaviour.'

John-Joe felt confused. 'I thought it was O'Connell who fought and won Catholic emancipation forty years ago?'

O'Malley pulled a face. 'O'Connell? What did O'Connell ever care for the Irish people? He cared about himself. He wanted temporal power. As a Catholic, short of changing his religion, his only means was to force the issue of emancipation so that he, as a Catholic, could be given permission to go and sit in the English Parliament. O'Connell was just a place-man and a pension seeker. In his day four million of our people spoke the Irish language, including O'Connell himself. He actively promoted the language of the conqueror, he taught his followers that they should endeavour to stop their children learning Irish. Today scarcely a million-and-a-half speak the language. O'Connell!' he sneered. 'Do you know that when Robert Emmet led his followers in the uprising of '03, a few Irish Catholic landlords volunteered to fight their fellow countrymen on England's behalf . . . one of them was O'Connell!'

'But he is called The Liberator!'

'Liberator!' O'Malley's face was red with emotion. 'Look around you, *mo bhuachaill*. Then tell me what O'Connell liberated!'

They continued on in silence for a while and then John-Joe asked, 'Will the people take any notice of what the priest said?'

'There will be some, of course,' admitted O'Malley. 'There are always spies and informers about, people eager to pick up easy money. But Father Shenton and his ilk have preached the same gospel of national subjugation for years. In my grandfather's time it was Archbishop Carpenter of Dublin who fiercely defended the English conquest. It's the same old sermon, a tired sermon. It was used against the United Irishmen in '98; against Emmet and against the Young Irelanders in '48. Now it is used against the Fenians. God help us if the Fenians fail to liberate Ireland because it will be trotted out for use against the revolutionaries of tomorrow. That's the way of it.'

'We must not fail!' John-Joe said vehemently.

'And yet the year is almost over and there is no word from the Military Council,' sighed O'Malley. 'This year was to be the year of the rising. I believed it. You have met *An Seabhac Siúlach*. What is he waiting for, Devlin? One can be over-cautious. In waiting until things are right, one can miss the best opportunity. Better to strike while the people are willing than wait until they are demoralized. Another series of arrests such as those last September and the people will fall away believing that the cause is lost.'

'The people will fall away in any case when the Church preaches sermons of the type that Father Shenton delivered,' complained John-Joe.

'Don't over-estimate the power of the Church. It's a strong force right enough but people can only stand so much political hypocrisy. They are intelligent enough to differentiate between what they owe to God and what they owe to Caesar. And Ireland owes England nothing. An allegiance born of conquest is no allegiance.'

'But priests like Shenton are spiritually blackmailing the people.'

'There are many priests who support the Fenians against the dictates of their hierarchy. But I would say be careful of a priest until they prove whose side they are on. When I was a boy there was a priest in Navan, which is not too far distant from here, who not only gave information against his parishioners but actually led the English soldiers to arrest them. Priests prate a great deal about the celestial power of the Church but I'll tell you this, Devlin, the majority of priests are more concerned with their temporal power and security. I couldn't name you one priest, aye and that includes the Pope in Rome, who would obey the command of Christ and give away all their worldly power and goods and go naked into the world to preach.'

He halted and glanced sideways at John-Joe.

'Now here's young Murna waiting for you. We'll be meeting after Christmas. I'm sure the word will come from Dublin soon.' He raised his voice. '*Dia duit, a Mhurna. Conas tá tú*?'

Murna, standing waiting for them, smiled shyly and bobbed her head.

'*Dia's Muire duit, a mhúinteoir*. I am well, thanks be to God. I was waiting for John-Joe.'

O'Malley halted and swung himself up into the saddle of his horse. 'I'll be off,' he smiled. 'It's been a good talk, Devlin. But talk's cheap enough. It's action that is wanted. *Slán libh*!' He raised his hand in farewell and cantered off along the track.

'You look worried, John-Joe,' Murna commented.

John-Joe shrugged. 'You heard what the priest said.'

'Don't pay mind to priests when they speak of politics. They have to say what they have to say. Father Shenton is from Dublin and has not been here long.'

'But doesn't he know that this is an Irish-speaking parish?'

'He knows well enough but he disapproves of the language.'

'Disapproves?'

'He considers it to be a badge of ignorance and barbarism.'

'That's ignorance in itself,' exploded John-Joe.

'Ah, and we must pity him for it. But that's the way it is,' the girl said in resignation.

The grey skies had deepened and the first harsh, cold splatters of rain began to fall.

'We're going to get wet, Murna,' muttered John-Joe staring up at the skies.

'There's an old cave up the hill. Come on, follow me or you'll be drowned dead.'

With a sudden laugh she ran lightly up across the stubbled heather, moving swiftly up the hillside, scrambling over the bare granite rocks so that John-Joe was hard pressed to keep up with her. She came to a hole big enough for a tall man to squeeze through and disappeared inside without a backward glance. John-Joe followed her more hesitantly and found himself inside a musty smelling cave. He looked about him in astonishment.

'Why, this is man-made, Murna.'

The girl was peering out through the over-hanging gorse watching the rain sheeting down.

'We were just in time,' she said, turning to smile at him.

John-Joe was busy examining the stone slabs of the chamber, for that is what it was; a chamber dug out of the side of the mountain and lined in granite stone on which there were strange, spiral engravings.

'What place is this, Murna?' he asked.

'I don't know exactly,' she shrugged. '*Múinteoir* O'Malley once told me that it was the burial chamber of our ancestors many thousands of years ago. You can see scores of cairns marking the places where such chambers are all over Slieve na Callaigh.'

John-Joe grinned. 'It's the first time I've taken shelter in someone's tomb.'

Murna returned his smile. 'I am sure they'll be watching us with a kindly eye,' she said solemnly. 'I'll offer them a decade of my rosary this night.'

He sat down on one of the stones and smiled up at the girl. 'Are you happy here, Murna?' he asked.

'Happy?' He could not quite see her expression in the gloomy interior of the tomb.

'Wouldn't you like to live in a fine house for example?'

'My own father's house was good enough,' she said softly.

'I don't insult his house,' John-Joe said quickly. 'No, what I mean is, wouldn't you like to see America?'

The girl was silent a moment and then she said; 'It must be a wonderful place surely. I'd like to see it right enough. But there is work to be done here.'

She glanced through the entrance and began to move out. 'The rain has stopped. We can go.'

John-Joe bit his lip in disappointment. Damn the rain, he thought as he pushed his way out behind her. He had wanted to say so much to the girl. He had never been in love before and it was a painful emotion, a bitter ache, disagreeable and disturbing. He did not know how to deal with it.

As he emerged from the chamber she was standing staring across the valley to the distant mountains. Her green-flecked eyes danced with merriment as she pointed to where the pale December sun was trying to break through the clouds.

'There,' she exclaimed triumphantly. 'It's clearing. It will be a pleasant walk we'll be having now.'

John-Joe sighed as Murna began to trip lightly down the mountain-side. It was too late. The opportunity was lost.

Chapter 27

Christmas was a fairly lonely affair for Gavin Devlin that year. He spent it in Albany working at General Sweeny's secret headquarters in the state capital. Since joining 'Fighting Tom's' staff, Gavin had been occupied with maintaining a record of the growing military strength of the movement. Under the orders of Sweeny, companies and regiments were being raised, each unit named and numbered – infantry, cavalry, scouts and even artillery companies. In addition, there was the matter of purchasing arms and ammunition for this secret army and the United States War Department, with the approval of the President, presented no problems in the matter of selling war surplus to Sweeny's commissariat. However, artillery batteries were more difficult to come by, although certain well-placed officers were not slow in promising their aid in the matter. Horses were simply impossible to get, let alone trained war-horses. After the devastations of the war and the carnage among cavalry units, the price of horses was incredibly high and the Union Army held a monopoly on all purchases even forcing the requisition of mounts from outraged ranchers. It was part of Gavin's task to co-ordinate the purchases for the Fenians and organize secret dumps across the country.

Father MacMahon kept in touch with Gavin during this period and travelled frequently to Albany as a messenger from the Union Square headquarters to General Sweeny's staff headquarters. It was through Father MacMahon that Gavin kept in touch with his family. Aideen Devlin was bearing up to the absence of her two sons with the same quiet fortitude with which she faced all the trials and tribulations in her life. Manus had become unobtrusively proud of his two sons, especially of Gavin's apparent conversion to the Brotherhood. There was little news, however, from John-Joe. Another letter had been received simply stating that he was well but that was all. One piece of news that MacMahon brought made Gavin cynically amused.

Stead McHale had announced the engagement of his daughter, Rosaleen, to Brock Delancey. They were to be married in the spring. Gavin had not finished with the Delanceys yet; he would not be finished with them until he had broken them. When he said as much to Father MacMahon, MacMahon urged him to forget the Delanceys for the time being at least. With lack of proof about the family's activities, Gavin would simply be throwing himself against an insurmountable wall or even worse. There had already been one attempt on his life but, with nothing definite to link it directly with the Senator or Brock Delancey, there was no authority which would help Gavin. With the Delanceys' highly placed friends no one would lift a finger against them. It was wise that Gavin remain lying low in Albany. After some initial argument, Gavin accepted the logic of Father MacMahon's advice. He would wait; but he would wait only until he had the power and means to topple them. At least December brought one piece of welcoming news. Slavery had finally been abolished in every part of the United States by a Thirteenth Amendment to the Constitution in spite of every effort by Senator Delancey to stir up opposition.

Christmas was a particularly joyless affair as Gavin absorbed himself into the work of the Brotherhood. However, his nightmares grew less frequent and he came to believe that he had accepted the death of Nora Quinlan while simply pushing it to the back of his mind and occupying his conscious thoughts by hard work. The more he became involved with the Brotherhood the more he persuaded himself that he was doing the right thing, that this was the cause he needed and that this was the solution to the ills that troubled him. The prospect of securing a homeland for the Irish, whether in the New World or in an independent Ireland, became a preoccupation which filled his waking thoughts. After all, the Jewish people were constantly agitating for a homeland and bemoaning their diaspora, the scattering of their people to the four corners of the earth. Yet what of the Irish diaspora? Since the English conquests of the seventeenth century the Irish people had suffered a dispersion of immense proportions. They had been shipped off in tens of thousands to the Barbados and other slave-owning colonies. Men, women and children had been taken in raids on their villages by the English soldiers and thrown on board ship for unknown destinations. Tens of thousands of others, who had constituted the last armies of Ireland, had been allowed to ship to Europe to take service with foreign monarchs in the Irish regiments and brigades that were to be found in the armies of France, Spain, Austria and even Russia. William III's Penal Laws had opened the flood gates for Catholic and Dissenting Protestant alike, precluding them from using their natural talents in their native land, they had been pushed to the far corners of the world in search of religious freedom. They had spread the world in their millions but nowhere did they congregate in such close communities and in such numbers as in America.

Gavin now believed that were Ireland to become free, the heartache and sorrow of her people would be over. The Irish would nurture their own. The floodgate of migration would be closed. He concluded that Roberts and Sweeny were right in their belief that the only way the Brotherhood in America could help force the independence of Ireland was by securing a piece of territory on the American continent on which to raise the flag of an Irish Republic and use it either as a bargaining counter with England or as a base to strike at English rule in Ireland. It would be an Irish Republic-in-Exile where, until Ireland was free, the Irish immigrants could find sanctuary and be protected from the poverty and exploitation inflicted upon them by others.

The belief was one not shared by the Brotherhood's titular head, O'Mahoney. His criticism of his senate became strident, especially after his defeat over his objection to the renting of the Union Square headquarters. A further dispute had arisen in November over finances when Patrick Kennan, in charge of raising money by Irish Republic bonds, resigned. O'Mahoney decided to have his own name engraved on these bonds without calling a meeting of the senate to obtain official approval. It was another example of the numerous arbitrary, constitutional decisions that O'Mahoney was taking to assert his authority. Roberts had called an emergency meeting of the senate on Saturday, 2 December, to discuss O'Mahoney's action. O'Mahoney, in turn, declared the senate session illegal. Roberts responded by charging O'Mahoney with violating his oath of office, ignoring the constitution of the Brotherhood and slandering the senate. O'Mahoney stormed out of the meeting, accusing the senators of being bribed by English gold to disrupt the movement. All his frustrations at his loss of power within the Brotherhood reached a head and his attack on Roberts and the senate became hysterical.

O'Mahoney found himself in a minority. America's most influential Irish newspaper, the *Irish-American*, declared its support for Roberts and the senate; so, too, did the powerful *New York Tribune* and the *New York Herald*. The support of such powerful publicists enraged O'Mahoney further, who called his own special convention of delegates of the Brotherhood in New York. Many delegates did turn up mainly out of respect for O'Mahoney and his reputation, but the vast majority of the Brotherhood obeyed Roberts's call to stay away from an unauthorized meeting. General Sweeny attended O'Mahoney's meeting in an attempt to appeal for unity against any split in the Brotherhood. O'Mahoney's supporters shouted him down and he was forced to leave. O'Mahoney's convention claimed that they were the official constituted Irish Republican Brotherhood with O'Mahoney confirmed as 'Head Centre', ruling the Brotherhood with an advisory council of five. All the policies adopted at the Philadelphia convention were to be overturned and a publication, *Irish People*, would be set up in New York to become the mouthpiece of O'Mahoney's wing. The senate policy of an invasion of the provinces of British North America was rejected. It was declared that, in spite of the recent set-backs in Ireland, the strike against English rule would be in Ireland and no where else.

Roberts and his senate remained outwardly impervious to O'Mahoney's split. After all, hardly ten percent of the Brotherhood had chosen to follow O'Mahoney and the senate quickly issued a statement reiterating that there was only one official Irish Republican Brotherhood as democratically formed at the Philadelphia convention. It had an elected senate which was firmly committed to the programme approved of in Philadelphia. Privately Roberts tried to mend the breach but publicly he lost no time in pointing out that O'Mahoney's group were pursuing a course of total inaction which would lose the Irish Republic. The arrests of the leaders in Ireland and the reinforcement of the English garrison there had put an end to the prospect of an immediate uprising in the country. That very fact put Roberts and his senate wing of the Brotherhood in a strong position. A few days after O'Mahoney's breakaway convention, Roberts's senate met on Thursday, 18 January and not only confirmed their support for Roberts as president of the Brotherhood in place of O'Mahoney as well as the senate but agreed to the principles of the plan which General Sweeny had drawn up for the invasion.

In a secret session Sweeny had proposed a three-pronged invasion of the British provinces. This invasion would rely on a rising of the Irish-Canadians in Montréal and the active support of the French-Canadians with whom links had been established and who were willing to supply the Fenian army with horses for their cavalry regiments. Sweeny suggested that if his troops could take advantage of the lakes and rivers which were now bridged with ice, he estimated that a minimum force of 10,000 with three batteries of field guns could accomplish the initial tasks of the invasion force. The troops would have to be furnished with 200,000 rounds of ammunition with 500 rounds for each field piece. If the invasion was left until spring or even summer, when there would be no ice bridge into Canada, then he estimated that twice the amount of men and artillery would be needed. The estimated cost for equipping this army would be $450,000. In the discussion which followed, the senate felt that it was too late to prepare for such a campaign while the lakes and rivers were still frozen and that the invasion would have to take place after the snows melted. The general terms of the plan would be taken by members of the senate to various meetings of the Brotherhood in order to obtain support before calling a convention at Pittsburgh on 19 February to have the plan officially endorsed.

News of the plan to invade the provinces of British North America had been widely circulated as far back as October when the Philadelphia convention had give its support to the idea. Attacks from the newspapers in the provinces and from the pro-British journals within the United States were predictable. Most of the loyalist newspapers in British North America, especially in Toronto, Ottawa and Montréal, poured scorn on the idea and dismissed the Fenians as hare brained. Behind the façade of scorn and contempt, the loyalist politicians were troubled. There was a great deal of unrest within the provinces and much hostility to the plans to unite them into one big Dominion under the British crown. The French-Canadians were openly hostile and the more extreme elements of the *Parti Rouge* were calling for Lower Canada, or Québec as they called it, to become either an independent republic or be annexed as part of the United States. What concerned the loyalists even more was the fact that the Irish constituted one of the biggest elements among the settlers in the provinces and their loyalty was undoubtedly in question. It was well known that the Fenians had been successful in recruiting 'circles', or branches, within the provinces and they felt that there was a need for these Irish communities to be won over to the cause of confederation.

The British North American loyalists found their spokesman in an Irishman, Thomas D'Arcy McGee, who had once been the darling of the Irish Republican Movement and one of its leading intellectuals. After the failure of the '48 uprising McGee had fled to New York where for some years he had preached revolution and the establishment of an Irish Republic by armed force. Then he had moved to

Montréal and declared, 'The British provinces of North America are not necessarily miserable and uninhabitable because the British flag flies at Québec!' He stood for the Legislative Assembly which governed Upper and Lower Canada as an independent, appealing to the Irish electors of Montréal. As soon as he had won the seat he blandly declared that the monarchy, and English monarchy at that, was the only form of government best suited for Ireland. The declaration caused a riot to break out in the Irish quarter of Montréal. It came as no surprise when McGee was subsequently appointed to the cabinet and renounced his claim to be an independent, joining the Conservative Party and becoming minister of agriculture.

During the Civil War, McGee hoped for a Confederate victory and warned the people of British North America that the United States had declared its belief in 'a manifest destiny to overspread the continent'. They had seen the Americans tear away the huge lands of Texas, Arizona, New Mexico and Upper California from Mexico in 1848. By threat of war they had forced the British to give up Oregon and pushed their western boundary to the 49th parallel of latitude. If the United States survived the war of secession, where would their manifest ambitions lead them? Had not the *New York Herald* warned that when Richmond fell the United States would throw the British out of America? Thomas D'Arcy McGee was already committed to the idea of uniting all the provinces of British North America into a Dominion of Canada which would, theoretically, be strong enough to thwart the ambitions of the United States.

Now he was persuaded to see the plans of the Fenians as an extension of Washington's policy towards the British. The Fenians were acting as mercenaries for the American government and, in the name of Irish grievances, were simply tools of 'eagle-screaming' American imperialism. The Brotherhood, according to McGee, was now 'the worst obstacle the devil has ever invented for the Irish, an irreligious revolutionary society in which patriotism takes the form of indifferentism or hostility to religion. This is the enemy of the Irish cause in our time and it is this that every man should combat first and foremost'. In using religion to attack the Fenians, McGee found ready support from the leading Catholic bishops. Bishop John Farrell of Hamilton declared that 'Fenians are not Catholics, being cut off from the Church, condemned by it and despised by all decent society'.

Following the news of the meeting of Roberts's senate on 18 January and its decision to press for the invasion of the British provinces, McGee launched a particularly scathing attack on Roberts and Sweeny as 'not honest men gone astray but dogmatic and anti-clerical demagogues, strong in their pride of opinion and eager for propaganda. . . .' They were, declared McGee, irreligious dupes of United States's imperialism. After the speech in the Ottawa Legislative Assembly, McGee allowed himself to be interviewed by journalists in a private sitting room of his hotel on Sparks Street. The correspondent of the London *Times* was direct and none too caring of McGee's finer sensibilities.

'As a one-time Republican and revolutionary yourself, do you expect people to take you seriously when you denounce your former friends and comrades?'

McGee blinked, his face colouring. 'I do not deny that I was once a Republican. But I say now that republicanism is no answer to the ills of the world. It has not worked in the United States nor will it work in Ireland.'

'Yet you took up arms against the British government in Ireland and preached rebellion. You were still preaching armed rebellion until you were elected to the Legislative Assembly for Montréal.'

'I do not deny it,' McGee replied gruffly.

'And you would have the world believe that you have renounced your past and your former friends?'

'The Fenians, the Republican movement of today, are not the same as the Irish revolutionaries of former times. The revolutionaries of '98 or of Emmet's Rising or, even, of '48, had a just cause because the British government denied the vast majority of the Irish nation any say in their own government. The Irish were a tongueless nation. They could not use a ballot box and so they took the only course of action left to them. They rose up and fought injustice. But the Republican movement of today is composed of cunning and treacherous men, men who aim to overthrow religion in Ireland. They are *sans culottes* – Communists.'

The Times correspondent leaned forward quickly. 'Communists, you say?'

McGee smiled thinly. 'I have it on good authority that James Stephens, the Fenian leader who escaped from jail in Dublin a few months ago, is an active Communist and a member of their International which has its base in London and is run by a collection of emigré German Jews. Such men have no love of Ireland, only a love of power.'

The reporter for the *National Intelligencer* of Washington coughed dryly.

'Haven't you sought power and position by changing your political beliefs, Mister McGee? At least the men whom you now so roundly condemn have maintained their beliefs and principles in spite of all vicissitudes.'

McGee whirled angrily. 'What power and position I seek are used to the benefit of the people of these provinces of British North America.'

'And Ireland, sir? What of your own people?'

'Ireland will not benefit from Fenian communism!'

'Where is the proof that Fenianism and communism are synonymous?'

McGee was fond of dramatics and drew a newspaper, almost theatrically, from his coat pocket and unfolded it. 'I have a copy of the *Irish People*, James Stephens's own newspaper printed in Dublin. Let me read you a passage. . . .' He cleared his throat and began; 'We make no appeal to the aristocracy . . . they are the willing tools of the alien government whose policy is to slay the people or drive them like noxious vermin from the soil. The people must save themselves. . . ."'

'Sounds like good Yankee democracy to me,' muttered the correspondent of the *National Intelligencer*.

McGee scowled and continued:

> Something more than even a successful insurrection is demanded. And what is that? An entire revolution which will restore the country to its rightful owners. And who are these? The people. Every Irishman and woman has one simple object to accomplish. It is to rid the land of robbers, and render every cultivator of the soil their own landlord, the proprietor in fee simple of the house and land of their forebears and which will be an inheritance worth a free person's while to bequeath to their children and worth the children's while to enjoy. We aim to make this nation a community which bows to no power under the heaven.

He paused for a moment. 'And here, gentlemen, is the proof of their irreligion and anti-clericalism,' he said before continuing.

> The people must be taught to distinguish between the priest as a minister of religion and the priest as a politician before they can advance one step on the road to emancipation. . . . Our only hope is revolution but most bishops and many of the clergy are opposed to revolution. Then priests turn the altar into a platform from where it is pronounced a 'mortal sin'

even to wish Ireland to be free, from where priests call upon the people to turn informers and spies . . . from where, in a word, bishops and priests do the work of the enemy. It is our duty to tell the people that those bishops and priests are bad politicians and worse Irishmen. Emancipation as secured by O'Connell was a measure calculated almost exclusively to benefit the upper and middle classes of Catholics. Emancipation simply separated them from the cause of independence and has turned out to be simply a means of bribing or corrupting wealthy and educated Irish Catholics from the nation.

McGee sat back, refolded the newspaper and smiled smugly at the newspapermen. 'Do you need further proof of communism or irreligion?'

'It is gratifying to note the firmness with which the Irish Catholic bishops have discounted all sympathy with the Fenians,' agreed *The Times* correspondent.

'But you, sir, were once a republican,' the *National Intelligencer* reporter pressed. 'You now say that Ireland must have no truck with republicanism, a creed you not only advocated but were driven into exile over. Now you say that Ireland should remain under a British monarchy.'

'For the time being,' agreed McGee. 'Don't forget that it is only thirty years since the Irish Catholics obtained the vote. . . .'

'Not the majority of Irish Catholics,' the *National Intelligencer* reporter observed dryly. 'Only those who prove their voting qualifications by virtue of their property. Universal suffrage is still an ideal in Ireland.'

'We have the same franchise as operates in England itself,' snapped McGee.

'The English voting qualifications also leave much to be desired. It is hardly the universal suffrage which the Republicans seek.'

'Universal suffrage? That old pipe dream from the days of the French Revolution?' scoffed McGee. 'Why, you will be telling me next that women should obtain a vote! That also is part of the Republican manifesto.'

'That will come in time, sir,' replied the reporter. 'But tell me this, if you will, what good will the current voting franchise do for Ireland?'

'Most Irish Unionists tend to sit with the English Tories at Westminster,' replied McGee. 'Most Repealers, Nationalists if you will, support the Liberals. Whichever side is in power, Tories or Liberals, the corresponding Irish group wins some favours. But I can see a day coming, and not far in the future, for it has already been spoken of in some Irish political circles, when a specifically Irish Party will be formed to go to the English Parliament and represent the Irish nation. That is what the vote can do for Ireland.

'The Fenians are an archaic anachronism. They harp back to the days when Ireland had no other course because they were denied the ballot box. The Fenians now prate about invading these provinces in order to establish an Irish Republic-in-Exile. Stuff and nonsense! We can see the hand of Washington behind them. But the American government has a strong sense of self-preservation and will be prepared to let the Fenians take all the risks. It is an idea born in evil, an idea invented by those who merely want to exploit Irish emotions for their own self-aggrandisement. They are robbers, sir, nothing more and nothing less.'

The performance was a good one and Thomas D'Arcy McGee secured himself a warm invitation from certain highly placed Unionists in Ireland to return to the land of his birth and talk further on such themes. A guarantee of military protection was also offered. Even the moderate *Irish-Canadian* of Toronto dismissed McGee as a raving 'Goulah', naming him after Goulah Sullivan who had betrayed his friends and comrades of the revolutionary Phoenix Society of Cork in 1858. More dramatically, a reward of $1,000 for the head of McGee was announced by a leading Fenian businessman, Patrick O'Day, head of the Brotherhood in the border town of Buffalo, New York. It was a theatrical gesture but it summed up the intense bitterness of the Irish at what they saw as McGee's Janus politics.

Chapter 28

The New Year started with a heavy snowfall on the Meath countryside. It happened during the early hours of the morning and had been followed quickly by a frost. When people awoke and peered out the snow not only lay thickly across the valley but so heavily and cold that the fir boughs were forced to touch the earth and froze there. Later, the sun rose in a pastel sky, glinting off the white surfaces so that people had to screw up their eyes to gaze out. A wind came in the afternoon to continue the work of the sun in melting the snow. Then the frost came again in the night to halt the process. So the early days of January continued with little to do in the evenings save huddle round the turf fire for warmth and comfort. It was not long after that first snowfall that John-Joe was sitting with Murna practising his growing knowledge of Irish when his attention was roused from the smoking fire by the wild, melancholy two-noted call of a bird.

'It's an omen of bad weather,' smiled Murna.

A second sharp call came through the evening air.

'We call it a *crotach* . . . I don't have the English for it. They nest about the lake shores this time of year. Whatever it is, the weather will be bad.'

The girl was right for, after the snow flurries and frosts in the early part of the month, the weather settled down to a series of downpours of heavy rain, heavy enough to stay any frost and make miserable the lives of those who had to toil in the muddy slush of the fields of the Mountcarrick estate. The rains were interspersed by north-easterly winds blowing across Slieve na Callaigh which buffeted the cabins without mercy. Yet work had to continue and Thady Connor, the overseer of the estate, came to the village to collect workers for the ploughing. John-Joe could not join in this communal activity lest he be questioned by Connor or the haughty Captain Dashfort. Instead, when he was able, he worked on Finucane's small patch of ground which provided the only sustenance for the family. The stoney patch with its solitary, long-suffering cow, produced a scrawny heifer before the month was out. Now and again, the villagers of An Bhaile Dearg would lead their few cows down to the pasture in the valley below the village which was, in fact, a Mountcarrick field. There they would be let loose among the rich grass and succulent clover. But this was a dangerous practice for Captain Dashfort was known to have no compunction about confiscating any animals found grazing on his domain. But the cows needed the feed and the clover was also gathered by the villagers for their own consumption, for meadow trefoil formed the basis of a traditional dish. That year, so Peadar Finucane told him through Murna's translation, the ploughing was not hard. The days were wet and misty but the rain made the ploughing easy with scarcely a frost to harden the ground. On those few days when frosts did occur Thady Connor took the men to the woods for the collecting of 'fell' wood which was sorted into faggots for firewood for Castle Mountcarrick while the stouter wood was cut for hurdles and fencing.

The long evenings were put to good use for they were spent with Murna teaching John-Joe the language and, with the aid of the old dictionary, he began to hear the sounds of the language rather than unintelligible noises. The progress in this task made him happy for not only did it constantly place him in Murna's company but he was beginning to have courage to hold brief conversations in Irish. Of course, the training sessions with Dualta's company continued and it was one night when the weapons were safely packed and Seán Ó Cleirigh, usually the last to leave, bade him his usual, '*Oíche mhaith agat* – goodnight!' that John-Joe found Dualta waiting to speak to him.

'Are you in love with Murna?' he demanded without preamble.

John-Joe coloured in embarrassment. 'What makes you ask?' he said defensively.

Dualta sighed in annoyance. 'You've become like a cow mooning after a lost calf.'

John-Joe frowned in angry embarrassment but before he could make a suitable retort Dualta asked, 'Have you told her?'

'No.'

'Why not?'

He stared at Dualta trying to work out an explanation but how could he explain when he did not know himself? He was scared;

scared of revealing his emotions in case the girl might laugh at him or, worse still, might pity him. His youth was against him. He wanted to appear strong in her estimation and wouldn't confessing his love present a weakness?

Dualta watched him for a moment and then shook his head sadly.

'Murna is a woman, John-Joe,' he said softly, almost as if he were able to read the confused thoughts in the young man's mind.

'What does that mean?' John-Joe frowned.

'It means that you cannot fool a woman. But if you don't tell her what she already suspects then you are storing up more trouble for yourself than you realize.'

'Has . . . has she said anything?' John-Joe asked, his expression slackening in confusion.

'*A thiarcais* – no!' Dualta was emphatic. 'But haven't I been coming into Peadar Finucane's house regularly with eyes as well as my other senses? Murna's not some ancient goddess of Ireland. She's just an attractive young woman and I can see that she is set upon you. Yet you disguise your feelings by silence.'

John-Joe felt a stab of pain as Dualta hit the point. It was true. He had placed Murna on a pedestal, made her a personification of his romantic ideals. *Murna na Muineál Báine*.

'I don't want to interfere,' Dualta said. 'It is no place of mine but do not play with the affections of a woman like Murna. You must be honest with her.'

John-Joe felt stung by the unjust rebuke. 'I am not playing with her affections!' he snapped. 'She is too far removed from me for me to tell her what I feel.'

'Removed?' Dualta gaped.

'Her world, her culture . . . yours, damn it! I came here with a dream of being Irish and realized that I am just an American. The villagers call me *An Ghall*, the foreigner. How can I be accepted by Murna when I am not accepted as being Irish?'

'*Ó, ó, ó, mo bhuachaill*,' breathed Dualta, shaking his head. 'You are not the suit of clothes you walk around in. Do you think it matters if your hair is yellow or black? You are what you are and there is an end to it. It is the person inside you that matters and if you are in love with Murna Finucane and not her image then you're damaging the both of you.'

The first day of February was a mild, damp day but the people of An Bhaile Dearg gathered to celebrate the feastday of St Brigid. John-Joe was amazed at the way the saint was venerated, being hailed by the people by the same titles as the Virgin, Queen of Queens and, more often than not, as Mary of the Gaels. What he found fascinating was that her feastday was celebrated with ancient symbols of fertility and, at one point, a ewe was taken from the small flock and given a blessing before it was ceremoniously milked. It was O'Malley, during one of their encounters, who told him that there had once been an Irish goddess of the same name who was goddess of poetry, wisdom and fertility, whose festival of *Oímelg* had been celebrated on the same day before the coming of Christianity. Brigid had been the daughter of Dagda, supreme god of the Tuatha de Danaan, one of the first peoples of Ireland. Not long after Christianity arrived in Ireland, a girl called Brigid had become a convert to the new religion in spite of her father being Dubhtach, a druid of Newry, in County Down. Brigid had founded the first women's religious communities. The Church, instead of suppressing the worship of the old Celtic goddess, simply allowed the image of goddess and saint to become merged into one with her feastday grafted on to the old pagan festival of fertility.

There was dancing in Ó Buachalla's barn that evening for it was too wet to hold the celebrations outside on the *moínín*, the centre of the village. The dances were complex and John-Joe felt a jealousy that he could not join Murna in executing their intricate steps. He watched while the young men and women of the village gathered in pairs as a fiddler struck up a tune. Murna had chosen young Seán Ó Cleirigh as her partner. The dance began with all the young people participating but, gradually, the other couples fell away until only Murna and Seán Ó Cleirigh were dancing. They were completely complementary in their dance; one performing while the other was in repose, mixing feminine grace with masculine vigour. He exhibited quickness, dexterity and poise, while she stood still, a slight smile on her lips. The fiddle music quickened as he drummed his feet on the ground to ancient rhythms expressing the joy of living, the gaiety rising through his feet to his body, his hands hanging loose at his sides and his face a sphinx-like mask. Then he paused and Murna took up the challenge. John-Joe caught a lump in his throat as he gazed at her beauty, her purity. She seemed everything to him; goddess, mother, lover and aspiration. Her movements conveyed an ineffable sense of female dignity – light and graceful, her steps seemed to float across the ground, effortlessly the steps quickened in mystic movements, spurred by the ancient sounds of the fiddle. Her face betrayed the pleasure of her soul.

Then the dance ended with abruptness. John-Joe watched with tingling jealousy as Seán Ó Cleirigh reached forward and, laughing lightly, pressed the girl's hand.

Then someone called upon her to sing and a man, drawing his straw whistle from his pocket, set an air. Murna's voice was clear and sweet and it was to him that she turned to gaze as she sang.

> *Do gheallais domh-sa, ní nárbh fhéidir,*
> *Go dtúrfá laimhnní do chroiceann éisg dom,*
> *Go dtúrfá bróga do chroiceann éin dom,*
> *Is c'luith don tsioda ba dhaoire 'nÉirinn.*

Dualta, standing just behind him, bent forward and whispered softly in his ear.

> You promised me a thing impossible,
> That you would give me gloves of fish-skin,
> That you would give me shoes of bird-skin,
> And a dress of the richest silk in Ireland.

John-Joe glanced at him nervously, trying to read the message in the words. Dualta smiled. 'Isn't she trying to tell you that she doesn't want things impossible? Don't surround her with dreams. Give her reality.'

He frowned as Dualta walked away to join the dancers.

Murna joined him a moment later. 'Isn't it hot in here?' she asked.

'Would you like some air?'

She smiled.

'We'll take a stroll to the wood and back.'

They left Ó Buachalla's barn as the fiddler was striking up a jig and turned along the track, walking in silence, listening to the receding music. They said nothing as they followed the darkened twisting path to the valley floor, just below the village, where the stream from the mountainside gushed and gurgled its way under a small stone bridge.

'Let's sit awhile,' the girl said as they came to the low parapet.

They sat and John-Joe cleared his throat awkwardly. She glanced at him quickly in the darkness and suddenly felt for his hand. The contact was like electricity.

'Do you know a song called *An Draighneán Donn* – The Blackthorn Tree?' she asked breathlessly.

He shook his head in bewilderment.

'There is a verse, I will try to translate it for you.' She paused a moment and then her voice came softly.

'Tis but folly to scan holly or more lofty trees,
When in the bushes where water rushes we find heart's ease.
Though the rowan so high is growing, its berry is tart,
While near the ground fruit sweet and sound will charm the heart.

She hesitated. 'Do you understand, John-Joe?'

'I think so,' he said slowly.

'I'm not a lofty tree, John-Joe, just a small bush by the waterside.'

He tried to see her expression in the darkness. She moved her face close to his and said clearly, 'If you do not kiss me, I shall die of shame.'

He took her awkwardly in his arms and, after a while, they broke breathlessly apart. The girl squeezed his hand.

He kissed her softly again on the lips, a chaste kiss with more meaning in it than the sensual, passionate embrace of a moment before.

'I've been a fool,' he muttered, 'thinking you were beyond my grasp.'

'Isn't it the problem of most people?' she replied. 'Those that think things are beyond their grasp are condemned to self-imprisonment. I'm not beyond your grasp, John-Joe. I never have been.'

He felt a surge of happiness. He had never experienced such happiness before.

Chapter 29

Two days after the feastday Thady Connor, the overseer of the Mountcarrick estate, rode into An Bhaile Dearg and, without descending from his horse, called in a loud voice for the people to come out and hear him. The heavy jowled overseer carried himself with an air of importance and as the villagers gathered round he extracted a piece of paper from his pocket.

'I have a notice from Captain Dashfort,' called Connor, using English and pausing for a moment for his words to be translated by those who could do so. 'One week from today, the rents and tithes which you pay to Captain Dashfort as land agent to Lord Mountcarrick are to be increased.'

A ripple of surprise and consternation ran round the people.

''Tis a high enough rent we pay now,' complained one man.

Connor glared about him. 'Complaints?' he jeered. 'It has been some time since your rents were increased. The captain has noticed that you have made many improvements and alterations to your cabins here. You cannot expect to live in luxury at the old rents.'

'But where will we get money from to pay the increase?'

'From the same place you took the money to make improvements,' replied Connor readily enough. 'There will be a general increase of your rents by the sum of two-thirds of the current sum. Do you understand that? For those who pay three shillings a month, they will pay five shillings. Is that understood. *An dtuigeann sibh mé?*'

'We understand you,' It was Seán Ó Cleirigh who replied. 'But how can we pay? No one can pay an increase the like of that.'

'I am not repeating myself,' replied Connor. 'The new rent falls due one week from today. Those that do not pay may expect to face the consequences.'

'Eviction?' cried Seán Ó Cleirigh.

'I suppose you expect Captain Dashfort to accommodate yous rent free for the rest of your miserable lives?' jeered Connor. 'Doubtless yous will then expect him to feed and pay yous wages for being idle?'

His mocking gaze swept around at their pale, drawn faces. 'A week from today,' he repeated before he turned his horse and trotted out of the village. There was a silence before the noise of angry protest rose.

'Can Dashfort do this?' demanded John-Joe of Murna.

The girl looked puzzled. 'He is the land agent for Mountcarrick.'

'But you must have some protection in law? It's pure feudalism and feudalism is dead.'

'He is the law, John-Joe. It is his right.'

'But there must be an appeal?'

'To whom? He is the lord of this land, John-Joe.'

'He and his kind are foreigners who stole this land by armed conquest.'

'And, until the people can regain it, it is his. He is still the lord of the land and there is no protection in this country for us against the likes of him.'

Peadar Finucane asked Murna what upset John-Joe and when Murna translated the old man replied in a resigned tone.

'My uncle says there is no protection for the Irish in their own land. Even during the Great Hunger the landlords demanded their rents from the peasants and that was why the Irish starved to death in their tens of thousands. Fear of eviction is the greatest of all the fears that beset our people.'

Peadar Finucane gazed unhappily at John-Joe a moment and then shrugged expressively.

'My uncle says there is nothing one can do. The choice is between paying or leaving the land and searching for work in the cities or beyond the waters. Perhaps one day our time will come and the landlords and their agents will be no more. Until that day comes the new rents have to be found. As you see, John-Joe, we live a conquered people in a conquered country.'

Two days later John-Joe met O'Malley with Dualta in Ó Buachalla's barn.

'Have you heard about the new rents in An Bhaile Dearg?' he demanded.

The schoolmaster nodded morosely as he pulled out his pipe.

'Not only in An Bhaile Dearg but in every village on the Mountcarrick estate. Dashfort is raising all the rents.'

'It's true,' Dualta waggled his head in emphasis. 'I was talking to one of Dashfort's stable lads who came to drink in the Green Man and he says that Dashfort has increased the rents everywhere on the estate. But the lad also heard that Dashfort is anxious to make a cattle run through the valley so that he can take the herds to the lochs beyond for watering. An Bhaile Dearg lies in the path and so he is anxious to clear the area and move the people elsewhere, perhaps across to Árdeas, one of the other villages.'

John-Joe stared in horror. 'You mean that he is deliberately raising the rents hoping that people can't pay so that he has an excuse to evict them?'

O'Malley shrugged indifferently. 'It has happened before. Who knows the truth of it?'

'But the people have lived in An Bhaile Dearg for centuries. It's their home.'

'They live on the sufferance and goodwill of the estate,' replied O'Malley.

John-Joe experienced a feeling of utter helplessness. Nothing had struck him so harshly about the realities of living in a conquered country as life in An Bhaile Dearg.

O'Malley saw the burning indignation on his face. 'Let me tell you a political reality, John-Joe,' he said quietly. 'It was not until the reign of the Tudors that the conquest and subjugation of our people was made a central policy of the English state. During the seventeenth century our people made two significant attempts to fight back against that conquest. You have heard of Cromwell's policy which was nothing less than the elimination of the Irish nation? By a certain day in the year 1654 all the Irish were to move into a reservation west of the River Shannon and their land was given to the English colonists. Any Irish person found on the east side of the river after that day could be executed immediately. An English soldier could collect a reward of five pounds for the head or scalp of an Irish man or woman or even more by selling them off to the slave-owning colonies in the West Indies or the Americas. Whole villages were rounded up and shipped abroad in that fashion.'

O'Malley leant forward intently. 'Yet, John-Joe, our people are resilient. They recovered and rose up again. But with the coming of William of Orange and the final Irish defeat at the battle of Aughrim, Aughrim of the Slaughter, the Irish nation went down into the twilight of conquest. The intelligentzia were dispersed, forced to go abroad, and the schools and universities were destroyed. The remnants of the Irish armies were allowed to go abroad to serve foreign monarchs. Our once great culture, our language and literature through which we taught the pagan English the Christian religion and spread the Christian teachings through Europe during the Dark Ages, was suppressed. While books in our language were smuggled in from Europe, many were discovered and destroyed. Irish was saved only by the stubborn will of the ordinary people, it was kept alive by underground poets. The eighteenth century was the age of the English ascendancy, the political and economic subordination of Ireland to England with the catastrophic confiscations and the inpouring of new colonists, the creation of a new English land-owning aristocracy which now owns ninety per cent of the land.

'You are upset about Dashfort's treatment of An Bhaile Dearg. Mark it well, John-Joe. That is typical of life in rural Ireland. The mass of our people are alienated from the landowners by language, culture, tradition and religion. They are serfs who have only a precarious hold on their land . . . their land? Should I not say the land they are allowed to live upon and from which they can be evicted at the whim of the landlord or his agent? Rural poverty and distress are a commonplace of Irish life. This is the reason why our fight for liberation must succeed. We must not only free our country but we must free the people so that they become an independent people in an independent country.'

O'Malley paused breathlessly and his eyes were shining with excitement.

'I am committed to that,' John-Joe whispered.

Dualta nodded smiling. 'Aye, we're all behind the Brotherhood in that.'

'Our liberation must be a social liberation as well as a national one. Fintan Lalor, the only real revolutionary of the Young Irelanders, knew that, John-Joe.'

John-Joe shook his head. 'I've never heard of him.'

'He was dead within a year of the Young Ireland rising,' replied O'Malley. 'But he held that no movement had the right to call itself an independence movement which neglected to end the frightful social misery which our people are suffering. Social and national freedom are not two unrelated issues but part of one great democratic principal.'

John-Joe nodded emphatically. 'That is why we must do something about the rent increase for the people can't pay and they will be evicted.'

'The Brotherhood cannot become individualistic, John-Joe,' O'Malley said with a sigh. 'We can do nothing until we hear from the Military Council. We must wait until we hear word of the rising.'

'But men like Dashfort are an irresistible flood tide engulfing and suffocating the people of Ireland,' exclaimed the young man.

O'Malley smiled thinly. 'There's a proverb: *níl tuille dá mhéad nach dtránn* . . . there's no tide so strong it doesn't ebb.'

A few days later O'Malley sent Dualta to John-Joe with some copies of an old newspaper called *The Irish Felon* which contained some articles by Fintan Lalor who had been acknowledged the theoretician of the Young Irelanders. John-Joe read them by the light of a tallow candle before going to sleep. The words written nearly twenty years before stirred his soul with an aching fire. For the first time he began to think clearly about the abstract concept of freeing Ireland and crystallized what such freedom meant. Fintan Lalor had said:

> The entire ownership of Ireland, moral and material, up to the sun and down to the centre, is vested of right in the people of Ireland; that they, and none but they, are the landowners and the lawmakers of this island; that all laws are null and void not made by them, and that this full right of ownership may and ought to be asserted and enforced by any means which God has put in the power of man.

The words caused him to shiver, caused his blood to tingle. The romantic image of Ireland began to fade in John-Joe's mind and from the words of Fintan Lalor sprung the practical application of freedom. He began to realize, too, the nature of the enemy he was fighting and, indeed, what it was he was actually fighting for. The Dashforts, which England has sent into Ireland as feudal barons, could only be fought if the people united, if every person refused to pay all rents and arrears of rent and fought against every attempt to invoke the law of eviction. John-Joe discussed the idea with Murna one evening.

'There are a great many "ifs" in your argument. It's a dreamer's word, John-Joe.'

He felt annoyed at what he thought was her flippant dismissal of his argument. 'Is your uncle going to pay the new rent?' he demanded.

'What else can he do?'

'And the others? Those who can't afford to pay?'

The girl bit her lip. 'Perhaps Captain Dashfort will lower the increase. Seán Ó Cleirigh is taking an appeal to him on behalf of Cáit Ní Nualláin. She is a widow with only one son, Diarmuid, and him not old enough to work. She is infirmed with the bronchitis. Dashfort will not be able to evict her.'

'Perhaps you're right,' John-Joe agreed. 'But I doubt whether you will be allowed to stay in your cabin now.'

'Would I like this America of yours?' Murna suddenly asked, turning the conversation.

John-Joe gave the question some thought before he replied. 'I don't think you would like New York. It's a big city with many people.'

'But you have freedom there?'

'I've never really considered it.'

'Not considered it?' Murna raised her eyebrows in astonishment. 'You came all the way here to Ireland to fight for freedom and you have never considered whether there is freedom in your own city?'

John-Joe smiled ruefully. 'I didn't quite mean it like that. Yes, there is freedom there surely. What I meant was that I've never really considered whether it was the freedom I wanted.'

'Are there so many different forms of freedom?' she smiled.

He nodded seriously. 'I'm only just beginning to realize that fact. I think I came to Ireland seeking the freedom of the old days; the days when Ireland was a centre of European learning, when her High Kings ruled; when students from all over Europe attended her famous medical schools and universities. The time when even the English petty-kings thought it prestigious to be educated in Ireland. The time when Ireland sent out her missionaries and scholars to help spread literacy and learning to Europe recovering from the destruction of the Dark Ages. I came to see an Ireland renown for her philosophers like Eriugena, her poets like Ó Siocháin and her geographers like Diciul. I came to find the freedom which made Ireland a bright jewel of European civilization; I came to rediscover that soul and raise her up again.'

'The days of the High Kings, the sagas and the poets and great centres of learning are gone, John-Joe,' Murna sighed. 'You can never return to the past.'

'But out of the past we can build a new future,' asserted John-Joe. 'The important thing is to stop people thinking they are what other people tell them. It's a slave mentality, a condition of mind. When Irish people stop thinking that they are slaves then they will be free and no tyranny in all the world can put them back into bondage. If only people would think themselves into freedom.'

Murna chuckled gently. '*If* only. . . .' she murmured.

'If only,' John-Joe laughed self-consciously. 'It's a wish, that's all.'

Murna smiled broadly and began to chant a wild melody.

> I wish, I wish, I wish in vain,
> I wish I had my heart again
> And vainly think I'd not complain
> *Is go d-téidh tú, a-mhuirnín, slán!*

Laughing, she leaned across and kissed him softly on the lips.

Chapter 30

Towards the end of January Gavin travelled from the New York state capital to the border town of Buffalo. He was pleased to get out of the confines of Albany. Initially he had been happy to throw himself into the task of military administration but as the weeks lengthened into months he found the crowded office routine tedious, the atmosphere somewhat stifling. The dull routine began to make him fretful. He had no complaints with the Brotherhood except the work, the tiring paper work, was repetitious and uninspiring. He began to long for some action. Inevitably, his mind turned to brooding thoughts of Nora Quinlan and thence to the Delanceys.

Father MacMahon had little information of interest about the Delanceys. They appeared as formidable and invulnerable as ever. Apparently the engagement between Rosaleen and Brock Delancey had been hastily engineered by Stead McHale who seemed to have rejected the idea of acquiring an heir for his law firm in favour of having a multi-millionaire son-in-law and the prestige which a connection with the Delanceys would bring. Rosaleen apparently had not objected to her father's wishes. It was with some surprise that Gavin found the news excited no strong emotion in him. He was even able to hope that Rosaleen would not be hurt but as for Brock Delancey he experienced only contempt and a bitter hatred. In the loneliness of his room at the retreat run by Father Fitzgerald, he devised and discarded innumerable plans to expose and bring the Delanceys to justice. Eventually he turned to schemes of simple vengeance. His frustration about his inability to do anything to bring the Delanceys toppling from control of their empire and his increasing boredom with the work in the Brotherhood's offices had reached the stage where he seriously considered resigning and moving west. Four years of action in the army had produced a restless spirit in him.

When General Sweeny asked him to accompany President Roberts and himself on a visit to Buffalo where they were putting the outlines of the invasion plan to the local Fenian 'circle' for approval, Gavin had agreed with some enthusiasm. His enthusiasm increased when Sweeny quietly informed him that he wanted Gavin to volunteer for a special assignment which would take him across the border into Upper Canada for several months. Sweeny could not give him details. There was to be a special meeting in Buffalo, unconnected with the Fenian 'circle' gathering, which he wanted Gavin to attend with him too. The details would be given to him at that meeting. Gavin felt almost a relief as he agreed. The desire to do some physical action other than signing papers was strong.

Since Gavin had spent the previous three winters in the more temperate climate of the south he had come to regard the winters of his native New York as harsh. But he had never realized what coldness was until the train pulled into the depot at Buffalo. The city was scarcely a hundred years old, huddled beside the Niagara River which marked the frontier between the United States and the British province of Upper Canada. In its hundred years of existence it had grown from a small trappers' settlement to a city of 80,000 people, a centre of manufacturing and ship building for the Great Lakes. The early French trappers had called the Niagara, the beautiful river – *beau fleuve* – and it was from an English distortion of this that the city received its name.

In winter Buffalo was a prisoner of the harsh snows and ice storms which swept from the north on its unprotected buildings. The Great Lakes, even the turbulent waters of the Niagara River, with all the small creeks which fed them, became frozen. There was always work for able-bodied men in the city during the winter months shovelling snow and sweeping the sidewalks. The icy winds whipped and lashed at the city constantly, causing the dry snow to drift almost aimlessly this way and that burying buildings as it chose. Sometimes the city would become cut off for days or weeks at a time for there was only one link with the rest of the country when the lakes and rivers froze over and that was via the railroad but often the tracks would become obliterated by drifting snow or, worse, the ice would twist and distort the rails.

As the train drew into Union Station, Gavin was loath to leave the warmth of the carriage with his companions. Roberts left them at the railroad depot to go directly to his hotel while General Sweeny led Gavin to the special meeting. The cold wind tugged at their clothes as they turned down the wooden planking which served as a sidewalk, ignoring the shouted invitations from a few hardy cabbies, whose horses and buggies stood under the lee of the depot buildings, heavy blankets shrouding them in an effort to stop them freezing.

'It's not far,' Sweeny muttered through teeth clenched against the cold. It seemed to Gavin a long walk as they moved down Main Street to where the frozen Buffalo River emptied into the equally frozen waters of Lake Erie. Along the north bank of the river ran a thoroughfare called Ohio Street. A short distance along the street Sweeny halted before a small saloon which also proclaimed itself as an hotel. He pushed in, pausing to stamp his feet to clear the snow and slush from his boots. A thickset, fleshy-faced man with dark, brooding eyes, nodded with recognition at Sweeny.

'Good-day, General.'

'Hello, Mooney. Are the others waiting?'

'Upstairs,' acknowledged the man with a jerk of his head.

'Capital!' Sweeny handed his bag to the man and motioned Gavin to do likewise with his valise. Then, without another word, Sweeny led the way to an upper room and entered without knocking. The room was permeated with the odour of cigar smoke. There were four men inside, seated round a table. They stood up respectfully as Sweeny entered.

'Gentlemen,' Sweeny's greeting encompassed them all. He gestured to Gavin. 'This is Captain Gavin Devlin of my staff. Devlin, I'd like you to meet Brigadier Lynch, Colonel Hoy, Major Canty and Captain Hynes.'

Gavin knew their names and reputations. Brigadier William F. Lynch was young, not more than thirty years old, but he had achieved a formidable reputation and popularity in the Union Army. As the colonel of the 58th Illinois Infantry he had led his regiment to assault the Confederate stronghold of Fort Donelson on the Cumberland River. A few months later his regiment had been cut to pieces at Shiloh and Lynch had been captured, spending nearly a month in the notorious hell-hole of Libby Prison. Within that year, however, he had managed to get back to the Union lines and reorganize his regiment, commanding it under General Nathan Banks in the expedition up Red River into Louisiana. At Sabine Crossroads the Confederates had pushed Banks back to a spot ironically called Pleasant Hill where they inflicted 2,500 casualties on the Union Army within two days. Among the seriously wounded had been Lynch. Now he seemed bursting with energy, his handshake was firm, his expression reminding Gavin of a buccaneer, eyes twinkling with carefree merriment.

The second officer, Colonel John Hoy, was a native of Buffalo who had served with distinction in Colonel Rogers 21st New York Infantry and subsequently in the 155th New York Volunteers. Hoy, Gavin knew, commanded the 7th Regiment of Fenians which had been raised in the city. He was slightly older than Lynch, a quiet and reflective man.

Gavin also knew Captain William J. Hynes, a Bostonian and a member of Roberts's senate. He was a thin-faced man with the attitude of a bank clerk, a stickler for detail and method, who, as well as his political involvement, had been appointed assistant-adjutant of the military forces in the border area.

Only Major John Canty, a broad-shouldered, stocky man in his late thirties, was unknown to Gavin.

They re-seated themselves around a card table with Lynch pouring the newcomers drinks from a bottle that was already open on the table.

'To the Irish Republic virtually established!' Lynch smiled.

'The Irish Republic!' they echoed.

Without any other preamble, Sweeny turned to Canty and asked; 'What is your situation, John?'

Canty was a broad-faced man with a shock of red hair and a pleasant expression. 'I've rented a house across the river in the township of Fort Erie and installed my wife, Catherine, and children there. We seem to have been accepted by the local people without any problems. I had no difficulty in getting a job with the Buffalo and Lake Huron Railway. In fact, they've made me a section foreman.'

There were some smiles and chuckles around the table.

'Is the pay good then, John?' asked Lynch with a grin.

Even Hoy forced a thin smile, 'Aye, maybe you'll be in a position to give us a loan?'

Sweeny was serious. 'You are sure that no one suspects anything?'

'No,' Canty assured him. 'There's a lot of soldiers returning from the war who are looking for work. One more or less doesn't make a difference.'

'Aren't the people across the river suspicious or alarmed by McGee's warnings about an invasion?' pressed Sweeny.

'So far, the people I've talked with regard McGee as a pontificating windbag trying to frighten them into supporting the proposition of confederation,' chuckled Canty. 'There's quite a lot of opposition to the unification of the provinces.'

Sweeny looked thoughtful for a moment and then glanced towards Gavin. 'There is no need for me to tell you that an army is only as good as the intelligence it has,' he said.

'I take it that Major Canty here is our intelligence officer across the border?' Gavin replied gravely.

'Right enough, Devlin,' smiled Canty.

'Major Canty was an intelligence officer on Sherman's staff and scouted for him on his march through Georgia,' Sweeny explained.

Gavin glanced with new respect at Canty. Anyone who could serve as a scout deep within Confederate territory, especially in the vanguard of Sherman's march, and survive, deserved respect.

'This area will be one of our main crossings when the time comes,' Sweeny continued. 'We have to build up our intelligence in preparation for our move but, in turn, the enemy, having been forewarned of our intentions by the various reports which have circulated since the Philadelphia convention, will already be watching for our moves.'

'The British already have such a force watching the border areas, General,' Canty agreed. 'There's a special force of detectives operating all along the border under the command of a judge called McMicken.'

Sweeny whistled softly, 'Gilbert McMicken?'

'Do you know him, General?' asked Lynch.

'I knew of him,' Sweeny replied. 'During the war he ran an escape route for Reb prisoners who managed to get out of our jails and cross the border. Gilbert McMicken's men would help them get to the port of Halifax in Nova Scotia and put them on a ship bound for the south. After the Rebs embarrassed the British with their raid into Vermont just before the end of the war, they made McMicken head of a secret service keeping an eye on the Rebs and Reb sympathizers. He's a sly fox. We must not underestimate him.'

'I know all about McMicken,' Canty said grimly.

Sweeny grinned crookedly. 'I wouldn't have sent you across the border if you couldn't look after yourself, John,' he replied. 'However, you are only one man and, because of your job, you are mainly confined to the Fort Erie area. I want more information on the canal system and defences further inland.' He turned to Gavin. 'That's the job I want you to volunteer for, Devlin.'

Gavin had already guessed as much. He felt excited by the prospect.

Here was some action at last. 'How long would I have to operate across the border?'

'Until the word is given for the crossing. You would then join the invasion force on the intelligence staff. Until that time you will operate under the direct orders of Major Canty.'

'How long would that be?' insisted Gavin. 'When do we cross?'

Sweeny shrugged. 'Certainly not until after the thaw. Spring at least and maybe not until summer.'

'Six months?'

'At the outside.'

Gavin was thoughtful for a moment. What had he to lose? He had already committed himself to the principles of the invasion. He wanted action. Now he could commit himself to the practical aspects. He nodded his agreement.

'Good man!' Sweeny exclaimed approvingly.

'What exactly is it that you want me to do?'

Sweeny took a well-marked map out of his pocket and spread it dexterously, in spite of his one hand. 'There is a system of canals and locks that must be scouted. They start at a town called Port Colborne on Lake Erie and run north into Lake Ontario.' He glanced towards Canty and the major took over.

'You probably know that the Niagara River is not navigeable to large ships between the lakes because of some spectacular waterfalls – the Niagara Falls. The British decided to build a series of locks and a linking canal between the two great lakes. It was opened back in '29 and is in constant use by warships as well as merchantmen. It's a prime military objective, a major military and commercial route within the provinces.'

'We'd like to know the extent of the British military strength around those canals and locks,' interposed Sweeny. 'We want troop positions, fortifications and all the military information you can gather.'

'That would require me living in the area without falling under suspicion,' Gavin remarked wryly.

'There are plenty of small farmsteads in the area,' Canty smiled. 'You could move round the area claiming to be a farmhand looking for work.'

'Major,' Gavin pursed his lips, 'I'm a city man out of New York and trained to be a lawyer. I guess what I know about farming wouldn't impress a ten-year-old country boy.'

'Nevertheless, Major Canty has a good idea there', Sweeny agreed.

'The war has made some strange changes among people. There are numerous reasons why a man should seek work on a farm when he has never worked on one before.'

'Sure,' agreed Canty. 'Apart from farmsteading, there is little enough work around the Port Colborne area, at least none that would not attract attention.'

Gavin shrugged. 'I'll give it a try,' he offered.

'Good,' Sweeny was brisk again. 'I chose you for the task, Devlin, because you've been across the border before. I believe you are the man to carry out this commission.'

Brigadier Lynch and Captain Hynes had remained silent most of the time but now Lynch spoke. 'Why are we a party to this meeting, General?'

'Because, brigadier, you will be commanding this sector when the time comes.'

Lynch raised his eyebrows in surprise.

'John Canty will be your chief intelligence officer with Captain Devlin working under him. It is essential that you know these men. Similarly, Captain Hynes will be assistant-adjutant in charge of operations in the area. Colonel Hoy, as commander of the local regiment here, should also know what is happening in his command area.' Sweeny turned to Canty and Devlin. 'These officers will henceforth be your chain of command. You will report only to one or other of them.'

They each made an acknowledgement.

'I can only reiterate that this is an important mission, gentleman,' Sweeny said softly. 'When our troops move across the river, the lives of thousands of men, the ultimate success of our army may depend on what you find out and report to us.'

Canty grinned encouragement at Gavin.

'The canal is only about twelve or so miles from Fort Erie so that you may contact me in an emergency. However, I suggest we maintain a regular meeting for reports. Perhaps we should meet at noon every twenty-first of the month in the City Hotel in Fort Erie. It's a busy establishment run by a man named Henry Fitch. It's best to meet among crowds.'

Gavin repeated the time and place.

'Capital!' approved General Sweeny. 'Now we'll have another glass of that excellent whiskey before I join Roberts in addressing the Brotherhood meeting at St James's Hall.' He glanced at Canty and Gavin and added, 'A meeting, gentlemen, that you would be wise to avoid. You are now agents for the Brotherhood and in these roles you must avoid any connection or interest in it until the time comes.'

'That's okay, General,' Canty rose smiling. 'I'm sure Devlin and I will find something in the city to keep us occupied.'

Chapter 31

A few days after the meeting in Mooney's saloon, Gavin Devlin stepped from a train at Sherk's Crossing, a small halt on the Grand Trunk Railroad not far from Port Colborne and the Welland Canal. His crossing into Upper Canada had been visually dramatic; he had walked across the Niagara River from Buffalo, and the vast flat white wilderness was a breath-taking sight. John Canty, who had left Buffalo a day ahead of him, had told Gavin that the best way to cross was from Squaw Island and he had made his way along Niagara Street out of the city to approach the southern tip of the island whose long thin finger stretched close to the American shoreline. Standing on the elevated quayside Gavin could gaze across the river to the Canadian shore. An irregular and uneven line of people were moving in both directions, most with back packs and show-shoes, guiding themselves across the frozen river with the aid of a rope which stretched from shore to shore. He hesitated wondering how easy it was to cross.

'Thinking of crossing, mister?'

Nearby an old man sat before a brazier in the shelter of a wooden hut. He was wrapped in furs and smoking a long pipe.

'I suppose it's safe?' Gavin asked dubiously.

The old man removed his pipe and gave a wheezy chuckle. 'Guess you're a stranger, eh?'

'You guess right.'

The old man stabbed with his pipe stem towards the river. 'The ice is pretty safe if you follow the guide rope, leastways until the end of next month. Maybe the thaw won't be until late March. Anyhow, see the way the ice floes stack up along the shoreline? You see it's pretty thick, eh? But it's wise not to wander too far away from the rope line.'

Gavin pursed his lips. 'Everyone seems to have snow-shoes on.'

'Easiest way to cross, mister,' the old man grinned. 'You wanna buy a pair? I'll sell you them for a dollar. If you wanna hire, then it'll be a quarter and you give 'em to my friend on the far side.'

'I'll buy them,' Gavin said. If he was going into the country he would need snow-shoes anyway.

The old man turned into the hut and reappeared immediately with the eliptical frames of wood criss-cross by gut which was a standard form of footwear during the winter months. He took Gavin's dollar, spat on the coin and pushed it into a pocket.

Gavin eased himself down the wooden ladder from the quay and stood gently on the frozen ice of the river. He felt nervous, scarcely believing the ice of the river would be so firm in spite of the evidence of his own eyes. Then he bent to put on the snow-shoes, picked up his bag and began to shuffle towards the guide rope. He began to move forward with the curious shambling gait of a snow-shoer wondering how far it was across. Perhaps a thousand yards? His body was held tensely and his eyes darted here and there watching the ice before him and wondering whether at any moment there might come an ominous crack which would warn of the ice opening.

It was cold out on the river. Now and then a man passing from the Canadian shore would move by with a greeting but most people shuffled along with their heads down, muffled against the biting wind that blew across the empty expanse. To his left Gavin was aware of the great wilderness that was Lake Erie, a breath-catching panorama where white lake and white sky merged at the horizon in one bewildering vista. He was glad that he had on two pairs of woollen stockings beneath his boots. The thick blanket coat and woollen scarf around his face and the racoon skin cap were necessary to prevent the freezing gusts of wind cutting into him. About halfway across the river he paused, gulping in deep breaths of the shallow cold air, and stared in surprise at a figure sitting not far away on the ice. It was wrapped in dark Buffalo robes so that it was impossible to tell whether it was an Indian or a white man. The figure hunched before a circular hole cut in the ice, a string in its gloved hands. Beside it on the ice lay a couple of trout. Gavin shook his head in amazement and pushed on again. He did not envy the figure its task.

The township of Fort Erie, which lay opposite Buffalo, was tiny compared with the city on the American side. Untying his snow-shoes he climbed up on the quay. A few people were lolling about in front of a brazier. A thin-faced man with a fur cap and coat glanced closely at Gavin. He wore uniform trousers and boots and a rifle was slung on his back. He said nothing. Another man sung out to enquire whether his snow-shoes were bought or hired and then Gavin moved off down the shore road in the direction, which Canty had told him, of the railroad depot. The township lay almost buried in its winter coat. There were a few people about and the roads were just slush-filled tracks. He had to wait two hours at the railroad depot. Canty had given him a sketch map of the area showing Port Colborne and the canal area. Gavin had decided to make a start, searching for a job, around Sherk's Crossing, which was the nearest settlement to the east of Colborne. It had not been a long trip. The train halted at Ridgeway, a village some ten miles down the line from Fort Erie, and then he had to ask the conductor to halt the train at Sherk's Crossing some four miles further on. The crossing was not a regular halt. Canty had already warned him. It was just a small trackway in a wilderness of pine forest on the northern shore of Lake Erie. Many small farmsteads sprawled throughout the area and Canty had agreed that it was the most likely place to start looking for work. For a short while Gavin had been able to bask in the warmth of the railroad car as the train wheezed its way along the northern shoreline of the great lake. He was almost falling into a gentle doze when the engine slowed, with a tolling on its bell, and the conductor had tapped him on the shoulder.

'This is it, mister. Sherk's Crossing.'

Gavin was a little surprised at the sudden isolation as he was left standing in a white bleak wilderness watching the dark shape of the conductor's van swaying away along the narrow trackway through a passage of evergreens until it vanished from sight. He shivered slightly and gazed around. Tall black trees seemed to stretch endlessly on all sides. The landscape was predominantly white and black with the occasional patches of evergreens. The cold encased him like a glove, squeezing against his body. He bent to put on his snow-shoes again. Then he chose the northerly track and began trudging along it. It was half an hour before he came to the first farmstead and moved cautiously along the pathway to the log house. Immediately came the sound of a baying dog sensing his approach from within the cabin. A tall man wrapped in furs came out on the verandah and watched his approach, great clouds issuing from his half-open mouth as his breath was given form in the chill air.

'G'day, mister,' he called.

Gavin halted below the verandah and pulled down the wool of his scarf.

'Good-day, mister. I'm looking for work.'

The man looked surprised underneath the shroudings of fur. 'Work? Farm work?' His voice was incredulous.

'I'll try my hand at anything,' Gavin nodded.

The man shook his head. 'This is winter, mister. You'll not be getting work in these parts. Even when the snows begin to melt, I doubt whether you'll find much to do. The farmsteads around these parts are small enough. Subsistence farming in the main. These places barely keep a family alive, mister, let alone feed extra hands.'

Gavin sighed. 'Well, thanks, mister,' he began to turn away.

'Hey!' He turned at the man's call. 'Did you come off the train at Sherk's Crossing?'

Gavin nodded.

'Ah. I thought I heard it halt. Like a coffee before trudging on?'

'I'd not refuse.'

'Come along inside. Wife's got some cookies hot from the oven, too.'

Inside, the heat from the pot belly stove was intense. The farmer's wife smiled a greeting as Gavin threw off his coat and hat and eased out of his boots. The snow-shoes had been left on the verandah.

'Sit you down, mister,' the farmer smiled, pushing aside his dog, which stood gazing suspiciously at Gavin but slouched into a corner at the word of command, still watching, fangs slightly bared.

'Don't get much news this way during winter, mister,' the farmer said, almost apologetically. 'What's new?'

'Little enough,' shrugged Gavin.

'Are you from across the border?'

Gavin did not deny it.

'Ex-soldier, eh?' The farmer grinned at the unconcealed surprise on Gavin's face. 'A lot of ex-soldiers coming this way since that war of yours ended, mister. Lot of southern folk. But I guess you ain't a southerner?'

Gavin shook his head.

'Lot of talk about these mad Irish invading us too,' went on the farmer. 'You ain't Irish?'

Gavin was thankful that the heat of the stove had given colour to his burning cheeks.

'No,' he said shortly.

The farmer's wife pushed a steaming mug of coffee towards him.

'Hush, Wilbur,' she rebuked her husband. 'You've been asking questions ever since the poor man set foot inside.'

The farmer shifted defensively in his chair. 'Ain't no other way to learn 'cept by asking questions. What brought you this way looking for work, mister?' He smiled maliciously and nodded towards Gavin's hands. 'You don't look like a farm hand.'

'I've done some,' muttered Gavin. 'When the armies began to disband there wasn't much work in the States so I thought I'd see how things were on this side of the border. Are you sure there is nothing in this area?'

The man shook his head but his wife smiled across from the stove. 'There are plenty of small farmsteads along the Garrison Road. You could try there,' she said.

'Thanks ma'am,' Gavin replied.

'Most farmers have nothing to do in winter except a few chores like milking, chopping wood, repairing the harness, harrows, ploughs and the like,' the farmer said. 'Not the sort of jobs you need extra hands for. It's a bad time.'

'Where will I find this Garrison Road?' Gavin said, ignoring the man's pessimism.

'If you continue up the track aways, you'll come to the Garrison Road running west into Port Colborne,' said the wife.

Gavin spent a little while longer over the coffee and the cookies chatting about the prospects of confederation. The farmer was obviously a supporter of the scheme for he monopolized all the talk which pleased Gavin. He was there to learn.

'It's got to come,' the farmer said enthusiastically. 'Confederation has got to come. It will raise us from the position of a number of small, inconsiderate colonies into a great and powerful nation. Why, once we extend towards the west we will rival your States in land size. It will also throw down the barriers of trade and give us markets across the world. Then we farmers can develop and expand instead of existing on small crops.'

After a time Gavin thanked them and left. He tried two other farmsteads on the way, receiving similar answers to his enquiries about work. Then he came to a long stretch of white snow which marked the Garrison Road and turned west along it. It was cold now and he knew it would be dark very soon. He began to think that he would have to give up the idea of finding work on a farm and trek into Port Colborne itself. To the north of the road he saw several small farmsteads. He tried three of them but the farmers, while treating him with courtesy and hospitality, could offer him no hope at all for work. Winter was the wrong time; it was the season that all small farmers hated. Little or no work could be done while the snows lay thick and hard on the ground. At the last farmstead he called at, he was offered a bed for the night. The farmer pointed out to the fleecey sky, darkening in the east.

'Reckon it'll be snowing afore nightfall, mister, judging from the like of that.'

'I'll go on a little further,' Gavin told him, thanking him for the offer.

'Take care, then,' the farmer called after him. 'I've known people going down to their own barns to check the animals who wandered off the path from the house and clear froze to death.'

Gavin smiled at the man's imagination.

Half an hour later he was beginning to regret his hasty decision. He came upon a small creek which, like all the other creeks, was frozen solid, and halted a moment. Twilight was starting to descend and it would probably be dark in a short while. From where he stood, on a small bridge of rough-hewn logs, he could see a light winking through the trees. He wondered if this farmstead would repeat the previous offer of hospitality.

A thin, shrill cry caused him to whirl round. Along the creek a small boy came, moving swiftly on a pair of skates, yelling with pleasure. Gavin relaxed and grinned as he watched the boy who seemed an expert at the game.

The sharp crack meant nothing to Gavin at first until he heard a sharper cry from the boy. A cry of fear. Then there came a curious groaning sound followed by a noise like a pistol shot. It was over in a minute. The ice abruptly broke in the centre of the creek and the boy careered headlong into it with a scream of terror. His arms waved desperately trying to find support and then he was gone into the black, freezing waters.

Gavin dropped his valise and went at a shambling run down the bank. He knew that if the ice in the centre of the creek would not hold a boy's weight then he had little hope in getting out on the ice. He glanced round, his mind racing, looking for a fallen branch or piece of wood. Further up the bank there was an old spit rail fence. He wrenched off his snow-shoes, scrambled up and heaved at it with all his strength. The wooden rails were not secured but they seemed impossible to move, frozen so stiffly to each other with an adhesion that was just as firm. With a savage grunt he lashed out with his boots to loosen them. By this means he dislodged a fair sized piece of timber and hauled it down the bank to the cracked ice. The boy was still struggling but Gavin knew it took only a short time to freeze to death in such waters. He pushed the timber out, praying it would reach the hole. It did, with an adequate length to spare.

'Grab hold of the wood!' he yelled.

The boy's eyes were closed. Whether he heard or not Gavin could not tell. But his threshing arms came up, found the wood and seized it with the grip of a drowning person. Slowly, groaning in the exertion, Gavin began to haul carefully on the length of timber, pulling back slowly and gently. It took a while and he thanked God that the boy was not too heavy. He eased him from the waters and slid him across the cracking sheets of ice. Then, with the boy within reach, he leaned forward and hauled him on to the bank.

The boy was unconscious, his face a ghastly pale complexion. The breathing was agonized. Gavin pummelled the frail form for a few moments to restore circulation. He stared round helplessly. Then he saw the winking light through the trees again, threw the boy's body across his shoulder and ran back to the wooden bridge. He began to ascend the small rise through the trees towards the light. It did not take long to come to a gate in the half-hidden split rail fence, passing two gaunt, gnarled trees that stood like sentinels on either side of the gateway. There was a small log cabin, a farmstead with outbuildings hunched around it. A lamplight shone through unshuttered windows. Gavin moved rapidly up the pathway, climbed on to the verandah and banged at the door with the toe of his boot. Inside he heard a muffled exclamation.

'Who's there?' demanded a female voice.

'I need help! Open up!'

The door creaked open cautiously, the muzzle of a pistol poked through.

'What do you want?' asked a suspicious voice.

'A boy fell into the creek. He's in a pretty bad way.'

The door swung open. Gavin had the impression of a woman standing there, a pistol in her hand. He did not even stop to consider but pushed roughly by her into the warm room beyond. He saw a bunk bed in a corner and deposited the boy there. He began struggling to tear off the already freezing clothes.

'We need hot water and towels. Quickly. He's likely to freeze to death.' He heard a sharp intake of breath behind him.

'Oh God!' the woman wailed. 'It's Tom! Tom!'

'Alright, ma'am,' muttered Gavin, 'Your boy will be fine so long as you get the towels and hot water.'

A thick, rough wool towel appeared at his side and then a steaming bowl of water. Gavin had the boy's clothes off by this time, rubbing his ice cold body with the hot water and towelling him vigorously. A red warming glow began to appear and the boy started coughing.

'Got any whiskey, ma'am?' demanded Gavin, his eyes on the boy's face as he continued to massage him. 'Just a small shot.'

The glass of spirits was placed into his hand.

He raised the boy's head and tipped the liquid down. The boy coughed, near choked, coughed again and swallowed. He opened his eyes and stared at Gavin in bewilderment. Then memory caused him to blink. Then he focused his eyes on the woman behind Gavin's shoulder.

'Sorry, Katey,' he muttered and coughed again.

Gavin smiled grimly. 'Okay son, you have a good cough now. Guess you must have swallowed a gallon of creek water.'

The boy opened his eyes again and nodded. Gavin tucked the blanket around the boy and stood up. He turned expecting to see a matronly woman, the boy's mother. But the girl who stood there was scarcely more than twenty-one years old. She was slim and attractively built, clad in a man's check shirt and dungaree trousers. She had touzled auburn hair, with a pert nose and her jaw was slightly aggressive. Her lips were red, well shaped and her cheeks, on which there was the faintest sign of freckles, were dimpled. It was the eyes that fascinated Gavin; they were ice-grey with a hint of hazel in them, stirring to some hidden fire. The thought registered in his mind that he would hate to see the girl in an angry mood. She was not beautiful; there was too much of a tom-boy urchin in her face and manner for that; but there was an attractiveness which Gavin found required more than a cursory glance.

'Sorry,' he muttered, as he realized that the girl was staring back at him with an inquisitive look. 'Guess I was thinking that you are a little too young to be the boy's mother.'

She chuckled. 'That's because Young Tom is my brother. I'm Kate Dawtry.'

'Gavin Devlin,' Gavin said, stretching out a hand.

'Well, Mister Devlin . . . I'm . . . Young Tom and I, that is, are mighty indebted to you. You'd best take off your coat and boots before you catch a chill and I'll make a hot toddy.'

Gavin smiled. 'I'd better rescue my bag and snow-shoes from down by the creek first.'

It took him a few minutes to collect them and return to the farmstead. The girl had prepared the hot drink and it went some way to restoring Gavin's circulation. Young Tom, now wrapped in a cocoon of blankets, was in a deep natural sleep, a reaction to the changes of his body temperature and the strong spirits. Gavin threw off his coat and boots and took the chair before the stove.

'Lucky thing you were about,' the girl said as she handed him the hot toddy. 'It's not often strangers wander this far from the main road. Did you get lost?'

'I was looking for work, er . . . Miss Dawtry,' Gavin replied. 'I came off the train at Sherk's Crossing.'

She stared at him incredulously. 'Work? You won't get work on the farmsteads at this time of year. Probably not even in spring nor summer. Most farmers here are subsistence farmers. Little enough work about when the weather is good.'

Gavin nodded. 'I realize that now. I've tried six farms along the way. I decided to try one more before trekking into Port Colborne this evening.'

Kate Dawtry looked astounded. 'You'd freeze on the road before you reached there.'

Gavin shrugged. 'Not much else I can do.'

She gave him a glance of close examination. 'Why are you looking for farmwork, Mister Devlin?'

He frowned. 'Why?'

'You're no farm hand. I can tell that just by looking at your hands. You're from south of the border, aren't you?'

Gavin sighed. People were more astute here than he gave them credit for, even this young girl.

'Ex-army, Miss Dawtry. Thousands of men have been disbanded from both armies during the last year, all looking for work. Most of them have not had a civilian job in their lives. War is all they know.'

'That goes for you?'

'That goes for me,' he echoed.

Kate Dawtry searched his face with her grey-hazel eyes for a few moments and then went to examine a pot simmering on the stove, stirring it with a long wooden spoon.

'Pea soup,' she smiled across her shoulder. 'You're welcome to stay for supper. And to the cot in the spare room for tonight.'

'That's very kind of you.'

'Like I say, Mister Devlin, Young Tom and I are in your debt.'

'Won't your folks mind me staying?' Gavin asked.

'Ma died when I was twelve giving birth to Young Tom. Pa died just after Christmas.'

'I'm sorry.'

The girl raised a shoulder in an indifferent gesture.

'Isn't it tough to be here on your own?' pressed Gavin.

'I was born and raised on this farm, Mister Devlin. It's the only life I know.'

Gavin raised his eyebrows. 'You mean to continue to run the place?'

'I've not had much time to think about it since Pa died. But I guess I'll have to manage somehow.'

She turned to lay the table.

'Can I help?' asked Gavin.

Kate Dawtry smiled. 'You've done enough by hauling Young Tom out of the water.'

Gavin realized that the prefix 'Young' was obviously her name for the boy.

'Why "Young Tom"?' he queried.

'Got in the habit when Grandpa Tom was alive. He died soon after Young Tom was born. He was eighty-eight years old,' she added proudly.

'That's a good age,' Gavin smiled.

The girl nodded.

'Was he from these parts then?' Gavin asked.

'No. Grandpa Tom came here back in 1815 from Australia.'

'He was Australian?' Gavin was surprised.

'No,' responded Kate Dawtry. 'Grandpa Tom was a rebel. He had been transported to Van Diemen's Land in '97. When his time was up he brought Grandma and Pa, who was a baby then, to set up a farmstead here.'

'What had he done to get transported? Was he Irish?'

'No,' she smiled quickly. 'He was from England. But he was a Radical and a Republican. Grandpa Tom used to tell us tales of those times. He supported Tom Paine and the French Revolution, you see. Then he became mixed up in an attempted rebellion in England, went to Paris and returned with a French invasion army commanded by some American general. They attempted to set up an English Republic, so Grandpa Tom said. But he was caught and transported to Van Diemen's Land.'

Gavin shook his head in surprise. 'I never heard that story before.'

'Grandpa Tom liked to talk about it,' Kate Dawtry said. 'He was a stubborn old cuss, Radical and Republican to his dying day. They even put him in jail at Hamilton for three months back in '37. He was seventy years old but that didn't stop them.'

While she was talking she was laying out earthenware bowls and spoons and cutting freshly baked bread.

'What happened in '37?' Gavin asked, feeling there was something about the date he should remember.

'I forgot you were from the States,' admitted the girl. 'That was when the Patriots and MacKenzie tried to set up a Canadian Republic. Grandpa Tom was a supporter of Mackenzie, you see. Anyway, they finally let him out because he had done nothing more than read Patriot literature. People round here thought he was an eccentric and didn't mind him much. They're mostly Tories around here.'

'Your Grandpa Tom sounds like quite a character.'

Kate Dawtry agreed. 'Reckon he was,' she said, gesturing Gavin to take his seat as she served out the soup.

'I'm beholden to you, Miss Dawtry.'

'It's nothing after what you did,' she smiled, sliding into the seat opposite him. They fell silent as they ate. Outside the wind was whistling against the cabin, constantly changing direction. The girl paused in her eating and listened.

'It's going to be bad weather tonight. Maybe a wind storm.'

Gavin stared at her in amusement. 'How can you be sure?' he asked.

'You can't be much of a country person if you don't know the signs of the weather,' she replied accusingly.

'Four years' fighting in a war makes a man forget a lot of things,' Gavin countered weakly.

Outside the wind began to howl and shriek around the chimney stack and under the eves with renewed vigour.

Chapter 32

Kate Dawtry had been right. There was a snow storm during the night, piling the snow in great banks so that when Gavin awoke he thought it was still night for the snow completely covered the tiny window of the spare bedroom in which he slept. He lay for a moment in the warm cot with its comfortable corn-husk filled mattress. When the girl had shown him it last night in the light of a fluttering tallow candle she had explained that it had been Grandpa Tom's room. It was cold and she apologized for it. It had not been used in a while. It had taken Gavin some time huddling under a couple of heavy blankets to warm up sufficiently to be able to fall into a sound sleep. He had lain thinking about the girl for a while, contrasting her vivacious practicality to the pertness of Rosaleen McHale and the wistful sadness of Nora Quinlan before asking himself why he should be making that contrast.

The first sound that indicated that it was later than he thought was the clucking of hens and a distant plaintive mooing of cows. He swung out of bed. The room was bitterly cold, and frost had formed inside the windows as well as outside. He hurried into his clothes and went into the main room. He could relax here in the warmth. Someone had already built up the fire and buckets of water, brought in from the night before, stood next to it in order to thaw the ice which had formed on them. A kettle was simmering on the stove. The door opened as he stood undecided what he should do and Young Tom entered staggering under a stack of logs. Gavin came forward to help him.

'Feeling better?' he smiled.

The boy, who was about eleven or twelve years old, smiled shyly back.

'Thanks, mister. Thanks for pulling me out last night.'

Gavin could see he was none the worse for the experience and smiled. 'Where is your sister?' he asked.

'Down at the shed milking the cows,' replied the boy, stacking the fire.

Gavin felt guilty then. He had lain asleep while the daily chores of the farm were being carried out. He drew on his boots, coat and scarf and pushed open the door into the cold morning. The wind caught him like a knife. It was never this cold in New York City; never this cold during the winters he had spent campaigning in Virginia during the war. Pulling his scarf over his mouth he trudged through knee-high snow in the direction of the barn. By the time he reached it he felt he had trudged a thousand miles.

Kate Dawtry glanced up with a smile as she removed the bucket from beneath a patiently standing cow.

'Came to see if I could do anything,' Gavin said awkwardly. 'I must have overslept. The snow covered the window.'

The girl smiled mischievously. 'If you spend any time on a farmstead you'll soon get an inbuilt clock to tell you when to wake up no matter how dark it is.'

He did not rise to the comment. 'Can I do anything now?' he pressed.

'You can carry the pail of milk back to the house,' she said as she pushed the cow into its stall.

They said nothing as they trudged to the cabin. Gavin noticed with astonishment that by the time they reached it a thin sheet of ice had formed over the milk which had been warm enough when it had come from the cow. Kate Dawtry chuckled at his expression.

'I can see that you've never had a winter in these parts before, Mister Devlin. You'll get used to things freezing around here. I've seen my washing water freeze round the edges while I've been washing in it.'

She took the pail from him and put it down near the range. Young Tom had kept up a considerable blaze in the stove and was now laying the table for breakfast. Gavin sat awkwardly while the girl began to fry thick cuts of bacon and eggs. He noticed that the loaf of bread sparkled with ice as she took it from the cupboard and set it near the stove to thaw. As they ate he became aware that Young Tom was regarding him curiously.

'Have you killed many people?' the boy asked suddenly.

'Tom!' exclaimed his sister in outrage.

'Katey told me you were a soldier in the war,' went on the boy oblivious to her indignation. 'Have you killed many people?'

Gavin bit his lip, unused to such directness. 'Soldiering is a job, son, much like any other. It has rules – things you do and don't do. One of the things you don't ask a soldier is who he has killed or how many. Killing is not a thing to boast about.'

The boy stared solemnly at Gavin. 'But killing in war is all right, isn't it? The dominie was telling us about the wars in Europe. . . .'

'The who?' queried Gavin.

'The dominie,' interposed Kate Dawtry, explaining. 'The schoolteacher.'

Young Tom nodded. 'He says we have to be proud of soldiers fighting for their country and all.'

'True, son. If a soldier is fighting for a moral cause, fighting for his people in order to protect them, then one can be proud but that doesn't make killing a good thing nor a thing to be proud of. What you have to be proud of is that people are willing to die for certain principles. . . .'

He trailed off seeing the puzzled look in the boy's eyes.

'Hush up, Young Tom,' Kate Dawtry intervened. 'You'd better be off to school or you'll be late. Are you sure that you feel okay now?'

The boy nodded. He rose from the table and put on boots and coat and took a knapsack which his sister handed him.

'Goodbye, Mister Devlin,' he said solemnly.

'Don't go falling into any more creeks, d'you hear?' smiled Gavin.

When he had left Gavin asked, 'Is the school house nearby?'

'There's a school house down towards Sherk's Crossing, maybe three or four miles,' Kate Dawtry replied.

'It's a long way to walk.'

The girl chuckled. 'You were raised in a town, weren't you, Mister Devlin? Some kids have to walk eight or maybe ten miles to school in these parts.'

Gavin sipped his coffee awkwardly. He was not doing well in his efforts to merge into this society.

'I'll be chopping some wood for the night's lodging, Miss Dawtry. I noticed you were out of kindling.'

The girl nodded and sighed. 'It's been difficult since Pa died keeping up with the chores.' She bit her lip. 'Fact is, Mister Devlin, I've been thinking about what you said . . . about looking for work.

The thing is . . . well, there's a number of jobs to be done on this farmstead but I just can't afford to pay you.'

Gavin seized with enthusiasm the opportunity that she hesitantly presented. 'Forget about the payment for a while. I only need food and lodging.'

The girl looked dubious, holding her head to one side, her brows drawn together. 'Well, there's wood to be cut and piled; the spouts need to be got ready for tapping the maples; I need to rack off the cider and sort the potatoes in the cellar; there's fencing needing to be fixed and a harness wanting repair; some tools need fixing, too, before spring. Then I have to collect cions for the grafting. . . .'

'If there's work needs to be done, I can do it,' Gavin assured her.

She did not look convinced. 'You haven't worked on a farm before though, that's obvious.'

He shrugged as if it made no difference. 'You tell me what to do and I'll do it. I can turn my hand to anything after four years in the army.'

'It's not easy work,' she began. 'Also, it's folks I'm also thinking of. . . .' She hesitated and a colour came to her cheeks. 'Well,' she explained as Gavin looked perplexed, 'we're a small community here and there's only Young Tom and myself on the farm. Folks will gossip.'

Gavin smiled easily. 'Folks gossip no matter what,' he said. 'If you care about their talk, no matter. I'll go on into Port Colborne. But if you really want those jobs done then to hell with them.'

The girl returned his smile readily. 'To hell with them,' she agreed. 'But are you sure you want no more than food and a bed? I can't give more.'

It was a matter of indifference to Gavin if he received payment. The important thing in order to fulfil his mission for the Brotherhood was to get a place to stay and some work which would allow him to merge with the people and the landscape so that his presence would excite no suspicion from the authorities. He was almost eager when he said: 'I will work for food and lodging.'

'It's a deal, Mister Devlin,' she said. 'Leastways, it's a deal until spring. Once winter is out of the way then I shall decide what to do about this farmstead, whether to sell up and go to the city. All my life I've wanted to get away from this place. Then Pa died. . . .' she shrugged.

Gavin gazed at her. 'I can't see you in a city.'

Kate Dawtry laughed bitterly. 'I hate this place, Mister Devlin,' she said. 'I hate farming. This is no life, labouring all day long, sometimes all night as well, just to grow enough to feed ourselves. The only thing farming has brought my family is heartache and failure. Grandpa Tom had this dream of freedom, of being independent and he thought farming would bring it to him. It was just a sentence to a lifetime of slavery. Yet he wouldn't give up the dream. He was a stubborn old man. All my life I've seen farmers eventually give up that dream and move to towns in search of other work. Independence! I've seen a farmer setting out to be independent; seen his work horse die, hippozymosis the veterinarians call it; I've seen their crops rot in the fields because, with a horse dead, the farmer has no means to bring them in. I've seen a farmer become a beggar in a single day because of bad weather or crop disease . . . and what can be saved from the weather and crop disease is destoyed by wild animals. Independence! That's not the independence that I want for the rest of my life, Mister Devlin. I'm sick of such independence.' The girl's face was quite animated and she paused as if amazed to hear her confession to a stranger. 'But if you'll accept bed and food in return for helping with the chores,' she confirmed, 'it's a deal.'

'It's a deal, Miss Dawtry.'

'You might as well call me Kate,' she invited. 'Just so long as you don't call me Katey. Young Tom does it only to annoy me.'

'All right, Kate,' Gavin felt an exuberance. 'Call me Gavin. And I'll begin to earn my keep right now by getting you that wood.'

Two days later Gavin was felling some cedar trees to repair the split rail fencing that marked the boundaries of the farmstead. He had adapted quickly to the tempo of life on the farm, rising early and going to bed early and in between times carrying out all manner of chores that he had never thought himself capable of. It was the noise of bells that caused him to pause in mid-stroke and he straightened up to see a one-horse sleigh entering the gate. Its occupant was muffled in furs but handled the reins expertly, swinging the vehicle to a halt before the log farmhouse. As the bear-like figure descended and paused to hitch the horses to a nearby rail, Young Tom came running round the side of the building yelling in delight.

'Jim! Jim!'

'Hi, Young Tom!' The voice was a man's, a rich baritone carrying a vaguely familiar accent to Gavin's ears. He frowned, trying to place it. 'Where's your sister, son?'

'In the house, Jim. Come on!'

The bear-like figure turned, apparently catching sight of Gavin for the first time, and halted. Even though there was only fifty yards between them, the figure paused and regarded Gavin carefully, hesitated and then followed Tom into the farmhouse. Gavin bit his lip. He was sure that there was something familiar about the man. He tried to dredge forth some recognition from his memory. Eventually he gave up the task and resumed his attack on the cedar wood. He had been working another hour when Kate Dawtry emerged on the verandah and called to him.

'Coffee up, Gavin!'

Gavin laid aside his axe, swinging it hard into a block of wood. He wiped the sweat from his face and rinsed his hands in a bucket by the well before going down to the verandah where he stamped the snow from his boots.

'Hello, Devlin.' The man who had arrived was standing by the stove, divest of his furs, and grinning crookedly.

Gavin's mouth slackened as he stared into the pleasant-faced, handsome man with blond hair and twinkling blue eyes. 'Captain Taylor!' He had last seen the surgeon-captain at the victory celebration in Washington.

Kate had not been prepared for the recognition because she stared in astonishment from one to the other of them.

'You didn't tell me that you knew Gavin, Jim.' she accused.

Taylor shrugged. 'I wasn't sure myself if it was the same man, although I thought I recognized him outside. Your arm is obviously healed, Devlin.'

Gavin took Taylor's proffered hand but the handshake was quick, a formality with no warmth in it. 'Exactly as you predicted it would, doctor,' Gavin replied.

Young Tom was staring up at Gavin, his eyes wide. 'Were you wounded in the war, Gavin?' he demanded. 'You never told us.'

'Hush up, Young Tom,' admonished his sister. 'Just how do you two know each other?'

Gavin turned to hang up his hat and remove his boots. He let the Englishman tell the tale. Taylor eased himself into a chair. 'I treated Captain Devlin in my field hospital at Petersburg during the Twelve Days' Campaign at the end of the war.'

'Captain Taylor probably saved my life,' affirmed Gavin. His mind was working back over the memories. He remembered Taylor saying in Washington, 'I'm heading back to Upper Canada to set myself up again as a country doctor in a nice, quiet township by Lake Erie. Hope to marry, too.' It was a small world.

'I guess this is that quiet township you spoke about in Washington when we last met?' he asked.

Taylor inclined his head, remembering the conversation.

'And did you get married?'

Taylor flushed and glanced at Kate. So it was Kate Dawtry who was the girl that Taylor had intended to marry? Gavin saw the look and felt a strange pang of envy go through him.

'Not yet,' Taylor said stiffly.

'Jim is our local doctor here,' Kate said, ignoring the exchange as she handed them coffee. 'It's quite amazing that you two knew each other during the war. Of course, I knew Jim served in the Union Army as a surgeon but you didn't tell me that you were a captain, Gavin, or that you were wounded.'

Gavin shrugged, 'Not much to tell.'

'Well,' smiled the girl, 'it's a coincidence all the same.'

Taylor was looking at Gavin with slightly narrowed eyes. 'It *is* a coincidence, isn't it?' he pressed sharply. 'Exactly what are you doing here, Devlin?'

Gavin hesitated before the doctor's belligerent note.

'He's helping us out on the farm, Jim.' It was Young Tom who eased him through the awkward moment with boyish enthusiasm. But it had been obvious that Kate had already explained what Gavin was doing before she called him down to the cabin for coffee. Taylor had a suspicious frown as he stared at Gavin.

'You're no farmer, Devlin,' he said softly.

'Never said I was, Taylor,' Gavin stirred uneasily.

'Fact is,' Taylor pressed, 'I recall you said that you were a lawyer out of New York City, isn't that right?'

'Quite right,' he agreed, trying to keep his voice even in spite of Taylor's growing hostile suspicion.

'We don't often have New York lawyers round these parts looking for jobs as farm hands,' he sneered.

'Jim!' Kate was aware of Taylor's hostility now. 'Gavin saved Young Tom's life. You've no call to question him like this.'

Taylor's eyes did not leave Gavin's face. 'I think I do, Kate. Since your Pa died I feel responsible for you.'

'Well, I didn't ask you to,' she stormed. There was unbridled temper in the girl now. 'This is my farmstead and I hired Gavin. He satisfied me.'

Taylor coloured a little under her attack but he stuck to his guns.

'Perhaps he should satisfy me,' he said quietly. 'One old comrade to another.'

'Satisfy you about what, Taylor?' Gavin demanded, equally quietly. He recognized that Taylor was only being hostile and suspicious because he was in love with Kate Dawtry and for no other reason. Gavin could handle jealousy. He just hoped the man would not remember his service in the Irish Brigade and start making a connection with the Brotherhood.

'Kate is a young woman here alone. . . .' Taylor began.

'Jim!' The girl was really angry now. 'You are presuming on our friendship. I think you should leave and come back when you are in a better mood.'

Taylor sprung to his feet as if she had slapped him. 'Kate. . . .' he began.

She turned her head to look elsewhere. He bit his lip and scowled at Gavin. Gavin lowered his gaze in embarrassment for the man. He wished he had not made an enemy of him. He was aware of Young Tom gazing at them all in bewilderment. Taylor, tight-lipped, grabbed his furs and stamped from the room. Gavin moved to the window, watching as Taylor's sleigh swung truculently out of the farmyard.

'Perhaps it would be better if I left, Kate?' he asked. 'I don't want to cause problems.'

'No!' snapped Kate. 'Jim Taylor doesn't run this farmstead.' Then she caught her temper and lowered her voice. 'I'm sorry, Gavin. Jim's not usually like that. I can't understand his behaviour.'

Gavin smiled softly. 'The man is jealous, that's all.'

Kate Dawtry flushed again. 'He has no reason to be,' she said hotly.

'He thinks he has. That's what matters.'

The girl flung back her head. 'You'd best finish the wood for the fences before the light goes,' she said tightly.

Chapter 33

Three weeks into February the mild weather broke and a severe frost set in across the valleys and mountains of County Meath, lingering long and sharply around An Bhaile Dearg. The ground hardened preventing the ploughing and Peadar Finucane, with a fatalistic shrug resigned himself to tree felling for the next week. John-Joe volunteered to help Murna mend some thatch on her cabin which had been torn through by the chickens pecking on the roof. The skies were thick and heavy with a promise of more snow and yet newborn lambs were already at play on the hillside, their high-pitched bleats sounding loud in the stillness, while the feeding ewes appeared extraordinarily white against the dark mountainside. In spite of the sharp cold there were mistle thrushes, *smólach mór*, Murna called them, singing in a little group near the stone wall at the back of the house where some had built their nests and were hatching their first broods of the year.

'Will it snow today?' John-Joe asked, as he climbed on to the thatch with straw in his hand to repair the damaged area.

Below him Murna shrugged. 'The sky is ready for it.'

Perched on the roof, John-Joe frowned as he saw the figure of a horseman suddenly appear through the trees below the village. He screwed up his eyes.

'Who is it?' called Murna, hearing the sound of approaching hooves.

'Dualta, I think,' called John-Joe.

They waited as Dualta Hanrahan made his way up the track, halted his horse and slid off breathlessly.

'What's up?' demanded John-Joe sensing the tension in the burly ostler. An expectation rose in him. Was it word from the Military Council? Was it the long-awaited word of the rising? His hopes were dampened immediately.

'Bad news from Dublin, I'm thinking,' replied Dualta, glancing at Murna and then shrugging at John-Joe. 'Everyone will know soon enough. Devoy has been arrested, tried and taken to England for fifteen years' penal servitude.'

John-Joe stared at him with a cold, sinking feeling. Devoy! The young man's grim face, the cut of his iron jaw, came to his mind. He had placed his trust in Devoy; in Devoy more than the romantic figure of Stephens. Stephens was the dreamer. Devoy was the man of action; the one who could bring the romantic dream to fruition. But Devoy was gone; fifteen years' imprisonment. Who could survive that?

'Is there a dish of tea in the house?' Dualta was asking. 'I've ridden from Navan this morning with the news.'

Murna turned into the cabin and soon returned with the tea.

'*Go raibh maith agat*,' Dualta thanked her as he took it and sipped eagerly. He paused and glanced at the shocked face of John-Joe. 'There's worse to come. . . .' He hesitated.

'Worse?'

'Save for Stephens, General Halpin and Colonel Kelly, the entire Military Council are all arrested. Lord Wodehouse has suspended habeas corpus and Colonel Wood's Irish Constabulary are raiding the countryside and arresting suspects by the hundreds.'

'Damn it!' John-Joe smacked his balled fist into the palm of his hand in exasperation. 'We must rise now or the chance will be lost.'

Murna seeing his agitation tried to reassure him. 'Those in Dublin will know what ought to be done, John-Joe,' she said.

John-Joe climbed down off the roof and, ignoring Murna, stared hard at Dualta. 'Is there no word from Stephens?'

Dualta shrugged. 'He's promised that the rising will be soon. That's all I know.'

'Soon!' jeered John-Joe. He was about to say something else when Seán Ó Cleirigh came running up, panting in the cold air. He gasped something to Dualta in Irish before running back the way he came. His words were too quick for John-Joe to grasp any meaning to them.

'What is it?' he demanded.

It was Murna, pale faced, who replied. 'It's the police,' she whispered. 'Police on the town road with Dashfort and Connor at their head. Their halting at Cáit Ní Nualláin's cottage. *A thiarcais!* He means to start his evictions now!'

Cáit Ní Nualláin's cottage was below the village on the far side of the bridge. Ó Cleirigh had roused several of the people in the village and they were converging in a stream down the hillside towards the grey stone cabin. They gathered outside it, a small sullen crowd. The Constabulary stood in a semi-circle in front of the cottage, rifles held across their chests, bayonets fixed. Their eyes were cold and dispassionate under their helmets as they surveyed the crowd. Dashfort sat at ease astride his roan mare directing half-a-dozen men in civilian clothes throwing out the few pitiful belongings of the Ó Nualláin family. Young Diarmuid Ó Nualláin stood with his arm around his mother's heaving shoulders. The old woman knelt on the ground before her cabin, she was sobbing and her voice was incoherent. Two other Ó Nualláin children, no more than eight or nine years old, stood behind her, clutching each other's hands, frightened, fearful as they gazed up at Dashfort while he directed his men in nasal tones. As the thatch of the cabin began to be ripped off the woman shrieked aloud and scrambled towards Dashfort's horse on her hands and knees.

'*Nach bhfuil trua ar bith agat dúinn a dhuin'uasail? Níl an sneachta imithe ón talamh fós,*' she wailed. '*Cá mbeidh ár dtreo, gan díon os ár gcionn lenár gcosaint, gan bhia lem pháistí a chothú, gan teaghlach, gan tine lena ngoradh?*'

Dashfort stared down at the old woman with distaste on his autocratic features.

'*An bhfágfar ar leath thaobh bhóthair sinn agus bás leis an bhfuacht agus leis an ocras i ndán dúinn? Mhair mo chéile, sabhála Dia a anam, agus mhair a athair agus athair a athar roimhe, ar ndóigh, mhair a sheacht sinsear ar an talamh seo agus shaothraigh siad é.*'

'Get this old bitch to stop her gibbering!' snapped Dashfort.

Thady Connor, the overseer, slid from his horse and tried to catch at the woman's shoulders to drag her away but she shrieked even more loudly.

'*Nach duine de na Nualláin ar bhain na clocha chun na ceithre bhalla den bhothán seo a thógáil. 'Sé seo mo theaghlach féin. Níor theip orainn riamh an cíos a íoc, a dhuin'uasail, fiú amháin le linn an Ghorta Mhóir. D'íocamar i gcónaí, ach níl sé ar ár gcumas cuid ar bith den mhéadú cíosa a íoc, a dhuin'uasail. Glac trua dúinn. Cé'n fáth atá tú ag déanamh an ghníomh seo?*'

In a desperate effort the old woman caught at Dashfort's stirrup to stop Connor hauling her away.

'Stop that woman's jabber,' snapped Dashfort. 'Talk English, woman, like a civilized person, dammit!'

Diarmuid Ó Nualláin had sprung forward to seize Connor's arm to prevent his hauling at his mother.

'My mother has no English, captain,' he called, his voice shrill. 'She is asking you why you are doing this to us when our family have lived here generation after generation. She says that the cold of winter is still on the ground and, therefore, why are we to be cast out to die of cold and hunger on the roadside? We have always paid the rent even during the Great Hunger.'

Dashfort sneered down at the boy. 'You are not paying rent now, boy. That is reason enough why you are to be evicted.'

There was a terrific crash as the thatched roof of the cottage went plunging in. Dashfort looked up to where his workmen were completing their task of destruction and nodded in satisfaction.

'Set fire to the thatch,' he ordered sharply. 'We don't want these beggars crawling back and raising the roof again.'

A low murmur went round the circle of onlookers as a man fired a torch. Cáit Ní Nualláin's voice rose in a wailing cry of despair. John-Joe clenched his hands impotently and took an involuntary step forward but Murna's hand was on his arm. She gave him a warning glance.

Cáit Ní Nualláin, still struggling with Connor, wrenched at the stirrups of Dashfort's mount, her voice wailing a despairing lament as the wreath of smoke began to ascend and the crackle of flames was heard. Dashfort kicked out, sending her reeling backwards into the mud and slush of the ground. Diarmuid Ó Nualláin sprang forward only to meet a stony faced policeman who held his rifle at the ready, the bayonet not an inch from the boy's heart. Seán Ó Cleirigh reached forward and dragged the boy back whispering something which John-Joe could not hear.

Dashfort turned his horse and gazed at the sullen crowd. 'You might as well all know that I intend to clear this land to make improvements on behalf of Lord Mountcarrick's estate. This is Lord Mountcarrick's land and you only live on it by his sufferance and generosity. Let this . . .' he waved a casual hand towards the burning cabin, 'let this be a warning to you. If you can pay the new rents, I will ensure that you are moved to other accommodation on the estate. If you can not, then you must leave the estate and find work elsewhere.'

'But we have lived on this land for generations. Our families have been here longer than Mountcarrick,' cried Seán Ó Cleirigh. 'We have rights!'

Dashfort permitted himself a thin smile at the flushed-faced young man. 'Then show me your deeds, show me your proof that you are owners of the land you claim. Where are your rights?'

'We don't need a paper from Englishmen to prove Irishmen own Irish land,' retorted Seán Ó Cleirigh.

Dashfort glared down, hand on hip. 'Sergeant!' he called, to a pale-faced sergeant of police. 'Mark that man! I want him flogged and thrown off my land. He's a trouble maker. A Fenian, if ever there was one.'

There rose an angry murmur and the villagers closed in around Seán Ó Cleirigh in a protective motion, pushing him to the back, away from the line of police.

The sergeant's eyes narrowed as he stared around at the faces of the people. 'Perhaps you should return to Castle Carrick now, sir,' he muttered.

Dashfort dismissed the man's apprehension. 'We shall have little trouble with this vermin,' he said loudly. 'They need a strong hand. They need discipline.' He stared at the burning cabin and nodded in satisfaction as the flames rose higher.

'*Cacamas!*' cried a voice that sounded to John-Joe remarkably like Seán Ó Cleirigh's voice.

The lump of mud struck Dashfort on the shoulder, splattering across his nice clean blue coat, the little specks spreading over his flushed features.

'*Cacamas!*' cried the voice again. '*Scrios dearg ort!*'

Emboldened, Diarmuid Ó Nualláin, standing at the edge of the crowd bent to follow the anonymous thrower's example. Unfortunately, the boy was standing too close to one of the constables. Even as he rose with his handful of mud, the man jerked his arm and sent the butt of his rifle crashing against the boy's head so that he fell senseless to the ground.

'Damn these rogues!' snarled Dashfort. 'Take the boy up. I want him taken to jail at Kells, sergeant. The charge will be assault . . . no, attempted murder.'

Cáit Ní Nualláin let out a fresh wail of despair as two of the constables picked up the unconscious form of the boy. Some of the village women were firmly pulling her away from the scene as Dashfort signalled his men to move off. The sergeant called for his constables to form up and turned to the people.

'Get about your business now,' he cried, He hesitated as no one moved and then repeated in Irish, '*Amach libh as seo anois*!'

Still the crowd did not move.

The sergeant licked his lips. 'Company,' he yelled, 'present!'

The lines of policemen presented their rifles, the bayonets still attached glinted wickedly.

'I said, get back to your homes,' the sergeant called again.

They still stood there, silently watching the flames devouring the cottage which had been Cáit Ní Nualláin's home.

The sergeant's face was pale with tension. 'Company, aim . . . !'

The rifles pointed to the crowd without a tremor.

It was then that Dualta called something in Irish and the people let out a sigh, turned and began to disperse. A couple of them went forward to gather up the few pieces which were Cáit Ní Nualláin's belongings. John-Joe and Murna fell in step with Dualta as they climbed back towards An Bhaile Dearg.

'Well, you've seen your first eviction,' muttered Dualta grimly.

'My *first*?'

Dualta heaved a sigh. 'They're common enough. Cáit Ní Nualláin's eviction is not the first, nor will it be the last until the day when we can stop it.'

'But this can't happen,' John-Joe said helplessly. 'How can such feudalism exist here?'

'It's the way of it, John-Joe,' murmured Murna.

'Ay, it's what we are fighting to be rid of.'

'Irish tenants, must have some rights,' protested John-Joe.

'Do you know what the English say?' asked Dualta. 'Irish tenant right is English landlord wrong. Once we were free in a free land. That was before the confiscations. Now tenant farmers live and work the land under the patronage of the conqueror. They labour long hours for miserable wages. They can be evicted when the conqueror's patronage is withdrawn. You see our people, John-Joe. They are generally dispirited, disorganized and desperate. They rent their plot of land, often build a cabin stone by stone, trying to scratch a living from the poor soil which the landlord allots them. If they fall behind with rent, or if the landlord suddenly decides to use their land for his own benefit, then they are summarily and legally evicted without compensation for the improvements they have made to the land or their cabins. There is no recourse to any law for protection. We live in a conquered country, John-Joe. There is no denying it.'

John-Joe walked on in silence for a while and then he said, 'What will happen to young Diarmuid Ó Nualláin?'

Dualta shrugged. 'Dashfort is the magistrate hereabouts. He may send him to jail. He'll be a long time there. If the boy is lucky he might be transported. At least there is a freedom about labouring in the colonies. Shut up in a jail kills a man's soul.'

John-Joe was suddenly thinking about John Devoy. Fifteen years' imprisonment in a jail in England! He shivered. This was the face of conquest, then. Here was something tangible to fight against. All the songs he had heard in his youth about the old country, about Caitlín Ní Houlihan, the personification of Ireland, about liberty and freedom, strange, intangible emotions, suddenly crystallized into a hard fact. By the time he reached An Bhaile Dearg he knew what he was going to do.

'Dualta,' he said softly. 'Tell the men to meet me in Ó Buachalla's barn just before midnight.'

Dualta stared at him. 'What do you intend to do, John-Joe?'

'To teach these high and mighty lords of the land a lesson which might prevent them making further evictions.'

'Now, John-Joe,' cautioned Dualta, 'the Military Council will not approve of individual actions. We'd best consult with O'Malley.'

'The hell with O'Malley and the Military Council!' snapped John-Joe. 'You've just told me that they are all but arrested.'

'Yes, but others will take the place of those who have been arrested. They will know what is best.'

'What is best?' John-Joe gazed from Dualta to the worried face of Murna and back again. 'Do you want to see the entire village on the roadside in this winter weather? Do you want to see the children dead before spring?'

'Of course not, but what can we do?'

'Plenty,' snarled the young man. 'Plenty. Have the men in Ó Buachalla's barn just before midnight.'

Chapter 34

'Now we will strike back!'

There were eight men in Ó Buachalla's barn seated in the shadowy light of a storm lantern and watching John-Joe's animated features with a mixture of excitement and curiosity. Only Dualta looked uneasy.

'They are trying to break the spirit of the people,' continued John-Joe. 'Seán Ó Cleirigh will tell you what happened last week at Ballymeek.'

They knew the story well enough but they turned to Seán Ó Cleirigh for confirmation of it.

'I was visiting my cousin when a troop of hussars came riding into the village and ordered everyone out of doors. They lined us all up, men, women and even the children . . . the young as well as the old and the sick as well as the healthy. We were made to stand with our arms raised and all were searched. No officer rebuked his men when one or two of them hit the people. The priest, Father Farrell, rebuked them and a sergeant hit at him across the cheek with the flat of his sword.'

Seán Ó Cleirigh hesitated and wet his lips. 'The same sergeant said that the men must be searched properly and we were all made to strip . . . strip in the presence of the women. And when we had stripped many of us were beaten. They called us Fenian bastards, took what food they could find, all the liquor in the village and rode away. But that was not the end of it. Father Farrell rode into Kells to protest to the English commander there and has not been seen since. The people at Ballymeek are too scared to go to Kells to find out what happened to him.'

There was a silence.

'You all know what happened at Cáit Ní Nualláin's cabin this afternoon. They are trying to break our spirit,' John-Joe said again.

It was then that Dualta sighed. 'It has been going on in this country a long time, John-Joe. It is nothing new.'

John-Joe wheeled in anger. 'Is your spirit so broken that you sit back and accept it?'

'We must wait for the rising. . . .' began Dualta.

'Then we will wait for ever,' snapped John-Joe. 'In the meantime, the English and their paid servants are allowed to bluster and terrorize their way through this country, burning homes, evicting the old and the young, allowing them to die in ditches by the highways. They have robbed us, beaten us and killed us. Now we will strike back!'

The men stirred expectantly.

'Do you have a plan, John-Joe?' demanded Seán Ó Cleirigh.

'We must challenge our oppressor. He thinks he is strong and can ride roughshod over our people, making us obey out of terror of him. He thinks that because he has more weapons, a trained army and all the power of an empire behind him he need not fear us. We will answer his terror with our terror.'

Dualta thrust his face forward towards John-Joe. 'Words are easily spoken,' he said softly. 'What can we do that could strike fear into men like Dashfort?'

John-Joe glanced round and smiled thinly. 'This afternoon Captain Francis Dashfort burned the home of Cáit Ní Nulláin leaving her and her children to beg or starve on the roadside. Tonight we will burn the house of Captain Francis Dashfort as a reprisal, leaving him to suffer in the same way.'

A murmur of excitement went through them.

'Is it right?' demanded one of the younger men. 'Revenge is condemned by the priests.'

'It is not revenge that I am advocating,' replied John-Joe. 'It is retribution. Doesn't the Bible say . . . eye for eye, tooth for tooth, hand for hand, foot for foot, burning for burning, wound for wound, stripe for stripe?' His face was flushed now. 'Burning for burning is what we will give Dashfort and he will learn by it.'

Several of them growled their assent and John-Joe turned to Dualta. 'Dualta, this is your company. I have no right to command it but I shall unless you are with us.'

'What do you intend?' asked Dualta.

'There are eight of us. We will take some storm lanterns with us. Make sure they are filled with oil. Each of us must also be armed, although I want to avoid bloodshed. I am after Castle Carrick and not human life. If we strike at the houses of the rich, they will soon learn the message and pass it on to their police and soldiers. For every cabin that the military burn in Ireland, they will find one of their fine homes burning. The odds are in our favour in this exchange. We will soon stop their terrorism.'

'And the plan?' pressed Dualta.

'We divide into two sections when we reach the grounds of Castle Carrick. Dualta will take one company and go to the outhouses and barns to fire them. I will command the other company and we will fire the house. As soon as the place is alight we will disperse to our homes.'

'It seems simple enough,' Dualta nodded reluctantly.

'Then you're with us?'

Dualta hesitated. 'It should be cleared with O'Malley. . . .' he began.

'And O'Malley will say wait for the word of the rising. I say we must strike now.' He glared at Dualta and repeated: 'Are you with us?'

Dualta heaved a long sigh of reluctance. '*M'anam!*' he said eventually. 'I am.'

The night was bright. The moon shone from a cloudless sky illuminating the countryside in shades of blue and grey, causing the hedgerows and trees to send long black shadows across the roads and fields. John-Joe and his men paused behind a hedge and gazed down from the small hillock at the great sprawl of Castle Carrick. It was not a castle in any sense of the word that John-Joe knew but, as Dualta had told him, didn't the English call every moderate house they built in Ireland a 'castle'? Castle Carrick was, in fact, a mansion built with impressive Georgian elegance, a brick façade with imposing columns and many windows. The outhouses and barns were grouped at a respectable distance beyond the house and a mile along a trackway, which ran through spacious lawns, stood a lodge house which guarded the tall iron gates to the road that ran clear to Kells.

John-Joe examined the shadowy approaches to the building. There seemed no sign of movement anywhere. The house was in darkness. The silence was broken only once by the barking of a dog from somewhere behind the structure. He reached into his pocket and checked the Colt revolver that lay there.

'Ready?'

There were whispered assents in the darkness.

'Dualta, take your section to the outhouses. Wait until you see the flames from the lower rooms of the house before you fire the barns.

Don't forget, it is the house that I want burned. Guns are to be used only in self-defence.'

'It is understood, John-Joe,' Dualta said grimly.

'Then let's go.'

They split into two groups and moved quickly and silently down the hillside under the cover of the hedgerows until they came to the stone walls which surrounded the gardens of Castle Carrick. Without a sound they heaved themselves over. Once on the other side, Dualta and his section vanished in the direction of the outhouses. John-Joe with his three companions ran, half crouching, keeping as low as possible to the ground, towards the back of the building. Tall French windows opened at the back to a small lawn where, it was obvious, the family would take their meals in the more mild days of summer. The windows were closed and bolted now. John-Joe made his way to them, paused and reached for a clasp knife. It took him a few moments to lift the latch of the first pair of windows and ease them open.

'Who has the storm lanterns?' he whispered.

Seán Ó Cleirigh came forward with three lanterns on his arm. Nearby, a dog suddenly started to bark. John-Joe swore. The dog had obviously been roused by Dualta and his men. They stood hesitantly. An upstairs window abruptly scraped open and someone yelled to the dog to be quiet.

'Quickly now,' whispered John-Joe, grabbing one of the lanterns from Seán Ó Cleirigh. He pushed into the room, a library judging from the rows of books across the walls. He moved forward, splashing the oil from the lantern, ensuring that it fell across the furniture and over the books. He turned, took a second lantern from Seán Ó Cleirigh and emptied it as well. Then he gestured his companions back to the window.

The voice from the upstairs window had grown suspicious as the dog continued to growl and bark.

'Damn it! There's someone by the barn!' came Dashfort's voice. A moment later a pistol cracked and a voice started yelling.

John-Joe, standing by the French windows, seized the third lantern from Seán Ó Cleirigh, struck a light, and cried, 'Run now, boys!' It was no use trying to maintain cover. He lit the wick and then stretched his arm back and threw the lamp into the library room. It exploded with a great whoosh of flame. He stayed only a moment more, watching as the eager flames leapt hungrily across the room.

Then he turned and ran swiftly across the lawn towards the stone wall of the garden.

The house was awake now, cries and yells pierced the air. Further down towards the outhouses he saw flames leaping and shadows rushing from the barns. A moment later Dualta and his men joined them in the shadow of the wall.

John-Joe took in the scene with satisfaction. 'Dualta, you'd better cut across to the road and stop anyone coming up from Ballymeek to put out the fire. It needs ten minutes for the flames to really do their work. Then disperse your men.'

'There's no one in Ballymeek or An Bhaile Dearg who will volunteer to put out Dashfort's fire,' muttered Dualta.

'Isn't there a company of Constabulary at Ballycross?'

Dualta nodded, as he saw what John-Joe meant. 'Ten minutes,' he agreed. 'We'll hold the road for ten minutes.' He moved his section off into the darkness.

John-Joe signalled his men to climb the wall. A number of figures were spilling out of the house now in several stages of dress while some were still clad in their nightclothes. The flames were getting a firm hold now and sending out a fierce flickering light across the scene. John-Joe paused on top of the wall as he caught sight of Dashfort himself. The man had found time to tumble into trousers and boots, his white shirt hanging loose. He was running this way and that, his voice strident as he yelled for buckets of water. The servants were scurrying to obey him. It was only then that John-Joe realized that there was a well and pump just at the back of the house. He slid quickly over the wall to the waiting men.

'We must delay them using the well for a while,' he hissed. 'We'll fire a volley above their heads. *Above* their heads, mind. We just want to keep them away from the well.'

They checked their weapons and cautiously raised themselves above the stone wall in time to see Dashfort leading his servants towards the well with buckets in their hands.

'Ready?' hissed John-Joe. 'Present . . . fire!'

The crash of the three muskets and John-Joe's revolver came like a thunderous explosion against the crackle and roar of the flames. Dashfort and his servants flung themselves to the ground as they felt the bullets whistle over their heads in the darkness. Then Dashfort was up, a revolver in his hands, blazing angrily into the darkness, not sure of where the volley came from. The servants climbed to their feet hesitantly. John-Joe heard Dashfort scream at them to fill their buckets.

'Another volley, quickly,' yelled John-Joe. 'Present . . . fire!'

The weeks of practice had worked well. As the second volley rang out the servants dropped their buckets and fled headlong. The roaring flames were already eating up towards the second storey of the house now. The eager tongues of flames devoured with consummate ease the dry wooden timbers of the building. The barns, too, were one mass of fire and the flames were rapidly eating the buildings. Smoke swirled everywhere. There was no way that Dashfort could halt the conflagration.

'Disperse, lads!' John-Joe cried. 'Back to Ó Buachalla's barn, hide your weapons and then home.'

His three companions turned and went scurrying away into the shadows, away up the hill by the cover of the hedgerow. John-Joe hesitated hearing, far away, an uneven volley of rifle fire. He wondered whether Dualta and his men were in trouble. He turned and began to move swiftly across the fields away from the dry tinder box of Castle Carrick.

It was a feeling from the ground rather than any noise which made him halt and glance back. The horse came at him like a black shadow thrown into dark relief by the glare of the burning house behind it. A figure hung low on its back, clutching at a bridle but without a saddle. John-Joe leapt to one side as the horse charged by him. He caught a glimpse of a white shirt and an arm holding a revolver. The horse wheeled and the rider turned so that the glare of the flames fell on his ghastly face, the yellow-red flames making the man seem like some devil out of hell. Even in the distortion of the light, John-Joe recognized the features of Dashfort. Dashfort halted his horse and raised his revolver, his mouth working.

'Irish bastard!'

The revolver cracked and John-Joe twisted to one side, sprawling on the ground. He was still carrying his own revolver in his hand and he tried to scramble upwards as Dashfort urged his mount closer, trying to make more certain of his second aim. John-Joe raised himself into a kneeling position and levelled his own revolver. Dashfort seemed not to notice it. He came on screaming obscenities. John-Joe squeezed the trigger, jerking back to the recoil of the gun.

For a moment Dashfort sat on his horse, staring down in open-mouthed surprise. His revolver fell out of his nerveless hand and it seemed that some black stain was spreading across his white shirt, across his chest. Then he toppled sideways from the horse and hit the ground with a heavy thud.

John-Joe stood up shaking. His mouth dry. He moved slowly to where Dashfort's body lay crumpled on the ground. He lay on his back, an arm flung outward, eyes open and staring sightlessly at the night sky. John-Joe knelt beside him and felt for a pulse. There was none. He had shot and killed his first man. He had been expecting some emotion. He had been expecting some revulsion, some questioning of himself. He had taken a life. All he felt was an annoyance; annoyance that his plan had gone wrong. He had not meant anyone to be killed; certainly not Dashfort. He had wanted the man to live and learn the error of his ways. Dead men did not learn lessons and those that came after them merely repeated the same mistakes.

He raised his head, becoming aware of a shouting and shadowy figures moving. He stood up and set off at a trot into the darkness towards the hill. The others were waiting for him on its brow. Dualta heaved a sigh of relief as he appeared.

'There you are, *buíochais le Dia*! We heard some shots. . . .'

'It was Dashfort. He must have seen me leaving the grounds. He came charging after me.'

Dualta stared hard at him, trying to discern his expression in the darkness.

'Dashfort's dead,' John-Joe said after a moment's silence. Then, 'We'd better disperse now. There will be a hue and cry before long.'

There was no elation among them, no sense of exhilaration or success, as they silently made their way back to An Bhaile Dearg with the burning buildings of Castle Carrick flaring like a beacon into the night sky behind them.

Chapter 35

The month of February sped by so quickly that Gavin Devlin could scarcely believe that they were already a week into March with the crocuses and early buds making cautious appearances in spite of the white carpet of snow that still lay over the province of Upper Canada. Kate Dawtry said that the thaw was late this year and so far as Gavin could see the only sign of approaching spring, apart from the early buds, was the breaking-up of the ice on Lake Erie. Oddly, Gavin found himself not minding at all about the conditions. He experienced a strange sort of peace on Kate Dawtry's farmstead, even enjoying the physical exertion which was a contrast to his previous life. He cynically wondered what Rosaleen McHale would say if she knew of his new life-style. But the thought brought bitter memories to him and the frustrations he felt about the Delanceys. He wondered whether Rosie McHale had married Brock Delancey yet.

He tried to dismiss his memories of New York from his mind and gave himself over to the enjoyment of life on the farmstead. If he were honest, however, he would admit that it was the evenings that he enjoyed most of all when there was no more work to be done in the cold and dark, when he was able to return to the log farmhouse, wash up and enter the warmth of the living room where Kate would be preparing the meal for the evening. The evenings he enjoyed best of all, when young Tom had gone to bed and he and Kate could talk or read in companionable silence. The house contained numerous books, the inherited library of Grandpa Tom, the old radical rebel. Grandpa Tom had been a printer in London before his transportation to the penal colonies and literacy appeared to be a family gift, for Kate was especially knowledgeable about literature and poetry. She subscribed to several newspapers and journals and read them avidly from cover to cover.

'I suppose, if I had been able to choose,' Kate told him one evening, 'I would have been a schoolteacher. But, after Ma died, Pa wanted help on the farm and so I stuck here. Now I simply don't know what to do. I have Young Tom to think about as well. Some of the neighbours have suggested that I sell the farmstead. Mullan Naul, who owns the property around here, has already made me an offer for the farm.' She sighed deeply: 'I don't know what I should do.'

'Do you really fancy teaching in a school?' Gavin asked in some surprise.

Kate chuckled. 'There's little enough opportunity for a girl to use an education other than school teaching. To be truthful, though, I do have one ambition.'

She glanced at him coyly, as if wondering whether to reveal her secret.

'What's that?' he prompted.

'I'd like to write for a newspaper.'

Gavin saw nothing wrong in the ambition. 'I seem to recall that the Press Association of the Confederate States had two women reporters employed as war correspondents.'

She smiled shyly. 'You're the only person who hasn't laughed at that ambition, Gavin,' she said. 'Maybe one day I'll do something about it.'

In turn, Gavin found himself telling Kate all about his life, his experiences, even about Rosaleen McHale, Nora Quinlan and the Delanceys, using the Delanceys as the excuse why he had come to Canada and was not pursuing his career in law. He told Kate Dawtry everything except about his involvement with the Irish Republican Brotherhood or his mission into Upper Canada. He found himself sliding easily into a role at the farmstead, even developing a fraternal relationship with Young Tom. The boy would help him with the lighter chores as soon as he arrived back from school. Young Tom seemed to seek his company regarding him with almost a form of hero-worship. Gavin supposed that it was inevitable, since he rescued the lad and it was a fact that the boy had no father now, no man about the house to model himself on. Young Tom was obviously impressed that Gavin had been an officer in the Union Army, had fought in battles and been wounded. When Gavin gently pointed out that Doc Taylor had also been an officer in the Union Army, the boy dismissed the fact by saying that Taylor had only been a surgeon. As Kate observed, when Gavin told her, the romance and glamour in war, such as there was, fell on the people who took lives and not on those who saved them. She spoke automatically without thinking, flushing as she realized what she had said but Gavin found himself agreeing with her.

Doc Taylor himself was a fairly frequent visitor to the farmstead. The Englishman was so obviously in love with Kate Dawtry. His initial resentment of Gavin's invasion of what Taylor considered his territory modified. His anger and hostile suspicion gave way to an uneasy acceptance of Gavin's presence. Apart from his jealous attitude, Taylor was not an unsympathetic man. He shared with Gavin many reminiscences of the lighter side of the war and some evenings, after a meal, the three of them would spend time playing cards.

It was inevitable that Gavin became increasingly attracted to Kate. After all, she was an attractive woman and the circumstances of being more or less isolated on the farmstead threw them together in an intimate way. Gavin, however, strove to suppress his natural feelings of attraction. He tried to dwell on the memories of Nora Quinlan. Was it not her memory which had decided him on his entry into the Brotherhood? Yet now he was scarcely thinking of the Brotherhood. He had hardly done anything to fulfil his mission of spying out the land around the Welland Canal. He had gone into Fort Erie on 21 February and met with Major John Canty as arranged but he had no information to give him and neither had Canty any news to exchange. Now 21 March was approaching and he stirred in annoyance. Was he letting new found friendships and comfort allow him to forget his duty to the Brotherhood?

The matter was somewhat taken out of his hands when Kate announced one day she needed to go into Port Colborne to do some shopping and have some tools repaired.

'Hitch up the sleigh, Gavin,' she said. 'Young Tom can come with us. I can get him some new clothes for spring while you can take those tools into the smithy's there.'

As Gavin guided the horse-drawn sleigh into the streets of Port Colborne, Young Tom gave a cry of delight.

'Look at all the soldiers!'

Gavin's eyes had narrowed as he observed companies of greatcoated men with rifles and knapsacks marching through the streets while sentries patrolled here and there.

'What's going on?' Kate murmured wonderingly.

Gavin guided the sleigh to a tavern where Kate directed him and a stable boy emerged to lead the horse inside while Gavin helped Kate down. Arrangements were made for the horse to be unharnessed and fed and the sleigh stored until they were ready to head back to the farmstead later in the afternoon.

'You take the tools to the smithy while Young Tom and I go to the general store,' Kate instructed. 'We will meet back here for lunch at noon.'

Gavin watched the girl and her young brother trot off down the street. He took the tools from the sleigh but he did not proceed to the smithy immediately. First he turned into the bar of the tavern and ordered a whiskey.

'There's a lot of soldiers in town,' he observed, as the moon-faced barman poured the drink. 'Anything happening?'

'Just arrived?' asked the barman.

Gavin nodded, jerking his head to the tools he had leaned against the bar. 'Came in to get these fixed,' he said. 'I was just surprised to see all the soldiers. Don't get much news on the farmstead.'

'It's the Fenians. They say they're gonna invade Canada,' said the barman.

Gavin forced a chuckle. 'They've been saying that for a long time.'

'Well, rumour has it that it's gonna happen on 17 March – St Patrick's Day – that's a sort of national celebration for the Irish. So the militia has been called out.'

Gavin raised an eyebrow.

'St Patrick's Day is a week away yet,' he pointed out.

'The militia have been out across the entire province these last two days,' the barman said. 'There's rumours of an attack on the canal and on the militia posts.'

'There seems a lot of soldiers about simply for rumours,' Gavin commented.

'Four rifle companies and the Welland Canal Field Battery with Colonel Stephens of Collingwood in command,' the barman said. 'Men enough to give them damned Irish a scare. But the picquets are stationed out all day and night under arms. I've heard tell the poor lads are coming down with frost bite.'

Gavin pursed his lips. 'Do you think the rumours are true?' he asked.

The barman shrugged. 'Well, someone does, mister. Lord Monck, the governor-general, has called out 10,000 volunteer militia along with the regulars. If those damned Fenians are invading us . . . well, they sure as hell picked a fine time to do it.'

Gavin left the tavern with the tools and found his way to the blacksmith's forge. The smithy was not busy and said he would deal with sharpening the hewing hatchet immediately but the felling axe was beyond repair. Gavin examined the man's range and chose a new one. He also purchased an adze, a tool with a curved blade to smooth and shape wood.

'Are you a farmer?' grunted the smithy as he bent to the hewing hatchet.

'Farmhand,' replied Gavin cautiously.

'Got some new catalogues in for tools if you want to take one,' said the smithy, nodding to a pile of catalogues on a shelf. 'Everything the modern farmer wants, mister. Separators, combined reaper and mower, fanning mill, self-raking reaper, straw cutter . . . you name it and Massey of Newcastle will supply it. Got a good saw mill unit there – all complete with a twenty-four inch saw at forty dollars. Show the catalogue to your boss.'

Gavin grinned as he picked up the catalogue of H. A. Massey, Newcastle, Upper Canada, and flicked through its pages.

'Are you an agent for Mister Massey?'

The smithy looked up with an answering grin. 'Sure as hell am, mister. You don't think I sell his goods out of brotherly love, do you?'

While the smithy was finishing his tasks, Gavin carefully worked the conversation round to the rumours of the Fenian threat to the canal, picking up valuable information about the strategic points of the canal system. Having concluded his business, Gavin took the tools back to the sleigh at the tavern, loaded them, and then found he had time left to take a stroll through the town. From Port Colborne, which stood on the northern shore of Lake Erie, the Welland River ran northwards, parallel with the canal through a lock which was apparently the eighth lock in a series which followed the canal all the way north to Lake Ontario. Soon after Port Colborne, the river and canal divided to form a long island at the township of Welland itself before the river turned eastward to join the Niagara River. The canal pushed on for twenty-six miles, running through the series of locks at St Catharines which brought it, by gentle stages, to the level of Lake Ontario which was 325 feet lower than Lake Erie. There was still ice on the river and canals and, as yet, no ships had passed through the system since winter. Gavin's experienced eye was able to make careful note of the strategic points and the military positions around the town.

He returned to the tavern just after midday. It was crowded now, the air thick with tobacco smoke, raucous laughter and general hubbub. He stood by the door, stamping his feet, and peered round for Kate and Young Tom. He saw her almost at once and began to move towards her, loosening his scarf.

'We've been waiting,' complained Young Tom. 'I'm hungry.'

'There's a table reserved for us in the dining room out back,' Kate told him, leading the way. Behind the saloon was a tiny eating house, warm and cosy. They were soon tucking into bowls of onion soup followed by game pie.

'Were you able to get the tools fixed at the smithy?' asked Kate.

'Sure,' Gavin had been pleased with the morning's work. He had picked up a lot of information to pass on to Canty at their next meeting. He frowned abruptly, remembering his visit to the smithy. 'I picked up this for you, just in case there was anything you wanted.'

She glanced at the catalogue of farming equipment and wrinkled her nose. 'Pa would have spent hours with this. He was always talking about getting one of these Universal Cultivators for ploughing. Twelve dollars, though. That's expensive . . . especially if I decide to sell the farmstead.'

'Will you sell?' asked Gavin.

The girl raised a shoulder and let it fall. 'I've been thinking about the offer Mullan Naul made me but I don't reckon I'll take it. I don't like the man anyway.'

'Why not marry Jim Taylor?' Gavin suddenly asked, the question coming out without his thinking. He bit his tongue at his thoughtlessness.

Kate coloured, a deep flush that started from her neck. Her eyes sparkled angrily.

'Well,' Gavin tried to justify the question, 'he's in love with you, you know that. It would solve your problem. . . .'

'It's no business. . . .' the girl began hotly and checked herself.

'No business of mine, eh?' Gavin finished for her. 'No, I guess not, Kate. But you must agree that it would be a better life for you and it would get that farm from round your neck, wouldn't it?'

There was still a sparkle of angry fire in her eyes when Kate met Gavin's across the table.

'You're right,' she said coldly. 'It's none of your business.'

Young Tom, finishing a slice of raspberry tart, gazed across the table at Gavin and winked solemnly.

Chapter 36

During the first week after the attack on Castle Carrick the Irish Constabulary and the military swarmed across the surrounding areas in a series of raids on the villages. The newspapers laid the blame squarely on the Fenians, calling it 'the latest of their outrages against respectable landowners'. John-Joe spent most of the time hiding out in the tomb on Slieve na Callaigh in which he and Murna had sheltered from the rain storm on Christmas Eve. It was too dangerous to remain in An Bhaile Dearg because, once questioned, he would easily be identified as an American and arrested. Reluctantly, John-Joe spent his time hidden in the tomb with a few blankets to keep him warm but with plenty of food smuggled up by Murna or Seán Ó Cleirigh. In fact, Murna came and spent long periods with him and the days were not tedious in their passing. They spent the days day-dreaming of their future plans and John-Joe had insisted that they should be married in the fall, whether the Irish Republic was then established or not. Neither had doubts that the Republic would be in existence before the year ended.

Peadar Finucane was Murna's guardian and it was Peadar that John-Joe would have to ask permission of to marry Murna. He suspected the old man knew of their relationship already but he had not mentioned the subject so far because he wanted to make the request in Irish. He wanted to speak to the old man in his own language. It was a matter of pride. Therefore some of the hours in the cave at Slieve na Callaigh were spent groaning over a dictionary and trying to memorize the words and sentences which Murna was teaching him. But, mainly, the time in Murna's company passed with the two of them sitting together expressing the intensity of their youthful love, exchanging kiss for kiss, whispering the countless endearments of controlled passion. Once the passion threatened to erupt, yet it was John-Joe who stopped it going further.

'Ah, John-Joe,' Murna had breathed, 'I'm sick with the wanting of you.'

John-Joe had held her hands firmly and shook his head. 'Nothing must happen until we marry,' he insisted.

'I'm a woman, John-Joe,' Murna retorted angrily. 'I'm not some fragile dream. I thought you'd finished with your romantic notions long ago.'

John-Joe felt hurt but perhaps she had a right to anger. 'I love you, Murna,' he replied softly. 'I need you and want you as much as you want me. But it must be right for us. We must wait. For us, everything must be perfect.'

Her eyes were desolate but she finally nodded and gave a deep sigh. 'I understand,' she finally said. 'It will be perfect, John-Joe. I promise you that.'

A fortnight later the hue and cry died away. A number of suspects had been rounded up and released when nothing could be proved against them. There was talk that Lord Mountcarrick was despatching a new estate manager from England. In the meantime, Thady Connor was running the estate but, wisely, was not pursuing any of Dashfort's proposed evictions. Eventually John-Joe was able to return to his normal bed in Peadar Finucane's loft.

It was only a couple of nights after his return that he was shaken roughly awake and Dualta's voice hissed urgently in his ear.

'Get up! If you value your life, *mo bhuachaill*, get up!'

John-Joe came awake blinking at the man who bent over him, a candle raised in one hand while he shook him with the other. 'What is it?' he mumbled, still half asleep.

'You've been betrayed, John-Joe. The military and police have a description of you and know that you are an American officer. They know that you are in hiding in An Bhaile Dearg. There's a hundred pounds reward posted in Kells for your arrest.'

John-Joe sat up, staring at Dualta. Behind Dualta he could see the worried face of Peadar Finucane.

'Come on, man!' snapped Dualta. 'O'Malley sent me to warn you. There's a platoon of constables on their way to the village to arrest you. I'm to get you across the country to Drogheda and you're to catch a train to Dublin. You must clear out of the country entirely.'

John-Joe shook himself. 'What's the time?'

'*A thiarcais!* Five o'clock and I've horses waiting at the door. If you don't move soon you'll be caught and it'll be a rope's end for you.'

John-Joe sprang from the bed and reached for his clothes. 'Who betrayed me?'

Dualta bit his lip. 'We'll find out,' he promised grimly.

John-Joe grabbed his bag and stuffed his few belongings into it and then hastened down the ladder after Dualta into the main room of Finucane's *bothán*. Peadar Finucane stood nervously before the smouldering turf fire. His wife, Nuala, stood near, wrapped in a shawl which almost covered her threadbare nightdress but not quite. She looked anxiously at him. He was also aware that Murna was standing at the door, her face wet with tears.

Dualta muttered something, moving for the door.

John-Joe halted awkwardly before Murna. The girl's eyes were bright and her mouth was pressed into a thin line to stop its tremor. 'Murna . . .' he began, pausing as he tried to find words.

She tried to force a smile through her tears. 'You must go quickly, John-Joe. It will not take the police long to reach here.'

John-Joe glanced towards Peadar and Nuala Finucane. 'Will they be alright?' he asked.

'The police will not prove anything if you are gone.'

'Tell your uncle and aunt . . . tell them that I am sorry for the trouble I have caused them.'

Murna shook her head. 'They know the risks. It is their fight too.'

'*Íosa, Muire agus Íosaf!*' exploded Dualta from the door. 'The horses are waiting. We must go!'

'Yes, John-Joe,' the girl was trembling now. 'Please go.'

'I'll go,' agreed John-Joe. 'But I'll be back for you, Murna. Tell your uncle,' he glanced towards Peadar Finucane who stood staring silently, trying to guess what was passing between them, 'tell your uncle that I'm coming back to marry you. Tell him. . . .'

He turned desperately trying to gather the words from his poor vocabulary. '*Ba mhaith liom . . . ba mhaith liom . . . a phósadh an neacht leat!*'

Peadar Finucane's eyes widened a fraction and sought those of his niece. Murna's eyes were bright and fastened on John-Joe's face.

'I'll write to you, Murna,' he said, gripping her hands against his chest. 'I'll come back!'

Heedless of Peadar Finucane or his wife he bent forward and brought his lips against the girl's trembling mouth.

'Oh, for pity's sake go now,' she wept as she pushed him away.

'Tell me that you'll wait for me?'.he demanded.

'I'll wait,' she sobbed. 'But go now.'

'Tell you uncle that I mean to marry you.'

'He knows.'

He bent and brushed her lips again. '*Mo ghrá thú*,' he whispered. 'I love you.'

He swung to Peadar Finucane. 'Thank you for your hospitality.'

'*Go n-éiri an t-ádh leat*,' replied the old man, '*go dtaga tú abhaile slán*.' His hand was strong and in his eyes there was a smile of understanding.

Outside the *bothán* Dualta was already mounted and holding the reins of John-Joe's horse. John-Joe flung his bag up to Dualta and hauled himself up into the saddle. He gazed down for a moment at Murna's tearful face.

'*Slán go fóill, a rún*,' she tried to smile. '*Slán go fóill!*'

Five days later John-Joe boarded a train bound for Dublin's Amiens Street Station. Dualta had delivered him to a safe house in Drogheda, a coastal town north of Dublin. He had stayed with a doctor and his wife who were members of the Brotherhood. The doctor had been able to obtain a copy of the police journal *Hue and Cry* in which an accurate description of himself had been printed together with the news that one hundred pounds was offered for information leading to his arrest in connection with the murder of Captain Francis Dashfort of Castle Carrick, County Meath, and the burning of the castle. John-Joe waited anxiously until he heard that An Bhaile Dearg had been searched, its inhabitants questioned, but no one had been detained. He was thankful for that. Thankful that no harm had come to Murna or her relatives. A day or so later a message arrived from the Military Council requesting that John-Joe report to them in Dublin.

The search for him had passed beyond Drogheda and the doctor escorted him personally to the railway station without incident. To his amazement the Great Northern Railway station was packed with soldiers and when the Belfast to Dublin train pulled in there was no question of obtaining any seats, not even in the First Class compartments. Instead he found himself in the corridor jammed between a burly dragoon sergeant and a wiry corporal.

'Never heard anything like this in my entire service with the regiment,' the sergeant was grumbling. 'And I've been with the 5th Dragoons for twelve years. Served in the Crimea, I did. We were part of Sir James Scarlett's brigade at Balaclava.'

The corporal grinned at John-Joe and then spoke across him. 'Well, sarge, ain't everyone who had the pleasure of charging the Ruskies, did they? Leastways, not the lads they've arrested.'

The sergeant groaned. 'Thirty men arrested as Fenians. Half of my company! It's a disgrace, that's what it is. They'll have my stripes as soon as we are back in the Royal Barracks.'

At Amiens Street, soldiers milled around the station in greater numbers. John-Joe stood hesitantly outside the barrier wondering what to do. The doctor had simply told him that he would be met and taken to a safe house. He hesitated anxiously. It made him nervous to see so many soldiers.

'Johnny! Here I am!'

The woman's voice was shrill and made John-Joe turn in time to see a well-dressed young woman fling herself into his arms. She pressed her cheek tightly against his and whispered'; 'For God's sake pretend that you are pleased to see your cousin Jane.' She pulled back smiling up at him.

'Hello, Cousin Jane,' John-Joe blurted. 'It's nice of you to come to meet me.'

The young woman tucked her arm under his. 'The carriage is waiting outside.'

Bewildered, he accompanied her out of the station to where a coach was drawn up, its two black mares under the control of a liveried driver. The man picked up John-Joe's case and put it into the back before handing up the girl. John-Joe climbed into the coach after her. With a jerk the coach joined the traffic moving along the cobbled Dublin streets.

The young woman was chuckling apologetically. 'I swear that you must think me very forward, Lieutenant Devlin. I have been asked by Colonel Kelly to meet you and escort you to your destination.'

She smiled and then leaned out of the coach window to call up to the driver. 'The shortest route to Kildare Street, Christy.'

'Yes ma'am,' came the reply.

'Was your journey without incident?' the girl asked, turning back into the coach.

'It was fine,' replied John-Joe. 'May I ask who you are?'

'A friend, that's all you need to know,' the girl answered. 'Officially, I am just your cousin Jane.'

John-Joe glanced through the window of the coach and raised his eyebrows in astonishment as he saw companies of armed soldiers stamping noisily across the Tara Street Bridge and moving northward.

'What is happening? There are so many soldiers on the streets.'

'The English are moving their troops into new dispositions. Every day new boatloads arrive at Dublin Quay to reinforce the garrison here. Arrests are taking place daily.'

He bit his lip as he gazed at the soldiers while the coach swayed southwards over the cobbles, round the imposing buildings of Trinity College and south into Kildare Street. They stopped at a fashionable house almost opposite the Kildare Street Club which, as John-Joe already knew, was the centre of the most extreme Unionist faction in Ireland. The girl, seeing his glance towards the edifice draped with the English Union flags, chuckled.

'What could be safer?' she asked. 'No policeman would think of looking for a fervent Republican hideout opposite such a loyalist stronghold, would they?'

She dismounted and tripped gaily up the steps of a wealthy looking house. Someone was obviously watching for them for she had no need to ring the bell. A solemn-faced butler swung open the door. John-Joe followed the girl into an imposing-looking hallway.

A woman, whose features proclaimed her to be related to John-Joe's companion, came forward with an expression of relief.

'Jane, dearest, thank God you're back. Was there any trouble?' she glanced rapidly at John-Joe.

'No trouble at all, Mary,' smiled the girl addressed as Jane. 'I've brought him.'

'Come this way, Lieutenant Devlin,' said the woman, turning to him. 'My husband is expecting you.'

John-Joe felt bewildered. 'Your husband, ma'am?'

'Mister Stephens.' John-Joe's jaw dropped a fraction as the woman went bustling up the stairs calling him to follow. She led the way up to the attic and paused to knock on a door.

'Lieutenant Devlin,' she called as she ushered him through and closed the door after him.

The attic room was bathed in a dingy light permeating from a skylight. James Stephens had not altered much since John-Joe had seen him in November. He sat in an arm chair before a small cast-iron stove which glowed softly and sent a warmth into the room. He was clad in shirt sleeves and a waistcoat which was unbuttoned. He was more pale and strained than John-Joe remembered. There was only one other occupant of the room, Colonel Tom Kelly. Only Kelly rose to shake his hand.

'Good to see you again, Lieutenant Devlin.'

John-Joe smiled briefly and turned to examine the silent, almost moody, figure of Stephens.

It was Kelly who spoke. 'We've had a full report about the Carrick Castle affair.'

John-Joe said nothing.

'Do you justify your action, Lieutenant Devlin?'

John-Joe stared down at Stephens. 'Do I need to?' he said softly.

'Damn it, you do!' It was Stephens who broke his silence by snapping at him.

'Dashfort was planning to evict an entire village, probably all the villages on his estate. I heard that all but three of the Military Council had been arrested, including John Devoy. There was no word about any probability of the rising except the same platitudes. . . .' He paused to let his phraseology sink in '. . . the same platitudes I've heard for months – that it would be soon. I decided, in view of the circumstances, that something had to be done locally; some action to deter Dashfort. I took that action by burning his house as a reprisal for the burning of the cabin of a poor woman and her family which he had evicted. Dashfort was meant to benefit from that lesson. He was not meant to be killed.'

There was a moment's silence.

'Is that your justification?' breathed Stephens. His voice was still angry.

'That is my report,' corrected John-Joe.

Stephens glared up at him.

'Damn it, Devlin, do you realize that you could have placed our entire plan for the insurrection in jeopardy?'

John-Joe could not suppress a sneer. 'Insurrection? We have been promised that the word for the insurrection would be given for the past year and where is it? The people of this country cannot wait for ever while men like Dashfort trample on them and their rights. The Brotherhood is supposed to protect the people and not stand waiting idly by for a rising that never materializes.'

Colonel Kelly's face was strained. 'Listen, Lieutenant Devlin,' he said quietly, 'the life of a nation is at stake here. We cannot act without thinking. When John Devoy was arrested in Pilsworth's bar last month there were many others arrested along with him. It seems that we have an informer in our military wing. As well as civilian members of the Brotherhood, arrests of soldiers who have taken the Fenian oath are becoming a daily occurrence. What is more important is that the English are quickly removing the regiments which we have managed to infiltrate out of Ireland and replacing them by loyal English troops. The recruits we have made among Irish soldiers, such as those in the garrison troops here, are now of no use to us. The 10th Hussars and 5th Dragoons are under orders to embark for England while the 8th, 24th and 61st Foot Regiments and the 9th Lancers are being replaced. Our whole military organization has been severely damaged. Do you really want Mister Stephens to declare for a rising now?'

'Why didn't he declare for it last year?' retorted John-Joe. 'Why not early this year? The organization in the army remained in perfect shape until the end of last month. If he had declared for a rising any time up to February the whole Fenian body of the army, armed and trained men, would have been fully ready and set the English a far more formidable task to combat than the uprising in India a few years ago. Why didn't Mister Stephens act then?'

Stephens sat with an angry scowl on his face. 'I suppose you are the great expert in such matters, Devlin?' he asked sarcastically. 'You will benefit us with your wealth of experience, eh? I had taken part in a rising and was wounded in it, before you were even born.'

'Is that a justification for your present inaction?' demanded John-Joe angrily.

Stephens paled and rose to face John-Joe levelly. 'I have grasped more of the truth than any other man. While others may have dreamed of it, I created this organization. *I* did! I will not be criticized by any arrogant young. . . .'

Kelly stepped in hastily. 'Gentlemen, let us be calm.' He turned to John-Joe with a troubled expression. 'The situation here is critical, Devlin. The English have dealt us two great blows. The suppression of our newspaper, the *Irish People*, also resulted in many of our leading members being arrested and imprisoned. Now someone has betrayed our organization within the army. To try and declare for a rising now would only result in unnecessary bloodshed and the inevitability of our defeat.'

Stephens abruptly sat back in his chair with a low groan, his head cradled in his hands. John-Joe was shocked. For the first time he realized that Stephens was an indecisive, broken man, who was still trying to cling to power for his own self-esteem.

Colonel Kelly bit his lip and continued, 'You may have heard that there has been a tragic split in the Brotherhood in America. The great potential of that movement seems almost a total loss to us at this time. The arms and men which we desperately need are being diverted to another cause. The major part of the Brotherhood there has swung behind a man named Roberts who has a crazy idea to invade the British North American colonies and establish an Irish Republic-in-Exile there. There is no alternative but to delay the uprising in Ireland and for Mister Stephens to go personally to America to appeal for the movement to re-unite and support the insurrection in Ireland. In Ireland and no where else!'

John-Joe's face tightened. 'I see no insurrection in Ireland to be supported. I don't know what Roberts's plan is but at least it appears to be a plan for action and not inaction; a plan to strike a blow and not sit back while the English crush our movement and our people are pushed even further in oblivion.'

'You are entitled to your opinions, Devlin,' replied Colonel Kelly softly. 'But you are a soldier of the Republic. There is a description and warrant out for your arrest. It is no longer safe for you in this country. You are to return to New York. . . .'

An image of Murna flashed before his eyes. 'I can not,' he protested.

'That is an order, Lieutenant Devlin,' snapped Kelly. 'Stephens and myself are leaving shortly for Paris. Mister Stephens will then go on to New York and try to talk sense into Roberts and his men. You will come with us to Paris and then continue on with Mr Stephens to New York.'

'I have unfinished business in this country,' John-Joe said stubbornly.

Kelly stared at him. 'We all have unfinished business in Ireland,' he said coldly. 'We have unfinished business until Ireland is a free nation once again.'

John-Joe shrugged in resignation. Colonel Kelly was probably right. It was best for him to get out of the country. He could write to Murna. Perhaps he could send for her to join him in New York?

'We'll be leaving in a day or two,' Kelly said. 'You'd best get some rest now.'

John-Joe hesitated. 'If I wrote a letter to someone, is there any way I could ensure delivery? It's to a lady in An Bhaile Dearg.'

Kelly's features softened slightly. 'If that's the way of it, then your letter will be delivered safely enough. However, a word of caution. I would delay the writing until you are safe in Paris. I will be returning to Dublin after a while and you have my solemn word that I'll ensure its delivery.'

John-Joe paused a moment, meeting the steady grey eyes, and then accepted the honesty of the man. He turned to the silent Stephens and suddenly felt sorry for him. The strain showed on his face. Gone was John-Joe's romantic image of *An Seabhac Siúlach* – the shadowy Wandering Hawk that would lead an invisible army against the oppressors of Ireland. The man sunk in the chair before the stove in the attic room was just a middle-aged, stoutish man, whose figure was showing signs of fat and whose shoulders bore too heavy a responsibility. Care oppressed his face, lending dull shadows to his anxious eyes. Here was the man on whom a nation relied for its liberty; on whom the hopes of millions of Irish men and women rested. And the bitter truth was that James Stephens no longer was equal to their hopes.

From Paris on Tuesday, 18 March 1866, John-Joe wrote two letters. The first letter was to his parents.

Dearest Ma and Pa,
You may be surprised at receiving a letter from me in Paris. I arrived in the city late last night in company of certain other gentlemen whose names I will not mention. I expect to be in New York within a month and all the details will wait until I see you then. Suffice to say that there were pressing reasons as to why I had to leave Ireland. Indeed, I and my companions had to effect an escape for the English were out in force waiting to discover us. We were in hiding in Dublin until the evening of Thursday last when it had been arranged for a certain ship to transport us. That evening we made our way to the City Quay where the captain of the vessel sculled us in person to his ship which was anchored at the mouth of the River Liffey where we were taken on board. We were disguised as crew members and what clumsy sailors we proved to be.

Our ship slipped its moorings about 1.30 a.m. on Wednesday and our captain, who had an eye for devilment, sailed us out of harbour between two English warships, set to watch for escaping Fenians. Then we sailed into rough weather and for three days our little ship ran before a gale, finally putting in at a Scottish port called Ardrossan. We stayed a night in Kilmarnock and then took the mail train to London itself. I can boast of having visited the capital of the British Empire. The irony of it all was that we spent one night there at the Palace Hotel which is opposite Buckingham Palace where I looked in vain for signs of the little English queen. How she would have ranted had she known that three such desperate revolutionaries as us slept a mere stone's throw away from her palace walls?

We crossed to France yesterday and arrived in Paris that evening. We were met by John Mitchel, whose fame is well known. He is a strange, brooding man. I think he is greatly marked by his experiences and resentful that his half-baked theories on slavery have made him the object of great criticism among his own countrymen. Nevertheless, for all that, he remains an Irish patriot. He is now arranging our passage to New York where I hope to acquaint you with my news in detail.

I have heard no news about Gavin. I suppose he is married now and settled to the practice of law. Give him a warm embrace from me. My fondest wishes and love until I see you both again. John-Joe.

The second letter was addressed to Murna Finucane at An Bhaile Dearg in the County of Meath, Ireland.

My darling Murna,

Mo ghrá, mo chroi! How I wish I had the gift of tongues to learn how to be able to write such a letter as this in the language of my ancestors which is still your own beautiful speech. You will see from this, dearest Murna, that I have reached Paris safely. To my amazement there are many Irishmen here who are sympathetic to our cause. Even more astonishing is the fact that there are many children of Irishmen and great-grandchildren of those who once served in the Irish Brigade and Irish Legion of France. Among such prominent personalities is General Patrick MacMahon of the French Army who played host to a reception in our honour. He solemnly reminded us that the French army records show that half a million Irishmen gave their lives for France during the existence of the French Irish Brigade. He also recalled that Marshal of France Bernadotte, who became King of Sweden, so admired Irish mythology that he named his first-born son Oscar, after the ancient Fenian hero who was son of Ossian. Mister S. told me afterwards that Marshal Bernadotte's wife was actually the daughter of a Dublin merchant who had settled in Marseilles.

Soon, my love, we depart for New York. I hope the parting will be brief and that I shall soon be back with you in An Bhaile Dearg. But if the months pass and there is no prospect of me being able to return to Ireland in safety, then I shall ask you to bestow on me a blessed favour. If I cannot come to you in Ireland, will you come to join me in New York? I will ensure that you receive passage money and more to supply your needs to make the voyage in comfort. Be wife to me in America until such time as we can return to live in a free Ireland. God grant you send a speedy 'yes' to this letter. Write to me care of my father, Doctor Manus Devlin, in Greenwich Lane, New York City.

If you see my good friend D. convey to him my affection and to all I know in An Bhaile Dearg. To your uncle and your aunt please tend my sincerest respect and high regard. But to you and you alone I send all my love which will last until the great oceans become deserts. *Mo ghrá thú.* John-Joe.

Chapter 37

March in Upper Canada had continued cold with snow still carpeting the ground. There were still many jobs to be done, especially now that spring was approaching. Behind the farmhouse, for example, stretched a forest with many maples whose trees supplied Kate with sugar, syrup and the main ingredient for candies. Early March had been the time to tap the maple trees by draining their sap in pails. In spring, so Kate told Gavin, the best sap flowed on the south side of the tree but later, when the syrup season started properly, sap was taken from the north side. After collecting it, the cloying substance was boiled in kettles. Milk, eggs or even pork fat was added as a clarifier. When the syrup boiled, the dirt rose along with the eggs and was skimmed. The liquid was then boiled again until it was so thick it could be used as sugar. Candy was also made by taking spoonfuls of the liquid and dropping it into the snow where it hardened and became toffee.

As March progressed Gavin also followed the alarms concerning the Fenians through the columns of the newspapers. The province of Upper Canada manifested considerable anger against the Irish and the newspapers were full of scathing attacks. Every Irish-Catholic was regarded as a Fenian and the owner and editor of the moderate *Irish Canadian*, published in Toronto, was actually assaulted outside his offices. The fear of an invasion combined with an uprising caused the provincial government to cancel the St Patrick's Day parades and celebrations on 17 March, although this ban did not stop Michael Murphy, as president of the Hibernian Benevolent Society of Toronto, pressing ahead with a demonstration. Although Murphy had attended the Philadelphia convention of the Irish Republican Brotherhood, claiming to be head of the Brotherhood in Upper Canada, the fact seemed unknown to the authorities for Murphy was not under government scrutiny.

Both Upper and Lower Canada, along with the other provinces of British North America, were gripped by an invasion fever throughout the month. Leading newspapers, such as the *Toronto Globe* and *Toronto Leader*, put the blame squarely on the administration of President Johnson and called upon him to 'bring an end to the proceedings of the Fenian Society throughout the Union and prevent the threatened raids across the border'. Sir Frederick Bruce, the British ambassador in Washington, sought a private meeting with President Johnson to express the disquiet of Her Britannic Majesty's government and enquire about his attitude to the private army being assembled on American soil for the purpose of invading her neutral neighbour. With a brisk smile, President Johnson began to speak of the aid Britain had given to the Confederacy during the civil war, of the raids that had taken place across the border from the British provinces into the United States, of the warships that had been built in British shipyards for the Confederacy. Sir Frederick listened to the recital with ill-concealed annoyance. The government of the United States was willing, added President Johnson, to enter into a negotiated settlement for compensation from the British government. With a flushed, angry face, Sir Frederick left the White House.

In the threatened provinces a new and virile phenomenon was emerging . . . the force of nationalism with Thomas D'Arcy McGee rising as the self-appointed prophet of a new Canadian patriotism. The individualism of the provinces, the hostility to a central authority, was now fading as the concept of a single state, stretching from coast to coast, binding the people together as one strong nation, began to seize popular imagination.

The day for the meeting with Major John Canty, 21 March, fell on a Wednesday and Gavin asked Kate Dawtry if she would mind him taking the day off away from the farm. It was obvious that she was interested in where he was going but she did not ask the question and Gavin did not volunteer information. He arrived at the City Hotel in Fort Erie just before noon. Canty was already in the dining room starting on a plate of pork and beans and a glass of beer. Gavin hung up his coat and went casually to the table at which Canty was seated.

'Mind if I join you, mister?' he said loudly, for the benefit of those around. 'I like a bit of conversation when I eat.'

Canty took the cue and jabbed at the seat opposite, 'Help yourself.'

The proprietor came bustling up and took Gavin's order. Gavin watched the man move away and smiled dryly at Canty. 'I didn't bargain on the winter being so long and cold in these parts.'

Canty prodded at his food with his fork and glanced swiftly about him before saying softly, 'Have you been able to move about yet? The troop dispositions around Port Colborne and along the canal are becoming a matter of importance for headquarters.'

They fell silent as the proprietor came back with Gavin's meal.

'The main troops stationed around Port Colborne consist of a volunteer artillery company,' Gavin kept his voice low. 'They are the Welland Canal Field Battery commanded by a Captain King. The battery is only a hundred men strong. Half of them are stationed in Colborne and the others are at a place called Port Robinson, twelve miles north along the canal.'

'Artillery?' Canty's eyes narrowed. 'What pieces of ordnance do they have?'

'Two twelve-pounders were based at Colborne and two at Robinson. They had ammunition wagons and equipment housed in wooden sheds which were inadequately guarded.'

'You are using the past tense,' Canty observed quizzically.

'The artillery brigade-major of the district, a Colonel Villiers, decided that the guns were so inadequately guarded that he had them shipped up to Hamilton,' Gavin smiled. 'The Welland Canal Field Battery is now an infantry company.'

Canty chuckled. 'God bless Colonel Villiers!' Then seriously, 'Are there no regulars stationed along the canal?'

'Not unless you count a bombardier named McCracken of the Royal Artillery who is the drill instructor for the battery.'

'What about the rest of the canal? Surely they must have some regular troops along it?'

'No,' Gavin replied with a shake of his head. 'No regulars at all. There are only militia companies at Thorold and St Catharines.'

Canty whistled softly under his breath.

'So far as I could learn,' Gavin added, 'the nearest regulars are stationed in Hamilton.'

'That means that the whole Niagara frontier is wide open with only a few militia companies to guard it,' Canty said excitedly.

'That's about the size of it,' Gavin agreed. 'Now, what is the news from headquarters? The newspapers here are filled with Fenian fever. There are too many alarms for my liking. The militia seem to be in a permanent state of readiness.'

'Sweeny is concentrating on building up his strength, purchasing arms and gathering intelligence.'

'Is there any news of the rising in Ireland, though?'

Canty glanced at him in surprise. 'You haven't heard?'

'You have access across the river, major,' Gavin pointed out. 'The newspapers here carry little information about Ireland.'

'The English have suspended habeas corpus, more leaders have been arrested and they are transferring out of Ireland any regiment that contains Irish troops. It seems some informer told them about the extent of Fenian infiltration into the army there and the English went into a blind panic thinking they would have to deal with a situation similar to the Indian Mutiny.'

It meant nothing to Gavin. 'Remember a few years before the war when there was an uprising in India against the British? Thousands of Indian troops threw in their lot with the insurrectionists.'

Gavin vaguely remembered something happening in India before the war. It had not really concerned him, although he knew that his father had been excited by it.

'Anyway,' Canty was continuing, 'the word is that Stephens has fled the country and is now in Paris.'

Gavin's eyes widened. 'If Stephens has fled the country, what hope is there for an uprising in Ireland?'

'Precious little. It means now, more than ever, that the first blow in the fight to liberate Ireland must be struck here where we are strong enough to fight the British on their own terms.'

Canty began rising to his feet. 'Next month then, Devlin. Same time,' he muttered, nodding a farewell.

After Canty had gone, Gavin sat back and finished his beer leisurely. There was nearly two hours left before his train was due to depart from the local depot and he decided to use the time in a stroll through the township. It was a small enough place, a few streets and a population, according to a notice board, of scarcely 600 citizens. He made his way down to the quays to look at the Niagara River. There had been quite a change since he had last seen it when he had walked across it from Buffalo. There was still ice in the river but the current was flowing swiftly and several sturdy ships were already making the passage to and fro between the American and Upper Canada shores.

Gavin stood for a while on the wharves gazing at the river while he smoked a cheroot. He realized that he had been staring at a figure further along the wharf for a few moments before a vague feeling of recognition came into his conscious mind. The man was standing with his back to him watching the approach of a large steam ferry which was pushing its way to the shore against the blustery winds and squalls. It wasn't until the man turned slightly, so that Gavin could see his profile, that he realized who he was. There was no mistaking the copper-coloured hair, the thin, almost hawk-like face made ugly by bulbous lips. It was Hogan, Brock Delancey's hired killer.

Gavin's jaws clamped around the end of the cheroot, mashing it in his mouth. He raised a hand to his mouth and spat out the pieces of crumpled cheroot in disgust. Hogan! He backed behind a large pile of timber which stood on the end of the wharf. The ferry which plied between Fort Erie and Buffalo was a wood-burning steamboat and Gavin uttered a prayer of thanks for it, for the logs, piled high on the wharf in readiness to load on the ferry, provided him with an adequate cover.

Again he wondered what Delancey's man was doing here. Why here of all places? Perhaps he was waiting to cross back into the United States? It seemed such a coincidence. Gavin stood watching Hogan as the ferry came alongside and bumped gently against the wharf, rousing everyone with several short blasts on its whistle. Hogan was gazing up at the decks of the ship while the sailors made it secure to its moorings. A gangplank, bearing the ferry's name, *International*, on its sides in big letters, was slid out and passengers began to disembark. From his stance, Gavin realized that Hogan was apparently waiting for someone. A few moments later a well-dressed man of short stature with greying hair and dour features came down the gangplank carrying a valise. Hogan moved forward and they exchanged a few brief words and then, together, they turned from the wharf, passing within a few feet of the spot where Gavin hid.

Gavin did not know exactly what compelled him but, as the two men left the wharf, he pulled his hat down and began to follow. He had not forgotten his crusade against Brock Delancey and his father, the senator. Hogan might be the way of approaching them. Perhaps he would be the weak link which would bring their empire crumbling. But Hogan was a dangerous man. Even though Gavin felt a fear of him, he had to know what the man was doing and whether it was connected with the activities of Brock Delancey. He simply had to follow him.

Hogan and his companion, whose age Gavin estimated to be about fifty, walked into the township deep in conversation, neither looking to right nor left. They eventually halted before a prosperous-looking house, mounted some steps to the door and were allowed admission. Gavin waited for some time before it became obvious that they were going to be awhile inside. He wondered whose house it was? The answer was supplied in a simple way. As he hesitated outside the house uncertain as to what he should do, a maid came out with a basket of washing.

'Hey, what are you hanging round here for?' she demanded indignantly as she spied Gavin staring at the house.

'Looking for work,' Gavin's reply was automatic. 'Do you need a handyman here, ma'am?'

'We do not,' said the maid with a disdainful sniff. 'Be off with you!'

'But they told me that Mister Jones was looking for a handyman. This is his house, ain't it, ma'am?'

'This is Doctor Kempson's house. I know of no Mister Jones around here. Now be off with you, less'n you want to get locked up. Doctor Kempson is the reeve of this township.'

Gavin frowned a moment. Reeve? The local magistrate. Now what would Hogan be doing with the local magistrate? A distant clanging of a train bell brought him back to earth again. He gave up the idea of waiting to see Hogan come out and hurried back to the railroad depot. It was a mystery. What was Delancey's hired killer doing in Upper Canada at all, and here at Fort Erie, meeting with the local magistrate; The bell of the train clanged more insistently. There was nothing he could do about it now. He had no time to go pursuing Hogan. He boarded the train back to Sherk's Crossing with a sense of frustration.

The rest of March slid by quickly enough. The Fenian fever began to die a natural death although there was one more local scare. Doc Taylor called by one afternoon and told them about an alarm at Port Maitland, further along the lakeshore, west of Port Colborne, at the mouth of the Grand River. A story had spread that the Fenians had arrived by boat and captured the township. The nearest troops were the Barrie Rifles, a militia unit stationed at Dunnville, four miles up river from the port. The company were called out at midnight in icy cold weather with orders to march with all speed to Port Maitland. The road was in a dreadful condition, winding through marshy peatbogs and the night was dark and sleeting, a raw wind slicing like a cold knife. Some civilians from Dunnville acted as guides for the troops, going ahead carrying lanterns, but, in spite of this, the soldiers had to march through mud and mire, splashing through icy cold waters. It took them two and a half hours to cover the four miles to the harbour town.

Port Maitland was dark and quiet, sleeping in blissful ignorance of any invasion. Captain Mackenzie, the commander of the Barrie Rifles, who was a stickler for order and the rule book, insisted on rousing all the inhabitants, posting sentries, dousing all lights and ensuring an absolute silence was preserved while awaiting the coming Fenians. Four cold, miserable hours later the soldiers, soaked and shivering in the grey light of dawn, were still awaiting the non-existent invasion. The Barrie Rifles were finally marched back to Dunnville, sore, angry and frozen. There were some among them who whispered that the alarm and the fatiguing march had been a test arranged by some over-zealous senior officer.

For the volunteer militia of Upper Canada, March had come in like the proverbial lion, roaring defiance, rushing its troops here and there to the border in readiness for invasion; but it had gone out meekly like a lamb as many of the militia troops were disbanded, returning home to their civilian jobs. The idea of a Fenian invasion faded and became something of a joke.

Chapter 38

The snows vanished at the beginning of April with a surprising abruptness. There had come a warming trend in the weather bringing heavy rainfalls, swelling the small creeks to raging torrents and the rivers to mighty waterways which flooded the low-lying areas. The buds and shoots began to break through everywhere, following the cautious crocuses of March, and soon a carpet of spectacular colour was spreading across the countryside among the meadow trefoils and sprouting sumac shrubs. The deep green shades of spruce and hemlock were varied by the new growth and lighter shades of the beech, cedars and oaks. Black walnuts spread in profusion and cherry blossoms began to appear along the highway called the Garrison Road.

'Time to start seeding,' Kate Dawtry announced as she gazed out at the crisp blue skies. 'There was a fog on the fields when I looked out earlier this morning. That means it will stay sunny today.'

Gavin had seen enough of the girl's powers of weather observation not to argue with her predictions.

'We can put in the barley crop. . . .' she was saying, pausing at the sound of a horse turning into the yard. It was Young Tom, glancing out of the window, who announced the visitor.

'It's Mister Naul.'

The dislike in Young Tom's voice and the shadow which passed across Kate's face caused Gavin to observe, 'He looks like an unwelcome visitor.'

Kate nodded, biting her lip. Agitation showed on her face.

'I told you that Mullan Naul had offered to buy this place when Pa died. I told him to wait until spring for an answer. I don't like him. He owns five entire sections down towards Port Colborne.'

'What does that mean?'

'That he's a pretty powerful landowner around here. These are small farms and a section is one-and-a-quarter square miles of land.'

'Kate Dawtry!' The man called from outside, his voice harsh and unpleasant.

'I thought it was in your mind to sell the farmstead?' Gavin said quickly as the girl stood up and went to the door.

She glanced at him and made a face, 'Not to Mullan Naul,' she said. 'Not on his terms.'

Gavin rose and went to the window so that he could observe the man without being seen. Mullan Naul had not climbed down from his horse but sat astride it in front of the farmhouse. He was a big man with a bushy beard that came halfway down his chest. Above the beard Gavin saw the face was pock-marked, the eyes sunken and dark. The hair was uncombed, tumbling out from beneath a woollen cap. For once nature had apparently mirrored the inside of a man's character with a suitable outward appearance. Naul sat on his horse, leaning slightly forward, his huge hands resting on the pommel of his saddle.

'Spring time, Kate Dawtry,' he greeted the girl as she came out.

'A beautiful spring, Mister Naul,' she replied evenly.

'You survived the winter then, eh?'

The jeer made Gavin bristle slightly.

'It would seem so.'

'Guess you won't be wanting to spend another one here, eh?'

When Kate did not reply the man went on, 'My offer to buy still stands. Only, because of the deterioration of your property during the winter, I'll have to cut my price by a third. You wouldn't like me to make a loss on the deal, eh?'

'There is no deal, Mister Naul,' Kate said clearly.

The ugly man looked puzzled. 'You can't manage this farmstead and you know it,' he said sharply.

'That's my business. I'm not selling to you.'

'I'm doing you a favour, girl. You'll not get another offer.'

Gavin saw the girl's chin come up defiantly. 'A favour? You're not fooling anyone. You've bought out enough farmers in your time at way below market price, playing on the fact that they wanted to get out in a hurry. You've built up a big slice of property in these parts. Well, Mister Naul, my property is not on the market.'

'You'll regret this . . . !' began Naul.

Gavin moved quickly to the door. 'That sounds remarkably like a threat,' he said mildly.

Mullan Naul jerked his head towards Gavin, his eyes narrowing as he examined him. 'Ah . . .' There was a sneer in his voice. 'I've heard that you had hired help. Must have been a cosy winter, eh?'

Kate flushed at the insolence in his voice. 'You get off my property, Mullan Naul!' she snapped. 'Get off this minute!'

Naul spat reflectively, ignoring the girl. 'What's your name, mister?' His black eyes burned with an angry fire as he gazed at Gavin.

Gavin told him. Mullan Naul's mouth parted slightly, showing his teeth among the blackness of his beard. 'Devlin, eh? Gavin Devlin? That's a Papist name; a bloody Teig name, mister.' He looked towards Kate. 'You have a care, girl. If you are sheltering Fenian scum then like as not you'll be in for a visit from the Peep o' Day Boys. Remember that and I'll be back in a couple of days for a more . . .' he paused and smile evilly, 'considered reply to my offer.'

The man hauled his mount in a tight circle and trotted from the farm yard.

Gavin glanced at Kate, seeing her face was pale, and then frowned after Naul. 'What did he mean?' he demanded.

Kate turned and her face had an expression of incredulity.

'You don't know? I thought you said your parents were Irish?'

'Sure, but what did he mean about the Peep o' Day Boys?'

'Mullan Naul is a member of the Orange Order in these parts. There are a lot of Orangemen in Upper Canada.'

The Orange Order. Gavin knew the folklore history well enough. It had been formed by Episcopalians in 1795 as a society to maintain the English Ascendancy and Protestant institutions in Ireland. Prior to the Act of Union of 1801, the Orange Order had been violently against the Union with England but, with judicious wooing by the English government, after the Union they had become a society to maintain it. In 1834 the Order, which had been exclusively Anglican, opened its ranks to all Protestant denominations, allowing the majority Protestant religion in Ireland, the Presbyterians, to flood it. It became a tool to keep English supremacy in Ireland and from Ireland the Orange Order spread to the New World. Gavin had heard his father tell tales of hooded members of the Order riding out at night, burning and driving Catholic Irish from their pitiful hovels and homes.

'You mean the Orangemen operate here?' he asked.

Kate nodded. 'Everywhere in the southern part of Upper Canada, especially in Toronto, you'll find Orangemen parading on the Twelfth of July.'

The Twelfth of July 1691 was the day when the Williamites had finally destroyed the Irish armies and their French allies at Aughrim . . . Aughrim of the Slaughter where, in a single day, Ireland had lost 7,000 men and 400 officers in a battle which set the seal on the English conquest.

'My Ma came from Biddulph township,' Kate said. 'She used to tell me horrifying tales of what happened there because the hatreds of Ireland seemed to have been transferred to Biddulph. In March the Catholics would hold their celebrations and in July the Protestants would have their parades. One night a Catholic barn would be burnt down, the next night a Protestant barn would be sent up in flames. Cattle and horses would be maimed. Men in white masks rode the fields at night. Whiteboys were the Catholics while the Protestants called themselves the Peep o' Day Boys.'

Gavin stared at her grimly. 'And Mullan Naul is threatening you with the Peep o' Day Boys if you do not sell to him.'

'They wouldn't dare harm me,' Kate replied but she sounded worried. 'But you carry an Irish name, Gavin. He's just trying to blackmail me through you. I would have a care about Naul and his friends. I told you that he has a bad reputation.'

'But what are you going to do about the farmstead?'

Kate shrugged. 'I haven't decided exactly. One thing I do know is that Mullan Naul is not going to get his hands on it.'

The next day Gavin was fixing the split rail snake fence that marked the border of the farmstead on the concession road. Young Tom had a day off from school and was helping him by holding the tools and spike nails while Gavin lifted the split cedar wood rails into position. The fencing along the concession road was old and rotting in several sections. Around midday Kate Dawtry brought them some lunch from the farmhouse.

'It's a beautiful day so I thought you two would like to eat out here.'

'Good idea,' Gavin smiled, driving the last nail home and rising to view his work critically.

'How's it going?' asked the girl.

'Thanks to Young Tom,' replied Gavin, grinning at the boy, 'this section will be completed by supper time.'

Young Tom threw out his chest proudly. 'Gavin said he couldn't do it without my help, Kate,' he told his sister.

'Neither could I. It takes two men to put up these fences.'

'And you can help me, too, Young Tom,' said his sister. 'I forgot to bring a blanket down here to sit on. Run back to the barn and bring back one of the horse blankets.'

The boy went racing away.

'He's a good kid,' Gavin said as he collected the tools and stacked them.

'Sure, and you are quite a hero for him.'

Gavin looked worried. 'That's bad, Kate.'

'Why? Pa always told me that boys ought to have heroes, men to look up to and model themselves on. You saved his life, I'm not forgetting that, and so it's natural that he looks up to you. He enjoys having a man about the place and someone who he can pretend he is helping.' She grinned suddenly. 'And speaking of helping, the Svensons are holding a barn-raising bee tomorrow and the whole neighbourhood is invited. Everyone gathers to help build a barn and have a party at the same time. You don't have to come, but I'm going to help Mrs Svenson prepare the food and Young Tom is coming as well.'

'I'll come,' Gavin smiled. 'It sounds fun.'

'It's hard work,' pouted Kate.

'It still sounds like fun.'

The next day was the first warm day of spring, almost as if the weather had been designed for the Svenson's barn raising. Gavin drove Kate and Young Tom to the farmstead which was a few miles away, arriving to find women already laying out long trestle tables piled high with food and bottles. Three open fires were blazing away on which iron pots were simmering. Across the fields they could hear the 'gee' and 'haw' of men leading oxen teams as they moved logs to where others were waiting to saw them into suitable lengths. The partially built framework of the barn was already towering into the sky. Men were passing bottles freely to each other while children ran about shouting with laughter in spite of the fact that now and again a man or woman would raise their voice to scold them.

The barn raising was an excuse for a great social gathering among the farmsteaders in which all the neighbours were invited to help in the erection of a new barn. Each neighbour brought tools but all the materials necessary for building the barn had already been obtained or made and placed ready. More importantly, two or even three days had been spent on the preparation of the food for the feasting and dancing which followed the actual work. That preparation seemed even more important than the work itself. Only one man in the community received payment for his labour on that day, that was the framer. Everyone else volunteered their help because they knew that when their turn came for building a barn or a house then their neighbours would come and help them too. Even Doc Taylor was in attendance in case of accidents in the construction.

A fiddler was supplying music while the work was being carried on. Young Tom had run off to join the children playing while Kate went to help with the cooking. Gavin, taking a hammer and handsaw, joined a group of men and was quickly set to work driving the long iron spikes into wooden planking. It was not hard but simply monotonous and soon he had worked up a sweat so that when a bottle was passed to him in turn he did not refuse. The barn was rapidly taking shape. The beams and posts were jointed by mortise and tenon, held in place by wooden pegs. Then the completed sections of the barn frame were raised into place by men on the ground using long poles while the men standing high on the frame itself guided the sections upwards. Each section was joined by beams and joists until the barn frame was completed. The beams were thick and strong and had to be so in order to support the weight of several tonnes of hay which would later be stored in the loft of the barn as cattle feed in winter.

At midday came the call to lunch. The men washed in the nearby creek and then headed for the trestle tables, laughing and shouting, to feast on hot bowls of pea soup, legs of pork, venison, eel pie with plenty of potatoes on the side. There was raspberry pie to follow and huge iron kettles full of tea or jars of whiskey to wash it down with.

It was only after he had finished eating that Gavin realized the dour Mullan Naul was one of the thirty or so men who were working on the barn. He caught the man watching him sourly and gave a mental shrug, turning away to search for Kate. He saw her standing with Doc Taylor and his spirits fell as he watched her animated face gazing up at the handsome features of the doctor. He had an uncomfortable feeling of resentment. He knew Taylor was in love with Kate and it was obvious that Kate had a high regard for the doctor. He knew he was attracted to Kate. Who wouldn't be? But he had no right to be jealous. He turned back to his work with a sigh.

The call for the afternoon break for tea brought Young Tom over with a steaming tin mug. He ruffled the boy's fair hair fondly and went in search of Kate. Before he saw her slight figure, poised in a defiant attitude, he heard the harsh voice of Mullan Naul. The voice was loud and carried.

'You *will* sell to me!'

Kate replied something he could not hear but, in answer, Naul seemed to make a threatening gesture. Before Gavin could act Doc Taylor pushed the girl to one side and faced the big, black-bearded farmer. Naul, with heavy set and broad shoulders, seemed to tower over the slight figure of Taylor. People, sensing trouble, were quickly converging towards them.

Birger Svenson, the elder of the Svenson brothers who owned the farmstead, was tugging at Naul's arm.

'Go home, Mullan,' he was cajoling. 'This is not the time for business argument nor bitterness. This is the time for neighbourliness and good spirits. The women have worked hard to make this a kind day.'

'Yes, go home, Naul,' Taylor echoed. 'I'll accept that the drink was in and the wit was out.'

Mullan Naul spat in anger. He stood swaying slightly, one hand tousled his black hair as if he were making up his mind what to do. Someone laughed. Naul's movements were slow, deliberate, but unexpected. He swung at Taylor, sending him spinning to the ground.

Kate gave a cry of fright while Birger Svenson and his brother Stefan tried to catch hold of the big farmer but Gavin saw Naul raise his boot to impact with Taylor as he struggled up.

Gavin reached the group almost as the blow landed and pushed his way through just as Naul shook himself loose from the Svensons' grip with an angry growl, like a bear shaking loose worrying dogs.

'You should have taken good advice when it was given, Naul,' Gavin exclaimed softly.

The man glared at Gavin, his eyes were red from drinking. He frowned a moment and then chuckled. 'The bloody Teig!'

Birger Svenson caught hold of the man again but Naul gave a backward sweep of his arm sending the anxious farmer stumbling against the crowd who had gathered. The men were laughing and cheering at the idea of a fight and only the women and children standing in the background watched with serious expressions.

Kate had knelt down to where Taylor lay, cradling his bloodied head in her arms. The doctor had been knocked unconscious.

Naul ran at Gavin with a roar, his fists flailing in his charge. So suddenly did he come that one of his fists caught Gavin a blow on the side of the head, knocking him backwards. Naul followed up by lashing out with his boot. Gavin twisted aside, his own boot catching Naul at the back of the knee as he balanced on one foot. With a scream of pain the big farmer measured his distance on the ground. Clambering back to his feet, he began to circle Gavin warily. Again he charged forward suddenly, without warning, lashing out with his boot again. This time Gavin was ready, side-stepped and driving his fist as hard as he could into the big man's black beard. It impacted slightly higher than he had anticipated, smashing against Naul's nose with such force that it lifted him from his feet and sent him crashing to the ground. The man lay still.

Birger Svenson moved forward and stared down at Naul in disgust. 'That's enough,' he growled. 'Will anyone here take Naul home?'

A thin, red-faced man named McBain came forward with a degree of embarrassment on his features and helped the burly farmer to his feet. Naul groaned as he recovered consciousness and shook his head, his red eyes trying to find Gavin.

'I'll get you, you Teig bastard!' he hissed through his bloodied mouth. 'I have your mark and. . . .'

'Shut up, Mullan!' muttered McBain sharply. 'I'm taking you home.'

Gavin watched as McBain hauled the big man towards the carts, hitched some horses and drove away.

Doc Taylor was on his feet now, groaning a little and swaying. Kate was supporting him. 'You shouldn't have intervened, Devlin,' glowered Taylor resentfully. 'It wasn't your fight.'

Gavin grinned wryly as he glanced at the doctor's discoloured forehead still bearing the imprint of Naul's boot.

'I didn't think you were in a condition to mind my intervention,' he replied evenly. 'Anyway, I'm working for Kate and any threat to her is my fight.' He turned to the girl. 'Are you all right?'

She smiled quickly but looked anxious. 'What about you? Did he hurt you?'

Gavin was aware of a throbbing temple but he smiled. 'No,' he lied. 'I'm fine.'

'Good.' It was Birger Svenson. 'In that case we can get on with what we are all here for. Let's get this party going, everybody.' He began to shepherd the people back to the tables and ordered the fiddler to strike up again.

Kate was still worried as she looked at Gavin. 'Mullan Naul is a bad enemy to have.'

'It's your farmstead that he's after, Kate. Not me.'

'Naul will have to deal with me first,' Taylor said, anger still in his voice. 'And I can fight that battle without your help, Devlin.'

He pulled his arm from Kate's support and stood swaying slightly. Then he shot her a look of acrimony and tried to stalk away. His path was a little erratic but the girl made no move to help him.

'If you want to go after Taylor, Kate,' Gavin suggested, 'I can look after myself.'

He was surprised at the blaze of anger in her eyes. 'Oh yes, all you little boys can look after yourselves,' she sneered. 'Well, you can mind your own business, Gavin Devlin, and I'll mind mine.' She strode away to join the women preparing tea.

Chapter 39

From the time of the split in the Brotherhood, the majority of Fenian circles in British North America moved their support to the O'Mahoney wing and turned against the plan of invasion put forward by William Randall Roberts. The milder comment on the plan was 'visionary and unproductive'. However, the activities of the government in Upper and Lower Canada throughout March, the calling out of 10,000 militia and the assaults on moderate Irish Catholics, forced those moderates to contemplate more extreme viewpoints. Thomas D'Arcy McGee, in his hysterical denunciations of the entire Republican movement, was unwittingly acting as one of the best recruiting agents for Roberts's wing of the Brotherhood. It was McGee who had pressed the governor-general, Viscount Monck, to ban the St Patrick's Day celebrations. It was McGee who demanded tougher measures against suspected Fenians and it was McGee who persuaded John Joseph Lynch, the Catholic Bishop of Toronto, to issue a pastoral letter denouncing all Republican Irish as lawless and godless men. And when the month of March passed without either the rumoured uprising or the threatened invasion, it was McGee who invited the governor-general to a celebration in Montréal to congratulate the Irish community there on their loyalty. And it was McGee who lost his temper when some of his 'loyal Irish' refused to stand or remove their hats during the singing of 'God save the Queen'. As he ranted, a member of the audience shouted that he was spitting on the graves of his ancestors and the men of '98.

'The men of '98 were fighters for freedom and liberty,' replied McGee without aplomb. 'The men of the Fenian Brotherhood are no more than assassins, plunderers and terrorists for by terror they seek to impose their political will. To use physical force to obtain a goal is a crime when one can go to the polls. Force and terror never achieved anything.'

'It achieved the conquest of Ireland!' yelled an indignant voice.

'I'll not address Fenians!' sneered McGee.

'You are not addressing Fenians,' came the reply.

'You differentiate between the terror of the conqueror to maintain power and the terror of the conquered to achieve liberty,' declared a young man from the audience. 'Why is the terror of the conqueror good and why is the struggle of the people for liberty evil?'

'I'll not speak here any longer,' stormed McGee, leaving the platform in a rage.

The audience hissed and booed as he left and then spontaneously broke into 'The wearing of the green'.

On 9 April, Michael Murphy, the Toronto Irish leader, who was also the 'head centre' of the O'Mahoney wing of the Brotherhood in Upper Canada, was arrested with several of his followers on a train bound for Montréal. Murphy and his men were found in possession of a quantity of guns and a considerable sum of money. A few days later the astonishing news spread that the Fenians had attempted to invade the province of New Brunswick. The astonishing part was not so much that the invasion had been attempted – an invasion that a few days before was being dismissed by the *Irish Canadian* as a threat which was a 'mere waste of words and time' – but the fact that the invasion had been attempted by O'Mahoney's wing of the Brotherhood which had always argued against such a venture.

In a desperate attempt to regain his lost prestige and the backing of the majority of the Brotherhood who supported the senate wing, O'Mahoney had allowed his lieutenant, Bernard Doran Killian, a New York lawyer, to gather 1,000 men at Calais and Eastport in the state of Maine in an attempt to cross into the British province of New Brunswick. The object was to seize an island called Campobello in Passamaquoddy Bay, an island whose sovereignty had long been disputed by the United States and Britain. O'Mahoney had managed to buy a warship *Ocean Spray*, purchased as war surplus from the US Navy Department. Killian had arrived in the border town of Calais and announced that the Fenians were there to wreck any ideas of uniting the provinces of British North America into one country.

Some 5,000 British regulars and militia were immediately entrained for the border under the command of Major-General Sir Hastings Doyle. An eighty-one gun warship, HMS *Duncan*, with 700 regulars on board, together with HMS *Pylades*, was also despatched into Passamaquoddy Bay. Vice-Admiral Sir James Hope was placed in command of Royal Navy operations while Major-General Sir Fenwick Williams, newly appointed lieutenant-governor of Nova Scotia, hastened to the border on his own account to volunteer his services. One political observer dryly commented that bringing such senior officers to the border would give the Fenian rabble much cause for boasting how seriously they were taken.

The newspapers were full of despatches from New Brunswick. The Fenian invasion had come at last and was proving no threat at all. The thousand Fenians, hastily organized, were already hemmed in, unable to cross the border because of the threatening guns of British warships and the large number of regular troops awaiting them. And in political terms those who supported the proposed union of the provinces were now able to make Confederation a matter of loyalism. Through all the provinces the strong feelings against the idea of a united Dominion of Canada began to ebb. Nowhere was this more apparent than in New Brunswick whose provincial government, until the appearance of the Fenians on their borders, had been against Confederation. The Fenians, in declaring their intention to thwart Confederation, caused the collapse of the provincial government. To support the prospect of Dominion was now to prove one's loyalty. To be against the Dominion was to be a Republican and a Fenian. The new provincial premier, Leonard Tilley, speaking of the Confederationist victory in the New Brunswick House of Assembly, while the Fenians still hesitated on the border, said, 'My honourable friend has referred to the Fenians, and asks if their coming had some effect on the election? I think it had, and a most decided one, for when they came and said they were prepared to assist the Anti-Confederationists in preventing Confederation, the feeling in favour of Union at once became more general, for the people saw that in that alone was safety.'

On 16 April, as the news of the O'Mahoney faction's gathering on the New Brunswick border was being published, Roberts's senate met in their new offices on Broadway. O'Mahoney had succeeded in having them evicted from the mansion on Union Square which had become his own headquarters. All fifteen members of the Brotherhood's senate attended and were sitting nervously around a green baize-covered table, when Roberts opened the meeting and came directly to the point.

'You have heard the news about O'Mahoney? That vain man has thought to pre-empt us by conducting his own excursion into British North America. It is an attempt without preparation, without thought and with only a handful of men. He is pinned down already on American soil, unable to cross the border because he faces forces of five to one and the heavy guns of two British battleships.'

Senator J. W. FitzGerald, who represented Cincinnati, cast a bleak look towards General 'Fighting Tom' Sweeny who sat at the end of the table, head bowed in thought.

'I proposed that we take immediate steps to push forward with our own plan before O'Mahoney steals our thunder,' he said.

Sweeny looked up and grimaced in irritation. 'We are talking about the invasion of a country here, senator. It takes time and organization. I will not react to reckless pressure brought to force me into premature action.'

FitzGerald raised an eyebrow. 'General, I have been touring across the country. I can assure you that unless you take the field at once with your army then the dissolution of this Brotherhood will be inevitable.'

Roberts sighed deeply. 'I'm afraid FitzGerald has a point, Tom,' he said. 'We don't know what the outcome of O'Mahoney's attempt at New Brunswick will be but, whether it is successful or not, our organization is demanding action. I have received numerous telegraphs from our circles across the country. FitzGerald is right. It is preferable that we face honourable failure on the battlefield than witness the disintegration of the organization.'

Sweeny moved uneasily in his chair. 'The funds at my disposal are hardly one-fourth of the amount needed. Our arsenal is not over 10,000 stands of arms and two-and-a-half million ball cartridges. As to the field pieces . . . we have no artillery to speak of.'

'And men?' demanded Roberts.

'In volunteers we have done better. We can make an army of 25,000 but we will have to rely on the French-Canadians to equip our cavalry regiments.'

Roberts looked around at each member of the senate in turn.

'Well, gentlemen, you have heard an estimate of our strength. Do you still insist on immediate action?'

It was Senator FitzGerald who spoke for all of them. 'Yes.'

Roberts glanced down the table at Sweeny. 'You have your orders, Tom.'

Sweeny rose and bowed stiffly. 'Very well. Action it shall be, gentlemen. It will take a month to bring our men up to the assembly points along the border and transport our arms and equipment. In anticipation of your decision today, I have already drawn up a number of general orders which will result in the Irish Republican Army crossing into the provinces of British North America on 31 May.'

There was a general muttering of approval.

'Can you tell us the main plan, General?' asked FitzGerald.

Sweeny exchanged a look with Roberts who nodded slightly. 'I have provided for three armies. Our left will be commanded by our Adjutant-General, Brigadier Charles Tevis, who will muster his troops around Chicago and Milwaukee. The centre army will be under the command of Brigadier William Lynch. This army will gather at Buffalo, Dunkirk, Erie, Cleveland, where Lynch will establish his headquarters, Sandusky City and Toledo. In other words, along the southern shores of Lake Erie. Our right wing will be commanded by Brigadier Sam Spear whose headquarters will be in St Albans, in Franklin county, Vermont. Attached to Spear's force will be our main cavalry force commanded by Brigadier Michael Murphy with his headquarters in Malone.'

The senate were fascinated as they listened to Sweeny.

'The overall strategy is this, gentlemen: we will make a descent from the Great Lakes simultaneously with the crossing of the boundary on the line of St Lawrence. General Tevis's army will number 3,000 troops and move twenty-four hours in advance of the rest of our forces. They will proceed by Lakes Michigan and Huron into Upper Canada and march on Stratford and London, threatening Toronto from the south-west. Twenty-four hours later, General Lynch's army of 5,000 will cross Lake Erie from Cleveland and the Niagara River from Buffalo in two columns, one securing Port Stanley and joining Tevis at London, while the other will secure Paris, Guelph and Hamilton. This will compel the British commander-in-chief to believe we are threatening Toronto and he will concentrate his forces about the meridian of Toronto believing that to be our objective. As soon as the British begin to rush their troops to the area to meet our threat, our auxiliaries, members of the Brotherhood acting with the French-Canadians, will rise and destroy St Ann's Bridge at the junction of the Ottawa and St Lawrence Rivers on the Grand Trunk Railroad and the Beauharnois Canal. This will effectively cut off all communication between Upper and Lower Canada.'

Sweeny paused and smiled at their mesmerized faces.

'And the main attack?' FitzGerald asked quietly.

'The main attack will come from our right flank and will consist of General Spear's army which will number 16,800 men, consisting of seventeen regiments of infantry and five regiments of cavalry. Our main thrust will be against Montréal. Brigadier Murphy and his five cavalry regiments from Malone will begin this movement by threatening Cornwall on the border and also Prescott. He will move up on both sides of the Richelieu River and seize the garrisons of Isle aux Nois, St Johns and Fort Chambley, or, at least, cut them off. He will occupy La Prairie and threaten Montréal by the Victoria Bridge, holding it until our infantry come up. By this time, he should be joined by a strong body of French-Canadians and members of the Brotherhood from the city. However, if he has to fall back, he must destroy the bridge.

'Simultaneously with this movement, a detachment of cavalry will be sent forward along the line of the Grand Trunk Railroad to seize Point Levis opposite Québec. Point Levis will be our main port to the Atlantic. We now have three warships armed and fitted. However, if Montréal and Québec cannot be secured, then our army will concentrate between the Richlieu and St Francis Rivers and the town of Sherbrooke will be declared our headquarters from which we will proclaim the Irish Republic-in-Exile.'

Sweeny stood stiffly looking at their undisguised excitement with satisfaction.

Roberts stood up, his voice uneven with emotion.

'Gentlemen, 31 May, it will be a day that will go down in history.'

Three days later, after consultation with emissaries from Roberts' senate wing of the Brotherhood, President Johnson ordered the victor of Gettysburg, General George C. Meade, to move into Calais and Eastport with regular American troops and put an end to O'Mahoney's threatening postures. The USS *Winooski* joined the British warships in Passamaquoddy Bay. Invoking the laws of neutrality, General Meade seized O'Mahoney's arms and supplies and forced the dispersion of his 1,000 men. O'Mahoney's threat at Campobello was apparently over and the British provinces heaved a collective sigh of relief. The *Canadian Freeman* was able to publish a lengthy article which it claimed was an obituary on the subject of Fenianism.

The same day Chief Justice Draper opened the Spring Assizes at Toronto with a vehement attack on the Brotherhood warning that if any further attempts to invade the provinces came, 'thank God it will not find us divided among ourselves, or unprepared to resist the invader . . . whatever our national origin, we are all Canadians. To a profound and zealous adherence to our constitutional rights and liberties, we add a personal devotion to our Queen, honouring her as the head of our government, loving her as the mother of her people, praying God for the prolongation of her reign and for her domestic happiness and welfare. . . . There can be but one reception for the invaders, a stern and pitiless opposition to repel aggression, striking for Queen and country, for law and liberty, for wives and children, and may God defend the right!'

In spite of the bellicose warning, the threat seemed to have disappeared and the militia were ordered to their homes while the regulars stood down. The *Sarnia Observer* breathed a sigh, 'so far as any fear of a Fenian invasion is concerned, the whole frontier force might be disbanded; for we do not believe the Fenians will venture across the border.' The premier of the united provinces of Upper and Lower Canada, John A. Macdonald, wrote to the head of his border secret service, Gilbert McMicken, 'I imagine that the Fenian war may be considered as over.'

Gavin had been shocked and confused by the reports of the Fenian attempt at Campobello and waited with impatience until the 21st of the next month when he was to go into Fort Erie to make contact with Major Canty again. They met at the City Hotel and went for a walk along the river shore in the direction of the stone fortress which gave the township its name. Canty was bubbling with indignation.

'That idiot O'Mahoney! That stupid egocentric idiot!'

'Then it wasn't Roberts who was responsible?' Gavin stared at him in surprise. 'But O'Mahoney was always against the plan to invade the British provinces.'

Canty grimaced eloquently. 'O'Mahoney thought he would steal a march on Roberts. When he saw our movement had obtained widespread support for the invasion, he thought he'd make the first move himself and grab the limelight.'

'The point that worries me is that President Johnson sent in American regulars to invoke the neutrality laws. I thought that he had indicated to Roberts that he would not do so.'

Canty tapped the side of his nose with a forefinger. 'The agreement with President Johnson was with Roberts, not with O'Mahoney and his pathetic group of hotheads. The Eastport fizzle will not interrupt our plans. Johnson will stand by his agreement with us.'

'But hasn't O'Mahoney damaged the entire movement? Those that were against Confederation are now preaching the union of the provinces. The *Canadian Freeman* is comparing the Fenians to Barnum's Circus and even the *Parti Rouge* in Montréal are saying that the

Fenians have played into the British pro-Confederationist hands. That's the reverse of what we hoped to achieve.'

'According to Senator Hynes, who I saw across in Buffalo yesterday, O'Mahoney has worked to our benefit.'

'I don't see how,' said Gavin.

'O'Mahoney has succeeded in distracting the British attention from our own preparations and reports of our strength and intentions have simply been discredited by his pathetic demonstration. The British think that the entire Fenian Brotherhood were licked at Campobello. All that has happened is that O'Mahoney has lost his arms, supplies, his money and whatever prestige he had left. Now there is only one Irish Republican Brotherhood in the field – the official senate wing and support from those disillusioned with O'Mahoney is coming in to us daily. The British are sitting smugly back now and they will have no idea of our existence until we strike.'

Gavin raised his eyebrows. 'And when will that be?'

Canty smiled slowly. 'At the end of next month.'

Gavin paused and stared in surprise. 'Is it true?'

Canty nodded. 'Our armies move across on the night of 31 May. On 1 June we shall raise the flag of the Irish Republic on British soil!'

They turned and strolled back along the river to the township while Canty explained to Gavin what details he knew. They went into the bar of the City Hotel. It was crowded and Canty ordered drinks, moving in search of a more secluded quarter of the taproom. Suddenly he paused and he tensed for a moment. He turned with a worried grimace.

'What's wrong?' demanded Gavin.

'The big wheel himself,' Canty whispered. 'McMicken.'

'McMicken, the secret service chief?' Gavin glanced over Canty's shoulder towards the two men he had indicated with a jerk of his head.

'The little man with the greying hair is Gilbert McMicken.'

Gavin felt a wave of astonishment. The man Canty indicated was the same who had met Hogan from the ferry the previous month. There was no mistake. It was the same dour little man with greying hair and a heavy brown overcoat. The sight of the other man standing talking to him made Gavin turn quickly. It was Hogan himself.

'What is it?' demanded Canty. 'Do you know McMicken?'

'No,' Gavin said. 'But I know the other man. A man called Hogan who is a hired killer out of New York City. Works for Brock Delancey, Senator Delancey's son. He tried to kill me once.'

Canty gazed at him in surprise. 'Are you sure that the little man is McMicken?' pressed Gavin.

'I know more about that little sonofabitch than anyone else outside his own family. I told you back in Buffalo that he ran an escape route for Rebs escaping from Union jails across the border and helped them to get back to the Confederacy. After the Rebs raided St Albans a group of officers were selected to slip across the border to assassinate certain people who were aiding the Rebs . . . I and a couple of men were chosen to eliminate McMicken.'

Gavin pursed his lips, 'What happened?'

'Lincoln found out about the scheme and forbade it. He even revoked General Dix's orders to his troops to pursue the Reb raiders into British territory and drag them back into the States without bothering about the neutrality laws. Dix was a general who believed in an eye for an eye. Lincoln thought he could coax the British with kind words and gestures of reconciliation. Reconciliation has to be a two-way affair.' Canty sighed. 'Anyway, we spent some time studying McMicken's life and habits before the scheme was cancelled. He's pretty rich and powerful. Came here from Scotland when he was nineteen years old and made a fortune out of a shipping business in Chippewa. He had a hand in building the Suspension Bridge below Niagara Falls and was instrumental in putting the first telegraph line across the Niagara as well. He's a member of the Legislature in Ottawa for this area and a prominent pro-Confederationist.'

'Did the British go along with all his pro-Reb activities then?'

'After the raid on St Albans they became kinda nervous. The fact that the Rebs were losing the war and that the Union Army might start conducting retaliatory raids made them hesitate. Two months after St Albans McMicken was instructed to use his network to watch the Rebs and their sympathizers and prevent any more attacks. He now runs the entire British secret service along the border.'

'Hogan's leaving!' Gavin whispered quickly.

'Right,' Canty said briskly. 'You keep an eye on McMicken and I'll see where Hogan is off to.'

As Canty left the City Hotel, Gavin shifted his position in order to keep a casual eye on the dour little man. McMicken had taken a table near the door with his back to Gavin and was ordering another drink. Nothing happened for about fifteen minutes and then there came the sound of the clanging of an engine bell across the hubbub of the taproom. Gavin saw McMicken raise his head.

'Is that the train for Chippewa?' he called across to the man polishing glasses behind the bar.

'Reckon it is, Mister McMicken,' the barman replied.

The little Scot stood up, drained his glass, put on his hat and left. A moment later Canty came in and slumped down beside Gavin.

'McMicken's catching the train to Chippewa,' Gavin said.

'Going home, I suppose,' Canty muttered. 'McMicken has a big house in Chippewa.'

'What about Hogan?'

'Went to the stables and took a horse. He's gone riding up the Garrison Road in the direction of Port Colborne. How dangerous is this man, Hogan?'

'Very,' Gavin said emphatically.

'Well, we'd best have a care. He is obviously a McMicken man. I guess McMicken must have his men watching this crossing. Maybe he has men along the entire river section.'

'But Hogan works for Brock Delancey,' pointed out Gavin. 'He's just a crook.'

Canty shot him a wry grin. 'Since when has being a crook precluded a man from being a spy and informer?'

'Are you reporting this to Hynes?'

Canty nodded. 'But nothing can stop us now,' he said. 'Not McMicken nor the entire British Army in Canada. Report here on Wednesday, 30 May, Devlin. And by 1 June there will be an Irish flag flying on top of this hotel.'

He turned to signal for a refill of their drinks and when the barman had supplied them he smiled and raised his glass.

'*Saoirse*!' he said.

It was one of the few Irish toasts Gavin knew. 'To freedom!' he echoed.

Chapter 40

Gavin spent a long while turning over in his mind the idea that Hogan was an agent working for McMicken's detective force. But he thought that John Canty must surely be wrong. Hogan was Delancey's man; a hired killer and no government would employ such a man even to do their dirty work. However, the sighting of Hogan at Fort Erie had brought the matter of the Delanceys into his mind again. He had not heard from his father nor from Father MacMahon since he had entered Upper Canada and he wished he had some contact with them. He wanted to know what was happening in New York. He supposed that Rosaleen McHale was married to Brock Delancey by now. That was a mater of indifference to him. What frustrated him was his inability to do anything about the Delanceys. Everything would have to wait now. Within a few weeks Sweeny's army would be crossing into the provinces. The realization of that fact left him somehow confused. All the while the invasion had been an abstract idea it had seemed so logical, without fault. Yet now he had lived with the people of this province. To them Ireland was a world away. They knew nothing and cared even less for Ireland and for the Irish immigrant slums of New York. He had witnessed the stirring of their patriotic feelings fired by the new concept of a Canadian nation, defending it against all comers. How would the Brotherhood be able to seize this territory and hold it against such a hostile population? That would simply be imitating what the English had done in Ireland.

A few days after he returned from Fort Erie, Gavin had to drive Kate into Port Colborne to pick up some supplies and new seeds for the spring planting. With summer approaching Kate Dawtry still had made no real decision about selling the farmstead except that she was determined not to sell out to Mullan Naul. Neither did it seem to Gavin that she was dealing with Jim Taylor and his desire to marry her. Taylor still visited frequently, treating Gavin with hostile wariness. The two men seemed to circle each other like suspicious mastiffs vying for teritory. Gavin had become convinced that Kate would finally accept Taylor's offer of marriage, in spite of her protests. He wondered why the thought stirred such resentment in him. What right had he to be jealous? The attraction he felt towards Kate, which had persisted and grown since he started working at the farmstead, was a feeling that he tried to dismiss. He was unwilling to explore its existence trying to sustain himself in the belief that he was still in love with Nora Quinlan, with her ghost or her memory. The hurt from her loss and the grief could surely never be repaired; yet the image of Nora Quinlan was fading in his memory. He tried to tell himself that any man would feel attracted to such a pretty and appealing woman as Kate Dawtry, especially a man alone who was confined on the same farmstead for three months. But there was something other than obvious physical attraction about Kate. She was intelligent, well read, with a personality that Gavin had never encountered in any of the women he had known, an ease of character with which he could relax and not feel discomfort. With whom he did not have to play a part rather than simply be himself. Yet, surely, he was not falling in love with Kate Dawtry? That would make life too complicated and the human mind could not be so fickle.

As they entered Port Colborne his speculations were chased from his mind by the ominous thunder of drums which rose from the quayside. There seemed to be a large number of people milling in the town and there were several uniformed militiamen standing under arms along the streets.

'Better pull up over here,' Kate advised him as they reached the tavern.

Gavin wondered where the groups of people heading towards the thundering drums were going.

'See the orange banners,' Kate nodded. 'It was the wrong time to come to town. There's a gathering of the Orangemen.'

Gavin hitched the horse to the rail listening to the strange rhythmic thundering of the drums, rising and falling but insistent. 'I want to see this,' he said but he found Kate's hand on his arm, staying him.

'Best keep out of sight while I collect the things from the store,' she muttered. She was clearly worried by the Orange demonstration.

Gavin waited until she had disappeared into the store before joining the people drifting down towards the calling drums. His curiosity was strong. Too strong to take note of Kate's worry. Manus Devlin had told him about the Orange mobs but he had never encountered an Orangeman until he had met Mullan Naul. He was not impressed. Down by the quayside, near the entrance of the Welland Canal, a platform had been raised which was draped in Union flags and orange banners. In front of the platform stood half-a-dozen young men, some mere boys, pounding away on great drums with sticks, sweat pouring from their faces as they created a continuous, monotonous, threatening roar. On the platform was a group of men, each with an orange sash. The first person that he recognized was the big, black-bearded figure of Mullan Naul. Gavin tilted his hat over his eyes so that he would not be recognized and stayed towards the back of the crowds.

Abruptly there came a silence which, after the rumble of the drums, seemed almost painful for a moment. Then Naul's harsh and strident tones crashed upon the air. The big farmer had moved to the edge of the platform, straining towards the crowd.

'People of Upper Canada! The country is in danger! It is in danger from the followers of the Papish Harlot of Rome! It is in danger from those envious and resentful men south of our border, those who begrudge the happiness and prosperity that we enjoy here under the beneficence of the blessed Queen of England. It is in danger from the covetous government of Washington which has had to resort to armed force to maintain their government over their own countrymen. It is in danger from the Papish malcontents that we nurture in this province of ours!'

There was a muttering as Mullan Naul paused for breath. He waved an expansive hand to a thin, pale-faced man whose black broadcloth proclaimed him to be a minister.

'You all know Reverend Renfrew. He has a few words to say before we parade through the streets of loyal Port Colborne. After he has spoken we shall move off with our banners flying, our drums beating, as a proclamation and a warning to any who harbour thoughts of disloyalty and sedition against our Queen. Fenians, beware!'

The minister moved forward, his voice shrill and reed-like; a wailing scream which Gavin found almost uncomfortable to listen to.

'You have heard how the treacherous Papists called Fenians have dared to gather on our borders for the purpose of invading our peaceful provinces? Yes, you have heard. Shall we tolerate it?'

A few of the young men with drums shouted 'No!' but the crowd did not seem stirred to respond by more than a half-hearted shuffle of their feet and embarrassed looks at one another.

'No! No! No!' the minister punctuated the words by jabbing movements of his hand, spots of red anger on his cheeks. 'Of course we shall not tolerate it. But what we do tolerate, in our blind magnanimity, is the fact that Teigs, Fenians, Papists – for they are all one – come freely into these provinces and settle among us. Yes, freely! Out of our population of two-and-a-half millions in the united provinces of Upper and Lower Canada, do you know how many are Teigs? A quarter of a million! Yes, one quarter of a million. Their perfidious temples, filled with graven images, are everywhere. They even have schools for training their pagan priests . . . not far from here in the township of London is such a seminary . . . a centre for the training of Papist priests. It is an evil and yet we, blinded by liberality, tolerate it.'

He paused. There was a soft murmuring but no general reaction.

'You all know the Roman Churches in this province. What do you see if you go into them? Legions of graven images! What does the Good Book say? "Thou shalt not make graven image, or any likeness of any thing that is in Heaven or the earth beneath or the water under the earth"! Yet the Papists, claiming to believe in that Good Book, ignore the teachings of God and make such images. There they are in their temples – gaudy legions of images. These are the trappings of the Scarlet Woman, the Great Whore of Babylon. It is rank in the nostrils of decent Christians, nauseous to their senses. The graven images, the foul-smelling sanctuary-lamps and candles placed before the idols, which is nothing more or less than worship of gaudy effigies expressly forbidden by God.

'We Protestant people, who stand for King Jesus, turn our backs on such blasphemy. We go forward with Christ, with fire in our hearts and the cry "No Popery here!" God save our Queen!'

Gavin watched the proceedings with a mixture of amazement and disbelief. He turned away sickened by such appeals to blind ignorance and hate in the name of religion. Mullan Naul's voice followed him from the platform, deep and ominous, 'Let this be a warning to all Teigs . . . we will not tolerate sedition! The cleansing fire of Christ shall sweep them from this land. Let them be warned!'

The drumming, remorseless and more threatening than before, started.

Kate was waiting for him by the buggy, her face pale and anxious.

'Didn't I tell you to stay away?' she demanded, half-angry, half-fearful. 'Don't you know how dangerous it is with those men about?'

Gavin began to help her load her purchases on to the buggy and grimaced 'If all they can offer is a load of emotional ignorance then I can't see anyone is in any danger from them. People aren't that stupid.'

'You don't know what the Orangemen are like,' Kate muttered as they left the township and began to take the Garrison Road back towards the farmstead. They could hear the drumming for quite some time after they left Port Colborne. As they were turning up the concession road to the farmstead, they met Birger Svenson.

'We're having a barn dance to celebrate the completion of the barn this Saturday,' the farmer greeted. 'You are both invited, you hear?'

'Guess I'm not much good at dances,' Gavin said as they unloaded the buggy. It was a shock to remember that the last dance he had attended was the Fourth of July celebration for the Irish Brigade in New York. That was long ago. How different things had been then.

Kate misinterpreted his reticence. 'Nonsense!' she said brightly. 'I'll teach you how to dance if you're unable.'

Gavin smiled quickly. 'I'd appreciate that, Kate. But you won't want to spend the time with a lame duck like me. They'll be plenty of partners waiting to dance with you.'

'Oh?' The syllable was uttered in an odd voice.

'Taylor will be going,' Gavin offered.

'Jim Taylor!' her voice snapped. 'Between you and Jim Taylor you seem to have my life sewn up for me.'

'Taylor is in love with you, Kate,' Gavin pressed.

'That's his problem,' the girl flushed testily and turned into the farmhouse.

Gavin was woken by someone shaking him roughly. He blinked and stared into the darkness and heard Kate's sob of frustration.

'For God's sake wake up, Gavin!'

'What is it?' he mumbled, rubbing the sleep from his eyes.

'There's horses coming and they're not farm horses. I can hear them coming along the concession road.'

The fear in her voice was catching. Gavin swung out of bed, hauling on his trousers.

'You think it is Mullan Naul keeping his word about the Peep o' Day Boys, don't you?' he demanded. 'Is that why you're scared?'

He saw her nod her head in the darkness.

'Get Young Tom and hide in the potato cellar,' he ordered, leaning towards his valise and rummaging inside until he found his army holster and extracted his Colt revolver and box of ammunition. Kate started to protest. 'There's no time to argue,' he snapped. 'Get down to the cellar.'

He moved to the window and eased it open. The moon was full, shining with an ethereal gleam across the yard and the fields beyond. He could hear the horses approaching rapidly along the road. The riders were making little effort to hide themselves for harsh voices were shouting and some of the men gave loud whoops. He suddenly saw them, jumping their horses in the moonlight across the low, split rail fencing into the yard. A dozen or so riders. Gavin gripped his revolver and checked to ensure the chambers were loaded. One of the riders came up to the verandah.

'Hello the house!'

Gavin saw, by the moonlight, that the men had white hoods on their heads, with slits cut for eyes. He could also see that most had long barrelled revolvers thrust in their belts.

'Hello the house!'

Kate had feared correctly. There was no mistaking the tones of Mullan Naul.

'What is it, Naul?' Gavin called back.

He saw the man stiffen in his saddle as if he had not expected recognition.

'So you're awake, Teig?' came the sneering reply.

'What do you want?' demanded Gavin.

'You, you Papist bastard!' cried one of the men, only to be snarled at by Naul.

'We'll be doing no harm to Kate Dawtry or her property if you come out, Teig.'

Gavin smiled thinly. 'What then, Naul? Are you inviting me out for a dram and a talk about the old country?'

Naul roared with laughter and slapped his thigh. 'That's the spirit, Teig. You come on out.'

'You can roast in hell, Naul. And hell is where you'll be if you don't leave here pretty damned quick.'

Naul turned in his saddle. 'McBain, you take the barn and start killing Kate Dawtry's razorbacks.'

Gavin clicked back the hammer of his gun.

'Kill one pig, Naul, and it'll have you for company.'

Naul grunted scornfully. 'You heard, McBain.'

Gavin aimed just above Naul's head. The shot was unexpected and caused the horses to plunge about in disorder, the hooded men were cursing and trying to control them.

'Now get off this land, Naul.'

The riders had drawn back and were holding a whispered conference. Some moved across to the barn. Then Naul's voice came again.

'Hey, Teig.'

'What is it?'

'You come on out now. We have the boy. Caught him trying to sneak off. Guess he was going to get help.'

'I don't believe you!' snapped Gavin, feeling a coldness round his mouth.

A piercing shriek answered him. It was Young Tom's voice. At the same time Gavin heard Kate scrambling out of the cellar. He ran into the main room just as she was reaching the door and caught her wrist.

'Get back in the cellar, damn it!'

Her eyes were wild. 'They've got Young Tom and it's my fault,' she sobbed. 'I told him to run off to the Svensons for help.'

'Get back to the cellar. I'll deal with it,' Gavin replied firmly.

She hesitated, then moved back reluctantly.

'Teig! Do you hear?'

'I hear!' yelled Gavin.

'The boy won't be harmed if you come out now! Throw out your gun first!'

'I'm coming out!' he answered. Gavin glanced round the room and saw an old iron candlestick. He opened the door and sent it into the bushes.

Naul chuckled. 'You've good sense, Teig. Now come on out!'

Gavin was already moving swiftly, cat-like, through Kate's bedroom and opening the window at the back of the house. He slipped through it into the darkness and then, crouching low, began to circle towards the barn so that he would come up at the rear of the hooded men. He could hear Naul shouting something but he did not pay attention. He had killing in his mind now, his hand tightly gripped around his revolver. He paused at the corner of the barn and glanced towards the group of men. Several of them had dismounted and were taking cover behind the corn-crib. One of them held a small struggling figure, twisting an arm behind it. Another had a rifle aimed at the door of the farmhouse, obviously awaiting his appearance from that direction. The corn-crib gave them plenty of cover. It was a small construction on stilts, built with wooden slats in the yard and used to keep the corn dry.

'Tell your men to drop their guns and release the boy, Naul,' he called harshly.

Naul and his companions froze.

Gavin moved forward a pace. His last thought was of something striking him from behind. When he came to he was being dragged to the barn by two hooded men who held his arms in a tight grip. He immediately lashed out with his legs.

'Get the bastard!' came Naul's savage voice.

Gavin felt a rain of blows on his head, felt them striking at him with fists, sticks and boots until the blood ran from his mouth, his head and nose. He writhed and twisted, moving like a wild animal in his desperation to get away until he slipped into unconsciousness again. The savagery of the beating seemed to satisfy a couple of Naul's men.

He came to and heard someone say, 'Let's leave it and have a drink, Mullan.'

Another voice, a vaguely familiar voice, cut in sharply.

'Finish it, Naul. Get a rope.'

He heard Naul's voice filled with uncertainty. 'What about the boy, Hogan? He's a witness.'

'Now he is, you bloody fool!'

'He's right,' said another voice. 'Too many names have been bandied about tonight.'

'Damned be!' came another voice. 'It's all very well to beat the hell out of the Teig but hanging's not right.'

'Shut up!'

Gavin dispassionately recognized Hogan's voice. He was surprised that he felt no fear only a terrible resignation. He could expect no mercy from Hogan.

'What is the Teig but a bloody murdering Fenian?' It was Hogan who now held their attention. 'Are you going to wait until the Fenians march across the border and burn your farms, rape your women and steal your money before you strike back? The only way to treat them is put the fear of God into them.'

'Hanging the Teig is one thing,' protested another voice. 'What about the boy and his sister?'

The crack of a rifle was like a tremendous explosion. The man who was holding Young Tom, still crying and struggling, gave a scream of agony and fell back with red staining his shirt. He fell to the floor clutching at his arm and moaning in agony. Everyone froze in a weird tableau.

Kate's voice came clearly out of the darkness beyond the open doors of the barn.

'Tom? Run this way, quickly!'

The boy did not hesitate. He ran.

'Get going to Mister Svenson!' Gavin heard her instructing. Then, 'And none of you move, you hear?' To emphasize her words she fired another shot into the wood of the barn.

'We can't wait for the boy to bring Svenson. He's a militia officer,' Gavin heard Hogan's voice whisper urgently. 'It's only a girl out there, we can take her.'

Gavin's eyes flickered and he saw Hogan reaching for his gun. Summoning what strength he could, Gavin rolled across the floor and grabbed the man's legs, tripping him. Hogan twisted and fell on top of Gavin swearing violently. There was bedlam in the barn as Naul and his men seized advantage of the confusion and began to run for their horses. Kate was unable to fire for fear of hitting Gavin. Hogan suddenly tore himself away and kicked at Gavin's head stunning him. He stood over him reaching for his pistol and then realized he had dropped it in the struggle. With an oath he turned and leapt for his horse to follow the others. Almost with abruptness the farmyard was empty.

Then Kate was bending over him, her eyes round and frightened. 'Oh, Lord!' she murmured. 'Are you hurt bad, Gavin?'

He felt as if several horses had ridden over him. 'Guess I'll be fine if I lay here awhile.'

The sound of thundering hooves caused her to grab for her rifle again but she relaxed as two horseman, one with Young Tom hanging on behind came into the farmyard. It was Birger Svenson and his brother Stefan.

'Hot damn!' exclaimed Birger Svenson, leaning over Gavin and feeling for broken bones. 'We heard shots and were coming to find out what was wrong when we met Young Tom on the road. Who was it, do you know?'

'Vigilantes,' breathed Kate. 'Peep o' Day Boys.'

Svenson whistled and exchanged a glance with his brother.

'The leader was Mullan Naul,' Gavin muttered.

Svenson looked hard at the girl and she nodded.

'He was mentioned by name and we both recognized his voice.

Besides,' she nodded to the corner of the stall, 'one of them's laying over there.'

Gavin had forgotten the man Kate had hit in the shoulder. He had been thrown back into one of the wooden stalls and lay, groaning softly and clutching his bloody arm. Svenson stood up and yanked off the wounded man's hood.

'By damn! It's McBain, one of Naul's men.'

McBain let out a whimper. 'For Christ's sake get me a doc, I'm fair bleeding to death, mister.'

'I'll get you a doctor, if you answer my questions. Was Mullan Naul the leader of the men who did this?'

McBain bit his lip.

Birger Svenson took out his revolver and pressed the barrel against McBain's wounded arm. The man screamed.

'Yes, yes, for Christ's sake! It was Naul.'

'A revenge for the beating that Devlin gave him at the barn raising?'

McBain scowled. 'We were going teach the Teig a lesson.'

Gavin had eased himself into a sitting position with Kate and Young Tom's help. 'You were going to lynch me, McBain,' he grunted.

'Come on . . . .' Svenson said disbelievingly. 'A beating is one thing but a lynching . . . ?'

'Was that Naul's idea or was it Hogan's?' snapped Gavin at the wounded man.

McBain tried to shrug. 'I don't know no Hogan,' he muttered.

'Hogan was with you tonight. He was the one giving Naul orders.'

'I don't know no Hogan,' insisted the man.

Birger Svenson was looking worried. 'This guy is going to bleed to death 'less I get him to Doc Taylor,' he said. 'Stefan will stay here just in case Naul and his cronies come back. I'll take McBain down to Doc Taylor's place and then ride on to Port Colborne to get the constable. It's no use asking any more questions now. The man is too weak.'

While the Svenson brothers were lifting McBain on to Stefan Svenson's horse, Kate helped Gavin walk slowly back to the farmhouse. Gavin sprawled in a chair while Kate began to go to work on his bruises and lacerations. There were only a few abrasions but no broken bones. While she was tending his injuries Young Tom brought in Gavin's discarded revolver and lay it on the table. Kate glanced at the weapon with a worried frown. Gavin saw it and smiled thinly, 'A souvenir of the war. Lucky I kept it.'

She did not reply but turned to Young Tom and ordered him to bed while she fussed about the kitchen to prepare a glass of hot whiskey.

'You sip that,' she instructed.

As she went to fasten the window latch in the bedroom she said, 'I hope they catch Mullan Naul quickly. He's a bad enemy to have, Gavin.'

Gavin bit his lip thoughtfully. A bad enemy – yes; but not so bad as Hogan. But how had Hogan found him? He supposed through contact with Mullan Naul. But there was a lot he did not understand. How had Hogan persuaded Naul to take part in a lynching party? And was Hogan acting on behalf of Brock Delancey or was he really an agent for Gilbert McMicken as Canty claimed? It seemed improbable and yet . . . . Before he could reach any conclusions he had fallen into a sleep of utter exhaustion in the chair. It was a few hours later that he woke to find a blanket wrapped around him, the room in shadows, lit by a still glowing fire. Kate had apparently gone to bed. He stretched, feeling the ache in his limbs from the cramped and awkward position. He made his way back to his bedroom and fell asleep almost immediately.

Chapter 41

By Saturday Gavin had sufficiently recovered from the beating to be able to accompany Kate to the Svensons' celebration. The newly erected barn had been transformed and was lit as though every candle and candlestick in the country had been made available to light it. Along one side of the barn a series of trestle tables had been arranged, each covered with spotless white linen and piled with colourful mountains of food and drink. There was bunting reflecting the Union flag everywhere and there were several flags which Gavin did not recognize but guessed they were mementoes of the 'old countries'.

Gavin had driven Kate to the Svensons' place, with Young Tom, in the buggy. When she had emerged from her room that evening to show off her dress, Gavin had been astonished. He was used to Kate Dawtry dressed in old dungaree trousers and boots and men's checked shirts. Now she emerged the equal of any of the wealthy young ladies he had seen at dances and other social occasions in New York. She wore a gown of light blue, he guessed it must be silk, which came off the shoulders with dark royal blue trimmings. It was gathered tightly at the waist. Her usual unruly curls were drawn back with a bow of dark blue. Around her throat was a single strand of pearls from which a cameo pendant hung. She stood smiling shyly, assessing the surprised admiration in Gavin's eyes.

'Well, do I pass?' she asked gaily, twirling before him.

'Oh,' he coughed and cleared his throat. 'I guess you'll pass fine.'

She laughed at his awkwardness. 'They were my mother's. The dress and the pearls, I mean.'

'I'm honored to be your escort, Kate,' he said, feeling suddenly ashamed by his own appearance. He realized that for the first time he was not attending a dance in a well-cut, tailored uniform with gold braid and tassles. He was, in fact, dressed in a suit which had belonged to Kate's father and which Kate had spent the previous day altering to fit him. Gavin had no extra clothes apart from the utility clothing he had packed into his valise and the brown paper parcel which contained the green Fenian uniform that his mother had made for him. He had it hidden at the bottom of his valise with his boots, gunbelt and sword. Kate had seen his anxious glance in the mirror and smiled.

'You look fine, Mister Gavin Devlin. I bet I know a few girls in the district who will be trying to get you to dance with them tonight.'

Gavin grinned ruefully. 'You promised to teach me how to dance,' he reminded her.

'So I did,' she murmured demurely.

On the way to the Svensons' their buggy was joined by wagons and carriages packed with men and women, girls with chaperons and escorts, all moving in the same direction, shouting, laughing, exchanging news and jokes. Among them Gavin saw a few red-coated soldiers and some men in dark green uniforms. When he asked Kate what the uniforms meant she told him that several of the militia units had adopted green uniforms.

The children were despatched to play in the Svenson farmhouse under the eagle eye of a few of the more elderly women while everyone else retired to the barn. A makeshift band was gathered and began tuning their fiddles, whistles and drums. People were crowding about, shy young girls, eager matrons, cynical spinsters and critical older women. The men moved in chattering, drinking groups who never wandered far from the bowls of punch or corn whiskey jugs.

Birger Svenson, resplendent in a militia lieutenant's uniform, rose to call for quiet, standing on an old wooden box at the far end of the barn. First he introduced the local reeve, a fat-faced prosperous-looking merchant who was cramming his corpulent form in the latest tight-cut fashion. He uttered a few embarrassing words congratulating the Svensons on the new barn, on the local people for their help and then, as if in afterthought, made an appeal for more volunteers for the militia. As he stepped down, to Gavin's utter surprise, the musicians burst into what he thought was the old Confederate anthem.

> Hurrah! Hurrah! For Southern Rights hurrah!
> Hurrah for the Bonnie Blue Flag
> That bears a single star!

He gaped in surprise as those around him took up the words. It was only when he listened carefully that he realized that they were singing a different set of words to the Reb song.

Hurrah! Hurrah! For Volunteers hurrah!
For Queen and Country we will fight, and not for soldiers' pay.
Hurrah! Hurrah! We're English soldiers brave,
If the war will come to join us, the Union Flag shall wave.

There was a spontaneous burst of cheering as the song ended. Gavin glanced around him and saw an almost fanatical glow on the faces of the people, the moist eyes full of pride, the smiles as they gazed upon the wearers of the militia uniforms. It occurred to him that these people believed in their cause with every bit of sincerity and fervour as the Irish believed in theirs. God and truth were on the side of these people as He was on the side of the Irish. There was something strangely wrong. These people believed in the freedom that they had and their hearts surged with devotion, pride and self-sacrifice. To them, the Fenians were some strange, threatening animal; a drunken mob intent on plunder. The thought hit him with deep depression: how could these people, secure in their own concept of freedom, hope to realize the hunger and yearning which made Irish men and women, young and old alike, hazard everything to secure the liberty of Ireland? The same flag that flew over these people also flew over Ireland. How could he explain that it did not therefore follow that the same freedom and liberty enjoyed here were enjoyed in Ireland?

He was aware of a tugging on his sleeve and glanced down with a frown.

Kate gazed up at him with a perplexed expression. 'You were day-dreaming, Gavin Devlin,' she rebuked. 'That is very ungallant of you.'

He started to apologize but she cut him short.

'I promised to teach you to dance,' she said, holding out her arms.

He was aware that the band was playing a slow waltz. Unthinking, he took her gently and stepped smartly away on to the floor. She gasped in surprise and indignation.

'Why . . . you *can* dance!'

He blushed sheepishly. 'I didn't mean to deceive you.'

'I forgive you,' she answered with a broad smile. 'After all, you dance extremely well.'

When the music stopped Birger Svenson was on his feet again.

'My brother Stefan and I just wanted to thank you folks,' he gestured awkwardly. 'We appreciate your help with the barn here.'

Someone let out a cheer and everyone applauded.

'The boys will play some reels now,' Svenson smiled. 'Pick your partners. The reels will be followed by some scottisches and end with a polka.'

Gavin felt a hand on his shoulder and turned to meet the even gaze of Doc Taylor. 'Guess you won't mind if I claim this dance, Devlin?'

Gavin glanced at Kate, nodded stiffly and moved from the floor.

He stood watching the doctor and Kate Dawtry romp away to the opening strains of the reel.

'Handsome couple,' remarked a voice behind him.

He turned to find Birger Svenson watching Kate and Doc Taylor, his face grave. 'Yes sir, folks round here have been expecting Doc and Kate to get hitched ever since Doc returned from that damned Yankee war. Do you think they will?'

Gavin frowned. 'Isn't that up to Taylor and Miss Dawtry?' he asked.

Svenson pursed his lips. 'Suppose so, but there's been talk . . . well, you know how folks love to talk? Anything in their talk?'

Gavin frowned in anger. 'Not knowing what they gossip about, Svenson, I couldn't say.'

'Forgive us, Devlin. You see we all like Doc and Kate. Wouldn't like hurt to come to either one. We're a close community.'

Gavin turned to faced Svenson. 'Sure you are,' he said softly. 'Didn't I have a taste of that a few days ago? Your close community didn't care much about Kate or Young Tom then. Some of them damned near killed them.'

Svenson winced. 'Mullan Naul has always been something of an outsider here, Devlin. He's not a good man.' He shrugged. 'Me, I'm a member of the Swedish Lutheran Church. Go to church every Sunday. But I don't press my beliefs on anyone else, don't force my neighbour to try to think as I do. That's why many of us left Europe, to find religious freedom. Mullan Naul believes that he has some divine order from God to change the world and destroy that which can't be changed.' He smiled. 'Are you a Catholic, Devlin?'

'I was raised a Catholic but I can't say I practise any faith any more, not after the war.'

Svenson sighed. 'Yes, the war. That changed many people's attitudes. Still, it doesn't really matter what religion a man is so long as he is a moral man. We are taught that Christ is Reason in which the whole of mankind shares. Those who have lived in Reason are Christian, even though they call themselves atheists. It was as true among the ancient Greeks as among the ancient Hebrews. . . . St Justin said that. The Spirit of God is not just inside a building called a church, not just inside a particular building dedicated to a particular church. Where the Spirit of God is, the Church is. No man has a better path to God than any other. Lutheran, Presbyterian, Baptist, Catholic, Anglican, Jew . . . we each follow the path that comes best to hand.'

Gavin smiled tightly. 'You sound like a minister, Svenson.'

The farmer chuckled. 'So I was . . . in the old country. Now I am a farmer and have widened my ministry.'

His face became serious. 'Just the same, speaking of Mullan Naul, I'd beware of him. There are many of his kind who share his intolerance to men and women of your origin. I heard that the constable was unable to arrest him because he has disappeared. Neither could he get McBain to identify anyone else.'

'At least McBain will go to jail.'

'It's Mullan Naul that you need beware of.'

Gavin started thinking about Hogan again. He tried to concentrate on what Svenson was saying.

'The constable says that Naul has probably taken to the bush. He hasn't been seen near his farmstead for the last few days, not since the raid on Kate's place. My guess is that he is hiding out locally, so be careful.' He leaned close and lowered his voice. 'If I were giving advice, Devlin, I would say, do not stay long in this area. Not with Mullan Naul around.' He glanced back towards Doc Taylor and Kate. 'Wouldn't it be best to move on . . . best for everyone?'

The music ended and Kate came smilingly towards them. Taylor had turned aside and left the barn, a scowl on his face.

'My dance, I think,' she said to Gavin.

They were playing a slow waltz again as he led her on to the floor.

'Where's Taylor gone?' asked Gavin.

An expression of annoyance swiftly crossed the girl's features. 'He's left.'

'A problem?'

'Not for us.'

Gavin did not press her further; there was something implied in her tone. It was later when she explained; when they drove back to the farmstead in the buggy with Young Tom curled up in a blanket on the back seat with the warm fragrance of the late spring night around them.

'Jim asked me to marry him again,' she said.

Gavin felt a dryness in his throat. He grunted non-committally.

'It's not the first time he's asked,' Kate added.

Gavin was drawing the buggy up before the farmhouse. He was silent.

'I told him that I did not love him. I've told him that several times before. Tonight I told him that I could never marry him now.'

Before Gavin could say anything she had clambered from the buggy and ran into the house. He paused in a moment of confusion. Then he lifted Young Tom from the seat and carried him, still sleeping oblivious to everything, inside and laid him on his bunk. Kate had gone straight in to her room and closed the door. Gavin hesitated and returned to the buggy, leading the horse to the barn.

It was only a while later, as he lay falling asleep, that he realized the inflection which she had given the sentence, 'Tonight I told him that I could never marry him *now*.' Before he could quite work out the meaning of the stress on the last word, he had fallen into an uncomfortable sleep. The nightmare which had not visited him for so long returned. Yet it was not quite the same. The faces had changed and kept changing during the dream – the faces of Nora Quinlan, Rosaleen McHale and Kate Dawtry swirled through his unconscious thoughts until all their features merged together and he awoke moaning in fear as the first grey light of dawn filtered in through the shutters of his room.

They did not speak much the next day and, during the afternoon, when Kate had taken Young Tom to deliver a pie to a widow on some neighbouring farm, he sat in the barn, trying to repair a harness, and work out his feelings for the girl. The sound of a carriage coming along the concession road made him reach for his revolver. He always carried it, or kept it close, since the raid. It was not Naul that Gavin feared as much as Delancey's hired killer, Hogan. He moved cautiously to the barn door to see a buggy turning into the farmyard. It was Doc Taylor. He replaced his revolver and emerged into the open.

'Afternoon, Taylor.'

Doc Taylor jumped down from the buggy and hitched his horse to the rail.

'Are you alone, Devlin?' he asked frowning.

Gavin nodded.

Taylor came across to the barn and sat on a straw bale watching Devlin resume his task of repairing the harness.

'Do you plan to stay here?' he demanded sharply.

Gavin glanced up at Taylor's flushed features. 'Reckon it's my business,' he said.

'You realize that I love Kate Dawtry?'

Gavin sighed wearily. 'I'd be deaf, dumb and blind not to realize it.'

'Before you turned up here I was planning to marry her.'

Gavin nodded. 'Sure, but doesn't Kate have to agree to that decision?'

Taylor's mouth quirked. 'I'm egocentric enough to think she would have eventually agreed to it had you not come along.'

'Oh?'

'She's in love with you.'

'Has she told you so?' Gavin's eyes narrowed.

'I can read between the lines,' snapped Taylor. 'She's besotted by you. The mysterious stranger,' his voice was a sneer. 'The war hero!'

Gavin said nothing.

'Why don't you move on, Devlin?' Taylor said. 'Right now. There's no better moment. I'll give you a lift into Port Colborne and settle with you the money Kate owes you for the work on the farmstead. I'll even toss in a few extra dollars to help speed your passage. You can get a train to most anywhere you like from Port Colborne or a ship to take you back across Lake Erie to the States. What do you say?'

Gavin stared incredulously at the doctor's eager face. 'What I say is . . . no! Trying to get rid of me won't alter Kate's ideas about you.'

Taylor's expression did not change for a moment and then he shrugged in a resigned fashion. 'I suppose I expected that, Devlin,' he said slowly. 'Matter of fact, I was half hoping that you would say it because it would mean that you were not simply playing with Kate's affections. I had hoped for Kate's sake that you weren't, not for mine.'

Gavin regarded him curiously.

'Do you love Kate?' Taylor pressed.

'I . . . I think I do,' he said hesitantly.

Taylor stared at him for a long while and then rose to his feet.

'I hope you do, Devlin,' he said. 'Or, by God, I'll kill you myself.'

Gavin suddenly realized the depth of feeling Taylor had for Kate

Dawtry and he was slightly awed by the realization. He stood up to meet the man's gaze levelly.

'I'll promise you one thing, Taylor,' he said slowly. 'I'll never do anything to harm that girl.'

Taylor blinked and half nodded, 'That's good enough for me. But just one more thing. . . .'

Gavin was totally unprepared for the weight of the fist that crashed squarely into his mouth sending him reeling backwards across a hay bale on to the floor of the barn. He lay there momentarily stunned, feeling the blood in his mouth. He saw Taylor standing over him.

'That's just an expression of my personal feelings, Devlin,' Taylor said tightly.

Gavin rose to his feet, shaking his head to clear it. He grinned wryly at Taylor, the blood trickling down the side of his mouth.

'I guess you were entitled, Taylor,' he said.

Taylor nodded. Then he thrust out his hand. 'You might be all right at that, Devlin,' he said. 'I'd like to think that I didn't save your miserable skin back at Petersburg for nothing.'

'Perhaps we should crack one of Kate's cider jugs to honour this occasion,' Gavin said solemnly.

When Kate Dawtry arrived home with Young Tom a few hours later she found Gavin Devlin and Doc Taylor stretched on the floor of the barn snoring peacefully together. There were three empty cider jugs beside them and the air was permeated with the fumes of alcohol. She gazed down in bewilderment as the two men lay cheek by jowl, blissfully unaware of her presence.

'Go on up to the house, Young Tom,' she snapped.

The tone in her voice forbade any dissension from the boy. She went to the well and drew up the bucket of ice cold water and hauled it back to the barn. The cold water woke the two men as nothing else would have done. Gavin gave a cry and came struggling forward like a wrestler while Taylor moaned and rolled over as if to escape the deluge. Both men had difficulty focusing on the figure of Kate Dawtry as she towered over them.

'Two grown men, drunk as lords!' she jeered. 'And on my cider! That'll be deducted from any money you've got coming, Gavin Devlin! Do you hear me?'

'I hear you, Kate,' murmured Gavin, rubbing his head to ease the buzzing that seemed to come from within it.

'Don't Kate me, you lummox!' snapped the girl. 'As for you, Jim Taylor . . . *Doctor* Taylor . . . words fail me!'

Taylor gave such a pitiful moan that the girl had difficulty controlling her features.

'You two get up to the house and clean up. I'll have coffee ready soon.'

She turned quickly, unable to stop the smile that spread across her features as she strode up to the farmhouse. She had a feeling that things were going to be fine.

Chapter 42

John-Joe arrived in New York with James Stephens during the second week of May. The journey from Paris had not been exactly a pleasant one. Apart from the heavy seas and squalls which made the physical aspect of the voyage unpleasant, Stephens had proved a morose and mercurial companion given to fits of self-pity and bouts of bombast and self-praise. There was little doubt in John-Joe's mind that the blows suffered by the Fenian Brotherhood in Ireland had nearly broken the man. The romantic days of *An Seabhac Siúlach* – the Wandering Hawk – were gone. The Brotherhood would never be the same. It was obvious that Stephens could no longer control the movement and lacked a steady nerve and judgment. Stephens's company grew embarrassing enough for John-Joe to avoid the man as much as possible on the voyage and no sooner had the vessel passed the quarantine island than he slipped away to the house on Greenwich Lane.

Bridget opened the door and let out such a scream of delight that it brought Patsy-Mike running through the house with a kitchen knife thinking an attack was taking place. Then John-Joe went in to see his mother. Aideen Devlin greeted her young son with her usual self-control, a quiet hug and kiss although she could not disguise the trembling of her mouth and the tears that lay on her cheeks. Doctor Manus Devlin was out and returned home to find John-Joe ensconced in the kitchen with a whiskey, the subject of rapt attention as he recounted his tales of Ireland to his mother and the servants.

It was only later that evening, after a celebratory dinner which, judging from the amount of dishes produced, seemed to indicate weeks of preparation rather than the few hours Bridget had actually taken, that Manus took John-Joe aside in his study. It was then that John-Joe pressed Manus for news of Gavin for, when he had asked previously, the answer from his father had been almost brusque.

'We haven't seen him since September,' Manus replied as he offered his youngest son a cigar and port. 'He had to leave the city for certain reasons.'

John-Joe was puzzled.

'I thought he would be settled down with Rosie McHale by now and a junior partner in her father's law firm.'

'Rosaleen McHale married Brock Delancey, the senator's son, last month.'

'You mean she rejected poor old Gavin?'

Manus shook his head. 'Not exactly, although I don't know all the details. Your brother seems to have had an . . . well, an affair, I suppose, with a girl who died in September.'

'Poor Gavin,' John-Joe breathed, feeling an overwhelming sadness for his brother. 'So he didn't go into the law business?'

'How could he?' Manus asked. 'No, he joined the Brotherhood.'

His younger son's eyes rounded in astonishment. 'But Gavin was against the Brotherhood! The lectures that he gave me . . . he tried to stop me going to Ireland.'

'I don't think he was ever against it,' Manus said defensively. 'At least he was not against its principles. It just didn't mean much to him at first. I believe that I was instrumental in changing his mind; Father MacMahon and I.'

'Where is Gavin now?' asked John-Joe.

'I'm not sure.'

John-Joe raised his eyebrows in surprise. 'Father MacMahon has kept in touch with him until the last few months. He is away on Brotherhood business.'

John-Joe was increasingly surprised. 'Father MacMahon? How is that old rebel?'

'Active as ever,' admitted Manus. 'You have doubtless heard about the split in the Brotherhood here?'

'I know something of it.'

He listened while Manus supplied the details. From Manus Devlin's viewpoint there was only one Brotherhood and that was Roberts's wing.

John-Joe listened in silence to his father's recital of events since he had left for Ireland and then he said, 'I escorted James Stephens to New York. He plans to throw his weight in support of his old friend O'Mahoney. I believe he is going to address a series of meetings across the country to speak out against Roberts and the plan to establish an Irish Republic-in-Exile.'

Manus shook his head. 'He won't be able to do much damage to the Brotherhood.'

'He still has a reputation, Pa,' John-Joe pointed out. 'The Wandering Hawk, the personification of the rising in Ireland.'

'Times change, son. No man remains a hero for ever.'

'But he could do a great deal of damage by speaking against Roberts and swinging support behind O'Mahony.'

'O'Mahony's influence is finished after the fiasco at New Brunswick. Now his group are just a small coterie of bitter, frustrated men caught up in a debate over details of doctrine and policy – whether it is right to insert such and such a word in a proposal or whether another word is more fitting. Our people want action and only our senate wing holds out that hope. Besides, John-Joe, I can tell you confidentally that Stephens won't have time to do much damage.'

John-Joe shot a look of inquiry at his father.

'I have it on good authority,' Manus Devlin lowered his voice, 'that our movement into the British provinces starts in a few weeks' time.'

John-Joe gaped for a moment. Action! At last here was action. 'Then I'm with Roberts all the way, Pa.'

'That's the spirit son,' nodded Manus Devlin approvingly. 'We're in the process of making history. We have a large army, trained and waiting to strike for Irish freedom. The men are eager but restless. That's why senate has to strike soon lest they grow dissatisfied and gradually fall away and the entire movement be lost. Now we are on the move. We'll establish a state across the border which will be recognized by all governments hostile to England and, God knows, there are plenty of those. There will be an Irish state which will become the champion of the Irish people until the day that England decides to leave Ireland.'

'Is it really going ahead? No delays? Are we really invading?'

His father nodded eagerly. 'I've been serving on our navy committee, son, and we already have three men-o'-war at our disposal. The third is being refitted in the Brooklyn dockyards at this moment.'

'A man-o'-war?' John-Joe was astounded. 'An Irish man-o'-war?'

'The one we are currently refitting is an iron sidewheel steamer of 600 tons,' Manus grinned. 'I've been over to have a look at her. She's old but pretty sprightly. The irony is that she was built on the Clyde, a British ship which the US Navy captured while it was blockade running to the Confederacy. They refitted her and used her in the Gulf Squadron until the end of the war.'

'How much did the Brotherhood pay for her?'

'I'm not supposed to say, son, but I'll tell you. About $30,000 including the six guns broadside and a pivot gun forward. The purchase included the breeching bolts, shell rooms . . . just about everything. She's capable of doing thirteen-and-a-half knots. She'll be ready to join her two companions and take to the high seas once we've secured our seaport up north. She'll be able to strike at the English Cunard ships and harass her shipping generally. An Irish Navy striking at the English for the first time since the days of the Irish Confederacy in the seventeenth century! Think of it, John-Joe!'

'If only the people in Ireland knew about it. It would give them such heart.'

Manus Devlin reached forward to refill his son's glass. 'If you are going to join up with Roberts, it might mean leaving New York immediately.'

'You'll have to explain to mother,' John-Joe agreed. 'There is another thing though, Pa. . . .'

Manus gazed expectantly.

'I'm going to get married. To an Irish girl.'

Manus raised his eyebrows in astonishment, paused and then chuckled softly. 'And do we know the young lady?'

'No. I met her in Ireland. Her name is Murna Finucane.'

'And are you both in love?'

His son nodded emphatically. 'I promised that if I was unable to return to Ireland by the fall, I would send for her to join me. I doubt whether this will be over by the fall, Pa.'

'Wouldn't it be wise to wait awhile, son?' asked Manus, stroking the side of his nose. 'With the coming troubles it might not be such a good idea to marry immediately.'

'I will not wait beyond the fall,' John-Joe said.

Manus smiled at the flat resolve in his younger son's voice and heard his own stubborn attitudes mirrored there.

'All right, son. We'll tell your mother. We'll find some way of sending her the passage money to bring her to New York. I have a friend in Dublin who can arrange such things.' He smiled broadly. 'It will be nice for your mother to have the prospect of a daughter-in-law. She was more upset than she would say when Gavin and Rosaleen . . . well, when it broke up. The idea of a marriage will concentrate her mind away from the troubles.'

'She must be worried, not knowing where Gavin is,' John-Joe observed.

'Yes. She worries a lot about Gavin.'

'Wouldn't Father MacMahon know how to get in touch with him?'

'If he does, he probably would not say unless it was in the Brotherhood's interests.'

'Well,' John-Joe rose to go to bed, 'wherever Gavin is, let's hope that he is well and happy.'

'Amen to that, son,' agreed his father.

It was the first really warm night of the year. Young Tom had been in bed for some hours but Gavin was seated on the verandah of the wooden farmhouse gazing into the velvet stillness of the night. It was balmy but too early for the mosquitoes and sandflies to come swarming attracted by the light of the lamp which stood on the table by his side. It was a peaceful evening and yet it made Gavin sad. It would not be long before he would have to leave the farmstead to report to Sweeny in Buffalo. Not long and yet he had not resolved his relationship with Kate Dawtry in spite of his talk with Doc Taylor, nor had he been able to think much beyond the approach of 31 May. Rumours and alarms about the Fenians were constantly appearing in the newspapers. Only that morning a newspaper had carried a report that all marine insurance companies were refusing to insure cargoes being shipped through the Welland Canal in case of a Fenian attack there. An American line of steamers, the Northern Transit Company, which ran ships through from Lake Erie to Oswego on Lake Ontario, had stopped all their vessels heading through the canal.

The door opened behind him. Kate Dawtry, having finished her chores in the kitchen, came out with a shawl around her shoulders and stretched as she gazed up to the pale moon.

'It's a grand night,' she said, perching herself on the rail of the verandah.

'Do you still hate it?' asked Gavin suddenly.

'What?' She did not understand.

'You told me once that you hated all this . . . the life of farming.'

She shrugged. 'It's bearable in spring and in summer and even in the fall. But being bearable doesn't mean I can come to like it, Gavin. What about you? You're not going to be a farm hand all your life.'

Gavin fumbled in his pocket and started to make a cigarette. 'I've not been thinking much about the future, Kate.'

'You're wasting your talents and education here. You know that.'

'Maybe. Maybe some day I'll put down some roots and start to practise law. It's what I always wanted. When I realized that circumstances had stopped me from practising law in New York, I thought, for a while, I'd go to San Francisco. It's a new town, a city, opening up there.'

Kate smiled. 'San Francisco? Even the name means warmth to me. All year round warmth. That's my dream, Gavin. If ever I had the courage to get rid of this millstone of a farm, then I'd like to go to the west, to somewhere like San Francisco. I don't want to feel the cold any more, don't want to wake up on a winter's morning and hack my way through ice and snow to the barn to milk cows with the milk freezing in the pail as fast as it comes from the udder.' She glanced at him. 'I envy you, Gavin. At least you have a profession if you wanted to take it up. There's no need for you to stay here. God, I wish I was a man!'

'I'm glad that you're not!' Gavin said fervently.

Kate smiled in amusement.

Suddenly Gavin realized that he'd been waiting a long time for the opportunity that was now his, waiting, rehearsing the words he would say. He knew that he had to say what he felt but he was tongue-tied.

'If you did . . . did sell the farmstead. . . .'

She sat staring at him with a small, quizzical smile. 'Yes?' she prompted.

There was a scuffling sound which made her turn her head and peer into the darkness. 'Oh Lord!' she cried, leaping disconcertedly to her feet. 'Racoons in the turnip patch!'

She seized a yard broom from nearby and went dashing into the night. With a suppressed curse, Gavin rose to follow her. He could see the dark shapes of the racoons moving among the turnips as Kate ran down on them brandishing the broom above her head and yelling fiercely. This way and that sprang the ring-tailed creatures, sprinting towards the trees where they usually clung when danger threatened. The breeding season had just passed and now the nocturnal little carnivores were emerging from their dens in the hollow trees and logs and crevices in rocks to grab whatever edible things they could forage. Thumping her broom, Kate ran after them trying to chase them from the garden.

Whooping, Gavin followed her lead and attempted to scare the 'coons out of the trees so that they would not simply climb down and attack the turnip patch again when it was safe. As he ran he caught his toe in a protruding root and went sprawling face down on the earth. Kate, who was just behind him, measured her length across him with a small scream. Gavin turned over, gazed up at her and began to chuckle. She stared down at him in the gloom, indignant for a moment until the humour of the situation caught her and she, too, began to laugh. For a while they lay full length on the damp, pungent earth among the turnips, laughing as if it were the funniest thing ever. And then Gavin reached slowly up, letting his fingers touch her earth-smeared cheek, gently wiping away the dirt. At the touch of his fingers she stopped laughing and stared down at him. She made no effort to rise from the warmth of his body. His hand gently encircled the back of her head and drew her face down to his. Their lips touched, soft and cold upon each other; touched and parted and then touched again more certainly. It was a slow, gentle embrace but it contained a passion which startled both of them. It was a long while before they broke apart.

'Kate?'

'Yes?'

'If I did go to San Francisco . . .' the idea was only just taking a definite shape in his mind. 'If I did . . . would you . . . you and Young Tom . . . come with me?'

There was no hesitation. 'Yes.'

Gavin felt an inextricable thrill of pleasure surge through his body.

'I love you.'

'I'm glad,' she whispered back. 'I've loved you for quite a while.'

He held her tightly, yet the contentment and happiness which surged through him was overshadowed, was threatened by the coming of 31 May. He tried to stifle the thought and succeeded for a while. They broke apart when Young Tom's voice called from the verandah of the house.

'Hey! I got woken up.'

'What is it, Tom?' demanded the girl breathlessly, as she tried to brush the earth from her clothes.

'What are you doing out there?'

'Chasing racoons,' replied Kate. Then she glanced at Gavin and began to giggle helplessly.

Chapter 43

The headquarters of the senate wing of the Brotherhood was a throb of activity. New offices had been established above Roberts's store and warehouses on Broadway in January when O'Mahoney had the senate supporters ejected from the building on the legal technicality that it was his signature on the lease of the Moffat Mansion on Union Square. The new offices were improvised and crowded. As he entered, John-Joe was asked to prove his identity before being escorted up a stairway to a pokey office in which William Randall Roberts was crammed. Roberts was hunched behind a desk crowded with papers. Perched on a corner of it was a stocky, bearded man in civilian clothes but whose empty right sleeve made John-Joe recognize him as General 'Fighting Tom' Sweeny. Roberts rose and shook John-Joe's hand before introducing Sweeny.

'We're delighted that you have decided to join us, lieutenant,' Roberts said as he slumped back into his chair. 'Your father and brother are among our most committed supporters and we value their services highly.' He hesitated and then added, 'We don't want you here under false colours so I must emphasize that James Stephens has declared himself totally opposed to our movement, claiming that we are the breakaway group and that O'Mahoney's movement is the official Brotherhood. You do understand that?'

'I do,' John-Joe said. 'I know all about the split.'

'I acknowledge that Stephens has worked miracles in the past by organizing the Brotherhood and, indeed, he has built it and guided it to a point where the Irish nation stands on the verge of victory. It has only to reach out and grasp freedom. But,' Roberts grimaced, 'for some reason best known to himself, Stephens is holding back and while he is holding back the Brotherhood could be destroyed and lose the historic moment.'

Roberts paused and glanced at Sweeny.

The one-armed general smiled at John-Joe. 'You have spent some time in Ireland, lieutenant. What would you say the mood is there?'

'One of frustration,' replied John-Joe immediately. 'The English have been able to take advantage of Stephens's delays by using their informers. The Military Council in Dublin have been almost all arrested. Only General Halpin and Colonel Kelly remain at liberty and Kelly is trying to rebuild the Military Council with men equally talented to the ones that have been lost by the arrests. That is a Herculean task. The English have moved all the regiments containing Fenian suspects out of Ireland and sent them to other parts of their empire. Some 8,000 trained and armed soldiers have been lost to us in this move. New English regiments have been poured into Ireland and the Brotherhood can rely on no one in the military garrisons.'

John-Joe hesitated. Roberts bent across the desk and prompted him to go on.

'I don't wish to denigrate Mister Stephens. I acknowledge that he created the Brotherhood. However, it is my opinion that we have lost the main chance in Ireland. By vacillation, by not giving the word, Stephens has allowed the enemy to take the upper hand and deal a severe blow at the organization in Ireland. Had the Brotherhood there risen in September I have no hesitation in saying that success would have been ours. Even as late as November and up to January a euphoria surrounded Stephens's escape from Richmond Jail which would have created the conditions for success.'

Sweeny grimaced. 'To what conclusion are you drawn, lieutenant?' he asked.

'That the plan to create a Republic-in-Exile from which either to bargain or strike at the English where they are weakest is the only hope for our people. It will instil new backbone into the demoralized movement in Ireland.'

'And you are willing to take part in the venture?' asked Roberts.

'That is why I came here.'

Sweeny smiled briefly. 'I am assigning you to General Lynch's army, lieutenant. There are three wagons of Springfield rifles and ammunition stored at Yonkers under the charge of six volunteers. You are commissioned to take charge of them and transport them by the quickest possible means to Buffalo. They are to be delivered into the charge of Patrick O'Day, the head of the Brotherhood in Buffalo. He has auction rooms on Pearl Street. Those rifles are a valuable acquisition and General Lynch must have them by the end of the month.'

'Very good, sir. And after that?'

'Report to General Lynch or his adjutant, Captain Hynes, for assignment.'

Action. Excitement tingled in John-Joe's body. The interminable waiting had stopped. He took the regulation military pace backwards, saluted and swung smartly for the door.

They were sitting eating a midday meal having spent the morning hoeing the potato field when Gavin decided to tell Kate. He did it without premeditation, on the spur of the moment.

'I'll be going away at the end of the month.'

He saw her figure tense. 'Oh?' It was a sighing breath of a question.

'I'll be coming back just as soon as I can. But I have to go away for a while, Kate.'

She raised her head and stared at him, her gaze steady. 'Where are you going?'

'I can't tell you,' he replied hesitantly. 'It is something that I am obliged to do, that's all.'

The hazel in her ice-grey eyes flickered with a curious fire. 'I'm no fool, Gavin,' she said softly. 'Jim told me that he suspected you were a Fenian when you first came here. Was he right after all? Are you a Fenian?'

He wanted to deny it; the denial sprang readily to his lips. Instead he quietly said, 'Yes.'

Her shoulders drooped a little. 'I'm confused, Gavin.'

'There's no confusion in the fact that I love you, Kate. I want to marry you.'

'And you a Fenian?' There was a slight bitterness to her voice.

'That has nothing to do with the way I feel for you.'

The girl sighed deeply, sadly. 'I wish I could understand. Everyone says that the Fenians are a bunch of drunken marauders who are going to raid the country, robbing, looting and God knows what else.'

'That's not so, Kate.'

'Then what's the truth of it, Gavin? I've grown to love you while trying to suppress the suspicions I had. Even Jim has come to believe that you cannot be a member of that band of cut-throats.'

'Let me tell you why I became a member of the Brotherhood, Kate. Will you allow that?'

She nodded almost reluctantly.

He began where it had always begun – with Jack Quinlan, with

Quinlan's death. He told her stories, many half-forgotten of his family, of Ireland, of the poverty among the immigrants in New York and somehow out of the whole he wove his *raison d'être*, the causes which had brought him to a conversion; a struggle against misgovernment, injustice and wrong-doing, a rationale of the seething anger at the injustices of society. And particularly of Nora Quinlan, whose death had been the trigger which had projected him into the movement. Kate watched the ingenuous passion on his face, his infectious sincerity of compassion and idealism. He reminded her so much of Grandpa Tom who had suffered the same indignation against the wrongs perpetrated by uncaring governments, woven into an imprisoning web of society. Yet she could not accept his cause, did not feel any conversion as Paul had been converted to Christianity by a momentary vision on the road to Damascus. She could accept that, if Gavin was right, then the people of Ireland were justified in calling for freedom . . . but what had that to do with Canada?

'The provinces of British North America are colonies of England,' Gavin insisted. 'They fly the English Union flag and do homage to the English Queen. There is an English army and navy which guards these colonies. England is the implacable enemy of Ireland and the Irish people. She has conquered Ireland and holds the country by force, by an army of occupation. The Fenians' fight is with England and until England relinquishes Ireland and allows the people to govern themselves she will continue to fight England.'

'Then why not fight the English in Ireland?' demanded Kate. 'You know the people here, our friends and neighbours – people like the Svensons. What do they know of Ireland? Why do the Fenians want to invade this land whose people have no interest in Ireland?'

Gavin shook his head. 'The same people who rule this land rule Ireland. It is as simple as that, Kate. Ireland has a right to pick her own battlefields, just as England has done in the past. England chose North America as the battlefield on which to fight her wars against France and Spain. What had North America to do with those countries? What had North America to do with England's wars in Europe? While the English government, the English flag and an English army maintain themselves in this country then Ireland is justified in striking here.'

'And if the people of these provinces want to be ruled by the English and the English Queen, surely that is their right?' retorted Kate.

'Then let England give up Ireland and she can keep Canada.'

Kate pursed her lips. 'It is not as simple as that, Gavin,' she said. 'Don't your leaders know it.'

'Kate,' Gavin reached forward and took her hand tightly. 'You don't think that I want to fight people here, the Svensons, Doc Taylor and the others? They are good people. They have fought nature to carve themselves a life in this wilderness and I honour them for it. God! If the Irish people had the same freedoms in Ireland as you people have in these provinces then we would have no quarrel. But the Irish have no freedom at all and England must be forced to give them the right to govern themselves because she will not do it voluntarily. The Fenians have to use English possessions as bargaining pawns in the game of chess that will force the issue.'

'Have you thought of this?' Kate said. 'When the Fenians cross our frontier they will not simply find English regular troops facing them but members of the volunteer militia; young farm boys, students, sons of colonists from countries who have never even heard of Ireland? They'll be fighting to defend their homes and families with the same depth of feeling which you claim for the Fenians.'

Gavin smiled bitterly. 'And with the farm lads there will be the Mullan Nauls and the Peep o' Day Boys.'

Kate sighed, 'Yes, I grant you that. But they are so few, Gavin.' Her voice rose abruptly harsh. 'God, haven't you had enough of war and killing?'

It was a brutal thrust and he winced. 'Yes, I have. But standing back now will simply store more bloodshed for future generations.'

'You are determined to join this mad scheme?'

'I owe it to my people,' he said simply. There was no pretension in his statement. It was merely one of fact.

'You are so like Grandpa Tom,' she muttered angrily. 'Stubborn, high minded – a Don Quixote going out to tilt at windmills. Don Quixote. That was one of Grandpa Tom's favourite books. It suited his character. Like him, you want to save the world but the world doesn't want to be saved.'

'I think it does,' Gavin said quietly.

'So did Quixote. There's no reward for a Don Quixote in this world, Gavin.'

She swung away and then turned back abruptly, her eyes moistening. 'I love you, Gavin Quixote Devlin. Can't you give up this madness and let's go to San Francisco now? Tomorrow, today, immediately?'

He shook his head gently. 'I cannot. I would not be able to live with myself if I deserted my people having come this far.'

She stiffled a sob and lowered her head. 'I cannot believe in what you stand for but I know that you are sincere and for that I can't condemn you nor can I betray you.'

She sprang to her feet and walked back towards the potato field. Gavin watched her go feeling the pain of conflicting emotions struggling within him.

When John-Joe arrived at the livery stable in Yonkers, where he was to pick up the six volunteers and the three wagonloads of weapons, he spotted a familiar figure waiting for him. Standing by the stable doors was a priest in his late forties with steel-grey hair and a sharp scrutinizing glançe.

'Father MacMahon! What are you doing here?'

The priest came forward and gripped John-Joe's hand firmly. His eyes crinkled. 'Didn't they tell you now? I'm one of your volunteers, son.'

John-Joe was shocked and showed it. 'But, Father. . . .' he hesitated.

'Aye, I'm a priest, is that it?' supplied Father MacMahon. 'Sure, and wasn't I a priest when I charged alongside you boys in the Irish Brigade?'

'But that was different. You were a chaplain in the Brigade.'

'And I'll be a chaplain again. There's a lot of lads up in Buffalo who will soon be needing a priest.'

John-Joe was contrite. 'Sorry, Father. I hadn't thought about it.'

MacMahon changed the conversation. 'How's yourself anyway, and how are your parents?'

'My parents are well, Father.'

'And you've returned from the old country. How is she?'

'Pretty bad.'

Father MacMahon shrugged. 'Ah well, who knows? Perhaps it won't be long now until we see a parliament sitting in Dublin once again.

> Life has conquered; the wind has blown away
> Alexander, Caesar and all their power and sway;
> Tara and Troy have made no longer stay;
> Maybe the English too will have their day.

John-Joe looked at him in amusement. 'Your own composition, Father?'

Father MacMahon chuckled and shook his head. 'My own translation from the original Irish which was composed about a hundred years ago.' He turned into the livery stable. 'I'd better introduce you to your fellow desperados who'll help transport your weapons of war to Buffalo.'

'One other thing, Father,' said John-Joe catching him by the sleeve. 'Do you have any word of Gavin?'

Father MacMahon shook his head. 'Not for a while. The last I heard was that he had gone north of the border to hunt.'

John-Joe's jaw dropped a fraction. 'To hunt?'

The priest chuckled at his astonishment.

'Sure, isn't that what we are all going to be doing shortly?' He winked broadly, turning into the stable before John-Joe realized exactly what he meant.

The three wagonloads of guns and ammunition had been stored by the livery stable owner and the weapons had been packed in crates marked 'furniture'. The crates were placed in the wagons under tarpaulins. In addition to Father MacMahon there were five volunteers to drive the wagons and a team of two mules to draw each one. John-Joe, assuming command, divided the men into pairs while he rode with the lead wagon. The early stages of the journey were easy enough for the wagons and their loads were taken by commercial barge as far as Albany, the state capital. The wagons were then loaded on to a freight train for Rochester, on the shores of Lake Ontario. From there John-Joe took his charges by roadway to Buffalo. They reached the outskirts of the city three days before the end of the month.

Patrick O'Day, the 'head centre' of the Brotherhood in Buffalo, had his auction rooms at 20–22 Pearl Street. O'Day had built up a thriving business in the city, having established himself there on his arrival from Ireland. He was well connected among the Buffalo business community, had a large house at 112 Jersey Street and he, his wife Bridget and their seven-year-old son Patrick James were regular worshippers at the Church of the Holy Angels in Porter Street. O'Day had been an early convert to the Brotherhood. He worked tirelessly and spent a great deal of his personal income in the furtherance of the cause. When Thomas D'Arcy McGee had lived briefly in Buffalo producing his Republican newspaper, O'Day had been an ardent supporter. Since McGee had set himself up as a British loyalist and the scourge of Irish Republicans, O'Day had become his vehement enemy, even offering a reward for McGee of $1,000.

John-Joe found the auction rooms without trouble and O'Day introduced him to Captain Hynes, General Lynch's assistant adjutant. Hynes was a small harassed-looking man who reminded John-Joe of a bank clerk. Father MacMahon had apparently met him before because they exchanged a friendly greeting.

'Delighted you made it with the arms, Devlin,' Hynes smiled as the wagons had been hauled into the stables, the tarpaulin stripped and the crates stacked by men wearing an odd assortment of Union and Confederate army uniforms. 'Our men will be needing these Springfields.'

O'Day was making notes on a manifest. 'I don't suppose you heard anything at headquarters about the field guns that we have been promised? There was also some word that we may get some Gatling guns.'

John-Joe shook his head. 'I was simply told to deliver these for General Lynch by the end of the month and then report for further duty.'

Hynes sighed morosely. 'A couple of Gatlings would stand us to the good. A five-barrelled Gatling can fire 700 rounds a minute – think of that! General Lynch said that he was promised a couple.'

'I'm sorry, sir. I know nothing beyond what I have told you.'

'No matter,' muttered Hynes, changing the subject. 'Now, you'll be billeted at Mansion House Hotel, that's on Main Street. You will have to share the room with another officer. Father MacMahon, we have a room for you at the Revers House Hotel.'

Hynes glanced back at John-Joe. 'Do you have a uniform?'

Aideen Devlin had presented John-Joe with her hand-made uniform, based on the one she had made for Gavin, as a parting gift. John-Joe had it in his luggage. He nodded.

'Well, do not wear it until the word is given and make no indication of who or what you are or your intent. We have many friends in the city but we also have many enemies. Watch what you say and who you say it to, remember the British are just across the river.'

'Is there anyone in particular to watch out for?'

'Everyone and anyone. The mayor of this city, John Wells, for example, is not kindly disposed to the Brotherhood. And a few weeks ago a new superintendent of the city police, David Reynolds, was appointed and he seems just a little too friendly with Hemans the British Consul here. Vigilance and security are the watchwords.'

'So something is really happening?' John-Joe asked with satisfaction.

Hynes raised an eyebrow. 'You doubted it?'

'I've just come back from Ireland,' John-Joe explained. 'It was all talk and little action.'

'You came back with Stephens?'

John-Joe nodded.

'I hear the man is scheduled to speak out against our invasion at a meeting in Philadelphia on Friday night.' Hynes's face suddenly cracked into a broad smile. 'Stephens has picked an ideal moment.'

'Why?' demanded Father MacMahon.

'Because that's the very night we cross the border.'

Chapter 44

Far off a bugle sounded.

The earth was cold, icy cold, and the mud clung to his shivering body like anxious hands, caressing him with frosty fingers. The smell of the earth was a sickly stench, permeated with the odour of decaying corpses, the purient smell of decomposing flesh. The earth was full of death; was death itself. He lay in the mud with the night black sky oppressive above him. Clouds like shadows hid the moon and stars, racing in their low masses swiftly across the sky. It was quiet; deathly still yet he knew what was to come.

Far off a bugle sounded. The thunder of explosions, regular and monotonous, the belch of flame and roar of the enemy's cannonade, began even as he knew it would; began with every shell aimed at him, screaming towards him like devils from the infernal region. Explosions ripped the mud all around him, mingling it with the warm red liquid from those who had crouched around him. Even as he knew it would, the figure stood up.

Ready the flag!

Jack Quinlan's resonant baritone urged the men upwards, upwards and onwards. Men screamed in fear and pain as explosion after explosion rocked the earth around them, showering them with mud and wet, sticky flesh as limbs were torn from bodies and flung in abandoned fashion.

Ready the flag!

In lines, in serried ranks, they began to move forward, moving in lines under the cracking of their silk battleflags. Drums beat the marching pace, the single monotonous beat as they moved through the blackness, rifles held forward, bayonets glinting here and there in the smoke-filled gloom. Far off a bugle sounded! Shrieking, crying, weeping incoherently, they began to run with the mud clawing at their legs as if it were trying to aid the enemy in holding back the charge. The cannonade poured into their serried ranks with its remorseless message of death.

Ready the flag.

The voice of Jack Quinlan rose to a scream. He was all alone then. Suddenly. All alone on the green sward by a gushing silvery creek. She was kneeling beside him, smiling down at him. He tried to focus on her face. The pale, emaciated face of Nora Quinlan . . . no, not quite. It was difficult to focus, so difficult. The green shimmering silk that draped her body fluttered in the breeze, blowing across her face so that he could not see the features.

'Who are you?' he whispered hoarsely.

Her laugh was a sighing echo of the gurgling stream. 'Who do you think I am, Captain Devlin?'

'Are you . . . are you Fand, Pearl of Beauty?'

'You know I am not.'

'Nora . . . Nora Quinlan?'

'Is it Nora Quinlan that you want?'

He struggled to see her face.

Laughingly she bent towards him, the green cloth shimmering away from her features for a split second.

'Kate Dawtry!'

'What, is it her you want, Captain Devlin?' came her mocking voice.

He tried to struggle upwards, towards her, and found himself meeting the dark, haunted eyes of Jack Quinlan. the stark figure on a small wooden cart, the bloody stumps of his severed legs dripping red on the green grass, a claw-like hand thrust towards him. He opened his mouth to scream at the haunted eyes that accused him. He tried to turn his head away.

'If you can't spare a dime, you must pay in kind,' grinned the red slit of a mouth. 'Duty is duty. We all have a duty.'

Then Jack Quinlan's cart was moving backwards, swaying backwards into the red blackness of battle and the girl was walking slowly beside him. Only once did she turn back with sorrow in her eyes.

Gavin awoke in his cot in a cold sweat. Dawn's grey light was seeping under the shutters. He swallowed painfully and reached up a hand to wipe his forehead. It was Tuesday and tomorrow he would have to leave for Buffalo. He felt anxious and confused. He wanted to stay. It would be so easy, so simple, to stay. Did he really owe the

Brotherhood something? He shivered as he asked himself the question. Of course he did. He owed his people something. He owed his family. Owed Jack and Nora Quinlan and all the ghosts of the past. He owed them a moral duty. Not to go would be a betrayal which he could never live with. He owed it to his people, the Irish people whose collective consciousness had born him and given him character. In the dim recesses of his mind their ghosts were calling him. . . . Yet it would be so easy, so much simpler to stay.

He swung out of bed and sat for a moment rubbing his temples as if to chase away the ghosts. Then he caught sight of his valise. He had not opened the parcel since that first day in Father MacMahon's house. In it lay his sword and gunbelt. He took down the bag and opened it, rummaging down to the parcel and tearing at the string. Gently he lifted out that dark green uniform jacket which his mother had so carefuly sewn for him, his eyes wandering to the brass buttons with their imprinted shamrocks and the captain's bars and the insignia bearing the words *Fianna Éireann*. Obeying some inner compulsion he slipped the uniform jacket on, moving to stand in front of the cracked mirror on the dressing table. He stood, staring at the strange apparition who stared back at him.

He was so engrossed that he did not hear the door open. He heard the sharp intake of breath and turned to see the face of Young Tom staring at him with wide eyes. Gavin turned confused.

'Have you joined the militia, Gavin?' asked the boy peering at the uniform.

Gavin bit his lip and shook his head. He could not lie to the boy any more than he could lie to Kate.

Young Tom came closer, his eyes wandering over the green uniform jacket, taking in the badges of the sunburst and harp, the foreign lettering and the brass buttons with their insignia. Frank Leslie's *Illustrated Newspaper* had been too regularly packed with renditions of Fenian symbols for the boy not to know what he was looking at.

'You *are* a Fenian!' he gasped.

Gavin did not deny it.

Young Tom's face suddenly worked into a mask of tearful rage.

'You're a Fenian!' he cried shrilly. 'A dirty, cowardly Fenian!'

Gavin moved towards him, hand outstretched, but the boy turned and ran from the room, out of the house and away across the farmyard like a jack-rabbit. Gavin halted on the verandah. Kate, a pail of milk in her hand, was standing on the steps staring at his green uniform jacket.

'What's upset Young Tom?' she demanded.

'He came into my room as I was trying on my uniform,' Gavin said flatly. 'He's bright enough to recognize the Fenian badges.'

Kate, her face suddenly white, put down her bucket and looked closely at the jacket. In her eyes there was a question.

'It's time. I'll be leaving tomorrow, Kate. But I swear I'll be back.'

Her mouth quirked in emotion. 'Back?' Her voice was sharp. 'You'll be back bringing your conquering horde, I suppose?'

'I'll be back for you, Kate.'

She shook her head slowly. 'You'd better get inside and take that jacket off otherwise you'll be going nowhere. Did you have to let Young Tom see?'

'I'm not ashamed of what I am, Kate.'

'That's one thing. Trying to explain it to Young Tom is another. If I can't understand it, Gavin, why should Young Tom? My conscience tells me that I ought to go for the constable but my heart won't let me. I can't. I don't know what I should do.'

Her lip trembled and she raised a hand to her mouth.

'Kate. . . .' he began.

'Get inside and take that damned jacket off,' she snapped.

She followed him in as he took off the jacket and replaced it in his valise. He turned to her as she stood staring at him with tear-stained eyes.

'I shall come back for you, Kate. That's a promise.'

'And it's the one thing you can't promise, Gavin. It will not be in your control.'

'Then let's say that it is my intention while I'm alive.'

Her face crumpled abruptly. 'What you are doing is madness, Gavin,' she was sobbing and he moved forward to take her in his arms. 'You'll be killed! And for what, for what?'

'I've told you, Kate. I must go. It is my . . . duty.'

She stared up at him through her tears. 'You are just like Grandpa Tom, damn you! Damn all you idealists! You want to make the world a better place. You say you care about your fellow men. And yet your fellow men don't care a damn whether you live or die. You'll go out and get yourself killed or crippled. You could be caught and, if they don't hang you, then you'll spend the rest of your life in jail. Do you think that will really change the world?'

Gavin shrugged. 'I have to believe it otherwise there is no point in anything,' he said quietly.

'That's just it,' her gaze was imploring. 'Don't you see. There is no point in throwing your life away when nothing will change?'

'If that's the way it is, Kate,' Gavin said softly, 'if we are condemned to a life in which we cannot change things, then there's little use in living at all. Things must change, Kate. Things can be changed. They do change.'

She broke away from him and turned to stare out the window. 'Just like Grandpa Tom,' she sneered. 'What did he achieve? Him and his Liberty Tree? Where are the English Republicans now, those who wanted to usher in a bright new world of equal laws and opportunities? Those who survived ended their lives in exile or in prison. They were vilified as traitors and rebels, not as patriots and saviours of their country and their fellow men. Why, I doubt if anyone in England even remembers their attempts to establish an English Republic!'

Gavin placed his hands on the girl's shoulders and gazed into her eyes. 'Your Grandpa Tom didn't believe in the things he did, do the things he did, simply because of what people would say about him. He did not want to have the good opinions of society. He believed in what he did because for him it was the only moral thing to do, the only way forward, the only way to stop misery, poverty and suffering in the world.'

'Then damn you and your morals!' cried the girl.

Gavin glanced out of the window towards the two oak trees which formed the entrance gate into the farmyard. 'Didn't you tell me that Grandpa Tom planted those trees himself and called them his trees of liberty? The tree of liberty was once a symbol of mankind's hopes, the Rights of Man. I must go and plant my own liberty tree, Kate. Please understand.'

He drew her close again. For a moment she struggled and then came willingly into his arms, her lips seeking his demandingly. Then she pushed him away, smiling sadly.

'I cannot understand or approve your views, Gavin. I don't know enough. Ireland is too far away. I know nothing about it. Perhaps I could be persuaded what you are doing is right . . . but I don't know enough. I don't know. The only thing I can say is that I respect the sincerity with which you hold your views and I acknowledge your right to hold them.'

Gavin exhaled softly. 'I can't ask for more than that, Kate.'

'It's like a fever,' the girl said. 'I know nothing will stop you. Just like Grandpa Tom. Go out and tilt at windmills, Gavin Quixote Devlin. It will not achieve anything.'

'Even if it fails I can live with the failure. I will have tried, at least. I will not be able to live with myself if I don't try at all.'

Her body went tense and her eyes widened. 'We've forgotten . . . Young Tom! He's upset, Gavin. We must find him.'

Gavin was suddenly anxious. He had forgotten about Young Tom and cursed himself for doing so. 'I'll find him and talk with him.'

She laid a hand on his arm. 'Be easy, Gavin. He's had a shock. He has grown to look up to you, admire you. Now he has discovered that you represent everything he has been told to despise. He just won't be able to understand.'

Gavin tried to hide the pain he felt. 'I'll find him,' he promised.

'He's probably gone up to Bear Rock. He has a special place there where he goes. It's an outcrop of limestone about a mile into the bush due north from here.'

Gavin pulled on his shirt, took down the old hunting gun from the wall, and left the farmstead. He turned across the split rail fences, moving quickly to where the woods started beyond the cultivated fields. The crows were wheeling in spectacular aerial displays in the sky and sitting on the branches of the trees giving vent to their raucous series of mating calls. Some had already mated and were building nests of grass and twigs in the branches of the trees. He found a ridge of limestone which stretched like a tentacle through the countryside, rising up towards the distant Niagara escarpment which ran down the peninsula between Lake Erie and Lake Ontario. He moved quickly, anxiously. It was not long before he spotted the outcrop thrusting upwards through the trees – a careless heap of bare rocks basking in the sun.

'Tom!' Gavin's voice echoed against the thickly growing surrounding trees. There was no answer.

'Hey, Tom! We must talk.' He put his head to one side, hearing a slight scuffling sound. He glanced round with narrowed eyes, hardly moving his head, not wishing to alarm the boy. Then he slowly climbed towards the top of the outcrop.

'Gavin!' Young Tom's voice was full of fear.

Gavin jerked his head up just in time to see the black muzzle of a revolver pointing down at him.

'Far enough, Teig. Drop your gun.'

Mullan Naul was peering down at him with a thin, sneering smile on his coarse features. One hand held Young Tom by the scruff of the neck, the boy struggled, trying to hit out at the man with his small clenched fists. Naul's other hand held a revolver. The grip was firm and unwavering. Gavin shrugged and let the musket fall to his feet.

Naul nodded with satisfaction. 'Now climb up the rest of the way. Slowly, mind.'

Gavin did so, scrambling up to the flat-topped rock on which Naul stood. 'Everyone was wondering where you were hiding, Naul. I thought you might be with your friend – Hogan.'

Mullan Naul blinked but the smile did not leave his face. 'Hands where I can see them, Teig,' he snapped.

'Let the boy go.'

Naul chuckled. 'You just take it easy, Teig. I've spent weeks having to hide out because of you. Had to spend time up at Biddulph waiting until I could come back. I owe you, Teig.'

'Let the boy go,' Gavin repeated.

Naul suddenly gave the boy a vicious shake, releasing him so suddenly that Young Tom fell back on to the rocks with a sharp cry.

'There's no need for that,' Gavin protested.

Young Tom raised himself suppressing a sob.

'Are you all right, Young Tom?' Gavin asked.

'I didn't mean to call you names,' sobbed the boy. 'I don't care if you are a Fenian.'

'It's all right, son.'

'I'm going to get pleasure out of this, Teig,' Naul grinned, thumbing back the hammer of his revolver.

'Aren't you going to wait for your pal, Hogan?'

'Hogan? A lot of help that bastard has been since I had to go on the run. I'll meet up with Hogan after I've settled with you.'

'I thought Hogan was your boss?'

'Did you now?' There was a tinge of anger which crept into Mullan Naul's voice.

'Yeah. I wondered how much he was paying you.'

'I don't have to be paid to bump off a lousy Teig.'

'I forgot. You are the great Orange patriot. Are you sure that Delancey's gold had nothing to do with it?'

There was no response on Mullan Naul's face. 'I don't know what you are talking about, Teig. If you are trying to delay things. you can forget it.'

Gavin bit his lip. He watched, sweating a little as Naul raised the revolver.

It was then that Young Tom gave a cry and came running to him.

'I didn't mean to, Gavin . . . I didn't mean to say what I did. I was angry and . . .'

Mullan Naul swore violently 'Get the boy away or he'll be hurt too.'

Young Tom swung round, his eyes wide with fear.

'Better do as the man says, son,' urged Gavin. 'Naul, you let the boy go, d'hear?'

'I hear.'

The movement was almost imperceptible, a black, shaggy shape rearing on its hind legs emerged out of the rocks behind and a little to the side of Mullan Naul. Young Tom gave a soft cry of alarm while Gavin gripped him by the shoulder and pushed the boy behind him. Naul watched their reactions in hesitant curiosity.

'Move easy this way,' hissed Gavin.

Naul stared at him for a moment. 'Quit trying to play games, Teig,' he snapped.

Behind him the great female black bear, its fur a reddy cinnamon colour in the rays of the sun, must have weighed all of 500 pounds.

'Run, Naul!' cried Gavin, easing backwards.

Mullan Naul hesitated. Then he heard the ominous growl and whirled round just as the giant female launched her attack, her great paws swinging. Even as Naul tried to depress the trigger of his revolver, she was on him. The gun exploded and the bullet must have entered the body of the bear for she fell on the man shrieking and rending with her giant claws.

Gavin grabbed the boy and was scrambling down the rocks to where his discarded musket lay, sweating as he worked to load it, cursing the fact that it was an old fashioned muzzle loader.

Young Tom watched fearfully as Gavin started back up the rocks. He managed one shot straight into the muzzle of the bear. Whether the shot was the cause or whether the revolver shot had mortally wounded the animal beforehand, the bear rose, waving her forepaws in the air, let out a shriek, fell on her side, lay panting a few moments and then was still.

Gavin stood shaking, the sweat pouring from his brow. He did not need a close inspection to see that Naul was dead. His ripped and bloody body lay sprawled in a grotesque attitude. After a few moments, Gavin said, 'Tom? It's all right, son.'

The boy came up to him, his frail body shaking. Gavin laid a hand on his shoulder and Young Tom burst into a flood of tears, grabbing him around the waist in a childish embrace. Gavin knelt awkwardly, trying to comfort him.

'We'd better get back to the farmstead,' he said. 'Your sister will have heard the shots and be worried.'

'I'm sorry that I called you names, Gavin,' sniffed the boy, trying to control his sobbing.

'That's all right, son. You'll have to make up your own mind about things.'

'I don't care if you are a Fenian. You must have a good reason to be, so I don't care!'

Gavin swung round sharply at the sound of a soft growling among the rocks. He was gripping at the musket when he saw two small bear cubs snuffling between the boulders.

'Is there a cave up there?' he asked Young Tom.

The boy nodded. 'It's an old den. It's why the place is called Bear Rock.'

The cubs must have been three months old, born while the sow was in her winter sleep and now they had emerged to gorge on the fresh green grass before eventually switching to dead meat and fish. They shambled plaintively towards their mother's carcass. Gavin, musket in one hand and the other clutching the boy, turned and eased carefully down the rocks. Even at this age bear cubs could still be dangerous and unpredictable. Gavin had heard old hunters tell that black bears had killed and maimed more people than all the other types of bears put together.

'We will have to tell Jim, won't we?' asked Young Tom.

'We will,' Gavin agreed. 'What do you intend telling the Doc?'

The boy stared up at him. 'Is it true what everyone says about the Fenians? Is it true that they are just a bunch of murdering renegades who want to conquer Canada and rob us?'

'No, son. That's not true at all. Do you want to know why I am a Fenian?'

Young Tom nodded and listened quietly, without interruption, while Gavin explained simply without rhetoric.

'If you want the Irish people to be free to rule themselves, why attack Canada?' he asked at last. 'We ain't done the Irish no harm, have we?'

Gavin sighed, 'It's called strategy, Young Tom. Then it's up to the politicians to sort it out.'

The boy pursed his lips reflectively. 'The job of politicians is to settle problems by sitting down at a table and talking things out, eh? Like the reeve and the township council?'

'That's about right.'

'And wars are fought when politicians don't do their jobs so good?'

Gavin smiled broadly. 'I think you have a point there.'

'I'd better run and find Jim,' the boy said. His face was serious. 'Mullan Naul should have known better than to hide out at Bear Rock.'

They exchanged a look of understanding and agreement. Gavin watched the boy run off towards the farmsteads and slowly walked on after him. He wanted to stay . . . it was so much easier. Such a simple way of dealing with his conflict.

Chapter 45

Gavin descended from the train at the Fort Erie railroad depot and glanced about him. He had left the farmstead at dawn before Kate and Young Tom wêre awake. It was better that way. He had left a message, a hastily scrawled note on a scrap of paper. When it was over he promised to return. She would understand that his ties of loyalty to his family, his friends and his people were forged in iron. She would understand and by that understanding know that he was also tied to her, that he would return for her. That was his promise.

Their last evening had been spent in uneasy quiet. Doc Taylor and the constable had come by and Gavin had shown them Bear Rock. No one asked any questions. They accepted that Mullan Naul had been hiding out at Bear Rock when the incident happened. There had been several deaths in the province from bears over the years, especially at this season when the sows were emerging from their winter lairs with their newborn cubs. Gavin helped Taylor and the constable wrap the remains of Naul in a tarpaulin and carry them back to Taylor's buggy. After Taylor and the constable had gone the evening had passed in almost silence. Before she went to bed Kate had kissed Gavin with a fierce longing kiss as if she knew it was time to part. He had slept fitfully, rising in the darkness to write his note, gathering his belongings and walking through the early dawn light to Sherk's Crossing. It was eight-thirty when he reached Fort Erie.

John Canty was not at the meeting place. Gavin waited awhile until he heard the persistent whistle of the *International* ferry warning of its departure for the American shore. He hurried down to the wharf. There were a few people about but not many. A red-coated soldier sat on a bale smokiing an old clay pipe while two officious-looking customs men were checking some cases. One or two passengers were embarking. Gavin paused on the ferry wharf wondering whether he should go on without Canty.

'Excuse me, mister,' Gavin swung round as he heard Canty's familiar tones. The major was sitting casually on a wood pile. 'Can you oblige me with a light?' Canty's pale eyes carried a warning.

Gavin put down his valise and fumbled for matches. As he moved his head towards Canty in the act of shielding the spluttering match, the major whispered, 'There's a couple of McMicken detectives in town. One of them is your friend Hogan. I think I'm being watched. I won't cross over with you just in case. If all goes well with the landing I'll be joining you as soon as General Lynch comes across. Tell Captain Hynes. He'll meet you on the other side.'

Gavin felt a coldness. 'Is Hogan here?' he shot back.

'He's taken a room at the City Hotel. Don't worry, I'll handle it.'

Canty rose and said loudly, 'Thanks, mister.' He strode away without looking back.

The ferry whistle sent its piercing cry once more into the morning air. Gavin turned and hurried up the wooden planking.

The short crossing was peaceful enough. He found it hard to believe that only a few months ago he had actually walked across the frozen surface of the stately flowing river. Only after it had divided around Grand Island would its sedate pace increase as it raced towards the Niagara escarpment where its speed would reach thirty miles an hour as it roared over the edge and plunged downward in a frightful torrent. But here the great river moved almost peacefully.

It was not long before the ferry edged against the wooden jetty at the end of Ferry Street, Black Rock, which was a suburb of the city. Gavin recognized the short, clerk-like figure of Captain Hynes seated in a buggy at the end of the wharf. Hynes raised his hand in greeting to Gavin and then cast a worried glance around the faces of the other passengers as they descended from the ship.

'Where's Major Canty?' he asked as soon as Gavin climbed up into the buggy alongside him.

'He's staying across the river. There are McMicken detectives in Fort Erie and Canty thinks that he is being watched.'

'Damnation!' breathed Hynes. 'Do you think it's serious?'

'Canty thinks he can take care of himself. Says he'll join with us as soon as the landing is accomplished.'

Hynes glanced at Gavin as he flicked the reins of the horse and sent the buggy moving quickly through the streets towards the centre of town. 'How about you? Any trouble?'

Trouble? He had an image of Kate's tear-stained face and Young Tom's hurt, bewildered look. Trouble?

'No trouble,' he said shortly. 'What's the news on this side?'

'The men have started to muster but we're nowhere near full strength. I've booked you a room for tonight in the Mansion House Hotel on Main Street. I'll drop you there now but at four o'clock there is a staff meeting at O'Day's auction rooms in Pearl Street. I want you to attend to give us the latest intelligence report.'

Gavin nodded.

'By the way, you'll be sharing your room . . . your brother reported for duty yesterday.' Gavin turned to stare at Hynes.

'My brother? But he's in Ireland '

'If your brother is Lieutenant John-Joe Devlin, then he's in room 201 at the Mansion House,' Hynes grinned.

Gavin was too surprised to respond as Hynes guided the buggy through the crowded streets. He became aware of groups of men standing here and there, milling on street corners, emerging from bars or entering pool halls. Most of them wore odd assortments of uniforms. Union Army and Confederate. Some already wore green shirts or green sashes. Beside him Hynes cursed. 'Must they make it so obvious?'

'I guess it is pretty difficult to hide an army in a city without making it plain who they are,' Gavin reflected.

Hynes dropped him outside the hotel in Main Street and Gavin was pushing through a crowded foyer to the desk before he realized that he already knew his hotel number. He negotiated the crowded stairway to the second floor and hesitated before room 201. Then he knocked softly. A familiar voice called, 'What is it?'

Gavin grinned before composing his features. 'Retribution!' he called hollowly.

A chair scraped and the door was flung open. John-Joe stared at Gavin in astonishment. 'I was told that you were hunting across the border.'

'And I thought you were in Ireland.' Gavin's face broke into a grin.

The brothers locked each other in a bear hug, swaying and chuckling before they broke apart panting from their exertion.

'I've a bottle here,' John-Joe gasped. 'This calls for a drink.'

Gavin followed him into the room and heeled the door shut. 'Captain Hynes told me that you'd joined up with us. But when did you get back from Ireland? Have you been in touch with Ma and Pa? Have you . . . ?'

John-Joe held up his hand in protest. 'One question at a time,' he said as he poured the drinks and handed a glass to his brother. 'Up the Devlins!'

It was their boyhood war cry.

'Up the Devlins!' echoed Gavin. He tossed back the liquid, 'Now,' he said when he had blinked from its effect, 'when did you get back from Ireland?'

John-Joe started to refill their glasses. 'At the beginning of the month with Stephens.'

'James Stephens?' queried Gavin.

'The same,' John-Joe screwed up his face cynically. 'My hero. *An Seabhac Siúlach* himself – the Wandering Hawk. More like a fluttering sparrow now.' His voice was suddenly bitter. 'He's started to speak out against Roberts and Sweeny and preach O'Mahoney's philosophy. Wait. The time will come. Wait. Always wait!'

'I've heard that Stephens was an old friend of O'Mahoney. They fought together in '48. I suppose it's natural that he will support him.' Gavin sprawled on the bed and inspected his young brother with interest. 'There's something about you, John-Joe. You've changed somehow.'

John-Joe roared with laughter. 'I guess that I've grown up a lot, Gavin!' he said. 'I've seen a lot, too; done a lot.'

'Was Ireland as you expected?'

John-Joe hesitated. 'No, not exactly what I expected and yet . . . yet it was more than I expected. I went in search of the soul of Ireland and I've found it, Gavin. By God, I've found it. And do you know what?'

Gavin smiled at his brother's excited face and shook his head.

'The soul of Ireland is a woman! Yes, by damn! I'm in love, Gavin, and I'm going to marry her.'

Gavin's eyes widened. 'You did have yourself a time over there, didn't you?' he chuckled. 'You'd better tell me the whole story. When do you plan to marry this lady of yours? And if you were having such a time, why did you bother to come back here?' He saw a shadow chase itself across his young brother's face.

'I had some trouble,' John-Joe said quietly. 'I was ordered to return. I had to. You see, Gavin, I killed an English landlord and was betrayed to the authorities by an informer.'

Gavin stared hard for a moment and then exhaled. 'You'd better begin your story at the beginning, John-Joe.'

'It's a long tale, Gavin. Well, it seems we've both got long stories to tell each other so I'd better start first, eh?'

It was just before four o'clock that Gavin made his way across to Pearl Street and reported to Patrick O'Day's auction rooms. The door was opened by a man whom he recognized from his first meeting in Buffalo.

'Colonel Hoy, isn't it?'

'Come in, Devlin. We're expecting you,' smiled the man.

He followed Hoy through the rooms which were packed with cases, some of them were open and he could see the rows of rifles inside. There was a small office at the back, a smoke-filled room crowded with men. Gavin saw Captain Hynes seated at a desk, apparently trying to exercise the office of chairman. Next to him sat a flush-faced individual who was introduced as Patrick O'Day, the head of the local Fenian circle. There was another man seated in a corner whom Gavin recognized but could not for the moment place. Memory came to him abruptly. They had met at the Fourth July celebration in New York.

'It's Colonel O'Neill, isn't it?'

O'Neill was puzzled. 'Yes. I seem to recall. . . .'

'Captain Gavin Devlin. We met at the St Nicholas Hotel in New York last Fourth of July.'

'Ah,' grinned O'Neill. 'I think I recall your father more. He was a very bellicose gentleman, if memory serves me right? Is he well?'

'As far as I know, sir. But if my memory serves me right, you were not enthusiastic for the Brotherhood.'

O'Neill chuckled. 'Neither was I, Devlin. Not until they came off their fat backsides and promised action. Then I raised a regiment in Nashville and here I am, champing at the bit to meet with our enemies.'

Hynes coughed hollowly, trying to bring the meeting to some sort of order. 'Gentlemen, we were about to start. Can I have your attention now.'

'Surely, captain,' O'Neill replied. 'But where is General Lynch?'

'He has not arrived yet,' said Hynes.

'Our commanding officer has not arrived?' There was a querulous note to O'Neill's voice.

'He will be with us when the time comes,' O'Day promised soothingly.

'Well, what is the plan of action?' asked another officer who was apparently O'Neill's aide-de-camp, a Captain Roddy Fitzpatrick. 'Can that be explained to us?'

Hynes brightened. 'Of course. At midnight tonight General

Charles Tevis will start moving his army of 3,000 men from Chicago and Milwaukee across the lakes to attack the towns of Stratford and London threatening Toronto. Twenty-four hours later we shall be moving across the river with General Lynch and 5,000 men in support of Tevis.'

He waited until the muttering rose and died. 'Our main attack, gentlemen, is coming out of Vermont into Lower Canada. General Sam Spear will lead an army of nearly 17,000 men against Montréal where our countrymen there, together with the French Canadians, are to rise up and join him. That is where our Irish Republic-in-Exile will be proclaimed. Our attack on Toronto is just a feint to bring the British troops against us.'

Gavin felt a quickening of his pulse as he finally understood the plan. It was not a hare-brained scheme as he had feared. The job of Tevis and Lynch was merely to keep the British regulars pinned down in Upper Canada while the main Fenian army did the real work in French-Canada.

'But shouldn't General Lynch be here already?' asked Fitzpatrick.

Before Hynes could reply, O'Neill asked, 'What is the current strength of our men gathered here? From what I have seen I doubt whether we have 1,000 troops in the city let alone 5,000.'

O'Day turned a slightly irritable expression towards him. 'Be assured, the men are still coming in, colonel. Don't forget they have until tomorrow midnight to complete the muster. They are arriving steadily.'

'But what troops can we rely on now?' insisted O'Neill. 'My regiment, the 13th, were 350 men when we left Nashville last Sunday. We picked up some extra men at Louisville and Indianapolis. But we weren't originally supposed to come to Buffalo. My orders were to embark on a ferry at Cleveland to cross Lake Erie. Then I received a telegram from Sweeny to report to Buffalo. Don't tell me that we are going to have another failure on our hands because of confusion in planning?'

Hynes face was bleak. 'General Sweeny knows what he is doing,' he snapped.

'Sure, but do his general staff?' retorted O'Neill.

There was a commotion at the door and two officers pushed their way into the room. Gavin stared at the leading man in surprise. He was in his late twenties, a boyish, handsome young man with dancing blue eyes, a quick laugh and a shock of blazing red hair. He stood in an attitude of eagerness, like a greyhound straining at the leash. He was dressed in a smart green uniform of a Fenian colonel.

'Colonel Owen Starr of the 17th Regiment out of Louisville,' he announced, smiling around the company. 'This is my second-in-command, Lieutenant-Colonel John Spaulding.'

A sober and slightly older dark-haired man nodded across Starr's shoulder.

'*Dia duit, Eoin,*' chuckled O'Neill rising with his hand out.

Starr saw O'Neill and let out a whoop. '*Dia's Mhuire duit! Cén chaoi a bhfuil tú, a Sheáin?*'

O'Neill turned to the company and grinned. 'Colonel Starr and I know each other well.'

Hynes cleared his throat officiously. 'Be seated Colonel Starr, and you Spaulding. Have you brought your regiment?'

Starr grinned as he sat down. 'We have that. The 17th are raring to go. We came up by train but had it stopped just outside of town at the Union iron works. My men are waiting outside the city so not to attract unwelcome attention.'

Hynes cast a triumphant look at O'Neill. 'As I said, the men are arriving steadily. We will soon be up to muster strength.'

Starr frowned, picking up the tension. 'What's our strength then, John?' His queston was directed at O'Neill and ignored Hynes.

'I don't see us having more than 1,000 men. There is your regiment, mine and that of Colonel Hoy's 7th together with some odds and ends.'

'Only 1,000 men? But we were supposed to number five times that amount. Where is General Lynch?'

Hynes was angry as he intervened. 'Colonel Starr, I am chairing this meeting. Lynch will be here soon. The movement doesn't start until tomorrow night.' He paused, gazing round in ill-temper. 'I cannot see anything useful deriving from the continuation of this meeting. I adjourn it until tomorrow evening at eight o'clock. For the sake of security we shall transfer our general headquarters to the Townsend Hall on Main and Swan Streets. If anything stops our meeting there, remember that our secondary quarters and commissariat will be at Hugh Mooney's saloon on Ohio Street. When you gather tomorrow be in full uniform with all your equipment.'

They rose to disperse muttering among themselves.

Hynes called, 'Colonel Starr – Colonel Spaulding – I suggest that for the sake of security, until tomorrow evening, you wear cloaks over those nice new uniforms of yours.'

Starr scowled at Hynes and then glanced towards O'Neill and pulled an amused face. 'Very well . . . *sir*!' he said with punctiliousness, raising a hand in a smart salute.

He and Spaulding went out with O'Neill, their laughter echoing back through the door. Hynes was still glowering after them when Gavin went up to check if he had any further orders. It was obvious that Hynes did not like the flamboyant colonel from Louisville.

'I hope to God that young man is able to fight as well as he dresses,' he sniffed disparagingly.

Colonel Hoy overheard and he smiled grimly. 'I wouldn't have any fear about that, captain,' he said. 'Owen Starr might look like a young dandy, more at home in the sitting room of some lady of fashion than on a battlefield, but he was one of the best damned regimental cavalry commanders in General Hugh Kilpatrick's division of Sherman's army. He might be full of Braggadocio but he has fought in the toughest conditions any soldier can conceive. Sherman's march through Georgia was no picnic. Starr has a determined military mind which has steered his regiment into the jaws of hell and out again many a time.'

Hynes bit his lip disapprovingly. 'Well, the 17th Louisville does not happen to be a cavalry regiment in this campaign, mister. Let's hope Starr is as good on foot as he is in a saddle.'

Chapter 46

The Townsend Hall at the corner of Main and Swan Streets was crowded. Men rested on packing cases full of ammunition and guns ready for distribution. There were enough armaments crammed into the hall to blow the centre of Buffalo to pieces should anyone have thrown a careless match among the wooden crates. In a variety of uniforms, men crowded in. Eager and excited. In an upstairs room the officers were gathered for their final briefing. Everyone was in a uniform of some description, either in the full green of the Fenian uniform or in mixtures of Union and Confederate dress with green shirts, sashes or armbands to denote their new allegiance. The air was heavy with cigar and cheroot smoke as they crouched over a packing case on which maps were spread.

'But where in God's name is General Lynch?' O'Neill was demanding as Gavin squeezed in and took a place against a wall.

Captain Hynes was pale and he coughed in embarrassment. 'I regret to inform you that General Lynch is at Batavia suffering an indisposition. A recurrent fever induced by his wounds suffered during the late war.'

There were several loud gasps from those asembled. O'Neill leaned forward from his packing case seat. 'Is the crossing to be delayed then?' he demanded coldly. 'Are we now to wait until General Lynch has recovered from his . . . indisposition?' He paused purposely before echoing the word.

Hynes shook his head violently. 'No, sir. General Sweeny has been informed of the facts and is directing Colonel Sherwin here from Batavia to take temporary command. Brigadier Michael Burns has been asked to come here as soon as possible to assume command but that may not be for some days.'

'And when shall we expect Colonel Sherwin?' asked O'Neill.

'Not until tomorrow at the earliest, I'm afraid.'

There was a silence. It was O'Neill who spoke again. 'We were supposed to cross tonight and now we are without a commander until tomorrow.'

Hynes stilled the ensuing hubbub by waving a telegraph. 'I have express orders from General Sweeny that the crossing must go ahead tonight as planned. General Tevis's column must be supported. I am instructed to hand command of the centre army to the most experience senior officer available.' He turned reluctantly to O'Neill. 'You are that officer, sir. You are to be acting-brigadier until the arrival of Colonel Sherwin or Brigadier Burns.'

Gavin saw John O'Neill shift uncomfortably in his seat and then hesitantly stand up. The other officers were muttering their approval.

'Very well, Captain Hynes. But pray tell me what I am supposed to accomplish with only one-fifth of the men who are supposed to be mustered here?'

'You must transport them across as planned,' Hynes replied. 'The movement has already begun. We cannot delay.' He thrust the telegraph into O'Neill's hands.

'You may commence working,' read O'Neill. 'The message is signed with the initials S.W.T.'

'That's General Sweeny's initials reversed. It is the coded message to begin the invasion. All three divisional commanders now have it. We must move.'

'It is essential, colonel,' chimed in Patrick O'Day, 'essential that we establish a bridgehead across the Niagara River. Once established, Sherwin or Burns will soon be here and able to move the rest of the men to reinforce your position.'

O'Neill pursed his lips as he stared at the telegraph. 'We have about 1,000 troops and no field guns. Yet I am supposed to cross into Upper Canada and fight my way across the Niagara peninsula in support of General Tevis who may or may not be at Stratford or London.'

'No,' Hynes shook his head. 'You are simply to establish a bridgehead, as Mister O'Day says. Sweeny is confident that the full 5,000 men with field batteries will be here within two days. We must have that bridgehead established. We must draw the British fire in order to allow General Spear to move against Montréal.'

'We have 1,500 men already,' announced O'Day. 'I have news that another of our regiments has just arrived in the city. Colonel John Grace and his 18th Regiment from Cleveland.'

O'Neill bit his lip. 'Do we know for sure that Tevis has crossed?'

'The telegraphs have not been reliable,' confessed Hynes. 'No, we don't know for sure.'

O'Neill glanced at the map on the packing case. 'And all I have to do is secure a defensible area on the other side to prevent any British counter-attacks until I am reinforced?'

'You are acting-brigadier, O'Neill,' Hynes agreed. 'You have absolute command in the field.'

'Such power,' breathed O'Neill. He said it too quietly for most people to detect the gibe in his voice.

'Captain Devlin has been living across the river since January with Major Canty, our chief intelligence officer. Devlin will explain the terrain to you and will act as your guide until Major Canty joins you on the other side.'

'So, at least we have done some forward planning?' O'Neill was sardonic.

Hynes' lips thinned. 'More than the British give us credit for.'

'Let's hear your views, Devlin,' O'Neill invited.

Gavin stood up and moved towards the packing case. They all strained forward to see the map.

'When I left yesterday there were very few regular troops in the immediate frontier area,' Gavin said. 'The landing should be completely unopposed.'

O'Neill tapped at the map. 'But what about this fortress here, Fort Erie itself? Isn't that a garrison?'

'Yes,' Gavin said. 'But the garrison is a small squad of the Royal Canadian Rifles, probably less than a dozen men. I can't see them putting up any resistance.'

'And the township by the fortress?'

'A small township of about 600 people. There are a few customs collectors there, a constable and his assistants . . . that's a sort of sheriff and his deputies,' he added, seeing some puzzled faces among them. 'There are no militiamen there at all.'

'Sounds too good to be true,' O'Neill said, rubbing his jaw thoughtfully. 'From the map it looks like a key border crossing. You'd think that with all the alarms about invasion the British would have at least one line regiment posted there.'

'Perhaps they don't think it's necessary,' Gavin said.

O'Neill invited him to explain.

'Two railroads converge on Fort Erie. The Grand Trunk Railway which runs in from the west and the Erie and Ontario which comes down from the north. Both these railroads are potentially dangerous because the British can move troops along them fairly quickly. The first objective, therefore, in my opinion, would be to secure the railroad depot at Fort Erie, ensure all the telegraphs are cut immediately and destroy or keep a careful watch on any movement along the tracks.'

O'Neill was making some notes and nodding. 'It sounds like pretty good sense to me. Go on, Devlin.'

'If the purpose is to secure the area and wait for reinforcements,' Gavin's military training began to take over as he devoted himself to the problem as simply a martial question to be resolved, 'then the main threat will come from the British regulars being entrained along the railroads. This is an area of small farmers, most of them are intensely British loyalist but, being farmers, they are conservative and I don't think they will put up any organized resistance. Volunteer militia units are to be found only in the larger townships, although one or two of the farmers are members of such units. I would suggest that we form a battle front and hold it against any counter-attack until we are reinforced.'

'Do you have a notion where this battle front should be, Devlin?' It was Owen Starr who asked the question.

Gavin indicated on the map. 'Along the line of a fairly natural fortification. From here, Port Colborne, the Welland River flows out of Lake Erie. For a while, as it flows north, it is part of the Welland Canal, which has a system of locks along it and is the main transportation route from Lake Erie to Lake Ontario. It's a river highway that is of strategic importance to the British. Now here, at Port Robinson, the Welland River turns east to run into the Niagara River. The river, therefore, forms a natural front.'

The officers followed Gavin's finger tracing the line of the river and canal system. O'Neill's eyes were glistening with excitement.

'I think I see your point, Devlin. We march to the Welland River and take this town at its juncture with the Niagara, Chippewa. Then we move west along the river destroying all the bridges, particularly the rail bridge at Chippewa and the one at Port Robinson. At Port Robinson we can destroy the locks to prevent ship movement and then move south to Port Colborne destroying the rail link there.'

Gavin nodded. 'That's right. The British, without bridges, would have to wait while they gathered sufficient boats to cross and I can't see them making a successful crossing in that manner. We would be able to observe any build-up of boats on the river or canal banks and concentrate our forces to cut them to pieces before they crossed.'

'But surely the British have pontoons?' Owen starr pointed out.

Gavin shook his head. 'Major Canty has been working as foreman on the Grand Trunk Railway and has been picking up information from the soldiers. There are no pontoons available and the only form of transport the enemy could use is rowing boats or barges.'

O'Neill sat back, fumbling for a cheroot. He drew it from his pocket and lit it with deliberate slowness. 'But what about garrisons and resistance from the townships which will fall behind our defensive lines?' He jabbed at the map. 'Fort Erie? Ridgeway? Stevensville? New Germany? Presumably the main enemy garrisons will be in the townships straddling the river and canal – Chippewa, Port Robinson, Welland and Port Colborne? I want to keep the enemy before me as much as I can. We can't spare troops to do interior garrison work if we are to hold this line for any length of time.'

'The militia companies will be in front of you,' confirmed Gavin. 'The townships are all small, just small farming communities as I said. They'll leave the fighting to the militia or regulars.'

'And where are the nearest British regulars?' It was Owen Starr again.

'Mainly garrisoned at Toronto although there are some infantry companies quartered at St Catharines.'

O'Neill sat half nodding to himself and then he glanced at Hynes. 'How sure is General Sweeny that the rest of this army will gather here within the next day or so?' he said.

'Absolutely certain,' replied Hynes more sharply than was necessary.

'So that if we cross as planned tonight, leaving a day for consolidation before we secure our front, we could expect the new forces to join us within twenty-four hours?'

'That seems a conservative estimate,' agreed Hynes.

O'Neill glanced back at the map. 'Devlin, how long would you estimate that it would take to secure this front which you propose, along the river and canal?'

Gavin shrugged. 'It depends on how fast you can move your troops, sir. If, in taking the railroad depot at Fort Erie, you could capture some of the engines and rolling stock, then you could probably secure the entire front in one day. You could entrain your troops west to Port Colborne, from Port Colborne to Welland and Port Robinson and also north from Fort Erie to Chippewa. The only stretch along which the railroad does not run is along the banks of the Welland River from west to east into Chippewa.'

'It seems possible,' O'Neill muttered staring at the map.

'Possible, John,' chuckled Owen Starr, 'it's a certainty.'

O'Neill smiled at the red-haired young colonel. 'All right, Owen. Your regiment will form the advance guard. You'll cross first and secure the fortress, the railway depot, seizing any trains and rolling stock, together with the township itself.'

Owen Starr gave a little whoop. 'By God, we won't fail this time!' he grinned.

'Devlin, you'll go across with Owen's 17th Louisville Regiment. You'll be his intelligence officer until Fort Erie is secured. Then you'll report to my headquarters, wherever that will then be. Understood?'

Gavin nodded.

'I'll transport my regiment, the 13th Nashville, across next. Colonel Hoy's 7th Buffalo will come next and Colonel Grace's 18th Cleveland will form the rearguard.'

A tall, languid officer moved forward. 'What about my men, colonel?'

Hynes performed the introduction. 'This is Captain Hugh Haggerty commanding two independent companies from Terre Haute, Indiana.'

O'Neill rubbed his chin reflectively for a moment. 'It would be best if you reinforced Colonel Starr's advance guard.'

There was a knock on the door and a civilian pushed in, found O'Day and hurriedly whispered in his ear. The businessman's face looked suddenly pinched. He rose and cleared his throat.

'Two bad pieces of news, gentlemen,' he said slowly. They watched him expectantly. 'Our man at the telegraph office has just reported that Hemans, the British consul in the city, has sent a telegraph to the British military commanders in Ottawa and Toronto and warned them of our intention to cross.'

There were one or two cries of anger and a general concerned muttering.

'That means they'll oppose the landing,' exclaimed Starr.

'A warning of intention is not the same as saying that we've actually crossed,' Hynes said pedantically. 'Even if the message was acted on, I doubt whether the British would be able to rush troops from Toronto to oppose us before we cross.'

O'Neill sighed heavily. 'You said two pieces of bad news, Mister O'Day?'

Patrick O'Day hesitated. 'Our original intention was to use the steam ferry of the Buffalo and Lake Huron Railway Company, that's the *International*, as the main transport across the river. The ferry has been docked on the Canadian side for the night as a precaution and Norton, the collector of customs in Buffalo, has closed the main docks to all traffic. Furthermore, Mayor Wells, who is not noted as a friend of the Brotherhood, has asked that the fifty regular army troops stationed at Fort Porter on the edge of the city be deployed in the streets as a token force. Mayor Wells has also sent a despatch asking that the USS *Michigan* be sent here.'

'The USS *Michigan*?' queried O'Neill.

'A steam revenue cutter under United States Navy control,' O'Day replied. 'She's usually stationed at Erie and patrols the lake. I've met her captain, Commander Bryson. He's a fair man but strictly navy, does everything by the rule book.'

'Once she gets here she could do us some damage,' muttered Hynes. 'She's armed with stern cannons.'

O'Neill stared at Hynes. 'It was my understanding that President Johnson and his administration supported this undertaking. Are you now telling me that we have to fight the American forces as well as the British?'

'President Johnson gave clear undertakings to the Brotherhood. He said he would accept accomplished facts. He cannot give explicit orders for the American Army and Navy to help us and, naturally, there will be some zealous pro-British officials like Mayor Wells.'

O'Neill bit his lip. 'So is there an alternative for transporting our men across the river?' he demanded.

'We have an emergency plan,' Hynes informed him. 'Five miles north of here is a suburb called Black Rock. There's a big iron works there, Pratt's Iron Works which has a ferry dock. A few days ago I formed a contingency plan. Under the cover of arranging a works outing for the employees, a day's excursion to Falconwood,' he smiled smugly, 'we hired two steam tugs and four scows, that's the local flat-bottomed canal barges. They are currently moored at Pratt's Landing in preparation for the excursion tomorrow.'

Owen Starr whistled softly. 'If that's so, we can probably manage the crossing before the *Michigan* arrives.'

O'Neill was already briskly rolling up the map. 'Owen, start moving your men and Captain Haggerty's two companies. Move them in companies of fifty men and avoid the obvious routes. We don't want the British consul or Mayor Wells to see where we are heading. If you are challenged by any American regulars, use everything short of force or threat of force to extricate yourself from a position of surrendering yourselves to them. The enemy is across the river, not on this side of it. Oh, and Owen, as soon as your men are embarked send a galloper back. My regiment will come next and then the others in the order I have given. As soon as the men are across, Hynes, start sending over the commissariat. I want the ammunition and guns given priority. We can probably live off the land for the first twenty-four hours. Any questions?'

They had all risen with O'Neill and stood silently, a trifle self-consciously. 'Then, if there are no questions, our next meeting will be on British soil. I'm no speech maker, gentlemen, but I wish you luck. *Dia ar 'ach bóthar a rachaidh sibh!*'

There was a moment of emotion as they stood looking at each other. The days of dreaming, planning and arguing were gone. This was the moment; liberty or death! It was Owen Starr who made the first move, raising his hand in slow salute to O'Neill. As O'Neill returned the salute, Starr gave a shout of youthful exuberance. '*Fágaigí an bealach ag slóite na bhFian!*'

'Out and make way for the bold Fenian men!'

Outside the Townsend Hall John-Joe was waiting in the company of a shadowy figure.

'Is it on, Gavin? Is it happening?' he demanding, falling in step with his brother.

Gavin nodded. 'I have to go, John-Joe. We are crossing now. What command are you with?'

John-Joe grimaced. 'Hynes has posted me as assistant commissary officer. As soon as Brigadier Burns gets here I'll be bringing over the rest of the ammunition wagons.'

Gavin suddenly halted at the familiar shadow behind John-Joe. 'Who's that with you?' he demanded.

'Just me, son.' Gavin's jaw dropped as Father MacMahon emerged into the street light.

Silently they shook hands. 'What are you doing here, Father?'

'Coming with you,' replied the priest.

'With us?' Gavin started in surprise.

'Sure, you'll be needing a chaplain,' smiled the priest. 'And I would have thought I'd be having a warmer welcome from you.'

Owen Starr hurried by. 'Come on, Captain Devlin,' he called.

'Colonel, have we room for a chaplain?' asked Gavin. 'This is Father MacMahon.'

'We can always do with some spiritual reinforcements, come and be welcome Father.'

Gavin turned to shake John-Joe's hand briefly in farewell. 'I'll see you on the other side then, John-Joe,' he grinned. 'If anything happens, though . . . well, you know. Give Pa and Ma my love and tell them . . . hell! Just tell them!'

'Nothing will happen,' replied John-Joe. 'Up the Devlins!'

Gavin raised a hand and turned away. Father MacMahon fell in step with him.

'I've waited a long time for this, son,' the priest said.

'Is there any news from New York?'

MacMahon frowned. 'I take it that you don't mean news of your parents, son?' he asked softly.

'News of the Delanceys, I mean.'

'You know young Rosaleen McHale married Brock Delancey? Married in March.' The priest sighed. 'Son, I'd forget the Delanceys if I were you. There are momentous times ahead. Compared to our present undertaking the Delanceys are like chaff that will blow from the wheat.'

Gavin shook his head. There was a harsh vehemence in his voice. 'One of these days, Father, I want to provide the wind that will blow them away.'

Owen Starr's regiment were marching in orderly companies, rifles slung, with jaunty swaggers, a motley of strange green uniforms and banners. Along the streets of Buffalo, down Niagara Street and Sixth Street, bewildered citizens lined up to see them passing by in the flickering glare of the torches and lanterns.

'By crikey!' Gavin heard a voice cry in surprise from the crowd, 'them mad Irish be gonna take Canada! Did yous ever hear such a crazy thing?'

Chapter 47

Under the vigilant eyes of their officers, the men of Owen Starr's 17th Regiment from Louisville, Kentucky, and Hugh Haggerty's independent companies from Terre Haute, Indiana, gathered at Pratt's Landing. Under Captain Hynes's direction a train with nine wagons of commissariat materials, weapons and ammunition had made its way into the sidings by the rolling mill and began to off-load. Gavin, with Father MacMahon, attached themselves to Starr's regimental staff, waiting as the men were conducted aboard the flat-bottomed barges. They moved to their positions without fuss; quiet and determined soldiers who did not complain of the drizzle which had been coming down intermittently for the last few hours. When the soldiers did speak to their companions the talk was introspective; of things men usually kept to themselves; admitting of fears, hopes and talking of personal matters with unusual candour. Gavin heard one young man ask his sergeant in a pleading voice, 'Do you honestly think that we stand a chance, sarge?'

'Of course we do, Doherty,' came the firm response.

'What if I get killed, sarge?'

'Then you'll be a martyr, boy, with a nice little marble tomb all to yourself. They'll even put a Latin inscription on it – *dulce et decorum est pro patria mori.*'

'What does that mean, sarge?'

'It is sweet and right to die for your country.'

'It's sweeter and better to live for it,' came another voice. 'You're a goddam pessimist, sarge. Stop scaring the boy.'

'Don' ya worry, boy,' came a southern voice. 'This is gonna be like a night ride on a Mississippi river boat.'

Starr took his staff aboard the leading tugboat, the *J. H. Doyle*, and gave the order to cast off. As the tug and its trailing scow began to manoeuvre across the river, the rain ceased and the moon suddenly appeared from behind the clouds, round and brilliant sending its light across the rustling dark waters of the river. It lit the scene almost as bright as day, a still, peaceful night filled with long shadows. Somewhere in the well of the trawling barge, audible above the chugging of the tug's steam engine, a tenor voice struck up:

> Death to every foe and traitor!
> Forward! Strike the marching tune
> And Hurrah me boys for Freedom!
> 'Tis the Rising of the Moon!

Starr turned angrily. 'Shut that idiot up!' he growled.

'Ah, but it puts the lads in good spirits,' Father MacMahon intervened softly.

'Yes, Father,' replied Starr. 'And it's likely to get them killed.'

The two tugs with their large trailing barges were moving across the river now. Standing on the prow of the tug Gavin felt a shiver of apprehension as he saw the blackened silhouette of the Canadian shoreline approaching. A solitary light shone here and there in the darkness of the buildings of Fort Erie. They were crossing the river at its shortest point, a few miles downriver from the small border township. The tug seemed to be approaching the darkened bank very fast, the feather from the prow cutting through the water. Gavin's apprehension was not of the coming conflict neither was his mind filled with thoughts of the awesome grandeur of the moment, this strange moment in history which might be the one which would usher in a new dawn for the Irish nation, the moment of its liberty. He was thinking of Kate Dawtry. It would have been so easy to have stayed. He wondered if she lay asleep now? Or, by some strange bond, was she awake feeling his presence just a few miles away?

The swell as they approached a fisherman's wharf in the darkness was high and the tug missed the landing point and had to be manoeuvred into place while Starr fretted and fumed. The men, tense and ready for anything, were all for jumping for the wharf but Starr's quiet orders stayed them. They stood, staring at the blackened shore, half expecting to be greeted by a volley of gunfire. There was nothing but quiet; the quiet was almost as unnerving as the expected gunfire would have been. The moon, brillliant now with the rain clouds gone, bathed them in an eerie glow as the tug and its barge made fast and Starr gave the orders to go ashore. It was done silently and with speed. They formed up on the road which ran alongside the river, forming ranks to the whispered instruction of their sergeants.

The Irish flag and regimental standard were unsheathed and the colour party formed up. Haggerty's two companies lined up behind Starr's regiment under their own colours, held by a raw-boned giant of a man clad in the uniform of a colour-sergeant of the Union Army. Starr stood chewing nervously at an unlit cheroot until Lieutenant-Colonel Spaulding came up and saluted. 'The regiment is ready, sir.'

Starr nodded and glanced up anxiously towards the white face of the moon, wishing for better cover.

'Very well. Devlin, show us the way to the railway depot and the telegraphs.'

Gavin nodded, nervously adjusting his sword belt, and moved off down the river road to where the township lay sleeping before them. At a silent signal, the men began to march forward. Already the two tugs with their barges were moving back across the river.

From afar they suddenly heard shouts as if someone was trying to raise the inhabitants.

Starr, striding alongside Gavin, peered forward into the darkness. 'Do you think the troops in the fortress will put up a resistance?' he whispered.

'The British only have a squad of men there, colonel. An observation force from the Royal Canadian Rifles. I can't see them putting up a resistance.'

'Well, like it or not, someone's rousing the township,' Starr said as the shouting grew louder and lights began to blink here and there. A figure came running along the road towards them. Hands reached for revolvers but a voice cried, 'Up the Republic!'

Gavin recognized the tone. 'It's Major Canty, colonel,' he said. 'Major, it's me, Devlin!'

Canty came up. He was dressed in uniform. 'Hello, Devlin, who's with you?' he demanded breathlessly.

'This is Colonel Starr, commanding the advance party.'

'Good to see you, colonel. You'd best hurry to the railroad depot, though. A rider came in with the news of your landing. He went straight to the depot to warn them. They've four engines up there and a lot of wagons which we could use.'

Starr swore softly but Canty went on hurriedly, 'Can you let me have a company to arrest the reeve and the constable before they can organize any resistance?'

'Who?'

'The local magistrate, the law officer.'

Starr turned and snapped an order and a company of men fell out. Canty led them off into the darkness while Starr signalled a rapid advance, breaking into a trot.

They heard the engines getting steam up long before they reached the railroad depot. The sound was followed by that of shunting cars. The depot lay where the tracks from the north and from the west met at numerous sidings and sheds. Men were shouting and running hither and thither as they approached and the pale pall of steam rose into the moonlit sky.

'They're trying to get the engines away!' cried Spaulding, pointing with this sword.

'Regimental line of attack!' yelled Starr, not pausing in his stride.

The column of trotting soldiers, each carrying their rifles and muskets ready across their chests, swung out, company by company, to form a scything line. Gavin had time, even as he ran forward, to admire the disciplined precision of the movement. A sharp cry informed them that they had been spotted. They were still a hundred yards away when the black shadow of the engine began to move, sparks flying from under its wheels, and the escaping steam hissing from its boiler. It moved slowly, with an agonized groaning and banging of the cars behind it.

'Stand!' yelled Starr, halting in his tracks. 'Volley fire over their heads! Present! Fire!'

The volley came in one terrific crash. The engine driver gave a desultory whistle from his engine, as if mocking them, and the train began to gather speed dragging the other engines and cars which had been coupled behind it. Starr lead a desperate charge into the depot across the tracks. For a few moments the rear car of the train moved with tantalizing slowness before them, as if an extra effort on their part could have caught up with it. Then it was gone swaying into the darkness. Starr halted and swore.

'Captain Geary!'

A figure emerged from the shadows milling around.

'Take your company and see if there is any way you can catch up with that train and halt it. If not, be damned sure you destroy the tracks so that the British can't use the railroad to move troops back here.'

The captain moved quickly off, his company trotting down the tracks in the wake of the receding red lights of the train.

Starr watched them go and turned to Gavin with a shrug. 'No hope of catching it without cavalry,' he sighed. 'Still, if it has to halt to change points Geary might have a chance. It's worth pursuing for a while.' Then he smiled broadly. 'Have to hand it to those railroad boys, linking up all the engines and cars into one train. We could have done with one of those engines.'

Spaulding came up. 'All the railroad men have skedaddled, sir.'

'Small blame to them,' Starr smiled. 'Post sentries at the depot and tell them to watch for Geary's return. Warn them about being trigger happy. We don't want any accidents. And get those damned telegraph wires cut!'

He waved Gavin to accompany him. 'Where's the main telegraph office?'

'That would be the post office, it's a wooden house opposite the ferry wharf, just across from the depot.'

Starr led the way from the depot down to the riverside. The *International* ferry was still laying alongside the wharf where it had been docked for the night. There was a good deal of arguing and excitement among the crew and a small party of Starr's men had already gone aboard to secure it. An abrupt burst of rifle fire and shouting broke out farther along the wharf. Half a dozen of Starr's men were firing at a small rowing boat in which Gavin could just make out the dark shape of a man pulling across the river as if his life depended on it. A woman, with a robe flung over her nightdress, was shrieking and beating with her fists at the soldiers as they fired until a corporal caught her by the wrists and held her back.

'What the hell is happening?' demanded Starr.

'A man ran out of that building there, sir,' the corporal nodded, trying to control the screaming woman. 'I was told it was the post office. He was carrying a bag. He leaped into that rowing boat and started to pull away.'

Starr grunted, gazing towards the frantically rowing figure.

'Stop firing at the poor devil,' he ordered softly. Then, 'Who's the woman?'

The struggling woman, seeing the soldiers had stopped firing, pulled herself together and swore at Starr.

'Ain't pretty language for a lady, ma'am,' reproved the corporal. He grinned at Starr. 'Begging your pardon, colonel, I believe she's the man's wife, especially from the squawking she's been making.'

The woman spat at him.

'Your husband doesn't seem to be very gallant, ma'am,' Starr smiled, 'him rowing off and leaving you here.'

'You cowardly Irish rabble!' cried the woman. 'My husband was saving the mail from your thieving hands.'

Starr chuckled. 'It's not mail that we've come after, ma'am. Take her back to the mail office and destroy the telegraphs there, corporal.'

He turned away, ignoring the woman's abuse, and went back to the railroad depot followed by Gavin. They found Spaulding busy posting picquets and Starr told him to make sure that the *International* ferry was held at the wharf until further orders. Then he gathered two companies of men.

'Suppose you show us where the British fort is, Devlin?' he said.

'Not far along the river bank, colonel,' Gavin replied.

They marched in silence down the trackway which led towards the southern end of the townlands, across low laying marshy ground and a creek. Dawn was just over the horizon now and a few birds had started to sing in the sprawling forest which stretched away from the river bank. The dark walls of the fortress rose in silhouette against the broad mouth of the river where it met the even broader sweep of Lake Erie. As they approached it, its old stone walls looked impregnable and threatening. The original fortress had been raised in 1764 as a defence against Indian attacks and had been damaged twice in the winter months by ice pushing out of the river up the bank to smash its wooden walls. That was when it had been decided to build a new fortress of stone and its bastions had been raised in time for the war of 1812. The Americans had captured it before pushing across the Niagara peninsula. After their defeat by the British at Lundy's Lane, the Americans had pulled back into Fort Erie. They withstood a two-month siege, coming under heavy bombardment and assault, but inflicting more casualties on the besiegers than they sustained and forcing the British to lift the siege. Two weeks later they withdrew across the river.

Starr halted his companies some way from the fortress and took out a white kerchief which he attached to his sword. 'Will you come with me, Devlin?' he asked.

Gavin nodded.

Together they walked silently along the path which led up to the strong wooden drawbridge, crossing the earthwork ditches to the gate of the fortress. To Gavin's surprise the drawbridge was down and the gates stood wide open. At the gate stood a solitary figure in uniform. In the strange half light they could make out the white trousers, dark jacket and the blaze of a sergeant's chevrons.

'I wish to speak to the commander of this fortress,' Starr said.

'I am in command here, sir,' the man replied, his voice nervous.

'I am Colonel Starr, commanding the 17th Regiment of the Irish Republican Army. I call upon you and your men to surrender to my superior force.'

The sergeant's face looked comically woebegone in the strange light. 'Are you Fenians, sir?'

Starr smiled. 'Yes.'

'Do you mean to kill us?'

'You may be assured, sergeant, that you will be well treated by us.'

The sergeant paused for a moment and then shrugged. 'There are only six of us in the fortress, sir. Observation party of the Royal Canadian Rifles. There is little point in our resisting.'

'Do you surrender?'

'We do.'

The sergeant turned and called an order. Six men with sloped muskets, clad in uniform, marched out of the fortress and halted. One by one, at the sergeant's word of command, they stepped forward and dropped their muskets in front of Starr. The young colonel turned and called his men forward, taking his white kerchief from his sword point and sheathing the sword again. The Fenians let out a cheer at seeing soldiers in the hated British redcoats throwing down their weapons.

'Sergeant Dolan,' called Starr to one of his men, 'take a detachment and escort these prisoners-of-war to the township. Find adequate accommodation for them.'

He turned with a grin to Gavin. 'History, eh? This is the first British fortress to surrender to an Irish army since . . .' he shrugged, 'well, maybe not since the Williamite conquest.'

The fortress was no great prize, however. It was mainly derelict with only a small barracks in which the detachment of the Royal Canadian Rifles had their quarters. There was certainly no armoury to speak of. The only weapons in the fortress were the muskets surrendered by the men. The fortress had not been used in a proper military role since the British had reclaimed it in 1814 and the destruction of the siege was still to be seen along its war-ravaged walls and bastions. Starr climbed up to what must have been a gun enplacement and gazed towards where the bright light of the approaching dawn was silhouetting the city of Buffalo across the river. He took off his hat and looked thoughtfully towards the shore for a moment.

We've bent too long to braggart wrong,
While force our prayers derided;
We've fought too long, ourselves among,
By knaves and clans divided.
United now, no more we'll bow,
Foul faction we discard it;
And now, thank God!, our native sod
Has native swords to guard it!

He turned and smiled self-consciously towards Gavin. 'Let's get back to the township.'

Spaulding was standing with Major Canty outside the post office when they returned.

'The town is secured, sir,' Spaulding reported. 'Major Canty has brought in the chief magistrate, the reeve they call him, and the constable. They are awaiting in the mail office there. Also, Colonel O'Neill has landed and will be making his headquarters at a farmstead to the north.'

Major Canty cleared his throat. 'I have had a representation from a number of townspeople, sir. They want to take the ferry into Buffalo where they feel they will be safer. The captain wants to know if he can put across the river.'

Starr scratched his nose as he thought the matter over. 'He can transport anyone who wants to go across so long as he undertakes to bring back our men and supplies. I want a detachment to go with the ferry. Now, Devlin, let's go and meet the local magistrate.'

The post office was, in fact, the private home of the post master, George Lewis, who had left so hastily for Buffalo a short while before. One large room was given over to the business of the mail service as well as the small telegraph office. Inside this room a group of civilians stood with dour or angry faces, depending on their mood and personality.

'Good morning, gentlemen,' Starr smiled blandly as he entered. 'I trust that your sleep has not been too impaired by the current disturbance?'

A florid-faced man who carried himself with an air of authority pushed forward. 'I demand an explanation, sir! I am chief magistrate of this town.'

'I am Colonel Starr, commanding the 17th Regiment of the Irish Republican Army.'

The magistrate sniffed contemptuously. 'I am Doctor Tertins

Kempson, reeve of this township. And I will see you swing for this, you blackguard!'

Starr's face did not loose its smile. 'There'll be no swinging here, mister,' he replied evenly. 'The gallows is the one thing that the British can take with them when they leave our country.'

'Your country?' sneered Kempson. 'God save the Queen, I say!'

There was a murmur of approval from the other civilians.

'A good sentiment,' replied Starr. 'God save the Queen of England in her own country. But God damn her in Ireland, where she has no right to be. Now sir, let us dispense with these pleasantries. As chief magistrate of this town I am requesting that you summon a meeting of your local council or leading citizens and consider the following requisition orders: I need provisions for my men so that they may breakfast. All arms and ammunition are to be handed over to my forces. All horses are to be rounded up and handed over. My officers will give signed receipts for everything which is taken.'

Doctor Kempson's chin thrust out aggressively.

'Kempson,' Starr said quietly, before the magistrate could retort, 'we do not come among you as marauders and looters but we come among you as determined soldiers. I would advise cooperation in the circumstances . . . that is if you hold the well-being of your township in your heart.'

Kempson stared at the youthful and determined Irishman, saw his calm assurance and humorous good nature which carried an intent more deadly than if the man had stormed and raved and acted the bullying braggart.

'How can I collect the councilmen together to discuss the matter?' he asked stiffly.

'I'll assign an officer to escort you,' replied Starr. 'In addition, doctor, I would like everyone gathered in the main street in front of this building at six o'clock when a proclamation from the commander of the Irish Republican Army will be read.'

As Kempson and the civilians left, Major Canty returned. 'The ferry is departing, colonel.'

Starr nodded and fumbled for a cheroot. Canty supplied a light.

'I'd also like to borrow Captain Devlin, sir,' pressed Canty.

Starr nodded again. He sat down with an expression of utter weariness on his face and drew deeply on his cheroot.

As Canty ushered Gavin from the room he lowered his voice. 'The McMicken detective . . . your man Hogan . . . he's holed up in a room at the City Hotel. I thought you'd like to help me pick him up.'

A tingling burst of adrenalin ran through Gavin's body. Hogan! Hogan was his key to the door which would lead him to Brock Delancey and his father.

'I'm your man, Canty,' he muttered. 'Let's go!'

They moved quickly up the street towards George Fitch's City Hotel. Green-uniformed soldiers were everywhere now but there were only a few civilians about. Most of the citizens of the township of Fort Erie were keeping well indoors. Canty halted on the opposite side of the street to the hotel, a short way away from it.

'Do you know what room he's in?' asked Gavin, staring across the wooden façade of the hotel.

'The top floor. Do you see the window on the far left?'

The hotel had two floors. The window on the far left was half open, the curtains fluttering in the early morning breeze. Gavin thought he saw a glimpse of a shadow there. 'What do you have in mind?' he asked the major.

Canty shrugged. 'There's only one door into the room. We just go in and get him.'

Gavin hesitated.

'Got a better plan?' demanded Canty.

'Like as not he'll start blasting away when we try it.' Gavin's eyes narrowed as he stared at the small verandah which ran along the front of the hotel above which was a shallowly sloping roof just below the windows of the second floor.

'You make a noise approaching the door of his room. I'll slip through another room out on to the roof of the verandah and come up behind him through the window while he's distracted by you.'

'Fair enough,' muttered Canty.

'Hogan is dangerous, major. Don't take any chances.'

They crossed the street quickly and entered the City Hotel. The proprietor was in the main bar, he was pale faced and unhappy. 'I have no valuables, no valuables at all,' he cried as they came in.

'Shut up!' snapped Canty. 'Stay over there and keep quiet.'

Gavin unhooked his sword and discarded it, took out his revolver and followed Canty as he began to ascend the stairs. While Gavin moved noiselessly, Canty stamped his boots. They reached the landing and Gavin slipped quietly across to the nearest door opening towards the front of the building. He swore softly. The door was locked. He moved along the corridor until he came across another empty room, hurried across and clambered out of the window. He kept his back against the wall, revolver in one hand, and edged his way along to the window on the far left of the building.

Canty's timing was right. He was about a yard away when he heard the major give a thunderous rap on the door and heard his voice call. The next thing was the sound of two shots exploding in the room. Gavin crouched towards the window. The man was standing with his back to him, pistol in hand having loosed his shots off at the door.

'Drop it, Hogan,' Gavin's voice was cold.

The copper-haired man froze and let his pistol slide from his nerveless fingers on to the floor.

'Okay, major!' cried Gavin as he slid over the sill into the room.

Canty came through the door with his pistol in his hand. 'Good work, Devlin. And you, Mister Spy . . . back against that wall!'

Hogan turned and recognized Gavin, his face flushed with surprise. 'You!'

The word was full of venom.

Gavin smiled softly. 'Me, Hogan. Mullan Naul failed – twice. He's dead.'

The man's bright eyes narrowed. 'That's disappointing. Naul had a reputation in certain circles, especially with his Peep o' Day Boys and his raids on you Teigs.'

Canty was searching the man's pockets and found a pocket book with an identity badge inside. 'He's a McMicken man right enough, Devlin.'

Hogan stood against the wall indifferently, his hands raised at shoulder level.

'You've got some explaining to do, Hogan,' Gavin said coldly. 'You were just a two-bit tough in New York City, working for the Delanceys. How come you're now a British spy?'

Hogan grinned with self-satisfaction. 'Shows you don't know everything, Devlin.'

Gavin felt a surge of uncontrollable hatred for this man. The harsh emotions found fuel as the memory of Nora Quinlan was reawakened in his mind. He thrust the barrel of his revolver against Hogan's throat. 'I said, you have some explaining to do,' he repeated through clenched teeth.

A faint edge of fear came into Hogan's eyes as he gazed at the unbridled anger in Gavin's eyes. 'Sure I was working for Delancey,' he muttered. 'Why not? It was a good cover. McMicken had sent me down to New York to find out what I could about you Fenian bastards.'

Gavin thrust the muzzle of his gun hard against the man's neck causing him to wince with pain. 'Did you know that I was a Fenian, then?'

'Not at first,' replied Hogan. 'Not when I was in New York. I just thought you were some smart lawyer trying to ride a white horse. Delancey wanted you out of the way. Then I saw you in Fort Erie. You thought I had not seen you in the City Hotel when I was with McMicken. Your friend tried to follow me but I shook him off by pretending to ride out of town. I doubled back and followed you to the Dawtry farmhouse.'

It fitted. Gavin nodded grimly. 'That's when you raked Mullan Naul out of his sewer?'

Hogan was silent.

'You were one of his masked vigilantes, weren't you?' Gavin again shoved his revolver hard so that Hogan gasped.

'Yes, damn it!'

'Then I owe you this!' Gavin whipped the barrel of his weapon against Hogan's head. Blood gushed from the cut and the man staggered and nearly fell.

Canty reached out a hand to stay Gavin. 'That'll do, captain,' he snapped coldly. 'The man is my prisoner, whatever he's done. He'll answer for any crimes when the time comes.'

Hogan gazed into Gavin's face, his pale eyes blazing with hatred. 'You'd better kill me now, Devlin, or, sure as hell, I'll kill you!'

Gavin tried to control the rage he felt. For a moment he felt like pulling the trigger. His whole body was tensed. Then he forced himself to relax.

'No, I won't kill you, Hogan. You'll live and you'll swear out a deposition concerning the Delanceys – about Brock Delancey and his father – and you will put down all the dirty business that you know them to be involved in and then you will come to New York to be my witness against them.'

Hogan's mouth slackened. 'You must be crazy.'

Gavin smiled grimly. 'If you don't, Hogan . . . then you'll wish I had killed you now.'

'All right, Hogan,' Canty intervened. 'Let's get going.'

Hogan dragged his gaze away from the burning fire in Gavin's eyes and glanced nervously at the major. 'What are you going to do?' he asked.

'For the moment, you are a prisoner and you'll be placed with the other prisoners in the schoolhouse.'

Gavin collected Hogan's weapons and they marched him out of the room, Gavin picking up his sword as they left the hotel, watched by the astounded face of the proprietor. The local schoolhouse had been turned into a makeshift prison for the captured soldiers and officials. They left Hogan under the charge of the guards there and made their way back to the post office.

'Are you serious about Hogan?' asked Canty as they walked down the main street.

Gavin smiled mirthlessly. 'I've never been more serious in my life, major. Hogan is an evil and dangerous man but he's just a tool. I want to use him to destroy a greater evil that has caused much misery, suffering and death in New York. I've waited for months for an opportunity to smash the Delanceys and now Hogan will supply me with the means to do it.'

Canty glanced at him with a worried look. 'That's as maybe. Meantime, you'd better remember why you are here. Personal business has to come later.'

Personal business? Gavin hesitated. Then he nodded. Canty was right. The Delanceys had waited all these months. They could wait a little longer.

Doctor Tertins Kempson had apparently persuaded the council of Fort Erie that it was wise to cooperate with Starr and provisions were being collected from house to house and distributed to the men of Starr's regiment who had bivouacked along the wharves and in the old fortress, setting up campfires. As Starr instructed, at exactly six o'clock, in the full light of what promised to be a pleasant summer's day, the townspeople gathered in the main street opposite George Lewis's post office building. Doctor Kempson and his councilmen stood in front of the citizens with several companies of Starr's men, with shouldered arms, on either side. Starr's officers were lined up by the flag pole in front of the post office from which the British Union flag usually hung. At six o'clock Starr came out of the building and glanced around.

'Well, gentlemen,' he smiled at his officers, 'it's a pity we didn't bring across a regimental band for this occasion.'

Spaulding responded to his smile. 'The men are in good voice, colonel. Just give the word.'

Starr nodded. 'Pass the word to the companies then, John.'

Spaulding saluted and moved off. Then Starr turned to face the gathered townspeople. There was an expectant hush. Heads strained to see what strange animal this Fenian chieftain was who had dared the might of the strongest empire on earth to invade the Queen's favourite colonies. Starr glanced to where a lieutenant stood in charge of a colour party. With military precision, the lieutenant unsheathed his sword and snapped an order. A sergeant and two escorting men moved to the flag pole. A black ball was attached to the halyard. Gavin felt his pulse quicken as the sergeant's steady hands set it aloft. As if mesmerized the people craned forward to watch its progress. The lieutenant's sword flashed in salute. The entire company came to attention, with a crackle of palms slapping the wooden butts of rifles as they came to the present.

The flag broke open.

It was the tricolour, in green, white and orange. The flag which Alphonse de Lamartine, president of the French Republic, had presented to the Young Irelanders. A tricolour based on the flag of the French Republic, its green, white and orange symbolizing the unity of the peoples of Ireland. The townspeople stared at it in bewilderment, unsure of what was happening.

Owen Starr moved forward and swept off his hat. From his pocket he drew a printed sheet.

'People of British North America!' he cried in a stentorian voice.

The people tore their gaze away from the strange flag fluttering to stare at the young officer in his handsome green uniform.

'We come among you as the foes of British rule in Ireland. We have taken up the sword to strike down the oppressor's rod to deliver Ireland from the tyrant, the despoiler, the robber. . . .'

He paused and swept his gaze around them, making sure he had their attention.

'We have no issue with the people of these provinces, and wish to have none but the most friendly relations. Our weapons are for the oppressors of Ireland. Our blows shall be directed only against the power of England; her privileges alone shall we invade, not yours. We do not propose to divest you of a solitary right you now enjoy. . . .'

Again he halted as if to give emphasis to his words.

'We are here neither as murderers, nor robbers for plunder or spoilation. We are here as the Irish Army of Liberation, the friends of liberty against despotism, of democracy against aristocracy, of the people against the oppressors, in a word, our war is with the armed power of England, not with the people, not with these provinces. Against England, upon land and sea, till Ireland is free. . . .'

Starr's voice had risen a little in passion and he paused again to clear his throat.

'To Irishmen throughout these provinces we appeal in the name of seven centuries of English iniquity and Irish misery and suffering, in the names of our murdered sires, our desolate homes, our desecrated altars, our million of famine graves, our insulted name and race – to stretch forth the hand of brotherhood in the holy cause of fatherland and smite the tyrant where we can. . . .'

Again he stopped, choking on the note of suppressed passion in his voice.

'We wish to meet with friends,' he went on staring at the silent people before him, 'we are prepared to meet with enemies. We shall endeavour to merit the confidence of the former, and the latter can expect from us the leniency of a determined though generous foe and the restraints and restrictions imposed by civilized warfare.'

He raised his voice now.

'This proclamation is signed by Thomas William Sweeny, major-general commanding the Army of Ireland and secretary for war of the provisional government of the Irish Republic. God save Ireland!'

He glanced at Spaulding.

A tenor voice rose from the ranks of the soldiers to still the muttering of the townspeople. It was pure and melodic, almost operatic in quality. The notes rose softly in the muted early morning sunlight, drowning even the morning chorus of the birds.

When boyhood's fire was in my blood,
I read of ancient freemen,
From Greece and Rome who bravely stood,
Three hundred men and three men,
And then I prayed I yet might see
Our fetters rent in twain
And Ireland, long a province, be
A nation once again!

The chorus was taken up with fervour by a hundred enthusiastic voices:

A nation once again!
A nation once again!
And Ireland, long a province, be
A nation once again!

Gavin stood feeling hot tears stinging his eyes. He tried to choke back the confused, half-shameful sense of his own mawkish softness but he felt helpless, almost like a child, inadequate to control a deep inextricable ecstasy.

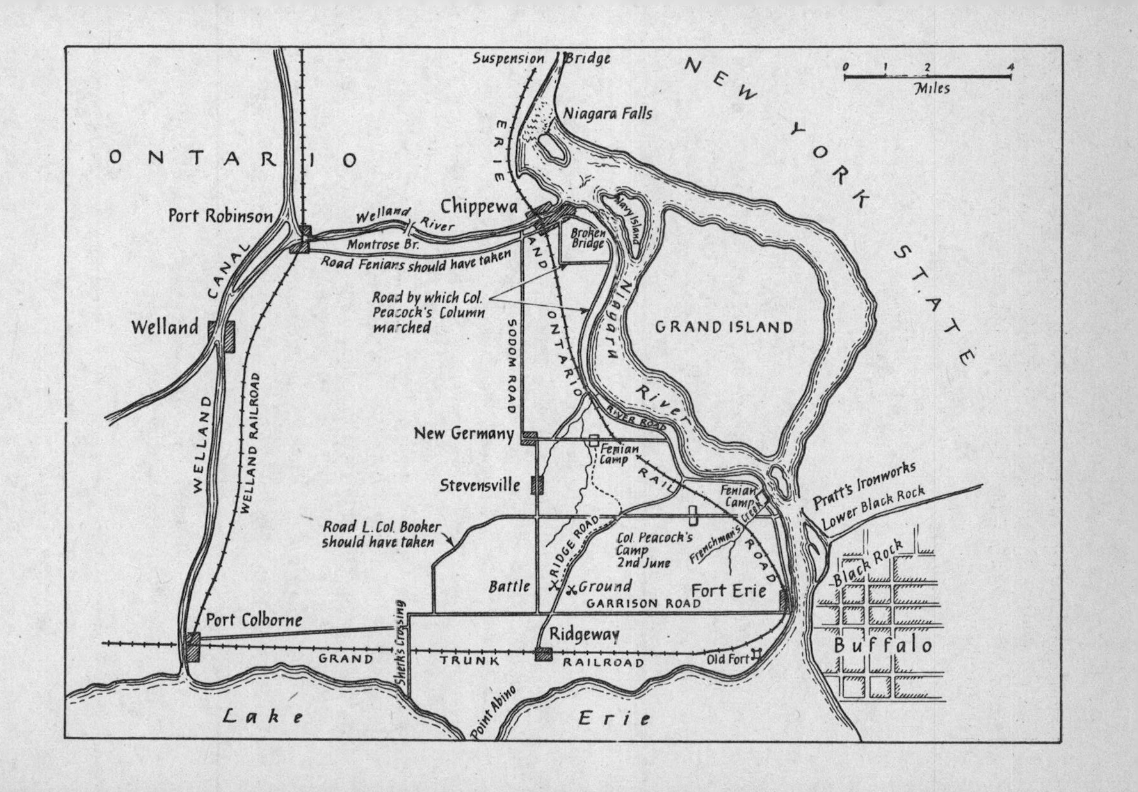
ONTARIO
NEW YORK STATE
0 1 2 4
Miles
Suspension Bridge
Niagara Falls
ERIE AND ONTARIO RAIL ROAD
Navy Island
Chippewa
Port Robinson
Welland River
Montrose Br.
Broken Bridge
Road Fenians should have taken
Road by which Col. Peacock's Column marched
CANAL
Welland
WELLAND
WELLAND RAILROAD
SODOM ROAD
Niagara River
GRAND ISLAND
RIVER ROAD
New Germany
Fenian Camp
Stevensville
Pratt's Ironworks
Lower Black Rock
Black Rock
Buffalo
Road L. Col. Booker should have taken
RIDGE ROAD
Col. Peacock's Camp 2nd June
Frenchman's Creek
Battle Ground
Fort Erie
GARRISON ROAD
Port Colborne
Ridgeway
GRAND TRUNK RAILROAD
Sherk's Crossing
Old Fort
Point Abino
Lake Erie

Chapter 48

His Excellency, the governor-general of British North America, Charles Stanley, Viscount Monck, was aroused by his servant soon after six o'clock that morning. Apologizing to his wife, Lady Elizabeth, who had also been disturbed by the discreet knocking, Lord Monck hauled on his silk dressing gown and rubbed the sleep from his eyes. It would not do for a governor-general to look bleary-eyed when the commander-in-chief of the army, the adjutant-general of militia and the first minister of the united provinces of Upper and Lower Canada, came calling on him. He paused to splash some water over his face and brushed his hair before following the servant downstairs. The mirror told him that he still looked tired; older than his forty-six years. But the lines were etched by anxieties over affairs of state. Since Lord Monck had thrown his support behind the confederation of the provinces, he had found that he had to work tirelessly against the considerable opposition to the plan. But now that opposition was beginning to crumble, and crumble rapidly. The first of the maritime provinces to change its opposition into positive support had been New Brunswick. That had been the crucial turning point. It looked as if both Nova Scotia and Prince Edward Island would follow soon although there was still considerable opposition in Newfoundland. But then Newfoundland had a strong Irish settlement which always dominated their politics.

'Sir?'

Monck silently cursed himself for daydreaming and followed his servant across the spacious foyer of Rideau Hall, the mansion he had selected as his official residence in Ottawa. The man paused in front of the library doors before throwing them open in a quaintly grand gesture and intoning, 'His Excellency, the governor-general.' He stood aside to allow Monck to enter and then closed the doors gently behind him. Two uniformed officers and a haggard-looking civilian stood in front of the fireplace. Monck took in their grim faces at a glance and made sure that the servant had withdrawn before he bade them good morning.

'Not so good, Excellency,' were the opening words from the civilian. John Alexander Macdonald was leader of the House of Assembly, first minister of the united legislature of Upper and Lower Canada. A fiery, impulsive man, in his fifties, he had been brought to Canada by his parents from their native Scotland when he was five years old in 1820. It was whispered that his father had fled during the suppression following the Scottish insurrection of April 1820, along with other radical leaders like William Lyon Mackenzie. Whereas Mackenzie adherred to his radical politics, eventually leading the uprising of 1837 and proclaiming a short-lived Canadian republic, the Macdonalds had prospered in business and John Macdonald had swiftly found a niche in the House of Assembly, rising to lead the Conservative government of the united provinces.

Monck waited, regarding Macdonald with a quizzical eye. It fell, however, to Lieutenant-General Sir John Michell, the commander of the army, to explain. 'We have received a telegraph from our consul in Buffalo. He reports that the Fenians have crossed the Niagara River during the night.'

Monck's expression did not alter although the news shook him. 'The consul in Buffalo?' he mused. 'That would be Mister Hemans, wouldn't it? Did we not have a report from him only last week saying that the Fenian project for the invasion of these provinces was virtually dead after the debacle at New Brunswick and suggesting that we disband Mister McMicken's detective force because the possibility of a Fenian raid was so slight that it did not justify the expense of its maintenance?'

Macdonald coloured at the even-toned rebuke. Although he was six years older than the governor-general, Monck always made him feel like a disobedient schoolboy. Only a few days ago he had told Monck that the split between the Fenian Brotherhood and the public argument now raging between James Stephens, newly arrived from Ireland, and William Randall Roberts had put an end to any prospects for an invasion. Monck's implied criticism of Hemans was therefore a veiled taunt at himself.

'There seems no doubt that a body of Fenians have crossed into Upper Canada, your lordship,' interposed Colonel Patrick L. MacDougall, the adjutant-general of militia. He was awkwardly hesitant. He had been in the country less than one year and was still unsure of himself, feeling a newcomer's nervousness. 'According to Mister Hemans's telegraph, they number 1,340 men with 2,500 stand of muskets together with six field guns. We have tried to get more precise information and telegraphed to Fort Erie for confirmation but the lines are reported down. Mister Hemans has informed us that reinforcements are waiting to cross the river to join the initial landing party.'

Monck raised an eyebrow and turned to Sir John Michell. 'Well, Sir John? This appears to be your province. Any suggestions?'

Sir John shifted his weight and cleared his throat. He was older than any of them, in his early sixties, and his uniform was covered by decorations and orders won in a lifetime of service to the British empire. 'Indeed, your lordship. But before any orders can be issued to counter this threat, I need your approval. Your authority as supreme commander in these provinces outweighs mine.'

'Quite so,' Monck muttered, wondering whether there was some veiled meaning in Sir John's comment. Final responsibility did lay with the governor-general but, surely, that was obvious. Monck felt a distinct unease whenever he addressed the general. Sir John Michell was an Englishman, Eton educated with all the privilege class and money could buy. Monck, on the other hand, had never been able to shake off the curiously defensive attitude of a colonial towards a native of the mother country. Monck had been born and educated in Ireland, a descendant of Cromwell's General George Monck whose army of Roundheads had carved their estates and privileges with their own swords. The restoration of the Stuart monarchy had blessed the Cromwellian conquest and colonization of Ireland. The Moncks found themselves elevated to the peerage. But the title was regarded as an 'Irish title' and the Moncks had become somehow less than Englishmen, even though the Union of 1801 had supposedly united Ireland and Britain into one nation. In spite of his graduation in law from Trinity College and being called to the Bar in Dublin, Charles Monck found he could not practise law in England without re-sitting all his exams in an English university and being called to the English Bar. On succeeding to the family title in 1849, he found that having an 'Irish title' did not even qualify him to sit in the House of Lords and so he had to fight his way to a seat in the House of Commons as a Liberal in 1852. The fact rankled with Monck and he always felt resentment when dealing with more privileged Englishmen; resentment and a feeling of inferiority. He became aware that Sir John was waiting politely.

'I'm sorry?'

'I have telegraphed to Major-General Napier in Toronto and given him full discretionary powers to make such deployment of troops which he thinks necessary to turn back the incursion. Nevertheless, I think it would be wise to put the entire army on alert in all the provinces, both regular troops and the militia. They should be brought to the nearest railheads for immediate entraining to the border areas.'

Colonel MacDougall was nodding his head in agreement. 'We can have 20,000 militia under arms within two days, your lordship,' he added.

Monck tugged at his lower lip. 'Are we to believe that this crossing is something more than a mere isolated incursion?' he asked.

Sir John Michell hesitated and weighed his words. 'It is my judgment, your lordship, that the Fenians may try to cross in several areas.'

At least Monck respected Sir John's military judgment. The old general had spent his life fighting 'rebels' against the empire. He had won his initial reputation in the 'Kaffir Wars' in Africa, had served with distinction in the Crimean War and then been sent to India to play a leading role in suppressing the 'Indian Mutiny' and bringing the sub-continent once more under the heel of the British Raj. It was his ruthless campaigning against the Indian insurgents, defeating them at Beorora, Mingrauli and Sindwaha, that had earned him his knighthood. He had been given command of a division in China when England had moved against Sinho and Peking. Sir John Michell had entered the summer palace of the Chinese emperors in Peking at the head of his troops in 1860. Now, nearing the end of his career but still an unrepentant fire-eater, feared and respected by his officers and men, he had been placed in command of the armies in British North America. If there were rebels to put down and destroy, then Sir John certainly had enough experience of doing so. Monck examined the general's expression carefully. Sir John was certainly not making light of the matter.

'As well as attempted crossings, do you think there will be risings in the cities?'

'D'Arcy McGee will be able to control the Irish in Ottawa and Toronto,' interrupted Macdonald.

Sir John shook his head. 'I am not concerned with those places. I think we should have a care of Montréal. The Irish and French have grown too close for my liking. I don't trust the radicals, men like

Papineau and his crony Dorian. The *Parti Rouge* has many among them who are Republican and several who advocate a union with the Americans.'

'Then it would be advisable to have the militia under arms at all strategic points in the city?' queried Monck.

Sir John nodded slowly. 'I would go so far as to suggest that we place a couple of regular regiments in Montréal and perhaps bring up a warship to train its guns on Verdun.'

Monck raised his eyebrows in surprise. 'You think the threat may be that serious?'

'I do, sir. Verdun is a nest of Irish, the one quarter of Montréal where a redcoated soldier can walk in peril of his life. If there is unrest in the city it will spring out of Verdun.'

'Then I agree to your suggestion. However, the immediate problem seems to be to discover the size of the force which crossed the Niagara River last night and to ascertain whether Toronto is threatened.'

'Napier is a first-class man,' conceded Sir John. 'The Napiers are a family of fine soldiers. He will soon have the rebels by the heels.'

'I don't doubt it,' Monck replied grimly. 'Well, pass your orders, Sir John. I will ratify them. Now, Mister Macdonald,' turning to the impatient minister, 'doubtless you will be wanting to issue civilian ordinances?'

'I will, sir,' Macdonald said stiffly. 'We must allay the fears of our civil populace. I will draft the proclamations presently. We must also make it clear to the Irish and French communities within our population that we will tolerate no disaffection nor sedition to the Queen's majesty. There is, as Sir John has pointed out, a great deal of sedition in Montréal in spite of the sterling work of Mister D'Arcy McGee. I believe that the Fenians may want to establish themselves in Montréal. They will strike into Lower Canada, mark my words.'

'But what of their movement across the Niagara?'

'A feint, sir. Nothing but a feint!'

Monck turned to Sir John. 'Would you agree with Mister Macdonald's military understanding?' he asked.

Sir John smiled thinly. 'Who knows what is in the minds of these Fenians. You are from Ireland, Excellency. You may have a better means of divination as to how these riffraff think.'

Monck felt a chill in his blood at the condescending manner of the Englishman. For a moment the blank mask of his face slipped. The corners of his mouth tightened.

'It is true I was born and raised in County Tipperary,' he said, measuring each word coldly. 'Does that make me, an Irishman, kin to the Irish rabble any more than it makes a white Canadian kith and kin to the aboriginal natives of this place? Next, Sir John, I will be led to believe that you consider Lord Wellington to be an Irishman simply because he was born in Dublin.'

Sir John's smile remained fixed. He was not unaware that he had touched on Monck's weakness.

'There was a stable lad on our estate in Tipperary who taught me some few words of native gibberish,' Monck continued. 'There was one phrase I learned. *An té a rugadh i stábla ní capal é*. Everything born in a stable is not a horse. I think, for once, gentlemen, the native gibberish of the Irish had some sense in it.'

He turned to a side table and picked up a small silver bell from it. 'If that is all for the time being, gentlemen . . . ?' he gazed at their bemused faces before he rang it. 'Good. I suggest we attend to the day's burden. We shall meet for a council of war at midday and discuss any developments. I shall be sending my aide-de-camp, Colonel Cumberland, to join General Napier in Toronto to ensure that I am personally acquainted with full details of the situation.'

It was six-twenty when Major-General George Thomas Connolly Napier was aroused by his adjutant and given a telegraph from the British consul in Buffalo. The general read the telegraph quickly and sprung from his bed calling for his servant to help him dress. He was a gaunt man of fifty-one years of age, the gauntness making him look stern and aggressive. His hook nose and swarthy appearance were part of a family inheritance. His uncle, Sir Charles, had been called 'Old Fagin' by his troops after the character in *Oliver Twist*. Napier had first arrived in British North America in July 1859, to be quartermaster-general. In December 1861, he had been appointed major-general commanding all troops in Canada West, the military designation of Upper Canada. The command was generally a peaceful one, even during the years when the civil war raged south of the border. Of course, there had been the occasional infractions of the neutrality laws by Confederate soldiers and sympathizers but these, on the quiet advice of certain officials, were generally ignored. During the last few months the rumours of a Fenian invasion had given Napier some worry but he had thought the threat had faded with the debacle at New Brunswick.

By the time Napier reached his office, his adjutant had received another telegraph, this time from Ottawa. Lieutenant-General Sir

John Michell was taking the matter of the Fenian crossing seriously; seriously enough to place all regular units in readiness to entrain anywhere along the border while all the volunteer militia were being called out. Napier's command consisted of 5,000 regular troops and about 10,000 militia units. Yet in the Niagara Peninsula, into which the Fenians were reported to have crossed, there were scarcely any regulars at all. He would have to order them down by train from Toronto.

An orderly brought in hot coffee and rolls while Napier peered at his large map of the peninsula. He was suddenly nervous. The ghosts of the entire Napier family seemed to be hovering at his elbow. Perhaps fate had ensured this curious destiny for him for the first stories that he ever recalled hearing in his youth were of Irish rebellion. His grandfather, Colonel Charles Napier, had obtained a large estate called Celbridge in County Kildare, ten miles from Dublin, and settled his family there in 1780. During the great insurrection of '98 Colonel Charles and his four sons, Napier's father among them, had fought grimly to defend their estates from the Irish rebels. He recalled hearing of how the countryside was littered with dead and wounded. His uncle Charles had been aide-de-camp to General Henry Fox in Dublin during Robert Emmet's uprising in 1803 and told stories of how the gibbet in Thomas Street was in daily use as captured rebels were made to queue to take their turn upon it. Perhaps this was his moment now; the moment to prove his worth as a soldier and measure up to the high standards that countless Napiers had set for him.

His father Sir George had fought with Wellington and lost his right arm at the storming of Ciudad Rodrigo. He had become governor of Cape province, was acclaimed the hero who stamped out slavery in South Africa and annexed Natal for the British empire. Napier had always felt in awe of his father's achievements as a soldier. Then there was his uncle Henry, a captain in the Royal Navy, whose ship *The Rifleman* had played such a dramatic role in the battle of the Bay of Fundy. His uncle Major-General Sir Charles, from whom he had heard most of his stories about the Irish rebellions, had served with Wellington, fought against the Americans, accepted command in India and conquered the northern territory of Sind and its capital Karachi to bring it under the empire. There were his cousins, the famous Napier brothers, Admiral Sir Charles, General Robert and General Sir Thomas. Napiers. Napiers by the score; generals and admirals every one, each playing their part to secure the empire. Napier suddenly felt their combined weight oppressive on his shoulders. When he had been appointed aide-de-camp to Her Majesty Queen Victoria in 1854, the little queen had smiled and said, 'We are extremely happy to see one of your distinguished name in our personal service.' Napier frowned at the memory. That too, had been a hot June day – 20 June 1854. He could recall riding to the palace as a newly promoted colonel alongside his grim-faced father who had just been given his generalship.

Napier remembered his father and remembered feeling somewhat of a fraud when, in turn, he became a major-general because he had not won the rank by fame and fortune like his father nor his other distinguished relatives; he had not acquired it by some dashing action or by annexing new lands to the empire. He had been given it as a reward for plodding, moving through the ranks by administrative ability, by an undistinguished career of hard work. The closest that he had ever come to seeing action was when he had been lieutenant of the Colonial Mounted Riflemen serving under his father in Cape Colony and dealing with the truculent Boers at the time when they began their Great Trek rather than remain under British rule at the Cape.

He blinked and realized that his adjutant was staring at him. He glanced guiltily at the clock ticking away on the mantleshelf of the room and coughed nervously.

'I beg your pardon. What was it you were saying?'

'Mister Carr, the city clerk, is waiting outside and tells me that the mayor is on his way here to discuss plans for the defence of the city. The rumour that the Fenians have invaded has spread like wildfire, sir. The proprietor of the *Toronto Globe* is also waiting for an announcement.'

'They can wait. What else?'

'A Colonel Dennis is also waiting outside.'

Napier frowned. 'Dennis?'

'Lieutenant-Colonel Stoughton Dennis, brigade major of the 5th Toronto Military District,' the adjutant said. 'He's requesting a field command against the Fenians. He seems enthusiastic.'

'He's a militia officer, isn't he?'

The adjutant nodded.

'Let him wait,' snapped Napier. He hated keen officers who volunteered for death or glory commands. 'We have more important things to organize. What are the nearest regular troops to the Niagara frontier?'

The adjutant checked a notebook. 'There are only two regular foot regiments immediately available, sir, the 16th and the 47th.'

'The 47th?' Napier turned quickly, interest in his voice. It was a good steady regiment which had distinguished itself at Alma and Inkerman in the Crimean War. 'That's Lowry's command, isn't it?'

'Yes sir.'

'Get Lowry here immediately.'

The adjutant's face fell. 'Colonel Lowry left Toronto last night, sir. I believe he went up to Georgian Bay on a fishing expedition with some other officers.'

'Damnation!' Napier swore. 'Get someone to ride after him and bring him back.'

'I'll send Lieutenant Dent, his adjutant, sir. But I don't think we will be able to get Colonel Lowry back before late this evening.'

'I know. I know. We can't wait for his return. I need another officer to command the field force until Lowry gets here.'

'Well, sir, there is the colonel of the 16th Foot.'

'Colonel Peacocke?' Napier pursed his lips disapprovingly. Peacocke had not seen action like Lowry. Lowry had already proved his mettle in battle. Peacocke was more of a staff officer. He had received his commission at the age of seventeen, attended the military academy at Sandhurst and returned to his regiment as a good administrative officer. By slow process of elimination he had been chosen to command the 1st Battalion of the 16th Foot. Just recently Napier had approved his brevet colonelcy of the regiment. Peacocke was a steady officer not given to flamboyant gestures. Napier stroked his nose thoughtfully. Perhaps that was what was needed to contain the situation until Lowry could take command? Peacocke would be capable of maintaining a holding action and not indulging in any grand gestures which would throw away the command and leave Toronto open to enemy attack.

'Where is Colonel Peacocke now?'

'Town of Hamilton, sir,' replied the adjutant quickly. 'He's there with a company of his regiment but most of his battalion are still quartered here in the city.'

'Some 200 men, eh? I need more than a mere 200 regulars. What other troops can be raised?'

'We can entrain the 1st Battalion of the 47th Foot, sir.'

'Who would command in place of Colonel Lowry?'

'Major Lodder, I suppose, sir.'

Napier snorted annoyance. He liked succinct positive replies. 'You suppose?' he commented, raising an eyebrow.

The adjutant consulted his notebook. 'Major Lodder will command, sir,' he corrected.

'Peacocke will need artillery support.'

'There's a battery of the Royal Artillery commanded by Lieutenant-Colonel Hoste available.'

Napier stared at the map before him, stroking his nose, '400 regulars and six field guns. It's not enough. Not even with the field guns. We'll have to enlarge the column with militia troops. Lieutenant-Colonel Currie's 19th Battalion are at St Catharines. They can join Peacocke. In fact, it might be best if Peacocke made the town of St Catharines his base of operations. Telegraph him to that effect and add that he may then make his own movements according to discretion. The Fenians must be contained as close to the Niagara River as possible.'

'Very well, sir,' the adjutant scribbled in his notebook. 'If the Fenians are at Fort Erie they will be within striking distance of Port Colborne and the Welland Canal.'

Napier turned his eyes to the canal system. His adjutant was right in drawing his attention to it. It was a fact that should have been obvious to him. The canals were a vital link through the Great Lakes. A prime military objective.

'We'll have to make up a second column from the militia to protect the canal. Raise Major Gillmor's 2nd Battalion and get them shipped across the lake to Port Dalhousie. They can then entrain directly to Port Colborne. Also order the 13th Battalion from Hamilton to join the 2nd Battalion at Port Colborne as soon as possible. They will be nominally under Colonel Peacocke's command but the senior officer present at Port Colborne must use his discretion to turn back any attack on the canal system.'

The adjutant nodded. 'There is a field battery there, sir, but without field guns. Shall I request they attach themselves to the 2nd and 13th Battalions as a supporting company.'

Napier inclined his head. 'In fact, issue a general order for all volunteer militia to assemble and await my further instructions.'

'Yes sir.' He hesitated at the door. 'And Colonel Dennis, sir?'

'Dennis?' Napier frowned. 'Oh, the brigade major who wants to see some action? Very well, send him in. . . .'

As the adjutant left an orderly entered and handed a paper to

Napier. 'Just arrived over the telegraph from Ottawa, sir. It's the governor-general's proclamation.'

Napier took up the paper. Lord Monck's proclamation was already being posted throughout the provinces:

> The soil of Canada has been invaded, not in the practice of legitimate warfare, but by a lawless and piratical band, in defiance of all moral right, and in utter disregard to all the obligations which civilization imposes on mankind. Upon the people of Canada the state of things imposes the duty of defending their altars, their homes and their property, from desecration, pillage and spoilation. The commander-in-chief relies on the courage and loyalty of the Volunteer Force and looks with confidence for the blessing of providence on the performance of this sacred duty which has been cast upon them.

Napier sighed as he sunk back in his chair. He found himself shivering and realized that he could not blame the morning chill for it. The stories he had heard in his childhood were about to become reality. He wondered how his father, Sir George, would have coped with the situation. How would he have issued his commands, made his dispositions and appointed his field commanders? Napier exhaled unhappily. He wished that he did not feel so inadequate. Would he be the first Napier who would fail to distinguish himself at the hour of his country's need?

Chapter 49

The landing of the main body of Irish had been completed before dawn but there were still many stragglers coming across the river. Gavin accompanied Major Canty along the river road in search of O'Neill's headquarters and was surprised to see the river dotted with all manner of boats and barges bearing uniformed Fenians and their equipment. From the Canadian bank more boats were putting out filled with civilians and their baggage heading for the security of the American shore, seeking escape from what they regarded as the inevitable mayhem and bloodshed that would follow the arrival of the British regulars. Both banks of the river seemed to contain a confused frenzy of people moving this way and that.

Gavin was filled with a grim satisfaction – not at the scene along the river banks but by the capture of Hogan. He had little doubt that he would, by some means or other, make Hogan do what he wanted. He would ensure that Hogan swore a legal deposition which would reveal the extent of the criminal empire of the Delanceys, the extent of their activities which had caused such suffering and misery and provided their wealth and power. Further, he would take Hogan to New York and use him as chief witness to indict Senator Delancey and his son Brock and bring their privilege and power tumbling about their ears. He would have his justice, his vengeance. It felt good to think about it. It made him feel exuberant and he walked with a spring to his step which he had not felt in a long time.

O'Neill had made his headquarters at the farmstead of Thomas Newbeggin, alongside a small stream called Frenchman's Creek six miles north of Fort Erie. Sentries had been posted and the main bulk of the Fenian regiments were encamped within and around the farm buildings and adjoining lands. Most of the men were stretched out trying to snatch a few hours' rest to make up for their sleepless night. Smoke from dozens of cooking fires rose into the air as some of them prepared breakfast. They were old campaigners who knew the value of eating a hearty meal where they could and sleeping when the moment offered.

As Gavin and Canty turned into the farmyard, Father MacMahon was setting up a small makeshift altar of wooden boxes for those who wanted spiritual solace before the coming fight, if there was to be one.

O'Neill was seated at a pine table in the farmhouse kitchen with his adjutant, Roddy Fitzpatrick, and three of his regimental commanders. The exception was Owen Starr who was still directing operations in Fort Erie. He looked relieved as Gavin entered and introduced Major Canty.

'Now we can get some proper intelligence,' he remarked, indicating to them to take seats around the kitchen table. An orderly was brewing coffee and brought them steaming mugs.

'The hospitality is by the unwilling courtesy of Mister Newbeggin, who owns this farm,' explained O'Neill. 'A doughty Scottish gentleman and a Justice of the Peace who, alas, has a bad habit of being somewhat outspoken with his views about Ireland in general and Fenians in particular. We have had to place Mister Newbeggin and his charming family in safe custody in a bedroom while we enjoy his hospitality.' O'Neill became serious. 'Were there any casualties at Fort Erie?'

Gavin glanced at Major Canty who now assumed his role as chief intelligence officer.

'None on either side, sir,' Canty replied.

'Excellent,' O'Neill nodded with relief. 'But it won't last. The enemy will soon learn of our presence and start his movement against us. We must begin to consolidate as soon as possible.'

Colonel Hoy of the Buffalo regiment removed a cigar from his mouth. 'The men were without sleep last night waiting for the crossing,' he pointed out. 'We must give them time to rest.'

'I know that, John,' replied O'Neill. 'But we can't afford to remain here beyond this afternoon. We must strike north to Chippewa and commence consolidating a front along the Welland River.' He paused and sighed. 'A pity Owen was unable to capture the engines and wagons at the depot. How far did Captain Geary pursue them?'

The question was directed at Canty. 'He followed the tracks for six miles until he came to a creek about six miles outside town. There was a wooden bridge across the creek, Sauerwine's Bridge I believe it's called. He tore up the rails and set the bridge alight before returning.'

'Six Mile Creek,' O'Neill muttered, peering at his map. 'So with the bridge and track destroyed there, the British can only use the railroad as far as this place . . . Ridgeway . . . to bring troops up?'

Canty nodded. 'I'd be surprised if the British used that route to attack,' he said. 'I would expect any attack to come from the north, from Chippewa.'

O'Neill grunted, noting the position on his map. 'By my reckoning, gentlemen, we have scarcely 1,000 men to secure the area until our reinforcements cross the river – 1,000 men and no field guns. True, there are stragglers still joining us but, from what I observe of them, many are not Fenians at all but merely riffraff from the poorer quarters of Buffalo, scavengers and looters, petty thieves and scroungers. We must be vigilant. I have issued strict instructions that no man in this command is to rob or despoil the civilian population. Requisitions for guns, horses and food are to be properly receipted. The crime of pillage and rape must not be levelled against us. If any man transgresses then he can expect to pay the full military penalty. Do I make myself clear?'

The officers muttered agreement.

'Spread the word to your officers and sergeants that a careful eye must be kept on unwelcome camp followers, those who think they will take advantage of the disturbances by following our army to rob the civilians. They will be punished as our soldiers will be.' O'Neill paused and added, 'Drunkenness is another crime that will not be tolerated by me. I have already ordered that all taverns and premises selling liquor in Fort Erie must be closed. Any man found drunk will be left behind and, if he is left, he can expect short shrift if captured by the enemy.'

There was an awkward silence and then Colonel Grace, commanding the 18th Cleveland Regiment, grimaced. 'Why should we be so particular? The British won't thank us and, in fact, will credit us anyway with all the crimes under the sun, real or imaginary.'

'We do it,' replied O'Neill icily, 'because it is morally right. The thing that separates us from our imperial masters is that we have moral right on our side. They have the right of conquest and power. We must never give up that moral right and adopt their standards.'

O'Neill paused for a moment, looking round the circle of officers, each in turn. Then he relaxed in his seat.

'What we are engaged in, gentlemen, is no narrow principle which involves one group of people or one nation. It is a principle that goes far beyond that. Freedom, both national and social, reaches out to all men, all nations, everywhere. Apparently, the other day at the Brotherhood offices in Philadelphia, one hundred negro soldiers, veterans who had fought in the Union Army, arrived to enlist in the Irish Republican Army. Why? Because, they said, the Irish had fought alongside them during the war for negro emancipation. Now they wanted to fight alongside the Irish for Irish emancipation.'

He smiled and shrugged, turning as an orderly opened the door to a nervous young lieutenant. The young man hesitated, staring round at the officers before picking out O'Neill and saluting him. 'I've just come across river, sir. Captain Hynes's compliments and I'm to inform you of the situation.'

O'Neill's mouth quirked. 'The situation?' he prompted gently.

'In Buffalo, sir. The USS *Michigan* has arrived and is moored at the foot of Ferry Street. So far, the authorities have made no attempt to interfere with the crossing of our men and supplies except . . . when the *International* ferry was preparing to return to the Canadian shore some customs officers tried to prevent some of our men going aboard. It was only half-hearted and the men simply ignored them.'

'What news of the reinforcements?' pressed O'Neill.

'Reinforcements are arriving and Colonel Sherwin is now in Buffalo. I have a despatch for you, sir.'

O'Neill took it with a sigh, ripped open the seal and glanced through it, chewing his lips thoughtfully as he did so. Finally he looked up and shrugged.

'The position, so far as we are concerned, remains the same. Sherwin says he will stay in Buffalo to coordinate the arrival of the reinforcements. Instead of instructing them to cross in a haphazard fashion, he will gather them in their units in readiness for General Burns who is expected momentarily. Our regiments are still to secure a bridgehead and wait until General Burns brings over the main force.' O'Neill drummed his fingers on the table. 'I would still like to double the force and have some field guns on this side of the river. Hell,' he snorted moodily, 'why didn't everyone turn up by the last day of May as they were instructed? It's a wonder we Irish bother to turn up at our own funerals.'

They waited in uneasy silence while O'Neill stared at the map again.

'Colonel Hoy,' he snapped, as if making a decision, 'I want you and the 7th Regiment to march out this afternoon and take the river road north to Chippewa. I will bring the main body after you within three or four hours. Our first task is to take Chippewa and then turn west, destroying the bridges over the Welland River. I want to be in Port Robinson on the Welland Canal by tomorrow afternoon.'

Major Canty caused them all to stare at him by suddenly saying, 'It's a damned good omen, sir.'

O'Neill raised a curious eyebrow. 'An omen?'

'Did you know they are burying General Winfield Scott at West Point today?'

Winfield Scott had been general-in-chief of the United States Army from 1841 to 1861. He was a legend whose military career had spanned the War of 1812, the Mexican War and had seen victory in the grim war between the States. The old general had died on Tuesday at the age of eighty.

O'Neill was perplexed. 'There is an omen in this, Canty?'

Major Canty nodded. 'I took the precaution of reading up on the history of the War of 1812, in particular the campaign fought in this area. In July 1814, General Brown crossed the Niagara and took Fort Erie in much the same manner as we have done. The British fell back to Chippewa where General Scott's brigade attacked them and broke their lines. It was the first action of the war in which American regulars faced and defeated British regulars. I say, it is an omen and what better tribute can we present to Scott's memory than capturing Chippewa as he did over fifty years ago?'

O'Neill chuckled approvingly. 'I believe Major Canty has a point. Let the password for the day be "Winfield Scott" and the countersign "Chippewa". Major Canty, you stay close by me. I shall want your advice.'

Gavin coughed anxiously. 'What orders for me, colonel?'

O'Neill thought for a moment, 'I'm putting you in command of a company of mounted scouts which will act in advance of the vanguard. We don't have many suitable cavalry nags but we are still requisitioning horses. I would give anything for a cavalry regiment,' he added with a sigh.

The young lieutenant who had brought the despatch from Colonel Sherwin blurted, 'It's reported the Colonel Denis O'Donoghue's 5th Maryland Cavalry is at Elmira on its way to Buffalo, 600 strong.'

O'Neill pulled a face. 'Elmira! That's about 150 miles away. I need a cavalry regiment now.'

The young lieutenant coloured, discomfited at the rebuke.

'Devlin,' O'Neill had turned back to Gavin. 'You'll find a mount in the stables. You'll also find a Lieutenant Boyd there with half-a-dozen men.'

O'Neill scribbled a few lines on a piece of paper. 'This is your commission,' he grunted, handing down the table. 'Your prime function is scouting. As chief intelligence officer, Major Canty is still your commander but when we begin our advance you will be going ahead of Colonel Hoy's regiment and reporting back to him.'

Gavin stood up and saluted.

Across the farmyard, in the barn, he found a group of half a dozen soldiers seated on boxes playing cards. A young man with pale, bony features glanced up as Gavin entered. He wore a grey Confederate uniform with a green sash. One by one the other card players glanced up. They were all in Confederate grey, a couple with green shirts, the others with green armbands. The uniforms were rumpled, some of them had tears.

'Yeah?' asked the young man languidly.

'I'm looking for Lieutenant Boyd.'

'You've found him.'

Gavin moved forward and pushed O'Neill's commission towards the man. 'I'm Captain Devlin,' he said coldly. 'I have been placed in command of your troop.'

The men around the packing case exchanged glances and then looked at their officer, watching his reaction. The young man rose reluctantly to his feet. He was tall, touching six foot, lean to the point of thinness. Gavin had seen many a 'Reb' in such conditions; their commissary had been poor in the last months of the war and malnutrition was a common factor in their army.

'Lieutenant Phil Boyd . . . captain,' he introduced himself with a deliberate pause before he acknowledged Gavin's rank. 'Late of Colonel O'Brien's Louisana Irish regiment, Army of the Confederate States of America.'

There was a challenge in his southern drawl, heightened by the sharp tones of his native Ulster which he could not disguise.

'Gavin Devlin,' Gavin replied evenly, 'Captain, Army of the Irish Republic.' He accepted the former Confederate's challenge and threw it back.

The blue eyes of Boyd clouded for a moment in hostility and then his pale face broke into a smile. He inclined his head in acknowledgment of Gavin's rebuff. The old animosities were dead and new challenges had to be met. Behind him, in acceptance, the card players dropped their cards and rose to their feet.

'This is your command, captain,' Boyd said. 'Sergeant Nolan here is . . . was . . . the best top sergeant in the Louisiana Irish.'

A muscular and stocky curly haired man straightened to attention. '*Dia duit, a chaptaen.*'

'Where are you from, Nolan?' smiled Gavin.

'Cahersiveen, County Kerry, sir.'

Boyd gestured to a corporal who seemed to have drunk a little more than was good for him for the dark eyes were clouded in his sallow face and he seemed to have trouble focusing.

'Corporal Collins. Best corporal in the regiment,' Boyd added hastily seeing Gavin's look of disapproval.

'I'll accept that,' Gavin nodded. 'But the order from the brigadier is no drinking, got that, Collins? If a man gets drunk he'll be left behind to the tender mercies of the English.'

'Don't worry about me, sir,' grunted Collins. 'I can handle myself.'

Gavin sniffed. 'I'm in command and *I'll* handle you, corporal. When I can't it will be time for you to worry.'

Of the four others he could not remember the names. They would come in time. All had been in the Louisiana Irish regiment and all had been members of the Brotherhood for some years. After the war they had come north together to join the Fenian army. They were equipped with an odd collection of requisitioned horses, none of which would have passed muster in any cavalry command. Nevertheless, they would be sufficient for scouting purposes.

'What are the orders, captain?' prompted Boyd, as he watched Gavin inspect the mounts.

'We'll be scouting in advance of our vanguard when we move off. That won't be until this afternoon so I would suggest you all get some sleep.'

He took off his sword belt and settled himself against a bale of hay near the barn door. Boyd moved over and sat down beside him offering him a cigarette. Gavin nodded his thanks and supplied a light. For a while they sat quietly, the smell of tobacco mixing with the scent of the hay and the fragrance of pine warming in the morning sun. A faint breeze ripped the needles on the tall conifers that surrounded the farmstead. Gavin thought of Kate and the Dawtry farmstead and experienced a strange melancholy; an almost frightening loneliness. A feel of momentary panic went through him causing him to shiver slightly. He wished he had stayed. It was so much more simple.

'It's not quite the banks of the Glendun nor the mountains of Antrim but it's a good country.'

Gavin turned to look at the lieutenant who had spoken softly. 'Antrim? Is that where you come from?'

Philip Boyd smiled. 'A small place called Cushendall. It's by the sea. Odd how you spend years somewhere and still miss home. I've been eight years in this country, since I was sixteen. Yet when it comes to the fall I get homesick for Antrim. That's when its painted in its best colours, the golds, russets and greens of autumn.' He paused and drew on his cigarette. 'Have you been here long?'

'Since I was a lad,' Gavin nodded. 'I can hardly remember anything of Ireland.'

'Ireland's a disease,' Boyd sighed. 'It gets into the blood and there's no cure except freedom. I remember the Sunday sermons when the minister. . . .'

Gavin's eyes widened. 'Minister? Then you're not a Catholic?'

Boyd chuckled. 'Presbyterian.'

'I thought most Protestants wanted to be ruled by England.'

Boyd snorted. 'You're an ignorant man, captain. Isn't John Michell the son of a Presbyterian minister?'

'I suppose I thought he was an exception. I didn't think there was anything but enmity between Catholics and Protestants.'

'Then you're a poor benighted heathen,' retored Boyd, with amused tolerance. 'Wasn't it Ulster Presbyterians who taught you poor Papists the creed of republicanism? Wolfe Tone, Robert Emmet, the Young Ireland leaders . . . did you think they were all Papists? Now tell me that you've never heard of Penal Laws.'

'I have,' Gavin replied, on surer ground. 'The English introduced them after the Williamite conquest. Catholics were forbidden by law to practise their religion openly, to receive education, to join any of the professions. They had no rights at all.'

'Catholics!' Boyd chuckled dryly. 'Did you know that the same laws that applied to Catholics also applied to all dissenting Protestants? It was only the Episcopalians who had religious liberty after the Williamite conquest in Ireland. A Presbyterian minister was liable to three months in jail for delivering a sermon and a fine of £100 for celebrating the Lord's Supper. Presbyterians were punished by law if they were discovered to have been married by a Presbyterian minister. All Presbyterians were excluded from holding office in law, the army, navy, customs or municipal government. The punishment for

Presbyterian ministers found teaching Presbyterian children was jail. Intermarriage between dissenters and Episcopalians was made illegal.'

Gavin stared at him in astonishment. 'Then the dissenters, the Protestants of Ireland, were suffering exactly the same as the Catholics were? I was never told that.'

'Sure they were. The Presbyterians, the majority Protestant religion in Ulster, have entertained a fiercer hatred for the English than ever you Catholics did. A quarter of a million Ulster Protestants came to America just before the War of Independence to find religious and political liberty. Without Ulster Protestant help I doubt that America would ever have become free of the English yoke.'

'What makes you say that?' demanded Gavin.

'Ulster Protestants produced nineteen American revolutionary generals, five signed the Declaration of Independence, four served in Washington's first cabinet, one was chairman of the committee which actually drafted the American constitution, and three out of the thirteen first state governors were Ulster Protestants. The creed of Paine's *Rights of Man* and the philosophy of republicanism grew out of Ulster Protestantism. Wasn't President Andy Jackson's father and mother from County Antrim? President Polk's family were from Derry; Buchanan's father was from Donegal. And look at President Johnson. His family are from Antrim, too. Ulster Protestants are natural Republicans not the Papists.'

'That's not what I've heard,' protested Gavin.

Phil Boyd heaved a deep sigh. 'I can believe that,' he said. 'Our English friends were quick to see that republicanism united Irish Protestants and Catholics under the common name of Irishmen. They were scared out of their wits when the Irish Republic nearly became a fact back in '98. They began to issue bribes and incentives to Ulster dissenters to establish them as a small élite, a privileged minority, in order to divide and rule.' He paused. 'To the shame of the Ulster Protestants they accepted the bribes. The people who gave birth to republicanism in Ireland became bribed, cajoled and propagandized into the population most strongly loyal to the English government and crown in Ireland. Yet there are still many among us who remember our real traditions and know that true happiness for the Irish people, all the people, lies in Ireland free and republican. We still have examples of men like Michell who refuse to be bought by English gold. You'll find a lot of Irish Protestants with us here. There's a Protestant chaplain, Lumsden, from Edinburgh, who has volunteered to serve with us.'

The sound of cannon fire caused Gavin to leap to his feet. There was a panic in the camp and cries of 'The British!' Then there came a second shot causing Gavin to go cold with fear, the images of terrible Confederate bombardments whirling like a kaleidoscope across his memory. Boyd had risen with him and stood, head to one side, frowning.

'Seems to be coming from across the river.'

O'Neill and his staff had hurried out of the farmhouse and stood gazing about them in uncertainty. Another explosion echoed from across the river. One officer, Gavin saw it was Colonel Hoy, focused a telescope.

'It's the minute gun from the USS *Michigan*,' he called.

By the sound of the fourth shot the officers had begun to restore order among the men, especially now it was apparent that they were not the subject of a directed bombardment.

O'Neill was perplexed. 'Just what the hell is the *Michigan* shelling? Are they shooting at our men trying to cross the river?'

The cannonade was continuing at regular intervals.

Colonel Hoy shook his head. 'It's a salute.'

'To whom?'

It was Major Canty who supplied the answer. 'I told you Lieutenant-General Winfield Scott was being buried today at West Point. The commander of the *Michigan* is simply paying his respects. A salute from the minute gun. It's midday now and that's the time when I believe they are burying Scott.'

They stood scarcely believing the coincidence, slowly counting the booms of the cannon.

'Fifteen for a lieutenant-general,' muttered Canty.

He was right. After the fifteenth roar of the cannon there was no more gunfire. Instead, the solemn tolling of the bell atop Buffalo City Hall came clearly across the river, sounding the civic salute to the old general.

O'Neill began to chuckle. 'Maybe Canty is right about the omen after all. Scott pushed the British back at Chippewa and, by God, that's what we are going to do!'

As O'Neill led his officers back into the farmhouse, Gavin saw Major Canty besieged by a small group of civilians. He moved across to see if he could help. It was apparent that they were members of the press. One man, who looked decidedly out of place, his hand straying nervously to his wire-rimmed glasses as he stared about him with an air of comical wonder, was raising his voice officiously.

'I am sympathetic to your cause, major. I recently chaired a meeting of the Brotherhood in Buffalo and like all Americans I am sympathetic to the cause of Irish freedom.'

Canty smiled thinly. 'Your position as editor of the *Commercial-Advertiser* and postmaster of Buffalo is well known to me, Mister Clapp.' There was humour in Canty's eyes for the *Commercial-Adverstiser* was hardly pro-Fenian.

'Is it true that the Grand Trunk Railroad is cut, sir, and a bridge destroyed to prevent the transportation of British regulars into this area?'

'That is so.'

Clapp scribbled hastily. 'And where is General Sweeny?'

'In the right place, Mister Clapp,' Canty's smile broadened.

'I thought he might be here?' prompted the editor.

Canty did not bother to answer.

'I'm Kean of the *Buffalo Express*,' called another man. 'I see that there is a lack of tents and commissary equipment among your men although, by the way they have bivouacked, it is evident they are veterans.'

'Most have seen service in the late war,' agreed Canty.

'Union or Rebs?' growled Clapp of the *Commercial-Advertiser*.

'Men of both armies, sir.'

'There seems no lack of food,' observed the man from the *Buffalo Express*. 'I have seen men cooking bacon, chickens, ducks and geese over their fires, preparing chowder. They seem well provided for.'

'Our men have to forage as they can for the time being, sir,' replied Canty. 'But all give proper receipts for what they take as is the custom of war. No personal possessions are looted. They have explicit orders on that point.'

'Yet, I am given to understand, sir, some unsavoury gentlemen have endeavoured to cross in the wake of your army for the very purpose of looting. What will be their fate?' demanded Clapp.

'Wherever our army is in control martial law will be imposed until our campaign is over,' replied Canty. 'Any civilians or soldiers, from whichever side of the river, caught ignoring the rules of war and good conduct will suffer the consequences.'

'Your general. . . .' began Kean.

'Colonel O'Neill, acting brigadier,' corrected Canty.

'He has assured the civilian population that any demands for property by his troops are unauthorized and that he and his officers will respect private possessions of every sort.'

'That is so, except for those required by the exigencies of war. That is to say, food, horses, arms and ammunition which will be requisitioned as necessary.'

'I am told he has closed taverns and liquor stores.'

'That is correct.'

'One more thing,' it was Kean who spoke, turning to look at Boyd who had joined Gavin watching the impromptu press conference. 'I see an officer here in the uniform of a Reb.'

Gavin saw Boyd tense slightly.

'I see an officer wearing the colours of the Irish Republican Army, sir,' Gavin intervened.

Kean gazed towards Gavin. 'Is there no animosity between you? I presume that you fought in the Union Army by the badge on your sword belt.'

'I did,' confirmed Gavin. 'But the reply to your question is that there is no animosity between Irishmen fighting for the common cause of the liberty of Ireland.'

Kean smiled cynically. 'I am sure Mister O'Mahoney and Mister Stephens would argue with you on that point, sir.'

Canty began to shepherd the reporters away. Boyd reached forward and laid his hand on Gavin's arm. 'Thanks,' he said shortly.

Gavin grinned back. 'Matter of fact, I meant to ask you . . . how did you come to join the Rebs?'

Boyd did not take offence. 'How come you became a Yankee?' he countered.

'Easy enough. I'm northern and I hate slavery,' Gavin replied.

'There were plenty of people who hated slavery who served in the Confederacy. I fought over the principle of secession. The war to me was about liberty,' Boyd continued. 'The right of people to govern themselves without coercion from anyone else. If it was merely about the retention of slavery, why did four slave states choose to fight for the north?'

Gavin was well aware that slavery had not been totally abolished in the north until eight months after the end of the war.

'I was in Virginia when the war broke out,' Boyd fumbled for his cigarettes. 'Virginia was not interested in the slave question but she did stand firm on the constitutional right of every state in the Union to enjoy sovereign rights and on that principal Virginians denied the claim of the Washington government to exercise coercion. When the seven southern cotton states broke from the union, Lincoln issued a call to arms to coerce them back into the Union. That's what pushed the other states in to join the Confederacy. Do you think that Robert E. Lee or 'Stonewall' Jackson were slave owners? Lee hated slavery. But he fought to defend the constitutional right of each state to secede. Lincoln denied that right by military coercion. That's what the war was about for me, and many like me.' Boyd smiled and stubbed out his cigarette.

'Reckon we should follow your initial suggestion, captain, and get some sleep otherwise we won't be much use to anyone by the time the order is given to march off.'

Gavin nodded, wondering why it was that nothing was just black and white, right and wrong. Why were there always so many shades of grey about every question? He was suddenly tired. Tired from lack of sleep; tired from constantly trying to seek out a simple method of living where there was no constant confusion, of having to ask whether something was right or wrong. The difficulty in life was choice. Yet there seemed no such thing as choosing a right path. A vague memory floated by. A line from Epictetus, 'It is your own conviction which compels you; that is, choice compels choice.'

Chapter 50

Far off a bugle sounded.

Ready the flag!

Ready the flag? It was dark. Dark and bitterly cold. Who would ever see the flag? Officers ran up and down the serried ranks yelling to still their own fearful heartbeats. With numbed fingers each man strove to fix his bayonet to his musket. Ahead lay sodden fields and swamps. The icy mud flats and rivers. Some wag shouted out he knew why the place was called Cold Harbor.

Ready the flag!

It was Jack Quinlan's rich baritone. He wished the man would shut up. The flag had long been ready. So had the men. They stood shuffling and coughing in the darkness. Now and again a low moan could be heard, a slow cry of fear like an animal in pain. Some men were relieving themselves where they stood, their urine adding to the sickly smell of the swamp around them.

Far off a bugle sounded.

Then it started like a raging torrent from hell, the shriek and whistle of the shells, the explosions, those terrible explosions ripping and blinding everywhere.

Ready the flag!

Oh God, not again! Slowly they began to move, rifles held tightly across their chests as if they were some magic amulet that would protect them from harm. They moved forward, silent for the most part. Pale faces, lips dry and compressed. At the end of the day their bodies would be a cypher in some adjutant's notebook, cyphers without names, ranks or personalities. Cyphers; not young boys and men who sweated, trembled and crawled on their bellies shaking with fear.

He raised his voice to cry out and started awake on the sodden straw of the barn. Boyd was shaking him.

'Major Canty wants to see you, captain.'

'What time is it?'

'After four o'clock.'

He sat up and rubbed his face with his hand. At least he had had a few hours sleep.

Canty was standing smoking a cheroot at the door of the farmhouse. 'Have your men fed and slept, Devlin?' he asked as Gavin approached.

'As far as we were able,' smiled Gavin wearily.

'Colonel Hoy and his men are moving off at five o'clock. They'll take the river road as planned. You'd better start out immediately and scout the road ahead. If the British have managed to entrain troops as far as Chippewa then we might be moving into an ambush.'

'I'll be careful, major.'

'Have each of your men collect one of the Henry repeating rifles,' Canty gestured to where a makeshift armoury had been set up by an outhouse. A sergeant was busy issuing weapons and ammunition. 'We had several boxes arrive an hour ago . . . part of the purchase Sweeny made from the Bridesburg Arsenal at Philadelphia.'

'At least we'll have good weapons to face the enemy with,' Gavin commented. The Henry repeater, with its fifteen-round magazine, was a much better weapon than the popular Spencer repeater with its seven-round magazine.

Canty shrugged. 'There's not many of them, that's why we're being careful as to who they are issued to. Mainly we have Springfield muzzle loaders and some Sharp's breechloaders.'

'Is there any news of General Tevis and his column?' asked Gavin, changing the subject.

'There's a rumour that he has crossed into Windsor and that Sarnia has been taken. But that's just rumour. We haven't been able to establish a telegraph link with his headquarters.'

'What about our main thrust against Montréal?'

'There's no news yet.'

Gavin raised his hand in a desultory gesture of parting and went back to rouse his men. They were ready and saddled in under ten minutes.

'What are the orders, captain?' asked Boyd as they mounted.

'We are a scouting party. No one is to shoot at anything unless shot at first. Keep your eyes and ears open and obey my orders without me having to repeat them. Understood?'

There was a mumble of agreement. Gavin swung his troop out of the yard and through the fields where Colonel Hoy and his second-in-command, Lieutenant-Colonel Michael Bailey, whom Gavin now knew by sight, were busy assembling their regiment for the march on Chippewa.

The late afternoon was hot, too hot to be really comfortable. Gavin guided his small troop along the river road, turning northward as it snaked along the bank of the swiftly flowing Niagara, which waters now reflected the peaceful blue of the June sky with only white feathers breaking here and there to hint at the rapids and the mighty falls which lay further on. Gavin spanned his men out on either side of the road, moving at a steady walking pace, passing the sullen glances of the civilians who were hurrying northwards too. Canty had told him that the area had originally been settled by Loyalists fleeing from the republican states during the War of Independence. Fierce British loyalism had dominated the area ever since; especially after the American incursions during the War of 1812. There was little comfort of local support to be had for the Irish in this part of the country. Gavin knew that already from his own experiences. However, he consoled himself that this was only a feint. When General Spear thrust into Lower Canada, the French-Canadians would flock to greet the Irish as liberators and not shake their fists and curse them as the people did now.

Gavin held his men on a tight rein as they moved through the lines of trudging people seeking refuge elsewhere. He could not afford to lose his mounted troop in any brawls. He was thankful that Boyd and his Confederates were disciplined. Only Corporal Collins worried him seeming too fond of the flask which he carried. Gavin kept a watchful eye on the man but the corporal performed his duty well enough and gave no cause for reprimand. There was only one incident when a shot gun blast exploded harmlessly in the air above them, but which caused them to scatter. It was Collins who saw the culprit first and, with a wild rebel yell, he jumped his horse over a low fence, drawing his sword and whirling it over his head.

An old man, who must have been in his seventies at least, was standing near a log cabin with a blunderbuss in his shaking hands. His face was a mask of hate and he ignored the approaching trooper as he strove to reload the ancient flintlock. Gavin, seeing Collins's swinging sword, gave a shrill cry of warning and jumped his horse after him. Collins glanced behind and drew up his horse unwillingly, trotting up to the old man and snatching the weapon out of his frail grasp. The old man's mouth was frothed with the spittle of rage.

'You bloody Yankees!' His cry was a croaking screech.

'What are you trying to do grandad?' demanded Gavin sternly as he came up.

The man's eyes were bright, an indiscernible colour. His face was like tanned leather. Gavin suddenly noticed that he had a bright silver medal pinned to his old chequered shirt.

'I aimed to get one of yous before you got me,' he spat.

Collins gave a bitter laugh and glanced at Gavin. 'Then I guess I'd better shoot the old varmint before he does any harm.'

The old man stared up defiantly. 'Cowards! Thieves! Looters!'

'Shut up, you old goat!' snapped Collins making a threatening gesture.

Gavin eased in his saddle. 'That'll be enough, Collins. Break the old man's blunderbuss so that he can't get into any more trouble.'

Collins rode forward and smashed it against the side of the house so that its stock was splintered from the barrel.

The old man glared with hatred at them.

'Guess it's no use trying to explain to you why we are here,' Gavin mused. 'Anyway, grandad, your war has been over a long time.'

'Not while you damned Yankees are over here. Chased you back across that river in '14 along with General Drummond. Do the same again now, yes, by crikey!'

Gavin smiled. 'Let me advise you not to go taking pot shots at our army, grandad, otherwise the next soldier who comes along might not let you get away so leniently. You might be hanged next time. You're still soldier enough to remember what happens to civilians caught in an act of war.'

'Yeah, you'll remember that too when they hang you,' spat the man.

'Collins,' Gavin turned to the corporal. 'Check the old man's house and see if he has any other guns inside.'

Collins grinned and slid from the horse. The old man stood by impotently, his gnarled hands clenched.

'Thieves!'

'Calm down,' Gavin said good humouredly. 'No one is going to steal anything from you, grandad.'

Collins reappeared. 'Nothing else in there, sir,' he said, as he remounted.

'Okay, grandad,' Gavin said. 'Behave yourself or you might wind up in trouble.'

As he rode back to the rest of the troop with Collins, the corporal muttered, 'Should have let me put the old bastard out of his misery. Let one of them Loyalists live and they wind up shooting you in the back.'

'That's not how we do things in this army, Collins,' grunted Gavin.

Boyd rode forward. 'Everything all right?' he asked.

'Just some crazy old man wanting to fight the war of 1812 all over again. Harmless enough.'

'No one's harmless if he can press a trigger,' Boyd replied seriously.

They turned and rode on in silence. The exodus along the river road was growing to a trickle and finally thinning out to nothingness. To the left of them, running through the shade of the tall conifer forests, they could see the railroad which led directly north into Chippewa. To the right, across the river, was the southern end of Grand Island.

'If the English have troops in this area then this would be a good place to set up an ambush,' Gavin muttered glancing around him. 'Sergeant Nolan!'

The big Kerry sergerant eased forward. 'Sir?'

'Take a man and go down to the railroad there. Follow its line and keep pace with us. Maintain a sharp lookout.'

Nolan raised a hand in salute and moved off.

The hot afternoon sun was beginning to lower behind the conifers so that only a flicker of bright light would stab through the trees as a wind rustled them. The air was full of the whispering forward urge of the great river, sometimes drowned by a bird able to make its cry sharp and distinctive from the nearby hedges or trees. They continued on in silence.

Five or six miles farther on they came to a curve in the road which abruptly opened up on a vista ahead of them. A group of mounted men were gathered perhaps two hundred yards away. Gavin's troop halted in surprise and before Gavin could give an order, the riders had spied them, and, with a shout, galloped off.

'Shall we pursue?' demanded Boyd.

'No,' Gavin said.

'Scouting party?' asked the lieutenant, squinting after the riders.

'Could be.'

'They were in civilian clothes though.'

'If I were the English commander I would send my advance scouts up in civilian clothes while I discovered our strength.'

Boyd nodded. 'I suppose we'd better report to Hoy? If they are scouts then the English troops could be close.'

Gavin dispatched one of the men back along the road to where Colonel Hoy's troops were making slow progress along the river. Then Gavin ordered Sergeant Nolan to listen to the railroad tracks for sounds of any approaching trains. Nolan bent his ear to the rails listening for a while before he stood up and shook his head.

'Come on, Boyd,' Gavin said. 'We'll ride up ahead to that point and see if we can spot anything.'

They galloped along the road about half a mile to the place where the group of horsemen had disappeared. The bank of the river bent inwards at this point giving a clear view across a bay-like curve. About four miles along the river road they could see some horses in a group. Gavin reached for the field-glasses which Canty had given him.

'Civilians, all right,' he muttered as he focused. 'But they . . . by damn! There's a redcoat with them. They're riding off towards Chippewa.' He turned to Boyd with a frown. 'That must mean that the English are already at Chippewa.'

Without another word he turned and, followed by Boyd, trotted back. He handed the field-glasses to Nolan. 'I want two men up at that point,' he ordered, pointing to where they had just come from. 'I want a sharp lookout on the river road and I want another man constantly listening to those rails for approaching troop trains.'

He waited until he was satisfied that his orders were being carried out and then he told Boyd to take charge. 'I'm going back to have a word with Colonel Hoy myself.'

It was Hoy's second-in-command whom he encountered first. Lieutenant-Colonel Michael Bailey was a pleasant-faced man in his mid-forties with a ready sense of humour. He had served as a company commander in the 100th Regiment of New York Volunteers during the war. He was commanding the advance guard and, hearing the report from Gavin's first messenger, had halted his companies. The men squatted where they had stopped, some resting on the bank of the roadside, others smoking cigarettes.

'I'm waiting for the colonel to come up before I proceed,' Bailey explained as Gavin rode up. 'What's happening ahead?'

'One redcoat with a number of mounted men in civilian clothes are on the river road ahead. They could be a scouting force sent down from Chippewa. The enemy might be near. What happened to my messenger?'

*

'I sent him down to Newbeggin Farm to let O'Neill know what was happening. We don't want to walk into a battle unprepared.'

The private railroad car was hot and stuffy and full of foul-smelling cigar smoke. It swayed alarmingly as the train rattled at speed over the points. It contained half-a-dozen Union Army officers and two civilians. One of the civilians was William S. Dart, attorney-general of the northern division of the state of New York. He was flustered and anxious.

'I simply can't understand it, general,' he said leaning forward and repeating himself for the tenth time since he had boarded the train at Albany. 'We have telegraphed Washington several times and so far there has been no response at all. Surely the administration must take some action over this violation of the neutrality laws?'

The major-general who sat casually opposite him, puffing on a cigar, his uniform jacket unbuttoned, was a stocky man in his late forties. George C. Meade, former commander of the Army of the Potomac, the victor of Gettysburg, and now commanding the United States Military District of the Atlantic, did not seem at all perturbed.

'We will be in Buffalo early this evening, mister,' he said reassuringly. 'We should have word once we get there.'

'But we must take immediate action if we are to enforce the neutrality laws,' pressed Dart. 'I cannot understand why the President does not make some announcement. We telegraphed the White House just as soon as the Fenian crossing became known.'

Meade shrugged dismissively, 'There will be some explanation for it. In the meantime, and in the absence of specific instructions from the administration, we will take our own action.'

On the other side of the compartment sat a colonel, a younger man than Meade, quiet and reserved. William Farquhar Barry was a New Yorker who had been Sherman's chief of artillery during the siege of Atlanta. He now stretched forward to intervene in the discussion.

'I thought we had a garrison at Fort Porter in Buffalo, sir?' he observed. 'Couldn't prompt action from the garrison commander have prevented the Fenian crossing?'

Dart gave a bark of laughter. 'Excuse me, Colonel Barry,' he said, 'but Major Duer has only fifty men at Fort Porter . . . I doubt he could have done anything to prevent the crossing of an entire army.'

Barry grimaced and sat back.

Meade was drumming his fingers on his thigh gazing thoughtfully out of the swaying carriage. He seemed to have made up his mind about matters and turned back to his companions.

'As of now I am devising a new military district of Ontario along the border. You are appointed to command, William, with a brevet rank of brigadier.'

Barry's expression showed no change. He simply nodded.

'We cannot wait for orders from the President,' Meade continued. 'We must begin to secure the border ourselves. Your task will be to preserve the neutrality laws by preventing the crossing of armed bodies of men into the British provinces; cut off their reinforcements and supplies; seize all arms, ammunition and stores which you have reason to believe are destined to be used unlawfully. Take all precautionary measures to prevent violations of our border agreements.'

'What about troops?' asked Barry.

'I'll issue the necessary orders for the transfer of infantry and cavalry into Buffalo immediately.'

In spite of the swaying of the train he drew out a notepad and began to scribble, handing each page to his adjutant as he completed it. 'Get them telegraphed at our next stop, Frank,' he told the youthful captain who served him. Then he turned back to the New York attorney-general. 'Did you say that the *Michigan* was already on station in the Niagara, Mister Dart?'

'Yes, General.'

'Capital. She can be brought into action and we'll see if we can find other gunboats to support her.'

Dart pursed his lips and sighed. 'I cannot understand the delay from Washington,' he repeated. 'Why hasn't the President issued a proclamation against these Fenians?'

Meade grimaced, 'Well, I know my duty, sir,' he said dryly. 'As soon as we reach Buffalo, I shall telegraph General Grant at West Point. He was attending General Scott's funeral there today. I shall ask him to come up to Buffalo, observe matters for himself and give his advice.'

John-Joe awoke to the clattering of horses and the unmistakable jangle of cavalry equipment. He had not gone to bed until midday having been up all night helping Captain Hynes organize the supplies for shipping across the river. He lay for a moment on his bed in the room of the Mansion House Hotel wondering what the sound meant. For a moment he wondered whether it was O'Donoghue's Maryland

Fenian cavalry coming into the city. He had heard that they were reported in Elmira not far away. He swung from his bed and peered down into Main Street. The street was filled with a column of Union cavalry, flags furled and sheathed. A few citizens were greeting their appearance with cheers of relief.

Frowning, John-Joe threw on his clothes and hurried from the room. He knew that Captain Hynes would be in Hugh Mooney's saloon on Ohio Street with Colonel Sherwin, who was now in command of the Fenians in the city. As he hurried through the streets he saw the green of Fenian colours everywhere. Reinforcements had been pouring into the city hourly. But the cavalry were regular Union army and perhaps that did not portend well. Hynes was sprawling in a chair in a back room of Mooney's saloon. Colonel Sherwin was reading through some papers with a perplexed frown. There was one other occupant in the room, Patrick O'Day.

'We know,' snapped Hynes as John-Joe entered. 'General Meade has arrived in the city and regular troops are beginning to come in. A Brigadier Barry has been appointed to command the border and close it. The USS *Michigan* has taken up a new position and armed sailors have put an end to the despatch of supplies and reinforcements. Soldiers are all over the docks. We are trying to contact Sweeny for new instructions.'

John-Joe's jaw slackened as he realized what it meant. 'Without supplies and reinforcements, O'Neill will be in a hopeless position.'

'We know that, lieutenant,' Colonel Sherwin said irritably. 'We're trying to remedy the situation. Burns hasn't arrived yet but we have another 1,000 men ready to cross. Colonel Stagg was about to take his regiment over when Meade cut us off.' His voice was bitter.

'I thought Roberts had reached an understanding with President Johnson?' demanded John-Joe. 'Why are the authorities enforcing the neutrality laws now?'

'We don't know what is happening,' Hynes replied. 'It may be that Meade is simply acting on his own authority.'

'Have Tevis and Spear begun their moves?'

'There is no word from Tevis, and Spear is still waiting for his men to muster,' replied Sherwin. 'If Tevis hasn't moved and Spear does not do so within the next few hours, then O'Neill will be on his own facing the entire British army – 8,000 regulars and 20,000 militia. And we will have no hope of reinforcing him.'

'Is there any chance that we could do a deal with Meade?' pressed John-Joe. 'Perhaps we could persuade him not to enforce the neutrality laws until he has had specific instructions from the President?'

'Meade the incorruptible?' sneered Hynes. 'I remember Meade objecting to some slight on his integrity by a newspaper correspondent during the war. He had the man placed backwards on his horse, a placard hung around his neck and paraded through the entire army to the tune of the "Rogue's March". The man was a civilian, mind, and not a soldier. No, when Meade is on his high horse about duty and right, it would take a brave man to suggest he turn a blind eye.'

'Then we must warn O'Neill of the position.'

'Sure,' agreed Sherwin mockingly. 'Do you want to volunteer to try to cross the river, lieutenant? The Union Army have issued a warning that they will shoot any men attempting to cross.'

John-Joe stared defiantly at him. He would show them where duty lay. 'Yes,' he said quietly. 'I'll take the message to O'Neill.'

They gazed at him in surprise and then Hynes said curtly, 'Well, you won't get across by boat. The river is completely cut off.'

Patrick O'Day glanced up with a hopeful expression. 'But there is the Suspension Bridge below Niagara Falls. It crosses into Upper Canada about seven or eight miles north of Chippewa. If the bridge hasn't been closed off you could take the wagons with supplies across as well. We have them stored at the Union Iron Works. It's worth a try. Better to make the attempt than to allow the supplies to fall into Meade's hands.'

'I'll not risk writing an official despatch, lieutenant,' Sherwin told him. 'We don't want anything to fall into the wrong hands if you are arrested. Simply give O'Neill a verbal account of what has happened. The situation might change if Meade receives instructions from a higher authority. Tell O'Neill that we are trying to reach Roberts to see if that higher authority is forthcoming. If we can do so, we will reinforce him as soon as possible. If not, then he must make his own decisions.'

Chapter 51

It was 8.30 p.m. before the messenger arrived from O'Neill. He was about to strike camp and move north after Colonel Hoy leaving only a few men in Fort Erie to direct any reinforcements that should arrive from Buffalo. He had dismissed the idea of an attack being launched by the British from Port Colborne as he had received news from Buffalo that a column of enemy troops had been passing through Niagara by train apparently heading for Chippewa. Observers from the American shore had been able to detect a battery of six field guns being offloaded at Niagara and these guns, with an escort, were now proceeding rapidly by road while the troops had continued on by train. The soldiers seemed to be regulars rather than militia. This had coincided with the report of the sighting of civilian scouts on the river road which Gavin had sent back to him. O'Neill had estimated that British regulars would be in Chippewa and probably preparing to use the Erie and Ontario Railway to move directly against his positions. Having consulted Major Canty, O'Neill estimated that the one weak spot on the railroad was where it crossed a bridge over a stretch of water which fed the Niagara called Black Creek. He ordered Colonel Hoy and his regiment to move up to Black Creek and destroy both rail and road bridges and wait for him.

Gavin rode back to his men and gathered in his outposts with the exception of Sergeant Nolan and the trooper listening on the railroad tracks. Now he knew that enemy troops were definitely ahead he must ensure that Nolan kept a careful ear open for vibrations on the tracks which would warn of any movement. With Nolan following the tracks and Gavin and his men on the river road it did not take long until they came to a creek which intersected their paths at right angles; a creek flowing into the Niagara. A rough trackway followed the bank of the creek and a wooden signpost pointed westward with the legend, 'New Germany: 3 miles'.

'This must be Black Creek,' Gavin said, halting his men.

Boyd glanced to his left, through the trees. The railroad tracks had diverged a while back and seemed to have moved a distance from the roadway. Gavin turned to Collins. 'Gallop down to Sergeant Nolan, corporal, and make sure that he halts at the intersection with the creek.'

'Is this it, then?' demanded Michael Bailey as the advance guard of the 7th Regiment came up.

'I don't have a map,' admitted Gavin. 'But I guess so. It's a creek and there's the road bridge right enough. The rail bridge seems to be a mile down this trackway.'

Bailey hesitated. 'I wish we had a map but I suppose you're right.'

He turned and gave orders for a company to fall out and commence to demolish the road bridge. It was a threadbare company of pioneers whose only tools were shovels and pick-axes. While they set to work with a will, Bailey sighed.

'If only we had some explosives. We could clear these bridges in no time.'

They were still working on demolishing the bridges when Colonel Hoy's main body came up and deployed along the banks of the creek in a thin skirmishing line to wait for the approach of the British troops.

It was nearly dark when an engine steamed cautiously into the railroad depot at Chippewa and let out three piercing shrieks on its whistle to bring the majority of townspeople crowding on to the streets in consternation. The chief magistrate of the town, Mister Kirkpatrick, quickly put on his coat and hurried across the road which separated his house from the depot. All day long rumour and counter-rumour had run through the township about the Fenian landing. Some of the old people, many of whom could remember the American landings in 1814, had gathered their belongings and were fleeing in panic. However, the train now shunting into the depot was arriving from the north and not from the south where the Fenians forces were. As Kirkpatrick hurried into the depot he could see the long line of cars behind the locomotive with uniformed men craning from every window.

In the leading car Colonel George Peacocke was feeling a momentary relief at not finding Chippewa in Fenian hands. Since he had received his orders from Major-General Napier and joined his command that afternoon he had been anxious. He made no bones about the fact that he felt himself best suited to administration rather than command of troops in the field. But here he was, in temporary command of a field force which had to contain an aggressive enemy. His special troop train had transported his men along the Great Western Railway from Hamilton to St Catharines. A force of 400 infantry regulars and six field guns. Yet, so it was rumoured, he was facing an enemy of four or five times his strength. At St Catharines he expected to be reinforced by volunteer militia but found they had not mustered. In addition to that problem there were numerous telegraphs demanding his immediate attention. The Fenians, whose numbers were reported to be growing hourly, were – according to some frantic civilians – marching on the Suspension Bridge below Niagara Falls with a column of 800 men and were only two miles from Chippewa. Peacocke realized that if the Fenians secured the Suspension Bridge, spanning the river from the American shore to the Canadian shore, then they could flood troops across the river at will. So grim was this prospect that he had abandoned hopes of waiting until the militia reinforced him and ordered his train to press directly on to Niagara Falls. The reports were incorrect. Niagara was peaceful. The Suspension Bridge was not threatened and, so it seemed, the Fenians had not even reached Chippewa.

Peacocke had ordered his battery of field guns to be offloaded at Niagara Falls because he was informed that there was no platform at the Chippewa railroad depot by which the guns could be removed from the train without difficulty. Lieutenant-Colonel Hoste was ordered to take the guns by road as rapidly as possible and join him at Chippewa. With the guns, and his 400 regulars, Peacocke thought he might stand a chance of fortifying the township before the Fenians attacked.

Mister Kirkpatrick, spotting the colonel as he left the train, hurried up to him to begin an officious speech of welcome but Peacocke cut him short.

'Is your house nearby, sir?' he demanded curtly.

Puzzled, Kirkpatrick gestured across the road to his large two-storeyed house opposite the railroad depot. Peacocke grunted in satisfaction. 'That shall be my headquarters, sir. I requisition its use.'

Kirkpatrick's jaw dropped. 'But I have a wife and family. . . .' he began to protest.

Peacocke's aide-de-camp, a solemn-faced captain, took Kirkpatrick's arm gently. 'We must all do our duty in this crisis, sir,' he reproved. 'Your house is requisitioned by order of the Imperial military authority. You may address any objections to the governor-general's office.'

Peacocke was already striding towards the house, his staff officers scurrying after him while others began shouting orders to get the men disembarked from the train. Kirkpatrick's wife and servants retired in confusion as the group of officers swarmed into the house with the chief magistrate, wringing his hands, in their wake. Peacocke chose the kitchen as a meeting room because of its big tables on which maps of the area were immediatelty spread.

Peacocke's aide was a sober and unimaginative officer of twenty years' service. Captain Charles Style Akers of the Royal Engineers was slow thinking, lugubrious and still carried the leisurely, easy pace of the rolling farmlands of his Kent childhood. His promotion in the service had been painfully slow. He had received his present rank in April 1859, and a commanding officer had then written of him that Akers was an excellent subordinate but did not have the flair of individual command. He would obey orders, did not have the ability to generate them and was easily swayed. Peacocke, however, found Akers reliable, able to carry out orders without panic or undue haste. He was someone who, Peacocke felt, would obey orders and only the orders given.

'It will not be long before Colonel Hoste's gun batteries arrive,' Peacocke announced, as he glanced at the plan of the township. 'When they do, I want them positioned around the bridge over the river to the south of the town. They will cover the road from which our enemy must make his attack.'

Akers made a conscientious note and then handed Peacocke a collection of telegraphs which had arrived at the railroad depot in advance of their arrival. Peacocke flicked through them and finally gave a grunt of satisfaction.

'Sometime during the next few hours, gentlemen, we should be reinforced by a further 800 men and two troops of cavalry. They are militia troops but they are better than nothing in the circumstances.'

Peacocke had no great love for militia.

In fact, at that moment a militia sergeant chose to enter the house in search of the reeve, Mister Kirkpatrick.

'I am in command here, sergeant,' snapped Peacocke. 'You may report to me.'

The militia sergeant looked momentarily abashed and then saluted the colonel. 'I've been down the river road as far as Black Creek, sir,' he said, clearing his throat. 'Some of our local militia, wearing civilian clothes, rode towards Fort Erie to inspect the Fenian camp down by Frenchmen's Creek.'

Peacocke pointed to his map. 'Point it out to me, man.'

It took the militia sergeant sometime to find the spot and point to it.

'Well?' Peacocke prompted.

'Well, sir,' the militia sergeant shifted his weight uncomfortably. 'We didn't get that far, maybe just beyond Black Creek on the river road, like I say. We saw the Fenians marching north along the river road.'

'How long ago?'

'Less than an hour, sir.'

Major Lodder of the 47th Foot leaned forward eagerly. 'Marching towards our positions? Do you think they'll make a direct attack, sir?'

'Perhaps,' muttered Peacocke, looking at the position on the map. 'Did you make an estimation of their strength, sergeant?'

The militia man was eager to make a good impression.

'Over 1,000 men, sir, and more reported to be coming across the river hourly.'

'You may dismiss, sergeant.'

As the sergeant left an officer entered with another telegraph in his hand and gave it to Akers.

'Confirmation that the 19th Battalion from St Catharines, the 10th Royals and another company of the 47th Foot should be with us soon, sir.'

Peacocke nodded absently.

'And there is news of a concentration of troops at Port Colborne,' Akers added.

The colonel found the township on his map. 'What troops are there?'

'The 2nd Battalion of militia from Toronto.'

'That's the Queen's Own, sir,' smiled Major Lodder. 'Major Gillmor's men. They are a cut above the usual militia battalions.'

'What strength, Akers?'

'Some 480 men. There are a further hundred men from the Welland Canal Field Battery which are stationed in the town and they are expecting to be reinforced before midnight by the 13th Battalion of militia from Hamilton. They would put their combined strength at nearly 1,000 men, sir.'

Peacocke chewed his lip thoughtfully. 'A thousand men? Plus our

1,000 troops here, once we are reinforced. Nearly 2,000 men? I do not think we can attack the Fenians with less. That means that our two columns must join forces before we encounter the enemy.'

'But the Fenians are marching on our position at this very moment, sir,' Major Lodder pointed out.

'We must hope that our field guns will deter them. Our next move will depend on the enemy's intentions, gentlemen. Until we know what those intentions are we must remain fortified in this townhship.'

John-Joe left Buffalo just before eleven o'clock. Captain Hynes had finally received a reply from General Sweeny. At 9.10 p.m. Hynes had sent a last despatch telegraph to the general at Albany, 'Our men isolated. Enemy marching in force from Toronto. What shall we do? When do you move?' Sweeny had replied, 'Reinforce O'Neill at all hazards; if he cannot hold his position let him fall back; send him and his men to Malone as rapidly as possible by the Rome and Watertown roads.' It did not look hopeful. Reinforcement was out of the question. The last contact Hynes had had with O'Neill was several hours previously when he had relayed the news from the scouts who had observed troop movements at Niagara. There seemed no way of pulling O'Neill back unless John-Joe was able to cross the river.

With the Suspension Bridge cut off, both at the Canadian end and on the American side, there was no chance of John-Joe moving the wagons of munitions across by that route, even if he did succeed in getting them through the ring of General Barry's troops which had just been thrown around the city. Nevertheless, John-Joe was anxious at the seriousness of O'Neill's position and, although he might not admit it, more so because of Gavin's presence. He determined to cross the river as best he could. An examination of the water front showed that all the small craft were firmly guarded by regular US troops while armed tugs were now patrolling up and down the river filled with marines and soldiers. The majestic threatening shadow of the USS *Michigan* lay just offshore. He tried to move northwards hoping to find an alternative method of crossing but the military patrols were frequent. The idea began to form in his mind when he saw the group of youths walking up the street; boys with long black hair, clad in doe-skin skirts and trousers. Indians. Wasn't the Tonawanda Reservation just a few miles north of the city? It was one of those facts that had been imprinted on his mind by a silly, unimportant event which had registered in his youthful prejudice.

Just after the war, while the Irish Brigade had been awaiting demobilization and its return to New York, a general named Ely Parker had visited the camp to ask for volunteers to serve an extra year in the west. Rumour had it that Parker was recruiting men to fight the Indians and when Parker arrived the men had been dumbfounded to find that the general himself was an Indian. Ely Parker had, apparently, been born Donehogawa, the Hasonoanda or Keeper of the Western Door of the Long House of the Iroquois Nation. He was a full-blood Seneca from the Tonawanda Reservation, who had been unable to speak English until he was twelve years old, but was now a trained lawyer, a qualified engineer and a lieutenant-general of the US Army.

John-Joe smiled in gratitude as he recalled the memory. If anyone knew how to cross the river without being observed it would be the Indians. He supposed that he would have to bribe them or pay them in some way but they were his best chance – perhaps his only chance – of crossing to warn O'Neill. He turned to hurry back to Hugh Mooney's saloon to ask Hynes if he could borrow a horse and rifle to ride up to Tonawanda.

Chapter 52

The atmosphere in the oval office of the White House was warm and stuffy. The air was made oppressive by the oil in the flickering lamps. The President sat upright behind his desk, hands clasped, resting them on the desk top before him, his eyes bright, watching the bleak face of the British ambassador as the man lowered himself into a chair before the desk.

'I regret the necessity of calling upon you at such an hour, Mister President,' Sir Frederick Bruce said, but his voice was hollow and without warmth.

'The telegraphs have been burning between here and Ottawa, Sir Frederick,' the President observed with a sly smile. 'I thought I might have the pleasure of your company before long.'

The British ambassador was irritable. 'Knowing that, Mister President, you have doubtless been appraised as to the situation and will know what is contained in this note of protest that I am compelled to hand you on behalf of Her Britannic Majesty's government.' Sir Frederick bent forward and placed a white envelope on the desk before the President. Johnson made no attempt to pick it up.

'Well, Sir Frederick?' he prompted softly.

'Sir,' there was a controlled hauteur in the ambassador's voice. 'At this very moment a motley band of armed cut-throats who call themselves Fenians have crossed into British territory from the city of Buffalo. Many of these men are citizens of the United States who have been allowed, unimpeded, to gather into an army with all weapons of war. Although your administration had the power to stop this invasion of our sovereign territory, you have been slow to act. Now Her Britannic Majesty's government demands that you enforce the neutrality laws and put an end to this affair.'

President Johnson suddenly relaxed, sat back in his chair and smiled. 'Mister Ambassador,' his southern accent became more pronounced, soft and deadly, 'our country has a mighty long border with the British territory in the north. It is simply impossible to police the entire border and prevent groups of armed men crossing as they will . . . during the late war of rebellion I recall that your government suffered similar disabilities in preventing rebel raiders striking into our territory from their safe havens in Upper and Lower Canada.'

Sir Frederick's face reddened. 'The crossing has been made over the Niagara frontier,' he said indignantly. 'There is no secret about the location of it, Mister President.'

'Of course,' nodded Johnson. 'But I cannot act solely on the intelligence and advice of the British authorities. I must await reports from my own commanders in the area.'

'His Excellency, the governor-general of British North America would appreciate your answer to this note of protest, sir.'

President Johnson glanced at the white envelope, still making no attempt to pick it up. 'Tell Lord Monck that I shall give my earnest attention to his note at the earliest opportunity. Thank you, Mister Ambassador.' There was a tone of dismissal in his voice.

Sir Frederick made a hasty effort to recover his poise. 'The matter is of the utmost urgency, Mister President,' he said rising stiffly.

'Just so,' smiled Johnson. 'And you can assure His Excellency that my administration seeks to pursue our agreement of neutrality to the best of our ability. We like to act with swiftness in response to all matters dealing with our external relations with friendly countries . . . just as I am sure Her Britannic Majesty's government seek to do.' Johnson paused and smiled disarmingly. 'I, personally, regret the delay which seems to have arisen concerning our proposal to Her Britannic Majesty's government for the establishment of a joint commission to negotiate the claims of these United States for reparation in connection with the loss of commerce and shipping suffered by the refusal of Her Britannic Majesty's government to adhere to the neutrality treaty of 1818 . . . the same treaty you are now . . . *demanding* we enforce,' Johnson carefully emphasized the word. 'The unfriendly actions of Her Britannic Majesty's government in recognizing the rebels as a legal government in our late civil war, in building and supplying warships and munitions, was hardly in the spirit of those same neutrality laws you invoke upon us.'

Sir Frederick's mouth tightened.

The President grimaced sadly. 'You may assure Her Britannic

Majesty's government that our intentions remain as they have always been, to comply with the spirit of those neutrality laws.'

'I seem to recall the *Trent* affair,' Sir Frederick said belligerently trying to score a point.

Johnson nodded seriously. 'Ah, yes. An unfortunate incident when a junior officer of our navy, set the onerous task of blockading the rebel ports during the late conflict, stopped a British mail steamer – which was blockade running – and arrested two rebels, Messrs Sliddell and Mason, I believe, whom he found aboard and en route to purchase arms and munitions in Britain. Lord Palmerston was quick to invoke the neutrality laws, claiming that we were in default for stopping a ship bearing the flag of Her Britannic Majesty and arresting people under her protection.'

Sir Frederick was quiet.

'We have always been anxious to maintain friendly relations with Her Britannic Majesty's government. In spite of the fact that the two men who were arrested were citizens of the United States then engaged in open, armed rebellion, Secretary Seward had them released into the custody of Her Britannic Majesty's government.' The President's eyes narrowed and he leaned forward. 'And yet . . .' his voice had a dangerous edge, 'and yet Her Britannic Majesty's government allowed a group of southern rebels openly to gather in Montréal, ride across the border into Vermont and attack the town of St Albans, murdering, burning and robbing our citizens. Those same rebels were then allowed to return in safety to Montréal.'

'They were arrested by British authorities,' Sir Frederick protested defensively.

President Johnson chuckled hollowly. 'Arrested, true . . . and then released by your Judge Coursell who ignored the plea of the extradition by Secretary Seward who had presented evidence that these United States citizens, in open and armed rebellion, had caused and participated in criminal acts on the territory of these United States.'

There was an awkward silence.

The President sat back and sighed. 'Indeed,' he said softly, 'we would be more than happy to have a response from Her Britannic Majesty's government on the question of negotiating reparation.'

A look of comprehension came into the British ambassador's eyes. 'Very well, Mister President. I believe I understand your trend of thought. Good night to you, sir.'

As the door swung shut on Sir Frederick, a side door opened and the Secretary of State, William Seward, entered.

'You heard?' Johnson asked without glancing up.

Seward shrugged indifferently. 'The British are not known for responding to pressure, Mister President.'

'Everyone responds to pressure, Will. What's the latest news?'

'Thousands of men and arms are pouring up to the border. The Fenians who crossed last night have not encountered the British forces yet but a clash is expected any time now. There's been a spate of telegraphs from General Meade and two from General Grant at West Point demanding to know what course of action you intend to pursue. Meade has already taken some action on his own account and appointed General Barry to command in Buffalo with instructions to cut off supplies and reinforcements from those who have already crossed. Everyone is waiting for you to make an announcement as to our attitude towards the Fenians, whether we enforce the neutrality laws or let the Fenians go ahead.'

Johnson grinned. 'We'll wait for the British response first.'

Seward bit his lip. 'Are you sure that they will make one?'

Johnson's glance was enigmatic. Then he said, 'Will, do you think those crazy Irishmen stand a chance of carving their Republic-in-Exile out of the British provinces?'

'Our reports show that there are thousands of men streaming for the border with all manner of arms and munitions,' replied Seward. 'Don't forget that it was men like these that maintained the Union. Yes, they have a chance if we do nothing to impede their crossing and their supply of arms.'

'If we know it then the British know it,' Johnson mused.

'What are we going to do then?'

'Let the British sweat.'

At eleven o'clock the captain in charge of scouts reported to Colonel Peacocke at Mister Kirkpatrick's house in Chippewa. The scouts had spotted the Fenians moving north but were conflicting in their reports. Estimates of their strength varied between 1,000 and 2,000 men. One report said the main body were entrenching at Frenchman's Creek in expectation of receiving reinforcements of a further 5,000 troops the next day.

Peacocke drummed his fingers impatiently on the table top as he studied the map in Kirkpatrick's kitchen. His staff watched him in silence.

'Gentlemen,' he said at last, 'the first great principle of war is always oppose the mass of your army to fractions of the enemy and ensure that your enemy is so placed that he cannot apply that principle himself.'

They waited while he gathered his thoughts.

'As I see it, there are three options now open to us. We can march by the river road to the Fenian encampment and, at the same time, order the column gathering at Port Colborne to go by the Grand Trunk Railway to Fort Erie and from there march up behind the Fenians. We would then be able to attack them from the front and rear in concert, forcing them between our two columns.'

A young ensign applauded enthusiastically. 'An excellent plan, sir.'

Peacocke looked at the young man pityingly. 'Such a plan would only receive approval in an unmilitary mind,' he sneered. The young officer coloured while one or two others tittered behind their hands at his discomfiture. 'If your enemy is in a superior force then one must not entrap him entirely but leave him a line of retreat into a neutral spot. If you entrap your enemy he may turn like a rat at bay and, in his desperation, fight with such courage and tenacity that the frenzy of his fight might win the day.'

Major Lodder nodded approval. He knew Peacocke to be an officer of undoubted courage but not one to risk the loss of his command for the sake of winning the doubtful reputation of bravery by a reckless management of his men.

'You said that there were three plans, sir?' he prompted.

'The second plan would be that we could concentrate our entire force in this town and wait for the enemy to approach. I do not believe that would be advisable as, hearing of our concentration, the enemy might march to other more vulnerable places such as Port Colborne or Port Robinson. I believe the enemy's intention may well be to disrupt the Welland Canal and destroy the locks. While we remain concentrated here, he could move on them at his ease.'

'The third plan, sir?' asked Captain Akers.

Peacocke tapped at the map. 'The column from Port Colborne must join us. Stevensville is the obvious place for the meeting of our two forces. It is ten miles from here and thirteen miles from Port Colborne. It is also ten miles from Fort Erie. With our men united at Stevensville we would therefore be in a central position whereby we could stop the enemy if he showed signs of either marching to Chippewa or to Port Colborne. It is a position which will dominate his movements and we would be able to fall upon him with the full force of our strength no matter which road he took. At the same time, we would be able to protect the Welland Canal.'

There was a murmur of approval from the officers as they appreciated the strategy.

'Who is in command at Port Colborne, Akers?' asked Peacocke when the murmur had died down.

Akers checked his notebook. 'There is a Lieutenant-Colonel Stoughton Dennis there commanding the 2nd Battalion.'

Major Lodder frowned. 'I thought Dennis was Brigade-Major of Toronto? Major Gillmor is in command of the Queen's Own.'

'Colonel Dennis has telegraphed us to inform us that he is in command,' insisted Akers.

'Well, tell him that if the *International* has put into Port Colborne for safety, I want him to place a detachment on board and send it round to patrol the Niagara River to prevent the enemy being reinforced.'

'Shall I also order him to prepare for the march to Stevensville, sir?'

'Not yet.' Peacocke bent over his map to prepare the final touches to his plan while Akers hurried to the telegraph office. He was back with further news within a short time.

'Colonel Dennis reports that the *International* isn't moored in Port Colborne. It put across to Buffalo and is still on the American side of the river. On his own authority he has telegraphed to Dunnville for the steam tug *W. T. Robb* to join him at Port Colborne. The tug is manned by the Dunnville Naval Brigade, sir.'

'Very well,' acknowledged Peacocke. 'Now I want you to go in person to Port Colborne.'

Captain Akers' jaw loosened a little in his astonishment. Go to Port Colborne? It meant crossing through countryside in dead of night with a potential enemy behind every tree and bush.

'I want you to take my orders verbally to Colonel Dennis at Port Colborne,' Peacocke went on, 'and explain why his command must march to Stevensville. I do not want those orders transmitted over the telegraphs in case the enemy is listening in. Do you understand?'

Captain Akers bowed to the inevitable. Peacocke had no worry. Akers was a man who could be relied on to carry out his orders.

'The column at Port Colborne must leave about first light and move north to Stevensville. I think we can safely set a time for the rendezvous at about ten o'clock in the morning. I have no idea of the conditions on the roads from Port Colborne to Stevensville so ensure that you instruct Colonel Dennis that, even if details of the plan have to vary by virtue of those conditions, it is essential that its spirit must be carried out. Do you understand? His column must rendezvous with mine at Stevensville by mid-morning.'

Captain Akers saluted. 'You may rely on me, sir,' he said.

Peacocke acknowledged the salute absently. 'I know that, Akers. Best of luck.'

It was just after midnight when O'Neill and the rest of the Fenian army arrived at Colonel Hoy's positions. O'Neill slid from his cream mare, which had been requisitioned from an indignant tavern owner, and came forward looking pale faced and annoyed in the light of a lantern held by one of his men.

'Damn it, Hoy,' he cried, 'you're in the wrong place!'

Hoy looked confused. 'Isn't this Black Creek?' he asked.

O'Neill was already spreading his map on a rock while his orderly held the lantern high.

'See here, you are below Black Creek. It's about a couple of miles further on downriver. This creek marks the township boundaries between Bertie and Willoughby. It must be Miller's Creek.'

Hoy looked uncomfortable but he wasn't one to blame his junior officers.

'We didn't have a map . . .' he began awkwardly.

Gavin, who had been standing with Lieutenant-Colonel Bailey, coughed uncomfortably.

'It was my fault, sir. I didn't have a map and thought this was the creek.'

O'Neill glanced at Gavin. 'A blunder like that has lost battles, Devlin,' he said softly. There was an embarrassing pause before he shrugged. 'Still, it can't be helped. . . .'

'Colonel!' Major Canty rode up and slid from his horse. 'Colonel, I've just heard from one of our sympathizers who has ridden in from Port Colborne. There is a British column gathering there about 1,000 strong.'

O'Neill swore softly. 'Two British columns to contend with! Is the man reliable? Is he sure?'

Canty nodded. 'He says that they were coming in from the north by train.'

'What troops? Militia or regulars?'

'The main body seem to be militia but he did see a unit with redcoats.'

'What about cavalry and artillery?'

'None that he could see.'

O'Neill swung back to his map, snapping to his orderly to keep the lantern high. 'They probably mean to catch us between the two columns,' he spoke half to himself. Then, 'Pass the word for the regimental commanders!'

Within a few minutes the colonels had gathered around him. O'Neill fumbled in his pocket and drew out a cigar, opened the shield of the lantern and lit it. He exhaled the smoke in a deep breath.

'The enemy has moved more quickly than I thought he would,' he announced, his lip drooping as if he were annoyed with himself for not realizing how fast the British could respond. 'We have one column in front of us at Chippewa and another behind us at Port Colborne. We are right plumb in the centre. My guess is that the enemy commander is an old hand at this game. He means to secure us in a pincer movement knowing that his combined strength far outnumbers what we can throw against him.' He paused and glanced to where Hoy's second-in-command was standing. 'Have your pioneers finished with the bridges over the creek, Michael?'

'They've done the best they could with hammers, picks and axes, sir,' Bailey replied. 'If only we had some explosive. . . .'

'If only we had a battery of field guns,' responded O'Neill wearily. 'We must make the best of what we do have. At least the enemy can't come down on us by train nor move his troops without let or hindrance by road. We'll bivouack here for a few hours to get some rest.'

'What do you aim to do, John?' asked Owen Starr.

'Close with the enemy,' O'Neill was grimly emphatic.

A murmur of expectation rose. Colonel Grace was pedantic, 'Which enemy, sir?'

O'Neill replied with a chuckle but his voice was brisk. 'I don't think that we have a choice, gentlemen. We must turn on one or other of the two columns sent against us. The northern column at Chippewa is reported to consist of regulars and have field guns. They may also be supported by cavalry. . . .'

Owen Starr saw his line of thinking and smiled enthusiastically. 'But the southern column at Port Colborne has no field guns or cavalry and is mainly comprised of militia.'

'Exactly so, Owen,' O'Neill said approvingly. 'We choose the weakest force first. If we can win a victory over the weaker column, it may demoralize the stronger one. By then, I hope, we will have received reinforcements from across the river. I could surely use the field guns which Sweeny promised.'

Major Canty was marking his map. 'How about dispositions for the bivouack tonight, sir?'

'We'll camp either side of this railroad track just in case the British attempt to move down during the night. I want Grace's men to bivouack on the river road to act as a rear guard. No fires. We sleep under arms until we are ready to move off. . . .' He glanced at his fob watch. 'Which will be shortly after three o'clock, gentlemen.'

'And the order of the march south?' prompted Starr.

'As you are so eager, Owen, you may take the vanguard.' O'Neill pointed to his map. 'We will move through these open fields on the east bank of this creek. Where it turns south-west we will keep due south and intersect with this roadway, moving directly across it to join this meandering road that runs down to that village . . . Ridgeway. That seems a good halfway point between Port Colborne and Fort Erie. We could meet the enemy anywhere around that spot.'

Owen Starr followed O'Neill's indications on the map. 'If I were the British commander, I would probably detrain my men at Ridgeway and march up this road to attack us in the rear . . . or, at least, what he thinks will be our rear,' he added with a grin.

Major Canty grunted approval, 'I know that road, sir. It's called the Ridge Road. It's slightly elevated on its western side most of the way along it which gives a good natural defensive position against attack from the west.'

O'Neill turned to Gavin. 'Devlin, you will take your troop of mounted scouts and proceed in advance of Colonel Starr's men tomorrow. You'll scout down this Ridge Road but remember that you may expect to encounter the enemy marching up it at any time.' He paused and added softly, 'This time make sure you have a map. There'll be a fight tomorrow and we want no mistakes.'

Gavin coloured slightly in spite of the gentle tone in O'Neill's voice. He knew the rebuke was deserved and that made him angry. Angry with himself. He had nearly ruined O'Neill's entire strategy by his stupid blunder that evening.

Chapter 53

Lieutenant-Colonel Alfred Booker was tired but the excitement kept him from sleep. Early that morning he had received orders to muster the 13th Battalion (Hamilton) Volunteers, a force of 265 men consisting of six rifle companies, of which he was the proud commander. His orders were to assemble his command and proceed by train from Hamilton to Port Colborne. En route he had increased his command by another 100 men when he picked up two additional militia companies, the York and Caledonia Rifles. Rumours had been many during the day but it seemed that the long prophesied Fenian invasion had come and that Colonel Booker's battalion was being ordered up into the front line.

Alfred Booker was looking forward to the encounter even though he had never heard a gun discharged in anger during his forty-two years. Nevertheless, he had a high opinion of his military capabilities. He was wont to boast that he was the first officer to receive a certificate of military competence when such certificates started to be issued by the newly established Department of Military Affairs in Ottawa. Booker was also proud of the fact that he had received a commendation from no less a personage than His Royal Highness the Prince of Wales who as commander-in-chief of the Army took a special responsibility for the military affairs of the empire. Yet Alfred Booker was only a weekend soldier and had never served in any other force than the volunteer militia of Upper Canada.

He was a taciturn, brooding English midlander, born and raised in Nottingham, the son of a strict Baptist minister. The family had emigrated to Upper Canada and settled in Hamilton in 1842 where Alfred began to establish himself in business as a merchant and an auctioneer, quickly acquiring a modest fortune selling real estate, horses, dry goods and specializing in purchasing the stock of bankrupt merchants and making exorbitant profits. He still found time to be prominent in the local Baptist Church and was also a leading freemason. It was not until his early thirties that he began to indulge his secret military ambition by purchasing a commission in the volunteer militia. Seven years later he received his colonelcy, serving as a staff officer before taking command of the 13th Battalion. His wealth and connections had secured the command of the battalion over the head of an officer due for promotion, James Atchinson Skinner, who was now his somewhat resentful second-in-command. Major Skinner carried out his duties according to the book but did no more than was expected of him. Skinner was content to watch and wait, hoping for the day when Booker would make a mistake which would remove him from the command which Major Skinner believed was rightfully his. But Booker was a cautious man, for all his boasted military capabilities. He never did anything borne of his own inspiration, preferring to seize other people's ideas and, when they worked, accredit them as his own. Such a man was difficult to entrap into an unwary action.

His train pulled into the railroad depot at Port Colborne about 11 p.m. He saw at once that the town was awake and restless. Militia sentries were on guard at every corner and all the street lights had been extinguished in case of a surprise attack. While his troops detrained Booker strode across to the station booking clerk's office where he was told the senior military officer had his temporary headquarters.

Booker knew John Stoughton Dennis having met the man at militia officers' training camps. Dennis, too, was a lieutenant-colonel and a year or so older than Booker but Dennis's commission was dated after Booker's commission and Booker knew it; knew, therefore, that he was senior to Dennis. From the way Dennis's face fell as he spied Booker, it was obvious that he also realized it.

Dennis was a land surveyor by profession although, in his militia uniform, he presented an imposing military figure with his heavy sideburns and moustache, Dundreary whiskers as they were called. Like Booker, he had never heard a gun fired in anger and had no practical knowledge of warfare. He was simply an enthusiast for military regulations and had been successful as brigade major of the 5th Military District of Toronto, receiving a princely sum of $600 a year plus small bonuses for his office. His superiors said that Dennis was a born staff officer. He certainly had as high an opinion of his own military abilities as Booker had of his. His bombast tended to create his own enthusiasm and carried everyone with him. That morning, as soon as the news of the Fenian crossing spread on the streets of Toronto, he had gone to General Napier's headquarters and demanded a field appointment. His enthusiasm eventually carried the general with it. Dennis was appointed commander of the 2nd Battalion (Queen's Own) in place of Major Gillmor, who had already embarked with the first detachment of the battalion on the *City of Toronto* steamer for Port Dalhousie. Dennis had followed with the remaining men to join Gillmor. The completed battalion, under its new, ebullient commander, had entrained for Port Colborne arriving early that evening.

John Stoughton Dennis was just beginning to grow used to his independent command at Port Colborne when Alfred Booker arrived. His face mirrored the disappointment but he saluted punctiliously.

'What troops are here, Dennis?' grunted Booker, his high, irritable voice an indication of his annoyance at finding Dennis there. Booker knew that Dennis was a hard officer to control. His bombastic enthusiasm and self-esteem was legend among militia officers.

'My own battalion,' Dennis savoured the phrase, 'the Queen's Own. Our strength is 480 men. There are also seventy men of the Welland Canal Field Battery commanded by Captain Richard King. We are shortly expecting the steam tug *Robb* from Dunnville with members of the Dunnville Naval Brigade on board. No more than thirty of them.'

Booker sunk into the chair reluctantly vacated by Dennis. 'What news of the enemy?'

'The damned rebels, eh?' corrected Dennis with a smile. 'An hour ago a man named Graham, who was a customs official at Fort Erie, arrived here and gave me the exact location of the rebel camp. It's at a place called Frenchman's Creek on the farm of a Mister Newbeggin. Graham says he went up to the farm about six o'clock this evening to have a look. He says that the Irish rabble are in a sorry state and have been drinking all day. There are scarce a hundred of them.'

Booker raised his eyes behind his rimless spectacles, then took off the spectacles and polished them with a sudden intensity. 'Do we have any other reports confirming that? I was told several thousand crossed the river. Civilians are liable to exaggerate.'

'The railroad superintendent here, Mister Lamont, confirms it. This morning the Fenian ragamuffins tore up the tracks and burned a bridge at a place called Six Mile Creek. Sauerwine's Bridge it is called. Lamont took a crew down there as soon as it was safe to do so, under the protection of Captain King's command, and repaired the line. Out of curiosity, Lamont moved into Fort Erie on a hand-car. He found that there were only a few drunken scum in the town and while he was examining the situation he met Graham. They both came back on the hand-car and reported to me.' Dennis smiled confidently under his moustache. 'May I make a suggestion, colonel?'

Booker sighed. 'What is it, Dennis?'

'Those Irish scum will fall an easy victim to a swift attack. They are drunk; no army at all, just a mob of armed thugs. We could take the men into Fort Erie by train and march up to their camp at Frenchmen's Creek, get there by dawn and round them up before they know what is happening.'

Booker shook his head. 'Colonel Peacocke is in command of the frontier force, Dennis.'

'Peacocke!' Dennis jerked his head up. 'With respect, Peacocke's regular army. I'll lay a wager that he is keeping the militia out of things so that he can claim all the credit for the regulars.'

'Credit?' frowned Booker wonderingly.

'Dammit, sir! For capturing the Fenian scum.'

'You seem pretty sure that they can be captured without much of a fight.'

'I know the Irish, sir,' Dennis smiled. 'They talk, brag and drink a lot but, by God, they'll run like rabbits when they come up against cold British steel!'

Booker was hesitant. He knew that Dennis had a reputation for visionary plans and an amazing lack of caution. He knew that it was easy to get swayed by Dennis's enthusiasm. But he also knew that it was flamboyant officers that won battles. What was it Napoleon had said? A commander must be lucky rather than prudent; unhappy the general who came on the field of battle with a system. Well, maybe Napoleon had been right. After all, he had conquered all Europe with his philosophy, hadn't he?

'Have you had orders from Colonel Peacocke?' he asked.

'Only to the effect of asking that a detachment be sent by ship to seal off the Niagara River. He wanted some men placed on the *International*, thinking the ferry might have docked here for safety. I telegraphed back advising that the ferry was still over in Buffalo and informed him that I would telegraph to Dunnville for the *Robb* and members of the Dunnville Naval Brigade to go forward to seal off the river.'

'And have you had no other orders from him?' pressed Booker.

'None, sir. It seems that we are to wait here while Peacocke and his regulars go into Fort Erie and arrest the Fenians.'

Booker hesitated. 'What do you advise, Dennis?' he asked wearily.

Colonel Dennis allowed himself a smile of condescension as he sensed he was getting his own way. 'I suggest that we entrain our troops, move straight to Fort Erie and attack the Fenians in their camp at dawn.'

Booker bit his lip and drew out his pocket watch to check the time. 'We must allow the men to victual first. We can entrain about one o'clock.'

'The sooner we attack the better,' Dennis pressed. 'Remember, colonel, we shall earn much glory if we drive off this drunken rabble before the regulars can step in.'

Booker pulled a face. 'I am only interested in doing the job to the best of our ability.'

'Just so, colonel,' Dennis said, twisting his haughty features into a superior smile.

It was scarcely an hour later when Captain Charles Akers of the Royal Engineers rode in from Chippewa with Colonel Peacocke's verbal instructions. At once Dennis questioned them, seeing his chance for personal glory vanishing.

'We have more detailed intelligence as to the Fenian position in Fort Erie,' he said. 'I think we should go ahead with our attack.'

Akers glanced uncertainly at Booker who shrugged unhappily.

'I cannot authorize your attack,' Akers said. 'Colonel Peacocke has received intelligence that the Fenians are far more in number and better equipped than you seem to believe.'

Dennis smiled and laid his hand on the captain's shoulders in a friendly, confidential manner. 'Look, captain, we have first-hand reports that the Fenians are simply a drunken rabble encamped at Frenchman's Creek. If we move our entire force into Fort Erie now we can catch them offguard and make short work of this whole affair.'

Akers was torn between his regard for the fact that this impressive-looking colonel was his senior in rank and the fact that the man was only a colonel of colonial militia.

'With respect, sir,' he said hesitantly, 'your proposal involves moving a large force by rail through wooded country at night and through an area not properly scouted. I must question the propriety of making such a deployment in close proximity to an active enemy.'

Dennis threw back his head and chuckled cynically. 'An active enemy? D'hear that, Colonel Booker? This officer says they are an *active* enemy . . . a goddam drunken rabble!'

Booker coughed nervously. 'Captain Akers, you say that Colonel Peacocke gave you verbal orders that this column must converge with him at Stevensville tomorrow morning so that the united force can proceed against the Fenians?'

'Yes sir,' Akers nodded. 'Those are my instructions.'

'It would seem obvious that Colonel Peacocke is erring on the side of caution. He plans to attack the Fenian camp at Frenchman's Creek with an overwhelming force. However, if our intelligence is right, a small force can bring off the coup more easily.'

Colonel Dennis grinned in triumph at Booker's advocacy of his plan.

'Exactly, sir,' he applauded. 'Peacocke is being too cautious.'

Booker was not completely happy with matters but he unwillingly felt that Dennis's plan had its merits and he only agonized a moment more before reaching a decision. 'I will carry out the plan that I have agreed with Colonel Dennis here,' he told Akers, 'subject to Colonel Peacocke's approval. I will telegraph him at Chippewa to that effect immediately.'

Akers bit his lip in indecision. He had delivered Colonel Peacocke's verbal instructions and surely no more could be asked of him? 'With respect, sir,' he said, 'I would be temperate in your wording in case the enemy have access to the telegraphs. The colonel sent me with verbal instructions because of that possibility.'

Dennis guffawed contemptuously. 'Your colonel is prudent to a fault, captain.'

Akers shrugged. He no longer wanted personal responsibility. 'I will place myself under your command, gentlemen,' he said.

While Booker was completing a draft telegraph Dennis had a further thought. 'Perhaps I can offer a further modification of my plan? Instead of entraining the entire command to Fort Erie, I could take a company on board the *Robb* when she arrives. We could sail to Fort Erie and make a reconnaisance along the river as far as the Fenian encampment. Just before dawn, you, colonel, can bring the main body into Fort Erie by train, join forces with me and together we can march on the Fenians.'

Booker was not completely satisfied. 'If Peacocke doesn't approve this scheme, Dennis, I shall have to disembark the column at Ridgeway and march north to Stevensville to join him as ordered.'

His telegraph to Peacocke was despatched. Almost immediately the steam tug *W. T. Robb* came into port. The tug was the proud possession of the Dunnville Volunteer Naval Brigade by virtue of the fact that it's master, W. T. Robb, was lieutenant and second-in-command.

In fact, the brigade numbered only twenty-two men under the command of a captain, Lachlan McCallum. Dennis proposed taking the seventy-strong company of Captain King's Welland Canal Field Battery with him and these were ordered on board the tug immediately. They waited awhile but there was still no answering telegraph from Chippewa. Dennis was getting impatient and felt he should leave immediately. Eventually Booker gave in to his demands.

'If Peacocke doesn't approve the plan I shall send the engine to Fort Erie to signal you on its whistle,' he said. 'Remember to take no aggresive military action until we arrive. If you hear the whistle you are to withdraw immediately and return here.'

It was 3.30 a.m. when the steam tug *W. T. Robb* pulled out of Port Colborne into the dark waters of Lake Erie. At the last minute it was decided that Captain Akers should accompany Colonel Dennis in order to act as his adjutant. Booker was slightly disturbed that Dennis, having persuaded General Napier to give him command of the Queen's Own, now abandoned that command again to Major Gillmor without a second thought. For a while Booker stood on the quayside watching the dark shadow of the tug until all that was visible of it was the red glowing ring from the top of its tall funnel stack. He fretted. He wished he felt more easy in his mind about Dennis's plan. Finally he turned to his adjutant, Lieutenant Henery. 'Are the men entrained?'

'Yes sir, some are a little the worse for a drop or two but that's to be expected. I have given orders for the officers to keep a careful watch on them.'

'They are nervous,' Booker admitted. 'I doubt whether any of them know what to expect.'

'Colonel Booker!' Out of the darkness emerged the railroad telegraph clerk.

'What is it?'

'A telegraph from Chippewa. Just arrived.'

Booker took the crumpled sheet of paper while his adjutant lit a match, shielding it with his hands, so that his colonel could read the message. It was very brief.

> Have received your message of 3 a.m. I do not approve of it.
> Follow the original plan. Acknowledge receipt of this.
> Colonel Peacocke

Booker gazed a long time at the telegraph and then turned to stare out to where the red rim of the funnel of the *W. T. Robb* was just a distant glimmer.

'Damn!' he said. Then again, 'Damn!'

Chapter 54

John-Joe paused and rested his horse in the darkness. It had taken him longer than he had expected to find the Indian territory at Tonawanda and now he was not sure exactly where he was. In the shadowy gloom of night he could see nothing of the countryside around him. The land seemed to stretch flat and marshy along the shores of the broad Niagara. Everywhere seemed empty of human habitation. It occurred to him that perhaps the Indians had left the area. He was unsure of their habits and way of life. He stared into the darkness wondering what he should do. It was only the slightly darker wispy column rising into the air against the night sky farther along the shore that made him pause. Smoke! He hurried forward and within a short distance came to a depression in which several vast buildings appeared. He halted amazed at the size of them, they stretched fifty to sixty yards in length and were perhaps four yards wide, rising to a respectable height at their apex. The strands of smoke curled from windowless constructions. A dim memory told John-Joe that they were Indian long-houses. He had heard about them from somewhere.

A voice spoke quietly from nearby causing him to start in his nervousness.

'What?' he asked, presuming that the voice had spoken in the Iroquois language. 'I don't understand.'

'What are you doing here?' repeated the voice in English. It had a hollow intonation. 'This is the land of the Seneca.'

John-Joe squinted into the darkness but could not see the speaker. 'I am looking for someone to take me across the river,' he replied without dismounting from his horse.

John-Joe waited but there was no response. He could see by the light of the moon, which now raced from behind the dark clouds, that he was in the centre of three or four of the long-houses which stretched along the river bank. The voice spoke again, even closer than before.

'You are a soldier.' It was a statement, not a question.

'That is so,' John-Joe said. 'I came to find someone who might be willing to take me across the river.'

'Why come here? You can cross in your own steel canoes at Buffalo.'

'But I wish to cross without being seen.'

A door in one of the long-houses opened and a woman's figure was silhouetted against a fire inside. There was a sharp exchange which he did not understand and then the woman disappeared. But he had seen the speaker standing in the shadow of the long-house.

'Do you own a canoe?' he pressed. 'I would pay you to take me across.'

'There is a big war canoe on the river. It stops all little canoes with its steam and smoke,' came the uncompromising reply.

'Yet a little canoe could cross in the darkness without being seen,' insisted John-Joe.

'Why is it necessary for you, a soldier, to cross the river?' countered the Indian.

'Because I must join my comrades.'

'Ah! Are your comrades those who make war on the people who live across the river?'

'We make war to drive the foreigners from our land,' explained John-Joe.

'Are the whites who live across the river on your land?' There was cynicism in the voice.

John-Joe tried to think of a way of explaining matters clearly and simply. 'Not exactly. Our land is a small island far to the east. Because strangers came and took it from us we were forced to come to this land. Now we are making war on these strangers, called the British, who also rule the land across the river.'

'I know the difference between American whites and the British whites,' came the reply. 'Yet when you examine them they are both the same – they are both whites.'

John-Joe thought desperately. 'The land of my people is dear to them, that is why we must fight the British whites and that is why I must join my comrades across the river.'

There was a movement further into the darkness and John-Joe realized that he was being watched by a second Indian.

'You speak strangely for a white,' came a more resonant voice.

'Not all whites belong to the same tribe or nation,' John-Joe tried to explain. 'Not all whites belong to powerful tribes. One tribe in particular has stolen many lands. The British have stolen our land from us, stolen our dignity. We must fight to get it back.

'This we can understand,' replied the second Indian. 'Our land was the dearest thing on earth to us. Then the whites came out of the east and we have let ourselves be destroyed. We have given up our lands, that which were bequeathed to us by the Great Spirit. The whites have forced us into little corners where the soil is poor, where the hunting is worse, where the fish are few. They have told us that this land they will reserve for us and when we say we cannot live on it in the way that our ancestors have lived they have told us, give up the ways of your ancestors and live like we do. They have given our young men liquor which makes them forget who they are. Surely, if we had descended on your lands, coming from the west to the lands of the whites, and seized the good land and tried to make the whites live on the poor land as we do, then the whites would have fought us to the last man?'

John-Joe nodded impatiently. 'Yes, yes, yes,' he said. 'That's the whole point, don't you see? We Irish are like you Indians. We had our own land, our own way of life, our own customs and laws and language. Then strangers came from the east and conquered us, driving us from the land.'

The first Indian spoke again.

'If this is so, why have you not profited by the experience? Why do you come here to our land and help these others drive us from it?'

'We want our freedom. . . .' John-Joe began.

'As do we.'

'Then help us and we, in turn, will help you,' he said desperately.

There was a silence. 'I am Cayuga, war chief of the Kaniengehaga . . . those you call Mohawks.'

John-Joe was puzzled. 'But this is a Seneca reservation, isn't it?'

The first Indian spoke. 'My wife's brother is from the Cattaraugus.'

The Cattaraugus Reservation lay twenty miles to the south of Buffalo.

'We of the Mohawk Cattaraugus fought against the British redcoats many times although some of our brothers from other clans have fought for the British,' said Cayuga.

'Then you'll help me cross?' asked John-Joe eagerly.

'I know of the Irish peoples. You are Catholics. That is good. We, too, are Catholics and so we believe in the same Great Spirit. That, too, is good. And, if you use words as more than sounds, we both believe in freedom. Tonight I return by the great river to Cattaraugus. But I will take you across. . . .'

John-Joe sagged with relief and slid from his horse.

'I will take you because I believe in the words of freedom. Yet we are on the land of the Senecas in which I am a guest. It would be appropriate to give my sister's husband a gift as a sign of goodwill.'

'I cannot take my horse across,' John-Joe said. 'Take it.'

The first Indian grunted and emerged from the shadows to take the horse by the bridle and lead it away. Cayuga turned and called softly. The door of the long-house opened again after a moment and the woman reappeared. There was a short conversation and the woman disappeared to re-emerge with a pile of furs.

'The great war canoe of the whites sends smaller canoes up and down river searching for you and your kind,' said Cayuga, taking the furs. 'If you want to escape from their eyes then blacken your face with mud and put these skins on you so that in the darkness you may pass for one of us.'

'Good idea,' John-Joe nodded eagerly.

The Mohawk turned to the woman and began to speak. Then the first Indian emerged and they spoke for a short while before they turned back into the long-house, leaving John-Joe alone with Cayuga in the darkness. The Mohawk waited while John-Joe smeared his face and drew the skins over his uniform. Cayuga examined him gravely before turning down to the river bank where a canoe lay drawn up on the mud. He pointed for John-Joe to get in and then pushed it forward into the current. The canoe rocked as Cayuga heaved himself aboard, took up a paddle and began to steer the canoe out into the river. They had not gone far when the Mohawk paused, head to one side listening.

'Get down under the skins,' he muttered.

John-Joe did so and a moment later a small steam tug emerged out of the darkness, a lantern bathed the waters around the canoe.

'Hey! Who are you?'

The Mohawk called back in his own language and John-Joe heard someone swear in the darkness.

'Jist some crazy Injun, cap'n.'

Through the gap in the skins John-Joe saw the lamp swinging and heard the noise of the engine of the tug as it swung away.

'That's lucky,' he whispered towards the dark shadow of the

taciturn Mohawk as the man resumed his powerful paddling motion, pushing the canoe further into the river.

'Stay under the skins until I tell you to come out,' came the stern response.

John-Joe was aware that they were skirting a stretch of land. He supposed it to be the southern point of Grand Island, which was still American territory. Then they were moving in the darkness towards the black and silent Canadian shore. There was no sign of movement; nothing. The nose of the canoe bumped silently against the gritty bank.

'Now you may climb out,' whispered Cayuga.

John-Joe threw off the skins and scrambled to the bank. Then he turned back to the dark shadow of the Mohawk. 'Thanks,' he said.

'Remember, Irishman, all men want freedom. All men want to see their land and people free. I will set myself to discover whether your people truly believe in such things and if it be so . . . if it be so then I, Cayuga, war chieftain of the Kaniengehaga will speak to my people and say, let us raise our war band and join these Irish people in their fight because they fight for what we believe in and our fight is but part of the same war.'

John-Joe smiled. 'Now that would be really something, Cayuga,' he said. 'Mohawks fighting alongside the Irish for Irish freedom.'

'Remember, all men want freedom,' came the Indian's voice as he back-paddled into the river. John-Joe watched until his dark shadow was gone into the murkiness of the night. He stood hesitantly for a moment and then climbed up towards the river road. Apart from the surge of the river, everything was quiet. Now and again an owl would hoot in mournful protest. He shivered slightly and guessed it was about an hour before dawn. He was cold and now that he had reached the Canadian shore he realized how terribly tired he was. He started down the road in the direction of Fort Erie, determined to find O'Neill's headquarters before his exhaustion overcame him. Without warning a horse and rider appeared on the road ahead of him.

'Who the hell are you?' came a fierce demand, as the rider sought to stop his mount from shying.

'Where are the Fenians?' asked John-Joe, trying to hazard whether the man was in uniform or not.

'The murdering bastards have gone inland,' the man snapped. 'They've gone . . .' He hesitated and peered closely at John-Joe.

'What's that uniform you're wearing . . . ? Hell! If you ain't a Fenian bastard yourself. Hands up! You're my prisoner!'

The man started to fumble for a gun and John-Joe turned in sudden panic, diving off the road and began to run through the trees and bush. There came a crack of a pistol behind him. He heard something strike a tree with a thud and he darted in the opposite direction like a frightened jackrabbit, twisting and turning through the muddy undergrowth with bushes ripping and tearing at him. He paused by the dried-up bed of a small stream. He could still hear sounds of pursuit and so he used the bed of the stream as a path, running along it until he was so breathless that he had to halt. He listened carefully but there were no longer any sounds of pursuit. He continued on for a while wondering what he should do. O'Neill had marched inland and he must obviously follow. But he was exhausted. He needed to rest for a while.

The dry bed of the stream led up to a railroad track and he saw the darkened shape of a barn on the far side. He just had to have a few minutes' rest, a brief sleep, otherwise he would be no good to anyone. He crossed the tracks and pushed the barn door open. It looked fairly warm and comfortable inside. There were bales of hay there. Without bothering to remove his belt or jacket, John-Joe flung himself down and closed his eyes. Sleep, the feverish sleep of exhaustion, came to him almost immediately.

A few miles from the spot where John-Joe had fallen into his sleep of exhaustion, his brother Gavin was wakening, shivering under the shelter of a hedge, his thin blanket hardly protecting him from the chill of the early morning air. He blinked. A figure was bending over him.

'Hello, Gavin. I'm glad I found you.'

'Father MacMahon!' Gavin sat up, rubbing the sleep from his eyes, and cast an anxious glance about. Men were moving in the darkness.

'What time is it?'

'About three o'clock,' replied the priest. 'O'Neill has just given the order to rouse the camp.'

Gavin rose to his feet and tried jerking his arms and stamping his feet to warm himself. 'What are you doing here, Father?'

Father MacMahon was a shadow in the darkness.

'I was thinking, there's bound to be a battle this morning . . . they'll be lads wanting the confessional before we leave. Perhaps . . . ?' He hesitated. 'Ah well, perhaps not,' he said when Gavin did not respond. 'We each have to come to God in our own way. I'll wish you luck, though.'

Gavin took the priest's hand. 'That I'll accept and welcome. The same for you, Father. You had no need to come with us, you know.'

The priest shrugged. 'Oh yes,' he said quietly. 'There was more need for me to come across with you lads than many others. When you help to wind up a clock, you should be there to hear it striking. I'll be about God's business then . . . may He go with you, Gavin.'

'Good luck, Father.'

Gavin watched his bowed figure vanish into the blackness. Then Boyd emerged.

'Captain, I've managed to scrape up some bread and cheese for you. There's only water to drink, I'm afraid.'

Gavin took the bread and cheese and suddenly noticed that his hands were shaking. It occurred to him that he was afraid. He felt a violent shiver rack his back and could not control it.

'A chilly morning,' he muttered, in case Boyd had seen.

That was not it at all. He was scared. He hoped that the British did not have field guns. He could face anything but a cannonade. He was surprised at the terrible certainty of the feeling. If the British had field guns then he would surely run. God, had he come this far to realize his own cowardice? Cowardice or was it merely that he had taken all he could? Was he not caught up in some nightmare? Should he not try to escape, back to normality, to Kate Dawtry? All he had to do was mount his horse and ride a few miles, an hour or two at most would place him in the farmstead again. He wanted to go there, to the peace of the farmstead. The desire came on him with a terrible aching. He wanted no part of this endless self-sacrifice, of continually pitting one's strength against insurmountable objects. Wasn't it easier to accept things as they were instead of climbing on white chargers and tilting at windmills? Peace. Peace was all he ever wanted in life. He wanted to go to Kate. *Home* to Kate.

'Anything wrong, captain?' Lieutenant Boyd was staring at him curiously.

Gavin shifted himself and shook his head negatively.

'You'd best eat that bread and cheese, captain,' Boyd said. 'You don't know when we'll be able to eat again . . . especially with a battle coming.'

Gavin nodded.

A bugle was sounding the call to assemble.

A moment or two later Gavin was leading his mounted troop out of the camp. Owen Starr had secured a map and Gavin now carried this in his breast pocket. He headed south through cultivated fields of wheat, following the creek. Gradually the darkness began to lighten and, as dawn came up, the occasional sleepy protest of an owl turned into a full-throated chorus of waking birds.

'There's a road ahead,' called Boyd.

They halted their horses while Gavin peered at the map. 'That must be Buck's Corner. The road O'Neill wants to take, the Ridge Road, starts on the far side.'

A dog howled in the distance as though sensing the presence of a large hostile body of men.

'There are some pleasant farms around here,' Boyd observed. 'It seems a real nice place.'

Sergeant Nolan suddenly raised a hand. '*Seachain*!' he hissed a warning, reverting to his native tongue for a moment. 'Look out! Horsemen!'

Three men on horses were coming along the road from the west. They were young men but in civilian clothes.

Gavin took out his revolver and signalled his troop to close up, easing forward across the field to intercept them. They were still a hundred yards away when one of the men spotted them. All three halted in confusion.

'Who are you?' cried one of the men.

'Irish Republican Army,' snapped Gavin. 'Halt!'

The three horsemen did not halt. They split into different directions. One of them turned and leapt his horse at a wooden split rail fence, clearing it with ease and striking out for the woods without a backward glance. Another of the riders turned back westward along the road while the third drew his pistol, let off a few shots and galloped away along a road which ran off southwards. Collins and another trooper, without waiting for Gavin's orders, unslung their rifles and let fly a half volley but without touching the man they had fired at. With a yell for them to cease fire, Gavin spurred his horse forward, clearing the fence into the roadway, and pursued the man who had fled south. After a few hundred yards it became clear that the man was mounted on a better nag. He was already out of sight. Gavin drew rein in disgust as Boyd came up to join him.

'He'll warn the British column,' Boyd said.

'We can't catch him,' Gavin muttered as the rest of the men arrived. 'Collins, ride back to Colonel Starr and tell him that we've made contact with riders but there's no sign of the enemy. We will continue down this road towards Ridgeway.'

The road meandered and twisted, unlike most of the straight highways in the area. It seemed to follow a natural ridge of limestone which gave it a slight elevation above the ground which fell away from it to the west. Small farms stood here and there with smoke rising from their chimneys as people began to rouse themselves to the chores of the day. From the way the sun was climbing, already warming them, this Saturday, the second of the month, was going to be another burning hot June day. They trotted slowly along the Ridge Road, as it was marked on Gavin's map, until they came to a sprawling tavern with a sign swinging outside which proclaimed it to be 'The Smugglers' Home'. It stood by a crossroads where the Garrison Road from Fort Erie to Port Colborne intersected the Ridge Road. Gavin estimated that it was only a few miles north from the township of Ridgeway. It was seven o'clock. He halted his troop at the crossroads wondering whether he should wait for Owen Starr's advance column to catch up with him or whether he should ride straight into the township.

Chapter 55

Colonel Robert Lowry gazed arrogantly at Major-General Napier. His uniform was spotless and he carried himself with the assured carriage of a man who knew his rank and privileges. He looked as if he had stepped out of some lady's morning room after taking coffee with her rather than a man who had ridden hard through the night to reach Toronto.

'Am I to command the field force then?' he demanded impertinently.

Napier returned the gaze of his junior critically, biting back his annoyance at the man's impudence.

'You've heard the news?' Napier said unnecessarily.

'My adjutant told me. The Fenian scum have finally crossed.'

Napier, despite his dislike of Lowry, knew that he had not made a mistake in choosing him as his field commander. Lowry had fought with the 47th Foot at Alma, Balaclava, Inkerman and Sebastopol. He had seen action and proved himself in the field. And Lowry had one other quality when it came to facing the Fenians. He was one of Ireland's biggest landowners with an estate of several thousand acres at Drumreagh, Dungannon, in County Tyrone. He was an Orangeman with a universal hatred of the 'native Irish'. He had all the arrogance of having been raised as a conqueror among the conquered. Dungannon's three baronies were widely Irish-speaking and many people spoke no word of English. The differences between the settlers and the natives were therefore marked. To Lowry, the Irish were merely a tribe of labourers and field workers who mumbled in unintelligible gibberish among themselves. A sullen and devious people. Treacherous and rebellious. Lowry believed in ruling them with a rod of iron. The evictions and clearances on his estate were well known and had made his name a feared and hated symbol among the Irish. The previous November Lowry's house in Toronto had actually been attacked by a mob. The Fenians were blamed and Napier was forced to approve a permanent guard of six soldiers to watch over it. Napier found himself nodding approval of his choice in sending Lowry against the Fenians. His hatred of them would ensure that he spared no pains to pursue and bring them to book. He could overlook the man's impudence for the moment.

'In your absence, I have placed Colonel Peacocke in temporary command of the Niagara Field Force,' Napier said. 'Peacocke is currently at Chippewa with 1,000 men and a battery of six field guns. There is a second column of 1,000 militia at Port Colborne under Colonel Booker.'

'Is Peacocke going to attack the Fenians?' Lowry asked anxiously.

'I think Peacocke will simply invest the Fenian positions,' replied Napier. 'If the Fenians attack him he will fight a holding action to contain them. He knows that you have been given command.'

Lowry relaxed. 'Excellent. What is my authority?'

'Your authority is total in the Niagara frontier area. I have arranged a train which will leave Toronto at two o'clock. You will take with you an additional field battery of four guns with Captain Crowe of the Royal Artillery.'

'Are there any other regular troops available?' Lowry demanded.

'Three companies of the 16th Foot's 2nd Battalion and the 60th Royal Rifles will be able to join the train at Hamilton. Also a militia unit, the Oakville Rifle Volunteers. Not much, but all we can get together in the time.'

Lowry nodded grimly.

'In addition to your staff,' Napier continued, 'you'll be escorted by Lieutenant-Colonel Cumberland, the aide-de-camp to the governor-general, whose duty is to keep His Excellency personally informed. Colonel Wolseley is also joining you as an advisor and I have Lieutenant Turner of the Royal Engineers available to consult with on any matter requiring engineering works. There are three civilians. . . .'

'Civilians?' Lowry's voice rose disdainfully.

'Messrs Clarke and Kingsmill, local men who know the country, and a telegraph operator named Hunter. They could be useful.'

'Very well, sir. But I am to have a free hand to crush this rabble?'

'Free so far as field operations,' Napier replied. 'You are in sole command there. Your task is to protect the lives and property of the citizens of the area and prevent the Fenians menacing Toronto.'

Lowry permitted himself a condescending smile. 'Then, by God, sir, I'll make sure that I smash these Papish carrion once and for all. I'll teach them a lesson which will make them forget their disloyalty and rebelliousness for the next hundred years.'

Lieutenant-Colonel John Stoughton Dennis was happy; happy that he had his own independent command again and that he was going into action with an opportunity to win glory and improve his career. He had ambition. He did not want to remain a land-surveyor all his life. He fancied himself in politics and distinguishing himself in a military role was one sure way of making a career in politics.

After his party had sailed from Port Colborne, the tug *W. T. Robb* had steamed along the lake shore through a fairly thick fog which hung on the waters. But, by the time they rounded Point Abino and started to move towards the commencement of the Niagara River, a fiery sun began to glow in the eastern sky and chase away the fog. The waters of Lake Erie were smooth, without a ripple to be seen except those created by the forward motion of the ship. Neither was there any sign of any other shipping on the lake. The shoreline looked peaceful enough. The only movement was the occasional smoke rising here and there from waking farmsteads.

The tug reached the headwaters of the Niagara River without incident. Captain Akers, whom Dennis had now appointed second-in-command of the expedition in deference to his regular army commission, suggested that the men should go below decks to disguise the purpose of the steam tug. Dennis appreciated that there would be numerous people on the American shore armed with all manner of telescopes and spyglasses waiting to signal warnings to the Fenians. He grunted his assent. There was a brief moment of panic when a steam yacht swung out of Buffalo harbour and seemed to be making for the *W. T. Robb* but it simply sailed by with only a dip of its ensign in salute.

'No sign of any movement at the old fort,' called Lieutenant Robb, the master of the tug. 'What do you want me to do, sir?'

'We'll proceed downriver as planned and examine this place Frenchman's Creek where the Irish rabble are reported to be,' Dennis replied.

The tug was starting to weather the point around the old fortress when Captain McCallum, the commander of the Dunnville Naval Brigade, called a low warning. Across the river the large black menacing outline of the USS *Michigan* was racing down on them.

Dennis's mouth tightened as he saw the ship's gunports open and the crews standing by.

A voice hailed them as the cutter swung, showing its 'Stars and Stripes' from its jackstaff. 'Ahoy steam tug! Identify yourself!'

'You may reply McCallum and break out the White Ensign,' ordered Dennis.

McCallum moved to the rail. 'This is the steam tug *W. T. Robb*,' he shouted. 'The steam tug *Robb* of Her Britannic Majesty's service. Captain McCallum, Dunnville Royal Naval Brigade in command.'

The ensign went fluttering up the jackstaff.

'Ahoy, captain,' came the same voice. 'This is Commander Bryson, United States Navy. What are you doing in these waters?'

'We are inside British territorial waters, commander,' replied McCallum, 'and on Her Majesty's business.'

There was a pause.

'All right, captain,' the voice sounded amused. 'It is my job to prevent infractions of the neutrality laws.'

'We appreciate that, commander.'

'Good luck to you.'

The black hulk of the American gunboat turned away and its wake frothed as it swung back to its own side of the river.

Dennis heaved a sigh of relief and sat back to watch the shoreline move slowly by as the tug continued its passage downriver. There seemed no sign of life anywhere, no sign of any Fenians in the early morning light. The *W. T. Robb* had moved as far downriver as Black Creek before Akers asked, 'What now, colonel?'

Dennis glanced at his fob watch and noticed the time. 'We'll turn back for Fort Erie and rendezvous with Booker as planned.'

The township of Fort Erie was still deserted as the tug nuzzled up against the wharf usually used by the ferry *International*. Only after they had made fast did Dennis spot a movement on shore and a challenge was issued. Two civilians, looking nervous and carrying shotguns, came hesitantly out from behind a wood pile.

'Who are you?' demanded Dennis as he came off the tug.

'Name's Schryer, mister. I'm the constable here,' volunteered one of the men.

Dennis peered at him disdainfully. 'Where are the Fenians?' he demanded.

The man shrugged expressively. 'Can't rightly tell you, colonel. There's a few about the township but the others marched off last night.'

'Dammit!' Dennis hissed. 'Which way did they go?'

'Last I heard they were off down the river road to Chippewa.'

'What about the others?'

'Them that's left?' Schryer grinned. 'Mostly drunk, I guess. There's a few sober ones guarding some prisoners in the schoolhouse.'

'British prisoners?'

Schryer nodded.

'We'll soon deal with that,' grunted Dennis. 'Do you know what's happening across the river?'

'There's a Yankee ship patrolling it. Elsewise, all communications are cut off.'

Dennis suddenly caught sight of a flag flying on a pole outside a wooden house near the wharf. It was a tricolour of green, white and orange.

'And what in hell is that?' he demanded.

Schryer hunched his shoulder again. 'Don't rightly know, mister. It's the flag them Irish put up yesterday. Flag of their Republic, so they do tell.'

'Damned insolent rebels!' cried Dennis. He turned to Captain Akers. 'Get that rag taken down at once.'

'Shall we disembark the men then, sir?' Akers asked.

Dennis hesitated. He gazed at the deserted streets of the township. There was not a living soul to be seen except the constable and his companion. Telegraph wires were strewn on the streets and there was an occasional discarded wooden box, smashed and emptied, which marked the passage of the Fenians.

'Yes,' he said. 'We'll disembark and free the prisoners at the schoolhouse. This man,' he pointed to Schryer, 'will show Captain King where the schoolhouse is. When the men are disembarked we'll divide them into companies and send them out to reconnoitre the township. I want to know where the damned rebels are. Anyone who cannot give a satisfactory account of themselves is to be taken into custody.'

Dennis took out his fob watch again. It was well after eight o'clock and there was no sign of Colonel Booker nor sound of a train approaching the railroad depot. Dennis was sure he could not have missed the prearranged signal, the train whistle, if Booker had been forced to change the plan. Perhaps Booker had forgotten the signal. Stupid fellow! He waited on the tug while Captain King led the men of his Welland Canal Field Battery to the schoolhouse. The half dozen Fenians who had been left in Fort Erie to guard the prisoners and direct reinforcements did not put up any resistance when they saw that they were outnumbered. Among the prisoners released from the schoolhouse were some men of the Royal Canadian Rifles and a number of prominent townspeople. The riflemen immediately volunteered to serve with Dennis and were given the weapons confiscated from the Fenians. Another former prisoner, a copper-haired man with almost ugly, hawk-like features, demanded Dennis's attention.

'My name is Hogan,' he said, showing Dennis a badge of identity. 'I am an agent of Mister McMicken, the police detective.'

'So you fell foul of the Fenians, eh?' Dennis smiled condescendingly.

'I want a chance to catch up with those bastards again,' nodded Hogan. 'I'd like to attach myself to your command, colonel.'

'I certainly have need of a scout, Hogan,' Dennis agreed. 'Can you take me to the Fenian encampment at Frenchman's Creek? I'm told the Fenians were last seen there.'

Hogan smiled viciously. 'If someone can give me a revolver, I'll be mighty pleased to take you there.'

'We'll form two columns,' Dennis turned to Akers. 'I'll command the right flank. You, Akers, will take the left. We'll strike northwards up to Frenchman's Creek, scouring the country on the way. Lieutenant Robb will move the tug downriver keeping pace with our passage on shore. Our two columns will converge at Frenchman's Creek.'

With Hogan guiding them, Dennis's column moved along the river road while Captain Akers moved inland, keeping within hailing distance. Captain King, who was a conscientious officer, suggested to Dennis that they ought to throw out skirmishers or flanking scouts. Dennis greeted the idea with a hoot of laughter.

'You are giving too much credit to these Irish for soldierly knowledge,' he rebuked. 'They are just a drunken rabble.'

It seemed that Colonel Stoughton Dennis was to be proved right for by the time the two columns converged again near Frenchman's Creek they had captured about thirty-eight men who could not give a good account of themselves, many of whom were the worse for drink.

Something sharp stabbed against John-Joe's chest. He stirred and grunted in his sleep. It stabbed again and this time John-Joe awakened realizing that the pain was not part of his dream. He had fallen asleep in a barn. He remembered that. His next thought was that he must have turned over in his sleep on to a pitchfork or something similarly sharp. He opened his eyes and found a weather-beaten face glaring down at him. The face was expressionless, the dark eyes fathomless. Only the cheeks moved rhythmically as the owner of the face rolled a wad of chewing tobacco from one side of his mouth to the other. The man wore a redcoat, white trousers and a white belt. In his hands was a rifle, the bayonet point rested on his chest.

'Well, lookee here,' drawled the owner of the weather-beaten face, spitting out a stream of dark brown liquid into the hay beside John-Joe.

John-Joe lay motionless waiting for the man to make a move, tensing for the movement which would send that sharpened bayonet into his body.

'Well now,' the man said again. Then he raised his voice, 'Cap'n!'

An officer appeared behind the man and stared down in surprise.

'Who is he, Corporal Reavley?'

'Guess I caught me one of them Fenians, sir.'

The officer stared hard at John-Joe's green uniform. The soldier with the rifle and bayonet chuckled with a high-pitched note.

'What do you think, cap'n? He was laying there all tucked up like a sleeping babe.'

The officer bent down and removed the revolver from John-Joe's holster, examined the mechanism, broke it open and emptied the shells from it. Having placed them in his pocket, he thrust the gun into his belt.

'Okay, Reavley. Let him up.'

'You heard the officer,' Reavley prodded him, none too gently. 'Get up!'

John-Joe scrambled to his feet.

'You're a prisoner, son,' the corporal said unnecessarily as John-Joe stood before the redcoat captain. The officer was examining John-Joe's green uniform with some surprise.

'What uniform is that?' he demanded finally, unable to suppress his curiosity.

'Army of the Irish Republic,' replied John-Joe trying to stop his tremulous voice by making his tone curt.

The captain's lip drooped. 'I know of no such army, no such country,' he sneered. 'Who are you?'

'Lieutenant John-Joseph Devlin, Army of the Irish Republic.'

The captain smiled thinly. 'I presume you mean that you are a Fenian?' he said. 'An Irish rebel, is that so?'

'I mean that I am an officer of the Irish Republican Army,' John-Joe replied stubbornly.

The captain gestured impatiently. 'What are you doing here?'

'Sleeping.'

'Where are the rest of your rabble?'

John-Joe shrugged trying to look indifferent.

'Where are the rest of you Irish scum?' shouted the officer angrily.

'I do not have to answer any other questions. I am an officer of . . .'

'Aw, stop that!' snapped the corporal, moving his rifle and bayonet in a threatening gesture. The captain raised a hand to stay him.

'Careful, corporal. The colonel will probably want to question this man. He's the first one we've caught who claims to be an officer among the rabble. Put him over with the others.'

The corporal prodded John-Joe out of the barn to where a group of redcoated soldiers stood grouped with a dozen dispirited-looking men in their centre. The corporal gave him an unnecessary push and he stumbled and would have fallen had not a man wearing Confederate grey, with a green scarf at his neck, moved forward and held him up.

'Take no notice of them, lieutenant,' he smiled. 'They'll soon be laughing on the other side of their faces when "Fighting Tom" comes across.'

John-Joe was about to retort that General Sweeny was not coming, that O'Neill was cut off, but he checked himself. There was no need to make things worse.

A moment later they were being marched forward under the watchful eyes of the guards. The march seemed to last for several miles. It was a hot day and no one offered them anything to drink in spite of the fact that they were forced across several small streams and a creek. John-Joe noticed that the sun was pretty high and he felt very hungry. He realized that he had not eaten since yesterday. None of the prisoners with him knew what had happened to O'Neill and the main body of Fenians. Several of them were stragglers and there were many who had no connection at all with the Brotherhood; petty thieves and scavengers who had followed in the wake of O'Neill's men hoping to pick up what plunder they could. They crossed a partially demolished bridge over a creek and John-Joe realized that the work of demolition had been recently done yet there was no sign of fighting having taken place. There were no bodies nor discarded material of war. It was at this ruined bridge that another group of prisoners were made to join them. They were guarded by what seemed to be a mixture of soldiers and sailors. At their head strode a colonel with impressive-looking moustachios and an overbearing manner with a voice which rose on such a note that caused John-Joe to be thankful he was not a junior officer in the man's command. The column of prisoners were finally allowed to rest and seize the opportunity to drink their fill at the creek.

After a while they were instructed to move north again, along the river road. Out from the bank, not exactly in mid-stream, a steam tug kept pace with them. At its bows, at the jackstaff, it flew a Royal Navy ensign.

There was an abrupt shout of command. They were halted and the tug edged near to an old wooden jetty whose wooden planking was in a state of decay. Helped by the none-too gentle prod of muskets, they were hurried on to the tug and ordered below decks.

Colonel Stoughton Dennis had observed a column of marching men moving towards him down the river road. Now he raised his field-glasses to study them more carefully, observing – with a tinge of disappointment – the redcoats and Union flags.

'They're our troops,' he muttered to Captain Akers. 'They seem to be turning west down that road ahead, away from the river.'

'That's the road to New Germany and Stevensville,' volunteered Captain King.

A mounted officer from the column, seeing them, came riding at a trot towards them.

'Hello!' he sung out and then, seeing he was addressing a colonel, threw up a hand in a confused salute.

'Who are you, sir?' demanded Dennis.

'Lieutenant Edward Parnell, sir, 19th Battalion of Volunteer Militia from Lincoln.'

'Where are your men going? What's going on?'

'We are part of Colonel Peacocke's command, sir. The rear guard. We are marching for Stevensville.'

'Can I get in touch with Colonel Peacocke?' asked Dennis.

'No, sir. He's far in advance along the road. You could send a runner but it will take time.'

'Have you any news of the Fenians? They were supposed to be at Frenchman's Creek.'

The young lieutenant shrugged. 'I've only heard scuttle-butt, sir. I understand that they are somewhere hereabouts and that we are to attack them as soon as we've joined with a column out of Port Colborne.'

'All right, lieutenant. Will you send a runner to Colonel Peacocke and tell him that Colonel Stoughton Dennis presents his compliments and is patrolling the Niagara shore, has captured several Fenians but has discovered that the others have deserted their camp at Frenchman's Creek. It may be, hearing of our approach, they have slunk back across the river.'

The lieutenant saluted and trotted off.

Dennis decided to move his troops back on to the tug and return upriver to Fort Erie. He would question the prisoners there at the same time as ensuring that the township was secured.

Across the Niagara River, gazing with a professional curiosity at the progress of the *W. T. Robb* through a pair of field-glasses, the forty-four-year-old commander of the United States' Army, Lieutenant-General Ulysses Simpson Grant had a clear field of vision along the Canadian shore. Beside him, also an interested spectator of the movements on the other side of the river, was his wife, Mrs Julia Grant. Grant's staff, including his aide-de-camp General Thomas, together with Brigadier Barry, stood grouped around him in a semicircle. General Grant and his entourage had arrived in Buffalo at 1 p.m. and eaten a light luncheon in Bloomer's saloon. The army commander had come to the city in answer to a telegraph from General Meade requesting Grant come to see the situation for himself. He had expressed astonishment at observing the thousands of Fenian soldiers waiting quietly in and around the city under the scrutiny of General Barry's regulars. What was astonishing was that there was no trouble, no rioting or drinking. They waited in disciplined groups. They were a disciplined army. Along the river front the same quietness and discipline did not apply as enterprising Buffalo citizens sought to organize a carnival. Those with telescopes, spyglasses and binoculars were doing a roaring trade charging twenty-five cents for an examination of the Canadian shore while others sold drinks and other refreshments. But, as Grant himself could see, there was little activity from Fort Erie apart from the progress of the steam tug. The township appeared deserted.

'Do you think that the British have matters in hand, General Barry?' Grant asked at length, lowering his field-glasses. 'I see no movement on the far bank to indicate any aggressive action on the part of the Fenians.'

Barry stroked his nose thoughtfully as he replied. 'The main body of Fenians have moved inland, sir. There are rumours of a battle about to be fought some distance beyond Fort Erie.'

Grant snorted softly. 'Well, that is a matter for the British to contend with. Our main task is to observe the neutrality laws. Have any Fenians attempted to contest the crossing with your men?'

'No sir,' replied Barry. 'The Irish seem good humoured and disciplined. They make no aggressive acts towards the United States authority. However, it would help, sir, if we had a clear indication of what the President intends. The local Fenians have been arguing that the President has actually approved this invasion and we are acting contrary to his promises to them.'

Grant grimaced wryly. He had heard the argument before. There were many rumours, and not just confined to Fenian sources, that Johnson was turning a blind eye to the Fenian plans. The fact that Johnson had not replied to any of his telegraphs gave credence to the possibility. The delay in not issuing a proclamation or statement clarifying the Administration's position was worrying. Grant could see the military being blamed by the politicians if anything went wrong. He had seen too many generals fall foul of the whims and fancies of politicians during the war.

'Until you hear differently, General Barry, your task is simply to contain the Fenians,' he replied. 'Contain them and prevent reinforcements crossing the river.'

'I believe that we are doing that, sir. There have been no men crossing over since yesterday. However, there are nearly 5,000 Fenians encamped in and around Buffalo now.'

'Have you sent for reinforcements?'

Barry nodded.

'You may call out the National Guard on my authority if you feel it necessary,' Grant added.

'As I have said, sir, so far the Fenians have shown no belligerence towards the flag of the United States. It would be a different matter entirely if we had to deal with an armed body of 5,000 hostile men. But they are well behaved and we are in close contact with their officers. Indeed, sir, many of their officers are old comrades who served in the same command during the war.'

Grant grimaced wryly, bringing his gaze back across the river. Damned President Johnson and his vacillation, he thought. How true were the rumours that he had come to an accommodation with the Fenians? If Grant made the wrong decision now, pre-judging the

President's attitude, his entire career could be at risk. There was a great deal of sympathy for the Irish revolutionary movement in general and the Senate and Congress in particular. Congressman Sydenham Ancona from Pennsylvania had been pushing to repeal the neutrality laws of 1818 which would allow the Fenians to move into the provinces of British North America without hindrance. Personally, Grant hoped that the Congress would allow no such thing. He passionately believed in maintaining neutrality on the borders, especially now that the north and south were still licking their wounds and only tentatively 'united'. A vast garrison army had to be maintained in the former secessionist states to prevent further rebellion and violence and, from what Grant had observed of the former Confederate states, the Union Army garrison would probably have to be there for many years, perhaps even for a decade. The United States could not afford to allow its territory to be used for any act of aggression which might plunge it into a new and bloody conflict. That might also result in a renewal of the secessionist war before it had recovered from the bloodiest years ever recorded in the country's history.

General Thomas leaned forward and whispered in Grant's ear. Grant nodded and checked his pocket watch, smiled at his wife and offered her his arm. Together with his staff they walked back to their carriages which would take them to the railroad depot. They were cheered along the entire route, even the Fenians, Grant noticed with irony, joined in and he acknowledged the compliment by occasionally raising his hat.

Colonel Stoughton Dennis disembarked his men at Fort Erie again and had the prisoners lined up outside George Lewis's post office building by the ferry wharf. The McMicken detective, Hogan, had persuaded him that something might be learnt by questioning them and Dennis readily agreed to the interrogation. Both Captain Akers and Captain King brought up the fact that it was a matter of concern that Colonel Booker had not kept the rendezvous nor sent a message. They both tactfully suggested that the command should return to Port Colborne to find out what was taking place. Dennis, enjoying the freedom of his own independent command, was not particularly concerned. Only when Captain Akers discreetly pointed out that Colonel Stoughton Dennis's command was actually the Queen's Own, and questions might be raised later as to why the colonel was out of touch with his battalion for such a length of time that Dennis pondered the problem seriously. He agreed that after the prisoners had been interrogated, he would escort them back to Port Colborne on the *W. T. Robb* leaving Captain King and the men of the Welland Canal Field Battery to secure the township.

John-Joe stood anxiously with his fellow prisoners watching as, one by one, his companions were taken into the wooden house at the corner of the main street. Each of the half-dozen men who preceded John-Joe into the building came out with their hands bound and cuts and red marks on their faces which had not been there when they went in. The man in the Confederate uniform, who had saved him from falling, was taken in just before him and came out with blood trickling from the side of his mouth.

'Watch out for the civilian,' he muttered as he was pushed by John-Joe. 'He's a mean bastard.'

A corporal marched John-Joe up the steps into what appeared to be the kitchen of the building. The colonel with the splendid moustachios was seated puffing on a cigar. He leaned back in the chair casually. Two soldiers stood on either side of the door behind John-Joe. A redcoat captain stood to one side with a note book. Standing beside the seated officer was a civilian, a copper-haired man with bright eyes and thick lips that were twisted into a sneer.

'This one is dressed up real fancy,' he jeered as John-Joe was pushed in front of the colonel.

'He claims to be an officer, sir,' supplied the corporal who escorted him in.

'Who are you?' the colonel asked softly.

'Lieutenant John-Joe Devlin, Irish Republican Army,' John-Joe drew himself up defiantly.

The colonel gazed at him scornfully and, for an odd moment, John-Joe felt he was staring into the face of Captain Francis Dashfort again, so similar did their expressions seem. It was that same contempt in the eyes.

The civilian sniggered as he moved to John-Joe's side. 'You are scum!' John-Joe, his eyes on the colonel, found the blow totally unexpected. It sent him staggering across the floor. 'You are a seditious agitator!'

Colonel Dennis took another puff at his cigar and watched indifferently as John-Joe recovered his balance.

'Quite so. As Mister Hogan says, you are a damned rebel and you shall be hanged.' He turned to the corporal. 'This prisoner is not secured. Tie him up.'

The corporal produced a rope and pulled John-Joe's hands behind his back. It was no use struggling. The man hauled so tightly on the rope that the bonds seemed to cut off his circulation. He winced as the harsh cord bit into his flesh. The man called Hogan perched on the edge of the table and smiled.

'Why are you dressed in that fancy get-up, mister?'

'I am a lieutenant in the Irish. . . .'

The flat of Hogan's hand caught John-Joe a crack across the cheek.

'Are you Irish?'

'Irish-American,' John-Joe mumbled shaking his head to clear the sudden throbbing.

'Are you a citizen of Her Majesty?' he asked unctuously.

'I am a citizen of the United States holding a commission in the Army of the Irish Republic.'

He expected the blow now but, strangely, it did not come. He didn't care. His arms were burning with numbness.

'Yes,' taunted Hogan. 'As you say, Lieutenant John-Joe Devlin. . . .' His eyes suddenly narrowed as he stared at John-Joe. Then he shrugged saying almost to himself, 'No, it would be too much of a coincidence . . . Devlin is a common enough Teig name.'

John-Joe replied, 'So is Hogan. Maybe you should think about your own people before you call people traitor and rebel.'

Hogan stepped back and smashed his fist straight into John-Joe's mouth. He went crashing back to the floor.

The redcoat captain moved involuntarily. 'Really, colonel,' he protested. 'I can see nothing to be gained by the beating up of a bound and helpless youth.'

Dennis glared angrily at the captain. 'Captain Akers, we are trying to gather military information.'

Akers's lips turned down in disapproval. 'Forgive me if I am mistaken, colonel. I thought we were simply allowing Mister Hogan to exercise his sadistic tendencies.'

Hogan swung round towards the captain but met the icy grey eyes and firm set jaw. He hesitated. Colonel Dennis waved a hand impatiently.

'You obviously don't know how to treat these Irish scum, Akers. Civilization has no impact on them. They swing between incredible ferocity and brutal obstinacy. They live in utter ignorance of our laws, our manners, our customs . . . some even are in ignorance of our language. They retain deep traces of superstitious beliefs from ancient times. Civilized? They are less civilized than the redskins hereabouts but are as crafty and as unforgiving.'

As Hogan hauled John-Joe to his feet with a grin, John-Joe whispered, 'That's you he's talking about, Hogan. Just as much as me. Maybe you'll think about it one day.'

Hogan gave him a shove. 'You'll hang with the rest of them, sonny, whether you talk or not.'

'Shall I remove the prisoner, colonel?' Akers cut in sharply.

Dennis's voice was disdainful. 'Very well. We'll get nothing out of the rogue.'

Outside, John-Joe was handed over to a sergeant and marched along the main street to the schoolhouse. There was a cellar beneath the schoolroom which had been used by the teacher for storing bottled preserves and cider in. It was cold, stone-flagged but the darkness was dispelled by a gloomy light which crept in through a small dust-covered window high up in a corner. There were half-a-dozen people inside. They were prisoners grouped on the stone flags. The sergeant pushed John-Joe inside and slammed the door behind him.

'Have they been treating you all right, lieutenant?' called an amused voice.

'I've been treated better,' replied John-Joe. 'Can anyone untie me?'

'We're all tied here,' the same voice said. John-Joe recognized it as belonging to the man in the Confederate uniform.

'My arms are numb,' John-Joe complained.

The man chuckled. 'Guess our bodies will be even more numb when they've done hanging us.'

John-Joe shivered slightly and he slid down to the floor beside the man.

'Can they do that?' he asked.

The shadowy figure of the Confederate turned his head towards another man. 'You tell him, mister,' he invited, turning back to John-Joe and adding, 'He's a lawyer; leastways he was 'til he was kicked out for malpractice.'

The lawyer's voice was heavy with alcohol.

'I was a good lawyer,' he said defensively. 'I was a very good lawyer.'

'So tell him,' pressed the Confederate.

'If you are Irish born ánd thereby a citizen of Her Gracious Majesty then you'll hang. High treason, you see, it's a hanging offence.'

John-Joe tried to rub his bonds against the wall to loosen them in order to ease his aching arms. It made no difference. The rope was too secure.

'But what if you are a citizen of the United States?' he demanded.

'Then they'll still hang you, son,' replied the lawyer cheerfully. 'The laws of this province says that a subject of any foreign state, then at peace with Her Majesty, who enters Upper or Lower Canada with intent to levy war on Her Majesty or to commit any such felony by the same, then such person or persons may be tried and punished by a military court or court of law and, if found guilty, suffer death or such other punishment as shall be awarded by the court.'

'Aw, shut yer yap!' snarled one of the other prisoners.

'Well,' John-Joe forced a smile in the gloom, 'he certainly sounds like a lawyer.'

The Confederate chuckled. 'Guess he does at that.'

'How many prisoners have they taken?' John-Joe continued after a while.

'I reckon about fifty, why?'

'Can they hang us all?'

'Yes, if they've a mind to, son. I remember my great grandaddy describing the mass hangings in Ireland after the '98 uprising. Numbers don't count to these folk much. They think that the more they hang, the better will be the lesson.'

'Maybe they mean to hang us as examples,' interrupted the lawyer. 'They've separated us from the rest. Why's that?'

'Bloody cheerful, aren't you?' sneered the Confederate.

'Then why have they separated us?' the lawyer demanded indignantly.

'Does anyone know what has happened to O'Neill?' John-Joe said hastily.

'He marched north towards Chippewa last night. A few of us had to remain behind to guard the prisoners and direct reinforcements after him if they arrived. That's all I know. There was some talk that two British columns were moving against him.'

John-Joe sighed. There was nothing to do. His fate was no longer in his hands.

'Well,' it was as if the Confederate sensed his resignation. 'We might as well make ourselves as comfortable as possible until they decide what they're going to do with us. Does anyone know a song?'

A portly man lying near the door let out an experimental hum.

The struggle is over, the boys are defeated,
Old Ireland's surrounded with sadness and gloom. . . .

'Didn't I want a song to cheer us up?' cried the Confederate. 'For the love of Christ, can't you sing something else?'

The man altered the melody to a jubilant quick time.

Oh! comrades, think how Ireland pines,
Her exiled lords, her rifled shrines,
Her dearest hope, the ordered lines
And bursting charge of O'Neill's men.
Then fling your green flag to the sky,
Be 'Limerick!' your battlecry,
And charge till blood floats fetlock-high
Around the track of O'Neill's men.

They joined him in bawling the lusty chorus.

Viva là, the new brigade
Viva là, the old one too,
Viva là, the rose shall fade
And the shamrock shine forever new!

There came a banging on the outside of the door. 'Shut up that caterwauling, you drunken bastards!'

Chapter 56

The shriek of a train whistle, two short blasts followed by a long one, caused Gavin's horse to shy fretfully. He and his small troop were still at the crossroads just outside the roadside tavern. The morning air was still and through its crispness they could hear the shunting and clanking of cars on metal tracks. Lieutenant Boyd pulled a face. 'A train,' he said unnecessarily. 'Troops maybe, eh, captain?'

'It's hardly likely they would be running a civilian train,' agreed Gavin dryly. 'I reckon that it'll be the troops out of Port Colborne. Ridgeway is only a mile or so down the road ahead of us. You keep the men here, Boyd. I'm going down to see if I can see anything. If I'm not back within ten or fifteen minutes, send word to Colonel Starr.'

He set off at an easy canter across the intersecting Garrison Road, continuing to follow the Ridge Road on its meandering course towards the small township of Ridgeway. It wound through open fields and clusters of woods among which houses stood sheltered from the winds that sprang off the great lake. Gavin realized that it would be impossible to observe the railroad depot without going right into the town. However, to his left rose a hillock and he turned his horse through a field and began to ascend it. He did not have to climb far before he obtained a view across the tree tops towards the low bright level of Lake Erie beyond. He could see the railroad from this elevated spot and see black smoke from an engine. He raised his field-glasses and focused. There were nine cars linked behind the locomotive which was standing at the tiny station hissing steam. He could see the diminutive shapes of men climbing out, caught the bright red of their coats and the flash of early morning sun on metal. There were many dark-coated figures, too; the dark green of militia. He could not count them for they were in their hundreds. In the still air came the distant shouting of orders. The soldiers appeared to be forming up, presumably to march north. O'Neill had been right. They were going to march north along the Ridge Road thinking to come up behind the Fenian army. That was all he wanted to know. He turned his horse and urged it back to the crossroads at a gallop.

Boyd watched his coming with interest.

'It's a British column right enough,' yelled Gavin. 'Let's warn Starr.'

The companies of Owen Starr's regiment were not far behind, moving down the meandering road at a brisk pace. Starr halted them as soon as he spotted Gavin and listened silently to his report. A glint of excitement appeared in the red-haired young colonel's eyes. He insisted on accompanying Gavin back along the road in search of O'Neill while Spaulding, his second-in-command, began to order the men into skirmishing lines across the fields.

O'Neill was only a mile behind.

'The stupidity of the engineer in sounding the train's whistle would indicate that the British commander has no idea of our presence here,' O'Neill observed as soon as Gavin had finished his report. 'Excellent! We'll form our lines here and let them march against us. Owen, your regiment and Captain Haggerty's men will form a skirmishing line along the Garrison Road.' They had dismounted and bent over a map to study the position. 'You'll fan out either side of this house by the crossroads . . . what is it?'

'A tavern, sir,' replied Gavin. 'An inn called "The Smugglers' Home".'

'Good. I want you well forward, Owen. My regiment will be the main reserve line and we'll hold this area behind that stone farmhouse on our left . . . there, among the orchards. I want Grace's men on my left flank and Hoy's regiment on my right. Is that understood?'

They all muttered agreement.

'What's the plan, John?' demanded Starr.

'The classic one,' replied O'Neill. 'The British will be marching north up the Ridge Road. Where it intersects the Garrison Road by this inn they will encounter your skirmishing lines, Owen. The correct response, if they have good officers, will be to throw out their rifle companies in flanking movements and begin to push on your front thinking that it is the main enemy force. As they push forward, you will fall back. But slowly does it, Owen. Make them believe that it is a reluctant retreat. You'll fall as far back as this brick farmhouse and re-group with my regiment. As you do so, Grace and Hoy will extend their flanks to form an encirclement.'

'It sounds simple, sir,' observed Major Canty.

'Simplicity usually works in these affairs, Canty,' O'Neill chuckled. 'Do you have your runners organized? I want men that we can trust with verbal reports.'

'I do, sir.'

'Good. Let's get to our positions.'

Father MacMahon caught O'Neill's attention. 'Some men will be dying before long, colonel. Is there any chance of being able to give a blessing and general absolution?'

O'Neill shook his head firmly. 'Sorry, Father. We must get into line before the British come. Perhaps you might say a quiet prayer on behalf of us all?'

Starr was mounting to return to his men when Gavin asked, 'Where do you want my mounted scouts, Colonel O'Neill? Shall I continued to support Colonel Starr?'

O'Neill shook his head. 'Do you see those orchards to the east, just behind the brick farmhouse? That will be my command point. Get your troop and report to me there. Your men are the only mounted scouts that I have and so you may be the arbitrators of this battle. Without mounted scouts an infantry man has no eyes or ears. I hope that fact will contribute to the downfall of the British. Let's pray that they remain in ignorance of our exact positions for a while longer.'

The British commander was, however, being given precise information about the Fenian positions at that very moment. Samuel Johnston, a customs official from Fort Erie, had managed to escape from the township just as the Fenians arrived. He had ridden to relatives in Stevensville and then with two friends rode in search of Colonel Peacocke's troops to volunteer their services. They had just had a narrow escape when they had almost ridden into the front of the Fenian army. Johnston's two companions had fled in opposite directions while Johnston himself had galloped south and found himself in Ridgeway as militia troops were detraining. He flung himself exhausted from his horse and was brought before the senior officer who eyed him suspiciously.

'The Fenians!' gasped Johnston. 'Two miles off and moving this way!'

Lieutenant-Colonel Booker was incredulous. 'But my information is that they are either at Frenchman's Creek or moving north on Chippewa.'

'No! No!' insisted Johnston. 'They are moving south against you. They are not far behind me.'

Booker was plainly sceptical. 'And do these Fenians have cavalry or artillery?'

Johnston shook his head vigorously. He was not ignorant about military matters for he had served in the 50th New York Volunteer Engineer Corps with General Sheridan during the Twelve Days Campaign.

'We could cut 'em to pieces with a hundred of your men, colonel,' Johnston suggested. 'You could march your men up to the orchards beyond Garrison Road and lie in wait for them. Ambush 'em, you see?'

Booker gazed at him in sour disapproval. 'Are you in command or me?' he said stonily. 'Anyway, who's to say where your loyalties lie? You might be a Fenian spy for all I know.'

'I'm as loyal a subject of the Queen as any man, damn it!' protested Johnston violently.

'Can anyone vouch for that?'

A local magistrate, who had turned out to meet Booker's column on its arrival, volunteered the information that he knew Sam Johnston and confirmed he was a customs official.

'Then may I suggest, Mister Johnston, that your best form of help is to leave me to do my duty,' replied Booker, turning away with a nod of dismissal. 'Gillmor,' he called to a militia major, 'you can give the words for the Queen's Own to march out as soon as they are ready. We will move north to Stevensville.'

The major saluted and instructed a bugler. The piercing notes of the fall-in were soon arousing those people in Ridgeway who had slept through the arrival of the train. Johnston stared at the soldiers in disgust. If the Fenians had not heard the blasts of the train whistle then they would undoubtedly hear the bugle calls. Why didn't the colonel simply order out a regimental band to greet the invaders?

The ten green-coated companies of the 2nd Battalion Volunteer Militia fell-in. Johnston experienced a feeling of outrage as he watched them. Two of the companies were no more than boys in uniform. No. 8 (Trinity College) and No. 9 (University College) companies were raised from students and officered mainly by their professors. Fresh-faced, eager youths, who had regarded being ordered from the colleges during the middle of their exams with something of a joy rather than trepidation. They were off on a spree, a chance to duck the hard work of cramming and pouring over books. Children pretending to be soldiers. Johnston recalled that the *Chicago Tribune* had recently described these companies of the Queen's Own as 'the pet children of Canadian aristocracy'. Well, he supposed all soldiers were someone's pet children.

Major Gillmor, back in command of the battalion since Lieutenant-Colonel Stoughton Dennis had proceeded in search of personal adventure, looked on his command with a feeling of pride. He was a stickler for order and a well-turned out appearance. He waited until the battalion had formed to his personal standard of perfection, letting the officers inspect and re-inspect the 480 men until they stood in serried ranks as if on drill parade. Since they were to form the advance guard of the march, Gillmor ordered Captain Edwards's No. 5 company to the front. The company were armed with the latest Spencer repeating rifles while the other companies had single shot breechloading Enfields. If there were Fenians ahead then they would be in for a shock. The Spencer was Major Gillmor's pride and joy. It carried a seven-round magazine firing a .52 calibre metal-rimmed cartridge. Gillmor had recently boasted in the mess that if his entire battalion were armed with the Spencer rifle he would take on the entire Fenian army with the Queen's Own alone.

Finally satisfied, Gillmor signalled the order for the companies to march off.

Booker turned to his adjutant, Lieutenant Henery, and asked him to tell the railroad engineer to take the train back to Port Colborne. It had completely slipped his mind that he had promised to send the engine towards Fort Erie to signal Colonel Dennis.

'What about the extra ammunition on the train, sir?' queried his adjutant. 'Shouldn't that be offloaded?'

'We can't carry it with us,' Booker shrugged as if it were of no great importance. 'Let the train take it back to Port Colborne.'

Henery went off to perform his task. It occurred to him momentarily that if there was to be a real battle then the extra ammunition would come in handy. But perhaps there would not be a 'real battle' after all. Colonel Booker knew what he was doing. He didn't seem to take the Fenian threat all that seriously.

Booker mounted his horse. It was the only horse in the column and Booker had insisted that it be brought in the guard's van of the train. After all, it would not do for the colonel to march with his men. While Booker was mounting, Major Skinner and Major Cattley were forming up the six redcoated companies of the 13th Battalion, 265 men proudly clad in the traditional British uniforms of red jackets and white trousers with white crossbelts. They were to march off next while Captain Davis's company of York Volunteer Rifles and Captain Jackson's company of Caledonia Volunteer Rifles, another hundred men, were to form the rearguard of the column.

The column began to march out of Ridgeway northwards. They marched with good discipline and high spirits. Each company had a drummer boy who beat the monotonous marching pace. Their banners cracked and fluttered bravely in the morning breeze. A few men in the ranks of the Queen's Own started up a ragged chorus to the popular refrain, 'Tramp, tramp, tramp, the boys are marching . . .':

> Shout, shout, shout ye loyal Britons!
> Cheer up, let the rabble come;
> For beneath the Union Jack
> We will drive the Fenians back
> And we'll fight for our beloved Canadian home.

Major Gillmor snapped an order to stop the singing in the ranks. Nevertheless, the column marched blithely on with light hearts and good cheer . . . almost heedlessly northward. Comfortable on his horse in the centre of the column, Lieutenant-Colonel Alfred Booker smiled complacently. He had not bothered to send out scouts nor flanking companies. What need was there? He had not believed that panic-stricken civilian, Johnston, for one moment. The Fenians were miles away and they were only a mob of drunken Irish anyway. With an easy, nonchalant step, to the beat of their drums and fluttering of their banners, the column proceeded on its way.

Colonel Owen Starr stood by the porch of 'The Smugglers' Home' tavern and stared down the road in the direction of Ridgeway. His mouth was dry with anticipation and his palms itched. Starr was a sensitive young man with a keen grasp of history. Even now he was experiencing a tremendous feeling of identity with the past. Not since the battles of the '98 uprising had Irish soldiers actually stood face to face with the British – as an army against an army. Neither the scuffles of Robert Emmet's rising in 1803 nor the skirmishes of 1848 could really be described as battles. This would be a battle. He ran a tongue over his lips to wet them and glanced anxiously to where his men were deployed among the outbuildings of the tavern and behind the hedges and trees that bordered the Garrison Road. Spaulding had already removed the tavern owner, Michael Hoffman, and his family, into the cellars for safety and placed riflemen at the windows. Yes, Owen Starr had a sense of history and he wondered what history would eventually have to say of this moment.

Far off came a sound. He held his head to one side listening. It was the muffled beat of drums, regular, monotonous, giving out the marching time. The sound was growing more distinct. Starr felt his heart surging. He unsheathed his sword. Not since the battles of Vinegar Hill nor of Tara . . . and he was privileged to give the very first order which could mark the beginning of the end of English rule in Ireland.

The front of the column swung into his vision along the winding road ahead. He stared, frowning at the ranks of dark green uniforms. Were they Fenians? He blinked. There was no mistaking the fluttering Union flag at their head. Hadn't Devlin mentioned something about militia uniforms being green? Well, there was the Union flag and their company standards. There was no mistake. He turned, realizing that his officers were gazing at him expectantly.

He raised his sword.

There was a shot. Damn! Damn! Damn! One of his men had moved into firing position without waiting for orders and had been spotted. The advancing British company had come to an abrupt halt, some kneeling, some standing and had commenced firing.

Starr swung his sword downwards. The roar of Springfield and Spencer rifles resounded like thunder.

The British were disciplined. Starr gave them that. They had halted to form a firing line. He could see companies beginning to double out to right and left to assume supporting positions. The rapidity of the British fire informed Starr that the enemy were equipped with repeating rifles . . . at least in their centre. The flanking companies seemed much slower in returning fire. Enfields, he thought. Muzzle or single shot breechloaders. It was curious how detached one became in spite of the fact that the air was alive with the whine and crash of bullets. Lead splintered the wood of the building where he was standing yet he made no effort to find cover. He pulled out his pocket watch and glanced at it with a thin smile. It was nearly eight o'clock. The first engagement of the war of liberation. Saturday, 2 June 1866. That would be an item for the history books in future years. He wondered what the British commander was thinking.

Lieutenant-Colonel Booker was in a state of shock. How suddenly it had begun. How abruptly. He had not believed the man, Johnston, when he had said the Fenians were close. Yet here they were; scarcely a mile out of Ridgeway and here they were. He sat on his horse almost frozen in inaction. Ahead of him, Major Gillmor had dealt with the opening movements of the encounter. He had ordered his No. 5 company to stay put in line of fire, keeping up a rapid reply with their new Spencer repeaters, while the rest of the battalion extended from the centre: No. 1 company moving to the left flank and No. 2 company to the right flank with the remaining companies deployed in supporting positions. By the time Booker was recovered from his shock, Major Gillmor had performed all the counter-measures necessary.

Booker's adjutant, Lieutenant Henery, went forward to consult with Gillmor and establish the enemy positions. Major Skinner, Booker's second-in-command of the 13th Battalion, suggested that the companies of the York and Caledonia Rifles should be deployed in the fields on either side as flanking protection. Booker waved a hand helplessly and Skinner took it as an assent. As the colonel sat in indecision, waiting for Lieutenant Henery to come back with a report, a railroad man came riding up from Ridgeway. He had a telegraph from Colonel Peacocke. Peacocke's column were delaying their departure from Chippewa until after dawn to await reinforcements. Peacocke suggested that Booker likewise delay his departure from Port Colborne. It was too late. The battle was joined and he was on his own. Booker found himself sweating.

Lieutenant Henery was back, his face flushed. 'Major Gillmor has engaged the enemy, sir,' he said unnecessarily. 'He reckons there are just a few hundred of them stretched around a tavern up by the crossroads ahead. He is deploying flanking companies and aims to push forward on the enemy centre. He will use the Queen's Own but suggests that the 13th Battalion should move forward in support behind his centre companies.'

Booker began to feel a degree of relief. 'A few hundred, you say?' he asked eagerly.

'That's Major Gillmor's estimation.'

'A few hundred bloody Irish rebels, eh?' Booker drew himself up confidently. Maybe this was Providence. Peacocke had not moved yet and Dennis was wandering around Fort Erie. He, Alfred Booker, was engaging the enemy. He would drive back the Fenian threat. He would attack and push the rabble back to Fort Erie where Dennis would be waiting for them. A few hundred drunken Irish! Dennis had been right. The only war the Irish knew was how to shoot at a man from behind a hedgerow. By damn! This would be Booker's moment of glory.

'Instruct Major Gillmor to press his attack, Henery. We'll sweep these bastards all the way back to the Niagara and pin them between Dennis and ourselves. Then we can crush them, by God!' His face was flushed with anticipated victory.

Owen Starr watched the deployment of the British with a grim smile. He watched the battalion and company standards and made notes in his notebook. Had the British fought four years of the type of warfare his Irish troops had fought, then they would not have made so free with their banners which showed the enemy not only where the troops were rallying but the points of attack. He turned to John Spaulding.

'The British are gathering for a frontal assault on our centre,' he said, almost casually, drawing out a cigar and lighting it with slow deliberation. He gave a few puffs. 'I think it's about time to get the hell out of here. They'll try to flank us right and left.'

Lieutenant-Colonel Spaulding nodded. 'Are our companies to fall back in alternate sections?'

'Damned right,' agreed Starr. 'Any wounded?'

'A few superficial wounds, nothing serious.'

'Dead?'

Spaulding shook his head.

'It won't stay that way,' Starr sighed. 'Those boys,' nodding to the British lines, 'are pretty handy with their toys. Tell our lads to stay low and keep with their companies.'

Spaulding moved off hurriedly.

The first lines of Starr's skirmishers pulled back fifty yards, covered by the second lines. The process was repeated. Slowly and carefully the Irish troops withdrew through the cultivated fields and orchards that spread on either side of the Ridge Road, moving towards the distant brick farmhouse where O'Neill and the main force were waiting. Owen Starr was the last to leave the roadside tavern with a small company of escorting riflemen. He walked among them calmly, smoking and chewing on his cigar as if out for a Sunday stroll with friends.

A bugle sounded harshly across the fields.

'The British are fond of their bugle calls, sir,' grinned Spaulding as he rejoined Starr.

'I'm pleased they are, John,' grunted the colonel. 'It tells us what they are doing.' He swept an arm to the fields on his left. 'Warn those companies over there to watch for British skirmishers coming through those woods.'

'The men there are confused, sir,' replied Spaulding. 'There are men in dark green uniforms there.'

'British militia wear dark green. Tell our lads to be careful. We don't want any confusion about who to shoot at.'

Starr brought his men into new lines taking advantage of a sizable copse just in front of the brick farmhouse. It was a large maple grove which gave them good cover and a commanding view over the cultivated fields.

Gavin, seated on his horse on the rise of high ground which O'Neill had made his command point, peered across the wooded countryside through his field-glasses. From his elevated position he could see the dark fluttering banners of the British moving forward. Around him those officers who did not possess spyglasses pressed him for information.

'They are advancing against Colonel Starr's new positions.'

O'Neill himself was excited. 'By God, Owen has executed his withdrawal brilliantly,' he enthused. 'The British commander has fallen for our ruse.'

'Redcoats!' It was O'Neill's adjutant, Fitzpatrick who swung his hand dramatically. 'The British are committing redcoats on our centre.'

Those who had glasses could see companies of redcoats doubling across the fields towards the maple grove where Starr had taken up his position.

'That means they've committed their regulars,' muttered O'Neill. 'Come on, Owen! Don't hang about there. Withdraw to this side of the farmhouse.'

Gavin noticed the movement to the right. 'Flanking movement, sir. Militiamen are moving up towards Colonel Hoy's position on our right.'

'He'll take care of them. But Owen is too far forward. He must fall back!'

'Flanking movement to the left!' called Major Canty, who was watching that area of the field. 'Skirmishers coming through the woods. Kilted, I think. That must be a Highland company down there.'

'Grace will halt them,' O'Neill replied absently. He was preoccupied with Starr's positions. The noise of gunfire rose deafeningly. Evidently, Starr was hotly disputing the advance of the redcoats who had taken over the centre attack from the green uniformed militia. O'Neill whistled softly in appreciation at the precision in which the redcoated troops pressed their attack.

'It's bravely done. Bravely done. We're facing good troops whether they be militia or regulars.'

'Only regulars wear redcoats, colonel,' offered Major Canty. 'I can't identify what regiment they are but I'd swear they must be regulars.'

'Whoever they are, they fight well.' O'Neill focused his field-glasses toward's Starr's position again. 'Damn it! Send a man down to tell Owen to fall back now. If he doesn't he'll be cut to ribbons. He must fall back to this side of the farmhouse and use the fencing along the road there as barricades.'

'I'll go,' Gavin offered.

'No,' O'Neill snapped. 'I want you here. Send one of your men.'

Corporal Collins edged forward on his horse, his face flushed. 'Be damned, I'll go, sir,' he offered.

Gavin repeated the message and watched the corporal gallop away towards the firing. Major Canty, who was watching the left flank, gave a cry of excitement.

'There's at least a couple of militia companies down there who have nearly outflanked Colonel Starr,' he called.

O'Neill swung round. 'Colonel Grace is engaging them. He'll hold them back.'

Behind them Gavin noticed that the men of O'Neill's own regiment, the 13th Regiment, were restless. O'Neill, also observing their restiveness, turned to them with a frown. 'Steady, lads!' he called. 'You'll soon get a bellyful of fighting if that is what you want.'

A growl rose up from the ranks.

'Give the order, Colonel John!' sung out a man in the ranks.

O'Neill grinned. 'Patience, men!' He turned back and bit his lip as he gazed down the hill. 'Starr isn't moving. Devlin, your man couldn't have got through.'

Major Canty eased forward. 'I'll go,' he said and before O'Neill replied he was sending his mount charging down, jumping the split rail fences, towards the maple copse. They watched his figure, crouched in the saddle, until it disappeared beyond the trees.

'Hoy's men are checking the flanking movement on the right,' called Gavin, turning to watch.

'I'm not concerned with the flanks,' flung back O'Neill. 'The British commander is putting all the pressure on our centre. He's only using the flanks as skirmishing lines and not building up an attack from them. If I break his centre attack then I shall break him but Starr has to pull back.'

They watched in silence for a while.

'Major Canty must have made it,' O'Neill's adjutant Fitzpatrick exclaimed, waving excitedly.

They saw the Irish companies begin to move backward from the maple copse, moving back to the roadway beyond the brick farmhouse. Gavin remembered from his map that this was marked as the Bertie Road which formed a crossroad with the Ridge Road just to their right where the brick farmhouse stood. The men of Starr's regiment were falling back in good order but the redcoats were pressing their attack now, sensing victory. They were raising a withering fire and even from this position they could hear the occasional scream of a man as he was hit.

O'Neill watched with critical impatience. Starr had moved back to the road, ordering his men to use the split rail fencing as breastworks. The redcoats had fixed bayonets, they could see the sun glinting as it caught on them, making them flash through the acrid smoke which drifted across the fields and through the woods. Bugles were sounding and the redcoats were forming into lines.

'They're going to charge, sir,' muttered Fitzpatrick.

'By damn,' breathed O'Neill, 'if that isn't one of the prettiest sights that I have ever witnessed.'

Gavin frowned wondering if he was being sarcastic. O'Neill was serious.

'It's a well-formed line and a brave advance, right enough,' Fitzpatrick was admitting.

'In line of battle in their redcoats they look almost beautiful,' O'Neill admitted.

'I wonder if Colonel Starr thinks so?' Gavin grunted.

O'Neill pulled a face. 'Your rebuke is well taken, Captain Devlin.'

The gunfire had become desultory. Now all was quiet as the British reformed their lines. It lasted a few moments before a bugle sounded and the crash of rifle fire started again. All the Irish units except O'Neill's impatient 13th Regiment were engaged. Starr's men were coming under the heaviest assault. Gavin ground his teeth as he saw bodies, like discarded rag dolls, sprawled here and there across the fields. There would be dead to be counted soon. There were always dead to be counted.

A soldier came running up the hill, panting and breathless. 'Colonel O'Neill!'

O'Neill moved forward. 'What is it, soldier?' he demanded.

'Colonel Starr's compliments, sir, but the British attack is too strong. He wants to pull back and form a new line.'

O'Neill uttered a profanity. Father MacMahon, watching with a couple of civilians – Gavin thought they were newspapermen – glanced to Gavin and grimaced wryly.

'By damn, no! You go back, son, and tell Colonel Starr that he is to hold on. Tell him that I am bringing Colonel Hoy's regiment over to press an attack from the flank.'

The man made to turn.

'By the way, son,' called O'Neill, 'why didn't Major Canty come back . . . it would have been quicker to send a messenger on horseback.'

The soldier frowned. 'Major Canty? Oh, the major on the horse . . . the horse was killed sir. The major's been shot through the chest. I think he's dead, sir.'

O'Neill bit his lip. 'Get that message to Colonel Starr then, son.' O'Neill glanced to Gavin. It was a moment of unspoken compassion and regret. 'You're chief intelligence officer now, Devlin.'

'Yes, sir,' Gavin said. He could not feel shock, nor even a sense of loss. He was back at war and four years of war had created a shell around his feelings, confining them into small recesses in his mind.

'Devlin,' O'Neill was speaking again, 'this is your moment, man. Take your troop and ride hell for leather across to Colonel Hoy's position. I want the 7th Regiment to break off its skirmishing lines and move up to Starr's right flank as if to build up an attack. That ought to ease the pressure from his centre. Understand?'

Gavin nodded.

'Make as much noise as you want when you gallop across. With any luck the militia companies might mistake you for a cavalry unit and be discouraged,' O'Neill added with a grin.

Gavin threw up his hand in acknowledgment and turned to where Lieutenant Boyd with the rest of the small troop stood waiting.

'This way!' he cried, leading them off at a fast canter down on to the Ridge Road and towards the crossroads to the Bertie Road. It would be easier to gallop along the road towards Colonel Hoy's positions than to attempt to cross the fields. It was dangerous but Gavin thought they might just get away with it.

Colonel Booker, still sitting astride his horse and using its elevated position to watch the progress of the battle, had taken up a position less than a hundred yards away from the crossroads on which the brick farmhouse stood. He was sweating freely with anxiety. This was not the quick decisive battle that he had imagined. He was facing more than a few hundred drunken Irishmen. At least he was not having to make decisions. Major Skinner and Major Cattley were moving the 13th Battalion on the enemy's centre while Major Gillmor had withdrawn the Queen's Own for a brief rest, ordering some of its companies into skirmishing positions on the flanks. The direction of the battle seemed out of Booker's hands. Now, as he sat, anxiously watching the points of the battle through his spyglass, Booker noticed a movement by the brick farmhouse. Sweet Jesus! The Fenian bastards had cavalry after all. Cavalry! They would all be cut to pieces. Booker slid from his horse in a fit of trembling.

'Bugler! Bugler!'

A young corporal sprang towards him.

'Sound, form squares! At once! At once!'

The bugler stared for a moment at the hysteria in Booker's voice.

Lieutenant Henery looked puzzled. 'Form squares, colonel?' he asked.

'Dammit! Yes, form squares! Form squares!' cried Booker. 'Get the men to form squares and prepare for a cavalry charge. I've just seen Fenian cavalry up ahead.'

Lieutenant Henery hesitated and then nodded to the bugler.

The notes were just beginning to sound when a young lieutenant from the Trinity College company came running up.

'We've seen horses ahead, sir,' he gasped. 'Our officer thinks it might be Fenian cavalry.'

Booker shot a look of triumph towards Henery. He was right. Of course he was right.

The bugle notes were resounding across the fields and the order was being shouted along the front, 'Form squares: prepare to repulse cavalry!'

From his command post O'Neill stared at the confusion in the British lines. What the hell were they doing, forming squares? Forming squares . . . ? He let out a great shout of laughter.

'Devlin's done it! Devlin's done it! Instead of frightening a few militiamen into thinking his scouts were cavalry he's frightened the whole damned British force into thinking it. They're trying to form squares. Come on, Fitzpatrick! Moment's like this are not sent often.'

He turned and moved back to the waiting lines of the 13th Regiment. 'Fix bayonets, lads!' he called, standing in his stirrups and unsheathing his sword.

There was a general movement along the lines and the sun gleamed and reflected on the glistening metal. An excited buzz went down the ranks to be silenced under a shouted word of command from the regimental sergeant-major.

O'Neill slowly raised his sword. '*Fág an bealach!*'

The cry was taken up by hundreds of voices. *Fág an bealach!* Clear the way! Clear the way! The ancient Irish battlecry; a cry that had driven the English from the field at Fontenoy in 1745 when France's Irish Brigade had inflicted the bloodiest defeat ever suffered by an English army. It was the battlecry of an ancient and free Ireland, an Ireland that had been and would, someday, be again. Clear the way! It was the fighting cry of the 69th New York Regiment of the Union Army. *Fág an bealach!* It had become the rallying call of the Irish Brigade. The cry was heard and taken up by Owen Starr's men.

'Fix bayonets!' Starr shouted.

And as the bayonets were fixed the cry became an echo of rolling thunder across the field. A cry of remembrance and of anticipation; a remembrance of a community of spirit with the countless exiles of the Irish Brigades who had fought for France, for Spain, for Austria, for Mexico and for America, men who carried the dream of Irish freedom to the four corners of the earth. *Fág an bealach!*

Colonel Booker's soldiers stirred uneasily, hearing the cry and not understanding it; to their ears it was merely a savage roar for none of them knew the meaning of the words nor the fact that they were words at all. Yet the menace of the cry was clear enough and they gripped their rifles anxiously as they peered forward.

O'Neill was marching his regiment forward now, line abreast, rifles and bayonets to their front. They marched slowly at first, down the incline to clamber over the split rail fences across the road and through the orchard, clearing the obstacles as if they did not exist. They marched forward confidently, an irresistable line of men with their standards, carrying the gold harp and sunburst on green fields, fluttering and cracking in the breeze. O'Neill rode before them with his officers, swords resting against shoulders.

Owen Starr saw their coming and raised his own sword.

'Standards to the fore!'

The colour bearers came forward, standing in full view of the redcoated squares before them. The effect was mesmeric. No one fired; no one from either side. It was a curious, strangely curious lull which sometimes occurs in battles where both sides come within reach of each other and stand realizing, perhaps for the first time, that the enemy is also human, that the enemy is comprised of individuals as well as they. Now Starr's men were clambering forward over the fences moving calmly into line as if on a parade, forming up behind their fluttering, cracking banners. Starr looked up at his regimental banner and muttered softly:

> We looked upon that banner
> And our memories sadly rose
> Of our homes and perished kindred
> Where the Lee and Shannon flows.
> We looked upon that banner
> And we swore to God on high
> To smite today the English might –
> To conquer or to die.

'*Fág a bealach!*'

They moved forward, running now, swiftly across the fields towards the redcoated squares, the cry rolling before them. Now the rifles began to crash on either side and men fell here and there but the irresistible line swept forward. It was the militia companies facing Colonel Hoy which lost their nerve first. Some of them had caught sight of Gavin Devlin's troop and whispered cavalry were coming. The cry of 'Cavalry!' caused them to turn in panic, turn running back, some throwing away their heavy weapons and knapsacks as they did so.

Hoy was quick to follow the advantage and called his men forward shouting that the enemy must not be allowed to reform. Clambering across the split rail fences, Hoy and Michael Bailey led their regiment of Buffalonian Irish surging across the fields. The militia companies who were facing them, the Trinity College company, with the York Rifle company broke before the wave. Gavin, with his small troop, following in Hoy's wake, paused to feel a moment of sorrow for the young men, students playing at soldiers. Yet all soldiers were young. It was the nature of things. Ahead of him was a young Fenian lieutenant, his sword flashing as he whirled it around his head, his battle cries lost in the mêlée. He reminded Gavin of John-Joe.

Edward Lonergan was celebrating his twenty-first birthday. He had never seen Ireland, having been born in Buffalo on 2 June 1845, where his father, Joseph, and his mother, Mary, had settled after fleeing from the poverty and death which would have been their portion in their famine-racked country. Joseph and Mary Lonergan had built a good home for themselves on Ohio Street, were devout Catholics and attended regularly at the Church of the Immaculate Conception. With the death of their eldest son, Thomas, in 1857, they placed their fond ambitions on their remaining son, Edward. With their daughters, Mary and Margaret, the Lonergans were an industrious and fairly prosperous family, able to buy an entire lot of 257½ square feet, Lot No. 98, in the Holy Cross Cemetery, the Catholic burial ground at Lackawanna, to ensure that the comfort they enjoyed in life would be maintained in death. Young Edward had worked on the long hulled ships that traversed the great lakes as a ship's chandler. During the closing months of the war he had served briefly in the 155th New York Volunteers. When the Brotherhood began to recruit its army he had not hesitated in volunteering to join Colonel Hoy's 7th Regiment being raised in the city of Buffalo.

Today was his twenty-first birthday. He should have been at home with his family celebrating his coming of age. Instead he was clambering over split rail fences, waving a sword and urging his men forward to a cry of '*Erin go bragh!*' That was when his life was brought to a sudden end by the discharge of a musket held in the trembling hands of a boy no older than himself, a youth dragged away from his examinations at Toronto's Trinity College. The ball smashed into Edward Lonergan's chest throwing him back against the split rail fencing with the cry of '*Erin go bragh!*' but short in his throat.

Gavin cursed softly. He could so easily have been John-Joe.

Colonel Booker wiped a trembling hand across his mouth. Around him confusion reigned. His men were running in haphazard fashion. The Fenian cavalry must be near.

'Sound the retire!' he cried hoarsely to the bugler.

'Sir,' urged Lieutenant Henery, 'wouldn't it be better to try to reform the lines?'

Booker shook his head vigorously. 'We'll fall back and then reform,' he shouted even as the notes of the 'retire' rose across the field above the crash of guns and the cries of the men. The strident notes of the bugle caused the redcoated square to dissemble. The lines of Fenians now appeared like some insuppressible force, like an unavoidable tide sweeping down. They turned in answer to the distant bugle and began to run helter-skelter into the lines of waiting reserves from the reformed Queen's Own who, catching the terrible feeling of panic, joined them in their headlong flight. Lieutenant Henery made a vain effort to stop them but Colonel Booker had already remounted his horse and was joining in the flight towards Ridgeway. Lieutenant Henery saw his colonel go, saw the soldiers swarming by in a surging, terrified mob, and cursed loudly. There was no way to rally them, no way to stop them. Their terror was too great. The enemy was remorseless.

O'Neill reached the brick farmhouse and its outbuildings and ordered his regiment to halt. He had seen the crumbling squares of British soldiers; saw them turn to flee; saw Owen Starr's regiment with Haggerty's companies in headlong pursuit. On his right flank, Hoy's regiment were moving after the fleeing militia. O'Neill was not given to useless gestures. He ordered his disappointed 13th Regiment to halt and ground their muskets.

Here and there across the fields groups of British soldiers were putting up a more determined resistance than their fellows. It depended on the ability of the officer, the non-commissioned officer or an individual soldier. O'Neill could admire their pluck. He saw Gavin and his troop returning down the road towards his position and waved gaily.

'Devlin, I want a couple of your scouts to ride back and see if there is any sign of the British column from Chippewa coming up behind us. Perhaps you'd better send Lieutenant Boyd. I want you to chase Colonel Starr and tell him to clear the field. He mustn't let the British reform . . . but tell him that he must not chase them beyond Ridgeway. Got that? Not beyond Ridgeway! If the second British column is on our heels, I don't want our men scattered all over the countryside.'

Gavin acknowledged and turned to issue orders to Boyd.

Colonel John Grace's 18th Regiment from Cleveland was beginning to push forward now. They had turned back the 10th Highland Company of the Queen's Own and were now pressing on the 9th University College company. For the soldiers of the University College company, their first time under fire had been disastrous. They had arrived on the field without their own officers, Captain Croft and Lieutenant Cherriman, both of whom had been detained at Toronto. Lieutenant Whitney of the Trinity College company had volunteered to take command of them. As soon as the engagement started they had been marched forward, ducking nervously at the sound of gunfire, moving through the woods to where the Fenians were supposed to be. Once they did catch sight of a man on a white horse, evidently an enemy officer, who seemed immune to the bullets which cracked around him. Every man in the company attempted to bring him down. Young David Junor, who held the company's medal for rifle shooting that year, was disgusted by his failure to do so.

The company had halted before a split rail fence and were told to take up firing positions. Abruptly they found themselves under fire from the rear as well as the front. In their dark green militia uniforms they had been mistaken for Fenians by other troops following them up. A runner had to be sent back and finally the firing stopped. Then they were ordered to clamber over the rotten wood fencing into a bare field and move up to the Fenian lines. They had hardly done so when they heard the call to form squares. They lay wondering what to do until a second call 'retire' came to their ears. They began to move slowly back. As they did so, they saw troops running helter-skelter in panic. A pandemonium raged behind them. The young soldiers of the University College company broke and ran just as Colonel Grace launched his charge.

Young David Junor, running beside his friend Will Tempest, saw his companion pitch forward with blood streaming from his head. Junor felt a fear that he had not previously known. Until that point in his life, the militia had been a game, part of the social ritual at university. It had impressed the girls in Toronto to be able to swagger along the streets in handsome uniforms. There was also excitement in the drills, the camps and the marching with flags and bands. This was different. As he saw poor Will Tempest die by his side David Junor was suddenly afraid. This was war. He ran; ran blindly, with the other members of the company. It mattered not the direction, only that it was away from the frightening, anonymous enemy behind them. By the time they reached the road to Ridgeway the company had lost three dead and four were seriously wounded.

On Starr's right flank, Captain Haggerty's two companies from Terre Haute were encountering some fierce resistance from Major Skinner's reformed companies of the 13th Battalion. Skinner had managed to hold his men in check in spite of the panic around them and the volley fire which he was putting up had forced Haggerty to halt his men. Private Thomas Lynch, a cavalryman who had joined the Indiana Cavalry Regiment only to find no horses available, had already been seriously wounded trying to storm Skinner's flank. Now Haggerty ordered a close quarter charge using bayonets. His colour-sergeant, Michael Cochrane, a big man from Indianapolis, raised the green flag and went charging forward, urging his men to follow. The last volley which Major Skinner ordered, cut Cochrane down, throwing him backwards and sending the flag flying through the air. A soldier running behind caught the flag as it fell and pushed it aloft again. The charge was overwhelming. Skinner ordered a withdrawal, slowly, firing each step of the way. His company was the last to leave the field with any semblance of discipline.

Behind them the University College company, or what remained of them, had reached the crossroads by 'The Smugglers' Home' tavern. Young David Junor was one of the last to reach it and as he did so he heard a voice crying from inside. He hesitated. The voice called again, 'Christ, help me! I'm wounded!' It was the familiarity of the agonized voice that made him pause and glance inside the inn. The man who had called out was one of his own company. In the taproom there were numerous men taking shelter or lying on the floor wounded. David Junor hesitated appalled at the bloody mess inside, at the bodies and the stench of urine mingling with the putrid smell of festering wounds. Near to the door there was a man from the Highland Company who lay with his arm nearly severed by a musket shot. He was moaning in pain and, seeing the frightened boy, called to him to get something to raise his arm on. David Junor hesitated, took off his coat and rolled it into a bundle. He placed it under the man's arm and this seemed to relieve the pain. A haggard-faced civilian, David Junor presumed it was the innkeeper, emerged from the rear of the taproom. His clothes were covered with blood and he was carrying some bandages.

'Are you a surgeon?' he demanded. 'Christ, we need a surgeon.'

Before David Junor could deny he was a doctor, a figure appeared in the door behind him. He turned to meet the levelled revolver of a fresh-faced young man in a strange green uniform. It was a boy, a fair-haired boy no older than himself.

'Surrender! In the name of the Irish Republic!'

Across the field the firing had died away. Only a solitary spasmodic shot sounded as the regiments of Hoy and Grace marched forward, having reformed their companies, moving down to the Garrison Road in the wake of Starr's pursuing troops. A pall of acrid gunsmoke drifted low over the fields which were now scorching under the midday June sunshine. The fragrance of summer grass, of earth and wheat, of flowers, mingled curiously with the stench of gunsmoke and death. There was a strange quiet broken by an occasional cry, the choking moan like an animal in pain, the heart-rending sob of anguish, of men hurting, of human beings in agony and wretchedness.

O'Neill rode down the Ridge Road with a grim face. He knew the sounds of the aftermath of battle too well to find any glory or splendour in it. He did not exult in victory. He felt only a sad satisfaction. It was necessary. A task that had to be accomplished. Now was the time to gather the dead and wound and, perhaps, time to utter a prayer of relief . . . of relief not of thanks.

Chapter 57

The noon day sun was fiercely hot. Gavin found the clothes sticking to his sweating body, uncomfortably heavy and damp. At least he was on horseback unlike the soldiers of Colonel Starr's regiment who were having to double-time across the fields in pursuit of the enemy. He cantered his mount down the Ridge Road, screwing up his eyes against the glare of the sun. The clustering flies were bothering his mare and he could do nothing to stop them except allow her to shake her mane now and then in an effort to sweep them away. But it created only a momentary relief. After a second or two they returned in their droves. As Gavin rode forward he observed the discarded rifles and knapsacks, an abandoned hat or uniform jacket, which lay strewn around. More poignant were the pathetic bundles of red and green which marked a dead or wounded man. Here and there were captured soldiers. Gavin passed a young redcoat weeping loudly and being chided with gruff humour by two of Starr's infantrymen. The boy was weeping and trembling in his fright. Gavin had seen such sights many times before in the aftermath of a battle. He sometimes wondered how he would behave in similar circumstances. All he felt now was an indescribable relief that it was over: that he had survived.

From the surrounding farms and houses civilians were beginning to emerge in bewilderment, frightened or angry as their character dictated. At one small wooden shack a woman ran out screaming at him and waving her fists, obviously thinking that he was in command of the Fenians by virtue of his horse. A man came running forward to take her arm and draw her away. Some children threw stones as he passed but they did not hit him. He ignored them. At the inn by the crossroads, 'The Smugglers' Home', a red-faced man, his shirt splashed in blood which was apparently not his own, sprang into the road before him and seized his bridle.

'Damn you! Damn you bloody Irish murderers! We need doctors. Get us doctors!' The man's eyes were wild and there was spittle at his mouth.

Gavin shook him from his horse and moved on. He tried not to think, not to dredge up his nightmares and merge them with reality. He tried to think of other things, not war or death. He tried to think of Kate, Kate Dawtry. He suddenly realized that during the conflict he had not thought of her once. It worried him. He had lived with death these last few hours and not once had he thought of Kate Dawtry.

At the crossroads beyond the inn he found Lieutenant-Colonel Spaulding forming up companies of the 17th Regiment to begin an orderly pursuit into Ridgeway rather than allowing a headlong run from the battlefield. Ahead they could hear an occasional discharge of a rifle or musket showing that not all the British soldiers had simply run away, casting their weapons aside.

'Sir!'

Gavin turned his head, aware that a young soldier was trying to get his attention. 'What is it?' he demanded.

'In the inn, sir,' the young man stammered, 'there's a lot of wounded. They need a doctor, sir.'

Gavin turned and saw a young man in uniform trousers and a white shirt. 'Who is that?' he asked.

'Britisher, sir. I think he's a surgeon. He was with the wounded.'

'These wounded will be protected, doctor,' Gavin told young David Junor. The student soldier nodded speechlessly. He felt relief that he had been mistaken for a surgeon. At least the Fenians would not kill him immediately if they thought that.

Gavin turned back to the Irish soldier. 'I'll try to find another doctor to help out,' he promised.

He turned and rode up to where Spaulding was about to march his men off.

'Where's Colonel Starr?'

'He's taken a few companies directly into Ridgeway.'

Gavin muttered a curse and turned his horse down the road. He found a veritable stampede before him. There was a confused mass of soldiers and civilians, men, women and children, on foot and on horseback and in a variety of vehicles – some even herding horses, cattle, pigs and sheep – moving in a disorderly, flustered scattering.

'Sir!'

A couple of soldiers emerged from a ditch dragging a civilian between them.

'Sir, we've a prisoner here who claims to be a doctor.'

The civilian was staring up at Gavin in speechless astonishment. Gavin gasped as he recognized the man. It was Jim Taylor. Taylor recovered first, his eyes narrowing.

'Are you with the Fenians, Devlin?'

There was no denying it and Gavin forced a harsh smile. 'As you can see, Taylor,' he acknowledged. 'What are you doing here?'

Taylor's scowl turned venomous. 'The noise of the battle was heard all along the lakeshore. I knew there would be wounded to care for. I gathered up such of my surgeon's kit as I had left and came to help.'

'Release him,' Gavin ordered. 'I know this man. He's a former Union Army surgeon.'

The two soldiers let go of Taylor's arms. One of them was carrying his bag. The other smiled apologetically at him.

'I'll look after your horse and buggy, doc. It may be that we'll have to requisition it, though,' he said good naturedly.

Taylor stared at the men contemptuously, his eyes wandering over their Union Army uniforms worn over green shirts.

'I'm sorry to see that uniform here. This is no place for it. I thought too highly of that uniform during the three years that I wore it to see it worn in such a wicked cause now.'

'Wicked?' Gavin smiled thinly. 'That's a matter of debate, Taylor, but it's a debate that must wait.'

Taylor scowled with hatred at Gavin. 'You made me a promise, Devlin. I shall kill you for this.'

The intensity of his tone disturbed Gavin. He remembered how they had become drunk on Kate Dawtry's cider once. 'If you are thinking of Kate,' he said brutally, 'she has known that I am a Fenian for some time. Even Young Tom knows.'

It was a stupid thing to say and Gavin regretted it immediately he said it. Taylor looked surprised and hurt for a moment before his face grew bitter.

'You're a liar, Devlin! A dirty thief, murderer and liar!'

The two soldiers moved in again with an anxious glance at Gavin. His face was white but he controlled his tautly stretched muscles. He pointed up the road to 'The Smugglers' Home'.

'There are men up there that are in want of a skilled army surgeon, Taylor,' he said tightly. 'Should you be called upon for assistance by the wounded of our army, I hope you will treat them as fairly as you would the British wounded.'

Taylor glared hard at Gavin, his anger deepening. 'I am a surgeon, Devlin, not a cut-throat marauder. I will scour the fields, roads and buildings, if I am allowed, and gather in all the wounded. I shall care for them without distinction.'

'Then you can start yonder, doc,' one of the soldiers said with a nod towards a nearby hedge. 'There's a British soldier in the field there that's in need of help.'

With a muttered oath, Taylor broke through the hedge to where a young man in a redcoat lay stretched on the grass. Gavin edged his horse up to peer over the hedge as Taylor examined the boy.

'Dead!' Taylor's bright eyes stared up towards Gavin. 'A boy,' he said, gesturing at the redcoated youth. 'A boy dead from exhaustion and heat. No glory, no wound. A boy dead because he was too frightened and exhausted to run further. Are you satisfied, Devlin? Does it make you proud to have overcome such a formidable enemy?'

'It's the fortunes of war, Taylor,' Gavin said hollowly, feeling as if he were chanting an empty formula. 'You should know that more than most.'

One of the soldiers nodded sagely. He could not have been more than twenty years old himself. 'All soldiers are boys, doc,' he said with grim humour. 'Except when they are dead then the enemy's dead soldiers become *men* while your dead remain as *boys*. It looks good in the newspapers.'

Taylor did not respond. Instead he continued to gaze for a moment or two into Gavin's face and then he said quietly, 'Damn you, Devlin! And damn all your Irish scum!'

Gavin let his lip droop sadly. 'If I wanted any Englishman to understand what we are trying to achieve here, Taylor, it would have been you.' He sighed. 'However . . . these two men will go with you. You are urgently wanted by the men . . . of both sides.'

He turned his horse abruptly towards the township. The encounter left him a little shocked and the predictable vehemence of Taylor's reaction at seeing him there had made him feel nauseous. He tried to stop himself thinking about Taylor and about Kate. He had to concentrate on the task in hand. Colonel Starr was at the Ridgeway railroad depot, seated on the raised platform, smoking a cigar and smiling. He greeted Gavin in high spirits as he dismounted and joined him.

'Ran like jackrabbits, eh, Devlin? That's a sight to be seen.'

Gavin nodded without enthusiasm and repeated O'Neill's orders.

'No need to tell an old campaigner,' smiled Starr. 'I've already halted the pursuit although I swear we could have followed them all the way up to Port Colborne and seized the town.'

Gavin noticed that Ridgeway appeared to be deserted of civilians. Many of the people had decided to flee after their troops, gathering whatever belongings they could on horse, mule and in carts and buggies. Someone reported that the British colonel had last been seen on his horse galloping down the railroad in advance of his fleeing troops. Discarded weapons and equipment trailed in the direction of Port Colborne. Starr's advance companies had been halted half a mile from the town and picquet lines had been established while the rest of the men had returned. Groups of soldiers were now entering the deserted houses in search of provisions and water. A couple of Starr's men were cavorting around two captured standards. Starr smiled across at Gavin.

'Not exactly battle flags but prizes none the less. Probably the first British flags captured by Irish troops since '98.'

'Whose are they?' asked Gavin not really interested but feeling he should respond to Starr's enthusiasm.

'We took them from two wounded colour-sergeants, poor devils. One is a company standard of the 10th company of a regiment called the Queen's Own and one comes from the York Rifle company. Our men have won their first battle honours.'

Gavin was thinking about Kate Dawtry again and did not reply.

David Junor had persuaded the civilian to help him take water to those still lying on the field of battle. He had done all he could for the wounded in the tavern and made them comfortable as possible. The two men, carrying buckets of water, began to walk across the fields. They had not gone far when they came across a young man lying with blood covering his stomach. The civilian with David Junor winced as he saw the wound and unctuously began to recite the Lord's Prayer while the young soldier tried to raise up his comrade's head and trickle some water into his mouth. The civilian had not completed his prayer when he suddenly burst into tears. 'I can't pray,' he cried. 'It seems so damned stupid just to pray when someone is dying like that. Can't we help?' David Junor shrugged. A moment later blood and water gushed from the wounded man's mouth and his head fell back.

'Come on,' the young soldier said in resignation as he rose and began to walk on.

A party of men in a motley of uniforms appeared from a small orchard and gazed in surprise at the two men. Their leader, a sergeant, saw David Junor's uniform trousers and raised his pistol.

'You must go with us, son,' the man ordered gruffly.

David Junor sighed and put down his bucket. The band of Fenians had several other prisoners with them, including a fellow student from his own company. The sight of his comrade made him feel better, not so lonely and isolated. They were all turned and marched back to the roadside tavern where a pleasant-looking man, obviously some sort of officer, gathered them together. 'You are prisoners-of-war,' he told them, his voice rough but kindly. 'You are prisoners of the Irish Republican Army. Behave yourselves and you will be well treated. Give us trouble and. . . .' He made a cutting gesture with his hand.

Gavin rode back to find O'Neill. Here and there the men were relaxing on the battlefield while companies detailed as medical orderlies moved about gathering the dead and taking the wounded to nearby houses. In spite of protests by a farmer named Weaver, who seemed to be spokesman for all the local inhabitants, O'Neill had designated some half dozen farmsteads around the Ridge Road as field hospitals and here the wounded of both sides were tended as best the circumstances permitted.

Most of the men were sitting or laying down, many taking a meal as no one had eaten since three o'clock that morning. They laughed and talked with one another in quiet self-conscious tones as if they spoke in a cathedral; indeed, there was something sacred about a battleground where men had died. Yet the tension of the fight was over, releasing in many a sense of macabre fun as their pent-up fears and anger were let loose and their talk was coarse and brutal, a black humour as they told stories to each other of how close death and mutilation had come or had, indeed, struck down their friends and comrades on that field. It was an expression of unconscious revenge for the fear that they had lived with.

Gavin saw O'Neill standing outside a wooden cabin where some wounded were being gathered. He hitched his horse to the rail and made his way up to the brooding commander. O'Neill was staring across the surrounding fields watching black crows flitting from tree to tree, croaking impatiently. He saw Gavin approaching and grimaced in acknowledgment.

'I've read that Napoleon was usually glad to look upon the dead and dying after a battle and sought to demonstrate a callousness as proof of his superiority, his magnanimity and fortitude.'

Gavin glanced at O'Neill, puzzled.

O'Neill shrugged. Somewhere, among the line of wounded who were being laid in a row outside the wooden cabin, there came a high wail of an Irish voice, reverting to its native language in pain and anguish, '*A bhean, a bhean, tabhair dom deoch! Tá mé nimhneach!*'

O'Neill's face was pale.

'*A Dhia, a Dhia, tabhair dom deoch!*'

The colonel grimaced angrily. 'Someone make sure that boy is attended to,' he called sharply to the orderlies.

He turned into the cabin and Gavin followed him. The smell was the first thing that struck him; the smell of urine where men in fear and pain had been unable to control their bladders; then the bitter-sweet stench of stomach wounds. Above all, there came the murmur of the wounded, the sighing and rising of their painful moans and the occasional scream of pain or hoarse cry for water.

'Is there a surgeon here?' demanded O'Neill, peering into the gloom.

Father MacMahon rose from across the room. 'No, colonel. A surgeon is what we need.'

MacMahon saw Gavin and smiled briefly in recognition.

'I saw a local doctor named Taylor on the field earlier. I think he may be down at "The Smugglers' Home",' Gavin said.

O'Neill glanced round, his face taut. 'We must have him sent up here.' He paused and looked down realizing he was standing by the bed of a wounded British officer. He bent down and smiled at the young man.

'Are you badly hurt?'

The man's redcoat was darkened with blood. He raised himself on his elbow slightly and grimaced in pain. 'Bad enough, mister.'

'What's your name?'

'Lieutenant Routh, commanding No. 4 company, 13th Battalion, Volunteer Militia.'

O'Neill's eyes widened. 'You redcoats are not regulars?'

'No,' the young man forced a determined smile. 'There were no regulars with us.'

'Then you fought bravely.'

'Thank you. You gave us a hard fight.' The man suddenly slumped back with a gasp of pain.

'Does your sword belt hurt you?' asked O'Neill in concern.

The man nodded. 'Take it off, mister. I am your prisoner. I suppose the sword is, by right of war, yours.'

O'Neill gently removed it, shaking his head. 'No. I will not take it, son. Its possession may be a solace to you . . . I will leave it by your side.'

The man gave a brief painful smile. 'Thank you, sir. You are kind. But someone less kind may come and take it.'

'Let me conceal it under the bedding,' suggested O'Neill, suiting his words to action. 'You and yours fought well, lieutenant. I wish you a speedy recovery.'

Gavin watched the joylessness on O'Neill's face as he rose to his feet with some surprise. This did not look like a man who had won a battle, the first battle against the British in nearly a hundred years. O'Neill had turned swiftly from the cabin.

On the far side of the cabin Father MacMahon was bandaging someone's bleeding arm. He glanced up. 'I'm glad you came through this safely, Gavin.'

'Thank you, Father,' Gavin replied gruffly. 'If I see the doctor, I'll send him along.'

Outside O'Neill was standing on the verandah of the cabin, his hands clutching the rail tightly, knuckles showing white. He sensed Gavin come up behind him.

'Damn it!' he breathed softly. 'Isn't it a saying that you cannot make an omelette without breaking eggs? When will these people learn that we don't wish to fight them? But we must be free . . . why won't they allow us to be free so that we can start living instead of . . . all this!'

Gavin did not reply. He had not the ability. A moment later Boyd, with the remainder of Gavin's troop, came trotting down the road and halted before them. O'Neill shook his head, as if to dispel his frustration, and a moment later was the professional commander again.

'What news of the column behind us, Boyd?' he asked as the lieutenant slid from his horse.

'Their advance guard has already reached Stevensville and are halted there. We were lucky. We fell in with a sympathizer from New Germany who told us that the main body was halted there.'

'How many troops?'

'Probably about 1,500, about a third of which are regulars.'

'And field guns?' O'Neill's voice was weary.

'A battery of six guns but they are expecting reinforcements hourly. There is talk that cavalry are expected and that a third column will be in Chippewa this afternoon with another battery of guns.'

O'Neill closed his eyes for a moment. His mouth crushed into a thin slit. 'Where's Major Canty? I need his advice.'

'Major Canty was reported killed, sir,' Gavin coughed uneasily as he gave the gentle reminder.

O'Neill's expression flinched and he sighed.

'Yes, yes, of course,' he muttered. He pulled a map from his pocket and, squatting down on the step of the cabin, spread it before him. Gavin bent over his shoulder with Boyd.

'The British have a column here, between Stevensville and New Germany. A second column will soon be at Chippewa. And then there is the remnants of the third column which will probably be back at Port Colborne by now. It might be rallied and turned to face us again. Our situation appears to be that we are outnumbered three or four to one without counting the enemy's field guns or the possibility of cavalry.'

They watched him in silence as he gazed at the map as if expecting a solution to spring from it.

'There seems to be only one direction in which we can go,' he finally shrugged. 'We must fall back on Fort Erie and form a defensive position around it. It will be the only way we can keep a secure foothold on this peninsula until our reinforcements are sent over.'

'Couldn't we move on Port Colborne and take it?' Boyd demanded. 'I doubt that the British could rally the men there in time, especially after this morning.'

'That would be a futile gesture with the column at Stevensville and a second about to start out from Chippewa. We would leave ourselves open to being cut off and isolated from our base at Buffalo. The column from Chippewa could simply move into Fort Erie. Then the only way we could be reinforced would be by the lake. No, we must go back to the river.'

O'Neill stood up briskly and folded his map. 'If you see any of my staff or the regimental commanders, tell them there will be an officers' call at the roadside tavern in half an hour. The men are to eat and rest. Those wounded who can be moved are to be loaded into wagons. The rest must be left behind. I want to begin a withdrawal to Fort Erie within the next two hours.'

He swung up on his horse and rode off. Watching his hunched shoulders, depressed with care, Gavin felt a sadness and sympathy for the man. He did not envy him the responsibility he carried.

Colonel Peacocke stared in disbelief at the unhappy, dust-covered subaltern who stood to attention before him. There was a tense silence in the taproom of the wayside inn outside New Germany where Peacocke and his staff were temporarily halted. The colonel was tired, his face yellow and puffy from lack of sleep. His eyes were dull and red-rimmed and he held his body with brittle tension. Shortly after sending his rebuke to Colonel Booker from Chippewa, Peacocke's command had been joined by a stream of reinforcements. Lieutenant-Colonel Villiers had arrived with another battalion of the 47th Regiment of Foot; Lieutenant-Colonel Currie's 19th Battalion of militia had arrived from Lincoln; the 10th Royals, commanded by Major Boxall, had also arrived and Captain Stoker's Volunteer Field Battery had increased his number of available field guns. The trouble was that the militia, in their eagerness to join Peacocke, had come without knapsacks or provisions. The furnishing of provisions had cost Peacocke a few hours' delay. Leaving Captain Stoker's field guns to protect Chippewa from any attack, Peacocke's column had not marched out until 7 a.m. The day was oppressively hot and his guides had taken the column by a longer route than was necessary. With the advance guard already in Stevensville and Peacocke's staff resting at a tavern outside New Germany, it was exactly 11 a.m. when a galloper from Colonel Booker's shattered command found the British commander.

'He withdrew from the field, sir?' Peacocke's voice was frosty with suppressed anger. 'You tell me that Colonel Booker withdrew from the field? Is that it, sir?'

The dust-covered young officer stared at his commander with wide, frightened eyes. It gave him an almost comical air. He could not bring himself to reply. Peacocke's staff officers exchanged nervous glances.

'Damnation, sir!' stormed Peacocke, rising suddenly from his chair and thumping the table. 'Booker and his men have fled the field. Fled! And now they are sheltering in Port Colborne like the wretched cowards they are!'

'Colonel Booker is in Port Colborne, sir,' confirmed the young officer unhappily. 'He has reformed the companies but the garrison is in a great state of confusion and all the troops that have been engaged in the battle are considerably exhausted from want of food and rest.'

'Battle!' sneered Peacocke. 'Battle, indeed! A mere skirmish.'

Lieutenant-Colonel Hoste of the Royal Artillery, feeling sorry for the young officer, broke in. 'Are there no reinforcements at Port Colborne?'

The young man shook his head.

Peacocke turned to his new adjutant. 'Are there any troops that can be sent to Port Colborne to put backbone into Booker's men in case the Fenians follow up with an assault there?'

A captain glanced at his notebook. 'General Napier has approved the despatch of the 7th Battalion, Prince Arthur's Own; thc Thorold Rifle Company, the Drumbo Rifle Company and four companies of the 22nd Battalion from Oxford. They should be arriving in Port Colborne sometime today, sir.'

The young officer from Port Colborne, eager to find favour with the commander, added, 'A defence militia is being formed by the local citizens, sir.'

Peacocke made a sound that was halfway between a laugh and a cough. 'Civilians! Though I'd lay a wager they would give better account of themselves had they been at Ridgeway this morning instead of Booker.' He sat back in his chair and signalled dismissal to the officer. His staff gazed anxiously at him awaiting his decision.

'Do we march on to Ridgeway and tackle the Fenians, sir?' Major Boxall of the 10th Royals finally demanded.

Colonel Peacocke shook his head. 'By this afternoon, gentlemen, I hope to be reinforced by the cavalry bodyguard of His Excellency the governor-general. Once they have joined us I shall march but not before.'

There was an exchange of glances.

'Cavalry, sir?' asked Colonel Hoste of the Royal Artillery. 'What do we need of cavalry?'

Cavalry were treated with scant regard by most of the general staff in the provinces of British North America; they were all infantry or artillery officers and consequently had little sympathy with the cavalry branch of the service. To such an extent was this prejudice imbued among the officers that the recruitment of cavalry was neglected and their use decried. The adjutant-general of militia, Colonel MacDougall, had gone so far as to state, categorically, that cavalry could not break a well-formed infantry square. He had added that the provinces were too divided with woods and fences to allow cavalry to manoeuvre and because of that fact cavalry had little place in guarding the borders of British North America. Peacocke had been one of the few officers to take note of the lessons of the war between the States and be reminded of the fact that Napoleon had hardly fought a battle where his cuirassiers had not overthrown infantry squares.

Peacocke glanced in irritation at Hoste. 'We need cavalry because I want to ensure our victory,' he snapped. 'We have just received news of the defeat of our troops at Ridgeway. . . .' He paused at the cries of protest.

'Hardly a defeat, sir,' Hoste had a superior smile on his face. 'A few militia withdrew after a skirmish. . . .'

'Colonel Hoste,' Peacocke replied evenly, 'a column of 1,000 British troops, whether they were militia or regulars, were driven off a field of battle at bayonet point by the enemy. They fled the field leaving the enemy in undisputed possession. However you might want to change the facts of the matter, that is a defeat.'

He paused and glared around at his officers who moved uneasily before his stern gaze. 'From the report we have received of our defeat at Ridgeway,' he went on, 'it should be obvious to everyone that cavalry would have prevented such a singular disaster. The cavalry are the eyes, the ears and the forage troops of the army. You may not recall it, gentlemen, but there are usually thirty days of marching, counter-marching and bivouacking for every one day of battle. During those thirty days a good commander relies for his information on his cavalry. Without cavalry a commander can learn nothing of the movements of his enemy and his infantry can never feel secure against surprise attack.'

He drummed his fingers on the table for a moment.

'As soon as our cavalry reach here we shall march against the Irish. Not before. Let us hope that we will then recover some of the honour we have lost by this morning's débâcle.'

Gavin and his troop of mounted scouts rode back to the brick farmhouse in whose grounds Owen Starr's regiment had made their stand against the redcoats. Groups of men were spread around, seated or sleeping, chatting or silent. By the split rail fences, before the farm orchards, the grass was streaked and stained with blood. Items of clothing and military equipment lay discarded. Orderlies moved here and there, gathering things together and collecting bodies on stretchers.

'Isn't that Corporal Collins's horse?' called Sergeant Nolan.

A bay mare stood tethered to a fence.

'That was his horse,' agreed Boyd.

They halted and stared at it, at the blood that was drying on the saddle. Then they became aware of a civilian in a white shirt and corduroy trousers regarding them apprehensively from the other side of the fence.

'Who are you?' demanded Boyd.

'I work at John Anger's farm, mister. That's the brick house across there,' the man replied worriedly.

'Do you know what happened to the soldier who was riding this horse?'

The civilian shrugged diffidently.

'Some wounded and dead have been taken to the farmyard.'

Sergeant Nolan grabbed the horse's bridle and they moved forward to the farm buildings. A group of soldiers were squatting around a fire in the farmyard preparing a meal. A few civilian men and women, obviously farm workers, were watching them nervously.

'Any dead or wounded here?' demanded Gavin of a sergeant who was roasting a chicken leg over the fire.

'Five dead over yonder, sir,' the man nodded morosely towards a corner of the yard. 'The wounded they do be taken down the road in wagons.'

Gavin dismounted and strode across to the bodies. His men watched him in silence. There were three bodies which lay stretched out in green uniforms and one in a redcoat. The last body was clad in a grey, tatty uniform. It was Collins. Gavin signalled to Boyd. He was turning away when he saw that one of the men in green, whom he had at first believed to be militiamen, was in fact a Fenian. A major. He could hardly tell from the head as it had been hit by several bullets and was not recognizable. Yet he knew instinctively that it was Major Canty. He dropped to his knees and fumbled in the man's jacket, taking out a pocket book. John Canty.

Boyd was examining Collins's body.

'I guess Collins didn't know what hit him,' he said with brusque cheerfulness. 'You can still smell the whiskey on him and the bullet went slap-dab through his chest.'

He picked out the man's pocket book and found a few letters and a silver dollar. 'I think he had a wife in Baton Rouge.'

Gavin didn't respond. He was remembering that Canty, too, had a wife; a wife named Catherine, and two sons, William and John, in Fort Erie. He had been dedicated to the movement, dedicated enough to risk his life to undertake the job of spy, dedicated enough to volunteer to give his life. He wondered whether Canty's sacrifice would be in vain, whether any one in future years would even remember that he had made it. There had been too many John Cantys, too many sacrifices.

'Devlin?' Boyd was trying to attract his attention. 'Devlin, the boys would take it kindly if they could bury Collins. He was a good man. A comrade. Three years in O'Brien's Louisiana Irish is a lifetime to be together in war.'

'It would be nice if we could bury them all,' Gavin sighed.

'The boys won't bury the British,' Boyd said quickly. 'You can't ask them to bury the British in the same grave with our lads.'

'I shouldn't think *they'd* mind,' Gavin gestured to the bodies. 'Death is a great leveller.'

'You can't ask it of them,' insisted Boyd.

'Hell, we don't respect men when they are alive. It's the least we can do to respect them when they are dead,' insisted Gavin. 'We'll bury all of them.'

Sergeant Nolan made the first move, breaking the awkward silence that had fallen. 'We'll bury them in that wood yonder,' he said as if settling the matter.

After it was over they returned to the farmyard to collect their horses. The other soldiers were finishing their meal, laughing and joking with one another.

'Do you know what's happening, cap'n?' demanded the sergeant who had been cooking chicken. 'Are the British surrendering?'

'Surrendering?' Gavin's voice was high with surprise. 'Why should they do that?'

'Didn't we beat 'em fair and square?'

Gavin signalled his men to mount up as he replied curtly, 'A battle doesn't win the war, sergeant. You know that. I guess the British haven't even begun to fight yet.'

Nearby, in the shade of John Anger's orchard, where the most intense part of the battle had raged, Mister Kean of the *Buffalo Express* sat with his writing block balanced on his knee, gazing thoughtfully at the surrounding countryside before commencing to write with enthusiastic speed:

The first battle in the Fenian-Canadian war was fought about two hours ago on and around the farm from which I write, and resulted in the decided repulse of the Canadian forces engaged . . . the forces on both sides fought with great bravery and showed admirable stuff. The Queen's Own from Toronto made several very gallant charges. . . . The Fenians fought magnificently.

Chapter 58

Colonel John Hoy's 7th Regiment led the march back towards Fort Erie along the highway called Garrison Road. He had placed flanking companies on the northern road which ran parallel towards the township. These were under the command of Michael Bailey, and Gavin, with his troop, were directed to join them for O'Neill believed that any attack on their column would come from his northern flank. If so, it would be up to Gavin to inform the rest of O'Neill's brigade as quickly as possible. Half an hour after Hoy's men moved off, O'Neill gave the order for the wagons containing the wounded to follow. The men of the 7th had insisted on taking the body of young Ted Lonergan with them in order to ship it back to his parents in Buffalo. Ted Lonergan had been more than a young officer to them; he had been something of a mascot and they felt they owed it to the boy and to his parents, waiting anxiously on the other side of the river, to take his body back for a decent burial. The rear of the column was brought up by Colonel Grace's troops.

The march back to Fort Erie commenced in good spirits, the men were still smiling and joking in relief following the initial shock in the aftermath of the battle. Several of them indulged in childish horseplay that was common among soldiers of all nationalities. Colonel Bailey, riding at the head of his small command with Gavin, allowed them to relax from the strict discipline with which he had previously held them. His men had suffered two dead and six wounded and those who had survived had earned the right to joke, laugh and rib each other. They had come through the baptismal fire of their ancient enemy and seen the hated United flag chased from the field. Several among the marching men started a song:

Seo chughainn na slóite 'teacht 'nuas druim a tsléibhe,
'S a mbrat ag croitheadh go hárd leis a' ghaoith. . . .

The voices rose and fell in beautiful harmony; slow and resonant, the words whispering with meaning. Gavin wished he knew enough Irish to appreciate the purposeful intent of the song. He turned in his saddle towards Bailey who was whistling the tune along with his men.

'What does it mean, colonel?'

Bailey grinned and glanced down behind him to a sergeant who was leading the company of singers. '*Cur Béarla ar sin*. Put English on it, Ciarán. Let's hear it in English.'

Without skipping a beat the sergeant's voice rose behind the counterpoint of the Irish chorus.

> See who comes over the red-blossomed heather
> Their green banners kissing the pure mountain air,
> Heads erect, eyes to front, stepping proudly together,
> Sure freedom sits throned on each proud spirit there.
> Down the hill turning, the blessed steel shining,
> Are rivers of beauty that flow from each glen,
> From mountains and valley, 'tis liberty's rally –
> Out! And make way for the bold Fenian men!

Throughout the marching companies, the song was taken up in Irish and in English as they marched slowly back towards Fort Erie.

Young David Junor, marching along with the rest of the prisoners behind the wagons of wounded, shook his head in bewilderment as he heard the singing. It had such a beautiful quality, almost like a hymn. They were surely mad, these Irish. One minute they were killing you, the next they were good humoured and friendly and singing like a choir of angels. Mad! No doubt of it. He stumbled. He had managed to pick up a military greatcoat to replace his lost uniform jacket but the coat had been made for a man of six foot and Junor was only five feet four inches. Even with the coat gathered at the waist and buckled with his belt, it formed a skirt that swept the ground as he walked. The guards were good natured enough but Junor's companions were nervous and silent. At one point they were halted and a Fenian sergeant brought them a can of buttermilk. Junor summoned up courage to ask the man where they were being taken. 'Fort Erie!' came the cheerful reply. At one farm some of the guards requisitioned a horse, buggy and harness and hitched them together. A dozen of them clambered aboard, shouting with laughter, and so overloaded was the shakey vehicle that it soon spilled them into the dust of the road, still chuckling. Yes, no doubt. The Irish were a mad people. Why were they always fighting?

The sound of gunfire was abrupt and shocking. The column was halted immediately. David Junor was awed by the rapid change of attitude of the Fenians from indolent good humour to brisk professionalism. He shivered nervously as he saw the determined way the men gripped their rifles.

It was about four o'clock that afternoon that Colonel Peacocke was roused from his brief nap in an upstairs room in the inn at New Germany. An aide told him that the Fenians were falling back along the road towards Fort Erie. There was a telegraph, too, informing him that Colonel Lowry had just left Toronto and would soon be in Chippewa with 1,000 men. As soon as Lowry arrived he would be in full command of the Niagara Field Force. Peacocke grunted with satisfaction as he clambered from his bed, splashed water on his face and hauled on his uniform jacket. With his aide hastening after him he went downstairs to join the rest of his staff, issuing orders as he went. They were to prepare to march for Ridgeway immediately. The orders were no sooner issued when he heard the distant sound of men cheering.

'It's the cavalry, sir,' announced Major Boxall entering the inn.

Peacocke went to stand at the door. A long column of scarlet-coated, white-plumed, cavalry troopers, came trotting down the road, the dust rising from their horses' hooves. A youthful major swung his mount away from the head of the column and clambered down before him, raising his hand up in salute.

'Major George Denison reporting, sir, with the governor-general's cavalry bodyguard.'

Peacocke acknowledged the salute. 'You have joined us at an opportune moment, major. The Fenians appear to be falling back on Fort Erie and I intend to follow them closely to prevent their breaking out again. Would you take your cavalry out to form an advance guard and scouting force?'

'What route shall we take, sir?'

'Directly into Ridgeway. If we encounter no surprises then I shall divide into two columns and move towards Fort Erie by the Lower Ferry Road along the lakeshore and by the main Garrison Road.'

The major saluted again and hauled himself back into the saddle, racing his horse a little to catch up with the head of his column. He raised his hand and the companies of cavalrymen increased their pace to a canter to take up their positions. The lines of infantrymen cheered loudly as they swept by. The enemy were retreating. They were pursuing. The idea appealed to them. It gave them a sense of superiority which they badly needed after the news that had downcast them this morning. The 10th Royals began to march off chanting the popular parody of the Confederate anthem 'The Bonny Blue Flag':

Hurrah! Hurrah! For Volunteers hurrah!
For Queen and country we will fight, and not for soldier's pay,
Hurrah! Hurrah! We're English soldiers brave,
If war will come to join us, the Union Jack shall wave.

'The men are in good voice,' observed Colonel Hoste as he watched the columns marching by the inn.

Beside him, Colonel Peacocke smiled grimly. 'Let's hope they fight as well as they sing,' he retorted. 'I'll lay a wager that their militia comrades went singing to Ridgeway this morning.'

'I'm sure the men will stand and fight, sir,' Colonel Hoste looked pained. 'I think you may rely on it.'

'Never rely on anything, Hoste,' Peacocke replied sourly. 'Certainly not on a man's courage. It's as variable as the wind.'

The standards of the column fluttered bravely as the multi-coloured uniforms of the regiments and battalions formed into a bright speckled serpent, twisting down the road towards Ridgeway.

As Colonel Peacocke was setting out, Colonel Stoughton Dennis brought his command to attention on the ferry wharf at Fort Erie. Twirling his Dundreary whiskers with a gesture of self-satisfaction, he cast a critical eye over his men.

'Well Akers, is everything ready? The Welland Canal Field Battery will be left behind to secure the township. The rest of us will embark on the *Robb* for Port Colborne.'

'I believe most of the prisoners have been loaded on board, sir,' Akers said.

A sentry called out further up on Main Street. They turned to see a civilian on horseback galloping down the street towards the wharf. One or two soldiers nervously brought their muskets to the present but Captain King barked a sharp order and then called in recognition to the approaching man. He went forward to greet him as the civilian almost fell from his horse and began talking volubly. Colonel Dennis stormed across in anger.

'Captain King!' he thundered. 'You seem to forget yourself. I did not give you permission to fall out. Perhaps you will be good enough to explain?'

King stared in surprise at the senior officer and then tried to collect himself. 'Begging your pardon, colonel, this is Lewis Palmer. He's a farmer from just outside town. Lewis, Colonel Dennis is in command here.'

Palmer, an elderly man with a sun-bronzed face, examined Dennis with bright, sparkling eyes which seemed to be amused by what they saw.

'Guess you'd better get your men on that tug of yours, colonel,' he gestured to where the *Robb* was drawn up at the wharf, waiting to load the remaining Fenian prisoners.

'Oh?' Colonel Dennis snapped irritably. 'Why is that, pray?'

'In about fifteen or twenty minutes the whole damned Fenian army will be here. They're marching for Fort Erie right now.'

Dennis smiled thinly. 'A contradiction in terms, wouldn't you say, Captain King? Fenian *army*?' His voice was pompously complacent.

Palmer seemed bemused at the colonel's reaction to his news.

'This Irish rabble hardly constitutes an army,' Dennis went on sarcastically when he saw an explanation was needed.

'Well now,' Palmer drawled, 'don't know how you define an army, colonel, but whatever you call 'em they've just had a shindig up at Ridgeway and chased 1,000 of our lads clear down to Port Colborne at bayonet point.'

Dennis stared at him in disbelief. He seemed shaken for a moment and then quickly recovered his poise. 'I'm not interested in rumours, mister. You are acquainted with military tactics, I suppose? A strategic re-grouping can become a retreat in the eyes of the uninitiated. You civilians make me sick with your rumours and exaggerations.'

'Lewis was a captain in the regular army, colonel,' interposed King angrily. 'It would be wise to listen to what he has to say.'

The commander of the Welland Canal Field Battery turned back to the farmer, ignoring the colonel's mortified expression and asked, 'It's true, is it, Lewis? Did the Fenians attack one of our columns and send them packing?'

The farmer grunted. 'True enough. There was a real sharp fight up by Ridgeway this morning, Dick. Pretty bad by all accounts.'

'I don't believe it!' snapped Dennis.

Palmer looked at him and shook his head pityingly. 'You'll find out the truth of it pretty soon, colonel, if you stay here much longer.'

'Indeed we will,' retorted Dennis. 'We will stay and meet this drunken rabble that you call an army.'

Palmer climbed back on his horse and stared in sad compassion at Dennis. 'Colonel,' he said slowly, 'you are either a very brave man or else a damned stupid one. A thousand Fenians will be marching down that street pretty soon. For myself, I'm getting the hell out of it. Good luck, Dick!' he added with a glance towards Captain King.

Dennis glared angrily after the man. 'Fenian *army!*' he gibed. 'You've seen the type of prisoners that we have been taking today. Do you suppose the others will be any different to them? They will be of the same slight material and of the same miserable character as the prisoners. Even if we have to resort to making a bayonet charge against them, our detachment is sufficient to deal with them. Our duty lies in making a stand against this rabble.'

'But, colonel,' King protested, amazed at the man's obstinacy, 'Lewis said. . . .'

'I'll not base my tactics on civilian rumours and gossip,' retorted Dennis. 'Rejoin your command, King.' He turned and raised his voice to the commander of the Dunnville Naval Brigade who was on the tug. 'Captain McCallum, get your naval volunteers off the tug.'

'Beg pardon, sir?' queried McCallum.

'Leave Lieutenant Robb on board with his crew and a few men to guard the prisoners. I want everyone else off and lined up on the wharf. I aim to fight this rabble.'

Hogan, who had followed the conversation with Palmer, intervened with a sly grin. 'I'll volunteer to go aboard the tug and stand guard on them prisoners, colonel. That will allow one of your sailor boys to handle his rifle along with you on the wharf.'

'Good idea, Hogan,' agreed Dennis, missing the duplicity of the man's intention.

Hogan was turning when he hesitated. 'Damnation! Guess we forgot about the prisoners in the schoolhouse. Give me a couple of men and I'll go and fetch them.'

A shouting made them stare up the main street. Another civilian seated astride an unsaddled plough horse was cantering towards them as fast as the heavy beast could move.

'The Fenians! The Fenians! Less than a quarter of a mile up the road!'

Dennis turned to issue orders and Hogan caught his arm. 'What about the rest of the prisoners?'

'Too late. Forget them. We'll soon have more than enough

prisoners once we teach these rebels a lesson. Get on board the tug and tell Lieutenant Robb to take it into mid-river just in case the Irish attempt to board it.'

Hogan glanced wistfully up the street to the schoolhouse. 'All right, colonel,' he shrugged. 'I guess I can come back for them.'

'Colonel!' It was Akers. 'I'll go to the railroad depot. They've opened the telegraph link with Port Colborne. I'll find out if the news about a fight at Ridgeway is true or not.'

Dennis acknowledged as the men of McCallum's Dunnville Naval Brigade joined the men of Captain King's Welland Canal Field Battery on the wharf. Colonel Stoughton Dennis turned towards them smiling and confident. He fingered his Dundreary whiskers absently.

'Well now, boys, fix bayonets. The regulars might be scared of a few drunken Irishmen but we volunteers are going to show them how this scum should be dealt with.'

Sergeant Nolan's face was slightly flushed. He had been sent ahead to Fort Erie but returned at a gallop.

'The British flag is flying from the town, sir,' he reported to Gavin. 'There's a tug with steam up at the ferry wharf. I saw a White Ensign on her jackstaff and there's about a hundred British soldiers lined up on the wharf.'

Michael Bailey looked surprised. 'One hundred men? No other troops?'

'Not that I could see, sir,' replied Nolan.

'Were they embarking or disembarking from the tug?' asked Gavin.

'They were just lined up on the wharf, sir. Lined up with fixed bayonets as if they were simply waiting.'

Bailey stroked his chin thoughtfully. 'The British must have sent troops round by the lake to land behind us. But one hundred is not many.' He turned and called Major Bigelow aside. Bigelow was his aide. They held a brief consultation and then Bailey announced, 'We'll move in.'

'It might mean a house-to-house fight,' Gavin pointed out.

Bigelow dismissed the idea with a chuckle. 'They'll surrender without a shot being fired when they see our strength.'

'It depends on how determined their commander is,' Gavin observed. 'I've been in a house-to-house fight before. A few determined men could hold up an entire army. I remember one small town in Virginia. The Rebs fortified it and were determined not to let it fall into our hands.'

'I don't think the British will fight for Fort Erie,' observed Bailey.

'If they do,' said Gavin, 'it could be pretty bloody. Each street and each house would have to be taken.'

'That shouldn't be difficult,' said Major Bigelow, 'when we outnumber the enemy.'

'That's what we thought when we went to capture the township from the Rebs. We lost nearly one hundred men before we winkled the defenders out. Know how many there were? Twelve!'

Bailey looked cynical. 'I can see that if you are moving through a mountain pass then there are dangers and a small company of men can keep you at bay simply by using the mountain sides as positions to rake your passing troops with gunfire. I can't see how a township would hold us up.'

'That's just it,' Gavin pointed out. 'What's a street but a defile, a narrow pass through which the troops can only move by narrowing their front? Defiles are difficult places for soldiers to manoeuvre and the sides of the defile are made up of houses. You have to take each house before your troops can pass through the streets.'

They came to the hill on the outskirts of the township, overlooking its buildings which spread down to the river bank where the broad blue strip of the Niagara flowed. They could see the steam rising from the tug and the small black figures of the waiting soldiers.

'Well,' smiled Bailey, 'let's see what their intentions are.'

He unsheathed his sword and took a white kerchief from his pocket. 'Have the men ground arms, Major Bigelow. I'll go forward and see if the British want to surrender.'

The afternoon sun was hot and the men were sweating freely from their march. Even Boyd, Nolan and the others of Gavin's scout troop were bathed in perspiration as they rested forward on the pommels of their saddles. There was a silence as Bailey, astride his white mare, trotted down the road towards the end of town, holding aloft his sword with its white kerchief. The street ran down a hill towards the wharves on the riverside where the black figures of the soldiers were lined up. Gavin raised his glasses and examined the rest of the town. There was no movement from it. It seemed deserted. Certainly there was no sign of any other British troops. Perhaps the commander of the unit had decided to surrender? He was certainly not ordering his troops into cover in preparation for a fight.

Bailey reached a corner, perhaps 150 yards away from the soldiers. They heard his voice call, 'Do you surrender?'

Gavin felt physical shock as there came a sudden crackle of rifle fire and both the white horse and Colonel Bailey went crashing down in the dirt of the street. There was a few moments of utter silent astonishment and then Major Bigelow began shouting orders for dispersal and attack. Gavin leapt from his horse and, unthinkingly, began to run towards Bailey's prone form. A captain named McGraw came running with him, moving from cover to cover as a fusillade of shots came from the direction of the wharf. The horse was obviously dead and Bailey lay bleeding profusely from his chest.

McGraw shouted a profanity and let loose a few shots with his pistol across the body of the dead beast.

'He's alive,' cried Gavin as he heard Bailey groan slightly. 'Let's get him to that brick house on the corner.'

They lifted Bailey between them and, half-carrying him, half-dragging him, they moved him to the cover of the house. McGraw hammered on the door with the butt of his pistol. There was a short pause and then a woman, with a white anxious face, opened the door a fraction.

'Our colonel is badly wounded, ma'am,' Gavin cried. 'He needs attention and a place out of the heat.'

The woman stared at him as if she did not understand. Behind her a man appeared and demanded what they wanted. Gavin repeated himself. The woman suddenly seemed stung to action. She swung the door aside and motioned them in and when the man raised a protest she shook her head.

'The man is wounded, dear. Doctor Elliott will have to be fetched.' She bent over Colonel Bailey and looked at the wounds. 'Bring him into the sitting room here.'

'Thank you, ma'am,' Gavin muttered as they laid Bailey on the couch. He glanced at McGraw. 'Will you stay with him? I must rejoin my men.' He hesitated at the door. 'Thank you, Mrs . . . ?'

'Stanton,' smiled the woman bravely. 'Mrs James Stanton.'

'I'll remember,' nodded Gavin. 'Thank you.'

Outside a fierce exchange of gunfire was taking place. A few yards away Gavin saw the blood-splattered body of Major Bigelow. He glanced around. The British were still fighting from the wharf while the Irish were using the cover of the buildings and pressing closely towards them. Colonel Hoy and the rest of the 7th Regiment had arrived by the Garrison Road and were moving towards the railroad depot and along the river bank. Outside the red-brick house of James Stanton, Lieutenant Boyd had found cover for the horses and the rest of the men.

'Pretty fierce,' cried Boyd above the crackle of gunfire.

'Let's get nearer,' replied Gavin. 'We'll leave the horses here.'

The six of them ran, keeping low, across the street towards a smithy's shop whose doors stood open. The smithy's fire was still glowing and the instruments lay where the smithy had abandoned them in his flight for safety. From the back of the smithy's shop they had a good view down to the wharf. Now they could see the enemy at close quarters and see also that they were in some disarray having realized the danger of their exposed position on the quayside. Behind Gavin, Sergeant Nolan muttered, 'Them sailor boys are giving a pretty good account of themselves.'

Part of the group were undoubtedly sailors and these seemed to have taken their own initiative for they were trying to move in a body down the river road, firing as they went. It was Gavin who realized that the steam tug was following them downriver and he guessed its intention.

'I think the tug is going to try to pick them up.'

'Leave 'em be, captain,' Boyd urged. 'They seem brave enough. It's the officer who gave the order to open fire on Bailey's white flag who I'd like to meet.'

On the ferry wharf the British soldiers now stood uncertainly. They had seen the tug drift downriver as the men of the Naval Brigade moved off under the guidance of Captain McCallum. He had not waited for Colonel Dennis's approval. The danger of the position was too obvious for McCallum to dawdle. Captain King, too, was beginning to realize that the tug was the only means of extricating his men from the countless Fenians who were flooding down on them. A mob of drunken Irish! He cursed Dennis for an idiot, or worse, and for placing them in such an exposed position under heavy fire from the front and flank. He turned to Dennis.

'We must withdraw, colonel!' he yelled above the noise of gunfire.

Colonel Dennis' face was a mask of horror. He was frozen into immobility, not even using his pistol to give answering fire. He seemed to neither hear nor see King. The captain turned away in disgust. Some of his men had broken ranks as their own sense of self-preservation took over. A number of them were trying to follow McCallum and his naval men.

From the cover of the smithy's shop Gavin saw the group of

soldiers attempting to join the sailors. The tug itself had edged in as close as it could to the bank. One or two men flung themselves in the water and swam towards it while others took long leaps from a wooden jetty in an attempt to land on its decks. A withering fire was being directed at the tug. It was then that Gavin noticed a man in civilian clothes crouching near the tug's wheelhouse and firing back. The copper of the hair caused Gavin to focus his field-glasses to confirm the recognition. Hogan! A surge of angry frustration went through him. Hogan must not escape. Not now. He must not allow it. He reached for his revolver.

'You won't reach the tug with that, captain,' Boyd warned.

He fired even though he knew Boyd was right. It did nothing to relieve his frustration. The fusillade from the Irish positions had caused the tug to give up its attempt at evacuation. The vessel was swinging out into the current, moving well into mid-stream and turning upriver towards the mouth of Lake Erie. A number of Hoy's men rushed down to the banks to take pot shots at the tug but the river was wide and it kept well out of shot. Gavin swore bitterly. Of all the men to escape he would have given anything to prevent one of them being Hogan. But there was no time to think about it now. The fight was continuing.

The sailors who had not made it to the tug had turned and were fighting with increasing obstinacy. The soldiers had split into various groups. One group was trying to fight its way along the river road with an officer, a tall man with magnificent side-whiskers, who seemed to be moving in a dream, oblivious to the bullets which whined and cracked about him. It was as if the man led a charmed life for no shot struck him. On the wharf another group of soldiers had remained and was fighting desperately using the fuel timber stacked for the *International* ferry as cover. Even as he looked Gavin saw their officer, a captain, go down with his leg shattered. Gavin admired the courage of the man for, from his prone position, he continued to fire his revolver at his enemies until it was empty. Then Hoy's men raised a cheer and were leaping forward with fixed bayonets. The bayonet charge unnerved the soldiers and they threw down their weapons but Gavin saw the wounded captain drag himself to the edge of the wharf and throw himself in the river in an attempt to escape capture.

Yet another group of soldiers, joined by the remaining sailors, was fighting its way towards a wooden house near the wharf. Gavin realized that it was the post office building where Starr had read

General Sweeny's proclamation to the people of the township . . had it only been yesterday morning? It seemed a thousand years ago. The group made it to the building and barricaded themselves in.

The crack of rifle fire and the harsh cries of command, the howls and clamour, caused John-Joe to struggle with his bonds in renewed vigour but with little hope of success.

'It's a battle,' muttered the Confederate. 'It sounds like our boys have come back.'

The door to the schoolhouse cellar burst open and two uniformed men appeared in the gloom. John-Joe's heart beat fast as he tried to identify them. From outside he could hear continuous firing and the occasional scream of anguish and pain drowned by the sound of whooping and cheering.

'Who the hell are yous?' came a broad Ulster accent as one of the soldiers stepped forward.

'Prisoners of the British,' cried several of the men. 'For Christ sake get us out of here!'

One of the soldiers came forward, slung his rifle, and stood gazing around in the gloom, shaking his head. 'Be damned!' he said mockingly. 'Now what are yous doing sat in this cold cellar when there's a respectable fight above?'

He took out his bayonet and began to hack at their bonds.

'What's going on?' demanded John-Joe waiting impatiently for his turn to be released.

'Steady, me boy,' replied the man. 'You'll be finding out soon enough.'

Gavin had moved his men closer to the post office building. The crash of gunfire was redoubled in its intensity. The British inside were apparently in no mood to surrender. Gavin waited until there was a pause in the firing before he raised his voice.

'Hey, you in the post office! Can you hear me?'

There was a short pause and a voice replied, 'Yes, Fenian. We can.'

'Let me speak to your senior officer.'

'This is Lieutenant Angus MacDonald.'

Gavin identified a Scottish voice. 'Your men are in a pretty desperate plight, lieutenant. Do you wish to surrender?'

'Not while we have ammunition, Fenian!'

To punctuate the reply came the crack of a shot causing Gavin to duck down as the firing was resumed. It was a withering exchange but little damage was actually done. Colonel Hoy's men were well emplaced while the British kept back from the windows. Hoy came crawling forward to Gavin's position to see for himself.

'We must take that building,' he muttered. 'The rest of them have surrendered but it will make things pretty awkward for us if we don't reduce that position. The building offers a good field of fire and a commanding position over the waterfront.'

'We could set fire to it,' Boyd offered. 'That ought to smoke them out.'

Hoy shook his head. 'I had a report that there were some civilians in there, women and children.'

'Well, if they hold out in there they can prevent any movement across the river,' Boyd replied.

The problem was still being pondered when the gunfire gradually died away.

'Look!' grunted Gavin pointing to the house. A white handkerchief had appeared fluttering from an upstairs window.

'Lieutenant MacDonald?' sang out Gavin.

'Aye!' came the Scots voice.

'Do you wish to surrender now?'

There was a pause and then the voice replied with tired resignation. 'Aye. We have no ammunition left.'

'Then send your men out through the door . . . one by one. No arms to be carried. Anyone coming through the door with a gun in his hand will be shot. Do you understand?'

'Aye. We understand well enough.'

Hoy stood up and shouted to his men, 'Keep your positions, boys, but don't fire. The British are surrendering. Don't fire!'

The door of the post office opened and a Naval Brigade lieutenant stepped outside. He was followed by a line of crestfallen men, a mixture of soldiers and sailors. There were about thirty of them with several walking wounded. They were followed by a number of civilians, mainly women and children.

Hoy moved forward, waving his men to stand up and follow him. They did so and quickly separated the civilians ordering them to move back to their houses.

'Are you in command?' Hoy asked the naval lieutenant.

'Aye,' the man replied morosely. 'MacDonald, Dunnville Naval Brigade.'

'Your wounded will be taken care of, sir,' Hoy assured him. He turned and ordered a sergeant to take some men into the house to check for anyone left inside and to bring out the weapons and any remaining ammunition. Then he told a lieutenant to take charge of the prisoners.

Gavin watched the proceedings feeling drained and exhausted. He lit a cheroot. The fight for Fort Erie was over as abruptly as it had begun. The familiar sight of the dead and wounded of both sides caused him to feel disgust. It had been such a useless gesture. He could not believe the criminal stupidity of the British commander. How could a colonel be so lacking in military knowledge and so dishonourable as to fire on a white flag? Hoy was still consulting with his officers when O'Neill rode down the main street with his adjutant, Roddy Fitzpatrick.

'So the British made a fight of it?' O'Neill observed grimly as he swung off his horse and surveyed the scene at the post office.

'They surely did,' Hoy replied. 'We didn't do too badly, though . . . three dead and about the same number wounded. But I guess that one or two of those won't make it until morning. Mike Bailey was shot. Some folks are looking after him.'

O'Neill pulled a face. 'Is he badly hurt?'

'Pretty bad,' Hoy assented.

'Well,' O'Neill sighed, 'set up field hospitals where you can. How about the prisoners?'

'We've taken nearly forty prisoners altogether.'

'Who was in command?'

'We picked up a Captain King. A game cove. Had his legs shattered but he tried to escape us by slipping into the river and hiding under the wharf. A couple of our lads hauled him out nearly bleeding to death. He is pretty vexed about his commanding officer. A colonel named Dennis.'

'What's he vexed about?' enquired O'Neill.

'The kind of words he is using about the man are "poltroon" and "coward". Apparently, this Colonel Dennis refused to heed warnings about our strength and placed his men on the deathtrap of the wharves. Just lined them up to be shot at. Captain King says the man simply froze when the attack began and was as helpless as a baby.'

'Do we have the pleasure of Colonel Dennis's company?' asked O'Neill with a grin.

'No, unfortunately. It seems the colonel has skedaddled.'

Gavin frowned and moved forward to join them. 'If Colonel Dennis is a man with side-whiskers then I saw him moving down the river road.'

'I'll order some patrols to look for him,' Hoy said. 'The man must be hiding somewhere in town.'

'He must be the officer who gave the order to fire on Mike Bailey's white flag,' Gavin said.

O'Neill raised an eyebrow. 'They fired on a white flag?'

Gavin quickly told him how the fight had started.

O'Neill's face was grim. 'Then I think we should indeed make an effort to find the gallant colonel.'

A group of men came hurrying down the road towards them. A sergeant leading the group called, 'Some of these boys were prisoners up in the schoolhouse, colonel. We've just released them.'

The first person Gavin saw was his young brother. He greeted him in astonishment, aiming a playful punch. 'What the hell are you doing on this side of the river?' he demanded.

John-Joe returned the greeting with a wry grimace. 'I'm glad to see you alive, Gavin. We heard that there'd been some fighting.'

O'Neill was gazing at the brothers in mystification. Gavin awkwardly introduced his brother.

O'Neill repeated Gavin's question. 'How did you get here, lieutenant?'

'I came across last night, sir, or rather early this morning. I have a message from Colonel Sherwin and Captain Hynes. Unfortunately, I was captured almost immediately I came across.'

'What was the message?' demanded O'Neill.

'Although all the centre army has now mustered in Buffalo, General Barry and the Union army regulars have also come in and stand guard over our supply routes. There is no hope of getting our men across without contending with the Union Army. Unless Barry gets orders from a higher authority and withdraws his men, Colonel Sherwin says he will only be able to move across by firing on the US flag. As he is not prepared to do that he feels there is no way he can reinforce you.'

O'Neill sighed wearily. 'What of the understanding Roberts and General Sweeny had with President Johnson?' he asked with bitterness.

'There has been no word from the President,' John-Joe said. 'No word either against us or for us.'

'Well,' O'Neill bit his lip, 'without reinforcements we are done for.'

He turned away to be with his own thoughts.

John-Joe hesitated and then, trying to ease the tension, whispered to Gavin. 'Did you capture the British commander, someone called Colonel Dennis? A man with mutton-chop whiskers who carries himself as if he is the reincarnation of the Duke of Wellington.'

'Colonel Dennis?' queried Hoy overhearing. 'No, we haven't seen him.'

'He's a bastard,' John-Joe added. 'Some of us were pretty roughly treated by him and an ugly-faced civilian named Hogan.'

'Hogan?' Gavin bit his lip in annoyance. 'Hogan escaped on the tug but I don't think the colonel did. I saw him running down the river road when the tug was already in mid-river and moving towards the lake.'

Hoy chuckled grimly, 'Well, if our bold British colonel is hiding in the town we will soon ferret him out.'

He turned and began to issue orders for a search.

O'Neill was leaning against a tree staring across the Niagara towards Buffalo. John-Joe exchanged a worried glance with Gavin.

'So near,' O'Neill muttered. 'So damned near and yet it might as well be a million miles away!'

Chapter 59

The last of O'Neill's stragglers came into Fort Erie by six-thirty that evening. John Grace's regiment was ordered to secure a perimeter around the town while the rest of the troops simply bivouacked on the streets under any shelter they could find. The prisoners were marched through the town and, together with those who had been captured in the fight for the township, were taken to the ruins of the old stone fortress by the lakeshore and held there under guard. They were supplied with a meal of biscuit, meat and water. O'Neill checked Grace's line of picquets personally, ensuring that his positions were protected by a semi-circular line stretching from the shore of Lake Erie to the south, through the low-lying woodlands, across the railroad and swinging around the edge of the town to the river road. He decided to gather his main force at the old fortress which he made his headquarters.

Gavin and John-Joe, accompanied by Boyd and Sergeant Nolan, made their way to Fitch's 'City Hotel'. The hotelier still had food to give them, especially when Boyd found a few silver dollars in his pockets.

'What were they saying on the other side of the river about our expedition, John-Joe?' asked Gavin as they tucked into the plates of rabbit stew. 'What do the American newspapers think?'

'I only saw the Buffalo newspapers before I came across. The *Commercial-Advertiser* said they could not credit the news and the *Express* was reporting that General Sweeny was in command and marching on Toronto.'

Boyd chuckled, 'I hope they've picked up a few facts since then.'

'But were they for or against us?' Gavin pressed.

'The *Commercial-Advertiser* thinks that we are going to be severely mauled by the British and that the idea of a Fenian success is preposterous. They dismiss us as being foolish and Quixotic.'

Gavin grimaced as the voice of Kate Dawtry sang in his ears. 'You are so like Grandpa Tom. Stubborn, high minded – a Don Quixote going to tilt at windmills . . . I love you Gavin Quixote Devlin. Give up this madness and let's go to San Francisco now, tomorrow, today. Immediately.'

He shook his head and tried to concentrate on what his brother was saying.

'The *Express* says that our plan can only be successful if the Administration in Washington takes a passive role and does not interfere with us. They are already hinting that the President has not issued a proclamation denouncing the crossing because of some collusion.'

'It seems confusing,' Gavin reflected. 'Washington is saying nothing but the military authorities in Buffalo are cutting off our supplies and reinforcements. Why doesn't Johnson make the position clear?'

'Politicians are famous for saying one thing and doing another,' Boyd remarked cynically.

'Was there news of the other movements, of General Tevis or General Spear?'

John-Joe shook his head negatively. 'There was no word up to the time I left.'

'Well, everything depends on General Spear's crossing now. If he can't establish himself in Lower Canada, where the people are sympathetic and should support us, then we have wasted time and effort to a wicked degree.' Gavin's face was worried. 'The people here don't really have any quarrel with us. They know less of Ireland than they do of . . . of ancient Egypt.'

'That's as maybe,' Boyd said, 'but we are here only to distract the attention of the British army away from Lower Canada.'

'And we've spent a lot of lives distracting their attention if nothing comes of our main plan. If the Brotherhood withdraw now and accomplish no more than a raid, it will be a criminal waste of lives, a criminal act.'

John-Joe stared at his brother in surprise. 'Nonsense!' he snapped. 'We've come too far to hesitate or turn back.'

'We may well have to, John-Joe,' Gavin replied. 'You say reinforcements can't come over the river? Then what can we do? We are outnumbered and surrounded.'

'O'Neill won't withdraw,' John-Joe said hurriedly.

Gavin found himself staring out of the window and thinking of Kate Dawtry again. He found himself thinking of the peace and tranquillity of the little farmstead just a few miles away . . . a few miles . . . The face of Hogan floated in front of him. Where was the man now? He immediately felt depressed. He was a prisoner of some remorseless destiny. He had never gone in search of his destiny, it had come in search of him and, where destiny blundered, his human prudence would not prevail. He was simply the prisoner of the accidents of life. It made him feel a sense of angry frustration.

When they had finished their meal they wandered down to the wharves. Reports and rumours among the men seemed to be changing from minute to minute. What appeared constant, however, was the news that the British had now surrounded Fort Erie and were closing in. The scavengers and looters who had followed in the wake of the Fenians with such eager delight were now hurrying back across the river as fast as they could. Military patrols on the American shore, or the three gunboats which now patrolled the river, were busy halting and arresting people who could not give a good account of their proceedings.

Along the wharves the men sat huddled, many of them smoking clay pipes or the occasional cigarette. They looked exhausted; two days and two nights with little food or sleep, and the constant game of chance with death, had made them pale and drawn. Yet the majority still held a sparkle in their eyes and there was a general good humour among them. Here and there a voice rose in song, songs of the homeland, chants of sadness, hopes of freedom.

'Gavin! John-Joe!'

They halted and turned as a figure hailed them while they were passing before a house near the railroad depot.

It was Father MacMahon. He stood smoking a cigar on the steps of the house, his hands clasped behind his back, looking for all the world as if he were standing in front of his own parish church. They went up to him and gripped his hand in turn.

'How is it with you boys?' the priest asked. When they had replied and asked MacMahon what he was doing he grimaced towards the house. 'It's John Canty's house. I've turned it into a temporary field hospital. I think he would have liked that.'

Gavin nodded, remembered how they had buried Canty in the little copse behind John Anger's farm at Ridgeway.

'Is Canty's wife inside?' he asked.

'Apparently he had ensured that Catherine and his boys were sent to Buffalo yesterday. But I've some wounded here. Some of them won't last long, poor lads. Poor brave lads.'

'Is there an English doctor called Taylor with you?' Gavin did not know what made him ask after Taylor. He had tried to put the vision of the angry doctor out of his mind and yet he found that he had been thinking on and off about Taylor and Kate Dawtry all afternoon.

MacMahon shook his head. 'We left him back in Ridgeway to take care of the wounded who could not be moved. He's a good man. Aye, even among the English you find good men. He used to be a surgeon with the Union Army.'

'I know,' Gavin sighed. 'I'm glad that he's safe anyway.'

'I was wondering if O'Neill has decided on his next move?' asked the priest. 'I understood that he was attempting to get a messenger across the river to obtain the latest information.'

'I don't know, Father,' confessed Gavin. 'We are just going down to the old fort now.'

'Well, it seems that poor Roberts may have been wrong to place his faith in President Johnson. He should have learned from history. Every time the Irish have relied on a power other than themselves to obtain freedom they have always been betrayed or deserted. It was the same when the Spanish offered to free Ireland from Elizabeth; the same when the French fought with us in the Williamite wars and the same when the French Republicans offered us aid in '98. We must learn to rely on ourselves alone.'

'Well, we're not beaten yet, Father,' declared John-Joe. 'It's not over yet. President Johnson may still keep faith with us.'

'Maybe so, maybe not.' Father MacMahon gazed thoughtfully at his flushed youthful face. 'From what I hear we are surrounded by 5,000 troops with field guns. We must either fight and die here or withdraw . . . evacuate across the river. Whatever happens some of these poor lads can't be moved. I must stay with them.'

'Is that a good idea, Father?' Gavin found himself worried for the priest. 'The British won't treat us as prisoners-of-war. Remember what happened after '98 and the Emmet Rising?'

'Yes,' Boyd interrupted for the first time. 'Look what the British did to the insurgents in Jamaica last year?'

The priest shrugged indifferently. 'I know what may happen if I fall into the hands of the British. We must expect that it is their nature to act against those they term "rebels" with cruelty and arrogance. A few years ago, when they crushed the uprising in India, I recall they strapped the unfortunate rebel captives across the muzzles of their cannons and fired them. When the civilized world expressed its indignation, the British justified their actions by saying that such terror was necessary to crush the rebellious spirit of the natives. Well, I will welcome martyrdom if it comes. The English share a proud conceit with all conquerors, past and present, and do not realize the strength of martyr's blood. Instead of intimidating those who hunger for liberty, it provides the very fertilizer which helps the seeds of insurrection grow. It sanctifies the cause of liberty and arouses the active support of many who have previously been quiet and complacent under the conqueror's heel. Every victim of a relentless and punitive justice will simply become an Irish John Brown whose soul will continue to march on to the final consumation of his interrupted mission.'

MacMahon suddenly paused and gave a self-conscious shrug. 'Perhaps I should save my sermons for my parishioners, though I do not think that I'll ever see that Indiana parish to which the bishop instructed me to repair. For the moment my parish is here, among the wounded.'

Roddy Fitzpatrick, O'Neill's adjutant, came riding by and hailed them. 'The colonel is holding an officers' call at the old fortress in an hour. He was asking for you especially, Captain Devlin.'

Gavin raised his hand in acknowledgment and then smiled at Father MacMahon. 'If this is goodbye, Father, then good luck.'

'Goodbye, Gavin. I hope that you'll never think ill of me for guiding you to this state of things. I believe that I did more than most in persuading you to join the Brotherhood.'

'If you guided me, Father,' Gavin smiled as he shook his head, 'then didn't I allow myself to be guided? I came to the Brotherhood for several reasons. Let us say that it was destiny.'

MacMahon pursed his lips: 'What was it Hamlet said, "There's a divinity that shapes our ends, rough-hew them how we will"? True enough, I suppose. Whatever God has brought about is to be borne with fortitude. Goodbye Gavin, goodbye John-Joe. If you see your father before I do, give him my kindest regards. God be with you both, and with you Lieutenant Boyd.'

They left the priest standing on the steps of Major Canty's house puffing at his cigar as if he were contemplating the evening air before his own home, deciding the manner of his Sunday sermon.

'The British ambassador is getting irritable,' Secretary of State Seward announced as he entered the oval study.

President Johnson looked up with a wry expression. 'Let him cool his heels a while longer. Have you heard the news from Buffalo?'

'Late editions of the newspapers are already printing accounts of the battle. The Fenians have given the British a bloody nose. The Irish in the city are already celebrating as if they've won a Gettysburg.'

The President's expression broadened into a smile. 'Maybe they have . . . maybe it's another victory for us. The telegraph wires have been burning between Ottawa and here. Shall we hear what Sir Frederick has to say?'

He reached forward and rang a silver hand bell.

A moment later Sir Frederick Bruce was shown into the office. He bowed stiffly and declined the offer of a chair.

'How are you, Sir Frederick?' Johnson greeted him jocularly.

'Well enough, Mister President,' the ambassador's voice was toneless. 'I am instructed by Lord Monck to reiterate his protest concerning the invasion of armed citizens from your country into British territory and demand your administration take action against the miscreants.'

'*Demand?*' Johnson's eyebrows shot up, his face paled. 'I seem to recall the gist of this message from yesterday, Sir Frederick. My reply is the same as yesterday. Our border is a long one.'

'Lord Monck refers specifically to the crossing at Buffalo.'

William Seward who had taken a watchful stance by the fireplace coughed and moved forward.

'With your permission, Mister President, could I point out to the British ambassador that this administration cannot be accused of lack of diligence in this matter? General Barry has already attempted to close the border at Buffalo.'

Sir Frederick did not bother to glance in his direction but kept his gaze firmly on the President. 'Her Britannic Majesty's government look forward to an early enforcement of the neutrality agreement between the United States and the provinces of British North America and the issuing of a clear statement from your administration declaring their intent.'

The President stared back at the bleak face of the ambassador. Were the British calling his bluff? He had thought he had made himself perfectly clear to Sir Frederick yesterday. He caught the ambassador's eyes and held them without saying anything. Johnson was a good poker player. There was a long, almost uncomfortable silence. Then Sir Frederick added reluctantly, 'Lord Monck instructs me to present his personal felicitations and wants me to assure you that he will give his earliest personal attention to the matter of instigating a thorough discussion of the dissensions that have arisen between our governments over incidents that occurred during the proceedings of the late war in your country.'

Johnson inwardly frowned trying to work out the precise formula of words. Then he smiled slowly. The British were wriggling. He had only to hold on a short while longer.

'Extend to His Excellency my personal regards, Sir Frederick. Tell him that I appreciate his assurances and will look forward to hearing from him as to precisely when we can proceed with such a discussion.'

The British ambassador waited, expecting the President to go further but Johnson had not risen through the ranks of the Senate with a lack of negotiating ability.

'In the matter of the violations of the neutrality laws . . . ?' Sir Frederick prompted hopefully. 'We have word that a very large Fenian force is gathering along the border throughout northern New York and Vermont. It is a matter of urgency. . . .'

The President rose, his face bland. 'And we are treating as such, Sir Frederick. Indeed we are. The neutrality laws are of particular concern to us and we have always endeavoured to maintain them . . . even in face of provocation. . . .' He deliberately let his voice trail off. Then he smiled briefly, without feeling. 'Thank you for coming in, Mister Ambassador. I am delighted to hear that Lord Monck is interested in a negotiated end to the claims for reparation which we have addressed to Her Britannic Majesty's government. I would certainly like the matter to be dealt with as quickly as possible.'

Sir Frederick bowed stiffly and turned for the door. As it closed behind him the President grinned towards Secretary Seward.

'I think we will hear from Lord Monck in a day or two. I can feel the British squirming.'

Seward shook his head cautiously. 'That's when the British are at their most dangerous, Mister President.'

Chapter 60

At 9 p.m. all O'Neill's senior officers and aides crowded into one of the rooms in the old stone fortress, one of the dormitory rooms set aside for the small guard of Royal Canadian Rifles which had been the ruined fortress's only garrison. O'Neill gazed around. He was looking old and tired. Gavin was amazed at the change wrought on the once debonair face of the colonel during the last few hours.

'Gentlemen,' he began, 'I will make no attempt to keep bad news from you. Earlier this evening I managed to get a messenger across to Buffalo where Colonel Sherwin is still in command. General Burns has still not yet arrived. The message I sent across was simple. I told Colonel Sherwin that the enemy will have us completely surrounded by dawn, if he has not done so already. He has at least 5,000 troops and is fully provided with field guns and cavalry. Our command here is now less than 1,000 men. It has no cavalry and no field guns. It cannot hope to hold out against a British attack.'

Owen Starr leaned forward pugnaciously. 'We won't surrender, John,' he said, a warning in his voice, a suggestion of disobedience if he was so ordered.

The others, Hoy and Grace among them, murmured their agreement.

'I have,' O'Neill said quickly, 'I have expressed my willingness to make this old fort a slaughter house if . . . by our sacrifice . . . we can buy time for General Tevis and General Spear. If the British have to thrust against us, then our defence will hold up their troops and artillery and perhaps allow our main objectives to be reached elsewhere.' He paused. 'I have now heard from Colonel Sherwin.' His voice was heavy.

Gavin suddenly became aware of a thin-faced man, with brooding eyes, sitting in the shadows in a corner.

'Surgeon-General Donnelly volunteered to come across and give me the message.'

Donnelly was on General Sweeny's staff and in command of all the medical units of the Fenian army. Donnelly cleared his throat.

'There are, at this precise moment, gentlemen, over 5,000 of our troops, ready and armed, in Buffalo and the surrounding countryside. A formidable army which is eager to get at the throat of the enemy. Yet there is no way of shipping them across the river without engaging General Barry's United States' troops. If our men move en masse to the river they will effectively declare war against the United States as well as on British North America. Colonel Sherwin's command is therefore bottled up in Buffalo and unable to come to your aid. They stand just a few hundred yards away, across the river.'

O'Neill gave a long deep sigh, his head bowed.

No one said anything. No one had any comment to make.

'Surgeon-General Donnelly tells me that Colonel Harry Stagg is willing to move his regiment of 250 men across the river under cover of darkness. Colonel Stagg is sanguine that his men can be floated across before the gunboats spot them. It is a courageous enterprise. I am forced to decline Colonel Stagg's offer. It will add little to the outcome of any attack by the British. Whatever we do, we must act alone now.'

'What about Generals Tevis and Spear?' asked Colonel Hoy. 'Have they moved yet?'

'I understand that there has been no contact with General Tevis. There is a rumour, and Surgeon-General Donnelly says it has been reported in the *Buffalo Express*, that Tevis has moved through Detroit and crossed over to take Windsor and Sarnia. As for General Spear . . . General Spear's army is still in the process of mustering around St Albans in Vermont. They have not yet moved across the border.'

Gavin ground his teeth. If any success was to come out of this, Spear had to establish himself in Lower Canada, among the sympathetic French-Canadians and the large Irish population of Montréal. He gazed across at O'Neill and felt sympathy as he saw the decision with which the man was faced. He could try to save as many of his men as possible, withdraw to Buffalo and probably be arrested by the United States authorities or he could order a last stand in this old fortress; a stand that would result in their annihilation. All the British had to do would be to bring up their field guns and systematically reduce the fortress to rubble without even closing within rifle shot.

'We must stand and fight!' cried the red-headed Owen Starr fiercely.

O'Neill smiled at his friend wearily. 'I have considered all the possibilities, Owen,' he said gently. 'Let me put them to you. There is a British column which has moved from Stevensville in pursuit of us. It is now about 2,000 strong, armed with field guns and cavalry. There is another column waiting at Chippewa, also with field guns and of similar strength. Additionally, there is the remnants of the column we defeated this morning at Port Colborne which has probably been reinforced by now and given a new commander. Call it 5,000 men, cavalry and field guns. There is a proverb in Irish, Owen. May I remind you of it? *Is fearr rith maith ná droch sheasamh.* Better a good run than a bad stand.'

Starr grimaced in a slightly sulky fashion but he was silent.

'I have decided,' O'Neill continued, his voice rising briskly, 'that we will evacuate during the night. I am sending Surgeon-General Donnelly back to Buffalo to ask Colonel Sherwin and Captain Hynes to arrange for barges to be sent across and brought to the wharves here. I don't think the authorities will stop them coming because the barges will be empty. Their object seems to be to prevent men and supplies coming across, not empty barges.'

'But they'll arrest us when we attempt to go back,' Starr pointed out.

'I'd sooner surrender to the American flag than to a British one,' O'Neill retorted. He glanced at his commanders. 'I want your various troops to stand ready soon after midnight and prepare to embark at the given order. That is all.'

As Gavin was leaving with the rest, O'Neill stayed him. He waited while O'Neill had a whispered consultation with Connelly. The surgeon-general left after a short while and then O'Neill took Gavin by the arm.

'You've done a grand job, Devlin, and so I am going to ask you to take on a new task . . . *ask*, mind you, and not order you.'

Gavin waited, wondering what O'Neill had in mind.

'As you are aware, we have had no contact with General Tevis. His column of 3,000 men were supposed to have crossed the lakes to menace Toronto. Buffalo has had no telegraph communication from Tevis but there are rumours that he has crossed and occupied Sarnia and Windsor as arranged.'

'What is it that you want me to do, sir?' pressed Gavin.

'If Tevis has crossed and captured Sarnia and Windsor then our withdrawal will ensure that the British will be able to throw the full weight of their troops against him. He has to be informed of our withdrawal from the field as well as the fact that General Spear has not crossed into Lower Canada as yet.'

Gavin saw what O'Neill was driving at. 'Are you asking me to volunteer to ride to Lake Huron? It's nearly 200 miles from here.'

'But if Tevis is there it is essential that he be warned,' O'Neill pressed. 'I don't say that it will be easy but you know this corner of the world, Devlin. The lives of Tevis and his men might well depend on them knowing that we have withdrawn.'

Gavin realized that O'Neill was right. It was sound military sense. 'I'll have to get rid of this uniform,' he said.

'That's right. Go as a civilian. I'd take the shore road, along the lake. There's enough woodlands there to avoid the British troops. Pass yourself off as a farmer. God knows there are enough of them about.'

'Would you mind if I asked Lieutenant Boyd and Sergeant Nolan to go with me? With three of us, one will be sure of getting through to General Tevis.'

O'Neill grunted assent, adding, 'I thought you might ask for your brother to accompany you.'

'I'd sooner John-Joe was safely back on the American shore,' Gavin said.

O'Neill held out his hand. Its grip was firm and steady. Gavin suddenly hesitated and stared straight into the Fenian commander's eyes.

'Has it . . . has it been worthwhile?' he asked.

'Worthwhile?' O'Neill's eyes widened a little. 'I believe so. If we have lost this campaign then we have not lost the war. And that war is old, Devlin. Remember that. It started when Strongbow landed on our shores and it will continue until the last English political administrator, and her soldiers who keep them in power, have left our native soil for good. The army who fight that war is refreshed with each generation that grows up and answers Ireland's cry for liberty.'

Gavin still hesitated. 'It's been troubling me, sir . . . just recently, that is. Was it right to come to strike a blow against England here instead of carrying the fight to Ireland?'

O'Neill stuck out his jaw. 'You have fought with the best of us, Devlin, and yet you have doubts?'

'More doubts than ever I had before the fight,' Gavin confessed.

'Well, let me affirm this principle; England rules Ireland by right of conquest only. That makes her government for ever a usurpation and a crime against humanity. England has no right in Ireland, never has had and never will have. Therefore the Irish people are justified in striking at England wherever England flies her hated flag until her grasp on Ireland is relinquished. Why should the Irish fight only by the rules England lays down? Why should we fight where England expects us to fight? I say that if we do no more than what we have done during the last two days, if we achieve no more, then at least we have kept faith with the past and handed the tradition to the future. If we had refused to fight then we would have admitted that we are truly a conquered people; that the English have a right to rule us, to dominate us, to destroy our language and hold us in subjugation until they have remoulded us in their image as quaint and provincial Englishmen. Every act of rebellion against that process is an assertion of our nationhood against the English conquest.

'What we have succeeded in doing at Ridgeway and Fort Erie is to demonstrate to the world that there is still an Irish nation which repudiates England's right of conquest and domination. In that we have won a victory. In future times there may be no monument to us at Ridgeway such as those the British erect on their victorious battlefields. But the men who fought at Ridgeway will know why they fought and what they gave their lives for. And while history is a capricious thing, perhaps future generations of Irish people will live in freedom and peace because of what has happened at Ridgeway. It will not be a great military victory that will be remembered but a moral victory and a moral victory is much more significant than a military one. To fight, to protest, is to win. To meekly submit is to lose.'

O'Neill's voice had risen in excitement and he paused. 'I hope you make it safely to General Tevis, Devlin. May we meet again soon. *Slán go fóill.*'

'Good luck, colonel,' Gavin said as he left. His last glance of O'Neill was of a man bending preoccupied over his map.

O'Neill had been absolutely right in one thing. The remnants of Colonel Booker's defeated column, recovering in Port Colborne, had been given a new commander in the person of Captain Charles Style

Akers of the Royal Engineers. He had just received confirmation of his appointment from Colonel Robert Lowry, newly arrived at Chippewa.

Captain Akers had gone to the telegraph office at Fort Erie's railroad depot to see if the wires had been repaired and if there were any confirmation about the reported disaster at Ridgeway. He had fully intended to return to Colonel Dennis. But the Fenians had arrived and he suddenly found a line of men in a motley of green, blue and grey uniforms spilling into the township. Skirmishers had already cut a line between himself and Colonel Dennis and the air was a thunder of crashing guns. Sweating in fright, Akers had seized an abandoned horse and buggy and whipped the poor creature to a gallop, sending the vehicle swaying down the shore road away from the fighting.

As he approached the bridge at Six Mile Creek, having managed to get through the Fenian lines, local farmers leaped out at him and forced him to stop. Recognizing him as a British officer, they demanded help in quenching a fire on the bridge and forced him to assist them in forming a bucket chain from a nearby well. It was from the farmers that Akers heard the full story of the Ridgeway disaster. With the fire out and now in control of his panic, Akers continued along the road, moving on to the Garrison Road. He stopped when he saw two redcoated soldiers lying wounded by the roadside. He managed to get one of them into his buggy but had to leave the other man who was too badly wounded to be moved. It was about 7 p.m. when he drove into Port Colborne to find a terrible confusion in the town. Soldiers lay about the streets or sat in exhausted groups, uniforms stained and powder burnt. The local doctor, with a couple of other physicians, had formed a makeshift hospital at one of the taverns. There seemed wounded men with bloody bandages everywhere Akers looked.

When he asked where the senior officer was he was directed to the railroad depot's telegraph office. He found Colonel Alfred Booker there. His own sense of shame at his panicked flight from Fort Erie faded when he saw the white face and trembling lips of the militia colonel. The man was a dreadful sight, overcome with anxiety and fatigue. He sprang up when he saw the regular army officer and seized him by the arm.

'Akers! Thank God! Thank God! You must take command here You must!'

Akers tried to pacify the trembling man but Booker kept mumbling, urging him to take the weight of command from his shoulders.

'I'd do as he asks, Akers,' said a copper-haired man sitting in the shadows. 'The good colonel is incapable of defending this place if the Fenians attack again.'

Akers stared in surprise at Hogan. He had last seen the civilian with Colonel Dennis.

'How in the world did you get here?' he demanded stupidly.

'On the tug. I brought the prisoners here. What about you?'

Akers flushed trying to forget his terrified flight. 'I managed to get out with a horse and buggy.'

'Your Colonel Dennis was an idiot,' the civilian replied complacently. 'He should have accepted the warning and cleared out before the Fenians arrived.'

'Did the Fenians take the town?' Akers pressed.

'Oh yes. We picked up a few men from Dennis's command and then made our way back here as fast as we could. I'm waiting for permission to take the prisoners on to Brantford Jail.' Hogan glanced with a sneer towards Booker, who stood mumbling and trembling still. 'You'd better take over, Akers. Otherwise we'll have another disaster on our hands.'

Akers glanced at Booker. It was certainly clear that the militia colonel had been totally unnerved by his experience at Ridgeway and so Akers agreed to accept command but only if the other officers in Port Colborne wished him to do so. He pointed out that there were many militia officers who outranked him although he was the only senior regular army officer there. The militia officers, thus consulted, readily agreed to Akers taking charge. They had been thrown into a state of confusion and anxiety at Booker's apparent breakdown as well as at the shock of the defeat at Ridgeway.

Colonel Lowry had now assumed command of the Niagara Field Force from Chippewa and Akers telegraphed him there for instructions. In the meantime he established a line of picquets from the shore of the lake on the eastern side of town, radiating a mile from the centre of Port Colborne to the Welland Canal in the north. The remainder of the troops were ordered to get what rest they could. Akers then sent out telegraphs for replacements for the muskets lost at Ridgeway as well as ammunition and food. He had just finished issuing the requests when a telegraph arrived from Lowry confirming Akers in command of the area.

Gavin, Boyd and Nolan walked their horses south of the Grand Trunk Railroad to the furthest picquet line established by Colonel Grace's men in the woods about a mile from the old fortress. John-Joe had insisted on accompanying them as far as the final sentry outpost.

'I wish I were going with you,' he told Gavin for the third time since his brother had told him of the plan.

'It's not going to be easy,' Gavin replied. 'Best that you get back across the river with O'Neill.'

'I still haven't fired a gun in anger,' John-Joe said bitterly.

'Maybe that's just as well,' Gavin smiled. 'You just make sure you get back safely across the river. We will try to cross into Detroit and join you later.'

They halted in the darkened forest. Through the trees to their left the bright June moon rippled the vast silver expanse of Lake Erie. Gavin found himself wishing that it was a cloudy night so that the moon would be obscured. They needed the darkness to hide in.

'Take care, John-Joe,' he said awkwardly. 'I'll bet you'll be in New York before me. If you are. . . .'

He left it unsaid. The brothers embraced and drew apart almost embarrassed. Then Gavin swung up into the saddle with the others and the three of them turned their mounts down the path along the shore of the lake. John-Joe watched their darkened forms until they became shadows flitting through the trees and were finally lost to sight. He heaved a sigh and turned back through the darkened woods, through the picquet lines towards the old stone fortress.

Barry Mallin was eighteen years old and he felt proud. Proud that he had stood under the withering fire of the British at Ridgeway; stood shoulder to shoulder with his comrades of Colonel Grace's 18th Regiment from Cleveland and returned shot for shot with the redcoats. Yet only four days ago he had not known how to shoot a musket, even less how to load and prime it. But Barry Mallin had fought his first battle and emerged unscathed. Ever since that morning he had felt a strange trembling in his body in spite of his pride. He laughed too sharply and too suddenly at silly things. He was slow to understand but quick to react. His sergeant noticed the thin edge of hysteria and had seen it many times before in young soldiers. It was not unusual. The boy would get over it; would get over it and become a veteran. At the moment the sergeant needed sentries. That was why Barry Mallin was now helping in the great work of Irish liberation by standing in a dark wood by the shores of Lake Erie holding a Sharpe's single-shot breechloader in shaking, sweating hands.

He tried to ease his nervousness by wondering what his father would say when he knew what his son had done. His father thought that Barry Mallin was in Toronto sitting an examination in University College. The boy had been born in the fever sheds at Point St Charles, Montréal, soon after his parents had arrived from County Kerry. It was in the fever sheds, close by the Lachine Canal, that Barry Mallin's mother had died giving birth to him; just another statistic of the tens of thousands of deaths among the newly arrived Irish immigrants. Nearly 10,000 had been buried in mass graves at Point St Charles along with his mother and yet, even there, in a consecrated Catholic burial ground, they were not allowed to find the peace in death which had been denied them in life. The mass graves had been levelled by the workmen of Peto, Brassey and Betts, employed in the construction of a bridge across the St Lawrence which would carry in the new railroad into Montréal from the south. The name of the bridge which arose from the mass graves of the Irish was ironically called the Victoria Bridge. Like the thousands of Irish who dwelt in the nearby quarter of Verdun, Barry Mallin had come to hate the very name Victoria, which now mocked the Irish dead as well as the living.

He had been eleven years old when the Victoria Bridge had been completed, completed even more ironically by the sweat of Irish emigrant labour. When the labourers had discovered that they were desecrating the graves of thousands of their own people they had refused to continue working, throwing down their tools and leaving the site. A spokesman was sent to the directors of the company to protest. The directors of Messrs Peto, Brassey and Betts informed their spokesman that labourers were plentiful. If the men did not resume work then they could starve with their families and others would be found to replace them. And so they were forced to return to work. They worked carefully, digging out what pathetic bones they could while the Catholic Church refused even to protest on behalf of the people and, by their passivity, condoned the sacrilege of a consecrated cemetery. Eventually, in an act of propitiation, the Irish workmen sought permission to raise a memorial to commemorate their countrymen, the women and children, who had once been laid to rest there. The commemorative stone, carved by their own sweat from a boulder excavated from the site, was erected at the entrance to the bridge.

Barry Mallin had grown up on Beresford Street, a short walk from the bridge. Each weekend he would walk to Point St Charles, gaze up at the rough-hewn black rock and recite a decade of the rosary in memory of his mother. He had grown up, like many children of Irish immigrants, with an intangible hatred of the people who had been responsible for the misfortunes of his kinfolk. That had been Barry Mallin's road to the dark, shadowy wood outside Fort Erie.

He peered forward nervously into the surrounding darkness. Hadn't the sergeant said that the British were all around them and might attack at any moment? Something was stirring in the wood before him. The young man licked at his dry lips and squinted. He glanced hastily round for the support of his companions but could see none. His mind began to race, trying to recall what it was that the sergeant had told him to do. He could hear the rustling in the undergrowth. The sweat began to pour down his face. His heart thumped so that it almost hurt his chest. He raised his musket and peered along its barrel. It felt as if it weighed a ton.

The leaves were rustling now; someone was coming. What was it that the sergeant had said? Something to do. Something to call out. No time to think about it now. No time.

One thought did come into his mind. A sentry should aim for the legs if he had no wish to kill. Barry Mallin remembered that almost at the last moment. Aim for the legs. He depressed the barrel of the musket. The figure emerged. He had a vague feeling that there was something else he should have done. A challenge? No time. Barry Mallin pressed the trigger and the rifle recoiled sharply against his shoulder, throwing him momentarily off balance.

Hiding in the darkness of the forest, Lieutenant-Colonel John Stoughton Dennis heard the single shot in the night and huddled further into the shelter of the thorn bush. It was cold and uncomfortable. The thorns tore at his flesh, pricking and irritating him. It must be time to strike out across country in search of Colonel Peacocke's camp, if the camp still existed. Perhaps Peacocke's entire command had been wiped out. Dennis shivered. In his mind he was already composing his report of the affair at Fort Erie, seeking to exonerate his conduct. 'There being little or no cessation in the fire upon us in retreat, I had no desire to remain under it longer than was necessary, and accordingly turned into the premises of a friend in the lower part of the village, where I lay concealed. . . .' Yes, that sounded good. It was better than admitting that a blind panic had seized him when he realized how he had underestimated the numbers and discipline of the Fenians. It was better than saying how he had seen his men falling, the enemy approaching so close that he could reach out and touch them. It was better than saying that, seeing his own capture inevitable, he had abandoned his men and turned, running along the river road until he was able to take shelter among the garbage and refuse of an ash-house. He had lain among the stinking waste until he had been able to find a better hiding place in a barn. There he had been discovered by the son of the barn owner and had prevailed upon the boy to bring him civilian clothes, water and a razor. Trembling with the fear of discovery, Dennis had thrown off his uniform, shaved his magnificent Dundreary whiskers, and clad himself in a well-worn suit of farmer's clothes, a cloth cap drawn well down over his face and a bandana kerchief around his neck. Dennis had waited until nightfall before slipping out of Fort Erie into the surrounding woods where he waited until he could summon the courage to start his trek to where he thought the British lines might be.

Already he was composing his version of these events: '. . . although the premises, where I lay concealed, were searched twice, the Fenians . . . ah, no . . . the *ruffians* stating their intention to come a third time, and threatening, if I were not given up, as they had seen me enter the gate, that they would destroy the property. Fearing another search, I dressed in disguise furnished by my friends and then came out and remained in the village until nightfall when I got through the lines and struck across country. . . .' He paused thinking that he had better not shift the blame for the defeat too much on the men under him. Best not antagonize any who had survived just so long as he was not blamed. 'My little command behaved most nobly in the affair during the afternoon at Fort Erie. I firmly believe that had I not ordered them to retreat they would have remained steady and fought until shot down in their ranks.'

He smiled. Yes. That sounded good. That exonerated him and would surely not incur the odium of the men.

The single shot cracked in the night and Colonel John Stoughton Dennis pressed more closely to the earth under the thorn bush.

The force of the .52 calibre ball threw John-Joe back with a grunt against the trunk of a cedarwood tree. He slid down and half rolled with a puzzled expression on his features. For a second he felt nothing but the jolt of the impact. Then he realized that there was a growing numbness in his groin. He heard someone cursing and the shouting of sentries. Someone came pushing through the undergrowth towards him. A match was struck.

'Jesus, Mary and Joseph!' muttered a voice. 'Get a surgeon!'

John-Joe stared up wondering why there was such a fuss. He tried to move and suddenly groaned at the spasm of agony in his thigh. A storm lantern had been lit and was being swung crazily above him.

'Make way for the doc,' called a voice.

A shadow was bending over him. He thought; what a damned silly thing to happen. Shot in the leg by his own side. What glory was there in that? What was the purpose? He became aware of a throbbing. The shadow of a man was bending over him pressing something hard into his groin. He wanted to tell him to stop it. It hurt; it hurt like hell. Then he saw Murna bending over him and smiling. He wondered how she had come to be there. He heard her soft voice and fought to understand the words of her song.

Cúig míle slán dom láimh bhí tharm 's nach mbeidh!

Five thousand farewells to the arm that was around me and will not be again!

He tried to reach up towards her sad, smiling face.

The truth shattered her image. He realized that he was going to die. How stupid, how useless, how bewildering. In the last split second of thought that was left to him he had a sense of indignation; of indignation and then of loneliness and fear.

The doctor sighed as he felt the pulsating throb of the severed artery slow and cease. He stared into the glazed eyes by the light of the storm lantern.

'Can't anything be done?' demanded Colonel Grace standing behind him.

The doctor swore vehemently. 'I can't raise the dead, mister. What do you expect me to do?'

Grace glared at the man for a moment, watching the emotion fighting on his glistening features. He did not reply but stood silently while the doctor wiped his brow and shook his head sadly over the body.

'He's only a boy.'

Grace shrugged. 'Who else dies in war, doctor? Not old men, that's for sure. Old men sit behind desks and sign papers or declaim to each other from platforms. It is the boys who go out to murder each other in order to settle the arguments of old men. And then the dead bodies are shovelled into holes as quickly as possible in case they offend the old men who will then present each other with gaudy decorations and declare how brave everyone has been and how generations yet unborn will never forget such sacrifices. But they do forget. Even the same generations. Indeed they do.'

The doctor, a Canadian who had lived all his life at Fort Erie, stared in amazement at the Irishman. 'I never expected to hear that philosophy from a Fenian,' he said cynically. 'Aren't you the ones who started this killing?'

Grace shook his head sadly. 'People who have always been free may never begin to understand the terrible passion that the dream of freedom arouses in those who are not free.'

The doctor gestured down at the body. 'One thing is certain, mister. . . .' he grunted. 'This boy is free now.'

A few yards away Barry Mallin swallowed tearfully. 'I didn't mean to kill him. I only shot at his legs. How can a person die if you only shoot at their legs?'

The doctor turned in his direction. 'You severed his femoral artery, boy,' he replied coldly. 'A person can't live more than a minute or two if that artery is severed.' He glanced back to Grace. 'Freedom or not, it was a waste; a bloody stupid waste.'

A sergeant was leading Barry Mallin away with rough but kindly words while the doctor returned to the township.

By the light of the lantern Grace saw for the first time that the ground was soaked where the blood had pulsated in great pumping spurts from the wound. He bent to collect some identification from the body, his eyes meeting those that gazed unseeingly upwards. They stared as only the eyes of the dead could, glazed in an attitude of bewilderment and fear.

Chapter 61

Led by Gavin, Boyd and Nolan rode in file along the shore of the lake, keeping close to the shelter of the woods. In the distance they could hear an occasional shout as a nervous sentry reported to his sergeant or made a challenge in the darkness. Once or twice they heard the ominous sound of shots being fired. Gavin planned to leave the lakeshore at Six Mile Creek, by the Sauerwine Bridge, in order to move inland thereby giving a wide berth to the township of Ridgeway. He felt a sharp pang in his chest at the thought that he would be moving so close to Kate Dawtry's farmstead. He would be so close and yet he would have to pass by without seeing Kate nor letting her know that he was alive nor where he was going. The forest was oppressively dark and only the infrequent scurry of some nocturnal creature or the mournful cry of an owl broke its stillness.

Riding immediately behind him, Boyd gave a low whistle of warning. Gavin halted and let him ease his horse alongside.

'There's a movement on our left,' he whispered.

Nolan was squinting into the darkness, listening for sounds. 'Cavalry,' he hissed.

Either the man had a good sense of hearing or some uncanny perception which Gavin could not apprehend.

'Where?'

'To your front and slightly to the left, sir.'

Gavin frowned into the blackness of the forest. Then, though conjured by magic, through the tall dark bars of the trees, he saw a group of dark shadows and heard the soft whinny of a horse. The three of them froze into immobility and waited for a while until the sounds of the horsemen died away.

'We'd better move inland now,' Gavin decided. They followed his lead, moving quickly and as quietly as they could through the shrub and undergrowth until they came to the railroad tracks and halted. Once again Nolan called a warning.

'Horses! Several of them, sir, coming this way along the tracks.'

They drew back into the shadows of the trees and dismounted, holding their bridles tightly while petting their horses' muzzles to prevent them crying in alarm. From their position, with the bright moon bathing the railroad, Gavin could see a troop of cavalry riding by in single file, bodies stiffly erect, almost in complete silence. British cavalry – professionals! They vanished as quickly as they had appeared. Purposefully and determined, only the dying sound of their horses' hooves thumping softly on the wooden sleepers of the track marked their passage.

The three of them mounted again and crossed the tracks into the woods beyond. After a while they came to a highway which Gavin recognized as the Garrison Road. They moved swiftly across, taking to the fields beyond. He thought they ought to be fairly near Ridgeway, near the battlefield from which they had departed victoriously twelve hours before. It seemed as if it had been in another life, another world. The moon was still high and had lost none of its brilliance, bathing the terrain in a pale light. There was enough light to recognize the fact that they were crossing the Ridge Road just north of where the roadside tavern had stood – what had it been called? The Smugglers' Home?

'Halt!'

Figures were moving ahead, the moonlight reflecting on burnished metal.

'Let's move!' cried Gavin, banging his heels against his horse's sides and laying low across her neck. The beast answered immediately to the pressure, springing forward like an arrow from a bow. He heard shouting but he could not discern the words. There were cries followed by shots. He was suddenly among a group of men, he saw the uniforms and the guns, but they were scattering right and left. He hoped Boyd and Nolan were following his lead. The horse thundered swiftly over the springy turf. The cries were fading behind him. He was safe.

He did not hear the shot. All he knew was that his horse seemed to have missed its footing and went slithering headlong into the turf. He felt its forward momentum; heard its sudden piercing scream of agony as it went down. He registered the thought that he must kick clear of the stirrups and throw himself away from the beast. Even as he registered the thought he was borne down by the threshing animal and rolled with it. The shock of the impact knocked the wind from him. He blacked out momentarily but then the agony, the terrible pain in his legs, brought him back to consciousness almost immediately causing him to shriek in the throb of burning torment. He immediately blacked out again. When he came to his legs were numb, there was no more pain. He was aware of the threshing beast lying half on top of him, its great breath rasping in agony. Someone was bending over him.

The British! He tried to struggle up but a hand rested on his shoulder.

'Still, captain. Stay still,' came Boyd's soothing voice out of the darkness.

Gavin became aware of cries and the occasional shot in the distance.

'Get away, Boyd,' he groaned.

'You stay quiet,' replied Boyd, grabbing the blood-flecked muzzle of the horse. Gavin saw him bring his hand to the high screaming mouth as it threshed in its agony. There was an explosion and the beast was suddenly quiet and still.

Gavin felt an excruciating agony as hands pulled at him. He was vaguely aware of Boyd saying, 'Don't worry. We'll get you away.' He groaned as he was hauled up on a pair of broad shoulders and then pushed stomach down across the saddle of a horse. There were more shouts now, getting nearer. Then someone had mounted the horse and he passed out as the pain of its forward motion caused a burning sensation to pass up his legs.

He came to in the bright light of early morning. He was lying on a mattress of soft grass which stretched by a small stream. He wondered if he were dreaming again and peered round expecting to see the green robed form of the girl, Fand the Pearl of Beauty. He was certainly laying on a mossy bank in a dell among beechwood trees. Odd he should notice the type of tree, he thought. Where was the girl? A figure stirred by the stream and he found himself focusing on the figure of Phil Boyd bending towards it and dipping a kerchief in its waters. He was not dreaming after all. He groaned, feeling his mouth thick and dry.

'He's coming round, lieutenant,' Sergeant Nolan's rich Kerry accent sounded just by his head.

Boyd turned and grinned at him. He came to kneel by his side dropping the ice-cool kerchief on his burning forehead.

'Where am I?' Gavin asked stupidly.

'Your guess is probably better than mine, captain,' Boyd replied.

'What happened?'

It was Nolan who answered his question. 'We ran into a British patrol. They shot your horse from under you, cap'n. We're probably four or five miles west of Ridgeway.'

Gavin tried to struggle up. The pain came at once. He grunted and sunk back.

'Steady, captain,' Boyd said. 'You smashed your leg under the fall of your horse.'

Memory came to Gavin sharply. 'Jesus! I can't move!'

Boyd looked down as if embarrassed. 'You'll be all right, captain. Don't worry.'

Gavin's next thought was of the mission. 'You'd better move on. Find General Tevis and tell him about O'Neill's withdrawal. I'll be fine here for a while.'

Boyd was too good a soldier to argue. 'We'll make you as comfortable as we can before we go. We can lie up here today and move on tonight.'

Gavin found the wall of blackness rushing to meet him again. He heard Nolan's voice saying, 'He's blacking out again. . . .' Then he seemed to wake instantaneously. He must have been unconscious for a while, however, for the sun was now high in the sky. He opened his eyes and looked around. Boyd was sitting with Nolan a short distance away. Gavin's mind was immediately filled with thoughts of Kate.

Boyd moved across as Gavin muttered his name.

'How are you doing, captain?'

'Did you say we were just west of Ridgeway?'

'Nolan did,' agreed Boyd. 'But I guess he is right.'

'Do me a favour, Boyd. Don't leave me here tonight. Get me down to the Dawtry farmstead.'

Boyd hesitated with a worried look but Gavin reached up and seized his wrist. He didn't want to be left alone. He wanted to be with Kate . . . safe with Kate.

'Please, Boyd! We must be fairly near a place called Sherk's Crossing. Just north of the Garrison Road is a farmstead; Dawtry's farmstead. You can't miss the entrance . . . there are two oak trees, one on either side of the farm gate. Leave me there.'

Boyd still looked dubious. 'Are they sympathizers? The first place the British will start searching are the homes of sympathizers.'

'Just leave me at Dawtry's farmstead,' Gavin begged, almost in panic.

The wall of blackness was rushing towards him again. He wasn't sure what happened next. Someone was heaving at him. He felt the pain of movement. It seemed endless; interminable. He swam in and out of consciousness. Then he was sure that he heard Boyd saying distinctly, 'He told us to bring him here, ma'am. Can you take care of him?'

A woman's voice answered. It was fearful, anxious, 'Is he badly hurt?'

'Reckon so,' came Boyd's voice.

The blackness oppressed him again. Faces swum before his eyes. Young Tom, pale and frightened. Kate, fearful with the stain of tears on her cheeks. Then the pain; pain so agonizing that it seemed his body was being wrenched apart. Taylor's face; angry, eyes full of hatred. Hands tearing at his body. Burning. Cold. Burning. Successive waves of pain alternated through his body. And then the fevered nightmares came and went in bewildering succession until he was not sure what was real and what was fantasy nor was he able to care. The images blurred and merged. Images of war. Images of poverty and death. The bitter sad face of Nora Quinlan. The claw-like hand of the legless beggar. The remorseless beating of drums. The call of a bugle far off. The world was in constant eruption, fire and death belched out of the darkness that surrounded him. The flames and smoke whirled and eddied. He swung from moments of lucidity to his world of dark phantasms.

He awoke from his fever with a strange calm; a tranquillity that he had not known since childhood. A man was bending over him. He blinked, focusing on the man's features.

'Taylor?'

Taylor drew back. He was in waistcoat and shirt sleeves. 'So you're awake, are you?' Taylor said sardonically. 'Welcome back to the land of the living.'

Gavin blinked again and stared around him in bewilderment. He was in his old room in the Dawtry farmhouse lying on his cot amidst the warmth of blankets. He felt drugged, as if he had slept for an age. He turned back to Taylor's graven features. Then he tried to move, becoming aware of something strapped to his leg. He twisted his head to examine it.

'Don't move,' snapped Taylor. 'You'll have to lie as still as you can for the next couple of weeks.'

Gavin became aware of the smell of camphor and the strong smell of pine wood which mingled with it.

'Did I bust my leg?'

'You don't remember?'

'I can't remember anything about getting here. Have I been here long?'

'About a week,' Taylor replied.

Gavin gazed at him foolishly. 'A week?' He tried to collect his thoughts. 'Have I been in a fever for that long?'

'You were busted up prettily badly, Devlin.'

He didn't take in the words. He was remembering the last time he had seen Taylor. It had been at Ridgeway.

'I suppose the authorities will be coming for me soon?' he asked with resignation, meeting Taylor's eyes for a moment.

'No,' Taylor said. His voice was sharp.

Gavin was startled; unprepared for the answer. 'You haven't told anyone that I was at Ridgeway, that I am a Fenian?' he pressed hardly believing Taylor.

'I may be all kinds of a fool,' Taylor glared at him bitterly. 'I may be disloyal to my Queen and country, but I have not told a soul. Neither will I. But don't think it is for your sake, Devlin.' Taylor hesitated. 'Kate is in love with you, God help her. When she sent for me after you had been left here by your friends I was going to bring the constable with me. Kate was willing to shoot me then. Willing to kill me to stop me betraying you.' His face twitched in anguish. 'So what could I do? I love her . . . damn you! You know that, Devlin. I love her. So what could I do?'

Gavin stared at Taylor feeling a tremendous compassion for the man. 'I hope that I am able to love Kate as much as you do,' he said quietly.

Taylor turned with an angry scowl and seemed to focus on the window. 'You'll have nothing to fear from me, Devlin. So far as I am concerned, I never saw you on that Saturday. Your present injury was apparently caused by a fall in the barn. That's all I know.'

His voice took on a softly vehement tone. 'But I'll give you a warning, Devlin. Stay around here for long and I may just forget that I am doing this for Kate's sake, especially if I find you continuing with your treacherous conspiracy. And let me add some advice. Kate doesn't want to stay on this farm. Get her to give it up and move away. That will be the only way that I will be able to stand the burden that I have shouldered.'

'All right, Taylor,' Gavin gently assured him. 'As soon as I am able, I'll be moving on . . . with Kate, if she'll have me.'

Taylor swung round to face him, his face still bitter. 'She'll have you right enough.'

'Then when can I get up and about?'

Taylor shrugged almost indifferently. 'It will be a while,' he said. 'You broke your leg awkwardly. I set it as best as I could but the break occurred in an awkward place to splint. The bone is not knitting back entirely as it was before.'

Gavin stared at Taylor's bland expression. 'For God's sake . . .' he found himself whispering, 'tell me the worst.'

'To be brutal, Devlin, your dancing days are done. I don't reckon that you'll be able to get by without a stick when you do finally get out.'

Gavin stared at him in horror. 'Are you saying that I am crippled?'

Doc Taylor pursed his lips. 'That's a state of mind not a clinical condition, Devlin. It's up to you. You'll be able to get around pretty fine but it won't be manual work for you. You'll have to get back to your law books again. Any job so long as you don't put a strain on that leg.'

Your dancing days are done! That's what Taylor had said, like an echo from the song, that damned song which had haunted him on and off since the Fourth of July celebration in New York. He could hear its mocking tones again hammering in the dim recesses of his mind.

> Where are the legs with which you run?
> Hurroo! Hurroo!
> Where are the legs with which you run?
> Hurroo! Hurroo!
> Where are the legs with which you run
> When you went to carry a gun?
> Indeed, your dancing days are done!
> Och, Johnny, I hardly knew ye!

Taylor was rolling down his sleeves and hauling on his coat.

'I'll be back in a few days, Devlin,' he said, picking up his bag. 'Meanwhile, just do everything Kate tells you to and, for your own sake, don't move.'

'I guess that I should thank you. . . .' Gavin began uncomfortably.

Taylor wheeled on him and Gavin flinched at the pain he saw burning in the man's haunted eyes.

'That's the last thing I want from you!' he said in a broken voice. 'I couldn't live with your thanks. If you want to thank anyone, thank Kate.' He stormed from the room.

A moment later the door opened and Kate Dawtry hesitated on the threshold. It seemed that they had last met in another life; it was so long ago. For a few moments they said nothing to each other. Then Gavin raised a hand and she came quickly to his side, pressing her damp cheek against his. It was a triggering mechanism. A well of anguish overflowed within him and he found the tears cascading unchecked down his cheeks. He could not stop them. He sobbed helplessly like a baby while she cradled his head in her arms, crooning softly to him, petting and comforting him. The emotion had complete control of him. He did not even know why he felt so desperate; so isolated from everyone. The words of the song kept echoing in his mind. He sobbed in his moment of wretchedness, unconsolable in his misery.

> I'm happy for to see you home.
> Hurroo! Hurroo!
> I'm happy for to see you home
> Hurroo! Hurroo!
> I'm happy for to see you home
> All from the island of Sulloon
> So low in flesh, so high in bone,
> Och, Johnny, I hardly knew ye!

Chapter 62

By the time Gavin was recovered enough to hobble to the verandah of the farmhouse and sit out in the late June sunshine, the attempt of the Brotherhood to establish an Irish Republic-in-Exile had failed. Gavin followed the rest of the story in the columns of the newspapers. O'Neill had been successful in withdrawing the main body of his troops back across the river during the early hours of Sunday morning. He had left behind him only those too seriously wounded to be moved together with volunteers, led by Father MacMahon, who offered to stay to nurse them. The main body had been towed across in two barges provided by Captain Hynes and Hugh Mooney. Other men, individually or in small groups, had made their way to the American shore in whatever transport they could find. The two barges, however, were intercepted by the armed tug USS *Harrison*, under the command of William Morris, and O'Neill and his men were escorted to Black Rock under arrest and placed under the menacing shadow of the USS *Michigan*.

At dawn that Sunday, Colonel Lowry's troops began to enter Fort Erie and by the end of the day some 5,000 troops had encamped in and around the frontier township. Those Fenians and other suspected people found in Fort Erie were immediately arrested. Colonel Lowry gave orders for several drum-head court-martials. At 5 p.m. on Monday, a soldier who had deserted from the 16th Regiment of Foot to join the Fenians was summarily shot outside the old stone fortress. A further execution of a second deserter from the 16th Regiment was held the next day. Stories swiftly spread into Buffalo that the British were systematically executing Fenian prisoners. Major-General Napier was forced to intervene to stop the execution of a member of the 2nd Battalion, Queen's Own, who had fought at Ridgeway but was arrested for declaring that the Irish had a right to fight for the liberty of their country. The charge of 'High Treason' was quickly dropped and the man was sent to Toronto in irons for uttering seditious statements. Major-General Napier made it clear that all Fenian prisoners and sympathizers were to be given over to the care of the civil authorities and the prisoners, including the chaplains Father MacMahon and the Reverend David Lumsden, were sent under escort to Brantford Jail.

Within twenty-four hours of O'Neill's withdrawal, James Speed, the attorney-general of the United States, issued a directive on behalf of President Johnson ordering the arrest of all prominent Fenians and anyone believed to be guilty of violating the neutrality laws.

On Wednesday, 6 June, as the British dead were being buried with all military pomp at Toronto, President Johnson issued a proclamation calling for the arrest of Fenians for 'high misdemeanours forbidden by the laws of the United States' and announcing his intention rigidly to enforce the neutrality laws. On the same day federal authorities arrested William Randall Roberts and a few hours later General 'Fighting Tom' Sweeny was captured at Albany.

On the same Wednesday O'Neill and his officers appeared before the Honourable George W. Clinton, Justice of the Supreme Court of Buffalo, at the Erie Court House, to be arraigned for violations of the neutrality laws. Seventeen of O'Neill's officers, together with Hugh Mooney, were given bail ranging between $3,000 and $6,000. O'Neill, who had on the Monday been officially promoted to the rank of brigadier by Sweeny, was carried shoulder high to the Mansion House Hotel where a crowd forced him to make an appearance on a balcony overlooking Main Street. His speech was short.

'Gentlemen, I am no speaker. The speeches I have been in the habit of making I suppose you are all acquainted with. It would not be prudent, under the circumstances, for me to say anything, nor would you desire me to do so. I thank you for the compliment paid the Irish Army through me.

'I advise all men under my command to remain quietly at their rendezvous and preserve the reputation they already have for discipline and good behaviour.'

Even as O'Neill was speaking, Brigadier Michael C. Murphy, formerly of the 69th New York Regiment, was mustering his Fenian cavalry regiments in Malone and crossing into Canada. General Spear, realizing that he had no time left to wait for his army to complete their muster, decided to press forward with what troops he had. There were several thousand Fenians troops along the border but, after the proclamation from President Johnson making an unequivocal stand against them, General Meade had begun to move to contain and arrest them. A battery of Fenian field guns was captured en route to the front at Pittsburgh. When General Spear finally crossed the frontier into Lower Canada out of Vermont, he had a column of less than 2,000 troops. Nevertheless, his men were able to capture and occupy Frelighsburg, St Armand and East Stanbridge. On Friday, 8 June a Fenian regiment commanded by Colonel Michael Scanlan engaged British cavalry at Pigeon Hill and drove them off with loss, capturing their flag. The next day a message was sent out from Pigeon Hill.

'We are in the enemy's country! The flag waves defiantly. We have captured Pigeon Hill, St Armand Centre, Slab City and the British colours. We are ready to advance. Hurry up the ammunition. Victory or death!'

However, the main thrust had been made too late for any hope of success with so few men. By 3 June there had been little likelihood of either the Irish in Montréal or the French-Canadian radicals rising in support of the Fenian invasion, even if they had wanted to. Two regular British regiments had been dispatched to the city and 10,000 militia had been placed under arms throughout the streets. From the river three British warships, with HMS *Pylades* as a flagship, menaced the city with their guns. On board was a special task force of Royal Marines ready to reinforce the troops already placed there. On Monday 4 June, a meeting was called in the City Hall at which loyal Irishmen were asked to express their support for the government. Thomas D'Arcy Magee was at his most strident.

'Without provocation, without pretence of provocation, crippled by the anathema of the Church and outlawed by the federal government, these deluded men dare to menace Canada . . . they dare to assail our frontier in the abused name of Ireland and the Irish people. The turbulent and the dissolute floating population of the large lake and sea port cities of the United States form the rank and file; all of them totally ignorant of the true state of Canada, crammed full of falsehoods as to the discontent of our population and the French-Canadians.

'I deny that they represent Ireland, to whom Canada has done no wrong. I would add that a more wanton, immoral, unjustifiable attack was never made upon a free people; and the fate of pirates and freebooters is all they can expect.

'We, the Irish, have a duty additional to the duty of others. We are belied as a class by these scoundrels, and as a class we must vindicate our loyalty to the freest country left to Irishmen on the face of the globe!'

But even D'Arcy McGee's usual bombast could not ease the tension that was felt in Montréal. It was a restless city under army occupation. Henry Starnes, the mayor of Montréal, who had called the meeting, confessed that he had been forced to dismiss a large number of city policemen of French-Canadian and Irish origin who, as news of the invasion spread, refused to renew their oath of allegiance which he had felt obliged to administer to all civic employees. The city was rampant with disaffection. The very day of the meeting, a regular soldier holding the rank of sergeant-major had been arrested for trying to stir up pro-Fenian sympathies among his men.

The Honourable John Rose, a member of the Legislative Assembly, declared that habeas corpus should be immediately suspended in Montréal in order to allow all those suspected of disaffection, or were already in arms against the government, to be arrested and executed immediately. There should be no shilly-shallying with trials and delaying sentences on legal technicalities. A drum-head court-martial was sufficient. If any person was arrested with a weapon in their hand on a Friday then they should be executed on the Saturday!

But there was no assistance forthcoming for General Spear from Montréal; no hope of successful insurrection under the menacing guns of the troops on shore and the warships out in the St Lawrence. Spear was isolated on the border. The British could turn the full weight of their troops against him. The position was impossible. Brigadier Murphy's cavalry had only penetrated fifteen miles across the border before it encountered a superior force and was pushed back to Malone with several losses. Spear reluctantly began an evacuation of his command across the border. His rearguard fought a harassing action with pursuing British cavalry suffering several casualties and losing three men as prisoners. At the border Lieutenant-Colonel Livingstone, commanding the United States 3rd Artillery Regiment, gave verbal permission to the British to cross the border in an effort to round up some of the Fenian stragglers, a few of whom were sabred while Livingstone looked indifferently on. One British soldier shot and killed a Mrs Eccles of Vermont as she stood on her own doorstep. The incident provoked a tremendous outcry and Livingstone was eventually reprimanded for allowing this infringement of United States' sovereignty.

General Spear's attempt to establish the Irish Republic-in-Exile in Lower Canada was over.

It was subsequently confirmed that Brigadier Charles C. Tevis, adjutant-general of the Irish Republican Army, had not moved from his headquarters in Chicago. His army, with its equipment, had mustered in the city and in Milwaukee as instructed. At his subsequent court-martial before the Brotherhood, Tevis denied that he had disobeyed orders and claimed that he had not moved because he had been provided with no ships to transport his army into Upper Canada. The fact that he had not replied to any of the telegraphs and stated his position caused his removal from office in the Brotherhood.

As General Spear was pulling his men out of Lower Canada, His Excellency, the governor-general, Lord Monck, having just sent an urgent despatch to England demanding a reinforcement of 8,000 regular troops, opened the united provinces' Parliament in its new building on Ottawa's Barracks Hill. After paying tribute to the militia force, Lord Monck said, 'The province has been invaded by a lawless band of marauders but I congratulate the country that they were promptly confronted and, within twenty-four hours, compelled to make a precipitate retreat. I deplore the loss of life and suffering inflicted upon the gallant body of Canadian volunteers in the engagement which took place, repelling so promptly the invaders who attacked the country; and I feel assured you will not omit to alleviate as far as may be in your power the miseries so wantonly inflicted on many families; but while I grieve at the individual loss, I congratulate the country that the first note of danger has shown Canada to possess, in volunteers, a body of men ready to peril their lives in defence of their Queen and country.'

Later that same day James Stephens, *An Seabhac Siúlach* – the Wandering Hawk, attended a 'Grand Reception for the Chief Organizer of the Irish Republic' in Washington. His speech to the assembled politicians, their ladies and other prominent personalities was brief and he read from a written text. The message was simple and clear: the proper place to fight the battle for Irish independence was in Ireland and in Ireland alone.

However, the senate wing of the Brotherhood had not yet admitted defeat. From Ludlow Street Jail, in New York City, William Randall Roberts was able to issue an appeal to his followers.

> Stand firm by the cause; be not dismayed by the obstacles you meet; you must surmount them. Let cowardice and ignorance desert and denounce

you. What of that? The true men are still a legion, and the struggle must not be abandoned now, though our soldiers should be compelled throughout the over-zeal of the United States officials, to abandon the present campaign. There is no turning back: no, my countrymen, our movement must and will advance. Retrogression would entail eternal infamy, and bring a deeper stain of slavery upon your country and race; and it is as legitimate for you to attack England's power in Canada as it was for England to attack France there, or France and America.

England, remember in union there is strength, and that union which has been cemented by the blood of our gallant brothers must be eternal and let the man be anathemized and banned who, with lying lip or evil heart, would have to weaken or dissolve it. Be true to Ireland, steadfast in the right, and undismayed by obstacles, and remember that

> Freedom's battle, once begun,
> Bequeathed from bleeding sire to son,
> Though baffled oft is ever won.

I remain, with unchanged determination and regard, Your countryman,
William Randall Roberts,
President, Fenian Brotherhood.

As Roberts was issuing his call from jail, Fenian sympathizers in Washington were gathering their forces, angered by the apparent volte-face of President Johnson. They now took their argument into Congress, where the Democrat congressman from Pennsylvania, Sydenham Elnathan Ancona, one of the most outspoken supporters of the Fenians, tabled a motion seeking the repeal of the neutrality laws in an attempt to stop the United States' authorities preventing the Brotherhood from moving troops and men across the border.

Whereas the Irish people and their brothers and friends in this country are moved by a patriotic purpose to assert the independence and re-establish the nationality of Ireland, and

Whereas the active sympathies of the people of the United States are naturally with all men who struggle to achieve such ends, more especially when those engaged therein are known friends of our government, as are the people of the Irish nation, they having shed their blood in defence of our flag in every battle of every war in which the Republic has been engaged, and

Whereas the British government against which they are struggling is entitled to no other or greater consideration from us as a nation than that demanded by the strict letter of international law, for the reason during our late civil war, that government did in effect by its conduct repeal its neutrality laws, and

Whereas when reparation is demanded for damages to our commerce resulting from the wilful neglect of Great Britain to enforce the same, she arrogantly denied all responsibility; and claims to be the judge in her own cause, and

> Whereas the existence of the neutrality laws of 1818 compels the executive department of this government to discriminate most harshly against those who have ever been faithless, not only to the general principles of comity which should exist between friendly states but also to the written laws of their own nation on the subject, therefore be it resolved that the committee of foreign affairs be instructed to report a Bill repealing 'An Act approved April 20, 1818.'

Congressman Ancona's arguments were forceful and persuasive but even with the debate in progress it was being whispered among the members that President Johnson was preparing to reach an agreement with the British government to enter negotiations to discuss the amount of compensation which Britain would pay in reparation for the losses suffered by the United states due to their recognition of the Confederacy during the war. The aides of the President pointed out that if Ancona's resolution were approved by Congress, then the delicate negotiations between the President and Her Britannic Majesty's government would be in jeopardy. The neutrality laws must be strictly enforced. As the debate continued it was soon obvious that even Congressman Ancona's oratory was not going to win the day for the Brotherhood.

Another supporter of the Fenians, Republican Congressman Robert Cumming Schenck of Ohio, sought a compromise and offered a new motion for the House to consider which would help the Brotherhood but which, in his opinion, would not endanger negotiations with the British.

> Be it resolved that the President of the United States, in the opinion of the House, should reconsider the policy which has been adopted by him as between the British government and that portion of the Irish people, whom in the name of Fenians, are struggling for their independence, and that he be requested to adopt as nearly as possibly, the exact course of proceeding which was pursued by the government of Great Britain in the civil war in this country between the United States and the rebels in revolt, recognizing both belligerents and preserving between them a strict neutrality.

But it was to no avail. The idea that President Johnson had already achieved a victory over the British government in the matter of securing compensation had become too firmly rooted. In some quarters it was also whispered that President Johnson had opened negotiations with the Russian Tsar to purchase the territory called Alaska whose attachment to the United States would act as a buffer against the total domination of the northern part of the continent by the British. The Fenian supporters among the congressmen were rebuked for endangering the best interests of the United States by seeking to support and aid the Fenian invasion. Both motions from Ancona and Schenck were eventually defeated and, in their stead, Congress accepted 'that the honour and good faith of the United States, imperatively demand a just and rigorous enforcement of the neutrality laws and that the House will entertain no proposition looking for their repeal, revision or violation.'

The lines of battle were now drawn entirely in the open. The Brotherhood and its army were still grouped at various mustering points near the border and, declared President Johnson, with the support of Congress, constituted an illegal private army. The United States' army, federal and state marshals and officials, were ordered to proceed at once with the confiscation of all weapons of war, munitions and supplies held by the Fenians, arresting leaders and placing all large bodies of men under observation until they could be dealt with. Any attempt by the Fenians to move across the border was to be met by such degree of force thought necessary to stop violations of the neutrality laws.

On Wednesday, 13 June, two days following the debate in Congress, Brigadier Michael Burns of the Irish Republican Army arrived in Buffalo and officially took over command from Colonel Sherwin. The city held its breath. Was the new Fenian commander about to attempt another crossing in order to test the new orders from Washington? Was he about to unleash the might of over 5,000 veteran soldiers gathered in and around the city? Was he about to make a demonstration of strength against Brigadier Barry's Union Army who would have to contest with him – former comrades clashing with each other. The tension heightened when some unexpected recruits to the Fenian army arrived in the city at ten o'clock that night – 500 Mohawk warriors, led by their warchief, Cayuga, volunteered their services to Brigadier Burns. Cayuga told him that they wished to fight for Irish freedom as the freedom of all men and all peoples was dear to them. The *Buffalo Courier* reported that these Mohawks had come from the Cattaraugus Reservation south of the city.

After a night of tension, General George Meade arrived in the city on Thursday accompanied by his staff. After a lengthy conference, the Fenian general announced that an agreement had been reached. A form of parole for all Fenian soldiers would be allowed. The Fenians quartered in the city resolved to abandon any expedition against the provinces of British North America, return to their homes and desist from any violation of the neutrality laws. In return, the United States' authorities would provide transport for them to any point they desired to go within the Union. By Friday, 15 June, some 5,166 Fenian soldiers gathered in the city of Buffalo had signed the parole.

The Fenian invasion was over.

It now fell to the British authorities to commence the trial of the Fenian prisoners held in Brantford and Toronto Jails. The trials were scheduled to commence in October and every prisoner, whether they were a citizen of the United States or a citizen of Her Britannic Majesty, would face capital sentences. The newspapers throughout the provinces were already demanding the death penalty for each and everyone. But against no one were they more vociferous than against Father John MacMahon who, as a Catholic priest, incurred their particular odium and prejudice. In noticing the report of the forthcoming trial, it was small comfort to Gavin to see that two other trials, this time courts-martial, were scheduled for November. Lieutenant-Colonel Alfred Booker had asked that a military court enquire into his conduct at Ridgeway. Lieutenant-Colonel John Stoughton Dennis, having been repeatedly accused of cowardice, especially by Captain Richard King of the Welland Canal Field Battery, who had lost a leg at the battle at Fort Erie, had resigned himself to a military enquiry into his conduct.

As the month of June drew to a close, it was the anti-Fenian *Buffalo Commercial Advertiser* which published a summary most people agreed with.

> There is no longer any reasonable doubt from the demonstration of Fenian strength and preparation, which have been vouchsafed, that, but for the prompt interference of our government, the Canadian provinces would today have been utterly and irretrievably vanquished and subjugated by the Fenian hordes. There can be no question that efficient Fenian soldiers would, ere this, have stood victorious on Canadian soil, but for the interference of the federal government. There is equally little doubt that their strongholds would have been captured, and a government improvised with an army and navy, a recognized base of action, and all the rights of belligerents. There is no doubt but that we should now be witnessing a mighty exodus of Irishmen from all over this country to join in a consolidated and harmonious movement upon the island Mecca of the *Fianna* . . . Ireland.

Chapter 63

It was on the second day of July, a Sunday not long after the martial law restrictions, which had been imposed by the government of the provinces, were lifted, that a familiar figure turned into the gate of the Dawtry farmstead. Kate was in the barn and Young Tom was on an errand to the Svensons. Gavin was sitting alone on the verandah reading the latest newspapers which had become his main preoccupation during his recuperation. At the sound of the gate swinging he glanced up and squinted at the figure curiously. There was no mistaking the lean six-footer with fair hair and the pale, almost boney features.

It was Phil Boyd.

He reached for his stick and made to rise. Boyd's smile of greeting froze a little and his eyes grew grave as Gavin limped forward. His greeting was nonetheless hearty for that.

'What the hell are you doing here?' Gavin demanded after they had clasped each other's hand and taken seats opposite each other.

'I'm here to see you, captain,' grinned Boyd as he settled himself and drew forth a cigarette.

Gavin grimaced uncomfortably. 'Enough of the "captain",' he grunted. 'It's not politic in these parts. Did you get to Sarnia? How's Nolan?'

'We reached Sarnia right enough,' Boyd replied grimly. 'You probably heard that Tevis, that yellow belly . . . well, Tevis was still sitting in Chicago too scared to move his men out. His entire damned army, 3,000 men with equipment and a couple of field batteries were still in Chicago and Milwaukee. When Nolan and I reached Sarnia we heard that Tevis was still across the border and so we managed to get ourselves over the St Clair River. We were back in Buffalo within a week.'

'But what possessed you to come across again?' Gavin was puzzled. 'It's still dangerous.'

'Well,' Boyd glanced at his feet awkwardly, 'Nolan and me, well . . . we decided that we might volunteer to go to Ireland later this year and help train the Brotherhood there. Nolan is waiting for me in Dunkirk, across the lake. I'm taking the ferry from Port Colborne this evening.'

'But you took a risk coming over,' Gavin said. 'The authorities are still looking for Fenians. There were some arrests in Hamilton a few days ago.'

Boyd was avoiding looking directly at Gavin. 'Captain Hynes wanted me to bring you some news,' he said.

'News?'

Boyd's eyes met his and then fell away. 'Your brother was killed just before O'Neill recrossed the Niagara.'

It was short and blunt. Gavin heard the words but refused to understand them.

'That's impossible,' he said after a few moments. 'There must be some mistake.'

'It was an accident,' Boyd said.

'It must be a mistake,' repeated Gavin.

'No,' Boyd went on. 'I was in Buffalo when they brought his body across. Your father came up from New York to claim it.'

'But I left John-Joe in Fort Erie so that he would be safe.' Gavin's voice was almost a whisper. 'It can't be true.'

'His body was brought to Buffalo two weeks ago.'

Major-General Napier had given his permission for the relatives of dead Fenians to claim their bodies and transport them back to the United States. The first body to be allowed back across the river was that of twenty-one year old Lieutenant Edward K. Lonergan. Although he had fallen at Ridgeway, Lonergan's men had insisted on taking the young man's body to Fort Erie with the intention of returning it to his parents in Buffalo. O'Neill's evacuation had made this task impossible and they had left it in the house of Major Canty with the other dead and wounded under the charge of Father MacMahon. When the British moved into Fort Erie on the Sunday morning they buried the Fenian dead in hasty graves outside the township. Edward Lonergan's father, Joseph, went to Fort Erie on the Monday to claim his son's body and was given permission to remove it. When the body was disinterred and taken back to Buffalo, where Coroner Edmunds examined it, there was outcry. Senator

J. W. Fitzgerald of Cincinnati told a packed rally in the Buffalo Opera House that evening – a rally in support of the Brotherhood chaired by Mister Justice James Ryan – that the body of Edward Lonergan had been horribly mutilated; the chest had been smashed in and the head had been scalped. Senator Fitzgerald accused the British troops of venting their rage on the Fenian dead. The report brought forth an immediate denial from Colonel Robert Lowry who was vehement that no indignity had been offered to the Irish dead. A few days later Colonel Hoy wrote an open letter to the *Buffalo Express* stating that claims that the body had been mutilated could be substantiated by sworn affidavits. Any further transfer of Fenian bodies was immediately stopped by the British authorities and Major-General Napier, in view of the affidavits from the American authorities, ordered an enquiry. The enquiry found that when the 10th Royals had entered the town, their commanding officer, Major Boxall, had ordered the burial of three Fenian dead found at Major Canty's house. The burials had been hurried and without coffins because of decomposition in the hot June weather. The injuries to the body of Edward Lonergan had been inflicted by the spades of the burial detail. An order was therefore circulated to all troops advising that, when such hasty field burials without the benefit of coffins were conducted, the dead were to be placed face downwards to minimise any such injuries. The explanation did not entirely satisfy the Brotherhood but the furore eventually died down.

It was therefore not until 14 June that the next body was allowed to be transferred; a young private named Buckley of the 18th Regiment was removed by the Buffalo city undertaker, Timothy Crowley, in preparation for its return to Cleveland. Crowley also brought back the body of John-Joe Devlin which had been claimed by Doctor Manus Devlin.

The depth of shock which Gavin felt, and the responsibility he believed was his for allowing John-Joe to remain in Fort Erie, was not immediately apparent. Boyd stayed a while longer and shared a meal with Gavin and Kate. He also offered to deliver a letter from Gavin to his father when he crossed back to New York. The conversation during the meal was awkward and monosyllabic but Boyd understood and, when Gavin had his letter ready, the former Confederate lieutenant thanked Kate warmly for her hospitality, clasped Gavin firmly by the hand and hitched a lift from a passing farm wagon into Port Colborne.

It was only after he had gone that Gavin told Kate why he had come. Since he had returned to the Dawtry farmstead, Gavin had never once mentioned what had happened during the four crowded days that he had been away during O'Neill's campaign. He had not even mentioned the Brotherhood to her, becoming introspective and morose, morbidly dwelling on his crippled leg and indulging in self-pity. Kate had attempted to shake him out of it but failed. Gavin simply buried himself in reading every newspaper the girl could buy. Now the news of John-Joe's death shocked him from his maudlin introspection. That evening he became a dam that had been breached. He let everything flood out in an action of confession, for was not confession the next thing to innocence? He wanted to be innocent again. And in confessing to Kate he found that his passion, the deep suppressed passion which had brought him into the Brotherhood, was evaporating; fleeing back to the fathomless depths of his mind and soul, or from whatever entity it had sprung. Telling it all to Kate left him tranquil. Not the grim, quiet satisfaction that he had experienced when he first made his decision to throw his energies into the Brotherhood after he came off the 10th Street pier in the misty rain of that dark New York afternoon a thousand years ago. There had been no tranquillity in that decision, merely a fierce determination whose passions effervesced just below the surface. He had never been sure where that burning fervour would lead him. It had sometimes occurred to him that it might have been a vengeance, perhaps a guilt. Or had it been merely confusion, some sort of delirium?

Yet the principles of his passion had surely been right ones? Lincoln had said that the doctrine of self-government was right – absolutely and eternally right. There was no confusion in that belief, no way of diluting its message or application. National and social freedom were beliefs well worth fighting for, the two sides of one great democratic principle, each being incomplete without the other. Freedom for the people of Ireland had to come, it had to come just as surely as the sun rose in the heavens. He would remain committed to that belief. It was merely that the passion was over for him, not the belief. He had to find another path, another way of expressing that belief.

For whatever reason had stirred the passion in him, he was grateful for it. It was an immortal passion fed by a surfeit of emotion for the plight of his fellow beings. It was a belief in an ideal which all men, whatever their circumstance or nationality, ought to hold dear. It was better to have been touched by that passion than never to have felt it at all. How did the old psalm put it? 'The scorching wind shall be a portion of the cup.' Well, he had been touched by the scorching wind, had felt its hot, heady breath and been enriched by it. He had done with that portion now. It was given only to a few to expend all their energies trying to enter the closed minds of men until, exhausted, they fell by the wayside, falling and yet passing on their eternal message to a new herald.

His passion was spent. He felt tired, almost old. The ghosts would remain; the ghost of his own brother joining with the others. But now he could accept them more philosophically, with sorrow and kindness rather than anguish and bitter thoughts of revenge. At least he knew them; knew their pain and suffering, their hopes and dreams; knew them and was better for it. He could now think of Nora Quinlan without guilt. He could think of the sacrifice and suffering of Jack Quinlan without a searing pain of remorse. And he could think of the thousands of graves, the countless Irish dead, of the Famine Years with only a quiet determination. Young and old, their bright, animated faces would not vanish; they would endure from generation to generation whispering the old songs, the ancient hopes until their dream became reality or until there was no one left to dream.

Kate listened to his confessional and understood. Don Quixote tilting at windmills . . . but even windmills grew ancient, crumbled and fell.

A few days later another visitor came to the farmstead.

Gavin was milking a cow. He had been sufficiently stirred from his self-indulgent inaction to commence doing odd jobs around the farmstead. Milking the cows, he found, was one of the few jobs he could perform comfortably. He could sit on the stool in the barn and milk without putting a strain on his leg. Kate had left him to the job while she went to prepare fodder for the pigs in the field behind the barn. Gavin was absorbed in his task when the shadow fell across him and a voice said mockingly, 'So it is true. I heard that you were still here but I couldn't believe it.'

Gavin felt a chill in his body as he recognized the familiar tone and he swung round on his stool. The copper-haired figure of Hogan leaned nonchalantly against the jamb of the barn door, arms folded as he grinned triumphantly down. The blood drained from Gavin's face. He had scarcely given the McMicken detective a thought since the moment he had seen him flee from Fort Erie on the tug. His only feeling had been one of regret that he had missed the opportunity to force Hogan to sign a deposition incriminating Brock Delancey. Even the bitterness he felt against Brock Delancey and his father, the senator, had somehow faded and become less important in his mind during these last few weeks. Seeing Hogan brought back all the fear, anger and bitterness in a wild surge of emotion.

Hogan watched the expressions chasing each other across Gavin's face and grinned. 'Surprised to see me?' he sneered. 'Well, it's mutual. I thought you would have skedaddled along with the rest of your cowardly friends.'

Gavin's eyes flickered to where he had laid down his walking stick but Hogan saw the movement. He jerked quickly away from the doorpost and pulled out a revolver in one easy motion.

'Don't even think of moving, Devlin,' he said quietly.

It was then that Kate came into the barn carrying a bale of hay.

'Gavin, did I hear a horse come. . . .' Her eyes fell on Hogan, on the revolver, and she dropped the bale to the ground. Astonishment and fear crossed her features. Hogan chuckled dryly.

'Well,' he drawled, 'maybe I can understand why you didn't quit the country after all.'

'Who are you, mister?' Kate raised her chin defiantly.

'Hogan,' Gavin replied for him, his lips dry. 'The McMicken detective.'

Gavin had told her all about Hogan. Her eyes grew rounded.

'What do you want here?' she demanded, trying to keep the fear out of her voice.

'Perhaps you can tell her, Devlin,' grinned the man.

'I guess that you are going to arrest me and take me up to Brantford Jail.'

Hogan chuckled mirthlessly. He shook his head and Gavin drew his brows together in bewilderment.

'Don't look so surprised, Devlin. The government here have enough on their plate without any more Fenian scum to spend time and money bringing to court for trial. I heard tell they have at least ninety Fenians to feed while they wait to hang 'em. No, you and me have a different account to settle. I remember Fort Erie.'

'What do you mean?' Gavin's fear had made his voice a whisper.

'I'm going to kill you,' Hogan replied evenly. 'I'll finish the job that Brock Delancey paid me to do in New York.'

Gavin bit his lip. 'So, you finally admit that Delancey hired you to kill me?'

'You knew it all along. McMicken sent me to New York to

involve myself with the Fenians. It was much more profitable working for the Delanceys.'

'You can't kill him.' Kate's voice was defiant now.

'Oh?' Hogan grinned mockingly at her.

'You won't be able to get away with murder, McMicken detective or not. I'll tell the authorities.'

Hogan began to chuckle again, it was an ugly sound. 'I'm going to shoot you, Devlin,' he said slowly. 'And then, you Fenian whore, I'm going to shoot you. That way, there will be no problems. Everything will be cleared up, nice and tidy like.'

'You bastard!' screamed Devlin, struggling to rise but his gammy leg sent him crashing to the ground. Kate gave a cry and ran to his side. Gavin tried to raise himself again. Hogan, still chuckling, raised his gun and drew back the hammer.

There was a movement in the yard, the soft whinny of horses, and someone cried out. But in the intensity of the moment Hogan took no notice, continuing to squeeze the trigger.

The pistol shot sent him crashing against a roof support, the revolver dropping from his hand. He swayed for a moment as if in drunken surprise before sinking slowly to the floor.

Gavin and Kate formed a numbed tableau, staring in growing disbelief at the sprawled form of Hogan, at the blood splattering his shirt.

Two men were dismounting at the barn door. They both wore militia uniforms. One, a lieutenant, was holding a pistol in his hand. He came forward hurriedly.

'Are you all right, Kate?'

Gavin and Kate turned to stare up at him.

'How about you, Devlin?'

The militia officer was Birger Svenson. He helped Kate to her feet and they both raised Gavin on to the milking stool while the second militiaman, a corporal, was bending over Hogan.

'He's pretty bad, sir.'

Svenson turned, his lips drooping. 'I only meant to catch him in the shoulder. He didn't answer my challenge. I had to shoot.'

Gavin and Kate were still staring in bewildered shock.

'Lucky we came along when we did,' Svenson was saying. 'The volunteers have been ordered to turn out and visit all the farms in this area to check up on suspicious characters. Searching for Fenians. We just happened by and saw this man about to shoot you.'

Gavin was recovering, wiping the perspiration from his forehead. 'Lucky for us you shot first, Svenson,' he muttered.

'Sir,' called the corporal, 'he's trying to say something.'

Birger Svenson dropped to Hogan's side. Hogan's eyes were open and he was trying to move his lips.

'He's . . . he's a Fenian bastard!'

Birger looked puzzled. 'What are you saying, man?'

Hogan coughed, a trace of blood appeared at the corner of his mouth. His pale eyes were bright with hate as they tried to focus on Gavin. He attempted to move his hand to his breast pocket.

'I am . . . am. . . .'

The rumble of a buggy coming through the farm gate caused them to turn. Taylor halted his carriage before the barn doors and swung down. His face was anxious.

'I heard a shot from the concession road. What's wrong? What happened?'

His eyes fell in bewilderment on Hogan's body. While everyone had turned to watch Taylor's arrival, Kate had moved to the wounded man, kneeling down and raising his head as if to make him comfortable. Hogan was gazing up at her with malice in his eyes but he could not speak because of a paroxysm of coughing.

'Ever see this man before, doc?' asked Svenson.

Taylor stared down at Hogan and shook his head. 'He looks to be in a pretty bad way,' he said, kneeling down and checking the man's wound. After a moment, he stood up and dusted his trousers, caught Svenson's eye and shook his head. Svenson knelt down by Hogan.

'You were trying to tell us something, mister. Something about Fenians. Are you one?'

Hogan made another attempt to reach his breast pocket. Kate's fingers were already there and she withdrew a pocket book.

'I think he is trying to give you this,' she said handing it to Svenson.

He took it and glanced through its contents. 'Man's name appears to be Hogan. There's a couple of letters addressed to him at a New York address.' He leaned forward. 'Hogan? Is that your name?'

Hogan tried to gather strength. He glared at Kate. 'Fenian . . . bitch!' His voice was weak and they had to lean close to hear him. 'He's . . . a Fenian . . . !'

He suddenly grunted and fell back. Taylor moved forward and made a quick examination.

'He's dead, Svenson.'

Birger Svenson stood up with a sigh. 'Check him over, corporal. There's not much in his pocket book.' He glanced at Kate and Gavin with a worried expression. 'He seemed a bit delirious. Thought you were both Fenians . . . or maybe I was mistaken. Sometimes I don't think my English is so good.'

Kate forced a smile and went to stand protectively by Gavin, the hand she placed on his shoulder was trembling.

'What can we say, Mister Svenson? The man came here and tried to hold us up. He wanted money.'

Svenson nodded absently, still glancing towards Gavin. 'I heard you had an accident, Devlin. What happened to the leg?'

'He fell off a hayrick,' Kate said, perhaps too quickly.

'Oh?'

Standing behind Svenson, Taylor caught the pleading in Kate's eye.

'Yeah,' he muttered. 'A fractured femur with extensive bruising . . . a broken thigh bone in layman's terms, Svenson,' he added as Svenson turned with a bewildered look.

The man grunted. 'Well, I hope you get better soon, Devlin.'

Taylor volunteered to take Hogan's body to the mortuary at Port Colborne and Birger Svenson, with the militia corporal, followed to make out their report. Kate watched their going and then drew a small shiny badge from her sleeve where she had hidden it. She stared at it in repulsion for a moment then moved hurriedly across to the well. With an air of finality she dropped it down into the well's black depths. Gavin knew what the badge was. He felt an abrupt lightness as if a heavy weight had been taken off his shoulders.

Chapter 64

At the end of July Gavin received a letter from his father, Manus Devlin. It was carefully and precisely worded so that if it had fallen into the wrong hands there was nothing to incriminate Gavin. It was obvious from the letter that the death of John-Joe had been a severe blow to his parents. The young girl whom John-Joe was to have married had arrived in New York two weeks after his burial. Manus, Aideen and the girl whose name Manus did not record in his letter, shared a period of grief together. Although Manus offered to find the girl employment in the city, she had decided to return to Ireland and had now left. It was the next item of news which brought a bitter sense of satisfaction to Gavin.

It had really started on that fateful 1 June when a cholera of a very malignant variety had been discovered among German immigrants landing at the quarantine islands from the ship *Union* newly arrived from Bremerhaven. The disease spread rapidly and Doctor Bissel, the health officer for the quarantine islands, had reported ten deaths on the first day of the outbreak. There was a wild panic in New York. Some 40,300 immigrants had entered the city there during the month of May alone and many of them had been able to find ways of getting ashore from the quarantine islands without the rigorous isolation period. It was not long before the contagion spread into the city itself.

The first death was that of a small-time lawyer, Mister R. A. Razier, who worked in an unsanitary basement near the waterfront and was apparently engaged in the questionable task of finding lodgings and employment for immigrants who lacked the necessary papers and clearances. A few days later his housekeeper, Mrs Reid, was dead and a German housemaid, newly entered into the household, was found to be suffering from the disease. During the week beginning Monday, 4 June, no less than seventy-seven people died of cholera in New York City. Brock Delancey was one of them.

Senator Delancey had been so shattered by the news of his son's death that he had suffered a stroke and had retired to his estate in Maryland. It was confidently expected that the senator would soon resign his seat and retire from public life entirely.

'Mrs Brock Delancey, Rosaleen McHale that was,' Manus wrote to his son, 'has left for Washington where I doubt that she will wear her widow's weeds for long, being still young and now very wealthy. On reflection, perhaps, you may accept that there is a just God in the Heavens when all is said and done.'

Manus Devlin ended his letter by permitting himself to add a plea for Gavin to return to the house in Greenwich Lane. It was a stilted sentence, a little reserved, but it was a plea nevertheless.

It was the letter which made Gavin decide that he should make a decision about his future. It was something which he had kept pushing to the back of his mind ever since he had awoken to the shock of his shattered leg.

'Remember how we discussed going to San Francisco before . . . well, before events overtook us?' he asked Kate. 'I think the time has come.' He glanced ruefully down at his leg. 'I guess that I have recovered as much as I am ever going to recover. It would be stupid to delay things any more. I want to go to San Francisco and apply to join the Bar there. The least I can do is get back into law and . . .' he smiled at her, 'start tilting at windmills again. This time, though, I'll use different weapons.'

Kate smiled and squeezed his hand. 'I'm glad you've come to that decision, Gavin. I was hoping you would.'

'But it's not fair that I should hold you to your previous promise, Kate,' he went on hurriedly. 'Not the way I am now. . . .'

Kate continued to hold his hand tightly. 'Don't think you can get rid of me that easily, Gavin Quixote Devlin. I want to come.'

'And the farmstead?'

She glanced around as if examining it. 'All I have known of love and security has been here on this land, in this house. The Liberty Tree. . . .' she nodded wistfully to the oaks which marked the gate of the farmyard. 'Grandpa Tom had so much faith in people; so much faith in his ability to fulfil his dream. Maybe that's not so bad. But life is change. Grandpa Tom used to say that the only permanent thing in life was change. What I am trying to say, Gavin, is that I shall be sad to leave here . . . in spite of my continual moans about the farm. But the time has come for change.'

Gavin caught her and held her tightly. There was no need to say anything more. Only when Young Tom came in did they draw apart with flushed smiles of embarrassment.

'San Francisco?' the boy frowned when Gavin put it to him. 'That's by the sea, isn't it? Is the sea as big as Lake Erie?'

'Bigger,' Gavin assured him. 'The Pacific Ocean is hundreds of times bigger than the lake.'

Young Tom looked disbelieving for a moment. 'It would take years to sail across a sea like that,' he reflected seriously. His eyes suddenly glistened. 'Could we live on the shore? Could we live by the sea?'

'Would you like that?' asked Kate happily.

The boy smiled from Kate to Gavin. 'I wouldn't mind,' he said self-consciously.

By the end of August Kate had sold the farmstead to Birger Svenson and packed what personal items and furniture she wanted to start her new home with. It would be an arduous journey. The railroad link which had been promised for completion soon after the war was still a year or two behind schedule. The trip would either have to be made via a series of train journeys and treks over mountain terrain by wagon, across plains where there were reports of wars with hostile Indians, or by the long haul by sea around Cape Horn. They decided on the latter route, taking a ship out of New York.

The short visit to Manus and Aideen Devlin turned into an entire winter at the house in Greenwich Lane. Gavin's parents took an immediate, almost desperate liking to Kate and Manus seemed delighted to have Young Tom about the place, insisting on taking him out to shows, to Barnum's and to the 14th Street circus. Bridget and Patsy-Mike also spoiled everybody enthusiastically. Yet the sense of gaiety in the house seemed forced to Gavin. He realized it only too well when he lay alone in the room which he had shared with his younger brother. It seemed that the household were trying to exorcise John-Joe's ghost by affecting good humour. He could not blame them. Nor could he help them. He had come to terms with it. His parents would have to find their own path.

He only submitted to one request that was against his nature, and that he did on Kate's insistence. He and Kate were married at Father MacMahon's old church of Holy Innocent on 37th Street. The ceremony was purely to please Manus and Aideen rather than any intention of a conversion to Catholicism by Kate or a renunciation of his views on religion by Gavin. Remembering the words of Father MacMahon, Gavin said, 'Well, so long as we lead good lives, happy lives, if there is a God, I guess he'll come to believe in us rather than us wasting all our time trying to convince ourselves to believe in him.'

When the thaw came and they were ready to leave, Aideen Devlin accepted their going with her usual quiet resignation and Manus Devlin, while he was inclined to bluster that San Francisco was a world away, eventually accepted their decision as well.

'Once the railroad link is made, you will both be able to come out and stay with us,' Kate assured them.

One task Gavin had to perform before they left the city. He went to the headquarters of the Brotherhood, above Roberts's store on Broadway, and resigned his commission. William Hynes, recently released from jail, was trying to pick up the fragments of the organization after the imprisonments which had followed President Johnson's proclamation. Roberts had also been released from prison but had gone on a trip to Paris to meet Brotherhood leaders there and discuss ways and means of uniting the two groups together to help an insurrection in Ireland. Hynes shook Gavin's hand awkwardly as he accepted the resignation, trying to ignore Gavin's gammy leg and mahogany walking stick. Gavin, he said, had a right to resign with honour and with no recriminations for he had served the cause conscientiously and with credit, suffering injury for it. It remained only to wish Gavin well for his new life in San Francisco.

In spite of Gavin's resignation and his determination to build a new life in the legal profession on the other side of the continent, he continued his commitment to the belief in Irish independence. He also continued to follow the aftermath of the invasion and bought every newspaper he could to follow the trials in Toronto that October. The first prisoner to be tried was a correspondent for the *Louisville Courier*, Robert B. Lynch, who, the prosecution claimed, was a Fenian colonel and one of the leaders of O'Neill's men. It spite of the evidence showing that he was simply a newspaper reporter and that he, coincidentally, bore a physical resemblance to a Fenian captain from Indianapolis, which confused several witnesses, Lynch was sentenced to be hanged on Thursday, 13 December. The prejudice of the judge and jury set the tone for the rest of the trials.

Father John MacMahon was next to be tried. Most prosecution witnesses admitted that the priest carried no gun and had actually nursed British and Irish wounded alike without discrimination, being there to render service only as a chaplain. But the prosecution found two witnesses to swear that MacMahon wore a revolver and gave commands to the Fenians. He was found guilty of levying war and sentenced to death. Before he was led away Father MacMahon warned the court that the executions would cry to heaven for vengeance. For several months the newspapers had been demanding MacMahon's blood, apparently on the sole grounds that he was an Irish Catholic priest. The anti-Catholic prejudice was revealed during the trial of the Reverend David Lumsden, the Protestant Fenian chaplain. In spite of the fact that papers were offered in evidence showing his signature as a Fenian chaplain, particularly requisition orders which he had countersigned under Colonel Owen Starr's signature, the jury declared him 'Not Guilty'. Father MacMahon's guilty verdict had been brought in on considerably less evidence.

Manus Devlin accepted the facts philosophically. 'Lumsden was a Protestant, you see,' he said to Gavin when Gavin remarked on the verdict. 'The British want to equate Protestantism in Ireland with Loyalism and Catholicism with republicanism and rebelliousness. They've been trying to do that since the turn of the century. Lumsden was an embarrassment to their propaganda. They would also have to explain why there were fourteen Protestant Fenians among the prisoners that are before their courts. Mark my words, all the Protestants that come to trial will be found "not guilty" or released before the trials take place.'

So it was. In all, twenty-two of the Fenians were sentenced to death. The governor-general, Lord Monck, issued an act of respite until all the trials were completed. In the meantime, a large American political lobby had formed into an Amnesty Movement and forced President Johnson to make representations to the British governor-general and colonial secretary. Eventually, on the orders of colonial secretary, Lord Carnarvon, all the death sentences were commuted to penal servitude for life. Then, as the pressure continued to be applied, the prisoners were gradually released one by one over the years. Daniel Whelan, wounded in the neck during the battle at Ridgeway, was the last of the Fenian prisoners to be released on 16 July 1872.

Gavin turned his interest to the court-martial enquiries that took place in November at Fort Erie. The first to be held was opened to enquire into the conduct of Lieutenant-Colonel Alfred Booker during the battle at Ridgeway. Three officers sat to hear evidence, the president of the court being the newly promoted Colonel George Taylor Denison who had commanded the governor-general's bodyguard. The court decided that the main fault of the Ridgeway disaster lay with the fact that Booker's men were young and inexperienced. Booker, in his own defence, said that he had given the order for the bugler to sound a withdrawal merely in order to regroup his forces and when the men started to flee from the field he could not hold them. The officers under his command, particularly those of his own battalion, the 13th, had a different story to tell. Nevertheless, Booker was exonerated and absolved of all blame for the defeat and panic-stricken flight that followed. Booker had already resigned from the 13th Battalion in July and now he was able quietly to resign from the militia itself. He no longer felt able to hold his head up in his native Hamilton, the home of the 13th Battalion, and so he established a new business in Montréal where he was not known and where he died four years later, a broken and embittered man, unable to live with the memory of Ridgeway, unable to prevent the gossip which followed him.

A few days after Booker's hearing, the court sat again to consider the allegations against Lieutenant-Colonel John Stoughton Dennis. There were six counts of cowardice and misconduct to be answered. After the evidence was heard, the court, by a majority vote of two to one, exonerated Dennis. The dissenting vote was, however, that of the president of the court, Colonel Denison, who issued a public statement announcing his dissension from the findings of his brother officers. The matter was sent to the governor-general, Lord Monck, who accepting the majority findings but, in an attempt to ameliorate Colonel Denison, pointed out that Stoughton Dennis had made an error in making his command engage the Fenian forces at Fort Erie. He had disembarked his men before he had made sure of the size of the enemy force. Lord Monck believed that Colonel Dennis's actions throughout had been rash but not cowardly.

A few years later Colonel Dennis was to be despatched to the Red River country, a territory which was ruled by the Hudson Bay Company. They had announced their intention of selling the area to the Ottawa government who would create it as a new Canadian province called Manitoba. Stoughton Dennis's arrogance and ineptitude was the spark which ignited the already explosive attitudes of the Métis, led by Louis Riel, who inhabited the land. Once more Colonel Dennis left his command in a dangerous situation, slipping away in disguise ostensibly to seek reinforcements. The Métis insurrection was crushed, Louis Riel was executed and Manitoba became a province of Canada in 1870. Stoughton Dennis yet again survived an enquiry into his behaviour and finally, in 1878, achieved his long cherished political ambition by becoming minister of the interior in the Ottawa government.

Initially, O'Neill's crossing had produced no great upsurge of anger on the part of the local people in the Fort Erie area. It was a fact which seemed to cause great annoyance to the civil and military government of the province and their supporters. The editor of the Conservative *Hamilton Times* wrote with indignation on 6 June:

> I was particularly struck with the mild-tempered feelings with which the Fort Erie people seemed to regard their invaders. They appeared perfectly willing that the latter should get away before the British Army arrived upon the scene to stop their escaping. To hear them talk one would imagine that the fighting had taken place between two opposing forces of foreigners on neutral ground entirely.

The Scots editor of the *Canadian Illustrated News*, Alexander Somerville, also heard nothing but complimentary reports of the military bearing of the Fenians and actually wrote to O'Neill to compliment him on the matter while expressing his abhorrence at the invasion itself. Even those who fought against the Fenians found praise for them. Colonel George Denison, writing an account a few months later, said:

> I spent three weeks in Fort Erie and conversed with dozens of people of the place, and was astonished at the universal testimony borne by them to the unvarying good conduct of this rabble while among them. They claimed food and horses, but they can hardly be blamed for that as an act of war, but can only be blamed because the war itself, which alone could give them the right to take these things, was unjustifiable and wicked. They have been called plunderers, robbers and marauders, yet no matter how unwillingly we may be to admit it, the positive fact remains that they stole but few valuables, that they destroyed, comparatively speaking, little or nothing, and that they committed no outrages on the inhabitants, but treated everyone with unvarying courtesy.
>
> It seems a perfect burlesque to see a ragged rabble without a government, country or flag affecting chivalrous sentiments and doing acts that put one in mind of the days of knight errantry.

However good-natured local attitudes had been to O'Neill, the main reaction across the provinces was one of alarm and near hysteria. The new nationalism became widespread. The former hostility to the plan for uniting the provinces into one big country ebbed and changed. The concept of a Canadian nation came abruptly into being, a belief in unity and strength which had not previously existed. In mid-June the *Toronto Globe* had commented, 'The Fenians have unwittingly done an essential service to the Canadian people, by inspiring them with a degree of confidence in their defensive strength which they did not before possess.' The proposal for the unification of the provinces of British North America received enthusiastic support. On 22 May 1867, nearly one year after O'Neill led his Irish troops across the Niagara River, the British North America Act was promulgated announcing that from 1 July 1867, the united provinces of Canada (Upper and Lower) New Brunswick and Nova Scotia would form a self-governing Dominion under the British Crown known as Canada. Upper Canada province would henceforth be known as Ontario and Lower Canada would become Québec. Manitoba would join the confederation in 1870 after the suppression of the Red River uprising; British Columbia would join in 1871; Prince Edward Island in 1873; Saskatchewan and Alberta would be created in 1905. The last province which was to join the Dominion was Newfoundland, the land where many Irish had settled and called *Talamh an Éisc* – The Land of Fish. Newfoundland finally joined Canada in 1949. The Canadian dream had been realized.

But of the politicians who had advocated that dream, one barely lived long enough to see the commencement of its realization. Thomas D'Arcy McGee, the former Irish Republican and revolutionary turned British Loyalist and Conservative, bitter enemy to his former friends and comrades, was returning home from the House of Commons in Ottawa in the early hours of 7 April 1868. The new Parliament had adjourned at ten minutes past two that morning. McGee put on his overcoat and top hat, paused to light a cigar, and walked down Barrack Hill to the corner of Sparks and Metcalfe Streets with a fellow member of Parliament, Robert McFarlane. The streets were lit by a full moon. Spring had turned the roadway into mud although a frost had laid a thin skin of ice across every puddle. McGee bade goodnight to McFarlane and turned down Sparks Street to the lodging house of Mrs Trotter where he and several other Members of Parliament stayed when in the capital. It was a few doors away from the offices of the Ottawa *Times*. McGee had barely reached the door when there was a loud report and he fell on the doorstep.

A moment later the street was filled with people but he was dead and the assassin fled. D'Arcy McGee had been shot in the back of the head with a pistol at such close quarters that the gunpowder had burned his hair. The bullet had gone through the base of his brain and emerged from his mouth, knocking out one or two teeth and his half-smoked cigar. A reward of $20,000 was offered by Prime Minister John A. Macdonald for information which would lead to the arrest of the assassin. On 11 February 1869, an Irishman, Patrick James Whelan, said to be a member of the Irish Republican Brotherhood, was executed having been convicted of the crime. The evidence against him was questionable and some witness afterwards admitted perjury. Those who knew Whelan discounted the claim he was a Fenian. Whelan was a drunk and a scoundrel but he had never been politically aware nor had he the nature to be a cold-blooded assassin. Later forensic evidence demonstrated that the pistol found in his room had not fired the fatal shot.

President Andrew Johnson, having succeeded in his purchase of Alaska for the sum of $7.5 millions from Russia, found his negotiations for compensation from the British government bogged down as one delaying tactic after another was used. Johnson survived an attempt to impeach him over his dictorial methods of government when the proposers of the impeachment proceedings failed, by a single vote, to get the necessary two-thirds majority in the Senate. President Johnson left office in 1869 to be succeeded by Lieutenant-General Ulysses Simpson Grant. Grant's first success in office was the payment of $15 millions in compensation from Great Britain in settlement of the United States' claims.

After the failure of the invasion and the subsequent uprising in Ireland during the following year, both William Randall Roberts and General 'Fighting Tom' Sweeny resigned office in the Brotherhood. General Sweeny was reinstated into the United States regular army and was able to retire to his home in Albany in 1870 with the brevet rank of major-general. The year of Sweeny's retirement, Roberts was elected to the United States Congress and also became an alderman of the city of New York. From 1885 to 1889 he served as United States ambassador to Chile. John O'Neill, whose popularity was enormous after Ridgeway, was elected to the presidency of the senate wing of the Brotherhood in 1868. He refused to abandon the idea of establishing an Irish Republic-in-Exile in Canada. On 25 May

1870, he made another attempt to lead a Fenian army across the borders of Vermont and New York only to clash with the Canadian militia and suffer heavy casualties. His plans had been betrayed by his adjutant, Henri Le Caron, who was, in fact, an English secret service man named Thomas Miller Beach who had infiltrated the Brotherhood soon after Ridgeway. A few months later, in October, O'Neill made his final attempt, crossing into the Red River country and seizing Fort Pembina in what was to become Manitoba. He offered Fenian aid to Louis Riel but, although Riel's secretary, O'Donoghue, was a member of the Brotherhood, Riel declined O'Neill's help. O'Neill returned to the United States, gave up the presidency and retired to private life, dying in 1878 a spent and wasted man. The little town of O'Neill, on the Elkhorn River, Nebraska, was named after him.

John O'Mahoney, whose individualistic attitudes had led to the split in the Brotherhood, died in poverty in New York city in 1877. And James Stephens – *An Seabhac Siúlach*, the romantic Wandering Hawk – was also to fade into obscurity. He had incurred such odium among the American Fenians, who denounced him as a traitor, that he returned to Paris to earn a precarious living from journalism and translation. Twenty years later, in 1886, under an amnesty from the British government and financed by a public subscription raised among his friends, the Wandering Hawk finally returned to Ireland to die there in 1901 at the age of seventy-six.

In January, 1868, Gavin Devlin, attorney-at-law in Point Lobos, San Francisco, received a letter dated the previous December in New York. It was from Lieutenant Phil Boyd.

'Having just arrived in New York, I took the liberty of obtaining your address from your father. He has informed me that you are well, married and that your wife expects a child in the spring. My felicitations to Mrs Devlin, to whom I wish to be remembered, and to yourself. I am delighted to hear that you have been called to the Bar and are highly regarded as one of San Francisco's emerging lawyers.

'For myself, I am well enough but much dispirited by my sojourn in Ireland. I have returned to this country in expectation of finally laying down my sword and taking up the pen, endeavouring to seek employment in the journalistic profession.

'You will doubtless have heard that the rising in Ireland is over and that the hopes for any successful outcome to the endeavours of the Brotherhood in that sorry land seem entirely remote.

'When I last saw you, I mentioned that Sergeant Nolan and I had volunteered to go to Ireland with the intention of training the Brotherhood there. We arrived at Queenstown, Cork, late in the fall and joined Colonel John O'Connor's command. The date for the rising was to be Monday, 11 February 1867. Soon afterwards it was changed to Tuesday, 5 March, because it was discovered that spies and informers had relayed this intelligence to the authorities. Alas, this Brotherhood of ours is so riddled with spies and traitors who sell their loyalty to the highest bidder that one is constantly viewing even one's closest friends with deep suspicion. The alarming thing was that news of the alteration of the date of the rising did not reach Colonel O'Connor nor did it, as I subsequently learned, reach Captain McAfferty's command in England. The result was very nearly disasterous.

'On Monday, 11 February, O'Connor ordered us into the field. Our task was to capture the military barracks at Cahersiveen, which is a market town on the Iveragh peninsula in the county of Kerry. It was the very town where Sergeant Nolan was born and raised. We began our movement sharply enough but found, among the prisoners whom we initially took, was an English soldier carrying despatches. Imagine our chagrin when, among those despatches, was information showing that the English not only knew of our plan but the fact that the Brotherhood's Military Council had postponed the date of the uprising. We dispersed immediately and O'Connor contacted the Military Council in Dublin informing them of events and demanding new instructions.

'Apparently, so I came to understand, Captain McAfferty fared worse than we did. I knew McAfferty well because he had served as an officer with Morgan's guerrillas in the Confederate Army. His expertise in this respect was much needed in Ireland but, instead, he was sent to England to take command of a group of men in Lancashire. Their task was to seize the arsenal at Chester Castle and transport the arms by ship to Dubliin. There was an informer among them . . . need I say it? The English thwarted the plan but McAfferty managed to avoid arrest and escaped to Dublin. Here, alas, he was taken and charged with High Treason. How, he asked, could he commit High Treason to England when he was born in Ohio and was an American citizen? According to the newspapers, he pointed out to the judge that, although England had supported the Confederacy during the war, he had never heard of an Englishman being arrested by the United States and executed for High Treason. The argument was lost on the judge and McAfferty was sentenced to be hanged. More enlightened politicians subsequently forced the court to commute that sentence to penal servitude for life.

'On 5 March the order came again to take the field. The men rose willingly enough in many areas of the country: in Dublin, Cork, Tipperary, Limerick, Kerry, Clare and Waterford. But in spite of our vaunted preparations, those who came out by their thousands to contest with the British were ill-trained and miserably armed. The vast majority were unaccustomed to meeting the fire of disciplined troops. Ah, had we only had O'Neill's brigade with us! In addition to the condition of the men, the day of the rising was bitterly cold and there was a snow storm which gave place to a howling maelstrom of hail and sleet. It was no weather for even veteran soldiers to be encamped in the field let alone the rawest recruits. This fiercesome weather continued for fully a week and would have dampened the ardour of even the most willing of volunteers.

'In spite of this, we gave a good account of ourselves. Military barracks were captured in Dublin, notwithstanding the large British garrison in the city, and at Tallaght there was a fierce battle. In Limerick I heard of fighting at Kilmallock and at Ardagh while in Cork our men cut telegraph and railroad links and destroyed one military barracks. As for O'Connor's command, we fought several engagements. We made an attack on the barracks at Cahersiveen, an impressive machicolated castle with a turreted tower, and seized it with few casualties. But one of our skirmishes took place with a regiment of English Lancers and poor Sergeant Nolan was pierced through the side. I was beside him when he died, God rest his soul. He died on the snow-swept slopes of the Kerry mountains just a short distance from where he had been born and raised. He had fought in the war between the States but went home to be killed by a foreign soldier. I remember that he mumbled a few words before he died. "*Tiocfaidh ár lá!*" Our day will come! Poor Nolan. He believed it with a quiet intensity and gave his all to make it so.

'Our men were pressed back to the mountain of Knockadobar, overlooking Cahersiveen, and we found ourselves surrounded by a Scottish regiment as we could tell from their kilts and glengarry caps. O'Connor ordered us to hold our positions until nightfall and then try to filter through the enemy's picquet lines under cover of darkness. The group I was with met no obstacles. I later heard that this regiment was the 73rd Regiment of Foot and comprised Scottish-Gaelic speakers; the language is only removed in dialect from Irish. Some of our men were challenged by the Scottish sentries and replying to them in Irish found that the Scots understood them. Many of these Scots sympathized with the Irish cause, having no love of the English for the many wrongs inflicted by them on their people after their defeat at Culloden. They therefore allowed the Irish to slip through their lines.

'I once heard a similar tale from my grandfather after the '98 uprising. When William Putnam McCabe, one of the leaders of the rising, was being taken to his trial in Dublin, he saw that his escort were Scottish soldiers. He appealed to them in Irish, observing that they ought to have more in common with his nation than with the English. The Scots responded by allowing him to escape. It is a fascinating story, yet perhaps I digress.

'Within a few weeks the rising was over. It was over almost before news of it had reached the Brotherhood in America. Yet I heard that the Brotherhood sent out one of its ships, the *Jackmel*, rechristened as *Erin's Hope* with 8,000 stands of rifles and ammunition and forty officers on board to teach their use. Alas, the ship arrived too late and was arrested by the Royal Navy.

'As the English began the inevitable round-up of prisoners, Colonel O'Connor hid in a house in Cork until he was able to get a ship for Boston. I, too, had to lay low for a while and many of my comrades were arrested. I believe that during those months of spring and early summer there were no less than 200 trials for High Treason at which sentences of death, penal servitude for life and transportation were common enough. One sad blot on my honour as a former Confederate officer was that a fellow officer turned informer to secure his freedom. Colonel Godfrey Massey, who had been placed in charge of securing Limerick Railway Station, was that man. Tom Burke, a former general in the Confederate service, was one of those that this wretched man sent to the gallows in order to save his own skin.

'Friends hid me while the trials continued and the English military were constant in their searching and raiding for arms and suspects. Arrests were a daily occurrence. The Irish bore it stoically. It is not the first time that England has brought them, as a nation, to obedience at swordpoint or cannon's mouth. Perhaps, though God forbid, it will not be the last time. But by such means each generation grows up more determined than ever before to drive the alien from their country.

'News of another disaster to our cause came while I was in hiding. Colonel Tom Kelly, late of the 10th Ohio Regiment of the Union Army, chief executive of the Brotherhood in Ireland, was arrested in the English town of Manchester, together with his adjutant Captain Tim Deasy, formerly of the 9th Massachusetts Infanty. The Brotherhood made immediate plans to set them at liberty. Colonel Ricard O'Sullivan Burke went to Manchester to organize the rescue bid. The attempt was made while Kelly and Deasy were being transferred from the court house to prison on 11 September. The prison van was ambushed by Burke's men. In the attempt a police sergeant within the van, bending down to peer through the lock in order to see what the commotion was outside, was shot and killed when one of the attackers called Rice attempted to blow open the lock with a pistol. Kelly and Deasy made their escape.

'In the aftermath of this, the police reacted with rage and bitterness. Many arrests were made among the large Irish community that lived within Manchester. Subsequently five men were brought to trial with indecent haste in order to appease the blood lust of the politicians. Among the five, ironically, was a Royal Marine called Maguire who had just arrived home on leave. The man Maguire was totally loyal to the British and entertained a hatred of the Fenians. Yet he was sentenced to death along with the others after a most appalling pack of lies ever told in a court room. Set before any decent judge those lies would have been instantly dismissed and those that told them branded perjurers. But the law was prejudiced by race.

'Another one of the five sentenced to death was an American citizen, Captain Edward O'Meagher Condon, who served with the 164th New York Volunteers during the war. You may have heard of this gentlemen for it was he who originated a plan to rescue some of the Fenian prisoners from Toronto by ambushing the prison van as it passed over the Don Bridge. I do not think anything came of the plan although I recall that one of the prisoners, a man named Ryan, did escape before he was brought to trial. Condon, however, was not even present during the rescue. The other three men sentenced to death for the Manchester affair were Allen, Larkin and O'Brien.

'In the end the British government baulked at the execution of a Royal Marine who plainly had nothing to do with the affair and so, to save face, they granted the man an act of pardon; *pardon*, mark you! As if the poor man had been guilty of anything other than being an Irishman. The findings of that farce of a trial were not overturned. Condon's sentence, however, was commuted to penal servitude after pressure from the United States' ambassador. But as for poor Allen, Larkin and O'Brien there was no reprieve. On 23 November they were publicly executed in Manchester while the mobs howled, cheered and sang around their bodies. I left Queenstown bound for New York on 4 December. When I left I found the reaction of the Irish people to the news from Manchester was one of unspeakable horror. The gulf between Ireland and England, always a considerable one, has never been so wide and so deep. Everyone knows that the three men, already called martyrs by even the most moderate Irish opinion, should never have been found guilty on such falsified evidence, with perjured witnesses and a blundering jury, spurred on by the hatred and invective of the English newspapers and politicians. I believe that there was a sinister intent to those executions. They were not an enactment of law but an example designed to strike terror into any Irishman or woman who dared whisper of liberty.

'Although I seemed to dissent from the general opinion within the Brotherhood, I feel that there is now a pause to the struggle while the Irish people recover from their setbacks, reorganize and consolidate their forces. Indeed, you may ask whether Ireland will ever obtain its freedom. I say, yes; as poor Sergeant Nolan said: our day will come. It is a belief held among all Irish people and it is a belief and hope that the English cannot seem to apprehend. They may strike down one generation but the next one rises up to challenge them again. Few English people that I have talked with can begin to understand that the Irish do not want to be ruled by a foreign power no matter how benign that power is, although no one who examines the record of English rule in Ireland could accord the word 'benign' to it. Ask an English person whether he would like his country ruled by a foreign country, with foreign administrators and soldiery speaking a foreign language. Would he not defend his independence to the death? Yet he cannot see how this applies to Ireland.

'Why do the English suffer such a peculiar blind spot so far as their relationship with their neighbours is concerned? I have heard several of our countrymen hold out the hope that the English people, once properly informed of what their government has done in Ireland over the centuries, will throw up their hands in horror and force their rulers to stop perpetuating these injustices. I am not so sanguine. I will admit that many English people are humane and progressive as individuals. Collectively, however, whenever the name of Ireland is mentioned they are, at best, indifferent. Most become superior and condescending, believing that England knows best how to govern such unruly, uncivilized barbarians. At worst, many of them are prejudiced with extraordinary intensity towards Ireland expressing the regret that Oliver Cromwell's plan to exterminate the entire nation had not succeeded.

'Even now the English newspapers are cluttered with racial hatred towards the Irish people. The little English Queen has publicly pronounced that the Irish are an 'abominable people', uncivilized and unfit to govern themselves. The editorial columns of one London newspaper I have before me as I write claim that the Irish are an inferior race and their extinction is not only a law of nature but a blessing to mankind. How can one attempt, therefore, to appeal for moral justice to such prejudice?

'Maybe, one day, the hate and intolerance will change to a more enlightened attitude. Maybe, one day, there will grow a friendship born out of mutual respect and understanding. As I see it, in spite of our long, troubled history, we have never hated the English *people* as they seem to hate us. Our hatred has always been reserved for their government, their soldiers and their landlords in our country. We have often appealed to the English people to educate themselves as to what is done in their name in our unhappy land. Surely a greater knowledge and understanding may eventually bring peace and friendship between us? Yes; maybe that day will come. One day. . . .

'Meanwhile, I am a pragmatist. I am an Irishman by birth and an American by adoption. I have declared myself an enemy to the power that holds my native land in the bonds of its tyranny. The statesmen of England have declared on innumerable occasions that the oppressed have a right to throw off the yoke of alien government and tyranny. Well, until the government of England commence to uphold that teaching in practice, as well as in pious political pronunciations and until they leave our island and its people to govern themselves in their own way, then the Irish people will continue to conspire against them, continue to conceive and devise the means to train its people, generation after generation, in an attempt to hurl the place-men and soldiery of England from the shores of their island. I say, along with poor Sergeant Nolan, yes, yes! *Tiocfaidh ár lá!* Our day will come!'

L'Envoi

The modern Irish Republic came into existence on 18 April 1949, and was recognized by the world community of nations. It became a full member of the United Nations Organization in 1955. However the country is partitioned with six counties in the north-east remaining under British control and being the source of bitterness and continued bloodshed. The re-unification of Ireland is a cherished aspiration for the majority of Irish people.

With the failure of the Fenian uprising of 1867, the Irish people turned to the new 'constitutional path' which had been opened for them by the Catholic Emancipation Act and Parliamentary Reform Act. An Irish Party was established to achieve self-government and during the next forty years this party held four-fifths of all the Irish seats within the British Parliament. In the first few years of its existence, the Irish Party presented no less than twenty-eight Self-Government Bills. The democratically expressed wish of the majority of Irish people was dismissed out of hand by successive British governments. The only success the Irish people were to achieve in this period was a measure of relief bringing the feudal alien landlord system to its knees by securing tenant rights and a 'fair rent' system. This relief was fought and won during the Land War (1879–1882).

In the general election of 1910, the Irish Party, having won yet another majority of eighty-four seats out of the 105 Irish seats, found they held the balance of power between the major English parties. It seemed inevitable that the Irish would achieve a measure of self-government after forty years of their democratically expressed wishes being contemptuously ignored. But the proposals for self-government were delayed and finally shelved when Britain entered the Great War in August 1914.

Fifty years after the Irish flag was hoisted by Colonel Owen Starr outside George Lewis's post office at Fort Erie, it was raised again.

This time it was hoisted over the General Post Office in Dublin on Easter Monday, 24 April 1916, when the Irish rose in arms once more to establish the cherished dream of a Republic. The 1916 uprising, like previous insurrections, was crushed. The Irish leaders were executed before firing squads over a protracted period to instil the maximum fear and obedience into the population. The last execution, that of the popular trade union leader, historian and political theoretician, James Connolly, who had been badly wounded in the fighting, caused a world-wide outcry against the British. Connolly was carried to his death on a stretcher and strapped to a chair to keep him upright in order to face the firing squad.

The British policy had a reverse effect to that intended. In December 1918, after the end of the Great War, a general election was held. Sinn Féin, a 'home rule' party, reconstituted itself as the new Republican party. Declaring its intent to withdraw from the British Parliament and set up an independent Irish Parliament in Dublin, Sinn Féin won seventy-three out of the 105 Irish seats. The old Irish Party won six seats plus a further seat in an Irish constituency in Liverpool, England. The Unionists held twenty-six seats, several of them won narrowly on split votes between the Irish Party and Sinn Féin.

In January 1919, the elected representatives of Ireland met in Dublin, issued a Declaration of Independence and affirmed the proclamation of the 1916 Irish Republic. The British government's answer was to attempt to arrest all the elected Republican Members of Parliament. One Irish leader observed that the entire Irish nation had been declared an 'illegal assembly' by Britain. British troops poured into the country and a guerrilla war commenced. The Irish War of Independence lasted from 1919 to 1921. The British government finally entered into negotiations and succeeded in coercing the Irish delegates, under a threat of the continuation of 'an immediate and terrible war', into accepting the partition of the country with the majority part recognized as a Free State being a Dominion within the British Commonwealth.

Faced with a *fait accompli* by their delegates, the Irish Parliament in Dublin split among themselves when asked to ratify this 'treaty'. A bitter civil war broke out lasting from 1922 to 1923 between those who accepted the treaty and those who maintained their allegiance in the declared Republic and the unity of the nation. The Republicans were defeated. The country was effectively partitioned.

Of the northern nine-county province of Ulster, militant Unionists had won majorities in only four counties and demanded separation from the rest of Ireland, asking to remain within the United Kingdom. The militant unionism was the result of a century of 'divide and rule' policy in which Irish Protestants were encouraged to forget their radical Republican roots and develop sectarian antagonisms against Catholics. Protestantism had now become equated with Unionism while Catholicicm had been equated with nationalism. However, as the four counties in which Unionists held a majority were not a viable or economic unit, two nationalist counties were arbitrarily seized to create a statelet called Northern Ireland, separated from the other three counties of Ulster and the rest of Ireland. A Unionist majority was guaranteed in perpetuity but further reinforced by the disenfranchisement of groups of Catholic voters, and segregation in all walks of life, especially in local and provincial government. The partition was, of course, undemocratic by any standard, born out of bloodshed and violence. Injustice was a tool by which the statelet was created and maintained and this has ensured that bloodshed and violence continues as a factor in Ireland's troubled history.

In the new Irish Free State, after the civil war, Republicans formed a new party called *Fianna Fáil* (Soldiers of Destiny) and won the general election in 1932. In 1937 the Fianna Fáil government adopted a new constitution which made the Free State into a Republic in all but name. In 1949 this constitution was tidied up and the state was formally declared to be the Republic of Ireland.

The Irish language

At the time when these events took place, one-and-a-half million people in Ireland spoke Irish of which 319,602 spoke no English. At the start of the nineteenth century, however, it had been estimated that two-thirds of the population were Irish-speaking of which the majority had no knowledge of English. The Famine Years (1845–49) had dealt a blow to the language which the planned efforts of the English administration to eradicate it had not been able to achieve. Among the immigrants to the New World, up to, and including, this time, Irish was the majority language. Several pieces of Irish have been included in this novel as part of the natural usage of the time. Usually the meaning of such phrases and words are made clear in the text. In a few places phrases and words have not been immediately translated not only as it would destroy the narrative flow but as it was the author's intention to demonstrate a lack of communication between English and Irish speakers. A crib of such words and phrases is provided to give non-Irish speakers an opportunity to share that extra understanding without destroying the intentions of the first reading.

chapter 3
page 34 *Ciúnas, a Bhríd! Tá tú ag geabaireacht.*
Quiet, Bridget. You are chattering.
Scread Mhaidine ort! Cacamas!
May you have the morning screech! (A curse) You shit!
Garsún.
Young boy.

chapter 4
page 46 *Cá bhfuil Patsy-Mike anois?*
Where is Patsy-Mike now?

chapter 8

page 82 *Dia anseo isteach . . . pionta, más é do thoil é.*
God save all here . . . a pint, please.
An bhfuil Gaeilge agat?
Do you speak Irish?
Is cuma.
It doesn't matter.
Tá tart orm.
I am thirsty.

83 *An teach mór; gabh ar dheis ansin . . . ar dheis . . . dheis.*
The big house, turn there on the right . . . on the right . . . right.
Ba mhaith liom gloine leanna anois!
I'd like a glass of beer now.

chapter 19

page 181 *Buíochas le Dia!*
Thanks be to God.

chapter 20

page 189 *Mo bhuachaill.*
My boy.
Maith an fear!
Good man!

191 *Ceart go leor.*
Right enough.
Marbhfháisc orthu!
Bad cess on them!

chapter 23

page 208 *M'anam!*
On my soul!

209 *A thiarcais!*
My goodness!

chapter 24

page 217 *Dia duit.*
God to you – standard form of greeting, e.g. Hello.
Tá an lá go dona. An bhfuil tú fuar?
The day is bad. Are you cold?
Ach, tá sé ag cur fearthainne anois. Isteach libh!
It's raining now. Inside with you.

220 *Suí síos.*

	Sit down.
	Ar mhaith leat cupán tae?
	Would you like a cup of tea?
	Go maith.
	Good.
221	*Mo bhean.*
	My wife.
chapter 25	
page 231	*Ciúnas anois, tá scéal le hinsint aici!*
	Quiet, now, she's going to narrate a story!
chapter 26	
page 242	*Dia duit, a Mhurna. Conas tá tú?*
	Hello, Murna. How are you?
	Dia's Muire duit, a mhúinteoir.
	Hello to you, teacher.
	Slán libh!
	Farewell.
chapter 28	
page 255	*Crotach.*
	Curlew.
258	*Moínín.*
	Village green.
chapter 29	
page 261	*An dtuigeann sibh mé?*
	Do you understand me?
chapter 33	
page 295	*Go raibh maith agat.*
	Thank you.
296	*Nach bhfuil trua ar bith agat dúinn a dhuin'uasail? Níl an sneachta imithe ón talamh fós. Cá mbeidh ár dtreo, gan díon os ár gcionn lenár gcosaint, gan bhia lem pháistí a chothú, gan teaghlach, gan tine lena ngoradh?*
	Have you no pity, sir? The snow is not yet gone from the ground and where will we go with no roof to protect us above our heads, no food to feed my children, no hearth nor fire to warm them with?
	An bhfágfar ar leath thaobh bhóthair sinn agus bás leis an bhfuacht agus leis an ocras i ndán dúinn? Mhair mo chéile,

sabhála Dia a anam, agus mhair a athair agus athair a athar roimhe, ar ndóigh, mhair a sheacht sinsear ar an talamh seo agus shaothraigh siad é.
Are we to be left on the roadside to die of the cold and hunger? My husband, God be merciful to his soul, and his father, and his father's father before him, and, indeed, all the generations beyond memory, have lived and laboured on this land.
Nach duine de na Nualláin ar bhain na clocha chun na ceithre bhalla den bhothán seo a thógáil. 'Sé seo mo theaghlach féin. Níor theip orainn riamh an cíos a íoc, a dhuin'uasail, fiú amháin le linn an Ghorta Mhóir. D'íocamar i gcónaí, ach níl sé ar ár gcumas cuid ar bith den mhéadú cíosa a íoc, a dhuin'uasail. Glac trua dúinn. Cé'n fáth atá tú ag déanamh an ghníomh seo?
It was an Ó Nualláin who raised the stones to make the four walls of this cabin. This is my home. We have always paid the rent, sir, even during the days of the Great Hunger. We have always paid. But we can pay none of this increase. Oh, sir, show some pity. Why are you doing this?

298 *Scrios dearg ort!*
Red destruction on you. (A curse)
Amach libh as seo anois!
Off with you now!

chapter 36

page 316 *Íosa, Muire agus Iósaf!*
Jesus, Mary and Joseph.
Ba mhaith liom . . . ba mhaith liom . . . a phósadh an neacht leat!
I would like . . . I'd like . . . to marry your niece!

317 *Mo ghrá thú.*
I love you.
Go n-éirí an t-ádh leat. Go dtaga tú abhaile slán.
Good luck to you. May you come home safe.
Slán gó fóill, a rún.
Goodbye for a while, my love.

324 *Mo ghrá, mo chroi.*
My love, my heart.

chapter 45

page 403 *Dia duit, Eoin.*
Hello, Eoin (Owen).
Dia's Mhuire duit! Cén chaoi a bhfuil tú, a Sheáin?
Hello to you. How are you (Séan) John?

chapter 46

page 412 *Dia ar 'ach bóthar a rachaidh sibh!*
God on every road you travel (good luck).

chapter 54

page 496 *Seachain!*
Look out!

chapter 57

page 542 *A bhean, a bhean, tabhair dom deoch! Tá mé nimhneach!*
Woman, woman, give me a drink. I am hurt.
A Dhia, a Dhia, tabhair dom deoch!
O God, O God, give me a drink!

chapter 60

page 578 *Slán go fóill.*
Farewell for a while.